Born in Tynemouth in 1919, C. L. Skelton's varied career included stage and film acting, war service in the RAF, seven years as a lay brother with a religious order, hunting the Loch Ness monster and selling insurance and brushes door-to-door in the Scottish Highlands.

Other novels by C. L. Skelton are *Hardacre*, *The Maclarens*, *Sweethearts and Wives* and *Beloved Soldiers*.

D1137222

By the same author

Hardacre

The Maclarens
Sweethearts and Wives
Beloved Soldiers

C. L. SKELTON

Hardacre's Luck

||| •PARRALLEL• |||

This edition published 1995 for
Parrallel Books
Units 13–17 Avonbridge Industrial Estate
Atlantic Road
Avonmouth, Bristol BS11 9QD
by Diamond Books
77–85 Fulham Palace Road
Hammersmith, London W6 8JB

Published by Grafton 1985
First published in Great Britain by
Granada Publishing 1984

ISBN 0 261 66689 4

Set in Plantin
Printed in Great Britain

CHAPTER
ONE

The last passenger off the Malton bus was a tall young man carrying a single cheap buff suitcase which swung lightly from his hand as if it were more than half empty. He was dressed in a sombre dark blue suit which, being slightly short at both wrists and ankles, gave the impression of something second-hand, and he carried an army greatcoat over his other arm. He hesitated for a moment, before stepping to the ground, as if he was uncertain yet that he had reached his destination. Then he descended the last step, one hand still resting on the dusty metal of the coach exterior. Almost reluctantly, he released his grip, and turned once around, swinging the suitcase easily. Then, like a homing bird, he set out with purposeful strides eastwards, in the direction of the sea.

The uncertainty he had shown in the bus station was gone now, and he made his way through the streets of the small seaside city with the assurance of a native. He turned a corner, and felt, as he had known he would, a burst of sea-wet air, and a sudden gust of salty November wind that cut through his clothing. He hesitated, then set the suitcase down and slipped the coat on over his suit, but left it swinging open as he walked, more quickly, towards the waterfront. When he reached the broad promenade he crossed to the stone wall facing the sea, set the case down once more, and stood leaning over the wall, his eyes on the darkening distance, where the lights of two fishing cobles bobbed on the rough sea's surface like early stars. He stood there, alone, for half an hour, drinking in the remembered delight of the sea.

It was getting dark, when he at last turned away. The

lights of the town were coming on, and they looked cheerful and warm. He was aware suddenly of the cold, and the need to find somewhere to stay. He was aware of hunger as well, and the startling necessity of finding a place to eat. He rubbed one long hand over the short stubble of his hair, as if uncertain how to go about the next move. For so long, the necessities of life had been provided, an unthought-of part of the smooth order of the days. To have to seek them out was distinctly odd. Walking more slowly now, he set out along the sea-front towards the Harbour, the sound of the sea constant to his left, while overhead a huge grey-backed gull shadowed him, crying mournfully, hanging in the air above like a kite on a string. The young man turned to look at it, before it swept away in a widening arc towards Flamborough. Loneliness descended upon him, as it departed, a loneliness as deep, and physical, as grief.

He found the café at the Harbour end of Queen's Street. It was a small, dingy affair, with tired black and white checked curtains half-shielding its windows, and dust and grime obscuring the rest. But its light shone out welcomingly on to the wet cobbles of the old street, and the tang of vinegar and hot oil drifted into the windy evening. The young man stopped, setting down his suitcase, and studying the front of the building. He did not remember it, and yet it was clearly of considerable age; not something that could have sprung up in the three years of his absence. He felt in his inner pocket for his new wallet, and glanced within, in the dim street light, counting the few bills carefully. He replaced the wallet, and reached into his trouser pocket, withdrawing his small collection of silver. He counted that, too, smiling wryly. Three shillings and sixpence. He replaced it, also carefully, picked up the case, and crossed the road to the café. From the look of it, he wouldn't likely find anything cheaper, anyhow.

Outside the door he stopped, looking up, surprised, and a slow smile spread across his face, lighting his dark, somewhat sombre eyes. Across the doorway an ancient wooden board was fastened to the brick wall, and on it, in peeling painted letters, was written the name of the café. Or rather *a* name of the café, since the window boasted a painted sign of its own, proclaiming, 'Charlie's Chips'. But the name above the door, disused and weathered, said simply, 'Hardacre's'. He reached up slowly, and touched it with the tips of his fingers.

Inside, the atmosphere was warm and steamy, smelling of oilskins and the fishy reek of sea-gear, and the air was thick with tobacco smoke. There were several small square and round tables, mismatched in size and finish, their surfaces marked with cup stains and cigarette burns. All but one were occupied by clusters of men in fishermen's gear, smoking and talking. They all stopped for a brief moment as he entered, and eyes followed him as he walked uncertainly to the small counter at the far end of the room, where a woman in an apron stood by a large brass cash register, totting up a bill. He waited while she finished her transaction, and gradually the conversations recommenced. The young man sensed he was being discussed. He had ventured into one of those establishments whose customers were so regular and unvarying as to comprise virtually a private club.

The woman, square-faced and unsmiling, handed him a stained, hand-printed menu from the limited fare of which he selected cod and chips and a pot of tea. She accepted his order and motioned to a solitary empty table beside the door to the kitchen. The young man sat, sliding his suitcase under the table, and swung open his heavy coat. He did not feel at home enough to take it off. While he waited for his meal he looked around, discreetly, so that the fishermen would not think him rudely curious. The room was shabby, the tiled floor grubby with boot marks. The upper walls were stained darkly yellow with years of smoke. The whole place was permeated with the stench of stale cooking oil. On the walls was a selection of seaside postcards of large-bosomed women and skinny men in preposterous situations, and a few fading framed photographs of the Harbour, the Priory, and the Old Town. Half covered over was an ancient poster, printed in red on deeply yellowed white: A HARDACRE CAFÉ WELCOMES THE FAMILY. Below the lettering was a Victorian romantic watercolour scene of fanciful children on a fanciful, long-ago shore. The young man studied it for a long while, and then turned away.

When the aproned woman brought his order, a grease-sodden portion of fish surrounded by limp barricades of chips on a smeary plate, he interrupted her hasty place-laying by pointing to the poster.

'Begging your pardon, but could you possibly tell me where that came from?' he said. The room stilled again, in response to his public-school tones.

'What, dear?' the woman said, not looking up. She used the word with tired, affectionless boredom.

'The placard. The Hardacre Café placard,' he said, pointing to it once more. She poured his tea for him, splashily, and looked up, vague eyes searching the wall.

'Oh, that. Was always here, best I can recall,' she said. She turned and was already making her way back to the kitchen when he stopped her again.

'Is this a Hardacre café, then?' he said. He was aware of the perversity of the question, in that he knew the answer, and was asking it, anyway, for reasons of his own. The woman stopped and looked queerly at him, perhaps in response to the faint note of displeasure in his voice.

'Happen it were,' she said, 'would it make any difference?'

She was defensive, and he quickly said, gentling his tone with a small smile, 'It might. Is it?'

She shrugged, more defensive and said, 'It were a Hardacre café when we bought.' And then, hedging, 'Mind, that were a while ago. My father ran it then.' She turned and hastened to the kitchen door, leaving the young man alone with his thoughts, and his cod and chips. He began to eat slowly, finding himself startlingly hungry and yet repelled by the quality of the food and the atmosphere of his surroundings. From time to time he glanced at the poster with something like annoyance. On one glance, his eyes met those of a big, weather-beaten man, with straggles of greying sandy hair plastered on his lined forehead, under his navy blue knitted cap. The man, dressed in yellow oilskin trousers and deep-cuffed fisherman's boots, was conspicuous for having but one arm. His left sleeve ended in an amputee's metal hook.

He said, without introduction, 'Now you've done it. Crossed our Mabel, you have. Be a long time before you get a smile out of her again, lad.'

'Since when have you ever got one?' a companion of the fisherman asked, over the pipe he was trying to light.

The young newcomer grinned, an engaging grin that won a responsive smile from the one-armed man in the blue cap. 'Sorry about that; I really meant no offence. Just curious, actually.' He was aware of the quality of his voice sounding distinctly out of place.

'Curiosity killed the cat,' the fisherman said. Then glancing to the kitchen door, from whence the sound of running water and clanging pots indicated Mabel's preoccupation, he said in a lowered voice, 'Aye, but you touched a sore point. Mabel might like to pretend that Hardacre sign's an accident, but we're no fools. Free bit of advertising, that is, and Mabel's not one for passing up anything free.'

'I don't understand,' the young man said, ingenuously.

'No, reckon you wouldn't. Now, you wouldn't know about this, seeing as you don't belong here,' he explained quickly, 'but time was when the name Hardacre over a café door meant something. Trippers used to come over from the West Riding and make for a Hardacre tea-shop first off.'

11

'Why?' asked the young man, finishing the last of his chips.

'You mean you never heard of Hardacre?' the man with the pipe said.

'And how would he?' the blue-hatted fisherman cut in at once. 'His sort wouldn't be eating in Hardacre's in those days. Reckon he's too young, anyhow, don't you? Been a long time since Sam Hardacre's day in the East Riding.' They discussed the young man pleasantly, as if he were not present. 'You'll have heard of Sam Hardacre, though?' the fisherman said then.

The young man nodded, sidestepping the question slightly. 'He ran tea-shops?'

There was a pause. The fisherman leaned back in his chair. 'Lad, in my father's day he didn't just run tea-shops. He pretty much run the East Riding. Mind now, them's bygone days. He was a reeght 'un, old Sam Hardacre. My grandfather knew him, down Grimsby way. My grandfather had a good herring coble and he knew Sam when Sam was just a quayside guttie. That's where Hardacre money come from, you know. Started out selling rollmops, at the race meets. Opened cafés then, like this 'un. Made a lot of money at it. Time went on, he got big, got into hotels, heard he got into railways too, but who knows? Men get big like that, they end up with a finger in every pie. Though I'll say for old Sam, he never changed much. Even when he was living in bluidy great house, down Driffield way, he still would come down to Grimsby and stand around harbour-side, chat to folk, like he always done. Was a good man, Sam Hardacre. Ran good decent places, too, not like this rubbish,' he waved a disdainful hand around the rudely decorated walls, mindful to keep one ear cocked towards the kitchen door and Mabel's domain. 'There was a day families could count on a Hardacre place, everything neat as a pin, clean, fresh. Used to say his wife, old Mary Hardacre, hersel' used to come and check up on all his cafés, and if she

12

found anything out of place, or a speck of dirt anywhere, she'd be down on her knees scrubbin' it up hersel'. Then old Sam would hear and there'd be hell to pay. He was a hard 'un to work for, but straight, straight as a die.

'Mind now, he'd turn in his grave if he could see this place, with his name yet hanging over the door. An' our Mabel pretending she'd not got round to taking it down in forty years. Reckon there's still the odd country soul comes into town is fooled yet, and if there's one penny left to be fooled out of someone, our Mabel will have it.' He laughed, swigging at his tea, but the young man didn't laugh with him.

'A course,' the man with the pipe put in, 'there aren't any real Hardacre cafés left. Old Sam pulled out just after the war, the first one. Went into other things, I suppose. And his son Joe were a different kettle of fish. A different kettle of fish entirely.' The first fisherman nodded sagely in agreement.

'Aye,' he said, 'Joe Hardacre. There was a reeght bastard, if there ever was one. Opened sweatshops all over t' place until his own father had to come and close 'im down. Ran off to America then and got hisself in so much trouble he ended up jumpin' out a window. Reeght funny how life is; two like that in t'one family. Still, it's the way uv things.'

'Aye,' the pipe-smoker laughed. 'Where there's muck there's brass, an' on t'other hand, where there's brass, there's muck.' They both laughed.

The young man did not join in the laughter. He finished his meal solemnly, and laid his knife and fork carefully down, with an orderliness that defied the casual clutter of the table with its ketchup stains and sticky-necked bottles of fruit sauce and vinegar. Before he finished his tea, a process he was dragging out to allow himself a little longer in the sheltered warmth, he turned around in his chair and addressed the two fishermen who had spoken, 'I wonder if you gentlemen could give me some advice?' He was aware of

13

the sideways glances from the other denizens of the café, as if any advice given must first be vetted by the entire company.

'Happen we could,' said the man in the blue cap, 'if it were the sort uv thing we'd know anything about.' He said it with a mixture of reserve and modesty that signalled to the young stranger that he might just be overstepping the bounds.

'Thank you,' he said, carefully. 'There are two things actually. I am needing a place to stay for a while. That's the first.' He paused, judging himself wiser to obtain the first answer before venturing the second query.

'Happen you're at the wrong end uv town,' the fisherman said slowly, tugging at one weather-reddened ear. 'Hotels uv t' sort you'd be wanting are all up t'other end. Mind, there's the Station just up t' road, but I don't reckon you'd go much on't.' He shook his head, and his companion nodded sagely.

'Actually,' the young man said, 'I wasn't thinking in terms of a hotel. Something more permanent. A guest-house, a boarding-house, really.' He paused, and then said quickly, 'Something a little less dear.' There was a silence, as the room took in this admission of financial insecurity, and the blue-capped fisherman appeared to be assessing it, uncertain whether he would choose to believe it.

'Something less dear,' he said at last, to be sure he heard right. The young man nodded and gave one of his bright grins, which on this occasion won no response.

The two fishermen whispered a moment together. 'Reckon Jean Hewitt might have a room. Clean enough there, anyhow.' They were talking, still to each other. A nod passed between them. The first fisherman again addressed the newcomer.

'Place up St Hilda Street, Jean Hewitt's, might do. Food's good, tariff's fair enough. Jean's a good sort, underneath. Mind you, takes a while to get underneath.

Still and all, her bark's worse than her bite. Jean Hewitt might do you. You're sure now, though, you'd not rather a hotel?' he added uncertainly.

'Quite certain,' the young man said, with another smile. 'I'll try Mrs Hewitt right now.'

They nodded, and one said, 'It's number eight. Will I show you how to find it?'

The young stranger shook his head. 'I'll find it,' he said. He rose to his feet, wondering if he'd asked enough questions for one night. He imagined he probably had, but time was pressing. 'And the other thing,' he added. 'I'm looking for work. Do you know of anything going?'

'Work?' they said together. 'You meaning a job?'

'Yes. Work. A job.' He grinned in spite of himself, wondering how they imagined people like himself to live.

'Oh, no, lad. There's nothing uv the kind uv work your sort would want around here. Just the Harbour and the fishing, and the arcades and cafés down this end. Nothing for your sort.'

The young man nodded. He'd have to find that answer on his own, it was clear. 'Thank you anyhow,' he said. 'I'll look around.'

'You won't find anything down this end,' they said again. He smiled, and as the venerable Mabel came, brows lowering, through the door, he reached into his trouser pocket for his three and sixpence, and paid out the one shilling and threepence for his meal. She took it, unsmiling, and rang up the cash register.

'Excuse me,' he said.

'Umm?'

'That placard,' he said.

'Now what about that placard?' she said with strained good nature.

'I want it,' the young man said.

'You *want* the placard now?' she repeated after him.

'Yes. What do you want for it?'

15

There was a moment's confused silence. 'For the placard?' she said. 'What do I want? Look, lad, I don't sell placards. What would I be selling that for?'

'Because I want it. And the sign outside. How much for the pair?' She stood with her rouged face impassive, but for her lowering, red-painted bottom lip. The young man was conscious of the listening ears at the tables all around. He would have to make the next move, for Mabel would no doubt stand there with lowered jaw forever. He reached into his inner jacket pocket and withdrew his wallet, a gesture that aroused a murmur of curiosity from the attentive room. Thinking quickly, with rash impulse, he withdrew a note and extended it, ostentatiously large, to the woman.

'Five pounds!' she exclaimed. 'For that thing?' Her voice rose to a shriek of amazement, and there was a quick muttering about the room.

'A deal then?' he said quickly.

'Sure,' she said, 'if you're as mad as that.' She took the proffered note quickly. 'And here's hoping there's more where you come from.' She laughed disdainfully and waved a hand towards the faded advertisement. 'Take it lad, it's yourn.'

'And the sign,' he pursued, 'the sign as well.'

'Take them both,' she said, laughing to herself as she folded the large note. 'Five pounds for that rubbish,' she muttered again, her voice echoing delight at her bargain and genuine disgust at his foolishness.

'Splendid,' said the young man. He strode across the room, suddenly lithe and athletic, and wrenched the tattered card from the wall. He tucked it under his arm and walked to the door, turning to salute the fishermen with a grin. Then he went out into the wet darkness and, with a sound that was audible within the café itself, he reached strong young arms to the old wooden sign and tore it from its mountings on the wall. Then he tucked the sign, too, under his arm, and strode, laughing, into the windy night.

The moment the door closed behind the young man, the attentions of the room, hitherto discreet and diverse, came to a sudden focus on his empty chair. There was a brief silence, in which eyes wandered from the chair to the one-armed fisherman in the blue cap, who had become, suddenly, an authority.

'Well, now,' said a fat, cheerful man in a thick-knit grey jumper, who had until now been apparently unaware of the whole event. 'What's t' make uv that?'

'Reeght queer, if you ask me,' answered the pipe-smoker. He tapped ash into a cheap metal ashtray and looked to the man in the navy-blue hat.

Mabel intervened. 'Daft,' she said, still showing her disgust. 'Got more money than sense and plain daft with it. Imagine putting out five pounds for rubbish like that.' She sniffed, slipping the note into the bottom tray of the brass register.

'Rubbish or not, you seemed happy enough to sell it,' the man in the blue hat said over his cup of tea. Mabel sniffed, slammed the drawer shut and retired through the battered door to the kitchen. Immediately the conversation in the room brightened and spread to include all aspects of the young stranger, his appearance, his manner, his accent.

'Now what d'ye make uv that,' one said. 'First he wants a rooming house an' a cheap one at that. Then he wants work on t' fish quay. Then he flings fivers about like they're going out uv style.'

'A fool and his money are soon parted,' said the pipe-smoker.

'Aye well. But if you ask me, there's more to it than that. He had a reeght peculiar look about him, that one. Clothes that didn't fit right, and a mouthful of marbles. "*Echtually, Ae need some advice, gentlemen*",' the speaker mimicked. 'I reckon he's a proper spiv, that one. Up t' no good, anyhow.'

'Seemed pleasant enough,' said the blue-hatted fisherman. He tapped the table with his one hand. The artificial one hung down at his side. The disability, the result of a savage encounter with a winch line, had cost him his working life, and he was ashamed of it and strove hard to keep it from showing. He was a thoughtful man, inclined not to judge others harshly, and he didn't like the way the conversation was going.

'Aye,' his pipe-smoking companion said. 'He would be that, wouldn't he. I'll tell you something I noticed. See the cut of his hair, reeght well shaved off, nay but a stubble it were that short. Now I can think uv just about one place where a man gets his hair cut like that.'

'Might be just out of the Forces,' someone put in, but he was countered easily by the pipe-smoker.

'War's been over near enough five years. Them that was gettin' out are all out long since. There was a time I'd have thought the same, mind; he had that look a bit. Mind how it was, in '46, every third lad blinkin' about wide-eyed in a de-mob suit, looking for work. Nay, not now. And I wager he's no professional just bought himself out, either. You can tell them a mile off, all spit and polish even in their civvies. Nay, boys, I know reeght off where *he's* been last year or two.'

'And where would that be?' asked his companion, his eyes on his artificial hand.

'Been inside.'

The fat man at the next table nodded sagely, and around the café there was a general murmur of interested agreement.

'I'd put money on it,' the pipe-smoker said, warming to his theme. 'An' what's more, he's no ordinary bloke got himself in a bit uv trouble wi' the law. Yon's a proper toff, son uv some big family gone bad. Worse kind ye can get,' he added darkly. 'Nay, Mabel,' he said to the sour-faced hostess who had reappeared at her doorway to listen, 'you'd be wise t' give that one short shrift, if he shows face around here again.'

'Bluidy rubbish.'

The pipe-smoker looked up from his discourse, surprised. His companion got clumsily to his feet, his false arm swinging loose. Painstakingly he thrust it through the sleeve of his yellow oilskin jacket that had hung over his chair back, and roughly pulled the jacket on. 'Of all the bluidy presumptious twaddle. You don't none of you know from anything a damn thing about t' lad and ye've well nigh got him tarred an' feathered. As fer Mabel's placard, well I'd pay a tenner myself ti see the whole damned place stripped uv all that rubbish and scrubbed clean. An' you needn't look offended, woman, the place is a damned disgrace. If lad shows up again it'll be his own misfortune, nay yourn. I'm off, anyway. Happen I'd rather talk wi' gulls.' He stalked out into the night, leaving a chastened silence behind.

Once outside he turned on his heel abruptly and made off with a still-angry stride towards St Hilda Street. He walked quickly, cradling his bad arm against his chest as he did when he was in a hurry and, as he expected, he caught sight of the young man with the suitcase before the latter had achieved his destination.

'Aye lad,' he shouted into the wind, 'hold on a moment.' The young man hesitated, looking round, and the old fisherman tried not to let himself read an undercurrent of edginess into the action. He lengthened his stride and caught up with the man with the suitcase at the corner of St Hilda Street.

'Sir?' the other said, politely questioning.

The fisherman was amused by the formality but said only, 'Summat come to mind, soon as you were gone, lad. Job of work needing doing. Mind now, Queen's Street, where we was,' he pointed back into the rainy night.

'Yes,' the young man answered, also peering into the darkness.

'Well, if you go harbourwards three or four shops, and

then across the street, there's another chip shop, newer place, run by West Riding folk, come over last year. Recollect now, their lass, who was always behind the counter, up and got herself married last week and left the place. Know for a fact they'll be needing a hand there, if'n ye'd not mind a bit of fish frying. Mind now, the wages can't be much; not when they're used to having family labour on the cheap.'

He looked doubtful, cocking his head to one side and studying the well-spoken young stranger in the wet street light, still uncertain what he was doing here. The young man's face broke into one of his broad grins and his dark eyes crinkled at the corners.

'I dare say I could fry fish with the best of them,' he said, laughing at some private joke. 'That's capital of you, sir. I can't say how grateful I am.' He glanced across the street at the friendly light of a pub with a ship's wheel motif on the hanging sign above the door. 'Could I stand you a drink, sir?'

The fisherman hesitated and then, catching sight of the old Hardacre sign still under the other's arm, he tapped it lightly and said, 'Nay lad, hang on to yer brass. You've spread enough about for one night.' He turned to go and then stopped and pointed up the road. 'Yon's Mrs Hewitt, number eight,' he said, indicating a tall, narrow-fronted building with a tiny garden edged by a low brick wall. 'You can tell her Mick Raddley sent you, fer what it's worth.' He turned and lumbered off, his gait uneven with the bad arm slung across his chest and his head bent towards the sea wind.

Mrs Hewitt proved to be a tall, thin body whose air of cultured haughtiness appeared a professional stance. Like the woven mat that said 'Welcome' on her scrubbed doorstep and the white lace half-curtains on her windows, it was part of the role.

'Yes?' she said, narrowing the vowel delicately. 'Can I help you?'

'I was looking for a room,' he said, adding quickly, 'Mr Raddley suggested I try here.'

'Mr Raddley?'

'Mick Raddley. He said I should say . . .'

'Indeed.' She eyed him as frostily as ever, but something in her voice had softened. 'I'm very much afraid my best rooms are all taken. I'm much in demand, you know. However, we might be able to find you a small accommodation. For a week. While we get to know each other,' she added darkly. 'Then we shall reassess.'

'A week would do splendidly,' he assured her rapidly, lifting his suitcase as she stepped backwards into the hallway to let him in. He was still carrying the sign, and tried now to conceal it against the sleeve of his greatcoat, knowing it would be difficult to explain.

She led him up two flights of narrow dark stairs, hung at fiercely regular intervals with small sentimental seaside prints. At the second landing she stepped towards the back of the house and opened a white panelled door. The room within, shabby in the dull grey of an overhead light, looked out on to a courtyard which revealed itself now only as a rectangle of black night bordered by thin pink curtains. She crossed to the window, tugged the curtains closed and indicated the bed, wardrobe, washbasin and small easy chair with a wave of one thin, beringed hand. On the floor an ancient square of carpet in mock-Persian design covered the centre of the room, revealing darkly-varnished floorboards at the perimeters. A small electric fire sat on the disused tiled hearth, its cord connected to a solid metal meter.

'Breakfast at seven, tea at five-thirty; I'll need your ration book, of course; tariff, five pounds per week. In advance.'

He was standing yet, looking bravely about the dismal room, trying to generate a homely warmth by force of will.

'In advance, Mr . . .'

'Yes, of course,' he said, hastily reaching for his wallet.

He withdrew a second fiver. One remained within the leather billfold. He extended it to Mrs Hewitt, and realized she was extending her hand vertically, as if to shake his. Quickly he transferred the money to his left and shook her hand with his right. Her fingers were dry and cold.

She smiled very slightly and said, 'Jean Hewitt, Mr . . .'

He looked at her blankly, as one searching for what to say. He cradled the old wooden sign closer and then, speaking hesitantly, he said, 'Hardacre. Sam Hardacre.'

She paused, her cold hand still in his, and bent her head back slightly. 'Mr Hardacre?' she said. 'Sam Hardacre?'

'Yes,' he said quickly, with more assurance. 'Sam Hardacre.'

'Interesting,' she said. 'That's a well-known name in these parts, you know.'

'Yes,' he said, with a sudden nervous grin, 'so I've been told.'

CHAPTER
TWO

The bright red MG TC roadster roared down the narrow Driffield road, scattering dry leaves in the November wind. Despite the month, the driver, a woman in a red headscarf that exactly matched the livery of her motor car, had lowered the hood and the wind whipped up strands of curling dark hair from beneath the scarf, blowing them forward over her face. She was a pretty woman in her late forties, her creamy French complexion only slightly marked by delicate and expressive lines of age. Her brow was furrowed in thought, or perhaps concentration, as the little car nipped happily round the stone-walled curves. At the big black iron gates of a great country house, the car skidded into a turn and roared off up the gravel drive. Madelene Bisset Hardacre was coming to tea.

Madelene jammed her foot down impatiently. The drive was always longer than one thought, winding at least a half-mile through tall elms and then a beech wood before one even glimpsed the house at all. It was scenic, and such driveways no doubt added to the dramatic impact of the mansion when at last it was sighted, but it was a tremendous nuisance if one was in a hurry. Madelene was always in a hurry. Today she was even more in a hurry than usual. The drive turned and dipped and Madelene, cornering hard, was confronted with a sudden splash of glorious moving colour in the centre of the roadway. She hit her brakes, skidding on gravel, and felt the rear wheels break free and come around. More angry than frightened she swung the wheel into the skid, over-corrected, swung the other way and slid, almost sedately, into the ditch.

For a moment she sat quite still, her hands on the wheel.

Then she carefully patted her face, adjusted her clothing, checked that her feeling of being physically unharmed was not an illusion. After another moment she was convinced that the only damage sustained was a small ladder in her left stocking, caused by the heel of her right shoe. She switched off the ignition and turned to open her door, awkwardly heavy since the roadster was tilted at a definite angle to the left. As she turned she came face to face with a large, scaly, beady-eyed head, and she screamed.

The head jerked back like a frightened chicken's.

'Zut,' said Madelene, pursing her lips and reverting to Gallic temper as always in times of stress. She was staring eyeball to eyeball with a peacock. Not just any peacock but the peacock responsible for her being in a gravelly ditch when she should be arriving to tea. Madelene abandoned the door and scrambled up on to the leather seat and over the side. She swung a vicious kick of three-inch heels at the bird, which staggered away with a noise like crackling brushwood as it dragged its heavy folded tail across the road.

'Stupid bird.' She thought of Harry, who treasured the ungainly glorious thing, and directed a mental kick at his posterior as well. 'Stupid Harry's stupid bird.' She walked around the car inspecting the damage while her temper boiled. It was minimal, but the car was well grounded. Noel would have to come with the tractor and haul it out. Meanwhile she was later than ever and faced with the prospect of a further quarter-mile walk in her tottering heels to the house. Madelene sat gingerly on the bright red right front wing as she pondered what to do.

It was not unlikely that, if she simply waited, someone would come along. The driveway, being the entrance to a working, if not precisely thriving estate, as well as a family home, must see its share of farm workers, tradesmen and sociable neighbours in an afternoon. If one could simply be counted on to arrive promptly. Madelene adjusted her red headscarf and crossed her legs, glancing impatiently at the gold wristwatch Harry had given her for their 'anniversary'. Her eyes lingered, savouring its precise detail and graceful design. The pity of having a lover was that one could never show off one's little trophies as a married woman could. She had told the ladies of her staff that it was the gift of a particularly grateful wealthy customer. Which of course only increased their pity for her and fuelled their efforts, as perennial as they were useless, to find the widowed Madelene a husband. Madelene had been a widow since the Great War. Considering her still striking attractiveness, that time-lapse alone should indicate that Madelene was making her own arrangements. But the ladies of Driffield were not a discerning lot. Madelene sighed, thinking of them with a faint amused pity of her own.

She knew they would never quite forgive her her connections, albeit by marriage alone, to the big house at the end of this gravelled drive. It was called after the family whose name Madelene Bisset had carried since 1916, 'Hardacres'. Not even Hardacre Hall, but simply the family name itself, aggressive and possessive, with which it had been rechristened on the exact day in the autumn of 1889 when it had been bought from the hereditary owners by the man known throughout the North as 'the Herring King'.

The ladies who patronized Madelene's dress shop, and patronized Madelene, called it nothing but the original name, 'Watton Manor', as a quiet way of keeping Madelene firmly in her place. She shrugged, wrapping her neat little fitted jacket tighter against a gust of leaf-swirling wind. Who knows, perhaps they were right. Perhaps they did not trust the Hardacres to establish the sort of dynastic firmness that is needed by those who are to be relied upon to make changes on the local map. Maps weren't drawn often after all, and in the context of a centuries-old manor house, what were the trifling years from 1889 to 1950? Who was to say the Hardacres would not prove a mere flash in the pan, retreating with barely sixty years' hold to leave the place once more in the hands of more traditional wealth. As things looked just now, such a possibility was not at all unlikely.

It saddened her, deeply. Not for herself – Madelene, even after all these years, was French to the core and English tradition meant nothing to her – but for Harry. Harry loved the place passionately and lived now in genteel poverty to maintain it, and yet Harry must know that if the icy grip of tightening financial straits did not get him then time itself undoubtedly would. For though Harry Hardacre had bodily heirs, and more than one, he had no spiritual heir. No one in the family regarded the old place as anything other than bricks and mortar, out of date and increasingly comfortless. Harry alone held within him the warm living soul of Hardacres and knew it would be extinguished on the day he died.

Madelene stared moodily at the dust-marked toe of her pale-beige calf shoe, feeling morose and sad for Harry to such a degree that she had almost forgotten her hurry and the reason for it. For the first time since yesterday, when Terry had telephoned, she had briefly forgotten young Sam.

The chastening thought of him flooded back, rekindling her haste. She jumped up and brushed down her swirlingly feminine beige New Look skirt. She would have to walk. She took two determined steps with the peevish stride of one who never ordinarily walks further than from the doorstep to the motor car at the kerb, when a distant sound broke through that of the rustling of leaves and squawking of peafowl; a sharp patter of hoofbeats down the gravel drive.

'Oh, thank God,' Madelene said, turning to the sound, knowing she was about to be rescued.

The horse, a tall bay with what Madelene, whose tastes ran to fast motor cars and pretty dresses rather than horses, would call 'black trim', cantered around the bend where Madelene had met the peacock. The rider, a woman in

26

precisely tailored hacking gear, reined in, and the horse came to a quick well-disciplined halt and stood puffing steamy breath into the frosty air. The horsewoman was Harry Hardacre's daughter Vanessa, a large-boned plain woman devoid of make-up, her shoulder-length greying brown hair worn straight and usually, as now, tied back tightly beneath a riding hat. She looked puzzled, and her eyes moved slowly from Madelene in her beige suit and high-heeled pumps to the red MG in the ditch and back to Madelene. She blinked once, in careful assessment.

'Having a spot of bother, old girl?' she said.

'I am in this stupid ditch because of your father's idiotic bird, and I am fifteen minutes late already, and it is more than a spot of bother,' Madelene declared.

'Does it still go?' Vanessa said warily, looking down at the immobile car. She had the same lack of interest in motors as Madelene had in horses.

'Whether it goes or not is not the point. I'll need Noel and the tractor to get it out. And I must see your father at once.' Vanessa blinked again. Madelene waited for Vanessa to suggest she ride off for help, but Vanessa was still engrossed in the grounded MG. She appeared to be considering the possibility of having to shoot it.

'Vanessa, I must get to the house. Could you possibly . . . ?'

'Give you a ride behind? Oh, I don't know, Gold Flake is not very keen on doubles. Liable to toss us both,' she added cheerfully. She returned her mournful gaze to the car.

Madelene shook her head. For all the years she had known Harry's daughter, she had found it impossible to make any point clear to her. Vanessa lived in a world of horses and tack and mucking out and bedding down and seemed to comprehend nothing else. At times Madelene had been most grateful for her obtuseness; at forty-four Vanessa, though a married woman and even a mother, had never imagined anything between Madelene and her father but familial loyalty.

27

'I have absolutely no desire to ride on that animal,' Madelene said. 'If you would be so kind as to ride up to the house and find Harry with the motor . . . ?'

'What a good idea,' Vanessa said brightly. 'Back in a jiff. Toodle-oo old thing.' She cantered off on her mission of mercy and Madelene sat down again on the wing of her MG. She watched the disappearing horsewoman and sighed. Thank God for Rodney, she thought, blessing Vanessa's husband, a man every bit as equinely inclined as Vanessa herself. Surely no one else in all of Yorkshire, or England, or the world, would have married the silly fool.

Fortunately for Madelene, waiting less than patiently amidst the beech wood, Noel Hardacre, Vanessa's elder brother, was at that moment clattering down the drive from the stable square behind the house on his tractor. He met his sister just at the point where the woods gave way to a long, dramatic sweep of lawn that drew the eye unerringly to the vast, square red-brick mansion at the crest of the hill. Vanessa had no eye for beauty and did not even glance at the majestic display of carefully managed greenery and softly ageing brick and stone. She had lived her entire life at Hardacres, apart from her school years of course, and it was utterly mundane to her. It existed for herself, and for Rodney, only as a spacious background for their equine obsession. There were rooms in the big house that she had not bothered to enter for years.

She reined in Gold Flake to a sharp trot and hailed her brother. Noel tipped his head, indicating that he had heard, was annoyed at being asked to listen and was not stopping, anyhow.

'Whoa, there,' Vanessa shouted to both her brother and the horse. She stopped directly in his path and, disgruntled, he stopped as well. She had not forgotten Madelene's abandonment, but a new thought struck her that was infinitely more important. She saw at once that Noel had the plough attached to the tractor, fierce blades swung up clear of the road. 'Where are you going with that?' she asked suspiciously, eyeing it.

'Bottom field,' he said. Noel, despite his gentle, scholarly father, and his public-school upbringing, had lived all his life as a Yorkshire farmer, seemingly only happy when physically engrossed in the tough struggle to make the once-lavish estate pay for itself. He worked with his hands every day of his life, and sought out the company of others who did so as well. As he aged, alone in touchy bachelor eccentricity, his accent coarsened, his dress grew shabbier, and even his face seemed to take on rough lines of its own. A year ago he had abruptly moved his uninspired belongings right out of the mansion house that he would most likely inherit and installed himself in a farm labourer's cottage on his own estate. It was just one more of his extraordinary and anti-social ways and at the time hardly caused a ripple of surprise among those who knew him well. Noel was beginning to be regarded by all around as 'a reeght queer 'un'. Vanessa was unimpressed either by his eccentricity or his renowned temper.

'And what, may I ask, do you intend to do with it in the bottom field?'

Noel screwed up his lean face in a slow amused grin. 'Aye well,' he said, still grinning, 'thought this tractor had the makings of a good point-to-pointer. Thought I'd set her at that big hedge Rodney's always putting horses over, and see if I can get 'er to jump.'

'Noel,' Vanessa spluttered, her face reddening. 'Noel, that is very unfunny. You know very well the Hunt uses that field every meet. What are you up to?'

'The Hunt *did* use it. Tomorrow she'll be my winter wheat.'

'Winter wheat?' Vanessa exclaimed. 'Since when do we grow winter wheat?'

'Since tomorrow. Come on now, girl, move that walking glue factory. Some of us have work to do.'

'Noel, you will not plough up our bottom field. Rodney

won't allow it. I won't allow it. I'll see Father. I'll see Father right now.' She turned the horse around in a dancing circle, muttering, 'Winter wheat in the bottom field. I've never heard the like.'

'Father'll allow it, all right,' Noel shouted over the continuing roar of his tractor engine. 'Father wants the bills paid.'

'Ridiculous,' Vanessa stormed, and then as Noel rumbled off she remembered Madelene. She galloped after Noel in triumph. 'Besides, you can't plough just now anyhow.'

'Can an' bluidy shall.'

'No.' Vanessa cut ahead of him again and he slammed his brake on and lost his temper.

'Get that bluidy useless beast out of my way or I'll run it down.'

'You can't plough today because you've got to haul a car out of a ditch,' Vanessa gloated.

'What bloomin' car? What ditch?'

'Down there,' Vanessa pointed an imperious finger. 'Madelene's in the ditch.' She paused. 'She's not very pleased.'

Noel stared down the silent, curving driveway. 'In the *ditch*? How the hell . . . ?'

'I think she was trying to miss a peacock,' said Vanessa in a small voice.

Noel stared. Then he slammed his fist on to the steering wheel of the tractor and shouted, 'Bloody damn women. Bloody damn animals. Horses, peacocks. Ye'd think I was running a bloody zoo.' He thrust the idling machine into gear and, still cursing, clattered off down the long drive. Vanessa gave a smug smile of satisfaction at his enforced detour, and whirled Gold Flake about and galloped off to her father and the rescue of the bottom field.

Harry Hardacre, Vanessa's father and bemusedly unassuming patriarch of the Hardacre family, was at that moment enjoying the special pleasures of a lovely autumn day from the quiet shelter of his favourite room: the oak-panelled, book-lined library. It was a room that, throughout his father's tenure of the house, had remained dustily abandoned, just as it had for the previous decades under the domain of the undoubtedly better-bred, but hardly better-read Sir John Wildebore. But when Harry inherited Hardacres the library became its heart. From boyhood, books had been his delight; and now, as old age approached, they were his refuge.

Harry rose from his chair by the fire and stretched awkwardly, shaking his bad leg, which stiffened always as he sat, and walked with a pronounced limp to the tall window that reached from knee level to near the twelve-foot ceiling. Watery thin sunlight came through, distorted by the natural deformities of the old glass, showing up dusty streaks on the interior of the pane. Harry looked at the streaks ruefully; they were a reproach, but one to which he was powerless to respond. The two ageing village ladies who, with Cook, now comprised the sum total of Hardacre household staff, could hardly be criticized for missing a window. They were, however, Harry would readily admit, precisely all he could afford. His only concern was that in the near future it was not impossible that one of them, too, might have to go. He put the thought from his mind, not wishing to dwell either on it, or its larger implications.

He let his eyes stray over the gardens again, his left hand gently caressing the broad depth of wall in the window alcove, feeling comforted by its ancient luxurious solidity. He glanced up to the high, beautifully moulded ceiling, finding it impossible to regret its graceful height, even though the house was proving daily more difficult to heat. He put that thought too, aside, and returned his eyes to the lawns, marvelling, as he always did, at how quickly they had recovered from their wartime devastation, when patriotic duty had obliged him to plough them up for corn. He remembered that day as if it were yesterday, himself on the tractor and Hetty and Madelene watching from the terrace. The thought of Hetty stirred him. He drew out his watch, wondering if he should wake her for tea or let her sleep. He decided on the latter. If he woke her, she would make a brave effort and come down to join them, but by dinner time she would be exhausted. Better those spare few hours in the evening, when they could laugh and talk over their meal and pretend everything was yet as it once was.

Hetty, or rather Hetty's failing health, was the one true cloud on Harry's horizon. All other concerns he could, with a practised talent, shove gently aside, smooth over with happier thoughts. But his wife's slow descent into invalidity was always with him, like the dull bone ache of his crippled leg. In the depths of his heart Harry Hardacre carried his wife's pain as if it were his own.

He could not remember even now when it had begun, at what point Hetty's general listlessness, her numerous unexplained small miseries, had crystallized into real ill-health. At times it seemed as if Hetty had always been ill, right from the beginning of their marriage. He could not honestly recall a day since he met her, when first she came to Hardacres as Nanny to his so recently orphaned children, when Hetty had displayed true bodily well-being. It was certainly true that within a year or two of their wedding day Hetty's complaints, her back, her 'female problems', her headaches, her nerves, had resulted in a retreat to separate beds. A less honest man than Harry Hardacre might have used that early estrangement as just cause for the long-standing affair with Madelene, as partial cause it certainly was. But Harry knew he would have loved Madelene regardless; indeed Hetty's health had been instead the one firm tie that had brought him hastening back from Madelene's bed again and again, on the bowed wings of guilt. He often wondered, had Hetty been tough and strong, as tough and strong as Madelene, would he have left her and Hardacres and all that was precious to him for the sake of love?

No matter now, he thought. Age had stilled his blood, as Yeats would have it, and now, ironically, he found companionship with both his women as gentle and loving as if each were his wife. Harry Hardacre, at seventy-two, was in many ways a more contented man than ever before in his life. Unlike poor Hetty, he had his health. Indeed his health was better than in his boyhood, when his childhood in poverty had taken its toll, and better than in young adulthood, when the Boer War wounds and the heart-wound of losing Judith had made him frail before his years. Now, like a thin old tree that had weathered much, he had grown surprisingly supple and resilient, able to take long walks over his estate with the aid of his stick, and to indulge in long nights of study alone into the small hours. He hardly needed to sleep at all any more, and was delighted with the spare time his wakeful nights allowed him. A few months ago he had commenced writing a book about his childhood with his itinerant parents and his long-dead brother Joe, just for the pleasure of freezing the past in words.

He had managed, over the years since his father's death, to keep both the family and the estate together, no mean feat, and even with finances a constant strain and his mixed bag of Hardacre offspring at odds he felt, just looking over the green lawns on a November afternoon, a distinct thrill of success.

Still, the need for money was a fact that would not go away, no matter how often he sidestepped it, as clear a fact as the undeniable descent of the Hardacre fortunes since the death of Sam Hardacre, the Herring King. How odd, Harry thought, smiling to himself, his hand still caressing the security of the two-foot-thick wall, that even living in a place like this one could need to worry about money. When he was a child, moving with his parents from rented room to rented room, or following the herring fleet in the old pony cart, sleeping nights in the countryside under the tarpaulin, he had thought that any human being who actually lived in a house at all was rich as Midas. Even a cowman's cottage, with thatched roof and crumbling chimney stack, was a palace in his boyhood's eye. Now here he was, Harry Hardacre, living in a brick Tudor mansion and he was one thing his father in all his life had never been: he was in debt.

Harry sighed and decided to use one of the few rich man's prerogatives left to him. He went to the old-fashioned velvet bell-pull by the fireplace and rang for tea. Even if it was only Mrs Bennett up from Driffield for the afternoon, she would bring a silver tray laden with the Crown Derby service, and when Madelene arrived they would sit before the fire and talk about the past and the future and the family as if nothing ever would change.

Thinking of Madelene, he glanced again at his watch, saw that she was even later than usual, and set to wondering again what the urgent matter was that she had refused to discuss in her telephone call earlier in the day. It must truly be urgent, too, or else she would not have come to the house at all. Usually they met in Driffield, where she kept her shop, or he went to her in her little cottage on the fringe of the Hardacre estate. As Hetty failed, Madelene withdrew. She had a great sense of justice and would not intrude upon a fallen opponent.

Harry strolled across to his desk, piled high with papers as always, and found his eye unerringly making for the stack of unpaid bills. He shuffled them wryly and then let them fall, with a soft sighing, to the dusty leather surface. Mentally he made another appointment with the bank manager, and mentally he broke it. The trouble with you Hardacres, the bank manager, a blunt man, had said, is you're all too good at spending money. And the only one of you any damn use at making it was old Sam. Harry wasn't offended. It was precisely the truth, a truth he had recognized long ago. Therein lay the source of the Hardacre dilemma. Sam Hardacre had begun his working life gutting herring on the Yorkshire fish quays. With wit and ingenuity and a tiny touch of sheer luck, he had moved from gutting fish to selling cooked herring at the racetracks, to owning cafés, and then owning almost every growing business in sight: hotels, railways, cotton mills. He was a young man in a country full of young, untrammelled industry – Britain in the 1880s, a country with fortunes to be made, crying out to be made. And Sam had all it took to make one. And then, Harry thought with a smile, he spawned a family as useless in that respect, as Sam himself was talented. Except for Joe, of course, Harry corrected a little painfully. His brother Joe could make money. Whatever his faults, that wasn't one of them. But Joe had got caught up in a different kind of country, a different kind of business, the frenetic world of paper money of the New York Stock Exchange. Joe got caught up and carried away, spiralling up and up to the vertiginous heights from which, with so many others, he came crashing down on a day in 1929. Joe Hardacre died in a bloody mess on a New York pavement, an ending that, to this day, his brother Harry found impossible to think about.

But Joe aside, there wasn't a one of them fit to stand in Sam Hardacre's shoes. Nor was there, ironically, room any longer in the Britain of 1950 for a man to step the length of Sam Hardacre's stride. From boyhood, Harry had known that he himself would never be his father's heir. Even when his inheritance was only a fought-for stance on the fish quays, Harry knew that. Joe was his father's son: tough, independent, fierce if necessary, though Joe, God help him, had always lacked old Sam's inherent decency. But Harry was his mother's child, a gentle, contemplative person who rose to challenges of the intellect, not the body. He was no coward and no weakling, having distinguished himself in his brief military career. But he was no fighter either, and Sam's world had been a fighter's world. Harry had sheltered serenely in the backwater of the role of second son until, of course, Joe's suicide thrust him unwillingly to the fore. Since that day, he had done the only thing he could do; he had conserved. But conservation, he was beginning to discover, was a fool's paradise, as his son Noel was always quick to point out. Harry did not mind that life, and changing fortunes made it impossible to advance. He had no wish to advance. What he did wryly resent was that there was no way, in the tumultuous, inflationary world of post-war Britain, simply to stand still. Death duties, rising taxation, rates, fuel costs and wages all chipped away at his fortune. Harry was left like a seaside child with his sand-castle under siege by the tide.

Harry thought it distinctly odd, if not downright unfair, that none of all the family had inherited the financial genius of his father, but it appeared none had. Of the original family, there was only himself and his younger sister Jane left, of course. Jane had done her best, actually, Harry thought with a smile, at least in the terms that their Edwardian coming of age had allowed. Jane had married money; old money, too, and a title, becoming the wife of the heir to the Macgregor of Strathconon. But Jane's husband Ian had died at sea in the First War; Peter, the son of her brief marriage, died in the air in the Second. The title and Estate had passed to distant cousins, and though Jane was well provided for, and even maintained a house in Strathconon yet, the Hardacre connections with Scottish wealth were more or less severed. In fact, two wars had dealt harshly with all the family, so much so that they had become a microcosm of the nation itself, which had by the end of the first half of the century lost so much of its wealth, territory and human potential, to violent history.

In fact, Harry thought, warming to the premise, it was quite possible that the wars, between them, really offered the answer to the decline of his family. What might have happened had Jane's son Peter lived? Or if Joe's son,

36

Arnold, had survived the 1914–18 conflict and taken his young French wife on into his father's business world instead of leaving her behind, a widow at seventeen? Harry scratched his head ruefully, recalling the long-ago entrance of the lovely black-clad young Frenchwoman into his household and his life. It would have made his own life, and Hetty's, very different, no doubt. Harry was sure the key lay with Arnold, for Joe's two daughters, Maud and Emily, had taken their own ways in life, and neither way had led to real money. Emily had married the detective Philip Barton and had led, until this year, a solid middle-class existence as he rose through the ranks of the London police; until, that was, Barton had taken this mad idea of owning a pub and had moved his protesting family, lock, stock and London accents, to The Rose at Kilham. Maud's marriage had at first promised even less financially than Emily's, when she had wed the father of her illegitimate daughter a year after the young lady's birth. Albert Chandler was then a hard-working, hard-up trumpet player, with as uncertain a future as possible. That had not stopped the artistic and romantic Maud, and for once the Hardacre luck held. Albert was in Hollywood now, with Maud and their daughter Janet, and though none of his film compositions had quite touched the heights of 'Theme for a Lonely Woman', there was hardly a major film made these days that didn't find his name on the credits somewhere. But that was nothing compared to his daughter, of whom he was, in his letters, understandably proud. Janet Chandler was exactly twenty-four, by Harry's information (although by Hollywood's she was nineteen for the third year running) and in her latest film, *Destiny's Daughter*, her name was above the title. The film had amused Harry no end; Sam's great-grand-daughter, with platinum hair and glowing lips, played a resistance heroine in wartime France, the poor child of a Breton fisherman. Still, Janet Chandler's almost unreal wealth would be of little use to Hardacres. It was a place she had last seen twenty-two years ago at the age of two, when she had been singularly unimpressed.

No, Joe's daughters would not provide the Hardacre heir nor, most certainly, would his own. Vanessa was the chief sinner his bank manager had in mind. She had been shovelling Hardacre money down equine gullets for the past ten years, with the able help of Rodney, her husband. The Gray contingent came down heavily on the debit side of the book.

And then there was Noel. Noel was the true enigma of the family. He had energy, toughness, an unimaginable capacity for hard work, untrammelled by the slightest trace of, say, Maud's romanticism, Harry's own conservatism, Vanessa's dim county pretensions, or the slightest touch of sentiment at all. Far from having to cry out for practicality, as Harry for ever was obliged to with Vanessa, with Noel he had to take constant blocking action or else Noel's ruthless practicality would have wiped every trace of dignity and beauty from the face of both house and land. Harry personally felt that Noel was never happier than during the war, when the national emergency enabled him to take progressive and destructive steps that peacetime would never allow. It was then, tearing out the centuries-old yew hedge, sowing the grand sweep of lawns in corn, turning Mary Hardacre's treasured grape arbours into impromptu chicken runs, that Noel had excelled. Hardacres to Noel was not a treasure but an adversary: he did not husband it, but raped it at every chance. Only Harry, hemmed in by debts, stood between Hardacres and Noel's full brutal intent. And yet Noel, and Noel alone, kept it running and made it grudgingly, and only just, pay. Even were Noel not his son, Harry knew he would never give in to the terrible temptation to send him packing. Hardacres needed Noel as it needed no one else, and like a battered wife it must cling to him to the end.

And yet Noel, Hardacres' grudging saviour, had brought

about the one disaster that would inevitably, Harry was sure, lead to its destruction. For, six months ago, Harry had made the first, only, financial coup of his life; a stroke of his father's wily genius descending in solitary splendour on his modest second son, as effective as it was uncharacteristic. And Noel, God damn his feisty temper, had in one moment tossed it away and, with it, their financial salvation.

Hardacres was a unique house. It stood in Yorkshire where great houses were built of stone and it had, for reasons lost in Tudor antiquity, been built in red brick. There wasn't another like it in the county. Artistically, that was no great loss; it was not and never had been a pretty house. It was square, massive, flat-roofed, graceless. Windows trimmed in sandstone were set in regimented orderly rows, like fussy buttons on a spinster's frock. The roof was festooned in chimney pots and circled by an illogical sandstone balustrade. It stood on an artificially enhanced small natural rise, like a big square brooding hen. But it had stood there for hundreds of years, while history rolled serenely by and Yorkshire winds and rain had weathered it to a soft colour impossible for man alone to create, and old trees had grown around it and fallen and regrown. It was as impossible to re-create, once destroyed, as an aged oak tree, and inspired the same, mortal awe. And in the late summer of 1949 Harry Hardacre quietly let it be known that he intended to tear it down.

Anyone who even remotely knew Harry would instantly take this announced intention for the bald lie that it was. But the officials of the National Trust didn't know Harry from Adam. They did know he was the son of a Yorkshire herring gutter and drew their own, ready conclusions about New Money. Whereupon they promptly marched up to Hardacres (alias Watton Manor by Great Driffield) and confronted the Philistine in his den. Wherein Harry Hardacre gave the sole theatrical performance of his life, a performance of such stunning veracity that the representatives of the Trust genuinely believed they were facing a heartless heathen who would shortly reduce the place to a massive heap of used brick and promptly build a bungalow on top. They argued; Harry pleaded poverty. They withdrew. Upon their return they made Harry an offer; the Trust would take over and maintain the property, allowing him and his immediate family the use of the West Wing in perpetuity. In return, Harry would stay execution. Harry dithered, hemmed and hawed and at last, graciously, over a glass of madeira, allowed himself to be thrown in the briar patch. It was a master work of which his father would have been justly proud.

And then Noel bought his Nissen hut. It was, in its way, the ultimate Noel purchase. He got it for next to nothing, at a military surplus sale at the nearby and now disused wartime aerodrome of Hutton Granswick. Not only that, but he managed to persuade a fellow purchaser to load the dismantled structure on to his own newly purchased army lorry and cart it to Hardacres, all for the price of a couple of pints. Proudly Noel returned homeward in his pre-war Vauxhall, tailing the lorry like a happy sheepdog. The whole procession arrived at Hardacres almost simultaneously with a clutch of National Trust officials and solicitors all about to attend the final meeting with Harry Hardacre, at which all necessary papers regarding the transfer of title deeds would be signed.

Unbelieving, they gathered in a wide-eyed pin-striped circle as Noel unloaded his treasure directly in front of the house. To be fair to Noel, he did not actually intend to keep it there; it was destined for the back of the stable-yard where it would become an instantaneous feed store, and the bargain of the year at that. But he was also genuinely very proud of it. He had saved a lot of money and got himself a tidy little much-needed feed store. He was fond of it. Noel was like that; he took fancies to things, and had favourites among his tools, his vehicles, his various farm structures. It was his pet, and now it was surrounded by a circle of citified dandies poking fingers at it and maligning it with well-bred narrow-vowelled tongues. It was late, he was tired and, deep in his heart, the sight of his father surrounded by the mockers of his new treasure was a little too much. Noel lost his rag.

Noel's temper was legendary through the pubs and auction rings and all farm gatherings of the North. He had thrown erstwhile companions through windows in his younger days, and was still known to fly into a towering rage at market if a favoured beast failed to make its price. Now Harry's little cluster of Trust members and solicitors got their first view of it. Noel raged, told them to get their hands off his property and their feet off it as well. He was huffily told the property was imminently theirs and while things were being got off it, he could start with his prefabricated abomination. Whereupon Noel announced the deal was off, Harry intervened in desperation, Noel threatened physical violence and a solicitor offered to telephone the local constabulary. Noel said he needn't bother since they were all just leaving anyhow, weren't they. An unfortunate Trust member suggested it might be wise if they withdrew for consideration, taking their documents with them. Whether it was a genuine move or a threat Harry never knew. Noel took it as a threat, which toppled what was left of his limited restraint. He suggested that the documents be rolled up tight and stored by the Trust member in an unconventional place. The delegation withdrew, quietly and for good.

Harry was left alone in the placid spring sunshine watching Noel construct his Nissen hut with delighted relish and counting the ultimate cost of that extravagant afternoon as the shadows of the great beech trees crept inexorably closer and evening descended on his great brick house. One day, he knew, that battered RAF pre-fab would prove to be the most expensive Nissen hut in the world.

Oddly, he forgave Noel at once. Something in his mindless attachment to his tin treasure reminded Harry of himself, clinging as desperately to three floors and forty rooms of ageing brick. They would go down together, his son and he, Hardacres both, in their separate ways. And unless the most unlikely occurred and his bachelor son decided at this late date, and nearing fifty, to wed, their going down would be the end of it. There was no one left beyond them to carry the Hardacre name. Except of course Sam and Terry, but their brand of bachelorhood was, unlike Noel's, no casual accident. And more even than Noel's, theirs was for keeps. Which as far as the family was concerned was more of a loss, Harry knew, than Noel. For they, Sam and Terry Bisset Hardacre, twin sons of Madelene and Arnold's fleeting wartime marriage, had always in his mind been the future. They alone carried the Hardacre name into the present generation. They alone, grandsons of his determined brother Joe, had within them the old verve and inventiveness and reckless courage that the rest of the family had lost. They were Sam's heirs in this world if anyone was and they, lively, bright, social, extroverted troublemakers throughout their youth had, in early manhood turned their backs on the world entirely. The Hardacre twins, famed through school for audacious pranks, through their army careers for outlandish devilment and no small degree of high living, the charmers of the family and its favourite rogues had, at the age of thirty, followed their mother's Catholic faith to its ultimate conclusion. Side by side, as they had done everything throughout their twinned lives, they entered the Benedictine Abbey of Ampleforth, and left all worldly inheritance behind. It was a turnabout that was, to this day, beyond Harry's comprehension.

Harry had accompanied Madelene to Ampleforth on that day. Hetty had refused to attend, not because of any resentment of Madelene but because the occasion was

Roman Catholic and Hetty's deep, wary distrust of Rome was the one remnant of her Yorkshire country background she could never shake. Madelene had wept, in a mixture of pride that her sons had given themselves to the Church, and sorrow over the lost hopes of grandchildren, and Harry, watching, said goodbye to Sam Hardacre's brief dream of dynasty. It was over. Two wars and half a century later the family of the Herring King was nearing its end.

A soft gravelly sound of horse's hoofs outside the window caused Harry to raise his head from his paper-strewn desk. Vanessa rode by the window at a brisk determined trot and a moment later he heard her author-itative 'Whoa, up,' followed rapidly by the clatter of the big outer front door and the solid click of riding boots on the tiled entrance way.

'Father?' she was shouting, even as she strode down the hallway, colliding in the library doorway with Mrs Bennett who had come in answer to his bell. Mrs Bennett attempt-ed to duck and scuttle rabbit-like away, as she always did when confronted by Vanessa of whom, for no logical reason, she was afraid.

'Just tea Mrs Bennett, please, when Mrs Hardacre arrives.'

'I can't possibly stay, Father,' Vanessa interrupted, un-aware that she hadn't been invited.

'For two, then, Mrs Bennett,' Harry said, with relief.

'Father, the most outrageous thing has occurred,' Vanessa continued, still panting from her ride, and her now full-blown indignation. 'The most unbelievable, out-rageous thing.'

'And what would that be?' Harry asked mildly, knowing it could be anything from a social gaff by some member of the Hunt, to another world war. Vanessa lacked propor-tion.

'It's a travesty,' Vanessa went on, 'a positive travesty.

43

The consequences would be sheer disaster. Disaster.' She shook her head, alarmed at her own thoughts, untying her blunt-cut hair and ruffling distraught fingers through its length.

'Consequences of what, my dear?' Harry asked, still mildly, fumbling for his pipe. 'And, by the way, have you seen Madelene? She's late.'

'I frankly doubt Rodney and I could possibly go on. We might as well write off the winter's meets right now. Just write them off. Tragic for Rod of course, and a complete disaster for Mary.'

Mary was Vanessa and Rodney's five-year-old daughter, and the entrance of her name into the catalogue of sufferers intrigued Harry to repeat, 'What, my dear? Consequences of what?'

To which Vanessa replied only, darkly, 'Noel.'

'Ah, Noel.' Harry was getting the picture. He found his tobacco pouch, unfolded it and plumbed its damp sweet-smelling depths with practised fingers. 'You haven't seen Madelene?' he asked again.

'Madelene?' Vanessa looked blank. 'Of course I've seen her. She's in the ditch.' Her tone of dismissive boredom seemed to indicate that the ditch was Madelene's natural habitat.

'Where?' Harry shouted, instantly alert. 'How? Has she had a smash? Is she all right?'

Vanessa blinked, looking surprised at his excitement and said in an ordinary voice, 'Of course she's all right. Do you think I'd be standing here if she wasn't?'

Harry thought solemnly for a moment and said, 'In your case, I'm just not sure. Why didn't you tell me she was in trouble? I'll go down for her right now.'

'You needn't bother. I've sent Noel on the tractor to haul her out. Everything is quite under control. You see, I am quite responsible,' she added, miffily.

'I'm sorry, pet,' Harry soothed, 'I was just rather taken

44

by surprise. Concerned.' He tried to bury his worries over Madelene. 'Now tell me, what's the trouble with Noel?'

At that instant there was a heavy thud on the closed door of the library as a fist was slammed against it, and a voice growled, 'That's right, baby sister, talk about me behind my back.' The door swung open and Noel, in his customary plus-fours and straw-covered tweed jacket stood glowering under his shock of grey hair at his father and sister at once. 'What's she been telling you, while I had my back turned, eh?'

'And why not? You'd plough up my bottom field behind my back, so why shouldn't I talk behind yours.'

'So it's *your* bottom field now, is it? Just when did you get the title deeds? Or have we turned the whole damned place over to your chinless pink-coated wonders for once and all?'

'Where's Madelene, Noel?' Harry pleaded, trying vainly to get the attention of either of his children. The door to the library, slammed behind him by Noel, once more swung, this time more sedately, open.

'Madelene is here,' Madelene announced, her voice delicate to the dangerous point of fury, as well Harry knew. He hastened across the room, extending his arms to her instinctively.

'My dear, you are not hurt?'

'Hurt? No. Angry, annoyed, humiliated, yes.' She glowered at Noel. 'Thanks to your foolish peacock and both your charming children. That one,' she waved a dismissive hand at Vanessa, 'leaves me waiting half an hour in the ditch, and that one,' she indicated Noel, 'hauls me out without so much as a word and tears off on his smelly tractor without waiting even to see if the engine will start.'

'Well,' Noel said sourly, 'it started. Or else you wouldn't be here.'

'So who should know that it would start or that it would not start, or go on fire or blow up and blow me to smithereens?' Madelene shouted. 'You could have waited a minute of your precious time!'

'To be harangued by two women in one day? No thanks. Engines don't blow people to smithereens, Madelene. Shotguns do that,' he added, glowering again at Vanessa. 'What have you said?' he demanded again, suspiciously.

'Only the truth.'

'And what is that?'

'That if you plough up the bottom field the Hunt will never meet at Hardacres again, and the last little touch of what all of us have stood for will be gone. Over. Finished. We might as well just pack up and leave.'

'What a splendid idea,' said Noel, and Vanessa dissolved incongruously in tears. It was a tactic she had employed at intervals throughout her life, usually to save some favoured pony from sale or, conversely, lure Harry into yet another auction ring folly. Noel was unimpressed.

Harry lit his pipe, hobbled to his fireside chair, and motioned to Madelene to take the other.

She hesitated, moved slightly towards him, and stopped. For the first time he noticed how pale she was, and how her delicately-coloured lips were set so tight that an unaccustomed narrow age-line appeared on either side of her slender nose. He saw her glance at his squabbling middle-aged children and knew she wanted to be alone with him. Searching for the most graceful words to achieve that effect he only managed to mutter, 'I don't believe the children will be waiting for tea.'

'On the contrary, Father, I feel the need of a cup very badly now,' Vanessa sniffed as Mrs Bennett entered with the tray. She hastened off for additional china, and Madelene suddenly sank into the chair by the fire, shook her head once at the hopeless intrusion of people all around her, and buried her face in her hands as she, too, broke into tears.

Harry clambered, astonished, to his feet, crossing the

fireside to stand beside her. Madelene's tears, an almost unheard-of rarity, were as genuine as Vanessa's were false. 'My dear, what is it, were you hurt?'

'Not me,' she sobbed. 'It is not me.'

'But what?'

'It's Sam,' she cried, shaking her head as Vanessa and Noel turned to stare.

'Sam?' Harry said, startled. 'Surely Sam's not ill?' The thought was incomprehensible. The twins were health and fitness personified, joint coaches of the Ampleforth school rugby team.

'No,' Madelene sobbed. 'Not ill. He's gone. Sam's gone. Terry telephoned last night. Sam's left.'

'Sam? Left Ampleforth?' Harry said. 'But where?'

'No one knows. He's just gone. He told the Abbot some months ago, and Terry yesterday morning. And he left, like that, alone. Oh Harry, where will he go?'

There was a silence, in which Vanessa stopped sniffing, realizing she'd totally lost her audience. Then Noel said, 'Where will he go? Here, of course. Where else? And that's all I bloody need. A bolting monk. A bolting bloody monk.' He turned on his heel and stormed out, slamming the ill-used library door once more.

CHAPTER
THREE

Sam did not return to Hardacres. Noel had misjudged him and later grudgingly admitted so. They had all misjudged him. Whatever his reasons for leaving, whatever his plans for the future, they did not include landing himself as either a financial or emotional burden on Noel, Harry, or any member of the family. Whatever he was doing, he was doing alone.

Madelene, with Harry accompanying her for moral support, motored to Ampleforth where a long, kindly discussion with the Abbot and a further long discussion with Sam's twin, Terry, did little to clarify the situation, although both managed in some way to ease her anxiety. The Abbot assured her that Sam's departure was amicable, the result of their mutual careful conclusion that the life of Brother Jude of the Order of St Benedict was not, after all, for him.

'He found he did not truly have a vocation,' the Abbot said simply. 'Many have found the same. That is what these first years are for. Still, they are not wasted years but years of discovery. Now we will see to what use he puts them.' He had smiled, offered sherry and then left them alone in the guest-room with Terry.

Terry, or more correctly Brother Erkenwald OSB, looking remarkably sedate in Harry's eyes in his flowing black habit, slowly turned his gaze from his mother to his great-uncle and back to his mother. Then with an expression reminiscent of the many times throughout their childhood when his brother had escaped unscathed from some mutual prank and left him holding the baby, he shrugged and grinned wryly. Apparently Sam, with whom he had shared

48

every secret from infancy, had kept totally to himself and the Abbot his momentous decision.

'He said, "I'm going." I said, "Where?" I thought he meant the pub or something. I just couldn't believe it. For a moment, you see, I wanted to go, too. That's why he didn't tell me, you know, until he was ready to leave. It took all his nerve to do something without me. And he knew I'd be the same. I still feel amputated. I keep talking to walls and expecting them to be Sam. It's like during the war, when I was in the bag. It's bloody awful being a twin sometimes, you know.' He paused, and sipped at the glass of sherry the Abbot had provided, and looked out of the window at the boys of the school on the playing field below. 'Still, it has its compensations. You needn't worry about him, Mother. He's quite all right. You understand.' He touched one finger lightly to the side of his forehead, a gesture that somehow evoked the uncanny communication the twins had always, like many twins, shared. 'I'll let you know if anything goes wrong.' He grinned at Harry and Harry was uncertain if he was joking or not.

'I do not understand, I do not forgive,' Madelene said slowly, 'that he did not let us know. Why did he not contact me? That was so unkind.'

'Because he knew I would,' Terry said logically. 'It's very hard, you must understand. It's rather like a divorce, I would imagine. Makes it terribly hard to face the family at first. He will. When he is quite sure. When he is sure enough that nothing can change his mind.'

A week of silence followed. Madelene went about her work and her daily life in a state of suppressed nerves that only revealed themselves when the telephone rang and she leapt for it demonically. It was never Sam. Harry, who did telephone regularly, reassured her each time that Terry was no doubt right and her errant son would make contact as soon as his mental state allowed, a viewpoint that Madelene found far from comforting. Harry himself, still convinced that Sam would turn up at Hardacres, jumped up at the sound of every arriving vehicle and Noel, with less friendly intent, cast each one a baleful glare until it vindicated itself by not producing the Prodigal Brother.

So it was that when, late on the following Friday afternoon, a large black taxi, followed directly by a blank-sided workman's van, pulled up in front of the main entrance, the entire resident family came instantly to attention. Harry, who had been enjoying a quiet glass of sherry with Hetty before Rodney and Vanessa joined them for dinner, hobbled quickly to the window and was joined there by his wife. Both leaned forward, pressing anxious faces against the glass. Vanessa and her husband had just appeared from behind the house and both, dressed alike in jodhpurs and hacking jackets, also stopped in their tracks and stared. Noel, who had just arrived back from Driffield with a load of feed-sacks in the shooting-brake, clambered out of that venerable vehicle and began striding purposefully towards the arrival, brows lowering ominously as he approached. The door of the taxi opened slowly, distractedly, as someone inside made some arrangement with the driver. Then a tall figure stepped down, tall, rangy, and unmistakably wearing a skirt. The woman straightened her back, smoothed a stray strand of dark-grey hair into the bun at the nape of her neck and came face to face with Noel, who hadn't had time to change his expression.

'My dear, don't look so frightfully appalled,' she said with a faint smile. 'I'm not *staying* or anything gruesome like that.'

Noel's dour face broke into a wide grin and he extended one work-grimed hand. 'Jane. How delightful. We didn't expect you, at all.' He was still grinning as Jane looked around her at the circle of staring faces, both in and out of the house.

'So I gather,' she said.

'No, please,' Noel continued, relief over his respite from Sam bringing out a totally uncharacteristic desire to make social amends. 'You must forgive us, but we're rather at loose ends around here. We were more or less expecting someone else. Sort of.' He tugged at a lank strand of his thinning hair, looking over his shoulder for help from his father, who was emerging from the front door.

'Yes,' Jane said, turning to greet her brother. 'And something tells me I can guess just who that might be.'

Quickly she embraced Harry, exchanging two affectionate cheek kisses. Lady Macgregor was a woman of sixty, a woman whom life, rich in experience and not without considerable misfortune, had sculpted to a point of high perfection, so that on the border of old age she was genuinely beautiful.

Jane was the only one of Sam and Mary Hardacre's three children to be totally at home in the world of the establishment; she alone had been born to it. Harry and his older brother Joe had each known the full depths of their parents' early poverty, and each had watched Sam Hardacre's extraordinary rise from the fish quays to country squiredom. Neither to Joe nor to Harry would Hardacres ever be anything but an extraordinary place, a fairy-tale handed them in their adolescence. To Jane it was simply home. She had been born there, like innumerable other well-born ladies of earlier times, had played about its vast gardens in childhood, and been sent out well prepared into an elegant world from its doors. If her marriage to the future Lord Macgregor had delighted and stunned her family, and perhaps outraged their detractors, to Jane it was only natural. Ian Macgregor was precisely the sort of young man she'd been schooled to expect and she made him, in their few years, an excellent wife, as comfortable at his side as her mother had been at the side of Sam Hardacre the guttie.

As a girl she had not been beautiful – she had inherited too much from her father for that – but was always thought attractive. Her strong-boned, honest face, and her direct blue eyes, surmounted by well-groomed luxuriant dark hair, glowed with character. Jane had enough tragedy in her life to have justified a retreat into sorrowful mourning but, too strong for that, she rose above it all, in time, and that character strengthened in her face until now, a tall, gaunt, handsome woman with a ready humorous smile, she caught and held the attention of anyone she wished.

In the years of her early widowhood women did not remarry, but later, after her son was grown and he too died in another war, there were offers of marriage, often from gentlemen of considerable standing. Jane turned them all down, good-naturedly but firmly. That part of her life was done, she would say, and she knew, even if others did not, when to let go of the things of youth.

Perhaps for that reason, Jane Macgregor had a tremendous affinity with the young, and her small house on the Macgregor estate was often filled with young friends, many of them the children, and even grandchildren, of her own contemporaries. Among the Hardacres she had fond friendships with Vanessa and Rodney's little daughter Mary Gray, and also with all three of her niece Emily Barton's young children, Ruth, Olive and Paul. Most family visits ended with Jane playing cards or billiards, or listening to modern dance music with the young, while her own generation were abandoned to their solemn adult state.

Before she would enter the house, Jane asked that her taxi-driver and the driver of the hired van be taken into the kitchens for a cup of tea, as she would be needing their services quite shortly and saw no reason why they shouldn't enjoy some refreshment while they waited.

'Of course,' Harry said, taking her arm. 'But surely you'll be staying for dinner.'

'No. On the contrary, I will be staying fifteen minutes. Oh, don't look so relieved, Noel, it's most ungracious,' she added with another grin.

Noel appeared genuinely dismayed and said, 'Oh please, Aunt Jane, do stay. Honestly, I'd like nothing better. I'll even change my shirt.'

'For that miracle, I could almost be persuaded,' she replied. 'But I really can't wait. I've promised Emily that I'll be in Kilham by five. I can assure you, we have a great deal of work to do this weekend. A great deal. Philip is out of his mind.'

Hetty had appeared at the door, in her customary tweed skirt and cardigan buttoned to the neck. She wore thick grey stockings and bedroom slippers of tartan wool. Jane sighed slightly at the sight of her, a sigh that had less to do with Hetty's ill-health than Hetty's dreary manner of dress. In Jane's view, feeling hellish was no justification for looking hellish and that, she was sorry, was that.

'Jane dear, how lovely,' Hetty murmured, extending woolly arms. Jane leaned forward for the customary kiss, feeling guilty about her recent thoughts because Hetty did look dreadfully pale and grey. 'What's brought you here?'

'A mission of mercy,' Jane said, as they entered the drawing-room, with Harry trailing and Rodney and Vanessa clumping along behind in their riding boots. Harry set about pouring drinks and Jane continued, 'I had a desperate telephone call from Emily. They had just arrived at this wondrous purchase of Philip's, after motoring for hours in the pouring rain, and she discovered that, wonder of wonders, he bought the place without ever looking at the upstairs.'

'Surely never,' Rodney said. He was a tall, bald man of near Jane's own age, considerably older than his wife, and his conversation, when not about horses, tended to such astonishments and little else. Rodney appeared permanently amazed by the world outside his stable-yard, a place of heathens and madness.

'I'm afraid so,' Jane said briskly. 'The roof was leaking, two ceilings were down, and none of the rooms had been decorated since the First War. Apparently Philip fell in love with the bar, checked it was stocked well, and left it at that. So there they are, ready to open to an eager public in a fortnight's time, may Heaven help them. I told Emily I'd come down via Edinburgh, drop into Jenner's for curtains, take the next train to York for the wallpaper and, well, here I am. What you see in that splendid little blue van out there is the entire interior of The Rose at Kilham. Pre-fab, so to speak.'

'Jane, you are awfully brave,' Hetty said in hesitant admiration.

'I'm awfully thick, if you ask me,' Jane dismissed. 'Still, I couldn't leave them floundering. And I am quite capable. I've just finished four bedrooms in the new inn, for Heidi, in Strathconon.'

Harry nodded. He had evidence of Jane's ability himself. Last year she had quietly saved him a considerable amount of money by redecorating the entire upstairs of Hardacres single-handed. He had never yet met a task of which she was not, if required, totally capable. During the war she had driven tractors on the farm with cheerful, inventive glee. For the one Hardacre born never needing to work, she was remarkably adept at all manner of it.

'How kind of you to stop in to see us,' Hetty murmured, adjusting her footstool in front of the fire, 'when you are so busy, after all.'

'Oh, I'm afraid this isn't exactly social, my dears,' Jane said at once. 'I have a message to deliver, you see, or else I am rather afraid I'd have given you all a miss.' She grinned again. 'Do tell, Madelene isn't by chance around?' She waited while the roomful of her relatives made their customary little silence whenever Madelene's name was mentioned in Hetty's presence. Jane was the only member of the family, other than the naïve Vanessa, who refused to indulge in this little hypocrisy, feeling as she did that Hetty had by now surely come to terms with the situation, indeed perhaps finding it in some ways to her advantage. It did, Jane was well aware, rather do away with that nagging question of bed.

'Oh, Madelene,' Rodney said blankly, as if he had just remembered who she was.

'I say, Jane, haven't you heard?' Vanessa blurted in her embarrassingly imperceptive way.

'Heard what?'

'About Madelene's Sam. He's bolted. Bolted and gone to ground. Quite the most extraordinary thing!'

'Quite,' said Jane with a slight twitch of her long, thin nose. She raised her glass of malt whisky, which she much preferred to the more usual lady's drink of sherry, and took a long, careful sip. She set the glass down. 'Yes, actually, I was aware. We had a long telephone conversation two nights ago, Sam and I. Please let Madelene know that he is in excellent health, and working hard at his new job.'

'Where?' Harry demanded. 'What job? Why did he telephone you, of all people? Is he in Scotland?'

'No. He's in Yorkshire. I told him I wouldn't say exactly where just yet, if you don't mind. He'd rather a little privacy yet. Do try to understand,' she said, echoing Terry, and sounding very like another young person trying to explain youth's vagaries to middle-age.

'What's he working at?' Vanessa asked. 'Imagine, "Defrocked monk seeks employment". It must have been awfully tricky.'

'Hardly defrocked, Vanessa,' Harry chided.

Jane smiled brightly and said, 'I suppose it wasn't easy. Anyhow he's managed.' She raised her glass again, as if in salute to the distant Sam. 'He's in a chip-shop. Frying fish,' she said.

Another silence fell on the beautiful drawing-room, as its occupants stood about with lowering jaws.

'Surely never,' Rodney murmured at last.

Jane looked at him, and then around the room, with her

55

slow grin spreading. Her eyes met Harry's and he also started to grin.

'What's t' bother then?' she asked. 'Happen us Hardacres 'ave done worse.'

CHAPTER FOUR

The Rose at Kilham occupied an attractive site at the end of the village, with its own small garden at the rear facing on to a small stream with tidy, grassy banks. Even in November there were flowers in the small borders, and a few remaining red roses on the tall climbing bush by the front door. The building itself, of native limestone, was long and low, so that the upper floor was barely full height, with shortened windows peering out under the lowering brows of the uneven, mossed-green slate roof. Jane pointed it out to her driver, who had recognized the pub already from the faded wooden sign above its door, and he pulled up in front of the many-paned bay window. The blue van drew up behind.

Jane got out of the taxi and, rather than approaching the door, stepped carefully out into the deserted street, peering in fading light at the faintly suspect slope in the roof-tree. She walked slowly around the gable end of the building and inspected the stonework, prodding a convenient piece of wood at the edge of one window, and casting a jaundiced eye upwards to one cracked chimney pot. 'Oh, Philip,' she said to herself. 'A lamb to the slaughter.' She imagined she could hear the faint chortling of the estate agent all the way from York.

Then squaring her shoulders unconsciously at the prospect of the mighty reclamation project ahead, she walked back to the front of the building and rapped sharply on the door. She was aware, as she stood awaiting a response, of the subtle twitch of lace curtains in the cottages across the street. She smiled to herself. Oh yes. They'd be laughing, too.

The door swung in suddenly and a tall, broad-shouldered

man with thinning sandy hair stepped half-out, staring blankly at her in the twilight. Then he recognized her and opened both arms out wide. He was dressed in a huge rough-knit jumper and tweed plus-fours, with thick stockings and brogues, and for a moment Jane found it hard to believe she was actually looking at Philip Barton.

'Jane,' he shouted. 'Eh, but it's grand to see you. Here lass, let's look. Aye, but yer lookin' gradely.'

'What?' said Jane, blinking. Philip of the London-tailored suits and life-long urbanity had suddenly blossomed into a salt of the Yorkshire earth.

'Oh Daddy, *must* you,' groaned a plaintive adolescent voice from behind him. 'You sound so impossibly gauche.' Philip stepped aside, looking faintly hurt, and Ruth, his fifteen-year-old daughter, squeezed past him as if afraid to let her stylish full skirt even brush against his offending tweeds. 'Oh, Aunt Jane, he's just intolerable since we've come here. I'll die if any of my London friends ever see him. Not that that's likely,' she moaned, with a mournful cast of her eyes heavenwards. 'I'll probably never see *any* of them again.'

She looked dimly up and down the narrow street, where the soft outlines of the cluster of little buildings now faded into furry dusk. 'Oh, this place!' She shrugged and grabbed Jane's hand, pulling her inwards as if to escape from some invading horror. 'Quick,' she cried, with mock desperation, 'talk to me. Is the world still out there? Stands Scotland where she stood? Oh God, Aunt Jane, I feel like Robinson Crusoe.'

Philip was still standing in the doorway, breathing ostentatious deep breaths. 'Smell that,' he cried, excitedly tugging at Jane's other arm. 'Nowt but good country air. Eh, lass, yon's t' life.' Ruth pushed the door closed, half on her father's brogue, with a grimace of distaste.

Ruth, until a week ago, had been a student at one of London's nicer girls' day schools. She was a tall girl looking, to Jane's eyes, surprisingly sophisticated in her soft dark blue skirt and pale blue twin-set. Her hair, dark brown like her mother's, was set in a smooth bob, just tucked in at the edges and held in place by a strand of velvet ribbon. She walked down the dark corridor leading to the kitchens of the pub with exaggerated care, conscious of herself and her new female grace. Jane followed behind, watching the bounce of soft curls on Ruth's shoulders with a small smile of pleasure. It had always delighted her to see the young come of age.

'How's your mother?' she asked.

'Frantic,' said Ruth. 'She's been scrubbing the kitchen cupboards all day. They were full of toadstools.'

'Dear me,' said Jane, treading carefully on a patch of wormeaten floorboard that sagged beneath her foot. 'And your brother and sister?'

'Out enjoying good country air,' Philip put in from behind.

'More fools they,' said Ruth.

Jane was about to ask the girl what arrangements had been made for her schooling when there was a sudden piercing shriek from the depths of the building.

'Good God,' said Jane. 'Is that Emily?'

'Aye,' said Philip, excusing himself past her. 'Happen we've got trouble.' He pressed on into the dark depths of the pub towards his wife's wails of distress.

'*Happen*,' said Ruth, with another grimace, 'we've more than you think.'

Jane smiled and patted the girl's shoulder and then hurried by to see if she could be of some assistance. She followed the shrieks, joined now by Philip's sharp barks of command, pure London now, his Yorkshire affectation sacrificed to the urgency of the moment.

She found a half-open dark-stained door and gave it a gentle push. Behind was a long, frugally furnished kitchen, with a large worn refectory table in its centre and a pair of ancient deep sinks, below which her niece Emily, generally a woman of definite elegance, was all but invisible behind a geyser of spraying water. Soaked from the top of her once neatly-waved hair to the toes of her good kid shoes, she was gamely struggling to cap the gushing pipe with her bare hands while Philip, a picture of manly fortitude, was dashing back and forth with a wrench in his hand shouting, 'Right, pet, I've got it now, pet, hold on!'

Jane stepped quietly into the rain of water, lifted the wrench from Philip's hand on one of his circuits of the scene, directed him out of doors to the mains water-cock, and quietly got to work.

Half an hour later, with everyone newly dried and freshly dressed, they were all sitting in the kitchen drinking tea, while Philip eulogized the astounding pressure of good Yorkshire water mains. Ruth's eyebrows rose regularly to brush her pert little fringe and Emily, her hair in pin-curls and a kerchief, sat stirring her tea with an expression of wounded martyrdom. Jane, contemplating the future of The Rose at Kilham, was privately giving even money that it would fall down in a cloud of dry rot or be burnt down by Emily, when the outer kitchen door banged open. She looked up to the refreshing sight of two smiling faces. Ruth's sister and brother, Olive who was thirteen, and Paul, just eleven, burst into the room, swinging conkers on strings and shouting in unison about entirely different subjects. Both were rosy-cheeked from the November air, and deliriously excited by whatever village games they had joined and Jane, for one, thought that in spite of Ruth's protestations the country was already doing them a world of good.

'Mum, I've met a super girl, her name's Ailey and she has a pony.'

'A cart-horse,' said Paul. 'And she's really frightfully stupid. She doesn't know anything. Eeh by gum,' he said in a splendid mimicry that his father must have envied, 'nowt but kintra yokels.'

'Don't mock the afflicted,' said Ruth. But Paul grinned, opened his mouth wide and began to sing in a delightfully clear childish voice,

> On Ilkley moor bar t'at
> On Ilkley moor bar t'at
> On Ilk-ley moor bar t'aat.

He danced around happily, his face rubbery with expression, swinging his strung conker in an arc about his head. 'Eeh, Da', what's t' matter wi' floor?' he cried. ''s all weet.'

'I think,' said Jane to Philip, 'the lad could teach his father a thing or two.'

Emily flared up suddenly and shouted, 'That's enough now, Paul. It isn't funny any longer. Just speak English like the rest of us.' She sighed, and turned to Jane with a wan smile. 'Oh, do let's talk about something other than Yorkshire. How's the North? How's Heidi? Has she opened the new inn yet?' She looked with pointed sourness at her husband and added, 'I do hope it's nothing like this.'

'Well, my dear,' Jane soothed, 'all old buildings have their little quirks. I dare say Heidi will have a few wrinkles to iron out, too.' Even as she said it she was inwardly thanking heaven that Heidi had had the foresight to have her small property in Strathconon thoroughly surveyed before she, with Jane's financial assistance, went through with the purchase. At least there weren't going to be two architectural disasters in the Hardacre ménage just now. Heidi herself, though perhaps Jane's closest friend, was no doubt the most distant member of the Hardacre circle, not family at all, but linked to them all just the same by a peculiar turn of fate, now almost forgotten by everyone. Jane doubted that Ruth, for instance, could even explain what relation her 'Aunt Heidi' bore to any of them, or why, since 1935, she had been part of their lives.

For Jane, the connection with Heidi Muller was much

older, and much deeper. Although they, too, met for the first time in a Munich ghetto in that year, Jane and Heidi had known of each other since the Great War, and had corresponded regularly throughout the twenties and early thirties. As was natural to women of their era, they had met through their husbands, who were both naval officers, Jane's in the Royal Navy, and Heidi's in the Forces of the Kaiser. It might be supposed that two such gentlemen, on the eve of the Great War, would be unlikely to speak, much less form a friendship, the ties of which would hold for forty years. But in truth, on the spring day in 1913 when Sir Ian Macgregor and his youthful bride entertained Lt Karl Muller of the German armoured cruiser *Scharnhorst*, aboard HMS *Monmouth*, riding at anchor off Hong Kong, no one knew themselves to be on the eve of anything. They were two small cogs in the world's two mightiest navies and each, proud of their own and respectful of the other's, regarded themselves as natural kin, with more in common than ever appeared to hold them apart. They had formed that sudden, brief, quicksilver sort of alliance that can occur between men of divergent backgrounds but common aims. Addresses were exchanged, promises made, healths drunk and an agreement made to surely meet again.

For the two men the meeting, or at least a meeting of the kind they envisioned, for they eventually 'met' indeed, in a grimmer way entirely, was never to come about. *Scharnhorst* sailed suddenly, leaving Jane and Ian with an odd feeling of a companionship untimely ended, and when next the two ships drew near together, it was October of 1914, in the South Pacific, over angry guns. *Monmouth* was the first victim but *Scharnhorst*, within days, met a similar fate in the South Atlantic. The two men who had been friends in Hong Kong now both lay in the Antarctic waters for ever, each leaving behind in their warring countries a young widow and fatherless child. Jane's Peter was born in November of that year, and in June of 1914 Heidi Muller, who had shared at a distance her husband's pleasure in his Scottish friends, had given birth to a son, whom his parents named Ian after Ian Macgregor. Throughout the year letters had been exchanged, letters filled increasingly with sorrow as war between their native lands loomed closer. Now, with both their husbands dead, the two women, one English, one a German Jewess, instinctively grasped and held the one link with their lost loves, a friendship that they refused to allow to die. Throughout the war they boldly, and each against the wishes of their husbands' disapprovingly patriotic families, sent letters through neutral Switzerland. After the war, Jane leapt at the chance to help Heidi, struggling in the chaos of her defeated nation, by sending parcels of clothing and food. Later, as years passed, she wrote encouraging letters, trying to comfort the young widow who found that in the new Germany, her status as honoured war-widow was more and more eroded by the acid of anti-Semitism. Concerned, but in truth not fully comprehending, Jane kept her steady stream of cheery letters and useful packages flowing until one grim day in 1933 first one, and then all the others were returned with a grim official stamp: No Such Person At This Address. At first assuming a mistake, later, something worse, Jane began a long campaign to learn the fate of her vanished friend. Letters, inquiries, visits to consulates, all in the end led nowhere. Eventually, with the feisty determination that had become part of her since Ian Macgregor's death, she packed her bag and with her son, now the young Lord Macgregor, set off for Munich in search of Heidi herself. It was a journey of discovery in many senses, where Jane saw with her own eyes what Heidi in her pathetic, frightened letters had been trying to tell her. It led in the end to the ghetto where Munich's Jews, Heidi among them, had been herded. She was alone, in desperate poverty, her young son Ian long since taken from her to some unknown prison for political offenders. Thus the two women, whose husbands had long ago been briefly friends, met for the first time and embraced like sisters, in a shabby room, on the eve of yet another war between their nations. Finding all official channels closed to them, Jane and Peter Macgregor smuggled Heidi across the Swiss border and home to England and to Hardacres, where for some time she had stayed, before moving North to the Macgregor estate with Jane. She had remained there ever since, saying she felt close to everyone she had lost there. She insisted on working, and had supported herself modestly by cooking in a local inn for some years until, with Jane's ready assistance, she had, just this year, set herself up in a business of her own, a German-style hostelry that promised hospitality among the Scottish hills with the added pleasure of good European cuisine. Jane had no doubt that she would succeed, certainly much less doubt, anyhow, than about Philip Barton's enterprise in the East Riding.

'I'm so glad for her,' Emily said with genuine feeling. 'I know it's been what she's wanted for years. You *are* a dear, Aunt Jane. And coming down here to rescue us, as well. I'm really most terribly grateful.' Emily was brightening under the effects of the warmth of the cheery fire in the old-fashioned kitchen grate, and the tot of whisky that Philip had poured in her tea. 'I suppose I am being rather a moan, aren't I?' she smiled at Philip whose face relaxed into a broad hopeful grin. 'It's really not such a bad place. The bar *is* lovely with the inglenook. And at least I have Philip and my children around me.' She paused, thoughtful. 'I could just weep for Heidi. Is she still trying to find him?'

Jane nodded. 'She always will be, I know. I'd be the same. I'm really far more fortunate. I mean, over Peter. Of course, I never . . .' she paused, swallowing a sudden surge of emotion, 'I never saw his body, never could stand at a graveside . . . but I did know at least for certain that he was dead. They saw him go down. I spoke, even, to the pilot who watched. I knew he couldn't have survived. It was terrible to hear, but at least I have that certainty. But Heidi, poor Heidi, will spend the rest of her days looking for her son. We all know he's dead. How could he not be dead? He was probably dead in 1933, the day the SS took him away. What chance would he have had? A nineteen-year-old, a Jew *and* a political offender. She had no contact from that day, and I've always thought they simply killed him. Oh, Heidi knows too. She must know, in her heart. But until she has proof she will keep searching, and any proof there ever was was certainly lost in the war years.'

'Perhaps she's happier that way?' Ruth ventured, her young face reflecting an innocent curiosity over these events of another era. 'Perhaps it's nicer believing he's alive.'

Jane shook her head sharply, 'No, my dear. It is not nicer. It is a slow twisting of a knife. That is all.'

'Did she hear again from the Red Cross?' Philip asked. 'I thought she was following some lead.'

'Yes, she heard. It was another Muller. And his first name was Isaac. The initials were all that they had in common. He was dead, too, anyhow.' Jane shook her head abruptly, not wishing to think any more, just now, about Heidi's hopeless search. 'Do tell, Emily, how is Maud?'

Emily laughed. 'Battening down the hatches, I suspect. Mother's coming to visit.'

'Is she indeed?' Jane said, interested. 'I thought she'd sworn off Hollywood.' She smiled to herself. Helen Hardacre, Joe's widow and Emily's mother, was possibly the only human being on earth for whom Jane had not a whit of sympathy. In fact, her own harshness towards the woman whom she had always felt had driven her oldest brother to a suicide's grave, quite frightened her. From time to time she tried, mentally, to dredge up the memories of Helen's past, her early youth as a factory girl, child of a brutal father, victim of one of Joe's own factories' harsh regime, to justify the woman she had become. But she was never able to make the trick work. After all, her own logic returned, Mary Hardacre too was the child of a brutal home, and as misused

65

as Helen had ever been, and Mary was kind and gentle all her days.

'Yes,' Emily said. 'We all thought that. It seems, you know, that the reason for that fracas at Dinardo's was Brannigan chasing some little blonde into the *kitchens* or some such place in full view of the assembled company. I mean, he *is* a fool. Surely he should know, if anyone, that Mother will stand for anything but public humiliation. You'd think he'd know which side his bread was buttered.' She stopped short suddenly, aware of the curious eyes of her children.

'What did Mr Brannigan *do*?' said Olive, who was young enough to actually ask the question that was gleaming in Ruth's eyes.

'Nothing, pet,' Philip said. 'Off you go now. See if the chickens are shut in,' he added officiously.

'Chickens?' said Jane. Ruth's eyebrows went up and Emily shook a bemused head.

'*And* ducks,' she said, resigned. When the children had gone she continued, 'It's really not the sort of thing the children should hear. I must be more careful. I mean, their own *grandmother*.'

'Helen,' Jane said drily, 'is hardly everyone's picture of a granny, though, is she?'

'Well, of course not. And naturally she's positively forbidden the children to address her as Grandmama, even in their letters. Isn't it pathetic? She's "Helen" to them, and the playboy of the western world is Mr Brannigan. Well, they could hardly call *him* Grandpa, could they?'

'Hardly,' said Jane. Mike Brannigan, Helen's husband, had been a business associate of Joe Hardacre before his death. Not all of Joe's businesses had been of the sort one would choose to brag about; before the First War he had invested heavily in the German armaments kings, Krupps, and after the armistice too, military dealings, with little regard to political consequences, had always formed part of his enterprise. Like his investments, Joe's associates were not always the most savoury. Mike Brannigan was typical, a tough Irish-American, whose past was subject to much speculation but almost certainly involved gun-running to Ireland in 1916 and, more recently, liberal dealings with all parties concerned in the Near East. He was rumoured to have taken part in the Easter Rising, less out of Irish patriotism than a belligerent delight in a good scrap. Whether or not the rumours were true, Mike looked the part, and in the late twenties, when the newly-widowed Helen Hardacre, having failed to wrest some of the Hardacre fortune back from Harry, returned to New York in search of a new protector, Mike Brannigan, a toughly handsome thirty-year-old, was not short of appeal.

In spite of a deliberate rich gilding of elegance, Helen Hardacre was, at the core, a woman very like Brannigan himself in character. They had sprung from similar sources, and fought their way up with similar gusto. Twenty years his senior, and far more experienced, Helen was able to convey to the brashly youthful Irishman an aura of sophistication and style he found irresistible, and he was already well involved with her before he realized he was entranced by fool's gold. She was no more lady than he was gentleman, but by then he was physically enamoured with her, a condition she did nothing to ease until her finger was once more sporting a band of gold. For Helen, at Joe Hardacre's death, was stony-broke, and indeed down to her last, borrowed mink, when Mike Brannigan, still convinced he was marrying wealth, led her down the aisle of St Patrick's. On their wedding night she satisfied his every desire. The following morning she taped her last bank statement to the bathroom mirror. It was a gesture of such black humour that, where she had expected to find him furious, she found him convulsed with enchanted laughter. Their marriage had, at times, a richness that surprised them both.

The marriage surprised Helen's British family even more,

partly because she neglected to tell any of them about it for years. In time, with her sharp and ruthless business wit backed up by Mike's brawn, she had managed to reconstruct a respectable semblance of Joe's old enterprise. Then with the advent of the Second War, while the Hardacres struggled in beleaguered Britain, the Brannigans built a fortune in armaments and the black market in America. Thus was Helen able, in 1946, to make an entrance of which she no doubt had dreamed for years. Arriving on the newly refurbished *Queen Mary*, she travelled up to London, her youthful consort on her arm, a monumental collection of matched luggage in tow, and booked in at the Savoy for a month. From there she issued invitations (Harry called them Royal Summonses) to the entire remaining Hardacre family, the greater part of which, out of a mixture of good manners and curiosity, came. There, in Helen and Mike Brannigan's sumptuous suite, they were treated to an evening of glitter and luxury such as none of them had seen since before the war. And which, quite frankly, in the new straitened circumstances of the country and their own fortunes, none of them was ever likely to see again. Champagne flowed, imported foods, some imported personally by the Brannigans to avoid rationing strictures, filled laden, white-clothed tables. Amidst her utility-dressed, post-war shabby in-laws, Helen glided, cool and delicious in oyster silk, sparkling with diamonds. The best of New York's cosmetics' masters graced her remarkably youthful features. Mike Brannigan, his muscular body still uneasy in its dinner-suit, was as handsome and devotedly attendant as a royal favourite. Emily, who had prided herself on being the family's one true sophisticate, was so put out by her mother's performance as to retire to the cloakroom at one point in tears. Harry maintained quietly to Jane that he'd like to check out Helen's loft for unusually aged portraits, but conceded gamely that his sister-in-law had definitely won this match. Only Madelene was unimpressed. 'Of course she is beautiful,' she said later, calmly. 'She is rich. A poor woman who grows ugly in time is unfortunate. A rich woman who allows the same to happen is a fool.'

Perhaps fortunately for family serenity, Helen withdrew once more to New York after making her point to the Yorkshire clan she always felt had looked down on her. Based there, with fingers of her complex and doubtful business empire reaching throughout the world, Helen grew richer and more stylish as time went by. Maud and Albert Chandler, whose company she occasionally kept, when operations on the coast required her personal attentions, maintained loyally that she was indeed still quite extraordinarily youthful for her age, though reading between the lines the family were able to discern hints of cracks in the armour. Helen did no doubt look ten years younger, even now, than she was, but she was still approaching seventy, relentlessly, and Mike Brannigan was in his prime.

'Do you know, Aunt Jane,' Emily mused, 'I actually feel sorry for her. She really is quite pathetic.'

'Like a crocodile, she's pathetic,' said Philip.

But Emily went on, 'No, truly. How long can it go on? Imagine having to keep your husband tied to your apron strings all the time, lest he run off with some platinum floozy. I imagine she has him practically manacled to her wrist for this Hollywood trip. She's going for Janet's new film's première. You can just picture the scene!'

'Oh, can't I just,' said Ruth, who had just returned from the garden with her empty chicken-feed bowl. 'She's too lucky for words. Imagine. Janet Chandler! And Don Madison! Oh, I can't believe she's really my cousin, and she really *knows* Don Madison. I bet she even gets to kiss him in the film.' Ruth sighed, sinking dreamily into a chair by the long table. 'Oh, why didn't we move to California to open a pub, instead of dumb old Yorkshire?'

'I very much suspect,' Jane said, 'that it is the purse strings to which the gentleman is tied and, if that is the case,

69

no doubt he will be content to remain just where he is. Anyhow, it's her life, and she's entitled to live it as she pleases. As for the rest of us, we simply must get on with making the best of our own.' She added, with a wink to Ruth, 'Tell me my girl, when was the last time you wielded a paint-brush?'

CHAPTER
FIVE

For once, Madelene was not late. In fact, so eager or, more correctly, so anxious was she regarding this luncheon that she had arrived at the sea front hotel in Scarborough a full half-hour early. The past four months, since Sam's departure from Ampleforth, had not constituted the most lengthy separation she had endured from her younger twin son, nor by any means the most worrisome; the war had provided both. But it was without a doubt the most frustrating and also the most hurtful. Here she was, living but a few miles away from him, communicating by wretchedly awkward telephone, when always within an easy familiar drive of a reunion, and unable to bridge that tiny geographical gap because of the emotional gap that had suddenly loomed between them. Madelene needed only a handful of words to bring her at once to the side of her son; she was not a spiteful woman; but they were words he persistently refused to speak. Until now. The invitation had come, in a brief telephone conversation on Wednesday when he had, at last, suggested they meet. She at once offered Hardacres as the logical venue, since it was Sam's childhood home, and as quickly realized, hearing the distancing of his voice, she had made a mistake. She left the choice to him, and he had designated this particular hotel, anonymous, neutral, devoid of association. Madelene restlessly paced its unfamiliar foyer, regarding its plush Victorian draperies with distaste. It had, in the last half-hour, come to represent the divisions between herself and young Sam, and she detested it. For the tenth time she settled in a chair by the window, looking out at the bleak winterscape imbued with the eternal sadness of summer resorts in winter, empty streets, tea-rooms and guest-houses dreaming silently in lace-curtained solitudes, empty beaches pawed by a restless, angry sea. Scarborough at least retained a fashionable dignity, unlike her more pedestrian sister down the coast, where Sam had chosen to live, and Madelene was not disinclined to enjoy a day's shopping here, or afternoon tea with lady friends. Sam knew that; knew she had her favourite hotels and tea-rooms for such meetings, and had deliberately chosen none of them. He was, even now, rejecting her, and the family, at every turn.

'Mother?'

Madelene whirled about, startled, blinking in the dim light after the brightness of the snow outside. He was outlined against the interior light of the building and his face was in shadow. For a chilling moment Madelene felt that, had he not spoken, she would not have recognized her own son. With no logic but the force of familiarity, she had somehow expected to see him in the black habit he had worn at Ampleforth. Instead, he was dressed in a casual mix of sports clothes, a tweed jacket, cavalry twill trousers, a worn-looking pullover and limp-collared white shirt decorated incongruously with the brilliant red and yellow stripes of an MCC tie. His hair had grown, naturally, in four months and had evidently not yet been graced by a barber's guiding hand. He was smiling broadly, and Madelene saw for the first time a startling resemblance to his great-grandfather who had smiled like that, and who also had never, in all his years as a country gentleman, learned how to dress.

'You look . . . horrible,' Madelene said, extending her neck slightly and turning her cheek for the habitual kiss.

Sam gave it more heartily than usual and grinned again. 'Thanks so much for the tact. I know. The combined talents of every second-hand shop in the East Riding. The alternative was army surplus and it was all a bit *déja vu*.'

'The tie is the worst. Take it off.'

72

'Mother,' Sam said firmly, 'the *tie* is really mine. From before, even. Besides, if I take it off they won't serve me lunch.'

'So?' Madelene said warily. 'You expect lunch, too, after four months of not even saying hello.' She was half-teasing, and half-not.

Sam smiled again and shook his head. 'Of course not,' he said. 'I'm taking you to lunch. You don't think I'd ask you all this distance for nothing.'

Madelene was taken aback and sorry for what she had said. 'Don't be ridiculous,' she replied at once. 'I was only teasing. Of course I will take you to luncheon.'

'No.'

She looked up, startled. His face was set firmly, and his voice had taken on that new, steady tone she had come to associate with his phone calls from Bridlington, which he always insisted on paying for, coin by coin.

'You can't pay for this,' Madelene said briskly, looking about the lavish surrounds.

'I'm not a monk any longer, remember, Mother. I can't expect to live on charity now.'

'Charity!' Madelene exclaimed, growing furious. 'Your mother taking you to lunch is not charity. Nor, for that matter, is your uncle's hospitality at Hardacres, or, or mine at home, or Philip Barton's at Kilham, or Aunt Jane's, or . . . or anyone else's that you've turned down in the last four months as if you never wanted to see any of us again.'

Madelene was quite red in the face from her sudden outburst of pent-up resentment and Sam, waiting until she had come to a spluttering halt, smiled once again and said, 'Sherry, Mother? Or a glass of wine?'

Twice more, during lunch, Madelene tried to persuade Sam to allow her to pay, but he was adamant. He had saved for weeks and weeks from his tiny wage, skipped meals and given up cigarettes so that he might arrange this meeting on his own terms; the terms on which he intended to base his future life.

'But what are you going to do?' Madelene demanded for the fourth, frustrated time.

'I told you. Fry fish, until I find something better.'

'You cannot fry fish for the rest of your life.'

'Why not?' Sam returned. 'Other people do.'

But his smile was hollow. Granted, in the first few weeks of his new employment the euphoria of actually earning his own living, paying his own way, triumphantly handing Mrs Hewitt the rent money each week (in advance) had been a kind of fulfilment in itself. Naturally enough, that childish glee wore thin as day followed day, and boredom set in, saturated with the pervasive reek of hot cooking oil. He felt he could smell the stuff on himself permanently, even after a bath and a shave and a change of clothing; it went with him everywhere, a new incense. He said again, 'I'll find something.'

'What?' Madelene pursued, and Sam, confidence faltering, let his gaze slide from hers, defeated, to the white cloth of the table. Like so many whose coming of age was greeted by the coming of war, he had trained for little but defending his country. A good public-school education and a single year reading law at Cambridge was all he had to offer the world, plus a not inconsiderable background of theology and philosophy from Ampleforth which, whatever its merits, lacked the worldly ring of practicality.

When he found no answer Madelene shrugged Gallically and said, 'It is a punishment.'

'A punishment?' Sam said, not sure he was hearing right.

'Upon me. For failing to support you strongly enough in the faith. Now you have lost your faith and Our Lady is punishing me.'

Sam leaned back in his chair and laughed so heartily and delightedly that his eyes watered.

74

'You laugh? I am distraught; you have abandoned the Church, and you laugh?'

'Oh Mother, sometimes you are so Catholic you are almost a heathen. Our Lady doesn't punish people. Anyhow, you supported me wonderfully, always,' he said, with such warmth and sincerity that Madelene forgave him his laughter. 'And I have not lost my faith. I have lost my vocation. That is utterly different. Or more precisely, I think I have found I never had one to start with.'

'Of course you had a vocation,' Madelene replied, indignant. 'You spent three years there. Three years. And Terry is still there, thank God, at least Terry still remembers you had vocations.'

'No,' Sam said, his voice once again newly firm. 'No, Mother. Terry had a vocation. That is why Terry is still there. I didn't. And that is why I'm here.'

'But if Terry . . .'

'I'm not Terry, Mother.'

'Of course not,' she said. 'But you are so alike. You are twins. Always you've done everything together. So why now this?'

'Just because something has always been done, it is not necessarily right,' said Sam.

'I don't understand,' Madelene said shortly, staring morosely at her half-finished trifle. 'I don't understand you at all. You've changed. You were never like this with Terry.'

'Blast Terry,' Sam said suddenly, startling himself with his own vehemence. Madelene looked up, appalled, but he held his course. 'I am *not* Terry, Mother. I'm me, Sam. I'm different. If you don't like me this way I'm sorry, but I'm going to stay this way. I'm going my own way. I love Terry and I love the Church, but I've my own life to live. I've followed Terry every day of my life. Until now. I followed him into the world, as you well know. You didn't even know I was there until after he was born. Then, surprise,

75

here comes Sam, number two, second-in-line, runner-up. Damn it, Mother, I followed him through school, into the army, out of the army, and into the monastery, and I never argued once. And now for the first time ever I'm taking one little step without him . . .'

'And look where it's got you,' Madelene said. 'A fish and chip shop in Brid. An achievement, I suppose?'

Sam was silent. He signalled the waiter and paid the bill, adding the precisely correct amount for a tip which he really could not afford. He rose from his chair and took his mother's arm gently. Out on the wind- and snow-swept sea front street he walked her carefully to her little red car. As he opened the door for her, he said, 'God would rather an honest man frying fish than a liar hiding behind holy vows. I have no vocation. I can't camp on His doorstep for nothing.' He bent to kiss her, and saw in her slight flinch that she still did not understand.

'May I drive you somewhere?' she said stiffly.

He shook his head. 'Thanks.'

'I didn't expect a yes or anything so gracious.'

'I love you.'

Madelene sighed, seated in the little car, looking up at the tall, handsome, black-haired man who was her son. 'Children,' she said. 'They think that will cure everything.'

'Won't it?' Sam said, with a small smile.

'Change that ridiculous tie.' She slammed the door, started the engine and roared away from the kerb, tyres spinning on slush.

'Drive carefully,' Sam called uselessly, from habit, as she tore off into the snow.

Within the week, on an equally cold day, Sam met the answer to Madelene's questions. Like most rare strokes of fortune, it was travelling incognito, and he did not recognize it at the time.

It was a stormy day in late February. Sam had risen

76

sharply for six o'clock weekday Mass at the Catholic church on Victoria Drive, as he did every day. Indeed, had Madelene Hardacre been able to observe the assiduous devotion with which he still maintained the religious life, she would have been less concerned about his loss of faith. And she would have been wrong as well, for Sam's daily attendance at Mass was less a virtue than a comfortable habit without which he felt lost. In an everyday sense, his life had not changed as much as one might suppose. He still began each morning in church, rising as early as he had ever done. He still ate frugally, and he still retired at an early hour to his bed in Mrs Hewitt's guest-house, whose guests' sitting-room maintained a starchy formality that produced in its inhabitants a fair imitation of the Grand Silence of Ampleforth. And as for the carnal life, he had not even considered it. He was less a bachelor than a widower in that respect, too stunned yet by the separation from the monastery to realize he was, in matters of love, once again a free man.

Sam's working hours did not begin until four in the afternoon, so he had a considerable length of day free to fill as he might choose. As he had made a custom, then, he walked from the church down Wellington and Trinity Roads, along Sewerby Terrace beside the Holy Trinity Church, coming out on the Alexandra Promenade overlooking North Sands. Then he turned and walked, as he had done on the day of his arrival, along the sea front, by way of Beaconsfield Promenade to the Victoria Terrace, from which he descended to the sands and walked out to the edge of the wildly angry sea, where a few early dog-walkers were his only companions. He tried with little success to summon up a summer-time image of the golden sands crowded with children and plump West Riding matrons enjoying the sun. Turning his back on the sea, which replied by casting spray up over the collar of his army greatcoat, he climbed up the damp, sand-strewn stone steps to the upper level of the

Terrace and continued southwards past the Floral Pavilion, snow-swept and deserted, on Royal Princes Parade, to the North Pier of the Harbour. He walked out to the end of the pier and stood for a while looking out over the sea, churned to a sandy brown colour by its own fury. Snow blew into his eyes and he narrowed them until he was peering through a haze of lashes, and eventually, admitting defeat, he turned and faced the gentler waters of the Harbour instead. The fishing fleet was still in, storm-bound, and there was little activity about the Harbour, where the yachts tossed restlessly in their sheltered moorings like bored thoroughbreds, awaiting summer.

'Aye, there, Sam,' a voice, rough and croaky in the wind, called over his shoulder. He turned quickly, having, in the stormy air, heard no approach. He recognized at once the unmistakable lopsided outline of Mick Raddley, the one-armed fisherman who had first befriended him on the day of his arrival. Mick crossed the windy pier with his rolling seaman's gait, his good arm across his chest, holding the collar of his navy jacket closed, the hook of his artificial arm hanging down from his cuff at his side.

'Cold day, Mick.'

'Freeze the balls off an Eskimo.'

Sam laughed softly. 'Cup of tea, Mick?'

'Aye, lad. I'll pay.'

'No you won't. You paid last week,' Sam said, and Mick, considering for a moment, agreed. Sam knew he was hard pushed for money but knew, too, he would insist on pulling his own weight or do without companionship. Mick was unemployed. He had been unemployed for four years, apart from occasional stints filling in on someone's baiting crew. It was a condition hard enough for any fishing man to bear, but harder for Mick, who had once skippered his own boat. She was the family boat, a Whitby coble that had been his father's before him. Mick, his brother and his son all had shares in her, and two young nephews were their baiting

78

crew. She gave a harsh, limited livelihood, but one he would have exchanged for nothing. They were line fishers, not yet faced with the competition of the newer net trawlers, and Mick was an expert at winding on and running out the long, many-hooked lines. But even an expert can make a mistake.

Mick's mistake was a fraction of a second's inattention as they winched in their long line. A frayed sleeve snagged on a flying hook, and in an instant he was dragged into the winch. His brother lunged to cut the line and stop the machinery. It was over in moments. Mick stood dazed on the bloody deck of his coble, his arm wrenched off at the elbow. 'Happen we'd best go in,' he'd said and his brother nodded and agreed. Together they brought the boat in, Mick's stump wrapped in a scrap of hessian sacking.

Some nimble-fingered surgeon, no doubt fresh from wartime casualties, patched up the stump, and in time fitted a mechanical substitute. It was six months before he was more or less normal again, though with a new one-handed normality, schooling his metal hook with surprising agility. By then, his coble, skipperless, idle and needing extensive work on her engine, was more or less in hock to the bank. They struggled on, Mick one-armed but efficient enough, for another year, but never recovered from their six months of debt. In the end Mick himself decided the boat must go. His brother hadn't talked to him since; as if the debt and the accident were things he'd chosen.

It was a bitterness that Sam Hardacre found hard to understand and Mick was unable to explain beyond saying, 'She were our Dad's afore she were ourn. Happen he thought I'd failed t' old man.' He would shrug and puff on his pipe. His brother had found work, grudgingly, with another boat. His son and nephews had gone their own ways.

'There's nobody wanting a one-armed skipper, lad,' said Mick, 'no matter if'n I can sail circles round t' lot. Who'll hire a cripple when he can have a sound man?'

79

Sam had known Mick for months before he had confided this story; it was not in the nature of the man nor his kind to speak over-freely with strangers. Sam had recognized this and respected it. They, the fishing men of the Harbour, were not unlike the Yorkshire farmers he had known as a child at Hardacres. They could be friendly enough, in their own gruff way, but they didn't like to be rushed about it. Sam left the approaches to Mick, meeting him from time to time by accident as both frequented the Harbour Top in the early morning, and over the months they had become, despite the gaps between them of both age and class, good friends.

They walked now, side by side, heads down and backs to the salty wind, to the Harbour Café, a small, waterside establishment long frequented by Mick and his compatriots. Inside, they sat in the steamy air amongst others also sheltering from the blustery day and the inactivity it obliged, sipping hot, sweet tea, with fingers wrapped around their mugs for warmth, while the February gale battered and shook the salt-crusted windows. They didn't talk much but savoured a shared, rather than a solitary silence.

A muffled boom suddenly broke the silence and, though Sam barely heard it over the roar of the wind outside, every other head in the café came up.

'That's the maroon,' someone said.

As Sam's eyebrows raised in question, Mick said, 'Lifeboat.' He was still listening, and the boom was followed by a second. 'That's standby,' he said, and a young man in a blue fisherman's smock, who had risen at the first sound, now grabbed his oilskin jacket from a hook at the door and ran out into the storm. There was a third boom, and Mick said, 'That's it. Launch.' He rose too, and so did Sam, instinctively. They ran out after the young man, gathering coats as they did so, and Mick led the way across the Harbour Top to the South Pier.

Below, on South Sands, beneath the pale outline of the Royal Spa Theatre and half-hidden by snow squalls, a flurry of activity and running figures concentrated on the lifeboat slip.

Sam's eyes travelled to the heavy surf in which they must launch and he said, 'I don't envy them that. What will it be, Mick, a fishing boat?'

'Nay, lad. Not if'n he's his head screwed on reeght. No business out on a day the like of this 'un. Reckon it'll be a freighter, summat bigger anyroad, run aground on the Smethwick or come in too close looking for shelter, an' got himself drove up against the cliffs.' He gestured north-eastwards where, beyond the North Pier, the grey chop of the sea vanished abruptly in a sheet of driving snow. 'Won't be the first, either.'

'Can't see a thing out there,' Sam said.

'Nor are you like to,' Mick grunted. He thought a moment, sucking at his unlit pipe. 'Tell you what, lad,' he said, 'bide a while, till we see her launched, and see which road she's gahin'. Then we'll lift my brother-in-law's car and run up the coast, see what we can see. Happen she's run right up ashore, an' they'll need a hand or two pickin' 'em out of the surf. Feel like a good drenching?' He grinned, showing tobacco-stained, crooked teeth and Sam nodded, his eyes still on the pounding froth of the surf and wondering just how long a man could survive in it to be picked out by anyone.

He looked back to the lifeboat slip where yet another man was arriving, running down on to the snow-covered sands from his car, left with one open door. Sam looked away again, down the length of the South Pier, grey and sullen under the storm. He imagined it suddenly as it had once been in his great-grandfather's day, crowded with gutties at their tables, their freezing hands numbly balancing herring and stubby knife, shuffling frozen feet, surrounded always by crying gulls and the salt-tangy stench of fish. A hard life; like any life connected with the sea, he reflected, thinking

81

again of the lost ship out there in the storm awaiting the help frantically gathering itself below on the sands. He wondered if he, witched back in time by a brutal magician, could work and survive in old Sam Hardacre's world.

It was gone now, the guttie's life. The benches were long since cleared, the last itinerant guttie long since shuffled off down some twilight road. Town officials had decreed the whole business untidy. Gutting was done aboard the boats now and the offal tossed into the sea. No doubt, Sam thought, eyeing its grey ferocity, it ate that as greedily as it ate anything; men, ships, Mick Raddley's arm. He remembered Mick saying over a pint of brown ale, 'Anyone says he loves the sea's a fool. The sea's a whore. A man might use her; he disn't love her.'

'There she goes,' Mick said emotionlessly, but Sam saw his jaw tighten on his pipe-stem and an involuntary twitch in his good arm as the lifeboat plunged down her ramp and hit the water within a great wall of thrown spray, plunging through the crisscrossing breakers out towards the open sea. He wondered, as they watched it growing smaller and fainter into the storm, if that tension were Mick's concern for the men aboard, akin to the Ave he silently offered or, rather, a restless desire to be among them.

The lifeboat cleared the end of South Pier and veered off northwards, abruptly vanishing into the storm.

'Flamborough,' said Mick. 'Come on, lad.'

Mick's home was up in the Old Town and his brother-in-law lived only a street away. Mick set off at a jogging run, a pace that, after they had left the waterfront and were climbing winding streets up into that higher district, Sam was surprised to see him vigorously maintaining. Mick had clearly not let his enforced idleness encroach on his fitness in the past years.

'Hey, slow down for an old man,' Sam panted, only half-joking, as he jogged at the old fisherman's side. Mick grinned and, if anything, speeded up.

They stopped in front of his brother-in-law's house, a small cottage that, were it not quite so battered and run-down, would be attractively quaint. But the doorstep was scrubbed and the brass knocker shining. Not that Mick used it. In time-honoured tradition he went instead up the narrow alleyway beside the house, leading to the back court and kitchen door, and disappeared around a corner, leaving Sam waiting in the street. In moments he was back, car keys in hand, making for a battered Austin mouldering at the kerb. Behind, a voice shouted, 'If'n ye bluidy prang her, ye bluidy well don't show up here agin.'

Mick grinned, pulling the peak of his flat cap down over his eyes, and clambered in, gesturing to Sam to do likewise. The car spluttered and grumbled and Mick slammed it, protesting still, into gear with the round base of his hook, and clattered away up the road. Sam hung on, wondering if he'd skippered his boat the way he drove. They went out of town by Sewerby Road and Sewerby Lane, running along the cliff tops from which Sam and, to his unease, Mick too, peered out to sea for a glimpse either of the lifeboat on its journey or the ship it sought. But not until they reached Flamborough Head itself did they catch sight of either.

Mick left the car, with motor idling, below the lighthouse and ran out, with Sam close behind, to the edge of the northern-most cliffs, an eerie experience, Sam found, with the blustering snow almost concealing the ragged edge of the chalky outcrop and whirling gusts of wind threatening to pluck them bodily from land and hurl them to the foaming sea below.

'There she is,' Mick shouted, having to cup his hands and direct his words almost against Sam's ear to be heard. Sam stared to where he pointed and saw nothing. Then, as a sheet of snow slipped past and momentarily thinned, he thought he glimpsed a dark shape, a thickening of water and air into an outline that he alone would never have recognized as a ship.

'You sure?' he asked.

Mick still peered north at the distant hulk. 'Aye. She'll be a freighter. Caught her belly on t' sandbar. Not close enough in for anyone to make it ashore either, from the looks of her. Lifeboat's got her work cut out.' He peered a few minutes longer and then abruptly turned and strode back to the car. Sam followed, his coat flattened against his back by the wind. He assumed Mick was abandoning his pursuit of the wrecked ship but when he climbed back into the car and shut the door against the storm, Mick said, 'We'll try the coast road. See how close we can get. She looks about half-way to Filey.' And he took off again, careening through the slush.

Midway between Scarborough and Filey they left the car and struggled across the snowy clifftops to the edge; and there, looking out due east, they saw her. Sam thought of that first sight, years later, like the first sight of a woman with whom one is destined to be in love and, even unaware, one feels yet something. Something tugged at him, part horror and part pity, at the sight of the wounded ship wallowing and rolling in heavy seas, but something else too, a sheer intuition that told him even then that his fate and hers were linked.

She was well aground, her bow down, grinding into the line of surf that marked the bar, her stern tilted unnaturally high and swinging back and forth like an awesome pendulum. She was listed heavily to port and the north-easterly gale battered against her partly-exposed hull while waves broke over her, cascading down her sloping decks. The distance was too great to make out any sign of life, but Sam assumed her crew were clinging to the raised stern, awaiting rescue, and hidden from view by the superstructure of the ship.

'She's finished,' Mick said, with the same dry dullness with which he'd spoken of the lifeboat launch. 'If she'd bury down a bit deeper she might have a chance but grinding like that she'll break up in half a day. Reckon her back's broken already.'

The words struck painfully at something in Sam that saw her as a living thing in misery. Then in the distance he saw a white splash of thrown water, repeated at intervals, that marked the approach of rescue through heavy seas.

Abruptly, Mick turned away. 'No use gawking about here,' he said gruffly. 'Might as well go home an' do summat useful.' He stomped off and Sam, with a last glance down at the distant stricken freighter, turned and followed him to the car. He understood then. The lifeboat crew were all Mick's friends and they were about to risk their lives against the sea and he was utterly powerless to help. Sam thought that, in his place, he would choose also not to watch. He was glad, anyhow. The slow destruction of the ship was something he wished not to see.

Mick dropped him at the top of St Hilda Street after a drive in which neither had spoken much. Sam knew better than to press the old fisherman in his present morose mood. Whatever was to be learned about the shipwreck would have to come later, or from someone else. He returned to his lodgings and sat at the window of his room overlooking the slushy grey courtyard and wrote a letter to his brother Terry at Ampleforth.

Later he went out to work. The chip shop, like everywhere else probably, was full of talk of the wreck, and rumours flew vacuously about. Some said that the lifeboat had saved everyone. Some said only two were saved, the rest lost to the surf. Someone arrived late in the evening to announce the ship had broken in two and one half had capsized. Sam concentrated on his work, battering cold slices of haddock and dropping them into the spitting oil, and deciding he would find Mick after the shop closed, if he could, and learn the truth.

The proprietor, a short squat West Riding man called Ormsley, who transferred his resentment for the daughter who had married and left him short-handed to the man who had replaced her, grudgingly agreed to close down at nine-thirty. There hadn't been a customer for the last half-hour, and as the gale had not relented but grown, if anything, worse with nightfall, it was hardly likely there would be any more. Sam scrubbed the counter, tidied the stacks of newspaper and swept the stone floor in the back room where the potato sacks were stored, and when Ormsley, who was ostenta-tiously mopping the black and white tiles of the shop floor, ran out of ways to squeeze his money's worth from his employee, he got his coat from the storeroom and went out into the night. Through the half-lit window he glimpsed Ormsley, back bent, short black moustache aquiver with muttered resentments, bearing his work like a grudge.

God, don't let me ever get like that, Sam thought, no matter how hard life gets. He turned and faced the easterly wind, impatient for its salty tang to get the stench of cooking from his face and hair, wondering how long before tedium and routine reduced him, like Ormsley, to sour pettiness. Still, losing an arm and his livelihood hadn't made Mick Raddley less of a man, he considered and, thinking that, decided to find Mick as an antidote to Ormsley and his chip shop.

He found him in the third pub he tried, one of his less-often-frequented haunts, a big establishment in the Old Town whose customers were less exclusively maritime men than in the others. Mick had cheered considerably since he parted with Sam in the afternoon and was now deep in conversation with a cluster of cronies. Sam recognized one as his brother-in-law and another, grey-bearded and wizened, as an ex-Navy man called Haines he'd met once before. They were seated in a little booth, crowded round a table laden with pint glasses in various states of replenishment. As soon as Mick saw Sam he signalled that he should join them, and a place was made by a hurried shifting of bottoms at the end of a bench.

'Alma, that's another round on me,' he said, gesturing to the multitude of glasses and to Sam as well.

Sam sat down, a little amazed and said, eyeing the old fisherman warily, 'You just won the pools?'

'Ye could say that, lad,' Mick returned, grinning, and there was a circle of laughter around the table. A pint of brown ale was placed before Sam and he drank it, still puzzled at Mick's sudden extravagance. When he offered, a little uneasily because of the size of the party, to get the next round in, he was quickly dismissed by more laughter, and he began to realize something was going on he didn't know about. He asked Mick, then, about the fate of the ship's crew.

'Safe and sound, lad, every one. Bit wet and cold, mind, but nothing that won't repair.'

Sam nodded, pleased, and said, 'And the ship?'

'Broke in two, just as they brought the last man off. Stern half's gone down on her side and her bow's breaking up on the rocks.' He paused, as if in respect, and then, surprisingly, his grin returned. 'Still 'tis an ill wind, lad, that blows no good.'

Again there was laughter and the Navy man, Haines, suggested another round. Mick looked at his brother-in-law and they made a little nod. Mick rose from his place, tapping Sam's shoulder as he left the table, and Sam realized he was meant to follow. Mick went out through an end door of the room into an alleyway beside the pub. Sam recognized the brother-in-law's car parked up the side street, and followed the old fisherman to the vehicle.

Mick flung the boot up and reached in for something shadowed and bulky. Then he paused and said, 'What d'ye say, Sam, does we give 'em salmon again, or d'ye think peaches fer this 'un?'

'What?' said Sam, mystified.

'I can give 'em this 'un, too, only your guess is as good as mine. Labels are so drenched it could be owt.'

87

'What could, Mick? What are you talking about?'

Mick stepped back and let the dim light of a distant street lamp fall on the car boot. 'These,' he said.

Sam leaned over the old fisherman's shoulder. The boot of the Austin was crammed with battered wooden cases, through the splintered boards of which he glimpsed the shine of smooth metal.

'Tins,' he said. 'Cases of tins.'

'Salmon, pears, peaches, pilchards and one of beans. Bit wet on t'outside, but reeght as rain within. Dandy thing about tins; don't mind a bit o' salt water at all.'

'Where'd they come from?' Sam demanded, and at the same moment he knew. 'The wreck.'

'Seas breached her forrard hold. Seems she come from Canada. Ain't seen so much good food since afore the war,' Mick grinned. 'An' t' sea weren't askin' for ration cards.'

Sam was silent, staring at the carload of booty. 'You've been paying for the drinks with this.'

'Two salmon and one of peaches. Alma says we can drink all week on yon.'

'But Mick, it's not legal, surely. I mean, these belong to someone, surely. The shipowners, or the shipping company.'

'Weren't no sign of any shipowners up to necks in t' surf that I could see.'

'But Mick . . .'

'Treasure trove, lad, finders-keepers.' Mick grinned again, slightly the worse for his night's drink, and then grew momentarily morose. 'Aw, lad, ye'd nay spoil our fun.'

Sam shook his head. 'It's not me, Mick. But if anyone finds out it could mean trouble. It is rather stealing, after all, isn't it?'

Mick was silent. He lifted out his case of tins, declining Sam's offered hands. He set it on the cobbles and closed the boot with a lonely click in the silent alley. The sound of the storm still moaned from the distant bay and the air was heavy with salt. Mick turned to face it and then turned back to Sam.

'Yon bitch,' he said, nodding seawards, 'owes me an arm. She'll needs toss a good lot more than this my way afore we're even.'

Sam nodded and said, 'I'm sorry Mick. I spoke out of turn.'

'Nay lad. You're most like reeght, leastwise where the law's concerned. What lies in her holds I'd nay touch. But the odd case on the shore's just flotsam. If'n it wisn't me, would be the next bloke, so it may as well be me.' He lifted his case and trundled it morosely off to the door of the pub and Sam hated himself for having in some way tainted the old man's night of glory.

When they returned they found the party had broken up, and only Haines and Mick's brother-in-law, Rob, remained at the table. They shared another round, and drank, but the high humour had gone, and each began to sink into inebriated somnolence. While they were sitting thus, in silence, a large man rose from his place at another table and walked with slow, heavy steps to their booth, settling without invitation at the end of Mick's bench. When he spoke his voice was surprisingly high, coming as it did from so big a body, and his tone was plaintive and sad.

'Friends gone already, Mick?' he said, and then when the distinctly drunken Mick made no answer, he said, to no one in particular, 'Isn't it always the way?'

'Erasmus Sykes,' said Mick, leaning heavily on Sam's arm as they made a weaving course for home from the door of the pub. 'Sorry to rush ye, but a night uv that 'un moanin' wud make an angel want to hang hisself.'

'Quite all right,' Sam said, laughing. 'I'd think we'd all had enough.'

'Aye,' Mick muttered. 'Happen Rob's had enough en'all, but he's still at it. Ye'd not catch me risking the wrath uv a woman with a tongue like Betty's. Still, Ah'd rather walk than listen to Erasmus tellin' how the world an' its brother 'as let him down again.'

'Who is he?' Sam asked, steering the wandering Mick in the direction of his own street.

'Erasmus Sykes?' Mick muttered with drunken surprise. Then he said, 'Sorry, I'm forgetting again you're not one of t' locals.' He grinned. ''E's one of *the* Sykes. You know, down the Promenade, Sykes Amusements, t' big Arcade smack in the middle of t' whole place.'

'Oh yes, of course,' Sam said quickly, knowing Mick would think him a total, not just a partial idiot, if he failed to identify it. An image of sleazy salt-faded signs over street-fronts boarded for winter gradually rose in his mind, where it had been imprinted by the sort of casual glance an uninterested adult would cast such a place. Sam smiled to himself, remembering how such Aladdin's caves of tinny joy had drawn him as a child upon visits to the seaside. Madelene Hardacre had invariably drawn him away with a disgusted sniff. Surprisingly, it was his great-uncle Harry, the most refined of all his family, who had gleefully led him on secret expeditions to those caverns of shadowed glitter, where ghost trains rode through mysterious tunnels on clanking tracks, and endless games offered wondrous rewards and tricked away the pennies in his pocket. 'Of course,' Sam said. 'The big old place. I remember it. I was forever trying to get inside when I was a child.'

'Aye, nay doubt. It were there as long as I can remember. Oldest and biggest in town. Erasmus's dad put 'er up. Erasmus an' his brothers run 'er. Made a pretty penny or two, the Sykes lot. Queer folk though, like gypsies, the Arcade folk. Like carney people the world o'er. Clannish, keep themselves ti themselves; nowt ti do wi' any other.'

'He seemed friendly enough,' Sam commented, nodding behind him to the pub and Erasmus.

'Yon's not friendly, lad. Nay. Just thought he'd the

chance uv a good moan. Moan ti anyone, just ti hear 'isself.'
Mick grinned again. 'Never met the like. All 'is life,
Erasmus 'as sung t' same tune; how poverty's got him by
the neck. In spite uv the Arcade, and the whole town
knowing what it brings in in t' summer. And never mind
the greyhounds he keeps and the string uv thoroughbreds
down Malton way, he's still poor as t' poor old church
mouse is our Erasmus.

'But then, back uv t' last year, old Erasmus gets hisself a
winner. Bonny wee mare, name uv Dainty Girl, wi' two
white feet an' a streak down 'er face an' she leaves t' lot at
ivry startin' post in the North. So Erasmus has a winner at
last. An d'ye know, lad, it's well nigh the end uv 'im? Nowt
ti moan about any more. Folk for ever coming up, all
cheery-faced, saying isn't it grand? Old Erasmus is like ti
drown in all yon cheeriness.' Mick stopped to light his pipe,
fumbling it with his one good hand, shielding the light from
the strong wet wind. 'Good lot of us thought 'twas the end
uv the old bugger. But nay, ye'll nay keep 'is like down.
Soon enough, Erasmus found a new song ti sing. Now it's
the sufferin' o' the wealthy in this greedy world. Beggars at
his door, taxmen climbing down his chimney, a' his friends
away wi' jealousy, a' his new friends just hangers-on after
the money. Nobbut t' same song, all reeght, wi' a new
tune.' Mick puffed at his pipe, grinning around its edges.
'Troublé with Erasmus, lad, is all 'is days 'e's had more
brass than wis good for 'im. 'E still disn't know what t' do
wi't.'

Sam smiled again, but in himself he felt sad. There was
something pathetic about the big friendless man lurching
with his imaginary sorrows from table to table in the pub.

He said, 'One feels rather sorry for him.'

Mick snorted. 'Lad,' he said, as they parted company in
front of his darkened house, 'the likes uv you an' I can't
afford t' feel sorry for the likes uv 'im.' He stomped off up
the shadowy close to his back door, but as Sam walked away

down into the town again, his thoughts were filled with the incongruous bulk of Erasmus Sykes.

Twice more in the following week Mick Raddley made forays down to the stony beach of the bay, in which the freighter lay wrecked, to search for more of her cargo washed ashore. On each occasion he added to his bounty with an extra crate and a scattering of loose tins amidst the splintered wood of their shattered boxing. But on neither day did he find the bonanza of the first, and on the last, on which he had brought along not only his ex-Navy friend, Pete Haines, but Sam Hardacre as well, the pickings were so lean that Mick announced that he'd not bother coming back.

'There must be more out there,' said Sam.

'Aye,' said Mick. 'An' it's staying out there, en'all. Leastwise, it's staying out there long enough that it sarn't be any use when it dis come in.' He shrugged. The bounty of the sea was as fickle as it was unexpected. He did not question beyond the obvious fact that there was nothing more to be had on the beach. He lifted one end of the crate and waited for Sam to take the other. But Sam was still looking out at the sea, where the starboard rail of the sunken freighter was barely visible, at low tide, as a line of disturbed, whitened water.

Pete Haines turned from the sack of loose tins he was gathering and called, 'Thinkin' uv swimmin' out for t' rest?'

Sam still stood looking out to sea. At last he turned to the two older men and said, 'Surely, it can be done?'

'What can? Swim for it?' Mick demanded, his bushy grey brows twitching as he chomped on his pipe-stem. 'Wouldn't fancy yer chances.'

'No, but surely there must be some way. Surely someone will try for the rest of it, won't they?'

'Who?' Pete Haines asked, with a shrug.

'I don't know. The shipowners, or the shipping company. It must belong to someone?'

'Sure it does. Or did,' Pete Haines said. 'An' they've had the insurance money by now. They'll be happy enough. Yon hulk'll be the proud property of Lloyds of London,' he added, with grandeur. 'Their latest acquisition.'

'What about Lloyds then?' Sam asked. 'Won't they want to try to salvage something from it? Get some of their money back?'

'Well, lad,' Pete Haines, getting settled into the conversation, seated himself on the crate that Mick had been about to lift, and launched into an explanation of the vagaries of shipwrecks. 'No doubt they'd like to. Now the question is, what's worth salvaging, and who can they find to do it? You see the thing about salvage is, it's summat uv a fool's paradise. T' sea is full uv treasure, but she's most tenacious about hanging on t' the lot. Now if'n they can find some blighter foolhardy enough to take up a contract, they might well have a go at her. Not that she's any use now for anything but scrap.'

'But the cargo?'

'Like Mick said, if'n it can be got out before t' sea gets at it, it might be worthwhile. On t'other 'and, it might not. It's worth a bob or two, nay doubt, but its nay gold either, lad. Job like yon'll take a few bob en'all, getting equipment out to her; ye'd need a salvage boat an' a diver, an' some grabs, an' yer compressors, a generator or two, yer winches . . . an' then ye've got t' bring enough up t' pay everybody's keep, an' just hope there's enough left over from what ye salve to make it worth yer trouble. An' if ye run into some snag, find her lying awkward so ye can't reach her holds at all, ye just may run out a' brass afore ye ever raise anything at all. Chancy business, lad, a bad 'un, if'n ye ask me.'

Sam nodded, chastened. 'Sounds it,' he said. 'And,' he added suddenly, 'one that you know something about. Am I right?'

'Reckon I should do,' Pete Haines said, with a reminiscent grin spreading across his weatherbeaten face. 'Spent most uv the war raising ships for His Majesty. He was forever droppin' 'em down in the damnedest places, too.' He leaned back with his hands on his knees, looking out to sea and the distant wreck. 'An' afore that, lad, I had ten years in commercial salvage. Raised everything from 2000 tons of freighter to a bloody Rolls-Royce some idiot drove into t' sea one fine night.' He laughed, remembering. 'Any road, during wartime I got my fill fer good an' all. Settled down ashore in the scrap business yince I got out, an' there's where I'm staying. A good living an' a nice dry one, at that.' He stood up, lifting the crate with Mick and edging with it back towards the difficult path leading up to the top of the cliffs and the road. 'Mind now,' he said, 'I won't say that I don't get tempted, now and again, when I see something like yon. It's like a lovely batch uv cream cakes behind t' shop window. Wouldn't be half as tempting if'n it weren't so damned out a' reach.'

Sam nodded thoughtfully. He hoisted Pete's hessian sack of tins on to his shoulder and, with one more glance at the grey North Sea curling around the curving white pebble shore, he turned to follow the two older men up the cliff path. At the top they set the crate down for the rest, and he lowered his sack to the wet grey grass.

'Mick,' he said, turning again towards the windy sea, 'I want to have a talk with Erasmus Sykes.'

'Do ye, by gum,' said Mick. 'Yer more uv an idiot than I thought.'

'Yes,' said Sam, with a small, rueful smile. 'And I want you there when I have it.'

'Bluidy hell,' said Mick.

CHAPTER SIX

Erasmus Sykes lived in a long, rambling flat above one segment of his sprawling amusement arcade. It was reached by two flights of narrow stairs, through the gloomy darkness of which Sam Hardacre climbed on the Sunday afternoon after the day of the shipwreck, with a protesting Mick Raddley in tow.

'If'n 'is bluidy dogs are there, I'm bluidy leaving,' Mick grumbled. 'Yappy wee buggers.'

'What dogs?' Sam asked, but Mick's reply was drowned in a sudden burst of shrill, sharp barking from behind the plain door at the head of the stairs. Over the torrent of yaps and yelps, Sam heard the high-pitched voice of their master cajoling, 'Hush, hush, Daddy's babies.'

'Hush, hush,' Mick imitated, prancing about on the stair landing behind Sam. 'Daddy's pains in t'arse.'

The door opened and Sam was deluged in small black poodles. Four of them, bouncing and scrabbling with stiff black claws, assaulted his trouser legs, worried his shoe laces, and then abruptly turned their attentions to Mick. Mick shuffled and fumed, detaching one and then the other while Erasmus Sykes stared mournfully at the mêlée as if it was totally beyond his power to control.

'Stand still, Mick, happen they're wanting your scent.'

'Happen they're wanting my leg, damn them,' Mick snorted. 'An' I'll nay spare them one. I'm an arm short already.'

Erasmus, still ignoring the chaos caused by his pets, extended a fleshy hand to Sam. 'Erasmus Sykes,' he said. 'And you'll be Mr Hardacre?'

'Sam Hardacre,' said Sam, shaking the proffered hand. A

95

faint smile momentarily crossed the wide, perpetually worried-looking face of his host.

'Reeght. The new Sam Hardacre.' He turned briefly to the circle of yapping poodles. 'Hush, Daddy's darlings,' he murmured to no avail, but as he led Sam, Mick and his little herd of woolly dogs into the interior of the flat he added, 'A name to live up to, lad.'

Sam said nothing, hoping Erasmus would not proceed on the obvious course and ask if he was of the same family. It was not an admission he chose to make, knowing how connections with supposed Hardacre wealth would make the proposal he hoped to make appear ridiculous.

Erasmus did not. He led them, instead, into the long sitting-room of the flat, and offered them seats on a huge sofa covered in dark red plush and ornamented with a multitude of lace antimacassars. The sofa was Victorian and ancient, sinking beneath their combined weight so that Sam found himself sitting with his long legs folded up and his knees nearly up to his chin. All the furnishings in the flat were of a similar era, chairs and other soft furnishings of the same red plush, and deep maroon velvet curtains looped heavily over the tall windows. Any light they allowed to enter was further screened by swathes of white netting, and the darkness was accentuated by layers of dark oriental rugs piled one on top of the other. Everywhere were small tables and glass-fronted cabinets and every surface was covered first in fading lace or fringed brocade and then with dusty ornaments of china and glass. For all its antique grandeur the room resembled, in Sam's eyes, nothing so much as a gypsy caravan of the older kind, all dark woods and fringes and velvet and lace, and he fancied that Erasmus could hitch it all up to his team of black poodles and draw it away down the road.

'You will have tea?' Erasmus said mournfully, as if their acceptance was at once both necessary and unfortunate. 'I'm afraid it will be nothing elaborate. I live alone.'

But tea, when it came on a great silver tray carried by their host, who pirouetted with amazing gracefulness among his still yapping dogs, was extraordinarily lavish, with scones, crumpets, sandwiches and cakes filled with great dobs of cream. Mick, compensating for his persecution by the poodles, loaded his plate with everything in sight and gobbled with evident satisfaction. Sam accepted tea, and listened quietly while Erasmus explained that now he had a famous winning racehorse many people came to call. People who in the past had no time for him at all.

'When the money goes, so will they,' he added morosely. 'I dare say, so will you en'all.'

Sam did not know what to say and eventually, as was his nature, plumped for honesty. 'All right, Mr Sykes, you've had your say. And you're right; I've come because you've a bit of money lying around.' He waited for a reaction, and saw the surprise he suspected would be there when Erasmus heard his own perpetual cynicism on the lips of another. 'But I'll tell you something else. I can't make your friends stay. That's for you to do. But if you'd like the money to hang around for a bit, I think I've the way to make that happen. If you're willing to take a chance.'

'I'm nay a gambling man, Mr Hardacre,' Erasmus said, with the stuffy defensiveness of one whose fortunes were built on games of chance.

Sam paused and then said, 'Neither am I, Mr Sykes. You see there are chances, and then there are chances.' As he spoke he seemed to hear his great-grandfather using the same words when he spoke of his own start in business. 'There's the kind when you invest in luck alone, and the other kind, when you invest in something more, skill, invention, wits. The things that make up a man. I'm not asking you to invest in luck alone, Mr Sykes. I'm asking you to invest in me.'

Erasmus sank in silence into his vast plushy chair, his small eyes growing smaller into folds of dreamy flesh. Mick looked sideways at Sam in amazement.

'What's all this?' he said, but Sam, willing him to silence, kept his eyes on the puzzled mournful face of Erasmus Sykes.

'Happen ye'd like to explain yerself,' he said at last.

Sam smiled a slow, spreading smile, sensing already he had won. He got to his feet, stretching out tall and unlikely in the plushy, over-furnished room. He winked at Mick, who was watching intently, his sharp blue eyes bright pinpoints under thick bushy grey brows. 'Happen,' he said, 'I would.'

He proceeded then to explain to Erasmus about the freighter *Louisa Jane*, and her cargo of tinned goods lying on the floor of the bay near Filey. He knew as he spoke that Erasmus, renowned local that he was, would have heard all about the wreck from other sources, but the large man made no sign that he had. He was clearly intrigued by Sam's purpose in raising the subject at all.

'It's a valuable cargo, Mr Sykes,' he said. 'At least until the sea has time to damage the tins. But it's not worth a fortune. Which suits my purpose.'

'Which is what, Mr Hardacre?'

'I want to raise that cargo,' Sam said. 'If I can, in a reasonable time, and at reasonable expense, there will be a respectable profit, not a fortune, but a respectable profit. From what Mick here,' he nodded to the one-armed fisherman, who was regarding him with a mixture of suspicion and new respect, 'and his associates tell me, there's not likely to be a great rush for the salvage contract. The margins are a bit narrow for the established boys. So I think I've a fair chance, if I act quickly.'

'And what if the margins are too narrow?'

'That's the risk, Mr Sykes. Still, barring any disasters, it should be possible to cut losses; any equipment we purchase could be resold, only the man-hours would be a dead loss. And even a partial success would redeem some of the investment.'

'What investment?' Mick said suddenly, chomping on his pipe-stem. 'Happen I got lost a while back.'

Erasmus Sykes passed over Mick's comment without response. Sam was aware of a sharp mind functioning behind the soft, pudgy, confused-looking face, a mind that showed only in the deep-set, muddy-coloured eyes, narrowed now to thoughtful little arcs. 'What's your experience, Mr Hardacre? What are you selling me?'

'None,' Sam said, looking straight at the shrewd arcs of eyes. 'Experience can be hired.'

'Wi' my brass.'

'Yes. With your money. I've none of my own or I'd not be here.'

'Bluidy honest, any road, aren't you?'

Sam said nothing.

'Let me get this straight, then,' Sykes said, almost smiling, patting the back of one of his overfed wiggly little dogs. 'You're asking me to invest in a salvage company run by a bloke what's nobbut an amateur an' hasn't a brass farthing uv his own to add to t'effort. An' 'e wants to raise a cargo t' proper salvage boys won't touch wi' a barge pole?'

'Eeh, hold on, 'rasmus,' Mick said, suddenly galvanized into defence of his young friend. 'It's nowt like that at all.'

But Sam ignored him, as Sykes had done before and said, 'That's right, Mr Sykes. That's just about it.'

'Ye must take me fer a bluidy fool.'

'No,' Sam said. 'I take you for a shrewd businessman who knows the gambling business like the back of his hand.'

'Ye flattering me?'

'I don't think so, sir.'

Erasmus sank down into silence. His eyes almost closed and his four dogs gathered on top of him in a woolly mound, whimpering, whining and pushing each other for the best place on top of his broad stomach. He stroked them idly, humming softly to himself. After a great length of time he opened his eyes slightly and his face regained its pathetic mournfulness.

He said, 'And if I do back you in your new business, Mr Hardacre, I suppose you'll be my friend then?'

Sam heard Mick's little catch of breath and felt him physically willing him to make the right answer to this vital question. But Sam only smiled a little and said, 'No. I'm sorry, Mr Sykes, but I won't be your friend just because you lend me money. I might one day for other reasons, but we'll just have to wait and see how we get on. But not for the money.' He heard Mick let his breath out in a long, raspy sigh and saw him shrug and instinctively reach for his flat cap, lying on the arm of the sofa beside him. Sam waited, quietly studying the complex, bruised-looking expression of his host. After a long, long while, he brushed his dogs from him, and as they tumbled and scrabbled to the carpet, he stood up and looked coolly at Sam.

'Eeh, but yer honest, noo. How far does yon honesty get ye?'

'As far as I want to go, Mr Sykes.'

'Happen it does,' Erasmus Sykes said slowly. Then he turned to Mick. 'Well, Mick,' he said. 'Reckon ye'd better take yer friend out of 'ere noo.'

Mick Raddley reddened beneath his stubble of grey beard and squirmed on the red plush of the sofa. 'Noo, haud on there, Erasmus, no sense getting all hot under t' collar.'

'Go on, Mick. Lad's got shoppin' to do. Reckon ye'd better go help him buy hisself a boat.'

It took Mick three days to find the boat. Sam spent the first of those days persuading Pete Haines out of his retirement and into Sam's embryonic team as salvage master. The second day, until four o'clock, he spent following Pete on a long trail that touched down at every scrap-merchant, marine-outfitters and military surplus outlet in the East

Riding, earmarking equipment for future purchase. Time was short for Sam in every way. He knew he had to have his bid in for the salvage contract within the week, and he needed the respectable semblance of a salvage company behind him to do it. Also, he was very rapidly going to run out of money to organize his assault on the *Louisa Jane*. He had given in his week's notice on the day he met with Erasmus Sykes, burning that small but useful bridge behind him. Ormsley had been less than pleased and would no doubt blacken his name accordingly and make finding another job that much more difficult. Sam didn't mind. He had decided something; he was planning never to be in anyone's employ again.

On the third day, Pete Haines produced the most necessary member of his crew: the diver. He was a man called Martin Raynor and they found him where Pete Haines expected to find him, on the floor of a pub.

'Great diver. Hasn't got a nerve in his body,' Haines commented as they walked a mumbly and protesting Martin Raynor up and down North Pier to sober him up.

'I should think not. Hardly room, is there, beside all the whisky.'

'Pay it no mind. Divers like their tipple. Do the job well enough, though, when they're sober.'

'When's that?' said Sam, staring morosely at the somnolent Raynor draped across a convenient bench.

'Leave him to me,' Haines said. 'Martin an' I've worked a fair share uv wrecks together. There's none better. Just leave him to me,' he added again, with grim confidence. Sam did, returning to the chip shop to complete his last days of work. When he finished, late that night, Mick Raddley was waiting outside the door.

'Found your boat,' he said with a wry grin.

The following day, in a tatty corner of a boatyard in Whitby, where even the oily water lapped pilings with an air of sullen despondency, Sam saw the reason for Mick's grin.

'That?' he said uncertainly, looking from the vessel Mick had indicated back to the old fisherman's face. Mick was giving nothing away. He stood studying an imaginary point somewhere just above the half-submerged bow of the boat.

'Aye,' he said, smiling to himself.

'That's her?'

'That's her.'

Sam nodded. He turned his eyes back to the boat, deciding he had better really look at her. Heretofore, his glance had but crossed her half-sunken hulk with perfunctory haste, convinced that she could not possibly be the vessel Mick meant for him to buy. His conviction flagged now; there was nothing else in sight and Mick was still looking dreamily across her unpromising bow. Sam was in a spot. He had never pretended to Mick any knowledge of the sea and matters maritime that he did not have. But on the other hand, he didn't relish the idea of having to reveal himself a complete idiot in that regard either. He glanced again to the mildly-smiling fisherman, wondering if Mick were playing an elaborate hoax to see if he was fool enough to agree to the purchase of a mouldering wreck. He studied her now with care. She was an old Keel boat, her black-painted steel hull surmounted by a stubby wheelhouse aft of her sixty-foot length. Actually, she didn't seem that much of a wreck, he decided. She wasn't so much sunken as riding very low in the water. Her paintwork was surprisingly fresh and a neat stowage of ropes and gear indicated she was still under some watchful eye, not yet abandoned to the harpies of the land.

'What's t' matter?' Mick said eventually, at Sam's long silence.

Sam took a chance. 'She looks rough,' he said.

'Happen ye were expecting t' *Queen Mary*? At price you set?'

'No,' Sam said, 'of course she'll be fine.' He paused. 'I say, Mick, isn't she rather low in the water?'

'Should be. She's on t' bottom.' Sam blinked. Mick was still gazing contentedly at the battered old Keel boat as he filled his pipe. He turned then to Sam, his sharp blue eyes crinkled up with amusement. 'You're the salvage-master, lad. Raise her.'

Sam smiled ruefully. He said, 'No, Mick. I'm not anything of the sort. I didn't even say that to Sykes; I certainly wouldn't to you. Pete Haines is salvage-master. You're my skipper. You raise her, if she can be raised. Give me your decision this afternoon and I'll buy her tomorrow.'

He turned and walked away from the water's edge, leaving Mick alone by his boat. After a moment he heard a shout, and turned.

'Eeh, lad, you're sore wi' me.'

'A little.'

'Now haud on. I was just havin' me bit o' fun. She's a good boat, a sound 'un. Nothing wrong wi' her that the odd patch and a bit uv pumping-out won't cure. I was right about the money, lad; she's nay the *Queen Mary*, but she's about t' best ye'll find at the price. I wouldn't have tricked ye. Nay fer the world.' He was standing with his one hand rubbing his chin in remorse, and his artificial limb hanging forlornly at his side, a solid, burly figure in his rough blue smock before the old Keel boat.

Sam's anger melted. He returned to the water's edge and stood looking at the boat. He said slowly, 'You know, Mick, it's not lack of knowledge makes a man a fool; it's lack of humility. I know I've a lot to learn about boats, the sea, salvage, all of it. I've *everything* to learn. I'm relying on you to teach me. You, and Pete Haines. I'm first to admit I'd never have started any of this without the pair of you. But,' he paused and smiled his slow, wide-spreading smile, 'I don't suppose the pair of you would have started this without me either, would you?'

'Never uv thought uv it,' Mick said honestly, at once. 'Would never uv crossed my mind. Funny that, too, because it's a simple enough idea, but I'd have just taken my crate of tins and left it at that. As for Pete, yince he'd hung his salvage hat up the whole thing were finished. Or so he thought,' he laughed softly. 'Haven't seen him so happy in years as he were when he come back from chasing after compressors and winches an' the like, wi' you. Mind noo, his wife's nay likely to be so pleased. Funny, too, here I am wi' a job, and there's Pete, back in his own trade, an' all because of you who doesn't . . .'

'Doesn't know his arse from his elbow, where the sea's concerned?'

'Aw lad, Ah've got yer back up, again.'

Sam shook his head. 'Truth doesn't make me angry, Mick. Trickery does,' he added sharply, and Mick winced slightly. 'I know I'm the innocent in this game. But sometimes it takes an innocent, someone on the outside to get the idea first. I know of a man who made a fortune by selling cooked herring to the crowds at race meets. Simplest idea in the world, only it just happened no one had thought of it before. Or at least, no one who had thought of it got around to doing it. There's the thinking, and then there's the doing. Nothing gets off the ground without both.'

Mick nodded. 'Well,' he said, 'I'm nay likely to be the thinker so I'd better be the doer. That's if'n I've still got a job?' he added warily.

Sam nodded. 'You've got one. Now we'll go and see the man who's selling this boat. I want her seaworthy in a week,' he said, to which Mick gave a small wince, but did not argue. 'And Mick.'

'Aye?'

'I want her name changed.' He was studying the lettering, *Susannah K*, on her bow. 'We'll call her *Dainty Girl*. After Erasmus Sykes's mare. The lass responsible.'

Mick laughed. 'Reeght. *Dainty Girl* it is. As long as ye don't name 'er after his damned wee curly-arsed dogs.'

* * *

Sam went back to Erasmus Sykes that evening with news of his find, and by ten o'clock the next morning with the ink barely dry on Erasmus Sykes's cheque, the *Susannah K* was his, and Mick and Pete Haines, with Martin Raynor yet in tow like a dog that needed watching, were at work upon her.

'See what I mean,' Haines commented, as Sam left them aboard his new acquisition, 'sober as a judge. He's nay touched a drop since day afore yesterday.' Haines smiled so beamingly that Sam suspected this was some sort of record where Raynor was concerned, and was less than comforted.

Sam drove Pete Haines's car to York where he had an appointment with a solicitor. By the time, four days later, when Mick was able to announce proudly that the newly-named *Dainty Girl* was afloat and watertight, his dealings with the solicitor and a firm of accountants had reached their own conclusion. *Dainty Girl* was no longer his but, along with the mass of hardware that Pete Haines had gathered and was storing now in a shed at his scrap-yard, was the property of a limited company formed for the purpose of raising the cargo of the *Louisa Jane*.

'Seeing as how it's my brass, ye'd think my name 'ud be in there somewhere,' mourned Erasmus Sykes.

'Your brass, sir, my company,' said Sam, with a grin. 'Hardacre Salvage. Or nowt.'

'Yer a hard man, Mr Hardacre,' Erasmus whined, but his shrewd little eyes were alight.

A day later, Sam Hardacre boarded a train for London. It was a week exactly since the sinking of the *Louisa Jane*. Sam had at his command a salvage company consisting of a skipper, a salvage master and a diver, a refurbished Keel boat, two ageing generators, two compressors, a Navy surplus hard-hat diving suit, a miscellany of air hose pumps, grabs and winches and enough financial backing from Erasmus Sykes to keep the whole operational for two months. He was dressed well in a new blue serge suit and belted trench coat, and carried in his pocket the five pounds spending money he had allotted himself, along with the new clothes, so that he might present an image suitable to a company director. Because the director of Hardacre Salvage had an appointment at four o'clock that afternoon with an underwriter at Lloyd's of London.

Mick Raddley saw him off at Bridlington station. 'Eeh, by gum,' he said, standing back. 'You look gradely.' He cupped his one hand over his ear and leaned Londonwards. 'I can hear 'em at Lloyd's already, ringin' t' bluidy Lutine bell.'

CHAPTER
SEVEN

It was three days later, on 9 March 1951, when Jan Muller arrived at the dockside of the Israeli port of Haifa. The ship was not yet in. He found himself relieved rather than impatient, and walked rather quickly away from the waterfront, back into the old Arab quarter where he might drown his unease in a bath of nostalgia. He had not realized until this moment how much he dreaded the coming meeting. Hannah had realized. As he walked he thought of her and her curious perception. She had not wanted him to come to meet Isaac at all and he had protested, saying she was heartless. But that was not the case. She had read his true unspoken reasons and knew what potential pain a-waited him along with Isaac Mandel on the immigrant ship from Cyprus. And because she knew and loved him, and did not know Isaac, her concerns were naturally for Jan.

Still Jan had ignored her and had travelled the dusty miles by coach from Kibbutz Aaron on the edge of the Negev to the humid heat of the Mediterranean city of Haifa, a city which of all places in his new homeland held traces of the indefinable heart-tug of home. It was to Haifa he had come sixteen years before in the late autumn of 1934, a refugee, penniless as most refugees, the son of a German war hero and a gentle German lady who was also a Jew. As he wandered deeper into the twisting shadowy lanes of the old souks, now pocked and shattered by shellfire, he felt he could actually come face to face with the ghost of himself, his old self, stumbling wide-eyed through those same streets, a startled European benumbed by the shattering changes in his country that had cast him unwilling into the gay, alien clutter of an Arabian city. A ghost amid ghosts, he thought sadly, for the Arabs whose city he had entered were gone, scattered by the violent birth throes of Israel, refugees now themselves beyond her borders. Haifa, the changeling child, had forgotten its parentage and rose up around him, a new, modern, western industrial city, irrevocably changed by its Jewish inheritors, of which he was undoubtedly one. Yet he mourned the old Arab city with a nostalgia that was undeniably perverse.

Jan was glad he was alone and that Yigel, his closest friend who had accompanied him on the coach journey, had gone off by himself this morning to poke about the museums with kibbutznik curiosity. Yigel would not understand his attachment to the Haifa of his memories; nor indeed would Hannah. She would grow hurt at what she interpreted as pro-Arab sympathies, as well she might. Arabs had killed both her parents, and he knew she must think of them as he thought of the Nazis. But Hannah was gentle, as the martyred often are, whereas Yigel, whose parents were alive and well and living in considerable comfort in Haifa itself, had nothing for Arabs but bitterness and hate. They were still to him the enemy they had been when he and Jan fought side by side in Haganah in the first days of Statehood, and so they would always remain. Jan did not argue. Yigel was a good friend, and Jan had learned in thirty-six years that it was possible to be friends and yet disagree. And so too, he thought again of Hannah, was it possible to be lovers. For she and he had so many chasms of strangeness, and alien culture, and language and belief to separate them that it seemed at times they had spent the last three years in one ceaseless argument shifting with lightning swiftness from German to Yiddish, to Hebrew, to French the better to express their differences. And yet they were, without question, in love.

Hannah's grandparents had come from Russia in the First Aliyah in the early days of the century; passionate and idealistic Zionists who had paid for their idealism with malaria and early graves. But not before providing Palestine with five Sabra children, among whom was Hannah's father who had founded the kibbutz of which both Jan and Hannah were members, and who had died beside her mother, defending it from the *fedayeen*. When Jan met Hannah she was a newly-orphaned fifteen-year-old with a long rope of sun-bleached hair and large dark eyes filled with a heart-wrenching combination of grief and determination. Within a year Jan was stunned to find himself her lover. He was seventeen years older than she, and her youth shocked him as much as it drew him. It was she, not he, who made every first move, with that frank-eyed Sabra candour that came so easily to young kibbutzniks, and so hard to the European born like Jan. At times, to amuse himself, he would recall his own adolescence, picturing himself at fifteen, a stiff, crop-haired blond youth in a dark suit and a stiff collar, sitting amidst his German aunts, drinking coffee and eating cakes by the coal fire of his mother's house in Munich. Then he would look at her, tumbling into the long grass of the kibbutz orchard, brown-legged in her rolled cotton shorts, her blouse half undone in readiness, her braids of hair flung out like a child's and her woman's arms opened to him. They might have grown up on two different planets, so unlike were they. And yet in all Palestine there was no place he felt he belonged more than in those sun-brown arms. 'Hannah,' he whispered out loud to himself, because he so liked the sound of her name.

A dark-skinned, dark-clothed woman passing in the street looked up, blankly and uninterested, at the sound. Her eyes took him in and dismissed him as the stranger he appeared. She was a Sephardic Jew, a North African immigrant, as were most of the occupants of the old Arab quarter. Eastern and alien, she had no more in common with him than had her Arab predecessors, and the dismissal in her eyes made clear she desired no further contact. But

109

for the continuing cataclysm called history Jan Muller and the Sephardic stranger would never have come within hundreds of miles of each other. Now they brushed elbows among Arab ghosts. Such was Israel, he thought, turning almost reluctantly back towards the harbour where another shipload of strangers sailed to join them.

Isaac Mandel, who should be among them, was Jan Muller's mother's cousin and, as such, the only Jewish relative he had ever known. His mother had been, like Hannah, an only child, and like Hannah an orphan at fifteen, though for no reason more dramatic than influenza. She had married out of the faith, a faith which her own family had only hesitantly practised, and had more or less left it behind, retaining only those aspects that cling to the apostate: culinary delicacies remembered from childhood and a faint aura of indeterminate guilt. Jan was raised in a Gentile household, among his father's German relatives, a quartet of blonde sisters whose mutual spinsterhood had been the legacy of the same war that had taken the life of Jan's father, a hero of the sunken *Scharnhorst*. Judaism, in the days of Jan's youth, was as alien to him as to his German schoolmates, except for a distant sense of connection. It, like the photograph of his father in the uniform of the German Imperial Navy, was a private possession, something unique that was his, and in both he took pride. Part of the pride, he realized later, was undoubtedly linked to Isaac Mandel, for as the one incarnation of Jan's Jewish family, he made a most striking and impressive figure. He was, in the time of Jan's boyhood, a bachelor of indeterminate age, handsome, dark, well-dressed, with a certain rakish style that whispered of experience. He stood out from the stolid German middle-classes of Jan's suburban home like a thoroughbred among dray horses; there was about him a panache that stopped just at the right side of flashiness, a glitter of wealth that fell short of ostentation, a glimpse of sharp intellect that yet evaded bookishness. He was a man of undefined power, a man for whom restaurant crowds stopped momentarily talking, and headwaiters whirled to attention by instinct, and when, on occasion, he swept into Jan's life from his home in Berlin, his big black Daimler attracting crowds of schoolchildren to their gate, his arms laden with expensive gifts, Jan's dull world lit up with a rare light.

There followed always family dinners, with the blonde aunts patting their coiled braids of hair and resting plump white hands on heavy bosoms, as Isaac talked of theatre and art. Then they would be taken out to the most fashionable restaurants for coffee and cream cakes, on balconies in the summer, or in velvety red interiors in winter. Jan's mother would blush, and glow, and protest that he did too much, was too kind, meaning it all because she was the most undemanding of women, and because of her sincerity Isaac would only redouble his efforts, and the presents and outings would increase. Jan, with boyish practicality, accepted all that was given, politely, and ingenuously waited for more. It was only when he was grown, and Munich was gone, and with it all their small world, that he really appreciated the generosity of this distant cousin who had done so much to make his mother's widowhood less lonely, and his fatherless boyhood less grim. Remembering that now, Jan knew that he was right and Hannah was wrong. She could not know, as he knew, what a lonely fierce thing it was to first set foot in an alien land, knowing it must become your home. If, for all that generosity of past years, he could in any way repay, it must first be in this way, to ease the awful loneliness of Isaac's first day in Palestine. Perhaps, he thought, as the harbour came in sight, and Hannah again flitted across his mind, perhaps he would be lucky and some god of conversation would prevent his mother's name from arising. Perhaps he could see Isaac off to his new destination without ever having to ask the questions he asked of all he met who had known Munich.

111

Have you heard? Have you seen her? Is she alive, is she dead? Those were the questions the Sabras could not understand; the questions that hung on the lips of every refugee from the charnel house that had been Europe . . . brother, sister, mother, father, child, lover . . . has anyone heard? For seventeen years Jan Muller had asked that question, and for seventeen years he had met no one who could answer. Not friend, nor family, old neighbour, or passing acquaintance, nor any of the great network of relief and refugee agencies who did their best to find the lost ones. Long ago logic had said she was dead and that same logic, he knew, was what drove Hannah to beg him to forget. But death was one thing, doubt another, and he was haunted forever by the image of her alone and seeking him, as she had sought him the foolish day he had run away from home at the age of seven. He fancied he could see her yet, walking alone down dark streets with no one, no husband, to help her, seeking her only child, calling his name into darkness. For seventeen years he had imagined her thus. It would be a relief, he knew, to learn at last she was dead. And yet it was a relief he found amazingly painful to face.

When he reached the waterfront again, the immigrant ship was just nosing into her berth, casting lines down on to Israeli soil. She was a rusty, unkempt old liner, but a long luxurious way from the battered sea tugs which he and his compatriots of Haganah had employed to run the British blockade in the days of the Mandate. Her deck railings were lined with crowds of men, women and children, silhouetted darkly against the morning light, straining forward towards their new home. Voices drifted down in a complexity of once-familiar tongues; Yiddish, German, Polish, French. As he caught and translated phrases, Jan realized suddenly that at last he had begun to think in Hebrew. He wondered how long before they would, too. He scanned the crowded railings, not really expecting to recognize anyone among such a crush, yet still looking. The men all seemed dressed alike, in shabby suits too warm for the humid heat of the morning, and the women, too, in their cardigans and cloth coats and headscarves had that displaced look of all refugees, self-conscious in other people's genteel cast-offs. He could not imagine Isaac as one of them and wondered if perhaps Miriam Krautz, who had written him of Isaac's arrival from her studio in the artists' colony of Ein Hod, had been wrong. Miriam had once been a neighbour in Munich, though she had moved away to Berlin long before the day of Jan's arrest, and she had heard, through the complex grapevine of the exiled German-Jewish community in Israel, that Isaac Mandel had been seen in a refugee centre in Cyprus and was on his way to Palestine. Dutifully she had informed Jan, whom she had met again some years ago in a half-constructed street of Tel Aviv, and with whom she had always afterwards kept in touch. He was grateful. It was from such frail links that the fragments of the past were slowly, painfully re-established. It was a process both necessary and agonizing, as each reunion invariably brought news of half a dozen deaths, as if by some cruel arrangement it was necessary to lose six to gain one. That was what it meant to be a survivor. The thought, the word, brought a damp shiver over Jan's shoulders beneath his sweat-stained cotton shirt, and he thought again of Isaac Mandel, the survivor. For Jan had escaped all that; his early arrest for what now seemed a ludicrously trivial political act, the defacing of a Hitler youth poster, had spared him, leading as it did both to his imprisonment and then his violent rescue by communist Jewish activists who destroyed his provincial prison cell with home-made explosive and smuggled him out of Germany. As the vice closed on all his Berlin family, Isaac Mandel first among them, Jan Muller was already building a new world in the desert of Palestine. Until Miriam Krautz's letter he had thought himself the only one, the last of his family, for Isaac with all the rest and no doubt his mother too, had been sent to the camps. But Isaac had survived.

The gangplank clanged, metal on metal on to the deck of the crowded ship, and at once its occupants poured down as if yet in doubt of their safety until they were truly on land. Once there, they milled about in the confusion of all disembarkings, looking for friends, relatives, each other, luggage, officials, road signs, lavatories. Children cried, bored already with the Promised Land, and an old, old man, in the antiquated dress of the Hasidim, solemnly sprawled full length amid the secular clutter of the quayside and kissed the concrete ground.

Through them Jan Muller wandered, looking for Isaac or, rather, looking for what Isaac might have become. As the pack of immigrants began to break up into small organized, determined groups, his search became more urgent. Like all Israeli events, the arrival of the immigrant ship was marked by a casual sun-washed informality. Open-shirted officials laughed and joked as they answered questions and directed groups in one direction or another. There was none of the paper and document and ink-stamp fuss that Jan associated with the officialdom of his native land, none of the concern for passports and identifications. But then in a land where the only requirement for entry was that one must claim Jewish identity, there was little need for documentation. It was not an identity, in the aftermath of the Holocaust, that anyone would lightly claim.

Still, for all its informality, the immigration procedures of Haifa had grown efficient with much practice and already a party of bewildered new Israelis were being led off by a broad, loud-voiced woman with the unmistakable agricultural authority of a kibbutz official, to a waiting lorry. Jan hastened after them, and had just ascertained that Isaac was not among them when, turning back to the ship, he saw him, standing isolated amidst the crowd, a single leather suitcase at his feet.

Isaac was dressed like the others on the ship, in a slightly ill-fitting, inappropriately dark suit and a battered overcoat, and wore as well a comically broad-brimmed white hat with a dark brown hat-band that, set above his drastically aged face and gold-rimmed spectacles, gave the impression of a kindly grandfather dressed as a gangster. He was studying a piece of paper in his hand, his eyes squinted up behind the glass of his spectacles, peering at the writing on it, obscured by the glare of the sun. As Jan strode through the parting crowd to his side he looked up and acknowledged him calmly, as if he had recognized him, without surprise.

'Isaac?' Jan called, 'Isaac, it *is* you, Isaac?' But the man only blinked in confusion, and Jan realized that it was not recognition that he had seen on Isaac's face, but a cautious acknowledgement of authority. He had mistaken Jan, unsurprisingly, for another Israeli official, and even an Israeli authority was awarded the terrible cautious deference that marked survivors of that world where a mistaken glance could bring arbitrary death.

'Please, I do not wish to cause trouble, but the lettering is difficult.'

'Isaac Mandel?'

The man nodded, more cautiously. 'I should not be here?'

'Isaac, I'm Jan. Jan Muller. Ian Muller,' he said, quickly remembering that Isaac had known him by the Scottish form of his name that his mother had given him in honour of a dead Scottish stranger. 'Heidi Muller's son, Isaac. I'm Heidi's son.' He reached to touch the man's shoulder but the other drew back as if expecting violence, or a trick.

For a long time he stood silently, as caution and amazement wavered in his eyes. He glanced once behind him, and once towards the doorway of the quayside building, where the two officials lounged, chatting to a pair of young immigrant girls. 'Ian?' he whispered. 'Ian Muller?'

'Heidi's son, Isaac. Your cousin's son. Surely you remember me . . .'

There was another long pause and then slowly, almost

115

without perceptible motion, Isaac made a nod of affirmation. He dropped his voice to whisper, 'Ian, a minute, can we talk . . . is it safe?'

Jan took Isaac away from the quay, up into the commercial district of Haifa, climbing away from the industrial clutter into the pleasant, almost European centre of parks and cafés, midway up the slope that led to the heights of Mount Carmel where the wealthy, Yigel's parents among them, lived. He carried Isaac's suitcase, so light that he suspected it contained nothing at all, in one hand, and kept his other linked through Isaac's arm. Isaac walked like an old man, shuffling and uncertain. On the way Jan assured him again and again that the converted lorry waiting to take him to the kibbutz to which he was assigned would not leave until afternoon.

'I asked especially, Isaac. Two o'clock. There is time yet. Time for lunch, coffee, whatever you like.'

'I would not find it, without the lorry, Ian. This piece of paper, I cannot read it properly. The print is small.'

'The lorry will wait, Isaac.'

'Do you have my case, still, Ian?'

'I have your case, Isaac.' Isaac nodded, shuffling on-wards. He still wore his heavy cloth greatcoat and Jan stopped and said, 'Let me take your coat, Isaac?'

'My coat?' Isaac looked up, his eyes suddenly frightened behind their gold-rimmed spectacles. Jan had a quick vision of those mountains of spectacles, shoes, black overcoats, the detritus of the death camps that the newspapers always showed.

'It's warm, Isaac. Let me carry your coat.' Isaac shook his head fearfully, and turned the lapels up around his ropy throat. Jan let him be. He found a café on the corner of one of the wide boulevards, where it was possible to sit at a table and watch the blue curve of the Mediterranean while the traffic went by. He seated Isaac, who asked that his case be put down beside his knees, where he patted it steadily as a child pats his mother's knee. Isaac did not wish to eat, but Jan ordered Turkish pastries with the coffee, hoping he would be tempted. When he turned from the waiter, a dark North African, Isaac was again peering at his piece of paper with the printing he could not read.

Jan took it from him gently, studying it momentarily. 'Yam Kinneret,' he said. Isaac raised a quizzical grey eyebrow, stirring in Jan a memory of that same brow, dark, sharp and wryly cynical, raised for some witticism. 'Yam Kinneret,' Jan repeated. 'The Sea of Galilee.'

'I am going to the Sea of Galilee?'

'A kibbutz. On the southern shore of the Sea of Galilee.'

'This is a camp?' Isaac said, patting his suitcase.

'No. No, not a camp.' Jan struggled with concepts and said, 'A farm, Isaac. A sort of farm where everyone works together.'

'I am to live on a farm?' Isaac looked incredulous, and when Jan nodded he made a small intake of breath and nodded again. His fingers scrunched up a small fold in the white tablecloth. The waiter came with their coffee and the plate of pastries and Isaac dropped his fold of cloth. He sipped his coffee solemnly, holding the cup in two hands, and reminding Jan of the old Jewish men he used to see in the parks of Munich sitting at café tables with chess-boards beside them. He wondered if Isaac, the old Isaac he had known, had really been like them after all, and the elegant gentleman he recalled only a creation of a romantic child's mind. Throughout the whole time since their meeting on the quay, Isaac had never once questioned Jan's presence in Palestine, nor even appeared to wonder how it was that Jan had known about his arrival and come to meet the ship. Perhaps curiosity, like youth and elegance and the old Isaac's broad, child-delighting laugh, was also a victim of the camps.

'Miriam Krautz told me you would be on this ship,' Jan

said then. Isaac nodded politely. 'You remember Miriam, don't you, Isaac?' Jan pressed. 'Surely. Miriam Krautz, the artist.'

'Ah, the artist,' Isaac echoed softly, but his eyes were on an Arab woman riding by on a donkey, and slowly widening with European astonishment. He said, 'What will I do on a farm, Ian?'

'You'll grow things, Isaac.'

'I don't know how to grow things,' he said pathetically.

Jan said, 'They will show you how.'

Isaac sipped at his coffee again and patted his suitcase, and Jan braced himself to ask of his mother, at the same time wondering if this new, lost, broken Isaac would have any memory of her. He opened his mouth to speak but Isaac said suddenly, 'Once, in Berlin, I grew a cactus. It was a pretty cactus with a red flower. But it died. Your mother gave it to me, the cactus with the red flower that died. It was no good, you see, me growing things. I am a goldsmith, Ian.'

'My mother . . . ?' Jan whispered, struggling for words.

'I put it on the window-sill, as Heidi said. But it died. First the red flower. Then all of it. Perhaps, on the window-sill was too cold?'

'My mother, Isaac, have you . . . heard of my mother? Since the war, have you heard?'

Isaac looked confused. He scratched his hair, behind his ear where the hot heavy hat yet sat on it. 'Heidi?' he said, uncertainly.

'My mother, Isaac. Heidi Muller, my mother. Do you know what's become of her?' Jan's voice rose, the words separate and sharp, small knives to cut through the fog in Isaac's befuddled mind.

'You do not know?' Isaac said. Jan shook his head, fighting back frustrated tears.

'Isaac,' he pleaded. 'Try to remember. I am Ian Muller. Heidi's son. I was arrested in 1933 for defacing a poster. I was sent to a prison, surely you heard.'

Isaac nodded suddenly, and said, 'Foolishness. And childish, too. A poster, you risk your life, your mother's security, for a poster.'

'Yes, it was foolishness,' Jan said, quickly, 'and you remember. I was in prison; a year, eighteen months. Men came, good men, Jews, and they freed me and brought me here. I wrote then, from Palestine, first to my mother and when letters were not returned I wrote to everyone I had known, but no one had seen her. The house was empty. I even went back, near the end of the war.'

'During the war?' Isaac said, jolted into reality. 'You were in Germany during the war?'

Jan waved away his incredulity, and said only, 'I was everywhere,' which was close to the truth. 'But where *was* she, Isaac? Before the war, she was gone already. Surely you heard? Surely you must have heard?' He realized suddenly that he was gripping the old man's cuffs, plucking at his wrists with his urgency, and Isaac's eyes were filled with fear. Jan forced himself to release his grip.

Isaac said, clutching his suitcase as if in a moment he would run, 'I tried, Ian, I tried to save her. After they came for you, and I heard, I went to Munich. I found her there alone, in a terrible state, and begged her that she should come away with me to Berlin and stay in my flat. Where, who knows, perhaps I can protect her. You see, what you and your friends were doing, it washed over on to everyone you touched. Who knows what they would do to her? But she would not come. Always she insists you will come back, and what if she is not there when you do? In the end, I go away to Berlin and she stays. One day, my letter is returned. I go back to Munich. The house is empty, boarded over, paint, things written on the door. You know how it was in those days. I go to the neighbours. They, brave people, have heard nothing, seen nothing. Heidi Muller? Who is she? I go away in the end. I drive around the city, that was before they took the car, and when we could still travel a little. I find a shabby street eventually. All the windows broken. Ah, I think, this is where Munich keeps her Jews. Yes, and I find Heidi, with two other women and many children in a flat. No water, no heating. Again, I beg her, come away. I think then, already I think of leaving Germany, funny how long before we think of it, how many years we think always it will stop soon, this craziness. Then of course, when wé know it will never stop . . . there is no way to leave, nowhere to go . . .' he trailed off and Jan gently prodded him.

'So she did not come to Berlin.'

Isaac shook his head. 'No. Again she insists she must be in Munich for you, when you return.' Jan nodded painfully and Isaac continued, 'Then, when I returned myself to Berlin, I find my flat locked, my home confiscated, all my property, some pretence, pretences were easy to find. Later they did not even bother with pretence. So then it begins. So, I cannot travel, I must stay in the ghetto with all the rest. I write to Heidi. Eventually the answers stop. What am I to think? And then,' he shuddered, shaking his head, his eyes feverishly alive with memory, 'then, Ian, it all begins. The hammering on the doors in the night. The journeys, the trains . . . and then those places.' He stopped, suddenly removed his hat and his spectacles, and leaned back in his chair in the café in Haifa. He closed his eyes, taking two long breaths. Jan saw for the first time the blue number on the back of his hand as his heavy coat cuff slipped up, almost as if it had waited until this moment to reveal itself.

'In August of 1944, in the place where I was, I met a woman who had stayed in that flat with Heidi. I say I met. I glimpse her beyond the dividing fence, where sometimes those who are unfortunate enough to have wives too in that place risk their lives for a word of greeting. I call to her, only the name. "Heidi Muller", and she calls back one word, before she sees the guard and must flee. "England".'

'England?' Jan whispered.

'It is the best day in three years. The best day for the remaining year. Heidi in England. Heidi safe. I think then I will never see her again, but it does not matter. Heidi is safe. And then, Ian, I see you there by the ship and I think all is well for Heidi, for surely she is here?' He plucked at the tablecloth, his old fingers fumbling past memories. 'Was it all a mistake, then, that woman in the camp? Was Heidi not saved?' Then he echoed what Jan had thought earlier, and said, 'What have we done, Ian, that we must pay always for one loved one with the life of another?'

'England,' Jan whispered again. Surely it was possible. It would explain everything. It was then he remembered Lady Macgregor and knew in that instant not only that she was in Britain but where in Britain precisely, she was. He leapt from his chair, threw his tough sun-browned arms around the old man's head and shoulders and hugged him passionately, kissing the thin grey hair.

When Jan arrived back home at Kibbutz Aaron it was late, after working hours, and he went at once to the dining-hall, where everyone gathered to make coffee and talk into the night, and found Hannah. His excitement, and his conviction that not only was his mother alive, but that he would at last almost certainly find her, had grown on him throughout the coach journey. He had not shared his thoughts with Yigel, and they had expanded richly inside him and now clearly glowed from his eyes and showed in his face. Hannah saw at once the change upon him, but she was guarded.

She went to the kitchen, behind the hall, and came back with coffee for him. It was the kind of domestic thing that she was inclined to do which, set against her farm-worker's strength and masculine ability with tractors and weaponry, so charmed him. Around him, in the communal warmth of the dining-hall, she yet spread another, more personal, more intimate warmth.

'Did you find him?' she asked. She was tentatively stroking one long, golden-brown braid. Her skin was creamy brown, pink along the cheek-bones. For her, all the exotic glory of Biblical poetry rose readily to Jan's lips; Daughter of Zion, Rose of Sharon. He smiled.

'I found him.'

She paused again, turning her cup around. 'What was he like?'

'Old.'

'You didn't tell me he was old.'

'He wasn't when I knew him.' He drank his coffee. 'Seventeen years. I wonder. Perhaps he would have been old by now, anyhow.'

'Where is he going?'

'Yam Kinneret.'

'Will he be all right?'

Jan shrugged. He said eventually, 'To be alive is to be all right. He is alive.' He looked down at the plain table, one of several, alike, utilitarian, and coffee-stained. 'It is hard for the old. For the young it is almost too easy.' He was watching, across the room, a middle-aged couple sitting alone, watching their young daughter going off for the night to the adolescents' house. She was dressed like the young Sabras, in rolled cotton shorts and a cotton blouse, a checked cotton scarf wound arab-style around her head and shoulders, her hair, like Hannah's, in a long plait. She swaggered a little as she walked, and flagrantly displayed affection for the youth at her side, her arm about his waist. Her parents, new immigrants from Poland watched still, torn between condemnation and pride. Daughter of Israel.

'I am going to England, Hannah,' said Jan.

Later, in the night, they made love. Not in his hut, a barren, unprivate place, but out in the fields, under the clear black desert sky, at the edge of the citrus orchard where the grass was wild. Hannah was all giving; she never cared for her own pleasure, only his, crying out for joy at his

122

coming, whether she came or not. Afterwards she stroked his hair and murmured over and over again that she loved him, wanting no answer. Hannah knew he had never loved anyone since the woman in France and the thing that had happened there, back in the war. Later, she cried.

He said, 'I'll soon come back. I'll bring her with me.'

She clung closer, shook her head, and wept.

On the morning Jan left Kibbutz Aaron, at the beginning of his journey to England, Hannah was in the fields. Yigel drove him away in the kibbutz car, and he leaned out of the small dusty window, watching her driving the tractor with a chain harrow rattling behind. Her back was to him, her strong young shoulders tense with strain. Her long plait of golden-brown hair bounced on her sweaty cotton shirt with the motion of the tractor. She was so near he could have almost touched her as she turned the machine at the roadside. She never looked back, spinning the heavy wheel around, raising between them a cloud of obscuring yellow dust. Yigel drove off down the long, rutted track and Jan whispered once, 'Hannah,' because he so liked the sound of her name.

A day later, he sailed from Haifa.

CHAPTER
EIGHT

'Hardacre Salvage?' said Heidi. 'It sounds terribly official, doesn't it?'

'Well, my dear,' said Jane drily, 'it takes little more than an afternoon's work to sound official. Though I wouldn't expect Sam to create a limited company simply for the fun of it. I imagine he has something practical in mind.'

'But what?' Heidi said, rising quickly to pour fresh coffee for Jane who said at once, 'Stay where you are and relax for one moment. I'm not a guest. Certainly not a paying one, anyhow.'

The two women were sitting in the empty residents' lounge of the Strathmore Lodge, enjoying a log fire and the surprising warmth of early spring sunshine shining through the many-paned windows. Outside, the landscape of bare fields, river and forested hillsides rising to barren moorland was still white with winter snow, though in the sheltered flower-beds of the inn's gardens crocuses and snowdrops were already in bloom. Jane rose from her chair by the fire and crossed to the window to look out.

'It really is lovely here, Heidi. You have a marvellous location, marvellous. I know you'll do well. What with the fishing and shooting, you can't go wrong.'

Heidi smiled. She was a small, thin woman whose ready smile saved her lined face from a look of severity. She dressed as Jane did, in tweed skirts and lambswool jumpers and looked, and spoke, almost exactly like a British woman. There was only the faintest touch of her German accent remaining with her, and at times Jane was quite certain that it was being superseded by a trace of Scots, from her many years in the North. 'The Macgregors have been a great help. I've had three parties from the castle already.'

Jane nodded. 'Quite right, too. I'm sure they are as pleased to have you here as you to have their assistance. Now that they are letting practically all the stalking, there's a stream of visitors wanting accommodation. It's not like the old days, when it was all friends and family and the Castle was always full. Rather sad now, actually, a lot of empty rooms and the family living in a single wing. Like Hardacres. I thought for a while it was just the aftermath of the war, but now I know it's more than that. It will never come back, the way we used to live. Even if the Tories get back in next time, it's all done with. Not that I mind that much. Rather exciting, actually.' She tugged down the hem of her green tweed jacket in a brisk, assured gesture. 'New times take new methods. A good time to be starting off in business, provided one's willing to work.'

'Oh, I'm that,' Heidi laughed. 'I've baked three dozen scones this morning, and done porridge and scrambled eggs for eighteen. And packed lunches. They're all off to climb the ben. No doubt they'll get as far as the first burn and turn back, but they'll feel they're real mountaineers. I think most of them prefer what comes after, the hot baths and brandies around the fire, anyway.'

Jane laughed, returning to sit again by the hearth. 'Oh, I didn't mean you, my dear,' she said, prodding with the brass poker at the edge of a burning log. 'Hardly. I've had my life's work cut out trying to get you to stop working some time,' and when Heidi shook her tight grey curls, she insisted, 'I have.' She paused, studying the fall of grey ash on the stone hearth. 'No, it's Sam I'm thinking of. I really do wish him well.'

She sounded doubtful enough for Heidi to ask timidly, 'Does he *know* anything about salvage, I mean, perhaps in the war . . .'

'I kept thinking of that, but no, I'm afraid he spent most

of his war in the middle of the desert. Not much to pick up there about marine salvage. No. As far as I'm aware this is just a bolt from the blue. All I've heard has been from Philip Barton who toddled down there one afternoon to have a chat and ended up in the middle of the North Sea, anchored over a wreck, hauling up crates of tinned salmon. Apparently he went home with his car boot full for his trouble, and Sam's number one in his books just now, I dare say. They've been living on leeks and neck of mutton since February.'

'Poor things,' Heidi murmured. 'But surely the business is not that bad?'

'Oh, no,' Jane said, turning towards the window at the sound of car tyres on the gravel of the front court. 'It's infinitely worse. Apparently Emily bridled at having men only in the snuggery, thereby destroying a thousand-year-old tradition of masculine solitude or whatever. The locals all walked out when she let the women in and haven't been back since. They've even threatened to take their dartboard out and meet somewhere else. The ultimate sanction, I gather.' She grimaced. 'Poor Philip's in the middle, his wife on one side and the pride of Yorkshire manhood on the other. I think there's someone coming to the door, my dear.'

'Oh, good heavens, I'm still in my pinny. Answer it for me Jane, will you please. I'll be through in a minute.' She jumped up and ran to the kitchen, divesting herself of her apron as she did. In a moment, Jane knew, she would re-emerge into the foyer of the hotel, neatly groomed, as manageress. Heidi was playing several roles in her little establishment, wisely limiting her staff to the bare minimum until the success of the venture were ensured. Jane rose, straightened her skirt, and went to the front door. If Sam Hardacre could work as hard as Heidi Muller, she reflected, he should make a fortune, whatever his unlikely new trade.

An ageing grey shooting-brake was parked a little way

down the gravel drive. Jane recognized it as the local village taxi, and nodded to the friendly wave its driver accorded her. A young man had stepped from the vehicle and was leaning in, conversing briefly with the driver. He turned, saw Jane in the doorway of the inn, appeared to hesitate, and then began walking quickly with a long, determined stride towards the door. He was tall and slim, dressed in a buff-coloured raincoat hanging loosely unbelted over sports trousers and pullover. He was hatless and the sun shone on strikingly blond hair. He looked about thirty, she judged, thinking automatically, 'about Peter's age'. It was a sad habit that never left her; she watched him grow older in the faces of his contemporaries, her son who would never age.

'Can I help you?' she called, as the man approached the small flight of stone steps leading up to the heavy front door, which stood open now, letting sunlight into the tiled small porch.

'*Ja*,' he replied, and Jane inwardly froze.

The young man shook his head as if annoyed with himself, and said again in accented, but correct English, 'Yes, please. Forgive me, I forget sometimes I am in England.'

'You're not,' Jane said, surprised by the coldness of her own voice. 'You're in Scotland. But we speak English too, if that's what you mean.' The coldness, which she found surprisingly difficult to control, was apparent to the blond young man, as well as to herself.

'I am sorry,' he said softly. 'I meant no offence.'

Jane forced a smile. *The war was over*. But she could not totally fight down the surge of resentment that rose at the sound of a German voice, other than that of Heidi who for so many years she had regarded as one of her own. Besides, he *would* stand there so healthily sun-bronzed at Teutonic attention the while, wouldn't he, reminding her of those blond young Nazis she saw in Munich with Peter, all those years ago. She always had wanted to kick one in the shins to see if they too would double up and hop about howling like ordinary mortals. She resisted a murderously strong desire to do just that to her young Aryan on the steps of the Strathmore Lodge.

'Scots people don't take kindly to being lumped in with the English,' Jane replied with a small smile. 'Offends their sense of nationalism. Something you Germans have always taken rather seriously, have you not?' The young man's eyes narrowed, and his face lost its essentially gentle cast, and Jane felt guilty. He was a potential guest after all, and she was being particularly unfair about his not uncommon mistake. Friends of her own in Yorkshire were quite accustomed to referring to everything beyond the border as 'North Britain', after all. She smiled a bit more naturally and said genuinely, 'How can I help you?'

'If you would be so kind,' he returned, retreating in a European way into correct manners, 'I wish to meet with Frau Muller. She is at this address?'

'Mrs Muller is occupied just now,' Jane said, 'but no doubt if you are wishing a room, I can organize that for you. Shall I ask the driver to bring your bags?'

'No,' he said, still speaking with careful politeness. 'That will not be necessary. I wish Frau Muller. That is all.'

Jane felt suddenly chilled, as if something from Heidi's frightening past had emerged to threaten her here, even, in the shape of a latter-day Nazi.

She straightened, looking severely down at the young man as if to impart to him, without words, her absolute solidarity with Heidi Muller, and her readiness to defend her friend against whatever unimaginable threat he might conceal.

'I will speak with her,' she said, and turned her back and walked into the inn, closing the door beside her. Once inside, she felt foolish. After all, what threat might this blond young German possibly offer in the middle of a gentle Highland spring morning? She walked through the long wood-floored corridor of the old building, back to the big kitchen with its ancient flagstone floors. At times like this she realized how deeply the war had affected them all, and why at times the young, blessedly free of its influence, did not understand them.

'Heidi,' she said, and Heidi looked up from her latest batch of scones, fresh from the oven, her face mirroring Jane's own concern.

'What's wrong?' she said at once.

Jane sat down at the kitchen table and smiled wryly. 'I don't suppose anything is, actually,' she said. 'I think I'm being a bit of a fool.'

'About what?'

'About nothing probably. Heidi,' she said again, slowly, 'there's a young man at the door, wanting to see you.'

'Oh, very well,' Heidi said, dusting flour from her hands. 'I meant to come right away, but I smelt these burning when I came in and quite forgot. We were so long over our coffee. I'm sorry, Jane, I'll go at once. I'll put him in number twelve, I think, it has such a nice view.'

'No, wait,' Jane said, and Heidi again looked startled.

'But why? He'll be wanting his room.'

'I don't think he wants a room,' Jane said. 'And,' she paused, 'there's more than that. He's German, Heidi.'

'German?' she looked surprised. Their visitors were almost always English, occasionally French or American. 'How unusual,' she said.

Jane was taken aback. 'Don't you mind?' she blurted out, and then softened it, saying, 'I thought perhaps . . .'

'That I wouldn't give a room to a German?' Heidi's worn, wise face twisted into a faint sardonic smile. 'So, if I start like that, one rule for one kind of people, one for another, where will I end up? Hmm? Will you tell me that?'

'You're very forgiving,' Jane said simply.

Heidi slowly lowered herself to a kitchen chair beside her friend. She laid her hands, small, neat, still dusted with

129

flour, on the smooth wooden surface. 'Forgiving?' she said. 'Jane, what was done goes so far beyond forgiveness that it is a mockery, a *travesty* to try to seek even a grain of retribution. What can all my petty little human vengeance do to balance that? No. I will leave that to God. Besides, Jane, my husband was a German, people I loved were German. *I* was a German once, or so I thought. Come, I will see your young man.'

She got up briskly, dusting her hands again, and Jane followed her brave little straight back through the doorway into the hall. She was sorry now she had shut the door in the face of her young visitor, leaving him alone in the spring sunshine. She hastened ahead to open it and found to her intensely renewed annoyance that he had done so himself and was standing hesitantly beyond the glazed inner door, in the tiled porch itself. She glimpsed him through the half-frosted figured glass, his hand hesitantly extended to that inner door as well, as if in some ill-conceived impatience he was already about to enter.

'Just a minute,' she called, quite harshly, 'I'm coming.' But he flung open the door and stood, tall and menacing, blotting out the bright snowy light. Behind her, she heard Heidi scream.

Jane leapt to protect her friend but Heidi, her hands clutched across her face burying the scream, was stumbling forward towards the man who ran to her, his arms out-reaching. They met and folded into a fused awkward huddle in which each seemed to be supporting the other from falling. The young man was so tall that he was bent almost double over Heidi's tiny frame and yet she, of the two, seemed the stronger. He raised his head, his eyes looking straight at Jane but unseeing through tears. He kept shaking his head and saying, 'You know me. I did not think . . . you know me.' Heidi drew back, releasing him only as much as she must so that she might look up to his face. She smiled her little wry crooked smile that Jane knew so well.

'I should forget a son?' she said. She kept shaking her head as he had done, bewildered, and turned to Jane, seeking in convention an avenue for unmanageable emotion, 'Jane, this is my son. My son Ian. You know, I have talked of him.' She nodded again, smiling, as if his appearance were the most ordinary thing in the world. Jane stood dumbfounded, and then utterly unable to find any appropriate words, she merely extended her hand.

'How do you do?' she said.

For days, Heidi and Jan Muller were utterly inseparable. From morning until night they spent every possible moment in each other's company, and Heidi went about the work of running the inn in a happily casual daze, totally uncharacteristic of her usual careful efficiency. The talk was endless, and each leapt over the other's words the more quickly to gain knowledge of the dark gap of years between them. Each statement, each name, each place mentioned, brought from the other a torrent of questions, and each hardly waited for answers in eagerness to question again.

When Jan learned of the role played by Lady Macgregor in his mother's rescue, he at once awarded Jane the same total devotion he accorded Heidi, so that she became almost a second mother. She, seeing in him the shadow of his father who had so many years before befriended her husband, was deeply touched, and felt that she too, in some small way, had regained a son.

Jane's only regret was that the reunion, joyful as it was, was inevitably tinged with the sorrow of uncertainty. Ian Muller, or Jan, as he over the years had become accustomed to being called, was an Israeli and Israel was a tremendous distance both in miles and ideas from the far North of Scotland that had become Heidi's home. Jane, in each of her visits from her home near Castle Conon, watched and wondered, afraid to ask. Would Heidi leave her adopted home after so many years and take up a new life in a new, raw, nation? Jane felt she would miss her friend desperately if she so chose, but her concerns were not those of self-interest. The more Jan spoke of the life he knew, a life of pioneering and no little danger, of complex mixtures of cultures and ideas, the less she could imagine gentle, European Heidi, so at home in the wet, cold northern hills, being at peace in that place of sun, idealism and strife.

It was Jan himself, in the end, who brought her concerns into the open. She had dined with them both, one quiet night at the inn, late, after the paying guests had been fed, watered and safely tucked up in the bar. Heidi left them to prepare coffee and Jan leaned towards her with that anxious wrinkling of his smooth, sun-tanned brow that she had come to associate with a troubled mind. It was the expression he wore whenever he spoke, and he spoke but little, of the war.

'What am I to do, Lady Macgregor?' he asked. 'I cannot leave her alone, and yet how can I take her away from here?'

'I have been thinking much the same, Jan,' she said. And added, 'Why don't you ask your mother?'

He shook his head at once, firmly. 'Oh no, it would only confuse her. It is my problem, for me to decide. I must wait until I have a good plan, and tell her then.'

Jane leaned back in her chair, her long bony hand held up to her chin, stroking thoughtfully down the side of her angular face. 'And yet, you spoke to me,' she said.

'But of course, Lady Macgregor. You are so . . . how do you say . . . so assured, so confident. You are a woman of position. But my mother, she is a simple person, only a housewife always . . . she cannot be expected . . .'

'She cannot be expected to know her own mind?' Jane said drily. 'Young man, you are falling into a fearful trap of the young, regarding their parents.'

'How so?' he said, surprised.

She replied, 'That happy conviction that your gaining of wisdom has occurred by some odd chemical process at the expense of theirs. Just because you are a man, and she your mother, does not guarantee your superior intelligence, your better judgement. Heidi has, all alone, supported herself and built a life for herself in a foreign country. She has a fine command of the English language, and has become a competent businesswoman. I suggest you do her the respectful service of according her at least a small say in whatever plans you have made for your futures. To your surprise, no doubt, she may have plans of her own.'

'Oh my, Lady Macgregor,' Jan said, leaning back as if in fear of physical attack, shielding his tanned face with his hands. 'You are formidable. Come, I have at last an idea. You will come to Israel with us, we all will be happy, and oh, such a kibbutz mama you will make.' He was laughing, but she could see he had listened to what she had said and later, when Heidi was once more with them, pouring coffee into demi-tasses, he at last broached the subject of their future.

She looked up, surprised. 'But there is no question,' she said. 'Your home is there, mine is here.' She smiled, with only a trace of regret. 'Perhaps in a different world it would have been different, but we cannot undo the years. My door is open always, to yourself and your,' she paused, blushed, 'your Hannah, should you ever wish to come.' She added, 'But I know the young must go their own way. My wise friend Jane has shown me that.' She stopped, studying the face of her son. 'You are not hurt?' she said. 'You did not suppose otherwise? You surely did not think that now we have found each other, we must turn love into a bond?'

Jan nodded gratefully towards Jane whose small quick up-turn of her chin reminded him that she had told him so. He said, 'Always I supposed if I ever found you, I would find you lost, desolate, with no one, like Isaac. I never thought you would have a life, friends, a place of your own.' He smiled ruefully. 'No, I could not dream to take you from this. You are more at home here than I ever have been

133

anywhere.' He looked away sadly, remembering all the places he had known and left, in his restless, moving life. He saw in his mother's contentment in the cold Scottish landscape the same contentment that glowed in Hannah's eyes when they surveyed the growing fields of Kibbutz Aaron. Perhaps there was never to be such a contentment for him.

Jane Macgregor had offered to drive Jan Muller as far as York on his return journey to Dover. She was planning a trip south, anyway, being accustomed to spending the early spring months in and about London, visiting friends. First, however, she would have a long weekend at Hardacres, and pay a fleeting, morale-boosting visit to Emily Barton at that renowned hostelry of the Yorkshire countryside, The Rose, at Kilham. 'I'll drop you at York. You can spend the night at the Station Hotel and take the first train south. No slight intended to the Highland Line, but I'm sure I can make your journey more interesting,' she said, with a wink to Heidi.

'Interesting!' Heidi exclaimed. 'It will raise the hair from your head, with Jane and that race car she has bought. Besides, there is no Highland Line, Jane,' she corrected. 'We have only the British Rail now.'

'So we have,' Jane agreed, mildly. 'Every time I turn around they've nationalized something else. You can't expect me to remember them all. I promise you,' she added, 'a most sedate and refined journey, and I swear to leave you safe and sound in York with all hair still in place.'

The motor car in question was a silver-grey Jaguar XK 120 that Jane, who for years had driven herself about in an ageing Morris, had taken a shine to one day in London and had bought outright on the spot. From having always treated her motor vehicle as a simple necessity, she was overnight transformed into a devotee, who was not above having a sporty suit tailored in a grey tweed to match her

134

new purchase. She, who had more often than not relied on the now nationalized North British and Highland Lines for her journeys between her two homes, now drove everywhere her petrol ration would allow, visiting friends she hadn't seen in years, just for the opportunity of a new, virgin road.

On the morning of Jan's departure she arrived in front of the Strathmore Lodge, the Jaguar's hood lowered, and herself wrapped snugly in a silver fox jacket. Her iron-grey hair was drawn back into a tight bun and covered with a silk scarf in silver and green. Jan emerged from the front door of the hotel, his arm about his mother, grinning.

'Ah, Lady Macgregor, it is magnificent. And you, too, are magnificent.'

Jane laughed. 'My dear, I am but basking in reflected glory, but at my age the setting of the stage is everything. If I'm to turn male heads now, it must be with such devices.' She smiled with satisfaction, patting the wood-rimmed steering-wheel.

'Why, Jane, that is not like you,' Heidi said, clearly shocked. 'Ian, she is a most proper lady, I assure you.'

Jan grinned again, loading his small hand-case in behind the seat. 'She is magnificent,' he said again. He turned then to his mother and Jane looked away, for they had suddenly arrived at the moment she was dreading and no manner of banter could make that moment go away. Jan stood with his hands at his sides like a small boy, his big tough body seeming to shrink into childish helplessness.

'Mama,' he said, 'I don't know what to say.'

'To say?' she said, her dark brown eyes warmly moist. 'So what is there to say? What families always say when they part . . . that you will write, and you will, but not very often, like all the young. That you will think of me. Of course you will think of me. That you will come back, with who knows, one day even a wife. Grandchildren. I know all these things, Ian. When you come, you will come. I will be here.' She laughed gently as he suddenly leapt forward and hugged her boyishly, all his grace reduced to bumbling by his own emotions. 'Ian, Ian, we have loved each other into a void for all these years. Surely you must know, if anyone, that it is not necessary to be together to love?'

Jane drove away fast, her eyes on the road, as Jan leaned over the soft top and waved with great broad strokes as if he could clasp from the air a symbol of his love. When the first bend in the road hid Heidi and the inn from their view, Jane kept her eyes firmly to the front, while Jan lowered his head on to his folded arms and wept.

Eventually he raised his head, shaking it at his own foolishness, letting the wind dry his face.

He grinned sheepishly and said, 'I am sorry, Lady Macgregor, I must embarrass you with my nonsense.' She shook her head, smiling, still looking forward at the winding road. 'Do you know,' Jan continued, 'for years I felt I had no emotion in me, after the war, some of the things that happened.' His voice dropped and levelled to a soft monotone. 'I used to think I would never feel anything again. Can you imagine?'

Jane nodded. 'After my husband was killed, I felt that way for over a year. And again, after Peter . . .'

'Oh Lady Macgregor, forgive me, I bring things back to you that should not be spoken of.'

'Of course not,' Jane said brusquely. 'There is nothing that should not be spoken of. And if you bring things back, then that is good, too.' She slowed the car, turned to look at him, briefly. 'Do you know, you are very like your father.'

He looked delighted, and said, 'Can you recall him? Really, can you? It is so long ago. But you know, I would like to be like him, I would like that very much.'

'You are. Quite identical. I look at you and I could be back all those years, before two wars, with my Ian still alive, and your father and I, the three of us, together in Hong Kong. Funny to imagine, isn't it?'

'What a strange world, Lady Macgregor, that I should at last meet someone who recalls my father, here, not in Germany, not in Israel, but in Scotland, a place I never thought to see.' He waved one hand with a bemused smile towards the barren hills still covered in snow.

'Or,' Jane Macgregor said, 'that I should drive through the Scottish countryside one day,' she smiled to herself, 'with Karl Muller's son. Do you know how strange that would have been, had someone told me this would happen, that day in 1913? And how strange all of it is, Jan. To be old,' she laughed at his instant dispute. 'No, Jan, I am old. Well-preserved like a good port, perhaps, but old. And of all the people who meant everything to me, who should remain but the son of a stranger met by chance in a foreign land.' She smiled gently. 'I think we shall be splendid friends,' she said.

In Inverness they stopped for lunch at the Kings Mills Hotel, and emerged to find winter had descended among the purples and yellows of the crocuses. They raised the hood of the Jaguar and drove out of the Highland capital into the snow. The journey thereafter rapidly became an adventure as they climbed up into the hills, reaching the Slochd Summit in heavy snow and meeting a real blizzard as they passed through Aviemore and climbed once more towards the barren heights of Dalwhinnie. 'Do you know, Lady Macgregor,' Jan said, 'for fifteen years I have missed seeing snow, and now I can't possibly imagine why.' He grinned gamely, as once more the Jaguar slowed to a slithering sideways halt and, as he had done twice already, Jan climbed out to dig their way out.

'Aren't you glad I brought the spade?' Jane said brightly as they pulled away once more into the storm.

'Delighted,' said Jan.

'I told you it would be interesting,' Jane sniffed, peering into shifting sheets of white haze. At Perth they gave up and settled for a good meal and two luxurious rooms in the

Royal George overlooking the River Tay. They awoke to find a spring morning, all traces of snow washed away, and continued on their journey once more at the speeds to which Jaguar and Jane were more accustomed. Jan hung on, thinking her driving style exactly like Yigel's with the kibbutz car over the rutted unpaved desert roads of home. He said nothing, suspecting she'd not like the comparison. They passed through Edinburgh and crossed the border in good time, so that it was still only early afternoon when they were already on the approaches to York.

'It seems such a shame to abandon you here with so much of the day left,' Jane said suddenly. 'I doubt there'll be a train, but you've still the whole afternoon. Of course, I suppose you'd love to see York; it is rather a gem, but I was thinking . . .'

'What, Lady Macgregor?' Jan said eagerly, because he too, was reluctant to end their cheerful companionship so abruptly and be left alone in a foreign city once more.

'I don't suppose you'd fancy a spin over to Hardacres with me? I could run you back in time for your morning train. Oh, forgive me, I am being a dreadfully selfish old bore, no doubt, but I have so enjoyed your company, and I would like you to meet everyone . . .' she trailed off, uncertain.

'But, Lady Macgregor, I would be so honoured,' he said.

With a grin of delight, and a resultant lurch that had Jan clinging to the smoothly polished door of the Jaguar, Jane spun the wheel and sent the car skidding round a sharp turn into a side road swathed in the grey spring mist of the Yorkshire countryside. As they roared off through the hedgerows and amongst low brick farm cottages, neither had the slightest premonition that that sharp turn of the road comprised as sharp a turn in Jan's life as the day forty years before that first linked their families in the colonial port of Hong Kong.

CHAPTER
NINE

Hardacres was in turmoil. After over five months of self-imposed exile, Sam Hardacre was coming home in style. Harry had received a telephone call two days before from a remarkably jubilant-sounding Sam, announcing that he had a weekend free which he would very much like to spend at Hardacres, and that he also would like to give a small party, 'in celebration' as he put it, for the family and a few select friends.

'Delighted, of course,' Harry said with his instinctive well-mannered hospitality. 'How many might it be for?' he asked then, with a premonitory flash of concern, hearkening far back to the pre-war days when a Sam and Terry party was something to give even the formidable pause.

'Oh, just an intimate gathering,' Sam said lightly, and there was a moment's silence in which Harry supposed him to be ticking off the guest list in his mind. 'A handful,' he said. 'About forty.'

'Forty?' Harry asked, swallowing hard, his mind leaping at once to the beleaguered store-cupboards of the Hardacre kitchens, and the gathered but meagre powers of the family ration books.

'Or fifty,' came Sam's complacent voice over the telephone. There was a brief silence and then suddenly Sam said urgently, 'You do understand that I intend supplying the food and all, don't you, Uncle Harry? You didn't think . . .'

Harry fought his sigh of relief into a whispering silence and managed to mumble, 'Oh, that really is too kind, Sam. Of course, it would help if you could manage part of it . . .'

'Everything, Uncle Harry. Everything.' There was

139

another pause and then Sam said, 'I do hope you all like salmon,' and on that cryptic note he hung up the phone.

The progress of the party was monitored by Harry over the next two days through a series of phone calls which came in at intervals announcing that this or that member of the family was absolutely delighted and would be sure to be there. Terry telephoned from Ampleforth saying he had permission to attend and sounding as enthusiastic about the social gathering as the old Terry of pre-monastic days. The Bartons, on Emily's insistence, agreed to close up The Rose for the day (not that anyone will notice, Emily added) and bring their children down from Kilham. Various total strangers with a vast array of startling accents telephoned or showed up at the door with vanloads of provisions for the kitchen. Harry felt rather like the guest of honour at a surprise party which, for all he knew of the event burgeoning in his own house, it might as well have been. Sam had said something about a celebration but had not obliged him with what had given him cause to celebrate.

Philip Barton, the only member of the family to Harry's knowledge to have been recently in contact with Sam, was hardly helpful. When Harry pressed him as to precisely what it was that Madelene's errant son was up to, he only answered, echoing Sam himself, 'Well, you won't be short of salmon, anyhow.'

Salmon came to haunt Harry. Mrs Dobson, the cook, had ventured upstairs after the most recent delivery and, in her hesitantly respectful way, had approached Harry.

'I thought I'd do some in a casserole. And some in a salad. And then there's t' mousse. But frankly, Mr Hardacre, it don't seem reeght. I mean, supposin' some folk don't care for . . .'

'Salmon?' Harry chanced. She nodded vigorously. 'I was afraid so,' he said, and left her to her own devices.

On the morning of the proposed event, Harry rose early, as was his custom, leaving Hetty sleeping on, and descended alone to the kitchens of Hardacres. Signs of preparation were everywhere, and Mrs Dobson was already busy baking fresh bread. She looked up in surprise but Harry, still in his dressing gown, murmured, 'Please, continue. I'll just make myself some tea. No, really, it's no trouble,' he added lamely, still staring at the mountains of food and cases of wine and spirits. He said, 'I just couldn't sleep. I suddenly had the most terrible suspicion.'

'Suspicion, sir?'

'About this party. I mean, has anyone actually heard from Sam again, after that first telephone call?'

'No, Mr Hardacre.' Mrs Dobson paused, wiping her hands down the floury front of her apron. She was a short round person with red country cheeks. 'I certainly haven't. Not that I would, mind.'

'No,' Harry said. 'But neither have I. You don't suppose it's one of his awful practical jokes . . . ?' Mrs Dobson's widening eyes, her expression first of amazement, then recollection, no doubt of the old days and a more youthful Sam, and then sheer boiling fury, drove him to insist hastily 'Oh, of course it wouldn't be, it was just a queer notion . . .' He retreated, still murmuring assurances, from the kitchen, and fled to his library and the comfort of the fire. He spent the morning there, peering cautiously out from time to time, hoping to see Sam, and fearing to see, unattended, a descending horde of unknown guests.

Promptly at ten o'clock, just after he had watched an oblivious Vanessa, who regarded the whole event as nothing to do with her, trotting off on Gold Flake, a large dilapi-dated grey-painted lorry came rumbling up out of the beech wood, crept self-consciously past the rolling sweeps of lawn, and came to a respectful halt well down the drive. It sat there, rumbling quietly and puffing diesel fumes conten-tedly into the country air until, eventually, a door opened and a man stepped down. At the distance between him and the lorry Harry could not recognize the figure, but he was

141

able to make out the lettering on the front of the lorry. It was new and bright, unlike the basic paintwork, and being set on a boldly painted patch on the front of the cab, it gave the impression of having been recently redone, perhaps over an earlier, obliterated sign. The large black letters on a red ground said HARDACRE SALVAGE.

'Who the hell are they?' Harry demanded of the velvet library draperies. And then he saw it was Sam.

In spite of the manner of his transport, Sam Hardacre was dressed very well, in a well-tailored business suit of navy blue, and as Harry, who had hastened outside, approached him, he was happily surprised at both how well the clothes suited him and how well he looked, lean and fit, and slightly weatherbeaten. Sam waved one leisurely long arm over his head towards his great-uncle and then turned back to the lorry, from which were descending two companions. A fourth member of the party who had evidently ridden in the open back of the vehicle was now rather shakily clambering over the metal side, rubbing a tousled head as if he had been asleep.

Each was, like Sam, dressed in a manner incongruous with the lorry in which they had arrived, most of all in the case of the gentleman who'd ridden in the back. Sam's companions, however, wore their party finery with something less than aplomb, and stood now looking about at the gracious setting of Hardacres with open nervousness. The one nearest Sam, a grey-haired, tough-looking man of late middle-age, conspicuous for his having only one arm, used his one hand to tug uncomfortably at his collar and tie. As Harry approached he heard him say, 'Eeh, lad, you've sure dropped us in it this time.'

'Harry,' Sam called, delighted, 'splendid to see you. Come, you must meet some friends of mine. Friends,' he added, with a grin, 'and business associates. Herein you see before you,' he encompassed his nervous, shuffling line of companions with a sweeping arm gesture, 'the full workforce of Hardacre Salvage. Mick Raddley, skipper of the *Dainty Girl*, Pete Haines, salvage master, and,' he paused, a cautious eye on the tall individual who had clambered out of the lorry, 'our diver, Martin Raynor.'

Harry nodded, still feeling vaguely confused, but dutifully shook hands, first with the one-armed seaman, then with Pete Haines, and lastly with the diver, a lanky man of uncertain age, with a beaky nose and a large Adam's apple giving him the look of a vast featherless fledgling bird. Harry felt distinctly that the diver, Raynor, was having difficulty focusing his eyes as he peered blearily out at his host.

'This is my great-uncle, Harry Hardacre,' Sam announced, and the three nodded and shuffled feet obediently.

Harry was swept with sympathy. He could see that they were utterly overawed by the house looming up behind him, and indeed by himself, looking the country gentleman that he had become. He wanted to say, 'Don't worry, I'm really just one of you,' but there was no way he could make himself believed, he knew. So he said instead, with instinctive kindness, 'The house is in a bit of an uproar just now, but I'm sure if we sneak in the back Mrs Dobson would give us all a cup of tea. Just the thing on a cold morning, eh?'

They relaxed, with grins and nods of agreement, and Harry led them off round the house, past the beautiful, now empty conservatory, and into the courtyard behind the kitchens. He felt their relief even as they entered that sheltered, homely spot, and he sympathized. He himself had always had a sneaking fondness for this more modest, less imposing entrance to the house and his mother, Mary Hardacre, had rarely used any other.

Thus it was that, over the broad pine table of the Hardacre kitchen, Harry first learned of his great-nephew's venturing out into the risky world of marine salvage, and his first, modest business success. Sam related the saga of the *Louisa Jane*, referring all Harry's queries of a technical nature to Haines and Mick Raddley whose confidence visibly grew once on their own familiar ground. Mick, in his turn, insisted on giving Sam full credit for the success of the venture.

'It were him that thought of it,' he said firmly. 'If'n it had been up to me and Pete she'd all be sitting there yet under t' sea.'

'And you've managed to raise the entire cargo?' Harry said, impressed.

'Near as damn it,' Mick said, adding a quick, 'pardon, ma'am,' with a glance to Mrs Dobson, who was laboriously laying out trays of food, with limited good grace, around her invaded kitchen table. 'Now's t' big job.'

'What's that?' Harry asked.

Mick looked to Sam who said, 'We've completed the contract for the cargo. Now we're thinking of having a go at the wreck itself, for scrap. We're all agreed,' he glanced at his three companions, two of whom nodded, while the third, the diver Martin Raynor, merely stared dreamily into his tea, 'we're all agreed,' Sam continued, 'to risk what we've made on the job on getting her up. Or at least getting the stern end up. Trouble is, I'm afraid we'll need more money. So we're waiting on Erasmus Sykes; you'll meet him today. If he decides to call in his investment, we can pay, but we can't go on.' He paused, tapping the table thoughtfully. 'Dashed pity if he does,' he said.

Pete Haines laughed. 'Look at him,' he said. ''E's got t' bug, all right. It's like gambling. Only wetter. Cream cakes in t' window.' He grinned at Sam and Sam grinned ruefully back.

'I rather suppose I have,' he said.

Harry smiled, and said, hesitantly, 'I really wish I could help . . .' but Sam cut him off brusquely.

'Good God, Uncle Harry, I wasn't meaning you. You're not a gambling man, thank God, or we'd not have this place any longer, would we?' He looked fondly up to the high beams of the kitchen of his childhood. 'No. It's a risky game, Uncle Harry. But Erasmus . . .' he grinned. 'He'll huff and puff, I reckon, but I doubt he can resist the bait.'

When Erasmus Sykes arrived, two hours later, Harry was not at all certain that Sam had judged his man right. He appeared at the front door, having arrived in an unprepossessing motor car which he had parked discreetly behind the Hardacre Salvage lorry, looking sadly about him as if the party were something he wished to enjoy and yet was certain that he was fated not to.

'Ah, Mr Hardacre,' he greeted Harry, after Sam's introduction. 'No doubt you have never heard of me. Little chance for the likes of you and me to meet.'

'Sykes Amusements in Bridlington, I understand?' Harry said helpfully.

Erasmus bent his heavy face into a wistful smile and said, 'My little enterprise indeed, famed so far afield?'

Harry was uncertain whether he was sarcastic or as genuinely pleased as he sounded, but Erasmus at once deflated his own pleasure by adding, 'But of course. Young Mr Hardacre will have explained!' His expression of resigned sorrow returned and he entered the house with slow, plodding steps. At once he was intercepted by Vanessa, who had been press-ganged into attending and who now barked at him an offer of sherry. Harry turned to go to his rescue, but other guests had materialized and he was obliged to leave Erasmus to his fate.

The Bartons had appeared at the door. Emily, slightly overdressed and over made-up, her eyes a little too bright with nervous excitement, cast an eager glance into the drawing-room of Hardacres, filled now with people, that was almost a look of hunger. 'Oh, it's so good to see you,' she said to Harry. 'So good to see everyone. So many people. Oh, do tell, has anyone come up from London, perhaps? Will Jane be here?'

'I'm afraid not,' Harry said, taking her by the elbow, with

145

a smile for her elder daughter Ruth, teetering on too-high heels. 'It's mostly Sam's crowd and a lot of new faces, too, from his,' he paused with a ruefully ironic grin, 'his business circle.'

'Nowt but good Yorkshire folk,' Philip bellowed and Harry saw Emily's mouth tighten with a wince that went beyond good humour. But Philip was away, glass in hand, pursuing Noel into the library, in what he obviously considered the proper Northern man's disdain for social fripperies. Noel, with his permanently jaundiced eye and his affinity with the locals, had become Philip's hero of late. The younger Bartons, Olive and Paul, stood self-consciously in corners of the drawing-room, sipping lemonade, and Harry dedicated himself to coaxing a smile back on Emily's face, with a tall gin and a long talk about the London stage.

'It's missing everything that I can't stand,' she lamented, but she brightened then and said, 'Oh, but Harry, I've the most splendid news. And I forgot to tell you. Albert and Maud are coming to London in July, with Janet, for the première of *A Lady in Love*. We're all invited. Isn't it marvellous? Everyone will be there . . . all the stars. I've started inviting my London friends already. It will be so wonderful, like a school reunion.' She stopped suddenly, smiling nervously. 'I must sound like a child.' Her lower lip trembled. 'I'd better put this glass down, Harry, if you don't mind. I think I've had enough.' She set it on the table and put her handkerchief to her lips, dabbing at nothing. 'Excuse me,' she said, turned away and walked, a little stiffly, to the drawing-room door. Harry heard her quick footsteps on the polished wood of the great main stairs. He stood sadly looking after her, sipping his sherry, and then suddenly remembered Erasmus Sykes and, recalling the obvious importance of that gentleman to Sam's fledgling company, he set out seeking him, feeling guiltily to have been lax in his duties as host.

146

His concern heightened when a survey of drawing-room, library, and the small study off the gunroom, all of which were occupied by happy crowds of chatting guests, did not reveal Erasmus. He poked his head round the edge of the dining-room door, where Mrs Dobson and three village ladies drafted for the day looked up in startled disapproval from their preparations of the large buffet luncheon. He waved lamely and dashed away, now really worried. Supposing the big sad man had just wandered morosely away, got into his dilapidated car, and driven off? Visions of Sam's future tumbling around his ears haunted Harry as he pursued his quarry even into the upstairs corridors of his house. Once there, passing a bedroom door, he was dismayed to hear the sound of a woman sobbing, and guessed quickly that it was Emily. He hovered helplessly, his hand on the figured ceramic knob, but slipped away. No doubt his presence would be more of an embarrassment than a help. Making a mental note to have a severe discussion with Philip, who he had last seen in the billiards-room with a renegade tankard of brown ale in his hand, Harry descended once more into the public rooms. He thought suddenly of the morning-room, where Hetty usually stayed during this sort of event, which invariably tired her. Surely not there though; the morning-room and Hetty were usually centres of feminine retreat, where the ladies stopped in to check their appearance in the large mirror over the fire and share feminine inconsequentials with their retiring hostess. Still, it was the last room he could think of. Unless Erasmus had simply retired to the gunroom and shot himself.

The door was almost closed as Harry approached, and he heard a soft murmur of feminine tones. Uneasily, he tapped lightly on the smooth panel and was greeted by Hetty's own voice, 'Come in.'

He entered hesitantly, still expecting to find a clutch of ladies annoyed at male intrusion. But there were no ladies other than Hetty, who was seated in the centre of a large

147

plush settee, at right angles to the graceful marble fireplace. The only other occupant of the room, perched with startling incongruity on a narrow, velvet-cushioned ottoman, almost at Hetty's feet, was Erasmus Sykes. He looked to Harry like a large brown bird that had landed by error on a much smaller bird's nest. He looked up and beamed a smile of genuine pleasure, which wrinkled up his face about his small shrewd eyes.

'Forgive me, Mr Hardacre,' he said, 'for monopolizing your utterly charming wife.'

'Oh, I'm so sorry, Harry,' Hetty said breathlessly, looking at the brass clock on the mantel. 'Are we late for luncheon? I'm afraid I've been so absorbed in Mr Sykes's conversation that I'd quite forgotten the time.' Erasmus beamed again.

'Not at all,' Harry said, with a mixture of relief and amazement. 'Plenty of time. Shall I get you both another drink?'

'No, I shall,' said Erasmus, getting at once to his feet. 'What can I get for you, Mrs Hardacre? No, no! You're not to move. I'll be back at once.' And with a confident nod to Harry, he plodded happily off.

Harry stood watching in astonishment until Hetty said, 'What a charming man. Do you know he's in business with Sam?'

Harry nodded. 'Yes. I had heard that.'

'It sounds terribly exciting. Raising ships from the sea. He was telling me all about his plans to save a freighter that sank off Whitby. Imagine. And Sam is helping too.'

'Indeed,' said Harry, swallowing hard. But Sykes had returned with a sherry for Hetty. He hastened about the room, finding just the right sized little table to set beside her before presenting her with her drink, and settled once more on the ottoman with his own.

'Oh, do continue,' Hetty begged. 'Just where you left off.'

'I suppose I'd best do the rounds,' Harry said lamely, but no one noticed and he slipped quietly away. Once outside the closed door of the morning-room he stood rubbing his thinning grey hair, smiling to himself. Of all the people to win the heart and attentions of the irascible Mr Sykes, who would have imagined Hetty? And yet, of course, who but Hetty? Erasmus Sykes, he realized with sudden insight, was lost, lonely and afraid despite his bulk, and his shell of cynicism and his posturing of misery was a complex screen. He was afraid of the world. But no one could possibly be afraid of Hetty. Weak, half-willed, as retiring as a small brown mouse, always half-lost in her own house, just as its previous mistress, Mary Hardacre, had been before her; Hetty would appear to Erasmus Sykes as something frail, needing his care, much as his famous black poodles needed the same. Her sorrows were self-evidently greater than his, her shyness more complete. In her company, Erasmus became a gallant, a knight, a protector. As unlikely a friendship as was ever to be found, Harry was sure, but also as sound. The effect on Sam Hardacre's future, he realized, was incalculable.

Still musing, Harry made his way to the main entrance hall, ready to meet any late arrivals. He glimpsed Madelene, on the arm of her son, being whisked into the drawing-room. He did not follow. On occasions like this, he and his mistress studiously avoided each other rather than practise the hypocrisy that the situation demanded. Harry was about to make a discreet retreat to the library when he heard, beyond the closed glass-panelled inner doors, the sound of a motor car on the smooth pink chippings of the drive. He made his way out into the large tiled entrance-way, with its elaborate wicker-backed watchman's chair and its array of walking sticks and hunting trophies from Strathconon, and stood just inside the open front door, trying to place the new arrival among the cluster of remarkably mixed automobiles before his house. It took him a moment to spot it, so low

149

and sleek that it was nearly hidden behind a tall Bentley. But a curve of gleaming grey wing revealed itself, and a flash and glitter of one wire wheel.

'I know that car,' he muttered to himself as a tall man appeared, straightening up from the low seat. He didn't know the man, however, and stared curiously at the handsome face, half-turned away towards whoever else was emerging from the vehicle. The most striking feature of the newcomer was his hair, a bright Nordic blond, almost white in the pale sunlight creeping through the moorland clouds. The other party then stood up into view beside her motor car.

'Jane,' Harry shouted, delighted. 'How did you know?'

'I'm most dreadfully sorry, my dear,' she called over the nose of the Bentley. 'I had no idea. May we gatecrash, or shall we scuttle off into the mist?'

Jane was not, of course, permitted to scuttle away. Her arrival could not have been more fortuitous for Harry for whom she held, as always, the position of favourite relative, the one person without whom no social gathering was completely satisfactory. She was to him still the little girl whose babyhood in his early adolescence had been the first occasion in his life of real love, that is, not the love of gratitude as to his parents, or desire as for a lover, but the love of caring, as parent to child. She would always be thus, his baby sister, in spite of the incongruity of their two grey heads, since age can alter only the individual, not his relation to others. He greeted her, as always, as if her arrival was the highlight of whatever event she was attending, and turned politely to welcome her companion as well. It did not surprise him to find his sister in the company of a handsome and youthful gentleman. Her companions were drawn from all age groups and he assumed himself to be meeting some past associate of her son, perhaps a school friend or comrade from the Forces.

'Muller,' the young man said, extending his hand, 'Jan

Muller.' Harry was shaking that hand and smiling politely up at the tall blond man, when the name sank into his consciousness. His smile altered from one of social good nature to one of wondering and he half-turned to Jane, who was suddenly overcome with emotion. She shook her head, blinking at tears.

'Heidi's son,' she said.

The party, then, that had begun as a celebration of the establishment and first success of Hardacre Salvage took a sudden swerve of course and re-emerged as a party in the honour of Jan Muller's return. No one was more pleased at the turn of events than Sam himself, whose long acquaintance with Heidi and long standing affection for her allowed him to quite literally share her rejoicing. He welcomed Jan into their midst as if he were a second brother, leading him about the house, introducing him to everyone in sight, and repeating again and again, 'You must meet Terry. I can't wait until he gets here, he won't believe this.' Harry had initially called all the guests into the dining-room, making the announcement of Jan's arrival a public matter and coincidental with the announcement of lunch. For the rest of the afternoon the guests were thus divided between those intimates of the family who knew Jane and Heidi and the entire story, and who now surrounded Jan, plying him with questions about the years of his absence and those more distant guests who had never heard of any of them, and therefore spent the afternoon asking each other what was going on.

The one exception was Martin Raynor, the diver, who occupied his time cruising happily from room to room sampling every manner of drink available, and there was a considerable variety and, from his assessment, an apparently unlimited quantity. The only cloud on his horizon was Mick Raddley who had set himself up as Raynor's watchdog and whom he was obliged to avoid. Seeing his approach, at one point, down the long passageway from the dining-room, Raynor panicked, and grabbing a handy bottle of Scotch and a glass he bolted out of the front door. He found himself in the tiled entrance-way, with the inner doors shut between himself and the party, and nothing now outside but patiently waiting automobiles and the occasional straying peacock. He shrugged, settled in the hooded watchman's chair with his bottle at his knee and gave himself over to serious drinking. An hour later, and with the Scotch bottle considerably lighter, he was still there. Within, the sounds of partying had grown quieter as guests replete with food and drink settled in comfortable groups around fires, in that pleasant hiatus before late coffees and farewells. Outside the light was beginning to fade, and the peacocks had crept away. A distant sound of an approaching motor car fell placidly on Martin Raynor's ears, but he did not stir. He must have slept then, briefly, because he had no recollection of the car's arrival, or the sound of closing doors, or of footsteps. When next he opened his eyes, reaching companionably for his bottle, a dark figure was standing in the open doorway, blotting out the light. Raynor started, leaned forward and his eyes opened in a widening stare. He had just taken in the flowing costume when his eyes settled on the face and, in the dim light, suddenly recognized it. With a howl of terror he leapt up, kicking over the clattering whisky bottle, and fled shouting through the inner doors, leaving them open behind him, and on into the body of the house.

Somnolent guests, aroused by the noise, stumbled out of various rooms, but there was only one that Martin Raynor wanted to see, and he howled louder.

'Mick! Mick Raddley! Help! Mick!'

'What the devil's with you?' Mick shouted, emerging from the billiards-room. He was glowering with suppressed fury and looked ready to tear the diver limb from limb.

'Mick, you were right. I'll nay touch another drop as

long's I live. I swear it. I swear it,' he moaned. He was shaking visibly and huddling into his rumpled jacket as if to hide in its depths somewhere.

'Talk sense, you bloomin' idiot,' Mick growled, still advancing ominously.

'It were him,' Raynor moaned.

'Who?' A curious onlooker gasped.

'It were him. I just saw him,' he glanced warily over his shoulder to where the main doorway was obscured now by the gathering crowd. 'I just saw t' boss himself, standing in the doorway.'

'So what?' Mick demanded.

'So what? So he were wearin' a dress, that's what. I just saw 'im, in a bluidy great black dress, Sam Hardacre, I'd know 'im anywhere.' But his eyes were widening again with amazement as he spoke, for the crowd had parted and Sam, in blue-suited normality was standing before him.

'It's you,' he moaned.

'You blitherin' drunken fool,' Mick roared.

'But it were . . . in a dress . . . I saw you . . .' Martin trailed off, looking about frantically for an avenue of escape.

Then the crowd parted behind him to allow someone's entrance, and he turned towards the door. Terry Hardacre was still standing there, looking faintly bewildered at all the commotion, in the long black habit of a Benedictine monk.

153

CHAPTER
TEN

Four days later, Jan Muller was still at Hardacres. In the confusion after Terry's arrival, Sam had lost track of Jan, and when he went looking for him, found him in a corner of the drawing-room, unexpectedly engrossed in conversation with Pete Haines, the salvage master. As he came within earshot, Haines turned and said matter-of-factly, 'Jan here thinks we'd be best to seal yon forrard bulkhead and try a tide lift, wi' pontoons, if'n we can find some old tanks or somesuch.'

'What?' said Sam, startled.

'I figure maybe summat from Army surplus.'

'Ellsberg used old gasoline storage tanks at Massawa,' Jan went on. 'Liberated them from Shell Oil. Of course you'd not need anything as large as that.'

'Ellsberg?' said Sam.

'Commander Ellsberg,' Jan replied, as if the name should readily come to anyone's mind. 'US Navy. Did the salvage work at Massawa.'

Sam looked blank and Haines said, a little proudly, displaying knowledge he had gleaned in the last fifteen minutes, 'That's on t' Red Sea. In Ethiopia,' he added, struggling slightly with the pronunciation.

Sam nodded, still looking puzzled, and touched Jan Muller's shoulder. 'Were you involved in that or something?' he asked.

'Massawa? No. I met Ellsberg in Oran, in Algeria. Clearing up the mess the Vichy French left behind.' His smooth, sun-tanned face lost for a moment its look of pleasant good humour, revealing a harder man beneath.

'Salvage work,' Sam said, just to be quite certain.

Jan Muller laughed, tossing his heavy forelock of white-blond hair back off his face. 'You could say. Twenty-seven ships sunk in the harbour, six blockships across the harbour mouth. It was, how you say, a balls-up.'

Sam grinned, still rather stunned at the coincidence, which he pointed out to Jan.

'Yes,' Jan said thoughtfully, 'I suppose it is surprising. But you see, it was just a small part of my life, and long ago. It only comes to mind as I talk with Mr Haines. I have done other things,' he added simply.

'E's done bloody everything,' Haines said with a grunt. 'An' been bloody everywhere.' He nodded towards the young Israeli with definite admiration.

'Yes, it seems that way,' Sam said, interested. 'How ever did you end up in Oran?'

Jan was silent. His forehead wrinkled with a look of almost painful thought and he said eventually, 'I was in France . . . I did some work there, with the Free French. When it became necessary for me to leave, I went first to Gibraltar, then North Africa.' He made a small circular motion in the air with one sun-dark hand, vaguely tracing the course of some long-ago journey.

He looked uncomfortable, and Sam sensed he should not pursue the conversation too far but, still curious, he said, 'As an Israeli?' because it seemed so unlikely.

'We were under British authority . . .' Jan paused, looking vague, and full of recollection. 'It was not unusual at that time . . . members of Haganah . . .' His voice faded again as if each phrase was wrested from a cavern in his mind into which he rarely ventured. 'There were others,' he said at last. 'It was not unusual.'

Sam nodded, knowing he must bring the conversation to an end. He turned quickly, spotted a tray of glasses left by one of the temporary staff and quickly uplifted it, offering drinks. Jan took one, nodding a double thank you. Sam understood. He knew many men who'd had the kind of war one didn't choose to talk of any more.

Sam did not raise the issue again and it would have remained just as passing conversation had it not been for a chance comment by Pete Haines, as the party was breaking up.

'Ain't it just t' way,' he said. 'First bloke I find in donkey's years can teach me a thing or two about salvage, an' he's just stoppin' over on 'is way to t' bluidy Near East.'

'You serious, Pete?' Sam asked.

'About what?'

'That he can teach you a thing or two?'

'Dead right he can. I mean, I know my trade, don't get me wrong. But he's worked wi' t' big lads. Damn, but I'd like to show him t' *Louisa Jane*, see how 'e'd handle her.'

'Yes,' Sam said, and by the fading look in his eyes Pete assumed he was no longer interested, and shrugged and turned away. Sam was the boss, anyhow, not him.

But Sam was interested, indeed, and his look of preoccupation was merely the reflection of a quick mental tally of ways and means of getting Jan Muller on to the *Louisa Jane*. He quickly settled, with shrewd confidence, on the one person he suspected of having more influence than anyone in sight on Heidi Muller's son: his great-aunt Jane. It didn't take much, actually; a heartfelt plea to Jane, with loyal Terry drafted in for support, an apologetic begging of further hospitality from his always hospitable uncle (fortunately with the less hospitable Noel out of earshot) and, by the time the last guests were leaving, the nucleus of Hardacres and their nearest and dearest were settling down to a country weekend. Except for the unfortunate Terry of course who, having added his sympathetic weight to Sam's request, was then obliged to return almost immediately to Ampleforth in time for benediction.

'Lucky devil,' he said, as he parted with Sam with a moment's boyish horseplay reminiscent of their earlier days, now oddly discordant with his costume. Sam ducked the light punch thrown by his brother and returned one for good measure. 'I can see a splendid booze-up building,' Terry went on, 'and I even helped to set it up. I'm jealous as all hell.' Sam grinned as the two stood alone facing each other in the empty hallway, both tall and lean, and astonishingly alike with their dark French eyes and hair, in spite of their radically different dress.

'Well, you needn't be jealous,' Sam said. 'This is business. Not pleasure.'

'The hell it is,' Terry muttered, swinging another light punch.

Sam ducked and fended.

'It is,' he said. 'It is.'

And it was. It evolved into the most exactingly businesslike weekend of Sam's life. By half-way through dinner, an impromptu affair based, unsurprisingly, around tinned salmon, he had concluded that Pete Haines was more than correct in assessing the man's experience. In a few short, hot, feverishly active weeks in Algiers, Jan Muller had had the kind of crash course in salvage that only military necessity can supply. Short of manpower, material and, most of all, time, he had, under the tutelage of true masters of the trade learned the kind of innovative improvisation that could make a small, shoe-string operation succeed where more conventional methods might, by sheer weight of responsible good sense, fail. Sam Hardacre, in charge of a new-born company operating on less than half a shoe-string, needed such a man, and with a single-mindedness that surprised himself he set out to get him.

In a very short while his intentions had escalated from merely getting Jan Muller aboard the *Dainty Girl* and over the wreck of the *Louisa Jane* for some first-hand observation and a gleaning of his valuable opinions, to inveigling him right into the company as a fully-working member. And that, considering Jan was a citizen of a foreign country with an established life far away, and a rapidly expiring visitor's visa, was not going to be easy.

He decided to work in steps and the visa, with its necessary restrictions on time, was the first obstacle to be overcome. Not for the first time, he fell back upon the resources of the ever resourceful Jane Macgregor.

'You want something,' she said bluntly, when he cornered her in the hallway when she was about to retire with Hetty and Vanessa for after-dinner coffee.

'Afraid so,' he said, grinning as engagingly as possible.

'You know, young man,' she said, looking severely down her long fine nose, 'you should realize by now that that gorgeous smile may work on twenty-five-year-olds, but not on ladies of sixty years.'

'Oh, surely no more than fifty,' he said, still grinning. 'And that I'll only accept because history demands it.'

'You *are* pushing your luck,' said Jane drily. 'Well, what is it this time?'

'A friend in the Home Office? Visas department?'

'And who says I *have* a friend in the Home Office?'

'Lady Macgregor, my beloved, you have friends *everywhere*.'

She had sniffed, lifting her still handsome chin with a slight twitching of smile. 'My coffee will be cold,' she said.

But he knew, as she strode off down the corridor, briskly adjusting her brief tweed jacket, that that much had been accomplished and official channels were now open. Now remained the much trickier task of the man himself.

Within half an hour of conversation Sam Hardacre had reached an important conclusion: Jan Muller was a man of action and, as such, would respond only to action. Words would invoke that pleasant European smile and ready agreement and neither would lead anywhere. Conversely, if he could just get the man on the wet, oily deck of the *Dainty Girl*, with the challenge of the North Sea all around, and the lure of the sunken ship below, the same excitement that charged him when he first saw the *Louisa Jane* would charge Jan as well. Which was why, without a word of consultation with either concerned party, Sam had volunteered to drive Jan to Bridlington in Jane Macgregor's car, for a day's reconnoitring of the salvage project, coupled with a dinner and overnight accommodation at The Rose at Kilham.

'You don't mind, Aunt Jane, do you?' he said anxiously, as he accepted the Jaguar keys from Jane's slightly imperious hand the next morning.

'Mind? Why should I mind? At least we're getting rid of you for the night.' She tilted her head sideways, watching her great-nephew climbing into the driver's seat, trying to conceal his eagerness to get her magnificent motor car on to the open road as he did so. 'Prang it and I'll have your head. I really will, Sam,' she said firmly, and with a dry smile added, 'I can't wait to see the welcome you get from Emily. Have you told her yet?'

'Shh,' Sam said, for Jan was emerging from the front door of Hardacres, graciously making his thankyous to Harry and to Noel, who had walked off in the middle.

Sam drove off docilely, down the long winding gravel drive, pointing out peacocks and the small inherited herd of fallow deer as they passed them. Once out on to the Driffield road, with Hardacres and Jane Macgregor thoroughly out of earshot, he put his foot down and let the XK 120 go. The surge of power satisfied all expectations.

'A superb lady,' said Jan Muller, thrown back in his seat by the acceleration.

'A gem. A true gem,' Sam whispered. 'I'd give my eye teeth for a car like this.'

Jan laughed, over the rush of wind and roar of the engine. 'No. Not the motor. I mean your Aunt Jane.'

'Oh,' Sam said, surprised. 'Yes, rather, now that you mention it. Jolly good sport, anyhow. Super of her lending the car.'

159

Jan laughed again. 'I think somehow she had little choice. You are a determined man, when your mind is on something.'

Sam glanced across at his companion, and back at the road. He drove on in silence, concentrating on the curving road and the rich pleasure of the Jaguar's response. He had underestimated Jan Muller. The ruse of the weekend had in no way fooled him. At last he said, 'That's right. I am.' He turned briefly, and grinned, his open, honest grin. 'Consider yourself warned.'

Jan nodded. But if he put up any interior defences, Sam saw no outward sign. He only relaxed back against the grey leather seat as if there was nothing on his mind but the enjoyment of the drive on a lovely spring day.

In truth his mind was in Palestine, with Hannah, in the dusty dry sun, awaiting his return.

To gain time, Sam talked about the project so far and his satisfaction in retrieving, with the diver and two mechanical grabs, virtually all of the tinned goods he was contracted to raise, with the exception of the half dozen partially damaged cases they had retained as 'perks'.

'Trouble is,' he said, negotiating a narrow blind bend by a tall brick wall as they passed through the village of Burton Agnes, 'half the tins in the damaged crates had lost their labels. The sea water unstuck the glue, and then they were anyone's guess. Of course they could still be resold as long as the structure was sound, but only at a fraction of value. Who's going to buy half a crate of salmon that might turn out to be peaches?' He shrugged. 'Anyhow, we made a reasonable profit from the rest. We're happy enough.'

'But not,' said Jan, 'happy to stop while, who knows, you are still ahead?'

'Do you think we're making a mistake?'

'What do the insurers think?'

'They're not involved. They're out of it now. The

contract was just for the cargo. The hulk was officially abandoned. She's up for grabs.'

'So,' Jan said, 'there is your answer.' He touched the side of his forehead with a gesture that Sam interpreted as 'a word to the wise'.

'The insurers' lack of interest doesn't negate the absolute value of the wreck,' Sam defended. 'It's maybe just not worth their while. There's not much in it, the ship was old and she's had a heavy mauling. I reckon they were content enough getting the cargo back.' He heard uncertainty in his own voice and did his best to suppress it.

'No risk to them,' Jan pointed out logically, 'if you were willing to take up the contract. No cure, no pay. That's how it's always done, am I not right?' Sam nodded. Pete Haines had explained that all to him at the beginning. 'However, supposing there was reason to assume that the wreck itself might become a nuisance. That's a busy piece of water, I understand, a lot of fishing activity, small boats, holiday-makers. Supposing you shift her and she breaks loose under tow, or whatever, and blocks the shipping lanes or harbour entrance. The owner might be obliged then to raise her at any expense. Much more expense than she's possibly worth.' Sam nodded again. He hadn't thought of that. Jan said, 'When insurers wash their hands of something there's bound to be a reason. They think with their purses, you see, not their hearts.'

Sam drove on in silence, feeling morose and faintly foolish. As they approached Bridlington, where Mick and Pete awaited them aboard the *Dainty Girl* in the harbour, he said, 'I know you're right. But somehow I think I'm right too. I've got a ready local market for her as scrap metal. I've got an abandoned slip in Whitby where we can tow her in and cut her up. Pete knows the scrap-metal business in this part of the world. He's got a million connections. I think you're right that she's scarcely worth bothering with for anyone else, but we're right here, on the spot, with all the facilities we need. I dare say I'd not travel half-way round Britain for her, but the *Louisa Jane* is on our doorstep.' He glanced across at Jan Muller, who was listening politely. 'And besides,' he said, grinning in spite of himself as, upon approaching the Harbour Top in Jane Macgregor's Jaguar, he caught sight of Mick Raddley watching with his jaw down to his ankles, 'besides, damn it, if I stop now, that will be the end of it. Hardacre Salvage will end up with a neat profit and no future. Mick and Pete will go their own ways, and I'll go mine, and in half a year the whole business will just be a queer episode in our lives we tell people about in the pub, or at dinner-parties. I don't want it to end already. I want more.' He was interrupted by a sudden loud burst of applause and looked up startled. It was Mick and Pete, and it was not his speech but his borrowed motor that they were applauding, but somehow the effect was the same. Jan Muller was watching with a faint, admiring smile, and Mick Raddley, approaching with an awed expression and his one hand extended to stroke one silken grey wing, spoke softly.

'Eeh boss, you tell now where it wuz you swopped a crate uv yon salmon for this, and Pete and I'll just be off to pick up ourn.'

Once aboard the *Dainty Girl*, the party fell at once instinctively under the leadership of Mick Raddley who, in his proper position of skipper once more, assumed a quiet but firm authority. Sam was glad to relinquish the continued seduction of Jan Muller to the old fisherman, and stood quietly beside the wheelhouse as, within, Mick could be heard shouting over the engine noise and the sea wind, pointing out one and another feature of the Harbour to their guest. Once out in the bay, the boat began to kick about in the rough uneven sea, and Sam was glad of a few moments' solitude, balancing against the shifting deck. Something had happened there, in his conversation with Jan Muller, that had shaken him. It was not, as logically it might well have been, Jan's cool-headed assessment of the financial risks of raising the *Louisa Jane*. Those were genuine problems, but already he sensed he could deal with them. At times like this, he found growing in him a shrewd intuition that no doubt came from his great-grandfather, the Herring King. He knew the odds were wrong and he knew as surely that he would win. It was perhaps superstition, but he did not care. He trusted it. But something else had grown upon him in latter weeks, as they struggled and then triumphed over the sunken cargo: an eagerness, a chafing at the bit, a desire for reaching further, and then further for an elusive goal. He had said it himself, without meaning to. He wanted 'more'. More what? Money? Undoubtedly, he admitted ruefully, thinking of his hands on the wood-rimmed wheel of the Jaguar. But more something else, something addictive perhaps, excitement, or success, or a risky combination of both. He'd known a man in the Forces who was a drinker, the sort of hardened drinker who was heading unerringly towards alcoholism. He remembered the look that man's face would take on at his first drink of an evening, a savouring, tantalizing look, as he held it a moment out of reach, secure in its nearness, but prolonging the delicious act of fulfilment as one prolongs the act of love. That look, that hungry excitement was, he realized now, the elusive yearning he felt when he had said he wanted more.

Chilled, Sam raised his eyes to the approaching white of the Flamborough headland. He thought of Terry, with an unaccountable feeling of distancing and separation. Not shame, as he thought would be sensible, having just admitted to a terribly earthly lust for wealth, but loneliness, as if an expanding physical distance was opening between him and the Benedictine monastery where Terry still remained. He huddled against the wheelhouse and was filled with a powerful desire to burst in, interrupt Mick's long, descriptive monologue, thrust Jan Muller aside, and turn the *Dainty Girl* and run downwind for home. But Flamborough Head slipped past as he stood, unmoving, and in the

163

distance he saw the familiar shoreline of the bay that held the *Louisa Jane*, and all his doubts flew and scattered like so much blown foam.

Sam Hardacre was discovering, like other men of business before him, that moral strictures were occasionally a luxury he would find difficult to afford. He did not like himself much in the discovering, but buried the thought under the concentration of talk and activity that the afternoon provided. They made fast to the same buoys they had used during the salvage operation, and Pete Haines launched into a detailed discussion of the size, condition and position of the stern half of the sunken ship. He brought out navigational charts and drew diagrams, and Jan stood on the tossing wet deck, nodding and listening and questioning and Sam saw, as he knew he would, casual polite curiosity strengthen into real interest, and harden into involvement and committed concern. By the time they cast off and headed back to the Harbour, Jan was oblivious to Sam Hardacre, wrapped up instead with Pete and Mick and the technical possibilities that lay before them. He seemed to have forgotten entirely that he was meant to be crossing the Channel in four days' time.

But he hadn't, as Sam discovered that evening after dinner at The Rose at Kilham. After their return to Bridlington Sam had taken the opportunity to telephone Emily, while Jan and Pete were still poring over diagrams in the wheelhouse of the *Dainty Girl*. He needed every ounce of the charm that had once won him WAACs at every turn, to persuade her not only to accept two uninvited, and unexpected guests, but to provide them with the sort of dinner one lays on to impress a would-be future business partner.

'I will pay, of course,' Sam said. 'I mean, business is business.'

'No, you won't,' Emily said morosely. 'I can't possibly let you after that lovely party and, what's more, you know it.'

'Aunt Emily, please, that's not so at all. I insist on

164

paying. I really do.' He was about to say they wouldn't come if he wasn't allowed to pay, but realizing that just might suit Emily nicely, he refrained.

'Oh, just shut up and come, Sam,' Emily snapped, 'before I change my mind.'

Sam hung up the phone, a little doubtful of what welcome he and Jan Muller could expect to receive, but with little he could do about it, considering that he had told Jan as early as that morning that the arrangements were all made.

'She can't wait to see us,' he said cheerily, upon rejoining Jan aboard the *Dainty Girl*.

Considering its less than promising beginning, the evening was a remarkable success. Emily, after her initial reluctance, chose to regard the event as a family dinner-party of the kind she had once enjoyed so in London, and consequently threw herself with manic fervour into the preparations. The inn was, as usual, more or less empty, and for once this annoying state of affairs was a happy convenience. She prepared the best two of the three bedrooms and, over the whimpering protests of all three children, converted two of the inn's squawking collection of hens into the makings of a luxurious *coq au vin*. She left a mortified Ruth gamely plucking both after the execution, and went into the kitchen to wash her hands with a certain satisfaction. Emily surprised herself at times with her own, albeit unwilling, adaptation to circumstances. It was an adaptation which her country-loving husband had not yet achieved: Philip always hid in the bar when a chicken or duckling was needed for the pot.

'Are they dead yet?' Olive mourned, looking up at her from under the kitchen table.

'As a doornail,' Emily said grimly. 'Go and pull some leeks. I'll make broth from the feet.'

'Yeeuk,' Olive said, turning upon her mother a look appropriate to a murderess, and plodded out to the garden on dragging feet.

By the time the grey Jaguar, open-topped in the evening

165

sunshine, pulled up in the narrow street before The Rose, the whole inn was imbued with a delicious mixture of scents, fresh bread, chicken in wine and subtleties of broth and spices, and Philip was standing in his plus-fours before the door.

Emily appeared behind him and, taking one look at Sam and his transport, said, as one would to a child with his big brother's best toy, 'Does Jane know you've got that?'

'Emily, you positive darling,' Sam declared, vaulting the door of the car. 'How marvellous to see you. Come, you do remember Jan?' He embraced his aunt with one arm, his uncle with the other, and led both across to meet his guest. After the politeness of greetings, with Philip leading Jan proudly off to his bar, she detached herself smoothly from Sam's embrace and said only, echoing Jane, 'You want something.'

'Just your company,' Sam declared honestly.

'I'm to be charming, am I?' Emily asked.

'You're always charming.'

'I'm not, Sam,' Emily said frankly. 'Not these days. But for you,' she relaxed into a small smile, 'I'll make an exception. What do you want from Jan Muller? Money?'

'No, far from it,' Sam answered at once. 'If I want money from someone I just ask for it.'

'Just like that,' Emily said, sniffing. 'You make it sound simple.'

'It is simple, compared to this. Investment is just a question of figures, and a bit of trust. But I want more than that from Jan. I want a commitment.'

'To what?'

'To Hardacre Salvage. I've got one more day to convince him that he wants to go to work for me, or with me, instead of going home to Israel.'

Emily paused, pursing her lips, tilting her yet pretty head back, thinking. 'Tall order, Sam. Now I've got to be more charming than a whole nation.'

Sam laughed. 'That's about it, my love,' he said.

Emily shrugged, but went off to the kitchen with determination. Sam, playing the evening by instinct, left all discussion of salvage strictly out of his conversation, during a long pleasant pre-dinner session before the log fire of the public bar, and throughout Emily's excellent dinner as well. He let the conversation follow its own natural course, unrestrained, touching on every subject from orange-growing in Israel to the forthcoming Festival of Britain, in the summer.

'You know Maud and Albert are coming, for Janet's film première,' Emily said to Sam, who nodded, remembering Harry or someone had mentioned something of the sort.

'You *will* come down,' Emily said.

'London?' Sam said, sipping his wine and only half-listening. But Emily looked so hopeful that he said, 'Of course. Of course I shall,' without really imagining that anyone would remember. Film stars, even those who were distant Hardacre cousins, seemed too remote from his present world to be real.

'She is most beautiful,' said Jan Muller suddenly. Everyone looked curious, until he explained, slightly embarrassed, 'The young lady, Janet Chandler. I see her films in Israel. She is very beautiful. I was most surprised to learn she is one of you Hardacres,' and then added quickly, 'until, of course, I see how lovely Hardacre women are.' He glanced at Emily, who made a mock scowl, and at the two young Barton daughters, who looked starry-eyed.

'Perhaps you would like to meet her,' Emily said to Jan, having quite honestly forgotten the proposed brevity of his visit. Then she remembered and blushed, as if she had revealed some secret plan, and said awkwardly, 'If you come back some time.' Sam said nothing. He had not found the right moment and was relying, as in the old days when he courted girls, on that intuition that would tell him the moment had arrived.

After cheese and trifle the children were sent to bed, Emily went away for coffee and Philip was called away unexpectedly to serve behind the bar. Sam knew his moment had arrived. So did Jan Muller. He met the look of questioning in Sam's eyes so directly that Sam only grinned, having no need to speak.

'No,' Jan said.

'I'm sorry,' Sam replied, toying with his port glass. He kept his voice casual. 'Still, I can't pretend I don't understand. It's risky. We're not all gamblers. Just as well perhaps.'

'It has nothing to do with that,' Jan said, defensive. 'I am not afraid of risks. What have I to lose?'

'I don't know,' Sam said honestly.

'Kibbutzniks have no possessions,' Jan reminded. 'A small initial investment which we are entitled to reclaim, should we choose to leave. In my case, I would feel obligated to forfeit even that. The kibbutz funded my journey to find my mother. I would feel I owed them that back.'

Sam made no expression but a nod, but he caught at once, from Jan's choice of words, the revelation that the man had clearly considered the consequences of staying on.

He smiled as a whimsical thought occurred to him. 'Rather like the monastery, actually. We have quite the same arrangement.'

Jan returned the smile. 'Logical,' he said. 'A similar enterprise in some ways. But in others,' he added slowly, 'entirely different.'

'So I would imagine,' said Sam.

'You see,' Jan continued, 'it is not that I would not enjoy working with you. I find it intriguing. But there is another matter,' he paused. 'A personal matter.' Sam looked steadily at his companion and then nodded again.

'A woman?' he said.

'A woman . . . a girl rather. No matter. She is there.'

'I see.' Sam was silent. He had been rather afraid of this possibility. He thought for a while and said, 'She wouldn't consider joining you here? I'm sure it could be arranged,' he went on, going out on a limb provided by Jane's friend in the Home Office.

'Never,' Jan said instantly. 'Never. She is a Sabra. Native born. Israel is everything to her. Everything.'

'I see,' Sam said slowly, because Jan had revealed in that description of his lover something too of himself. 'But not so to you?' he asked.

'I do not understand.' But he did, and Sam knew he did. Jan paused, uncertain, and said, 'I have determined to make my life there. With Hannah.'

'A lovely name,' said Sam. He said nothing more, watching the man war within himself.

'You do not see. She is so young, so vulnerable,' he shrugged, raising his hands in wordless apology. 'She loves me,' he said, again revealing more of himself than he imagined. Then Sam did something that would prick his conscience for weeks, indeed months to come. He did something that from the very start he had sworn he would not do. Later, alone in his bed with a weight suspiciously like guilt on his mind, he could not honestly recall why he had done it; only that it had fitted into the conversation too well to be avoided, and he had grasped it as a young man grasps the fatal line of flattery he knows will turn a woman's head.

He said, 'So does your mother.'

Jan was silent. He fingered an unused spoon on the linen tablecloth, reached for his port glass, found it empty, refused Sam's offer of the decanter. He shook his head, saying at the same time, 'Of course. Of course.'

Feeling already a regretful need to make amends, Sam said awkwardly, 'But of course she has many friends. I know she's very happy in Strathconon. Very happy. Jane always says . . .'

'I am lying to myself, am I not?' Jan said, his pale confident eyes suddenly made younger, more vulnerable, by doubt. 'I keep saying that too, but I am wrong.'

'Not at all,' Sam said, aware of his impotence to undo the effect of the thing he had said, and frustrated by it. 'Look, Jane knows Heidi better than anyone and she was the one who advised you to go.'

'Jane knows her better? And how can that be so? How can anyone know her better than I? I am her son.' He shook his head again, so that his heavy blond hair fell over his forehead, and angrily pushed it away. He rose suddenly and said to Sam, 'Will you possibly excuse me? I am suddenly very tired. This travelling always . . . could you speak for me to our kind hostess . . . ?'

'Of course,' Sam said, guiltily solicitous. He got up and stood watching Jan walking with bowed head towards the stairs. For the rest of the evening, Sam, relieved of the tension of business and, moreover, eager to forget some of what had passed, relaxed into the family party, assuring Emily that Jan's early departure was no reflection on her entertainment, and showing everyone by his own overt cheerfulness that the evening had not been the disaster that Jan's defection might indicate. He knew, in fact, that it had not. He suspected already that he had been successful and was filled with a hollow deadness, part aftermath of concentration, part guilt. He drank too much and stayed up too late, alone with a well-lubricated Philip, discussing the relative merits of a variety of local ales. In the morning he awoke with a hangover, a rare occurrence, and descended blearily to the dining-room to find Jan Muller already awaiting him.

Whatever his troubles of the previous night, Jan was in a buoyant and cheerful mood. He grinned at Sam's obvious suffering and said loudly, 'Come, such a splendid breakfast, your aunt prepares. Join me. What will you have, porridge, or boiled eggs?'

'Coffee,' Sam croaked, waving the rest away.

Jan grinned again. 'So, Mr Hardacre, there is evidence of a hard night. What a pity. I had thought we would start our work this morning. Nothing like some good sea air for a hangover.' He made with one hand the motion of rippling waves.

Sam closed his eyes. 'You serious?' he asked.

'But of course,' Jan said. 'Would I mock my new employer?'

From the start, Jan Muller was an employee in name only. Sam Hardacre regarded him, with his expertise and experience both in salvage and in the ways of the world, as more than an equal. He regarded him as a partner and had already decided that, were Hardacre Salvage to progress beyond this first job and become a company of genuine substance, he would make the financial arrangements in accordance with partnership. He told himself it was sound business practice, a practical thankyou to a valuable man and a good way of holding on to the same. It was, however, more likely a kind of apology, partly to Jan for winning him by devious means, but more to a lonely young girl far away; a girl called Hannah, whom he would never meet.

CHAPTER
ELEVEN

That summer, the summer of 1951, was one that Sam Hardacre would remember as uniquely pleasant, an un-British season of balmy days and sunshine. Whether his recollection was accurate, or the result of his memory falsely re-creating an appropriate climate for the springtime of his new enterprise he could not honestly say. Surely the climate in the rest of the country was less bountiful.

The heady wave of socialist ideals and nationalizing fervour that had swept over Britain in the immediate post-war years had now broken, and swirled about the feet of the stumbling Labour government in a muddled eddy. The pinch of rationing seemed as tight as ever and the monumental task of rebuilding both the physical structure and the industrial fabric of the nation seemed a terribly long way from finished. With the physical evidence of the recent war still painfully visible, British troops were again at war already, in Korea. In the words of Noel Hardacre, upon being requested to join in family and national celebrations of the Festival of Britain in London, conveniently coinciding with Janet Chandler's film première, 'Seems t' me there's bloody eff-all to celebrate.'

But as always when an economy is more or less in rubble, somebody is using the pieces to lay foundations. This time Sam Hardacre was determined to be one of those somebodies and the odds, for a man who just a year ago had been a penniless religious Brother, were looking surprisingly good. He was still pretty much penniless; he'd used all his profit from the *Louisa Jane* to purchase more equipment; odds and ends of military surplus, useful junk; but primarily another workboat, an open personnel carrier that had done service on D-Day. What he really needed was a small tug, but that would have to wait. In the meantime, he put what he had to good use.

For Sam, the Festival of Britain, and the much bally-hooed première of *A Lady in Love* stood out as two moments of calm in that hectic, sunny summer, whereas to Emily Barton, on the other hand, they were the most exciting and vivid times of the entire year. Perhaps their different attitudes could be ascribed to the fact that Sam spent what felt like every other moment of that summer on one or another wet, salty deck of a ship, floating half-sunken, or thoroughly aground, while Emily spent the equivalent period of time in the kitchen of The Rose at Kilham.

'I wish I'd been born a man,' she said enviously one afternoon when Sam, passing through Kilham with a load of salvaged slates in his new army surplus lorry, had dropped in unexpectedly at The Rose.

'I never knew you wanted to be a salvage engineer,' Sam sympathized. 'But I'm sure I could find you a place . . .'

'You know what I mean,' she said, giving him a friendly shove as she set tea before him in the pub's kitchen. 'Men get to do what they want. They get to choose. All women get to choose is who they marry. Then hope *he'll* do what they want, and not just . . .' she shrugged, looking about the busy scrubbed workroom that was her kitchen. Sam looked around as well, and the industrious cleanliness, the cared-for hardworking look of it drew his sympathy where her complaints alone might not have done. He had to say that for Emily; she knew how to work.

He said, 'What did you want to do, Aunt Emily? I mean, that you never got to do?' She looked surprised, then thoughtful and then suddenly forthright.

'Do you want to know really?' He nodded and she smiled slightly. 'I wanted to sing. I wanted to be a singer.'

'Can you sing, Emily?' he asked curiously, having never heard her do so.

She shrugged again. 'A bit. I could once, anyhow. I mean if I'd had training. Who knows? Oh I'd have probably failed, like Maud did at her sculpture, but I'd like to have tried. Of course, Mother wouldn't hear of it. I mean, one daughter in the "arts" was enough for her in those days.'

'I thought it was more up to great-grandfather what you did. You lived with him then, didn't you?'

'Oh yes, of course. And he would have indulged me, but that was it. It would just have been indulgence, like he used to indulge Jane before she married. I didn't need that, Sam. I needed someone who'd take me seriously. Someone who'd back me, believe in me . . . Then of course I married Philip and everyone was happy.'

'Except Emily,' said Sam. Sometimes he forgot he was no longer in the monastery and his words no longer veiled by the cloth.

She looked shocked, and then smiled wryly. 'All right Sam. I asked for that. I know. I married him, and it's all my own fault.'

'I never said that,' said Sam. He had parted with her there, in the silent kitchen, with a kiss and a promise to meet up in London at the family gathering. It was a promise which in the past he had made lightly, little intending to keep. Now Emily's large dark defeated eyes demanded sincerity.

'You won't be too busy?' she said. 'I'd understand . . .'

'Of course I won't,' he lied. 'What could be more important?' A million things, he knew, as Jan and Mick and everybody would point out to him, upon his return. But this was family, and family mattered to Sam, even now. In the end, when he went to London, he took Jan along as well, managing to create a meeting with a London scrap-merchant interested in the brass and copper fittings of an old wartime wreck he had his eye on, as justification. He had not forgotten Jan's enchantment with his theatrical cousin, and felt an introduction was the least he could do for a friend. It was, he later admitted in a moment of private remorse, the most unmitigatedly stupid thing he ever did in his life, but that realization was mercifully in the future. For now, his only interest in London, Janet Chandler and the Festival of Britain included, was to do an acceptable amount of duty to the family and get back North and back to work. Like so many of the pivotal points of life, that summer weekend in London, for Sam, passed somewhat unnoticed.

Once in London the Hardacre family, for all the outward pretence of a cosy reunion, in reality set up three separate camps. Sam and Jan Muller stayed, courtesy of Hardacre Salvage, in two rather sad rooms in a guest house in Earls Court and Sam worried about whether he could really afford that. Harry and Hetty motored down from Hardacres, with Vanessa and Rodney's daughter Mary being allowed to attend as a special treat. Vanessa herself announced that she couldn't possibly leave Yorkshire until something called Fancyfree had foaled, but swore she would 'pop down', Rodney in tow, at the first opportunity after the big event. Harry was just as pleased; Vanessa at Hardacres was trying; Vanessa in London, striding about overturning tables and braying, was unbearable. Harry set up his camp in Brown's, where he had traditionally always stayed, and worried now whether he could any longer afford that.

Helen Brannigan stayed at the Savoy and didn't worry about anything.

'Britain is finished,' she announced with flat cool satisfaction, standing at the window of her river-facing suite, gazing across to the South Bank and the lights of the Festival proclaiming back at her that Britain was on the threshold of a new beginning.

'Mother,' Maud said in her soft patient way, 'how can you say that? Why, everyone's trying so hard, working so hard. Already things have come a long, long way since the war's end, I'm sure.'

175

'Rather easy for you to say,' Emily cut in sharply, her voice surprisingly like her mother's in tone, 'watching it all from the safe distance of sunny California.'

Maud was unperturbed. She plucked gently at a piece of lint on her husband Albert's worn dinner-jacket collar and said, 'Well, never mind. That's all done with. We're back to stay.'

'Idiots,' said Helen, with contempt.

'Mother,' Maud pleaded. 'We've been through that.' Her husband Albert, placing a gentle hand on her knee as they sat side by side, dwarfed by the luxury of a huge velvet settee, interrupted in her defence.

'Now, Mother, there's no use laying into Maud over that. It's all because of me. All my fault. You know that.' He spoke very softly, with a faint twinkle in the dark eyes that used to enchant his audience with their quick, over-the-shoulder glance as he led his band.

Albert was impossible to rile, but he was not above a little gentle needling, and his use of the word 'Mother' in addressing his mother-in-law was a well-tried technique. It worked, as always. Helen froze, casting him a bitter stare, and turned back to the window, pouring her venomous look on the new Royal Festival Hall, across the Thames. Helen was one of those ladies who liked to be reminded that her daughters looked to be merely sisters of so youthful a mother. She did *not* like to be addressed maternally by an ageing bandleader, a romantic idol of the thirties. Granted, Albert Chandler was a good few years older than his wife; that was one of Helen's original objections to the marriage, an objection not loudly voiced, however, since Janet Chandler's birth had preceded her parents' marriage by several months. No fault of hers, of course, and very little of her parents' actually, but the result was that a marriage that would have been strictly forbidden between that well-known bandleader and Joe Hardacre's daughter went ahead with everyone's hurried blessing.

Blessings or no, it had proved a happy union, probably the happiest Hardacre marriage since poor Harry's brief idyll, so many years before, with Judith Winstanley. Maud, looking about her family with their many frictions and quiet dissatisfactions, thought perhaps there was truth in the old adage that good fortune in money could never be linked with good fortune in love. She smiled secretly. Well, if that were the case, she'd accept their own reduced circumstances without a second thought. They were small enough price to pay for her years with Albert Chandler.

She turned and looked lovingly towards him, a look that in its natural simplicity spoke touchingly of utter, almost childish devotion and disgusted her mother whenever she saw it. Albert Chandler had changed very little since the day, in the early twenties, when he and Maud had first met. That fact summed up both his personality and his career, and was at once both a compliment to his enduring qualities and a criticism of his inability to adapt.

He dressed and groomed his hair in precisely the fashion he had done when first working in the West End. The dinner-suit he wore was twenty years old, at least. He had a newer one, but it hung in his wardrobe. He preferred this, with its wide lapels and flapping trouser-legs tumbling in dusty black profusion over his polished black shoes.

'Too tight,' he always proclaimed of newer garments. 'Damned uncomfortable. Can't get a tailor who can cut a decent pair of trousers any more.'

Maud would smile; undoubtedly comfort was part of his reason, but nostalgia was more of it. To Albert Chandler, those bright and glorious days between the wars, when women were all ladies, men all gentlemen, and music a sweet soothing honey of horn and strings, comprised an unsurpassable halcyon era. Nothing after would ever match it. He still damped his hair and brushed it slickly back from his forehead, though it was too thin and too grey to create that smooth shining black cap, reflecting the lights of the stage like patent leather, that once it had been. He still wore the brisk little pencil moustache that no one ever noticed, but without which his face would have been utterly different, and infinitely more modern. When he dressed for day, no matter how informal a day, he wore a three-piece suit, a cashmere scarf and a belted woollen greatcoat which he had to be persuaded to discard even in the Californian heat. A kindly columnist in Hollywood had once said of him, 'Wherever he goes, we really know that Albert Chandler is still gathering lilacs down an English lane.' The columnist had, of course, known Albert well. Anyone who knew Albert, from his bandsmen to the favoured members of his audience, to all manner of the theatrical press, could be nothing but kind. He was probably the best-liked man in his profession, a profession not renowned for brotherly affection. But not everyone knew Albert, and not every columnist was kind.

Unkindest of all were audiences, those crowds of restless, unforgiving people, with no memories. Who was there in the West Coast sunshine who knew the Café de Paris, the Piccadilly Hotel, the Dorchester, the Grosvenor House? Who recalled Jack Johnson, Lew Stone and Bert Ambrose? Who had huddled over a wireless in a darkened British provincial living-room to catch the tinny translation of the heartsongs of the West End? Albert did not blame them. How could they miss what they'd never known? How could they not be seduced away by the bewitchment of black jazz, the American subtleties of swing?

But Albert Chandler remembered, and his memories, sweet and unrelenting, isolated him further, day by day, from his audiences until one day, recently, he had discovered they had nothing left in common. Like partners in a marriage gone slowly, slowly sour, they were left with nothing but a tired, baffled dismay. Albert was honest. He did not blame them but himself. He knew his music was ending even before he left London at the end of the war. It was ending, in a way, before the war ever began. The music of the dance bands had grown up with Albert Chandler, shared with him its heady prime and, by the end of the 1930s, was feeling already the chill of middle-age. He had been with it as a young trumpeter with the Savoy Orpheans. He had gone on to lead his own band, and broadened his fame by broadcasting from hotel ballrooms on the radio waves of the youthful British Broadcasting Corporation. He branched out into recording, coaxing from his ten skilled musicians the precision and accuracy required to produce three uninterrupted flawless minutes for the wax disc and posterity. Later there were more musicians, bigger bands. Later there was Variety, as well as the hotel ballrooms and the clubs. The money was good and the Chandlers lived well. But even then, when the nightly symphony of club-land, the endless stream of dreamy ladies in silk frocks and gentlemen in monochrome perfection, seemed as eternal as London itself, change was whispered for those who would listen.

Albert found it hard to listen. He went with others of his profession to The Nest in Kingly Street, for after-hours jam sessions with black musicians, but Albert was not one who fell under their spell. He listened politely, and politely went away. Perhaps, he thought, he was simply too polite. Music, dance music, to Albert Chandler was always sweet, perfumed and rustling like silk. He had no heart for the sweaty gusto of jazz, no soul for the disturbing rhythms of swing. He was, he admitted once, just too utterly English for it all, and he went on quietly playing his own kind of music as long as anyone would listen. But the big bands were doomed. They'd thrown their lot in with Variety, topping the bills from the Palladium to Prague, but Variety had grabbed them for the same reason it clutched at the strippers and the dirty-mouthed comics: it was on the way down. The big bands were hitching a free ride to oblivion. Albert saw it coming but could not avoid it. He saw, too, the coming of the war and, with it, the snatching away of his best musicians one by one into the Forces. That he weathered, bringing old friends out of retirement and back on the boards, drying out those virtuosi of the whisky glass for a last swan song. What Albert could not predict was the fickle discovery of their former employers, club managers, hotel owners, proprietors of the big dance halls that, as in wartime, any band would now do. The big names meant nothing any more, and the big money was not to be had. For the very best, and Albert Chandler's Band was one of the very best, it did not at first matter. He had a season, post-war, in the West End. The dancers were thinner on the floor, the lavish tips that had once been thrust into his hand with requests for favourite numbers were no more, the adulation of the audience only a memory. But he was in work. He adapted as much as he could. He added a vocalist, a pretty girl with a rich throaty voice and, when an invitation to tour the States appeared, he took it up, hoping to find in a new country the success now fleeing him in the old. It was a forlorn hope. He ended up in California with a string of half-empty houses behind him, a drunken tour manager, and a group of musicians in virtual revolt. But there, in a casual meeting at a party, he made the contact that had carried him through the last five years. An undistinguished gentleman approached him, glass in hand, and commented about a particular song in the repertoire of the Band. Albert thanked him for his appreciation. The man wandered off. He returned later and mentioned the song again. Albert thanked him again, and once more he ambled away. It was only on their third encounter in the same crowded room that the man had ventured to ask the composer. Albert explained that the song was his own. It was a piece of information he would never have thought to volunteer. For a trumpeter, Albert was exceedingly reluctant to blow his own horn. Too English to survive.

This time, however, he did survive. The gentleman was a

film director. He was looking for theme music. He thought perhaps that song, some variations, if Albert had the time. Albert had more time than he cared to think about, and less money. He sat up all night and wrote the score. The little tune the director had fancied became in the end his world-famous 'Theme for a Lonely Woman'. They lived off it still.

Albert had often wondered what would have happened had that chance meeting, and the new world of film scoring that it opened, not occurred. He had wondered, but not worried. Doubtless something would have come up; doubtless they would have scraped by. With a woman like Maud beside him, he knew he could do anything. He would have found a job playing for some other band or orchestra, or opened a guest house, or stood busking in the street. Maud, he knew, with her gentle, unruffled smile, would be there contentedly at his side. One bleak night, when their vocalist, a beautiful girl with a lonely penchant for drink, had simply vanished on the evening of a performance, Maud, with her gentle shrug, had donned the girl's costume and overcome her massive shyness to get up on their little stage before the band and sing. She had a pretty voice, prettier than Emily's, and absolutely no desire to perform. But she would do it, and still did it, from time to time, when gin got the better of their ageing *chanteuse*. Thus Emily's dream was Maud's patient penance, an irony that neither of them would ever fully understand.

'Ah, don't be an asshole, Bert.'

Everyone at once looked at the door. Only one person referred to Albert as Bert, and only one member of the family used words like that in mixed company, cheerfully and with no remorse. Mike Brannigan was standing in the open doorway between the palatial bedroom and the sitting-room of the suite. He had been dressing and was still struggling with his black bow tie. Helen rose at once, went immediately to his side and tied the tie for him, while he stood contentedly with his arms at his sides like a small boy.

181

When she went to straighten his collar and adjust the lie of his dinner-jacket, flicking dust from the lapels, he squirmed and fussed, also like a restless child and said, 'Aw, cut it out, Helen.' Emily, watching, wondered if her mother ever realized how much their relationship visually resembled that of mother and son.

Helen tucked her arm possessively into Mike's and steered him towards a chair beside the one in which she had been sitting. Well, not precisely handcuffs, Emily thought meanly, but we're getting there. Undoubtedly Helen had cause for possessive caution, if not concern. Mike Brannigan was indisputably attractive. He had, with advancing years, lost the stunning handsomeness of his youth. The sharply defined perfect features were blurred now, by drink, time, and the batterings of a few less than successful fights. Mike was not a big man, but he had a straight-backed cocky stance, as if he were bristling for a scrap, that led him, rather gamely, into physical combats he could not always win. He had grown jowly in the year or two since Emily had seen him last, and his black hair was now heavily greyed. But his eyes, the dark blue, black-lashed Irish kind, were unchanged, deliciously troublesome-looking and, even now, roved ever so gently over the youthful innocent breasts of Ruth Barton, dressed up in her first adult evening gown. Ruth blushed and looked at her feet, and Mike, remembering who he was and where, smiled a soft smile of mature condescension and patted her head as he passed. He was practising that attitude of fatherly appreciation very hard just now, hoping in time he'd convince himself.

'C'mon Bert,' he said, taking the drink that Helen had offered him, knowing she would have watered it, but not prepared to argue, 'you're not really telling us you're planning on staying in this dump?'

Albert sipped at his own drink and very quietly nodded. He looked more amused by Brannigan than offended.

'Well look, pal, if it's money's the problem . . .' Mike

waved an expansive, generous arm. He was always generous. Whether he'd have been equally so if the money involved were his own, and not his wife's, no one would ever know.

'I can earn my living, Mike,' Albert said.

'Well all right. If it's a job, I mean, I can fix that. I got friends on the Coast. One or two who owe me a favour. There's no *problem*.'

He seemed so genuine in his concern that Albert was actually touched and said, 'No, really, Mike. It's terribly kind. But it's not what I want.'

'We *want* to come home, Mike,' Maud said sweetly. 'We miss home.'

'This?' said Helen, a little unfairly, waving a dismissive hand about the lavish fittings of the room. Still, if it were the Savoy Hotel they were coming back to on a permanent basis there'd maybe be less cause for concern. Actually, Helen thought, the place, with its now dating thirties décor, suited Albert and Maud perfectly. Maud, like her husband, had not progressed in her manner or dress beyond that era either. She was wearing now a backless evening gown, with a broad ruffle over the shoulders and down the back, where it met a large, girlish bow. On her feet were the black, peep-toed, ankle-strap shoes that everyone had stopped wearing three years ago. Her hair, still a warm honey brown, was softly, modestly waved and ended in a row of curls at the base of her neck. She wore, as always, the one strand of pearls that Albert had given her for her first wedding anniversary and which remained ever after her favourite jewellery, worn always, regardless of costume. Helen took it all in, in its familiarity, and dismissed it with a shrug. She had given up attempting to make Maud fashionable twenty years ago. As far as she was concerned Maud, the Savoy Hotel, and all of Britain could age peacefully together, if they so chose. But Helen knew, too, that it wasn't to the sacred ballroom of the Savoy, where once he had reigned in triumph, that Albert Chandler was returning.

'You'll regret it, Albert,' she said at last, and swallowed her gin and lime in a long, less than ladylike swig.

'Perhaps,' he said, unperturbed, convinced that he would not. Maud only smiled. She was watching her mother, wishing she would not drink quite so much, wishing she would not dye her hair quite so severely dark, nor paint her lips and eyebrows on quite so fiercely. Maud occasionally, at times like this, thought of her grandmother, Mary Hardacre, in the little cottage on the Hardacre estate where she had ended her days. She wished her mother were like that, or that Mary Hardacre had been her mother, and then at once felt a flood of guilt. She tried to see Helen then, loyally, as no doubt Helen saw herself, and admired honestly her trim figure, slimmer than Maud's gentle curves, and the elegant fit of her black sheath dress with its slit skirt and fashionable flying panels. It was a beautiful dress. It really was. Helen looked quite remarkably like a young girl, if only from the back. Maud left her assessment right there, having taken kindness as far as honesty would allow.

'Hey, c'mon,' Mike Brannigan said, looking at his watch and beginning to pace restlessly, like too large an animal in too small an enclosed space. It was always his way in immobile situations, like cocktail parties. 'Let's get this show on the road, folks.' He looked at his watch again.

'There's plenty of time,' Helen said calmly. 'Anyhow we have to wait for Harry and Harry is no doubt being very British and late,' she added drily.

'Yeah, well, he better cut the crap and get here,' Mike said again. 'Janet's not gonna be exactly thrilled if we turn up late for her première.'

Maud said nothing, looking a little sadly at her peep-toed shoes. Janet, she was very much afraid, would probably not even notice. She had felt in the last two years an ever-widening gap developing between her astoundingly success-

184

ful daughter and the rest of the family, herself included. She did not resent it. Indeed, she understood. Janet Chandler's world was *not* their world, but it was a world Maud, through her years in Hollywood, understood well. Frenetic and frantic, selfish and solitary; it was not the world she would have chosen for her daughter. But Hollywood had chosen Janet Chandler, and Janet was not like Maud. Janet was like Emily. Or like Helen. It was a thought that Maud, in a rare lapse of candour, tried not to face. But it came upon her more and more. Even so, it was not for her own sake but for Janet's that she wished her different. Helen Hardacre Brannigan was many things, many of them much admired, but by no stretch of the imagination would anyone call her happy.

Harry Hardacre did arrive then, looking, in his faintly moth-eaten dinner suit and stiff wing collar, even more outdated than Albert, and a lot more uncomfortable. Harry, whose childhood had been spent on the fish quays, adolescence in a tatty public-school and university years at Oxford, and who, through marriage, had moved into the staid ranks of Yorkshire county gentry, had long ago lost any semblance of belonging anywhere other than the oak-panelled library of Hardacres itself. Only family duty, and his role as unassuming patriarch, could ever persuade him into a circle and setting such as that in which he now found himself. Hetty crept in beside him. She was wearing a pre-war gown of rose silk and the sort of fur wrap with its profusion of tails, paws and snouts that brought one in mind of a bad day with the local hunt. Emily put her lips together in exasperation and raised her chin in that gesture of hers that proclaimed she might be with them, but wasn't 'of' them. She was glad Philip had stayed in Kilham with the two younger children and the pub. By now he'd probably have been demanding a brown ale. Mary Gray, Harry's little granddaughter, emerged eagerly from behind Hetty and ran shrieking across the room to greet Ruth Barton with waves of giggles. She settled on a settee beside her cousin, with the skirt of her fluffy organza many-petticoated dress floating up in clouds about her. She sat with her feet together, pigeon-toed, and leaned and whispered in Ruth's ear, giggling the while. She was a pretty child with the black hair and blue eyes of her great-grandmother Mary Hardacre, whom everyone said she resembled, if Mary's one portrait was anything to go by. The portrait, commissioned by old Sam the year his family moved into the big house, showed a slim young woman, surprisingly young-looking if the painter was to be believed, who visibly shrank, even in oils, from the attention that portraiture demanded. Her features were indeed similar to those of this little girl, though Harry could not envision even that portrait as having anything to do with the gentle work-worn woman he had known. And this young lady, pampered and pretty, and totally unlike her own gawky mother, was a creature of another world. 'When do we *see* her?' she blurted out, and everyone knew she meant Janet Chandler.

Ruth Barton, every bit as eager, but determined to be mature said, 'It's really the film I'm eager to see. They say it will be a landmark of the cinema.' She had read the phrase yesterday in *Variety*, and rolled it lovingly off her tongue.

Mike Brannigan snorted and said, 'That means we get to see her in her slip for half a second before the lights go out. Big deal, first time *I* saw her she sat bare-assed on my knee.'

'For Christ sake, you big ape,' said Helen, 'she was three.' Mike shrugged, grinning at the two girls who sat wide-eyed and open-mouthed in fascination.

Mary Gray could be forgiven, no doubt, that Mike Brannigan was for her the most memorable person and event of both the première of *A Lady in Love* and the Festival of Britain. Older, wiser, more experienced women than she had been so affected. Mike's charms, by his own rueful admission, were fading. But they were powerful enough to enchant little Mary and fill her dreams for years to come. Perhaps because she would not meet him again for years, the spell was all the more powerful. He would be her first love, and she, albeit without his knowledge, his last conquest.

Ruth Barton had other dreams, more secret, less innocent and more ambitious. Ruth had borrowed her dreams from her mother, though she would never know it. Ruth's romance was not with a man, fantasy or otherwise, but with the theatre. And more, with what was still lovingly called 'the silver screen'. Ruth spent every moment of her spare time, and every penny of her pocket money at the cinema in Bridlington or, if that was all she could afford, upon magazines offering tales of cinema stars, doubly remote, being American and far away. The cinema queues were Ruth's one escape from the provincial monotony to which her father's longing for earthy roots had condemned her. Ruth would go to anything, as long as it was a film, and stayed from the first shorts, through the B picture, the main attraction and the Pathé News, right down to the credits. Not for her the quick exits while the film yet rolled and the heroine's joyful tears were still falling. Not for her the regular treks to the lobby for popcorn and sweeties, made by her little brother and sister. To Ruth the cinema was far too serious to be mere amusement. Willingly she chaperoned Paul to see Audie Murphy in *Kansas Raiders*, or Cameron Mitchell in *Smuggler's Gold*, or the weekly serial, tolerating *Atom Man Versus Superman* without complaint. Patiently she indulged Olive's surprising delight in war pictures, through *Tripoli* and *Mystery Submarine*. Ruth didn't mind. The lights went out and the dreams came up just the same and, best of all, her sisterly helpfulness pleased her mother and gave her almost a limitless ticket to the pictures of her own choice, as reward. And so she could sink, again and again, into the bliss of the red plush seats and crackling sweetie papers, as the lights dimmed into a rich velvety black and the unreal power of the score swamped her with its vibrant warmth. Then they came to her: Tyrone Power, Susan Hayward, Greer Garson, Yvonne de Carlo, Errol Flynn, Van Heflin, Maureen O'Hara. They were her saints; at night their fanciful names, reeking of self-creation and hence the possibility that even Ruth Barton might be created anew, were a litany whispered into her pillow. Lili Palmer, Jane Wyman, Van Johnson, William Holden and Ruth. Ruth something, certainly not Barton, boring old Barton, but Ruth. Brighter and more famous than even Janet Chandler, who would one day be known first and foremost as the cousin of the wondrous Ruth. Ruth had gone five separate times to see Bette Davis and Anne Baxter in *All About Eve*, and was on her way for a sixth when her exasperated father called a halt. That was alarming enough. More alarming still was that in all those five delicious visits, the lesson of the story had never reached home.

For Ruth had learned a trick, a daring and imaginative trick. If the story didn't end the way she wanted, she rewrote the end. Not always more happily, indeed Ruth liked a good morbid weep as much as the next youngster. She liked power in stories, and romance, and heaven help the film that went soggy on her; half-way through Ruth was already rescripting. And she didn't stop at the cinema. Ruth was quite capable of rescripting life. Already her future career and that of the unfortunate Janet Chandler, to whom she had ostensibly come to pay homage, were on collision courses, and Eve and Margo were angels by comparison to the participants of the heady conflict Ruth had already envisioned. Needless to say, being the scriptwriter, Ruth was plotted to be the winner.

Knowing the script made life much easier for Ruth. It made it easy to tolerate the oafish jesting of Mike Brannigan (whose effect on her was quite the opposite of that on Mary Gray) with a cool smile. It enabled her to ignore her mother's fussing over her dress as if she were still a child, and her grandmother's intensely annoying habit of mixing her up with her sister Olive (Helen was never any use at grandchildren's names). Knowing the script, Ruth could step with ease into the hired limousine for the journey to the Leicester Square Odeon. Limousines would play a large part in her life of the future so she might as well get comfortable with them now. Knowing the script, Ruth could smile calmly at the crowds outside the theatre, imagining those crowds as being for her, and the billboards plastered everywhere as picturing not Janet Chandler, blonde and radiant, but herself.

Most of all, knowing the script made it possible for Ruth Barton to tolerate the hideous guilty-by-association purgatory of being at this glittering occasion in the company of her family, that mismatched, boring, intolerably clumsy collection of social disasters that comprised her nearest and dearest. There was great-Uncle Harry in that ridiculous old-fashioned collar, and Aunt Hetty in her horrible fur. There was that revolting man Brannigan talking too loudly in his broad American accent and cuddling stupid little Mary Gray and she, silly ass, was shrieking with delight. And there even was her mother, too made-up and too old-fashioned, all at once. And Aunt Maud even worse, and Uncle Albert. The least they could have done was spruce up a bit, she thought, with a sudden upswing of loyalty towards her resented and famous cousin. Only her grandmother, sleek and slim in her black dress and her silver-blue mink, passed Ruth's severe test of elegance. And she, of course, was just too horribly old to think about. Ruth sighed, unsurprised when an over-officious official almost shooed the entire Hardacre contingent away before he realized who they were.

They were ushered in, then, to a glittering lobby, as laden with the crystal of chandeliers as a true theatre of the older kind, for this palatial cinema was as far removed from the grubby, chewing-gum sticky aisles of Ruth's haunt in Bridlington, as was the Albert Hall.

Milling about the lobby, awaiting the arrival of the stars of the film, the Hardacre family floundered, lit cigarettes, talked about the film, about which they as yet knew very little, admired the billboards, commented about the décor of the lobby, and felt more or less lost. Emily shone, particularly when a theatrical columnist cornered her and begged a personal viewpoint of her famous niece. She responded with animation, growing visibly younger and happier in the attention of the moment, and glowed with delight when the columnist, perhaps genuinely, commented that a family resemblance was markedly visible. Ruth, safe in her dreams, stood aloof. Mike Brannigan paced, watched admiringly by Mary Gray. And Sam Hardacre walked into their glittering formal midst in a blue lounge-suit and his MCC tie.

'Sam,' Emily gasped. 'You've not dressed.'

Sam looked down and up and grinned. Jan Muller, a few paces behind, joined them. He at least was properly attired for the occasion, in a dinner-suit; Sam's dinner-suit, to be precise. 'Sorry, Emily, but we only had the one between us, so I lent it to Jan. I'll stand behind him.'

'There's such a thing as Moss Bros,' Emily said, un-amused.

'Just what we intended,' Sam said, 'only we ran out of time. I was on a scrap barge in the middle of the Thames . . .' he glanced at his wrist-watch, 'forty-five minutes ago. Unexpected business,' he added with another, less confident grin.

'I am so sorry, Mrs Barton,' Jan said. 'It is no doubt all my fault.'

'Nonsense,' Emily snapped, 'it's his fault, and he's enjoying it.'

But she softened as Sam leant forward for a kiss, and whispered, 'You look ravishing, Mrs Barton. You'd better be careful. These film stars hate to be outdone.'

He slipped away then and greeted his grandmother,

whose welcome was no warmer than Emily's. It was when he turned from her to speak to her husband that he saw Mike Brannigan and Jan Muller facing each other in an isolated circle in the centre of the theatre lobby with a look on each of their faces of stunned, angry amazement, as if a pair of fighting cocks had been dropped into a ring.

The lobby, packed with strangers, suddenly seemed silent as their own little knot of people drew in closer, watching. Finally, Mike Brannigan spoke, grinning, but without humour, 'Well, well,' he said. 'The hero of Haganah has forsaken his tractor at last.'

'If you please, not *here*,' Jan said, in an angry whisper, retreating as always into icy European propriety. 'I am with friends.'

'Friends?' said Mike Brannigan, amusedly raising one thick dark brow. 'You, pal, are with my family.' Jan was stunned into silence, looking uncertainly to Sam, and to Helen. Helen slipped her possessive arm through Mike's and looked Jan Muller up and down with cautious care.

Sam Hardacre, confused, said quickly, 'Mike Brannigan, Jan. My grandmother's husband.'

'We've met,' said Mike, with a big, unfriendly grin. He extended his hand and Jan abruptly spun on his heel, turned and strode away. But he had gone only two paces when a subdued British cheer and a staccato of applause rippled through the crowded lobby and he was forced back by a backing wave of people.

Janet Chandler, exquisite in a lilac satin gown, stepped regally into the golden light beneath the chandelier.

CHAPTER
TWELVE

She was not as any of them had expected. Of course she was like her photographs, those photographs reflecting her everywhere so many times bigger than life. She was blonde, her eyes were that strong clear blue on the edge of green that marked so many of the Hardacres; so much was true to the camera. But to the camera, Janet Chandler was an object, blurred by soft-focus, tamed by gentle lights and gauze. And to a living audience Janet Chandler was not object, but subject. *Control*, Sam Hardacre thought, watching her, she's in such perfect control. It was that, the power, that struck him first. Her beauty came after, rippling like an after-shock striking him weakened already from the first blow.

Her eyes were wide-set, her chin strong, the lines of jaw-bone and cheek-bone both prominent, balancing each other with a geometry that was intriguing in its imperfection. They were wrong, and they were lovely. She turned briefly, widened her wide mobile mouth into a personal friendly smile that managed to touch each individual in the room with its private intimacy. *I am here for you alone.* Liar, thought Sam Hardacre, even as he unwittingly smiled back. She brushed by within inches. She was taller than he expected from her screen image. No doubt her co-stars were all tall men, or standing on soap boxes. But she was not as tall as she appeared either, he realized, as for an instant he found himself looking down on to the glistening divide of her smoothly-parted hair.

It was the slenderness of her figure that implied height, an almost boyish figure, narrow at the hips, and surprisingly broad at the shoulders, with a hint of masculine straightness about them that made the feminine sway of those hips all the more devastating. He smelled her perfume and, startlingly, her sweat. She was working hard at creating that shimmering fantasy, working up the same earthy smell familiar to his own body out on the decks of the *Dainty Girl*. That salty tang did more for Sam than the scent of Chanel drifting behind her with the last sleek fold of her frilled narrow skirt. As she turned to greet a photographer's shout her hair, softer than her lilac mink, whipped across his upraised wrist with a touch like candle flame. 'My God,' he whispered, years of celibate composure shattering in the white-blue explosion of the photographer's flash.

Then she was gone. A door had opened, black dinner-suits closed about her, an escort, a bodyguard, and like a queen in train, she left the crowded room empty in her passing. Sam became aware of his surroundings in a rush, like a man rising from a faint, and remembered first off Jan Muller and Mike Brannigan, as if recalling the last moment of consciousness before the dark. He turned, half-expecting to see Jan gone, but Jan was standing silent, his eyes on the door that had taken Janet Chandler, then he, too, seemed to stir from lost awareness. Mike Brannigan was standing virtually beside him; they had forgotten one another.

Jan glanced sideways to Sam and their eyes met. Jan looked away, shaking his head, embarrassed, and telling by his sudden confusion that his mind, too, had flickered through the same bedroom labyrinth as had Sam's. 'So beautiful,' he whispered at last, his accent suddenly heavy on his voice.

'Best bit of ass in the business,' said Mike, with something approaching paternal pride. He was grinning his cocky troublemaker's grin and Emily Barton, having watched and absorbed everything, now suddenly leapt into the fray, clutching Jan Muller's dinner-jacketed right arm and obliging him to unball the fist he was preparing for Mike's jaw.

She cried loudly, 'Oh do be my escort Jan. I feel quite lost without Philip.'

'Good God,' said Harry Hardacre, never thinking to have heard that, but as Emily successfully dragged Jan into the waiting auditorium Harry gathered up Hetty's arm and followed. He was as stunned by the vision of Janet Chandler as anyone else, but not for reason of her beauty. He acknowledged that; it was indisputable; but what had struck Harry silent upon seeing her was something far more private, something only Harry perhaps could see. It was the eyes of his long-dead brother, Joe, strong, determined and ruthless, looking out from a young girl's smiling face.

The crowd rapidly thinned. Sam Hardacre was left suddenly alone on an empty piece of lush carpet, with a slender young girl standing a few feet away, unmoving. It was Ruth Barton. She stood very still, her arms awkwardly hanging at her sides. Her shoulders were girlishly slumped, her dress, with its full ballet-length skirt and matching gauzy stole, looking suddenly too old for her. Her hair, in its fashionable urchin cut now looked merely dishevelled, as if mussed by a distressed childish hand. She was quietly crying. Sam crossed the room hurriedly, gently taking her arm behind the thin elbow.

'Hey, sunshine,' he said, leaning down. 'Did they go off and leave you? Never mind, I'm still here.'

He felt a real surge of anger for Emily, even though Emily had acted hastily and more or less on his own behalf. But when Ruth looked up to him, he saw in her wet eyes a grief deeper than desertion, a humiliation more crushing than childish discomfort.

'No, I'm quite all right, thank you,' she said. 'I'm not a child.' He believed her. It was not a child's voice, but the voice of a wounded woman. And so, to the woman, he spoke, in the words of the poet his Uncle Harry had read to him throughout his childhood,

194

'But I being poor, have only my dreams;
I have spread my dreams under your feet . . .'

Sam leant down over her, indicating the red carpet of the theatre foyer. He smiled and bent his handsome face down close and kissed her tear-stained cheek.

'Tread softly . . .'

Sam straightened and with his arm through that of Ruth Barton walked slowly into the darkened theatre where the screen was already flickering with its own tapestry of dreams.

Sam did not enjoy the film. He hardly saw it, and remembered so little that the discussions of its merits afterwards were an embarrassment. His mind was filled with other thoughts. Foremost was Jan Muller and his startling confrontation with Mike Brannigan. What were they to each other, he wondered, and where had they met? For there was no doubt that they had met and in less than friendship, that was also obvious. What their connection had been and, more pertinent, what it might mean now to his new enterprise he could only guess, and the guessing was both wild and disturbing. He had never had much respect for Mike Brannigan, and there was a family conspiracy of silence over his questionable past. He was, like someone's ill-trained but beloved watchdog, the sort of thing families put up with for each other. But only now did it occur to Sam that he knew even less about Jan Muller, and absolutely everything he knew came from Jan himself. It had never occurred to him to question the man's integrity. He was Heidi's son. Heidi's son whom Heidi had not seen for nearly twenty years. In that time, in the savage times that Jan had lived through, what might have happened to him and how might it have moulded him forever? He thrust the thought aside, ashamed, and yet it pursued him. His only escape was the moving imagery on the screen

195

before him, and that, he quickly realized, was no escape at all. For there was Janet Chandler, hugely overgrown and disguised, albeit by the character whom she played. But the disguise was like one of those lacy black masks that ladies wore to fancy dress balls, that covered only the thin ribbon of face that held the eyes and let the eyes themselves gaze out to deny their own mystery. It was a disguise that enhanced, that drew the eye, rather than deflected it. And whenever he looked he could smell that sharp tang of marvellously controlled effort and, whatever the virtues of the heroine on the screen, they were neither so bold nor so devastatingly romantic as the courage displayed by one young girl holding a room in awed submission to nothing but her own dream of herself. Sam knew he would see that girl, that dream-maker again, in the flesh, in hardly more than two hours' time, and the film became only a distraction, a veil between him and that moment and he wished suddenly he could brush it away like so many cobwebs and touch the real woman beyond. The desire was so strong, and so unnerving that at the end of the film he vowed he would go back to Earls Court alone, and not on to the promised party, rather than risk a meeting that threatened his own sure control of himself. But it was a vow, like his determination to turn the *Dainty Girl* and run for the safe harbour of home, that he knew he could not keep.

The party after the showing, a tradition as unavoidable as the champagne and the mindless kisses for everyone, was held at Claridges, where Janet Chandler and her entourage maintained a suite for their London stay. Whether her separate residence indicated a split with the Brannigans, or merely a variance in her taste in hotels was not clear. Maud and Albert would know, Sam realized, but Maud and Albert seemed quite unperturbed by that separation, as indeed they seemed quite unperturbed by everything. The glamour and the drama made no impression on their gentle calm. Maud smiled happily when people praised her daughter, and Albert watched with gentle dignity. Sam briefly wondered if the clamour and excitement tugged painfully at his memories, bringing him back to the London he knew once, the London that had once known him. But watching that straight-backed decency, that patient smile as foolish people gushed over him, asking him how he liked London, forgetting he was British, forgetting entirely when London had been his, Sam knew otherwise. Albert Chandler had survived the roller-coaster of the theatrical world all these years for one good reason: Albert had a seatbelt, called truth. He had been good. That was the truth. Never great, but good. Times and fashions changed; not his intrinsic worth. Sam, watching him walk, forgotten and content, from the theatre that worshipped his daughter on every hand, wondered if Janet Chandler was so protected.

Outside the theatre, in the crowds milling in the soft June darkness, Sam located Jan Muller and managed to steer him into one of the waiting London cabs, and sent the driver on his way to Claridges before anyone else could think to join them. He needed a few minutes with Jan alone if he was to hope to avoid a new eruption of the conflict Emily so deftly had fended.

'Where?' he said, as the cab pulled away from the kerb. Jan knew at once what he meant. He looked out of the window, avoiding eye contact as he did when he talked of the war. Suddenly that habit worried Sam, as he read potential new significance into it.

'Palestine.'

Of course Palestine, Sam thought impatiently, but only said, 'When?'

'During the Mandate.'

'Before the War?'

'After. The last days. I do not wish to talk about it.'

'Sorry, mate. I do.' Sam heard his voice as surprisingly sharp. So did Jan, who looked startled and slightly guarded.

'I am sorry. I was startled. I did not expect to see him . . . again. I lost control. It will not happen again. He is your family, I will respect that.' He raised his hands, open and weaponless, as a kind of pledge.

'I want to know what it was about,' said Sam. 'I have to know.'

'Why do you not ask him?' Jan said.

'I'm not sure I can trust him to tell the truth,' Sam said honestly.

'But you are not sure you can trust me, either,' Jan replied, at once. Sam was shaken. He had not realized it showed, his new uncertainty. He shrugged. 'Show me I can,' he said quietly.

Jan was silent for a long while, but when he spoke it was in a conversational tone, without undue emotion, 'You must understand that war is complex. It means different things to different people. One man's war is merely another man's opportunity. The life of a nation . . . a people . . . sometimes it is only business. One cannot, I suppose, blame a business man for doing business.' He spoke with careful logic, like a lawyer discussing degrees of murder. 'You do know his business?' Jan said cautiously, as if he feared revealing a secret.

'I know he deals in armaments,' Sam said. 'I assume that's what we're talking about.' Jan shrugged again.

'Armaments,' he said, delicately.

'All right. He's a gun-runner. Or he was. *I* didn't marry the bastard, Jan. My . . .' he paused, finding as always the term difficult to apply to Helen Brannigan, 'my grandmother did.' He looked out of the window at the slowly passing lights, thankful for the stream of heavy traffic. The black cab felt isolated from all the world. 'My family isn't all that close, Jan. But they are my family.'

'*They* were my family,' Jan said softly, as an echo. And he repeated, 'That is what they were. My family. My only family.' He looked up suddenly, meeting Sam's eyes with a steadiness that relieved Sam of his suspicions at the same time it unnerved him with its bitter intensity. 'You sell a man a coat; a bad coat with no lining, so,' he shrugged again, hearing somehow a distant echo of his mother's cousin, Isaac Mandel, 'so he is cold in the winter. He is not dead. He is cold.' His eyes darkened and never left Sam's face. 'But a gun, Sam, a gun for a man fighting a war, fighting for his homeland, his life, his children . . . a gun that does not work, a gun for which the spares are wrong, the ammunition wrong. A gun you do not deliver, but sell again to his enemies . . .' He was shaking suddenly and clutched Sam's wrist with his trembling hand. 'So, it is only business but they were my family, my only family, those young men, boys, and girls, girls too fought in those days. And they died. A bad coat, one is cold. A bad gun, one dies. Mike Brannigan killed them, Sam. Not the *fedayeen*.' He let go of Sam's wrist, coming to awareness of himself, as he had in the theatre after Janet Chandler had passed. He shook his head, and covered his eyes with one hand. 'I will respect your family,' he said.

'You gettin' out, guv, or staying the night?' said the cabbie. Sam looked up, startled, to see they had arrived at their destination and the taxi was idling before the main entrance of Claridge's Hotel. He looked once more at Jan, wondering if they should both go back to their rented rooms in Earls Court, much more their style anyhow, and avoid a confrontation.

'You have nothing to fear,' Jan said, as if reading his thoughts. And Sam nodded, opening the door of the cab and reaching into his pocket for the fare. He knew Jan's scrupulous, almost fastidious good manners would prevail, once his honour had been so pledged, as long as Brannigan also practised some restraint. That, of course, was subject to debate.

The party in Janet Chandler's personal suite was well under way when they arrived. There was music. There were tables laden with an after-show buffet supper. There were crowds of glittering strangers with the flamboyant cheerfulness of theatre people, and a small circle of Hardacre family, looking more lost than ever. Harry Hardacre was tugging at his wing collar and glancing surreptitiously at his watch. Hetty was sitting down, looking tired. Mary Gray was staring wide-eyed and sleepily at more famous people than she was ever likely to see again, Maud and Albert Chandler were holding hands in a corner, whispering alone like sweethearts, and Emily Barton was getting drunk.

Mike Brannigan was already drunk and monopolizing the company of a round blonde girl who lisped breathlessly in open imitation of Marilyn Monroe with a cockney accent, and Helen Brannigan was watching darkly from the corner of one dark mascaraed eye. There was about the entire company that restless feeling, akin to that of departure lounges of ports and railway stations, where people fill in time with half-hearted interest, while waiting for the journey to begin. Sam knew, just looking at them, that Janet Chandler was not here.

'Perhaps she will not come,' Jan Muller said at his shoulder, as if he had voiced his thought aloud. But Sam realized that Jan's thoughts were as much on the young star of the evening as were his own, and the thought disturbed him. He wandered off for a drink, keeping a wary eye on Brannigan, but Mike was too involved with the cockney girl's cleavage to pursue his argument with Jan. He chatted with his uncle Harry who wondered if he could, in decency, leave yet, and then joined Emily, trying and failing to deflect her from her too-steady drinking. He felt suddenly out of place in the crowded room, not because he was ill-dressed for the occasion, or among strangers, both circumstances that had rarely troubled him in the past, but because Terry was not there. Parties had always been a joint love of both brothers, and a remnant of the twinned existence he had forsaken. He felt suddenly too old, and too restricted,

200

at once, finding the smoky air intolerable and wishing he was back up north, out on the *Dainty Girl*, or tinkering with her grumpy engine, with Mick and Pete Haines. He thought of leaving, but saw that Jan was now deeply in conversation with Albert Chandler, and obviously not ready to depart. Bored, he reached for his pack of Senior Service and noticed, as he took out a cigarette, the address and phone number of the contact he had made that afternoon on the Thames. He remembered, then, having promised to telephone Mick with news of the day's business and realized Mick would be waiting at the Ship's Wheel, whose telephone they conveniently borrowed, for want of one of their own. Fumbling in his pocket for change, he went towards the outer door of the suite, glancing back to determine that Jan was still involved with the Chandlers. Once out in the corridor he made his way towards the lift shaft, intending to find a telephone in the foyer on the ground floor. His mind was on business now, miles away, with the wartime wreck off the Humber Estuary, the brass fittings of which he had earmarked for the London scrappie. When he heard the voices ahead of him, around a corner in the corridor, they hardly registered. But as he reached the turning of the hallway there was a sudden loud crash, as of something thrown, and a yelp of genuine alarm. He strode forward, rounded the corner and instantly dived against the opposite wall as a glass ashtray flew by, skimming his sleeve and shattering in blue-white splinters against the floor.

'Jesus Christ, Janet, you'll kill some poor bastard!' shrieked the yelping voice.

'Yeah, you snake's asshole, maybe *you*,' said the lady in the lilac gown. 'Maybe this'll be my lucky day.' She looked up then from the shrinking figure of a small, slim man in a maroon dinner-jacket who huddled against a door jamb and her blue-green Hardacre eyes met those of Sam. They widened for a moment, as if a vestigial dignity yet lurked there, engendering embarrassment, but she was far too angry for that. 'What the eff-all are you staring at, you big twerp?' she demanded. 'Screw off, this is a private fight.'

'Madam,' Sam said, his own eyes crinkling up with amazed fascination, and his slow grin spreading, 'could I possibly buy my way in? It looks the best game of the night.' Her mouth opened and closed once, like a particularly beautiful bullfrog, but she said nothing. The small man in the maroon dinner-jacket scrambled to a more upright position and approached Sam with outspread palms, shooing him back as if a wild animal was advancing down the corridor to the attack.

'Please, mister,' he said, 'I warn you, she's not gonna like that . . . Miss Chandler,' he straightened, reassuming an air of managerial dignity, 'has had a trying evening.'

'Shut up, Bernie,' the lady in lilac said, tilting her chin, so the delicious strength of jawline caught the light. 'The gentleman wants to play.' She looked Sam up and down, and where a moment ago he felt quite in control of the situation, now he felt less so. 'Let him play. Get us a drink, Bernie.'

'Aw, Janet, you promised . . .' Bernie whined sadly.

'A drink,' Janet Chandler repeated, with a quick cold glance of blue-green eyes that sent Bernie scuttling away and through a doorway. She looked at Sam again and suddenly she smiled, a wry, wise smile, older than her years.

'I'm plastered. Bernie's busy sobering me up for my entrance,' she shrugged towards the distant sounds from the rooms Sam had left. 'How's the party?'

'A party,' he said, not taking his eyes from hers.

'I was afraid of that.' She leaned against the wall, tiredly. 'Oh boy,' she said. 'Oh boy.' She appeared then to have an idea and said suddenly, 'Look, you, whoever you are, shall we have this drink in here?' she gestured towards the door behind which Bernie had vanished. 'I mean, the hall's

202

draughty and I'm not ready yet for . . . a party,' she added, with another wry wince. 'It's my bedroom,' she added, 'I'm just saying that so you don't do your nut when you see the bed. This is not a seduction,' she chanted, in a mock-Tannoy voice. 'Repeat. This-is-not-a-seduction.'

Sam grinned. 'I'll try to control myself,' he said.

She smiled, straightened up from the wall, trailing her mink after her in a slightly self-conscious gesture, as if she were playing the part of a film star like another role. Sam followed, meeting the eyes of the amazed Bernie as he entered the room with a nod and a brief smile. Bernie was fussing over the drinks cabinet.

'You needn't bother watering it, pal, I'm having coffee,' Janet Chandler said.

Sam had coffee, too. It was all he wanted. The company of the young lady in the lilac gown was intoxication enough. She sat on the floor at the side of the bed that dominated the inner room of the two-room complex and leaned her blonde head against the pink quilted satin of the coverlet. Sam, finding the superior height of a chair inappropriate, settled on the floor also, crossing his legs like a boy. She kicked off her shoes and drew up her knees and sipped seriously at her coffee. 'I'm Janet,' she said.

'I know,' he smiled. 'I'm Sam.'

'Sam who?'

'Sam Hardacre.'

She looked up, startled. 'That's my great-grandfather's name,' she said, almost possessively, as if Sam had no right using it. She blinked, with the perverse concentration of those too drunk to concentrate.

'What a coincidence,' said Sam. She blinked again, and then she turned quite suddenly to Bernie, her manager, or agent or aide-de-camp, Sam was never quite certain who he was. 'Out,' she said.

'Miss Chandler,' he ventured respectfully. 'The party . . .'

'Out,' she said again. 'Go on, Bernie, don't be a third wheel.'

He sniffed, and stalked to the door, and something in the stiffness of his short precise steps assured Sam that his position in Miss Chandler's bedroom was *only* managerial. 'We'll be waiting,' he said pointedly, and closed the door with a curt, peevish little slam.

'He's a darling,' she said absently, after he left.

'You don't treat him like a darling,' Sam returned. She looked up, startled to be reprimanded, but determined to be good-humoured.

'Bernie understands,' she said firmly. She looked hard at Sam and said, sounding very sober, 'You're my cousin, aren't you? Arnold's son. You're one of the twins.' Sam smiled again, his eyes still on her lovely face, cherishing even the smear of mascara on one slightly drink-flushed cheek.

Relationships, he reflected, family and all its ties and subsequent taboos, were learned, not grown. Whatever the blood ties between them, he and this young lady, years apart in age, thousands of miles apart in their childhood geographies, and even further in their cultures, were strangers.

'Kissing cousins, no doubt,' he whispered and, leaning forwards, carefully took the coffee cup from her slightly shaky hand and bent his head down over hers, his lips on her own. There was for a moment no response at all, and then an inquisitive softening, a momentary struggle, and ready surrender. He had tasted nothing so sweet in seven years. The taste was momentary, and the wine was snatched away.

A shout sounded in the corridor, perhaps Bernie, but then another and then the sound of running feet, a hurried argument, a woman's voice over Bernie's and a hammering on the door.

'Sam, Sam, are you in there?' the voice demanded,

slurred and hysterical. 'Sam, where are you?' It was Emily Barton, and desperation rather than drink blurred her voice. 'For God's sake, Sam, he's going to *kill* Mike.'

Sam ran. He leapt up, leaving a startled Janet Chandler still sitting on the floor in her satin gown, and crossed the two rooms, slamming the door open and bursting out into the midst of Emily and Bernie engaged in a hysterical and, on Emily's side, drunken, argument over the rights and wrongs of disturbing Miss Chandler. Emily's amazement at precisely where Sam had disappeared to flickered momentarily across her face, but was hastened away by more immediate concerns.

'It's Jan,' she cried, 'you've got to stop him.'

But Sam knew it was Jan and he was already running, eluding Emily's plucking fingers on his sleeve. In the months he had known him, he had never seen Jan Muller so much as raise his voice, and yet he was filled with foreboding. Bernie and Emily, and Janet Chandler too, followed after him, but he was utterly unaware of them in his haste.

The door of the party suite was standing open, crowds of its occupants had spilled into the corridor, those one or two afraid of adverse publicity for their own private reasons were already slipping surreptitiously away. Passing them in the corridors came a clutch of dignified, but efficient-looking hotel staff, homing in on the scene of the disturbance like dinner-jacketed prison warders. Sam pushed by a cluster of shrieking women and into the suite, where the sound of shattering glass and a young girl's high-pitched scream greeted his entrance.

The room was in chaos, one white-clothed table having collapsed across the floor, scattering its contents. The carpet was soaked with spilled wine and glittery with broken glass and mounds of multi-coloured mousses and terrines lay in moist heaps like wet sandhills. Guests were cornered into the outskirts of the room, standing on sofas and behind chairs, and the first person he recognized was Harry Hardacre, isolated by a ring of fallen furniture.

He was saying softly, 'I say, I say, really, chaps . . .' in a voice of courageous optimism, while Hetty cowered behind him, and Jan Muller and Mike Brannigan wrestled full-length on the sodden floor.

The room was clamorous with mixed voices offering advice to the combatants or shouting for help and, conspicuous in her silence among them, stood Helen Hardacre Brannigan, coolly smoking a cigarette and watching with mild disgust. Mike, who had no doubt instigated the conflict, had clearly put up a good fight; Jan's bloody face was evidence; but he was equally clearly losing now. He was older, paunchy, and more than a little drunk and, more important, Mike was an unruly brawler, sloppy and uncontrolled. Jan Muller, Sam recognized at once, was a trained guerrilla soldier. And he was angry enough to kill. Sam did the only thing he could; he flung himself into the middle of the fight, grappling with Jan, ignoring the outraged squeal of Mike, who wanted to finish the fight, even if it was going to finish him. Jan, as he knew he would, immediately turned on himself, and for the next few moments Sam was thoroughly occupied defending himself from the fierce blows of his outraged friend. Then the rest of the room, galvanized into action by Sam's interference, also waded in and separated all three combatants by sheer weight of numbers until, at last, they were left standing in silence, with Bernie clucking in circles in their midst like a broody hen.

Sam carefully, hesitantly, released his grip on Jan Muller's left arm, while a burly London film producer still held gamely to his right. Jan shook his head, wiping blood from his mouth with the torn sleeve of his borrowed dinner-jacket. The blonde cockney Monroe rushed, in motherly fervour, with wet towels for Mike. As she lisped sympathy and dabbed at his cut eyebrow and swelling mouth Helen said, 'Wrap him up and take him home, honey, if you want. It's all the same to me.'

'Aw, sweetheart,' moaned Mike, remorsefully.

'You stupid ass,' she said, and stalked out of the room, leaving the party, and her husband, to pick up the pieces of each other.

Sam turned to Jan whose face had a dreamy look as of one wakened from sleep. He again made that short, characteristic shake of his head, as if clearing his thoughts and said simply, 'I am so sorry. It was unforgivable. I do not know what I can say.'

Sam shrugged.

'I suppose he gave you reason.'

But Jan replied tiredly, 'He is filth. But it was no reason. I am sorry. I forget at times where I am, who I am. So much, learned so hard; so hard to unlearn.' He shrugged also, and Sam, who had had his own war, thought he understood. Jan looked about the shattered room, seeking someone to whom he might direct his regrets. There was no one; only a circle of confused guests before him and Janet Chandler, yet unseen, behind him in the doorway. So, facing Harry Hardacre, who throughout had stood straight-backed and unshaken by the chaos, he said, 'My behaviour was unforgivable. I extend my heartfelt apologies. I will leave you now.' Then he bowed, a short formal bow from the waist, and turned and walked out of the room.

In his dazed state he did not notice Janet Chandler standing just inside the door. She turned, her eyes following his back, and when she looked back into the room, it was Sam that she first saw. What intimacy had occurred between them, momentarily, in her bedroom was forgotten. She looked straightforwardly into his eyes, as if he were a useful stranger.

'Who is that man?' she said, softly awed.

Sam didn't stay around to explain. His duties, he felt, were towards Jan, who he had got into this mess, and he

207

hastened after him. His farewell to Janet Chandler was brief. He fully expected to see her the next day, when she and all the family were to tour the Festival site on the South Bank, pose for pictures and share a publicity-minded luncheon in one of the pretty temporary summer cafés. Besides, her dismissal of him, so soon after her unexpected momentary intimacy, shook him. He felt he was no longer talking to the same person and he felt, too, with faint resentment, that the reason was Jan.

No matter, he would sort that out tomorrow. But the tomorrow he had planned did not arrive. After escorting Jan Muller, moody and depressed after the violence of the evening, back to Earls Court, he slipped out to a phone box and made his call to Mick Raddley that he had never made from Claridges.

'Where t' hell have you been?' Mick growled, over a crackly line.

'Detained,' Sam said, shortly, not in the best of temper.

'Well, happen ye'd better get un-detained,' said Mick. 'Big nor'easter's blown up an' broke t'mooring lines on that barge we anchored over t' work site. Run her ashore.'

'The equipment?' Sam demanded, quickly tallying the load of the barge, which they had been using to attempt to raise the propeller of their wartime wreck.

'Pete an' I got most of it off, before, on to t' *Dainty Girl*. But the barge'll break up if'n we don't get her off. We're going out at first light if the wind drops.' He paused. 'Could use some help,' he said pointedly, and Sam could hear the familiar chomp of his yellowed teeth on his pipe-stem.

'I'll get the next train,' he said. 'And Jan, too,' he added, for reasons of his own.

And so, by one o'clock in the afternoon, while Janet Chandler, in a Festival of Britain jumper decorated with a futuristic Britannia, one small hand holding down her loose blonde hair, posed before the Skylon for the cameras of the world, Sam Hardacre was knee-deep in surf on a wind-battered North Sea shore, fixing salvage lines on a recalcitrant barge. The following day he saw Janet's picture in every newspaper, a stranger from another world.

He would not see her again for four long, active years and, before he did, his own life would have been irrevocably changed for ever.

CHAPTER
THIRTEEN

Everyone agreed the gardens of Hardacres were at their best in May, though March ran a close second, when the daffodils scattered chaotically across the wide lawns, and gathered in yellow herds in the marshy greenery down where the beech wood faded to lawn, by the Victorian marble tomb old Sam had built there for himself.

Sam was not its first occupant, however. Harry's youthful bride, Judith Winstanley, mother of his two children had been laid there first, a week after the birth of her daughter. Sam was second; Mary Hardacre third. And fourth was Hetty, in the early summer of 1953. She had come half a century before to Hardacres, as nursemaid to Harry's motherless children. And though she had spent the rest of her life there, first as nanny, and then as wife, she had never really taken possession of any of it. The children she raised there were not her own, her husband's affections forever only half hers. Once she shared him with a ghost; later with his mistress. The house itself eluded her, as if it, too, were living and faithless. She walked its corridors for fifty years, always with the hesitant tread of one who came first as a servant. Even on the day of her death, her requests and desires were couched in trembling uncertainty. So that when, upon retiring for her regular afternoon rest, she had asked Mrs Bennett for a cup of tea to be sent to her room, she had done so so diffidently that the request, like all Hetty's hesitant desires was, if not ignored, simply postponed throughout the afternoon until, when the tray finally reached her bedside, Hetty herself had gone. Harry was summoned, and found his wife quietly dead with her small hands clutching the edge of the coverlet as if about to draw across her lined face her own shroud. She had left them, as she had come to them, creeping like a small brown mouse into eternity.

But if Hardacres had been less than attentive throughout her life it, like a guilty spouse, made up for it at Hetty Hardacre's funeral. Harry himself thought he had never seen the old place quite so beautiful, brightly rain-washed under a blue flirtatious sky, filled with grey cumulous clouds rolling down from the moor, and respectfully piling up only in the northern sky, beyond the big red house, so that the sun might still shine on Hetty's burial.

Hardacre roses covered her coffin, and Hardacre family, gathered from diverse and distant locales, followed her to the church and back to the family tomb beneath the beeches. It was the largest gathering of the family since young Sam's party over two years ago celebrating the launching of Hardacre Salvage. Ironically, he was the only member of the immediate family who did not attend; urgent business kept him elsewhere. Although he sent his tele-grammed regrets and spoke at length with his bereaved uncle over a difficult line from the northwest coast of Scotland, his mother Madelene found his absence unforgiv-able. She had determined to tell him so, too, though Harry advised her gently not to do so. He was aware, as was she, that their influence on young Sam was lessened to the point of non-existence. Sometimes she felt painfully that she meant nothing at all to him, any longer. Terry, who alone of all the family seemed yet to truly communicate with Sam, insisted it was not so. But then Terry would defend his brother at any cost.

What made it all the more painful for Madelene was that in spite of the same business pressures that Sam had pleaded, Jan Muller had attended. And so, of course, had Erasmus Sykes, but that was less surprising since, while Jan Muller's mourning could hardly be more than good man-ners, Erasmus Sykes's grief was all too real.

Their friendship, begun so quixotically at that same party two years before, had blossomed into one of life's more unlikely liaisons. Erasmus Sykes had become a regular visitor at Hardacres, spending long Sunday afternoons in winter with Hetty before the drawing-room fire, or strolling in the summer gardens, with the lady of the house on his arm. It was really quite apparent to everyone that Erasmus had simply fallen in love with Harry Hardacre's modest and retiring wife. But so respectful, indeed worshipful, was his attitude, so caring for every courtesy and decency, so comically innocent in a man of near sixty years, that no one, least of all Harry, could dream of objecting. Far from it; Harry was intensely grateful for the bright, gentle pleasure Erasmus had brought to Hetty's final years. Of course, it was only in retrospect that the finality of those years was apparent although, also in retrospect, the signs were subtly there, as general invalidity turned almost suddenly to something more threatening, to whispered conversations with doctors, and inconclusive tests, and decisions not to operate, decisions also not to tell the patient of her plight. It was that deception, not the more obvious romantic deception of his long years with Madelene, that Harry regretted most after her death, since its secrecy had separated them in a way Madelene's love had never done. Once he had thought to confide in Erasmus, but decided against it, knowing he would only be easing his mind at the expense of that of Hetty's friend. He left them to their late-November romance, like two schoolchildren holding hands down some long-gone autumn lane. They had had such fun together, drawing from each other secret untapped resources, drawing each other out of their cavernous silent shells. It was Erasmus who had persuaded Hetty to take over the directing of the local village pageant, in that same Festival year of 1951 in which young Sam's salvage business first got properly under way. Hetty had stunned everyone with her emergence from her shyness and a quite remarkable theatrical talent. The pageant had featured historical figures from Britain's past and Erasmus, coy as a prima donna, had been coaxed into the role of Henry VIII, complete with black poodles. It was probably the highlight of his entire lonely life.

Hetty had done that, Harry reflected now, carefully dead-heading the tea roses in his mother's favourite rosebed. Quiet little Hetty. His respect for her, always latent, suddenly emerged and grew to tremendous proportions, now that she was gone. He supposed it to be a form of guilt, for guilt was what he had expected, guilt, lying in wait for him, was what he had braced for and, surprisingly, guilt, in open guise, had not yet come.

As if to test that premise, the sound, throaty and evocative, of a sports car engine purred up into Harry's consciousness, and he straightened his stiffening back and gazed down the long, curving pink drive. The sound grew and faded, a tremolo born of the twisting of the roadway and sudden copses of trees that blocked sound intermittently all the way up from the Driffield road. But then he caught a flash of red between two grey beech trunks and smiled in spite of himself. Perhaps he was simply too old to indulge in hypocrisy; Madelene had delighted him for over thirty years. She would not cease to delight him now that Hetty was dead.

She parked the car part-way down the drive, by the flowering cherry that Mary Hardacre had planted and which was now growing old and lichen-bound. She paused a moment before opening the door, and then stepped out almost hesitantly. He wanted to call out, to ease her way with words, but knew she must find her own pace back to him, and redetermine for herself her welcome. He stood among his roses, secateurs in hand, as she slowly, with dignity, approached. He thought of her suddenly as his bride, at last, coming to his home, and in the same instant tried to fathom by what method she had, over the years, justified their adultery in the lights of her faith to which she was so undoubtedly devoted. She was French; therein he knew lay the answer. Hers was a peasant faith, and the lady before him, for all the sophistication of her pearl-grey sheath dress, had had a peasant childhood in provincial France. From such childhoods comes the all-forgiving faith with which she was blessed. He wished suddenly his own youth had provided him with an equivalent malleable code that could absorb guilt so gently and reassure so heartily. Both his parents had been religious, in that they believed in God. But theirs was an odd God, wrapped up somehow with class and social status and propriety so that, although they wed in church, they did not return there, except for the christenings of their children, until Sam Hardacre's business success had borne them into a higher social strata, in which apparently they felt themselves more able to approach the Lord. It was almost as if they felt they must improve themselves in this world before they were fit to approach the next. And yet no doubt they had believed, and they had faced their own deaths with equanimity.

As for himself; Oxford, the Boer War, Judith Winstanley and his bitter loss of her; all had unravelled whatever fragile fabric of religion they had bequeathed him. He was not an atheist, nor even an agnostic, but a gentle humanist who tried to live according to a private code of decency that had more to do with the philosophies of his favourite poet and his own deep-rooted desire to preserve what remained, in a changing world, of grace and beauty, than with God. Perhaps, he thought bemusedly, that was what God *was* to him. Just as the animist found his Lord in trees and water, so Harry Hardacre found him in the slow heritage of two thousand years of civilization, and art.

'Harry?' Madelene called, still many yards away across the green lawn.

'Yes, my dear.'

'Do you wish to be alone?'

He smiled. 'Of course not.'

'Shall we have tea then?'

'Why not?' With his arm lightly on her shoulder, as much for his own balance with his bad leg gone stiff from his gardening, as for her comfort, they made their way up the wide sweep of steps to the semi-circle of gravel, and the front door of Hardacres.

Harry laid his secateurs on the inlaid Indian coffee table before the fire, and rang the bell for Mrs Bennett. His eyes met Madelene's, and there passed between them a look of both affection and apprehension. They might as well start now, Harry thought, though Madelene's dark eyes were filled with unease and vulnerability. Throughout their years together, she had been the object of a great deal of below-stairs fascination and gossip, but the existence of a valid wife above stairs had kept all such speculation firmly in its place. Now all was changed, and what little remained of their staff, coupled with the much larger field of village observers, would be waiting, perhaps with no little belated aggression for the next moves by the rival of their dead mistress. Hetty, gently forgiving, silently unseeing, had protected them. She would protect them no longer.

Mrs Bennett appeared. Her eyes darted from Harry to Madelene and then back firmly to Harry, refusing again to acknowledge Madelene's presence. 'Sir,' she said, shortly.

'Tea, please, Mrs Bennett.'

'For two?' she asked perversely, and Harry nodded patiently, 'For two.' 'Very good sir.'

She left them, closing the door behind her with a firm, pointed little clunk. Harry almost laughed. Outraged York-shire decency had managed at last to produce what years of gentle training had not. Mrs Bennett had finally achieved the brisk formality of properly schooled staff; losing, through disapproval, the too cosy country style that had long been her major failing.

'She detests me,' said Madelene forlornly. 'And she always will.'

'She's embarrassed,' Harry said gently, 'She doesn't know what to think. She doesn't know what we are going to do. Give her time. She'll come around.' He paused then, having touched a crucial issue, before he was really ready to face it. But having raised it, he felt he must pursue it. 'What *are* we going to do?' he said.

She shrugged, Gallic and unfettered. 'Does it matter?' she said.

'Of course it matters,' said Harry. She shrugged again. He paused, feeling this was neither the time nor the place, and resenting being forced to hurry a moment he had long savoured in advance because of the gossipy Mrs Bennett. But he said, 'Do you want to marry me?' She shrugged again, darting him a quick, uncertain, indeed almost hostile glance.

'I can't marry you,' she said at last.

'Can't?' he said, blinking, wondering in a totally insane way if she had momentarily forgotten that at last they were both free.

'Of course not. You're not a Catholic.'

Harry stared. He was not sure she was not simply joking. It wasn't always easy to tell with Madelene.

'I'm not a Catholic,' he repeated slowly, as if uncertain of having heard her correctly.

'No,' she said briskly, 'and you won't convert because you hate the Church. So I can't marry you.'

'I *don't* hate the Church,' Harry protested loudly. He was about to add, also loudly, that it was *Hetty* who hated the Church, in case she'd forgotten, but decided not to drag Hetty's name into any of this. Besides, Mrs Bennett's steps were sounding in the corridor and he did not wish to satisfy her morbid curiosity with a lovers' tiff. They both fell silent at the knock on the door and Harry bade Mrs Bennett enter. In silence they watched as she set down the tray and

216

adjusted the cups in readiness. Pointedly, she placed the handle of the silver teapot directly in front of Harry, no longer allowing Madelene that mistress's right she had so often been permitted before. 'That will be all, Mrs Bennett,' Harry said, tired of the pointed fussing, and Mrs Bennett, surprised by the unaccustomed harshness of tone, made a hasty, graceless exit.

'Silly cow,' said Madelene, anger reviving her old spirit.

'I don't hate the Church,' Harry repeated, as if the interruption had not occurred. 'If, as you say, I won't convert, it has nothing to do with hating the Church. I respect the Church, Madelene. Really I do. I sometimes feel quite envious, I mean, talking to Terry particularly.'

'But you won't convert.'

'How can I, Madelene?' he pleaded simply. 'I don't believe.'

She shrugged again, reaching deliberately in front of him to turn the teapot and undo Mrs Bennett's sabotage. She started to pour tea.

'I can't marry a non-Catholic.'

He shook his head, bewildered, and said suddenly with a dignity comically opposed to his words, 'It's hardly stopped you going to bed with one all these years. *And* a married one.'

'That's different,' she said.

'It's a sin, damn it,' he argued, '*your* Church says so.'

'Only God knows what is a sin and what isn't,' she returned, stubbornly.

'But if you married me,' Harry pursued, 'it would stop being a sin. All these years you've been sinning, and now you've got the chance to make it all legal you're refusing. The Church does allow such marriages. I'll talk to Terry. Surely there is some way . . .'

She shook her head firmly and Harry, in frustration, demanded, 'What's the matter with you? Do you *prefer* adultery or something? Have you simply got used to it? Why not please God when you've got the chance?'

'Do you think,' Madelene said, with a decisive clink of teacup on saucer, 'that God is so easily fooled?'

And so there it was ended. Harry knew he would not budge her from the position she had taken, and so acknowledged defeat. Whether she would live with him, or no, remained a future decision. But if she chose to, it would be yet in her familiar role, as mistress rather than wife. Dimly he wondered how he would handle the resulting social disturbance, but decided he was too old to worry about it. So be it; one aspect anyway was made easy for him. Wed or unwed, she still bore his name. Only those close to the family need know it had been given her not by himself, but by his nephew. She was Madelene Hardacre regardless.

Madelene dusted her hands together in a peremptory gesture, ending the discussion. 'I've heard from Sam,' she said, abruptly.

Harry paused, not as adroit as she at the quick change of mood. He said, slowly, 'Good. No doubt you'll be better pleased with him now.'

'Of course I'm not pleased,' she returned at once. She was, at times, hard to keep up with. Harry sighed patiently, and sipped his tea. 'Just because he's telephoned me now doesn't mean I'm any less angry about the other day.' By 'the other day' Harry knew she meant the funeral. He was slightly confused, actually, in which capacity Sam had been judged to have failed them. Was it as Hetty's great-nephew by marriage, or her husband's mistress's son? He decided it must be the former; precedents for funeral attendance by the latter were lacking.

'I wouldn't be so hard on him,' he ventured. 'He *is* terribly busy.' It was true. Since the disastrous gales of that January, Sam had had more work than he could handle. Harry wanted to add, also, that Sam was, as well as busy, making a great deal of money suddenly, and was generous with it. A recent attack of dry-rot in the perennially damp east wing had been dealt with and paid for by Sam before

Harry had time even to worry where the money was to come from. He opened his mouth to venture this defence, but Madelene was not in a mood to hear her son praised.

'I'll be hard as I like, thank you. It was a family responsibility that he be here.' Her lips were firmly set and traces of French matriarchy lingered in her aggrieved eyes. It was not just the English who cared about family and duty, Harry reminded himself. 'Besides,' Madelene continued, 'he has developed an alarming habit of assuming he can delegate others to carry out his duties. It's all very well in business. But not here.' She was thinking, clearly, of Jan Muller's attendance in Sam's absence. 'As well,' she continued, 'as a totally despicable tendency to use money instead of time. Just because he's invited us all to that warehouse he's living in for another of his abominable parties, we're all to forgive him everything. Well, I won't for a start. And you're not to either,' she added sharply. 'And, quite frankly, I'm really not at all sure we should even attend.'

'Attend?' Harry said dimly, as her diatribe ended. He couldn't remember what future event she referred to or even, alarmingly, if he'd already been told of it. Hetty's death had had a shattering effect on his mental processes. He suddenly found himself forgetting things for the first time in his life, as if senility had crept up and struck him as he stood by her deathbed. Madelene blinked, looking at him as if he'd gone mad.

'The Coronation,' she said. 'Of the Queen,' she added drily, 'in case you've forgotten.'

'Good God,' said Harry, because he had. June the Second, just three days away. The major event of the world's social calendar; the biggest piece of history of the year, most likely, and he had forgotten. To such private recesses does personal grief drive a man, in lonesome solitude. 'I had quite forgotten,' he said. 'Do you think I'm losing my faculties?' He said it with such honest concern that she softened, forgetting her row with her son. She rose and hastened to his side, and stood by his chair with her arms around his proud, straight old body, gently stroking his thinning white hair. She could remember it as dark as Sam's when she first saw him. He had seemed though, then, quite old to her, being so many years her senior and she just a widowed girl.

'Of course not,' she said. 'Forgive me. I forget what it is like. I, who should know better.' She was thinking of her own husband and her first mindless physical grief after his wartime death. A physical grief for the physical body, she thought. Even Harry would feel that; even for Hetty. The detachment of one human creature from the lifeless husk of another was a slow and surgical process, even when love between them had withered from passion to gentle familiarity and no more. 'When Arnold died,' she said slowly, 'I forgot everything. France, the War, my ruined village. Nothing mattered. My country itself seemed to die with him and, poor Arnold, he was not even French.' She smiled privately and Harry tried vainly to figure the logic of that last *non sequitur*. He gave up.

'We're to go and watch it all on Sam's new television then, aren't we,' he said tiredly.

'Only if you wish,' said Madelene. 'It does not matter.' Harry was silent, swamped suddenly by history, thinking of the other coronations he could remember throughout his long life. They, like the wars his nation had endured, punctuated his lifetime, like chapter headings. His childhood, in the long endless security of Victoria, the Edwardian years: the brief idyll of his first marriage, and the agony of his first widowhood. Then George V and the war years and Madelene; the brief, shattering uncrowned reign of Edward VIII and then, on the eve of the next great war, gentle, retiring George VI, the King everyone loved. Harry had not really expected to see another Coronation; surely this King would have outlived him. But then one day, in that same Festival year of 1951 that had brought so many subtle changes to the Hardacre family, he had chanced to be walking on a street in London used often by royal vehicles in non-processional royal journeys. It was late autumn; the King had undergone his lung operation in September. News was scanty, as it always was in those more formal, less inquisitive days, but it appeared a recovery was to be expected. But on that street, quite empty but for himself, Harry Hardacre found himself suddenly overtaken by a large black, royal car, discreet flags flying, and glancing into the windows glimpsed a face thin and pinched and bewildered as a boy's; the King on his way to Sandringham. To Harry, at least, his death in the following February came as no surprise.

And now, thought Harry, a new young queen, a queen who he remembered well as only a pretty child of the Duke of York, with no likelihood of succession, was to be crowned. A new Elizabeth and, with suitable romance, the tabloids declared a new Elizabethan age. Harry Hardacre looked round the slightly tatty grandeur of his widower's drawing-room, and wondered. But he said, aloud, 'Oh yes, I must see her crowned.'

* * *

THE BARTON KIDS
SPECIAL
CORONATION PERFORMANCE

The sign, boldly painted in red on the white card-back of a MacFarlane's Biscuits placard begged from the village shop in Kilham, was propped up beside the weathered stone of the Victoria Terraces. Olive, who was good at that sort of thing, had made a bunting of red, white and blue to drape over it, matching the special trimmings she had sewn, also, on to their 'costumes'. Ruth eyed it critically as Olive fidgeted hopefully, and awaited her too-rare praise.

'It's all *right*,' Ruth said at last, doubtfully, and Olive

221

beamed. From Ruth that was a high accolade, and Olive, unlike their brother Paul, cared terribly what Ruth thought. Paul, disinterested in the discussion, had wandered off down the beach, and was now engrossed in a long ribbon of seaweed freshly washed up on the pebbly sand. He watched some town boys, slightly older, or at least older-looking, walking with fishing rods over their shoulders, towards the harbour. They would be out for a morning's fishing from the pinnock steps, and he half-wished he was with them. He looked down at his bare legs, infuriated with his mother for keeping him yet in loose shorts, when the town boys were already in long trousers. He had lost any sophistication his early London years had given him, and was a little afraid of the Bridlington lads he met around the harbour. They had a toughness, a working man's short-spoken manner, in imitation of their elders that he envied. He kicked at a buried timber, part of a decaying bulwark. Even if they'd let him join, it was still no use. Ruth wouldn't let him go. And since he was only permitted to stay in Brid with Sam Hardacre if he was daily, hourly supervised by Ruth, he had no choice but to do what she wanted. It was that, or another long summer at Kilham, with his mother and father too busy with the pub to ever talk.

All of which put Ruth in a position enviable by many an impresario: of the three-member cast of her fledgling theatrical company, one was herself, one was a sister devoted solely to pleasing her, and one was a brother held in thrall by parental dictate. Of course, even that situation had disadvantages. The hero-worshipping of Olive made her emotional and vulnerable and Ruth was often regretful (for purely business reasons, so to speak) of her waspish tongue which could send her sister into panicky tears. And Paul, well aware of his key position as the one less than willing member of the troupe, was not above a bit of brotherly blackmail. Fortunately he could as yet be fobbed off with sixpence worth of broken lettered-rock from one of the multitude of seaside confectioners with which he held an addict's familiarity. Still, he knew his limits. One threat too many of 'I think I'm going back to Kilham next week' and Ruth would simply hit him. Paul Barton learned early that not even a star is totally indispensable.

For Paul was, undoubtedly, the star. Obviously, when Ruth first concocted the idea of a performing group to entertain the trippers on the summer shore, 'The Barton Kids' was intended merely as a vehicle for her own talents. It was a logical assumption: she was the oldest, she could sing, tap-dance, and recite. Olive, three years younger, could only make a pale imitation, childishly eager, of her big sister's smooth, well-practised performance. And of course Paul was just the baby. But Paul had only to open his mouth and music tumbled out, like the silver coins of some fairy-tale. His gift had been discovered only by accident when he overcame an initial early childhood shyness and happily regaled the dinner-table with the filthy lyrics of playground ditties in a voice as liquid and clear as birdsong. Had Emily more time, and Paul himself more interest, voice training would have been obvious, and indeed she always intended in a distracted way to 'do something' about Paul's extraordinary talent. But it was left in the end to Ruth to make use of it.

It was to her credit that Ruth never displayed any of the resentment she must have felt at having her starring role usurped, right from their very first performance. It was also a measure of her genuine devotion to the theatre, a devotion that would never desert her, even when the object of her love was less than kind. It was Ruth's great misfortune to first experience the bright kiss of the spotlight only in its brief sweep over her head to settle upon that of her brother. Heaven knows what would have happened had it been Olive who won their first audience's hearts; no doubt such unintended treachery by a pretty young sister would have been that much harder to take. But a brother, her baby brother at that, and one with a talent that delighted her even as she envied it, was somehow more acceptable. And yet, when it first happened, Ruth had been obliged to dismantle their little stage, and take away the costumes in a fretful hurry so that she might find comfort in tears in a darkened corner of Sam Hardacre's flat.

It had been late August, last year. 'The Barton Kids' had been performing now for almost a year. Ruth, bored even with the picture houses and her film magazines had conceived the idea of a little wandering troupe and developed it, scripting their jokes, choosing their songs, even constructing her little tap-dancing stage, all in two frenetic days. The next step had been to win permission from her mother for the jaunts to Bridlington to perform amongst the donkey-rides and paddling trippers. Sam Hardacre, her handsome and charming older cousin whose kind attentions to her at Janet Chandler's première she had not forgotten, proved to be her saviour once more. He had then only recently moved into a spacious, if unusual flat, the entire upper floor of an old warehouse down on West St, near the harbour, that he had recently purchased as a storeroom. He had divided the upper area into an extravagantly designed many-roomed apartment, doing half the work himself, using the carpentry skills he'd learned at Ampleforth, and hiring a motley collection of harbour hangers-on to do the rest. The result was an interesting and surprisingly pleasant home; the first home he had ever owned, and he was both proud of it and generous with it. The Barton children were invited to stay whenever they were in town, performing or otherwise. Emily, thus mollified, approved Ruth's scheme, and within a week Ruth was setting up her little tap-dance platform in a quiet corner of sand below the stone sea-walls of the Victoria Terraces.

Of course they were not half so sophisticated then as they were now: there was no sign, no playbills for Olive to deliver, no costumes to catch the eye. That had come later.

224

On the first day they had simply stood on their little plank stage, arms around each other and sung together, at the top of their lungs, until a crowd, small but curious, began to gather. They sang 'Home on the Range' because it was Paul's favourite song. Then Ruth did her tap-dance, and Olive played the ukelele, quite badly, and finally when Ruth had solemnly recited 'Gunga Din' and Olive had told some terrible seaside jokes, Paul was thrust on the stage, alone. He was supposed to sing, 'How Much is that Doggie in the Window,' but forgot the words and so he stood and sang the only thing he could remember, which was the favourite of Emily Barton's one daily 'help' at The Rose, delivered always in her warbling soprano, 'Oh, for the Wings of a Dove'. The audience, which had been watching and listening with that good-natured patience adults reserve for children's performances, suddenly began to really watch and really listen. Only once was there a sudden outburst of laughter, and that was aimed at Olive who had turned about in such comic amazement to stare at her own brother's unexpected new song. The laughter did not disturb Paul in the slightest, even though he assumed it was directed at himself. He hardly cared what anyone thought of his singing, anyhow. It was just a thing he could do, like standing on his head. But when he finished, and they clapped and cheered, he grinned happily and then made a dramatic bow which, like the song, he had learned from watching someone else, in this case a local village performer in the pub. Cheers came again, for the bow, and shouts for more. But Paul wouldn't do any more. He was bored then, and wanted to go and play on the sand. Ruth let him go, pride and envy warring in her heart. But she was as shrewd as any hardened vaudeville producer, and Paul Barton sang 'Oh, for the Wings of a Dove' every day of that summer.

'I'm sick of it,' said Paul now, coming only reluctantly from his retreat by the bulwark, with the seaweed still draped about his head and shoulders. 'It's a sissy song. Can't I sing something else?'

'Everybody loves it,' said Olive helpfully, but Paul didn't care about that.

'Well they can sing it themselves. *I* hate it.'

'Hey, look what I found,' Ruth said, drawing from her pocket a crushed paper-bag. Paul took it, suspicious.

'Gobstoppers,' he shouted. Ruth snatched it back.

'Hey, give it here.'

'Not unless you sing it.' Paul glowered. He reached for the sweets, but Ruth held them out of reach until he promised. He thought briefly of sabotaging the song with rude words, but knew he wouldn't. The truth was, when he was singing he forgot everything else, even being angry at Ruth or hating the lyrics. It was the liquid delight of his own notes that seduced him and obliged him to continue, following his own vaulting soprano into its own high, airy land.

'You'd better be nice to me, now,' he said, sucking a sweet. 'Next year my voice will change and I'll be no use at all. Like that croaky old frog in the pond at Kilham.'

'No. You'll still be able to sing,' said Ruth calmly, hoping she was right. Ironically, it was she, and not the possessor of that lovely voice, who cared. 'Just different songs,' she added.

'Roll on the day,' said Paul, extending to her a sugared pink tongue. 'Come on, let's get it over with, I want to go back and see the Queen.' Ruth had promised them an early morning performance only on Coronation Day, so they could gather, a little self-consciously, with the family about Sam's new television set to watch the great event. Paul was more intrigued with the television itself, a new thing in his life, than with the Queen's coronation, and would have happily watched even the blank screen.

In spite of their bunting, and Ruth's fervent recitation of patriotic favourites from Kipling and Henry Newbolt, in honour of the day, 'The Barton Kids' were a failure on 2 June. People had other things on their minds and were hunched over wireless sets, and crowded around rarer televisions, or simply reading and rereading the newspapers with their joint celebration of the royal event and the conquest of Everest. Only Paul's sweet soprano diverted them, and that only momentarily, and in the end Ruth gave up in ill-humour and packed up their gear to go home. Midway through she was obliged to drop everything and go running up the stone steps to haul Paul down off the high balustrade, twenty feet above the sands where he was prancing back and forth waving one of their Union Jacks and proclaiming himself Edmund Hillary on top of the world. But just as she reached him, tottering terrifyingly there, a tall man in a buff trench coat suddenly appeared beside the balustrade and snatched Paul off.

After a moment's surprised struggle he suddenly grinned and shouted, 'Uncle Albert. It's Uncle Albert, Ruth!'

He happily allowed himself to be swung in a wide circle and set, dizzy-headed, down on the pavement and began at once to babble questions about Albert's arrival, and the band, and his aunt Maud, because they were his favourite people. But Albert Chandler was busy talking to Ruth and only patted his head in reply.

'How'd the show go?' he asked, grinning. She looked away. She assumed he was teasing her, but replied seriously.

'Not very well. No one was terribly interested today.'

'I should think not. You're quite an attraction, young lady, but Her Majesty is putting up pretty stiff competition, today.'

'We'll get them back tomorrow,' Ruth said, without a smile.

'I'm sure you will, pet,' Albert said. He patted her shoulder but she shrugged away, fearing condescension. But it was not that, but sorrow that made Albert wish to draw a smile from that solemn, serious countenance. He had made no judgements of Ruth's theatrical promise; he had only once seen her perform at her parents' home and saw only a pretty child who reminded him faintly, in feature, of his wife, prettily displaying herself. She was too young, he assumed, to be seriously judged, but instinctively he felt the lack of real talent, disguised though that lack was by fierce determination. It was that determination, that solemnity, that worried him, and made him reach for the lightening effect of humour. He had seen that awful determination destroy so many young lives, in his years on the stage.

But as they walked together up towards the harbour and Sam's warehouse home, with Ruth and Olive each on an arm of Albert's, and Paul galloping around behind like a playful colt, they were suddenly stopped by a loud shout.

'Albert. Albert Chandler.' A tall lanky figure hurried up to them and extended his hand to Albert, who released Ruth so that he might take it. 'Albert Chandler, I knew it was you. Haven't seen you in donkey's years. Didn't know you were back in the country at all. By gum, those were the days, down at the Spa. They don't make music now the way you did.' Albert smiled. The children watched, waiting perhaps for Albert to introduce them, which he, as it was, could not do. The man was only one of the myriad of his long-ago fans who remembered him yet. There was no way he could be expected to remember them all, as well. The man seemed to understand that, because he took no offence, and even offered his name, to which Albert gave a polite smile, and another handshake, and made no pretence of having known it all along. The man continued with his praise, and then, realizing he had delayed them long enough, backed away, but suddenly caught sight of Paul.

'Eeh,' he shouted, 'it's t' little songbird.' Paul blushed, but Albert looked surprised, and then the stranger said, 'By gum, should uv guessed. Talent like that don't come from nowhere. He's one uv yourn, isn't he?'

'My nephew,' Albert said, looking slightly puzzled at Paul, who was ducking the stranger's affectionate tousling of his hair.

'Eeh lad,' the stranger said. 'Nay doubt ye'll be famous too, one day. But ye've a way to go yet afore you're Albert Chandler.' He strolled off, happy with his memories, and Albert stood looking after him, and then turned to his nephew who was waiting in an almost fearful silence for what he knew would follow.

'What's this about singing, lad?' asked Albert with a curious smile.

CHAPTER
FOURTEEN

The restaurant in Soho had an indisputable dinginess about its exterior that even Jane Macgregor's silver Jaguar parked before it could not dispel. But it was known and loved by this year's crop of London sophisticates for its excellent Italian food and discriminating wine list. Most of all, it was 'in'. Next year they would be somewhere else, when the tourists, creeping back to Britain after their long absence during the forties, had taken Mama Rini's to their hearts, and the provincials down for the day in t' Big Smoke settled their ample North of England posteriors on its small cane seats. For now, however, only those in the know would dream of coming here, and inviting their favourite elderly aunt to partake of luncheon behind its modest checked curtains. Sam Hardacre was 'in the know'. Suddenly, he was a Londoner again.

'Very nice, Sam,' Jane said, settling herself cautiously on one of the small chairs at Mama Rini's best table. She looked about and gave, involuntarily, her 'I'll wait and see' sniff.

'Wait until you taste the food,' Sam said, smiling.

'I said it was nice,' Jane defended, still looking about warily. But Sam was confident. He knew his restaurant, like he knew his city, the way he used to know that long-gone London of the war. Suddenly Jane's face brightened, and she began to smile broadly.

'I remember it,' she said.

'You what?' Sam was startled.

'The restaurant. It was the new name and the new . . . décor . . . that put me off. Of course. It's Valente's.'

'It's Mama Rini's,' Sam protested.

'*Now* it's Mama Rini's,' Jane dismissed with a wave of her bony hand. 'I remember it from the *thirties*, Sam.' She peered, childishly pleased, through the checked half-curtains, spotting landmarks outside on Dean Street. 'Valente's. I used to come here, years ago. Once I even brought Mother.' She smiled at Sam, conscious of having deflated his new discovery. 'London's a very *old* city, my dear. I think it was even here before you were born.'

'Touché,' said Sam. 'I should have known better than to try and impress you,' he added ruefully.

'Oh, but I am impressed,' Jane comforted, taking up the simple handwritten menu and studying it intently. She paused, and leaned back and said then, her voice lower, 'I came here during the war, too, Sam. Once. With Peter. And Mavis. I'd quite forgotten all about that. I think it was about two weeks before he was killed. They were so happy.' She shook her head, and looked back at the menu.

Sam said, 'Oh, I've picked a real winner this time. Sorry, Aunt Jane, I had no idea.' She laughed.

'Oh, not to worry. To be honest, I hadn't thought of that day for years. I must have put it right out of my mind. It doesn't really hurt any more, remembering. I mean, it's almost nice, savouring the good things. Such a pleasant girl she was, Mavis. Do you remember her, Sam?'

Sam ordered for them both and, since the waiter had suddenly appeared beside him, chose wine. Then he said, 'Certainly do. She was quite the looker, Mavis Emmerson.'

'They'd have been happy, wouldn't they, Sam?'

'I'm sure.'

Jane looked sad. 'I never understood why we never heard from her again. She just vanished after Peter died. After all, they *were* engaged.' She traced the outline of her bread knife on the cloth with a well-manicured nail. Sam watched her carefully.

'That was wartime,' he said simply, and she nodded, accepting it as explanation enough.

231

Sam used the restaurant a lot; it was just down the street from the small flat he had rented, for his and Jan Muller's use whenever either of them was in London. He was back and forth all the time now, or so it seemed, and a few weeks into the new year he had totted up his hotel bills and decided a flat would be cheaper. And more private. London, he had to admit, had more attractions than business alone. He had enjoyed rediscovering it, and rediscovering his bachelor ways.

Mama Rini herself came from the kitchen to make a big fuss of him. It was partly business, he knew, but the proprietress was genuinely fond of him and had taken a motherly interest in him ever since she learned he was a Catholic. He introduced Jane, who shook hands and smiled politely.

'And how is the young lady?' Mama Rini asked, just as Sam rather feared she would. Jane's beautifully defined black eyebrows rose one millimetre. Mama Rini beamed motherly interest, and Sam said, 'Very well,' hoping Mama Rini would not go into detail about either her, or any of the other 'young ladies' she might have noticed in Sam's company, over the months. The one in question had dined with him here just two nights before and he had bedded her after and to his chagrin he could not recall her name. There'd been a lot of that sort of thing lately and he wasn't proud of it, particularly not in front of Aunt Jane.

Fortunately Mama Rini was summoned to her kitchen before the conversation could go further and when Sam's eyes met Jane's she only smiled and looked away, dismissing the subject. He was glad. What had seemed only natural at twenty-seven seemed inappropriate at thirty-seven, with three years in a Benedictine monastery lying in between. He wondered at times if he oughtn't to marry and yet could not conceive of it happening.

'I think late marriages work best, anyhow,' Jane said, and Sam looked up amazed, as if she had read his thoughts, until he realized she was still thinking of her son Peter and his fiancée. 'I mean, even my Ian and I *could* have become a disaster as we grew older. Who will ever know? I look back on the child I was when I married . . .' she shook her head, 'it always amazes me.'

'But you were happy.'

'We were children together. Who knows where life would have led us?' She shrugged. 'All of us . . . Ian and I, Madelene and Arnold, Peter and his Mavis. War threw us together, or at least hastened things, like it did for Ian and me. And war separated us. Perhaps it was best. Such sweet memories. Like flowers, cut and pressed before they can possibly decay.' She sipped her wine. 'Don't possibly tell anyone, but I think Philip and Emily will divorce.'

'Oh, no,' Sam whispered, genuinely shocked. She shrugged again.

'Oh perhaps not. But I see it headed that way. They were children too. Or at least, Emily was. Now she's grown up and Philip's behaving like a little boy with his first train set.'

'What of the children?' Sam asked.

'Well, I'm sure they'll wait for the children to finish school. Anyhow Ruth only has this year, and Olive is at the High School too, now. And Paul spends more time with Albert and Maud than anyone. They're taking him along on their summer tour. It's just around the Northern towns, so he'll never really be far from home.'

'Is he singing with them?'

'Oh no,' Jane shook her head, firmly. 'No. Albert wouldn't allow it. He sees to the voice lessons, but no performing, absolutely. He's very firm about that, and Paul's just as pleased, you know. He's only a little boy, still, and Albert insists he's not cheated of his childhood, as he puts it, whatever the talent.'

'He's wise,' Sam said.

'Emily doesn't think so. But she doesn't argue. You know, she's afraid of Albert!'

'No one's afraid of Albert,' Sam said, over his lasagne. 'He's the sweetest guy in the world.'

'He's a tough one, when he knows he's right,' Jane said. She sighed. 'Maud, at least, was lucky,' she added with a smile. She glanced suddenly towards the kitchen where Mama could be heard, faintly, singing in Italian. 'And you?' she said disarmingly. 'What of you?'

'*What* of me?' he bluffed.

'The young lady?' she reminded.

'A friend.'

'Just friends,' Jane said, making sure she heard right.

Sam nodded, looking down. He said, 'One of many.'

'Ah,' said Jane. When she had finished her grilled sole, Sam ordered coffee and they sat drinking from tiny espresso cups. Jane said, 'Never met the right girl, Sam, or not the marrying kind?'

He shrugged. 'A little of both, I think.' He was silent and then said, hesitantly, only because he was closer to Jane Macgregor than to anyone other than Terry, 'I suppose there was one, once . . . but it never came to anything.' He was surprised at how boyish and shy he still felt over a woman he had met only once. It was March now of 1954; two and a half, two and three-quarter years ago, that meeting, to be exact. He doubted Janet Chandler counted the days.

'Who knows,' Jane said brightly. 'Perhaps it will happen anyhow. I can remember when we were sure Vanessa would never wed anything but a horse, and look at her now.' Sam laughed.

'How are they?'

'Splendid. Driving Noel mad of course. They've just bought two more mares, both in foal. It's funny, of course, but not funny too. The old place is really getting rundown. Except for the stables. Harry is facing another rates bill and quaking in his wellington boots.'

'Tell him not to worry,' Sam said quietly.

She eyed him carefully and said, 'I'm not sure you can afford to keep doing this.'

'I can afford it.'

'Really?' she asked, uncertainly.

'Really.' He paid the bill and rose suddenly. 'Come on,' he said. 'Let me show you something.'

'Where are you taking me?' Jane asked, smiling. She had suggested Sam drive, on the pretext, quite false, that she was uneasy with London traffic. She knew how much he enjoyed the car.

'Wait and see,' he said. Sam drove out towards the East End and after a while Jane was pleased enough that she had allowed him the wheel. He had lost her completely, down in twisting mazes of streets she had rarely, if ever, seen, among the warehouses and bombsites of London's dockland. Eventually he drew up at the back of a riverside building, blank-walled and decaying, and got out, helping Jane as well from the vehicle. Street children gathered to stare, and the bolder came up to gaze at their reflections in the Jaguar's gleaming wings.

'I feel like Marie Antoinette,' Jane said. 'Are you sure we're quite welcome here?' Sam grinned.

'We'll just be a moment,' he said. He took her arm and led her round the corner of the building and down a narrow cobbled alleyway, towards the river whose wet and sour smell drifted up to greet them. He seemed at ease and familiar in these surroundings, just as he had in the restaurant, so much so that the incongruity of the car, and her smart tweeds and his own well-tailored suit apparently did not occur to him. At the end of the alleyway they found themselves standing on the edge of a deep slip of oily water in which was moored a large vessel, a tugboat, rust-stained and businesslike, with huge padded bows, and her decks taken up by heavy winches.

She appeared unoccupied but Sam, leaving Jane comfortably seated on an overturned crate, said, 'Just one moment,' and clambered, uninvited, up the steel gangway extending from her deck to the dockside. He wandered off round the far side of the black-painted wheelhouse, and returned with his hand companionably on the shoulder of a man in dungarees who carried a paint bucket. 'Come aboard,' he shouted to Jane, who hesitated, and Sam ran down the gangplank again to assist her.

'Are you quite sure we're welcome?' she said again, but he only took her arm, without answering, and led her up to the deck.

'Stop fussing,' she said, annoyed, as he carefully helped her over the side. 'I was a Navy wife once, if you recall.'

'I'd forgotten,' he smiled. 'Forgive me.' The man with the paint bucket had wandered back to the starboard side and Sam led Jane after him. 'Where are we going?' she demanded.

He only smiled. There was a ladder propped up against the red-painted stack and the man she had seen was climbing it once more, paint bucket in hand. He recommenced his work as she watched, amazed, carefully filling in the last neatly stencilled letter of the name: *Mary Hardacre*.

'Sam?' Jane asked, uncertain.

'I'll name the next one after you,' he said.

On the drive back to Soho, Jane Macgregor really began to absorb quite how far Sam had come and where he was going. At first she simply repeated, almost to herself, what she had said on the dock.

'It's a *real* boat, Sam.'

'You mean not just the *Dainty Girl*?'

'Well, perhaps I do. I can't get over it. It's so *big*.'

'She's a sea-going tug, Jane. Not that big really, at 125 feet; she just looks big on the river. But she's powerful.' She was, too; 3,200 horsepower in her diesels, enough to haul a good-sized freighter through the North Atlantic.

'Is she really yours?'

'Most of her. She sank in the Solent. We raised her, and

then I bought her. I had to stretch a bit. I even sold something, and I don't like selling things. Jan was glad. He says I'm a squirrel.'

'What did you sell?' she asked, curious.

'A little haulage company.'

'I didn't know you had a haulage company,' Jane said, again amazed.

'Ah, you should watch more closely,' he teased. Then he said, 'I got involved last year shifting a lot of rubble from a couple of old aerodromes they were breaking up. Got a contract from a chap down in Sussex who was doing some construction, and needed some site-fill. Thought it was easier to do the transport myself, rather than pay someone else. Worked well, too. I had my contract from the RAF for taking the rubble away, and of course the chap I sold it to contributed as well, and I ended up with four lorries as well as my profit.'

'Do I understand you got paid twice for shifting the same rubble?'

'Not exactly. I got paid for clearing the site. Then I got paid for filling another. One man's broken up runway is another man's site-fill.'

'I think you're a rogue,' Jane said, but she smiled.

'An opportunist,' said Sam, chiding gently. Then he added, 'An opportunist is a rogue in a Savile Row suit.'

He stopped the car in front of the building on Dean Street that housed a florist's shop on the ground floor and his flat on the second. He got out and went round to open her door. He handed her the keys, and escorted her to the driver's seat. As she got in, he said quickly, 'Just wait,' and dashed round behind the car and into the florist's shop. He emerged before she had time to readjust her driving mirror, and was standing at her window when she looked up, holding out a single red rose.

'Sam.'

'Aunt Jane.' He handed her the rose through the open

237

window, kissed her cheek and stood waving in the middle of Dean Street, oblivious of traffic, as Jane drove away.

After the Jaguar disappeared round the corner into Old Compton Street, Sam stepped back on to the pavement and stood, hands in pockets, looking abstractedly at the traffic, while trying to decide what to do. He had an appointment at Lloyds at five o'clock, and a date for dinner and theatre with a young lady called Georgina something-or-other whom he'd met at a party the week before, at seven. But there was still an hour or two of afternoon left and he felt urgently he should do something with it. There was paperwork lying on his desk in the flat, and he had promised to telephone Jan with his decision over a sunken coal-barge in the Clyde. But the day was springlike and lovely and he seemed to be spending entirely too much time indoors of late. He wished he had a car in London, and wondered idly if Hardacre Salvage could afford to replace the old banger he used up north with something a bit more extravagant. The wood-rimmed wheel of Jane's XK 120 left its phantom shape yet in his hands, like the morning-after memories of a lover. He wandered off, slowly, down Dean Street. There was a Jaguar showroom not far from there that he had noted idly one day, and it was a perfect afternoon for window-shopping . . .

'Captain Hardacre!' A voice, amazingly like his financial conscience had it not been for the military form of address, grabbed his attention as only the sound of one's own name in a crowded street can do. He turned, uncertain, wondering who from his wartime past had spotted him. But there was no one he recognized on the street; no one with that cheerful fatuous grin of army pals the world over. Perhaps he had heard wrongly; perhaps they meant someone else. He stood looking about, hands still in pockets, when the shout came again, a little nearer, and accompanied by a rumbling sound of metal-rimmed wheels. 'It *ees* you. I know you any-where . . .'

There was still no one he could possibly know in sight, but his eyes were now obliged to seek out the source of the voice and settled, baffled, on the swarthy young face of a black-haired, dark-eyed barrow boy, pushing a cart laden with crates of sweet-smelling fruit down the crowded street. The rumbling of the wheels stopped and the young man, face beaming a happy, white-toothed grin, released the handles, lowered them hastily to the street and, mindless of the irate cab driver blocked behind him, ran towards Sam with his long, lithe arms outspread.

'Pardon?' was all Sam had time to say, before he was enveloped in a warm, Italian, garlicky embrace.

'Ah, *mama mia*, so many years, I never think I see you again. So, how ees life? Have you wife, bambini? Look,' he released Sam with one arm so as to point to his cart, still blocking Dean Street. 'You see, I am in beesness, as I say I will be. No? You remember?' He beamed happily, pounding Sam on the back with one big, surprisingly tough hand. Sam escaped backwards just enough to avoid another affectionate bear-hug, and finally managed to interject a phrase in the barrow boy's cheerful monologue.

'Who *are* you?' he begged. The beaming grin very slowly began to fade to uncertainty.

'Captain Hardacre?'

'I'm most terribly sorry, old boy, but I honestly don't . . .'

'You no know me?'

'I'm sure I *should* . . .' Sam ventured helpfully.

'You no know Riccardo?' Abject disappointment crowded the immensely expressive features. Behind the young man the taxi driver was leaning all his weight on his horn, and in the distance Sam caught sight of the tall black helmet of an approaching bobby.

'Look, old son,' he said, encouragingly, taking the now mournful-looking Italian by the elbow. 'What say we move this cart of yours and discuss this later, eh?' But the young man only shrugged. He looked at his cart then at the cab driver, who was now hanging out of the open door of the big black taxi screaming cockney abuse. The young Italian lifted a fist under his forearm in an expression of ethnic disapproval, but even the obscenity was delivered with disinterested dejection. Sam, feeling horribly responsible for ruining someone's day, even if the someone was, as he was certain now, a totally mistaken stranger, went himself to lift the handles of the barrow.

'Aye, aye, sir?' said the bobby.

'We're just moving it, sir,' Sam said, as Riccardo who-ever-he-was jumped to his aid. At the same time his mind was racing to the incongruous possibility of missing his appointment at Lloyds because of a charge of handling a fruit-barrow without a licence. But the bobby passed by with a nod as Riccardo trundled the barrow off the centre of Dean Street and round a convenient corner into a narrow cobbled alley. He straightened up after lowering the shafts to the cobbles and, brushing his hands off, extended one apologetically to Sam. 'Your pardon, sir, I beg. I do not mean to offend,' he said with a continental formality that reminded Sam comically of Jan Muller.

'No, wait,' Sam said. 'Surely there must be some explanation . . .' Because he realized there must be more to it than mistaken identity. The man knew his name.

'No, no. It no matter, now. Once, long ago, I know you, sir. You forget. You are big man. I do not intrude.' He stepped back as if to depart, and bowed briskly. His eyes were hurt but not angry. Nor was there any retreat in them from the familiarity with Sam's face they had first shown.

'You *do* know me,' Sam said uncertainly.

'Long ago, Captain Hardacre. The war. I am little boy, then. Just bambino. I bring fruit to the fence, no? You call me Ricco.'

'Fence?' said Sam.

'Big wire fence,' said Riccardo, gesturing high with his

hands. 'So big. But no good at bottom. I crawl under . . .
we play creekit . . . I still play. I very good now. Go to
Lords, see England. Hey, we play again and I bowl you out,
maybe yes?' He grinned again, his good-humour returning.

'Italy,' said Sam, thinking quickly.

'*Scusi?*'

'A prisoner-of-war camp? In Italy?'

'So?' said Riccardo, confused at why Sam was stating the
obvious.

'That is where you know me from?' Sam asked again, to
be sure. The young man beamed again.

'*Deo grazie!* So you remember Ricco?' The white grin
returned and Sam was pounded once more on the back by
the broad affectionate hand. He gasped for breath. No, he
didn't remember Ricco, or Riccardo, or anybody from any
Italian prisoner-of-war-camp. Sam had never been a prisoner-of-war. But he knew somebody who had.

'Terry,' he said.

'Terry Hardacre,' Riccardo shouted, delighted, as if Sam
had finally agreed to be the person Riccardo had known he
was all along. 'I tell you I come to London, make a good
beesness, no?'

'No, wait,' Sam cried, grabbing the bouncing Italian
firmly by both shoulders. 'Listen. I'm *not* Terry Hardacre.'

Riccardo looked at him. He raised one hand and slapped
it against his forehead and closed his eyes. '*Mama mia,*' he
said.

'You don't understand,' Sam protested. 'It was *Terry*
Hardacre you knew in Italy. I'm *Sam* Hardacre. We're
twins. Brothers. We look *exactly alike*,' he added with
emphasis, looking directly at the bewildered Italian. 'Exactly alike,' he repeated.

'*Fratelli?*' said Riccardo.

'Brothers,' said Sam.

'You, Terry Hardacre, *fratelli?*'

'*Twin* brothers,' Sam said again, wishing he could speak

241

Italian and make it clearer. But it was clear enough. Riccardo gave a whoop of joy and once again leapt upon Sam with his fervent embrace, this time embellishing it with a kiss on each cheek and a delighted cry of '*Fratello!*' as if Sam were not only Terry's brother, but his own.

Sam took him to Mama Rini's. It was the obvious place, all considered, and he would be able to rely on Mama herself for translations if Riccardo's limited English broke down entirely at any point in his related history. And so, with Mama Rini leaning over his shoulder prompting the young Italian from time to time, and with cup after cup of her good espresso coffee crossing the table in the quiet of the mid-afternoon, Sam learned the story of Riccardo Cirillo, which was his full name.

Riccardo had been born, just outside Naples, into a large family, happily blessed with a multitude of aunts, uncles, cousins and lesser relatives, in May 1936, the day before Mussolini's troops captured Addis Ababa and brought the Empire back to Rome. It must have seemed to many a propitious moment, but by the time he was five Italy was at war, and the Cirillos had more to sorrow for than many in the conflict that had engulfed Europe. Half their family was in England, three brothers and a sister of Riccardo's own father had emigrated in the twenties and by the time of hostilities were so involved with the London restaurant business, and London life in general, as to regard themselves as English. The Government of Britain regarded them differently, and the male members of the family spent the war in internment camps. Neither that fact, nor the aggression between the two nations that the family straddled much affected either their affection for one another, or their affection for Britain. Riccardo, raised on stories of wealth and opportunity, had set London as his goal by the time he was seven, war or no war, and when a party of British prisoners, captured in North Africa, were moved to a rather lackadaisical imprisonment centre near his slum home, he regarded them at once not as the enemy, but as compatriots. Among them was Terry Hardacre, whose delight in children, and dismay at the miseries wrought by war so apparent around him, both found an outlet in the skinny boy who wheedled his way past guards and through shabby fencing into the prison itself. No doubt it would be a lot more difficult for a grown man in British uniform to make the same crossing made by a cheeky boy, but Riccardo Cirillo made his own rules, and was soon a regular visitor. He brought fresh oranges and lemons, stolen no doubt, and whatever treats he could imagine, and was always delighted by the occasional bar of chocolate from prisoners' packages that found its way back with him. But he did not beg. He didn't want anything from them but communication; to practise his handful of English words and to play English games and to find an audience for his post-war, English dreams. And so, as soon as the war was over, and the restrictions on enemy aliens were at last lifted, Riccardo got on the first boat from Naples to Cannes, cadged lifts across France and wheedled his way into England and the 'care' of one of his now-released restaurateur uncles and his English wife.

'So,' he beamed, 'I am here.' He raised his hands, palms upwards. 'You see the fruit-barrow, that is my beesness, it very good, make lot of money already. I am here already three months, already rich man,' he laughed, stretching luxuriously in the cane chair of Mama Rini's, as if reaching out for how far he could go. 'But please tell more of Terry. He very good man, I think. Good man for God. Maybe he become a priest?'

Sam shrugged. He had not mentioned the years that he too had spent in Ampleforth Abbey. 'I think he is a good man, too, Ricco. Perhaps, who knows, perhaps he will become a priest.' It was a thought that had never really occurred to him and somehow it frightened him, both in its essential likelihood and the added distance it seemed to place between him and his brother. 'I will telephone him, and tell him all about you,' he said, and Riccardo beamed. Sam paused and then said, 'Tell me your plans.'

'My plans?' Riccardo said innocently, but his eyes were lively.

'You did not come all the way from Naples only to push a fruit-barrow.'

Riccardo grinned. 'No,' he said. 'I come to buy the Savoy Hotel, maybe.' He laughed richly and finished his espresso, protesting only lightly as Mama Rini refilled it. She went off to the bar and came back with a bottle of Sambuca liqueur and three tiny glasses, which she filled. Riccardo grinned again and lifted Sam's matches from the table and, striking one, carefully lit the surface of the liqueur, which flamed bluely. He nodded to his two companions and did the same for each of their glasses, and then he raised his, still flaming, in a toast.

'My new friends,' he said.

'To your ownership of the Savoy,' said Sam, in reply.

They all drank, Riccardo gulping the blue flames as well. He said then, seriously, 'While I work, I learn from my uncle. I have the barrow for daytime. At night I work in the kitchens, learn the way to do things.'

'When do you sleep?' Sam said.

Riccardo shrugged, 'When I am older, there will be plenty time to sleep. When I am dead, even more.' Sam smiled and Mama Rini fussed, saying it was no good, he would be ill, he needed good cooking and a wife. Riccardo only laughed, and Sam watched him, and slowly gathered together the threads of an idea.

There was still almost an hour left until five o'clock. Sam suddenly rose, thanked Mama Rini for her hospitality, offered to pay for the espresso and had his offer refused by a big friendly push from her fat, playful hands. He thanked her once more, as did Riccardo, and then he led the young Italian back out on to Dean Street. 'I want to show you something,' he said.

They walked for fifteen minutes. When he found the building he was actually quite relieved. He had only glanced at it in passing once or twice. Like the Jaguar showroom it was something he'd only taken faint note of for future reference. He had not really expected to need a London ground-floor site just yet. It was a small building, the plate glass windows whitewashed over, the abandoned door firmly locked and chained. He stood beside Riccardo, peering into the interior through a gap in the fading curtains still hanging from a brass bar midway down the window. The name of a vanished café was yet painted in faded red letters across the glass. He looked at Riccardo.

'There's no doubt a kitchen at the back. It won't be much. And I'll have to see that the lease is reasonable. But the main question is, could you make a restaurant out of this?'

Riccardo looked at him and at the tatty building, the delight in his eyes showing that he was seeing it in the rosy light of his own dreams. 'Of thees?' he cried. 'Thees is a palace! I could make a restaurant of a hole in a wall. From *thees* I make the Savoy Grill!'

Sam left Riccardo once more pushing his barrow on its interrupted journey along Dean Street. He had Sam's address in his pocket and was singing 'Santa Lucia' at the top of his lungs. Very badly, Sam thought, denying the cliché of the universal musicality of Italian tenors. Sam glanced at his watch, and hurried off to the nearest underground station, knowing he'd just have time for his appointment at Lloyds. On his way he passed the Jaguar showroom he had intended to visit before his meeting with Riccardo. He slowed for an instant and glanced in. She still sat there, pristine in British racing green, an XK 120, a twin to Jane's. He smiled at the smooth graceful swoop of bonnet, the curving wings, the fairylight glitter of wire wheels, the pale luxury of tan hide upholstery. He slowed to a stop. Whatever funds he had earmarked, even playfully, for its purchase, would go into the lease for Riccardo Cirillo. He smiled wryly.

'Later,' he whispered, and broke into a trot as he hurried on his way.

CHAPTER
FIFTEEN

The dreamy stillness of Ampleforth Abbey, Virginia creeper-draped grey stone against a blue May sky, was rudely shattered by the throaty roar of a healthy three-and-a-half-litre engine, as the black Jaguar drophead coupé roared away, scattering gravel with irreligious disdain. At the wheel, his black habit surprisingly appropriate against the black Connolly leather interior, was Brother Erkenwald, OSB, and, in the passenger seat, his twin brother, and the Jaguar's owner, Sam Hardacre.

'Oh, a bit of *all right*,' exulted the delighted monk, whipping through the gear change with a hand not at all rusty from lack of practice. He threw the car round one bend in the short steep driveway the schoolboys called 'the snake' and clipped a bit of privet hedge on the next.

'I hope Father Abbot is somewhere else,' Sam moaned, hanging on. Terry seemed oblivious, out on the open road, his eye on the next curve. Sam's eye was on the speedometer, touching sixty. 'You could at least bloody wait until we're out of the place!' he shouted. 'They'll never let you out with me again.'

But Terry was in a private paradise, slowing only briefly for the turn and then tearing off, with another sure-handed melodic climb through the gears, until they were flying eastward, towards the coast. Sam let him be. If there was one thing possibly he enjoyed even more than driving his new car himself, it was watching the joy it gave Terry. It was 8 May 1955, and they were on their way to The Rose at Kilham for the annual family gathering on the anniversary of VE Day. The custom, begun accidentally, like most customs, by a spontaneous party attended by all the family who could gather in London on that date in 1945, had genuinely stuck. Now, none of them would even consider not being together on that date. But, for the first time ever since '45 the venue was not Hardacres.

'Do you know,' Terry said suddenly, slowing as they approached Malton, 'it's ten years. Can you imagine?' Sam nodded.

'I've been thinking the same. It seems far longer, and, in a funny way . . .' he paused.

'And not as long,' Terry finished for him, in the habitual twinned way they had of completing each other's thoughts. 'So much has happened,' he added, driving almost sedately through the village, with the rumble of the Jaguar engine like the purr of an immense and impatient çat. It took off again as they left the last straggle of town buildings behind, with seemingly little encouragement from Terry. 'Oh this is a motor car,' Terry breathed delightedly. Sam nodded, childishly pleased that Terry was pleased. He liked giving things to Terry, and now that Terry was a religious brother without worldly possessions there wasn't much one could give him, other than temporal pleasures, like good meals, and the sensation of a superb motor car. Sam held, all his life, a conviction that Terry was a better person; a conviction perhaps rooted in nothing more than the simple fact that, although they shared much, their deepest consciousness must naturally be separate, and Sam never credited Terry with any of the less worthy thoughts and desires that crossed his own mind. In truth, Terry *was* a very gentle soul, and subject, in their childhood, to being the victim of pranks, and the inheritor of guilts and punishments meant for his brother. As ten-year-olds they had once fought, quite viciously, with the result that Sam had obtained a cut and bleeding lip which, in its healthy bloody flow, had terrified Terry, and Sam had played on that terror. In the end, to win a promise that the source of the wound would not be revealed, Terry had handed over his total financial treasure,

248

a shiny half-crown given him one Sunday by Uncle Harry. Sam had received the same, of course, but had spent his while Terry, entranced with its silvery round promise, had, as he often did, hoarded his own. Sam had accepted it, heartlessly, but kept to his promise of silence over the cut lip. Afterwards he'd spent it greedily, forgetting its source, and then later, regretting it, saved from his own pocket money until he could replace the sum. It took a long while and by the time he returned the half-crown, Terry could barely recall what it was for. Reluctantly, he accepted it, but Sam had found that his guilt was not so simply alleviated. He tried again. At Christmas he slipped a half-crown into Terry's Christmas pillowcase. At Easter the following year, he managed to present him with another. At odd occasions throughout their adolescence he would find some pretence to slip a half-crown Terry's way. He did it so subtly that Terry probably never guessed the reason why. Nor did he ever manage to clear from his mind that tiny, guilty debt. Some things could not be paid back, regardless of one's wealth. It was a lesson he had still not fully learned.

'I think you're being a bit unkind,' Terry said.

'Unkind?' Sam jested. 'Shall I drive, then?'

'You know what I mean.' Sam did, too. The change of locale of the VE Day gathering was Sam's doing entirely. It wasn't that he had any real objections to going to Hardacres. It was, more or less, his family home. He had been raised there. And now that his mother and Harry had made their unorthodox arrangements rather courageously open, he was in a real sense, the son and heir. Noel, to whom the place would one day undoubtedly belong, regarded it more as a wart on the landscape of his farm than anything. His own residence in his farm cottage was totally, ingrainedly established. The place, full of wellington boots and bachelor oddities, was no longer a stop-gap residence. It was impossible to conceive of him as ever again inhabiting the Big House. Terry, of course, had his own family at Ampleforth, and his stay there, too, now had developed a solidity. The uncertainties, like the bridal period of a marriage, were all behind. He had taken solemn vows now, and no one imagined any longer that he, like Sam, might leave there. He was growing older, in that peaceful, unlined way that members of religious orders aged. Oddly, he looked older than Sam, who was the one out in the battlefield of the business world, where stress and tensions were expected to take their toll. They'd taken no toll yet, on Sam. He thrived on them, and looked it, and had learned early on to balance the frustrations of paperwork and working luncheons with healthy doses of physical labour. When he got too much of anything, he'd go to sea with Mick and Pete and be totally unreachable for days at a time. Jan said it was no way to do business, but Jan was tense and irritable more often than not, and his lean, farm-worker's frame had softened slightly and developed the slight paunchiness of muscle gone to flab. And, anyway, the business was doing just fine. If he missed a deal, or lost out on an untimely shipwreck, by his North Sea sabbaticals, he gained in his relationship with the men who worked under him. There were more by far now than just Mick and Pete Haines. And their original diver had retired to professional rather than amateur alcoholism and been replaced by four others. The newcomers were businesslike and the whole, perhaps, lacked the careless camaraderie of the early days but, like most working men, they liked a boss who worked beside them, and did the dirtiest and most dangerous tasks as well.

And it was dangerous work. By definition, it meant going to sea in the worst of weathers; weather that caused shipwrecks. It meant playing risky games of tag round a floundering, disabled vessel, trying to get a tow-line aboard in a gale. It meant riding out such a gale on a powerless, and sometimes sinking, ship under tow. Even the tools of the trade were dangerous; high explosives for underwater de-molition, taut steel winch lines that could, in an instant of overstrain, snap and cut a man in two; and they used those tools always in the worst of conditions. It was the sort of work that demanded concentration, co-ordination and trust, and men working together in such conditions won one another's respect. Accordingly, they obeyed Jan Muller, politely, but they really liked Sam, and would do anything for him. So he continued in his own way, going to sea whenever he could, or whenever he felt the need, and leaving Jan to man the ship-to-shore radio, awaiting the calls of distress that meant work. It was a vulture's role, salvage, and that aspect was one he could neither get used to nor forget. Generally, he could thrust it aside; after all, it was work that needed doing. Shipowners needed salvage men even if they didn't always like them. And most of the time he was too busy to worry over emotional or moral implications. He was too busy, actually, to worry overmuch about anything, and that included, perhaps unfortunately, family.

'I really had to, Terry,' he said, 'I didn't have the time to spare. I haven't got *this* time to spare, damn it.'

'No one said you had to pick me up. Harry could have.'

'I *wanted* to pick you up. You're the one bit of family that really . . .'

'That really matters?' Terry glanced across, slowing the car, prepared to argue. Sam shrugged. 'Thank you,' Terry said. 'Don't think I'm not flattered.'

'Don't push your luck, mate.'

'I'm serious. I am flattered. I know we're close. And I'm glad we're close. You're my brother and I love you more than anyone with the possible exception of God. But the rest of the family has rights too, pal.'

'I *know* that. Look, I'm here, aren't I?' He raised both hands, in an annoyed gesture.

'Yes, here. You're not at Hardacres though.'

'So. We'll still be together.'

'May the Eighth is the biggest event in Harry's year. He looks forward to it for months. It's about the only social

251

event he *does* look forward to. You know how shy he is. But this is *his*. He's sure of himself in this. It's his yearly occasion for playing the patriarch. And damn it, Sam, he has a right to it.' Terry gunned the car with surprising vehemence.

'If you smash up my damned Jaguar I'll throttle you.'

'I'm not smashing anything.' They were out on the open road, crossing the moorland between Malton and Sledmere, and stone walls and hedges were making a May-green blur, speckled with the white of summer blossoms. The road was dry, and perfect.

'Look,' Sam said, conscious of labouring a point as one is inclined to when uncertain of one's position, 'if we had the party at Hardacres, it wouldn't just be the party. You know what Hardacres parties are. It would be the whole bloody weekend. And the weekend would have started on Thursday. And by the time we had the "just the family dinner" and the "everybody dinner", and the party itself, and the "day after the party just us again supper", God Almighty, it would be Wednesday. I have to be in London on Monday. And I *should* have been in London today. And once I *go* to the old place I can never get away. Harry wants me to see everything. And Mother gets furious if I don't do everything Harry wants.'

'What would *you* do if Noel Hardacre was your only son?'

'Shoot myself, but what has that got to do with anything?'

'Precisely. Noel's the biggest flop of a son since Cain. Can you blame Harry if he lets his paternal pride lap over a bit on to you. *And* he's only saying thank you. You do practically keep the place running, I gather.'

'Hardly as much as that.'

'You pay for everything,' Terry returned bluntly.

Sam shrugged again, 'I oil the wheels a little. I can afford it.'

'But you don't have to.'

Sam looked across at him again, and said, 'I don't

252

understand. First you're saying I don't do enough. Now you're saying I do too much.'

'No. I'm saying only that you'll do anything money can buy.' Terry glanced across, a knowing sharp look in his dark unpredictable eyes. Sam looked away. He started to protest but in glancing up saw a flash of bright yellow beyond a heavily foliaged chestnut tree at the bend in the road ahead. 'Watch it!' he shouted, clutching instinctively at the side of his door. But Terry had also seen it and hit the brakes, hard and skilfully, and the Jaguar, shrieking protest, came to a slithering but controlled halt in a shower of gravel just three feet from the tailgate of a fish lorry, wedged at an impossible angle across the road.

Terry let out a long sigh. 'Maybe you better drive,' he said.

'I don't see why,' Sam answered, hearing his own hard breathing shaking his words. 'You handled that well enough.'

'Didn't see it,' Terry whispered.

'Well, who the hell would have expected it?' Sam defended him. 'And what's it doing here, anyhow?' They both climbed out and walked round the front of the lorry, where they found a scene of busy chaos. It had apparently attempted to take a sharp turning in the road a fraction too quickly and had slipped into the off-side ditch, tilting enough to spill half of its precariously balanced load of crated fish.

'Phew,' Terry said, sniffing the aroma on the warm May air. 'If they weren't rotten when they started, they sure are now.' Broken crates and spilled contents littered the road surface, coating it with a greasy mix of broken fish, entrails, fish scales and thin sea-watery blood. The lorry was being further lightened by the removal of additional crates, which were being stacked by the driver and a couple of local farmers on the verge. A constable had arrived and when sufficient crates were cleared from the road, he signalled to

Sam and Terry that they might continue their journey. As always, Terry's clerical garb won him special deference.

'Just come along this way, right over to the verge, Father,' one of the farmers called. Sam buried his face in his sleeve to keep from laughing, as Terry solemnly steered the Jaguar through the fishy slime on the road and out beyond the scene of the accident on to the open road. He waited until the constable and respectful farmers were thoroughly out of earshot beyond two bends before he opened the throttle and the black car leapt forward once more. If he was chastened by the near miss with the fish lorry, it didn't show. Sam was still laughing.

'Father Terry, wad ya be after hearin' my confession?' he said in his best Irish accent. Terry slammed a free fist at him, missing.

'Anyhow,' he said suddenly, 'I'd be Father Erkenwald.' He grinned. Sam had never got used to Terry's monastic name. He did not return the grin, seeing something both teasing and secretive in it, like a challenge. Eventually, he took the bait. 'Oh, you're not really thinking of that?'

Terry shrugged.

'Come on. Tell me you're not.'

Terry said nothing. After a while he said, 'You know, I'm terribly grateful to you, leaving when you did.'

Sam looked up, startled. 'You didn't seem grateful at the time.'

'Of course not. I was really hurt. I shouldn't have been, but I was. The funny thing was, I was thinking of leaving myself.'

'You were?' Sam said, amazed.

'Of course. We'd been there three years. The honeymoon was over. Everybody thinks of leaving sometime. Usually about then.'

'Then why didn't you?' Sam said stiffly, still ill-at-ease about his own decision, even after all this time.

'Because you did. Naturally, I wanted to, but I couldn't

254

then. It would have been like all the other times, with me following you. I just couldn't let it happen again. I was furious. I felt you'd stolen my exit.'

'*You* following me?' Sam said. 'It was never *you* following me. I was the one doing the following. Always.'

Terry looked startled. 'Surely you don't mean that?' Then, when he saw that Sam obviously did, he just laughed softly for a long while, driving smoothly and easily down the narrow country road. 'I suppose,' he said at last, 'that's what being twins is. We were even alike in that. The blind leading the blind.' Sam was still too astounded by that revelation to say anything. Terry continued, 'But then, I thought I'd break away. I'd stay. And I was glad. I am glad. I've found my place. I know it now.' He paused, glancing quickly at his brother. 'I hope you've found yours.'

'You're going to do it, aren't you?'

'I've a long way to go,' Terry said. 'Ordination isn't just a snap of the fingers.'

'You smug bastard.'

'Please don't be like that. It won't make any difference between us.'

'Of course it will.' Sam turned away, glowering at the countryside fleeing past. Then he caught hold of himself and apologized. 'I'm sorry,' he said, and then laughed. 'Do you know, I feel jealous. As if you were getting married.' Then he laughed again, 'I should congratulate you, but I can't because I'm jealous as all hell. Do you remember that time you *were* going to get married . . .'

Terry turned briefly to face him, and blinked, and then turned his eyes back to the road, puzzling. Suddenly he recalled and shouted with laughter. 'Louise. Louise Scrimshanks. Oh my God, I'd quite forgotten. Do you remember she had the most enormous . . .'

'*The* most enormous,' Sam broke in.

'The most Enormous Tits in the World,' he and Brother Erkenwald chanted fondly, together. Terry smiled privately

255

and said, 'Oh, I was so much in love. I was nineteen. What a disaster that all would have been.' He was silent, remembering, and Sam felt the unreasoning jealousy and anger leave him. They would still be together, no matter what.

Terry said softly, 'You *are* right though. It is like getting married. It does cut you off in a certain way from the family. Though no doubt it joins you in another. That's why they lay off me, always, of course.'

'Who?' Sam said, puzzled.

'The family. You get the brunt of it. You're the unmarried son. For me, it really is as if I already had a wife. And if I'm ordained, it will be that much more so. They wouldn't think of objecting if my duties keep me elsewhere. So it all falls on you. I'm sorry. I've rather landed you in it, haven't I?' Sam shook his head, no longer angry at anyone.

'I'll try a bit harder,' he said, as if Terry really was already a priest.

'Nothing for it,' Terry said smoothly with a grin, 'you'll just have to get married, that's all.'

'Not bloody likely,' said Sam.

Upon their arrival at Kilham, Sam mischievously directed Terry to draw the Jaguar up beside Jane's silver-grey XK 120, and they left the two parked side by side. Sam went to the bay window of the pub, knowing the family would be gathered in the front room, drinking tea around the coal fire in the brick fireplace. He rapped on the window, was greeted by shouts of hello from the assembled company, and managed to gain Jane's attention. She glanced out of the window, nodded briefly and disappeared within the room, to emerge a moment later at the front door. She looked carefully at the two, near twin motor cars, and her two twin great-nephews.

'It's the new XK 140,' Sam said, grinning, in case she hadn't noticed. Jane had noticed. She looked it over carefully and sniffed.

'A little flashy in black, don't you think?' she said. Sam

just grinned, fastening down the tonneau. The May evening was warm and fine and no doubt they would return, as they had come, in the open air. Jane took Terry's arm, directed another haughty glance down her long nose at Sam and his Jaguar, and re-entered the pub. Sam followed, still grinning.

Inside, Harry was standing before the brick hearth, doing his best, no doubt, to recreate his patriarchal position in this new setting. If he resented the changed circumstances of the party he did not show it, greeting Sam instead with great warmth. Philip Barton was in his favourite place, behind the bar, holding forth about hill sheep in his yet inadequate Dales accent. Emily was nowhere in sight, and Sam suspected, guiltily, that she was in the kitchen, another consequence of the change of venue. He looked quickly around the room, assessing who had arrived and who was yet to come. Maud and Albert had an engagement in Brighton and had sent regrets. Rodney and Vanessa were yet absent; they always arrived everywhere last, usually via some market or stud farm where they would have spent half the day, enabling Vanessa to wear her usual mixture of perfume: Chanel and saddle leather. As always, she would be in workaday tweeds and headscarf and, as always, she would apologize profusely, as if such apparel had never been known before to grace her back. As he thought of her, Sam heard the familiar rough note of the Hardacres Land-Rover arriving outside and smiled. Across the room, Heidi Muller, seated at a small table and in earnest conversation with Ruth Barton, caught the smile and smiled back. Sam crossed to her. She stood in her formal way and shook his hand.

'So good to see you again,' she said, shyly. Heidi did not often venture down from her inn in Strathconon. This was their first meeting since the same day, a year ago. 'I trust my son will soon join us too.'

Sam nodded. 'If he's late, it's my fault. There were one or two points to clear up about a tow job we've contracted for, so he might still be on the telephone to Holland. Some of these people aren't that easy to contact.'

'You for one,' Philip put in. 'Tried to ring you all last week, where were you?' Sam sat down beside Heidi and thought a moment. His days were so busy that it was often difficult to remember a week back.

'Tuesday?' he asked.

'And Wednesday and Thursday. And Friday.'

'Tuesday in London. Wednesday, Thursday and Friday on the *Mary Hardacre* off the Aran Isles.'

'How lovely,' said Ruth Barton dreamily. 'The Aran Isles.' Sam looked properly at her. She had changed. Her face was older, set already in faint shadows of Emily's own lines of disappointment. She made up too heavily, like Emily, and dressed too fussily. As always she tugged at his heart, making him wish to reach out to her and turn her again into the little girl she should be yet, not the sad woman she already was.

'They *can* be lovely, sometimes,' he said. Not in a Force Ten gale with a bad-tempered barge in tow, however, but he decided not to spoil her picture of them.

'I'd like to go to sea sometime,' she said. Sam grinned, pretending flirtation.

'You'll have to run away with me then, when your mother isn't watching.'

'Oh, I couldn't do that,' she said solemnly, shocked. She was not a girl to jest with, he remembered, a little late.

'Who's that trying to seduce my daughter?' a voice called from the kitchen doorway. Emily emerged, arms out-stretched, hips tilted forward, shoulders back, in her dramatic way of greeting people she really liked. Ruth blushed again, receding into her corner. Flirtation worried her; flirtation on her mother's part, no matter how innocent, even more. But Sam knew the part he was expected to play and leapt up to accept Emily's embrace. He liked Emily, anyhow, but he knew she must have her moments of

258

glamour or the evening would be misery for her. So he made much of greeting her, pretending to hustle her out of Philip's glance for a mock-passionate kiss. Philip never noticed anyway.

'Too late,' Emily crowed, 'you've lost your chance.' She pretended to brush Sam off and turned back towards the kitchen. 'I've found a new love,' she said, winking over her shoulder. She was dressed in black, with a striped, neat apron over her cocktail dress, and her jewellery flashing incongruously in the late afternoon light. Sam followed the conspiratorial wink, letting her lead him into the kitchen, where he expected to find young Paul, or perhaps the old gardener, Bemrose, as the object of her 'flirtation'. He bent his head beneath the low lintel of the hall and followed Emily's quick high-heeled footsteps down the dark corridor. The kitchen door stood open and to his amazement he heard a man singing, Italian accented and with a terrible voice,

> Bless thees house, Oh Lord we pray
> Make it safe by night and day . . .

The last notes were strung out in a horribly off-key tremolo. There was only one person who could sing that badly.

'Riccardo?' he guessed, astounded.

'Ah, there she ees, my lovely one, my little cabbage, my . . .'

'Oh, do shut up,' Emily said, her eyes glowing, pleased with herself. She shoved him roughly in the ribs, but he only engulfed her in his long lithe arms, still singing over the top of her head. 'Riccardo's helping with the meal,' Emily protested, her voice muffled against his shirt. Sam looked hard at Riccardo. Riccardo grinned, his white beautiful teeth showing a devastatingly rakish look of innocence.

'So I see,' Sam said, not sure what to think. Riccardo was twenty, or twenty-one, no more. But he was also Italian,

259

and street-wise. He'd no doubt had lovers since he was barely old enough to do up his own fly buttons.

'She is wonderful woman,' Riccardo protested suddenly, reading Sam's gaze. Emily caught his eye and for an instant read his suspicions. She looked shocked. It was clear that what was going on in the kitchen was only play in her mind, whatever it was in Riccardo's. 'I come up to do the pasta, and the feesh. It is a big meal. I think she need some help.'

'Of course,' Sam said. It was none of his business, anyhow. And Emily looked so happy, playing like a girl. 'What a kind thought.' Riccardo audibly breathed out. He rushed forward, and shook Sam's hand.

'My pleasure,' he said, still nervous. His restaurant business, thriving though it was, still was utterly dependent on Sam Hardacre and the thought that he might have offended an unexpected streak of prudishness in his principal backer had shaken his nerve.

'How's business?' asked Sam.

'Oh, she is splendid. Splendid. I find just the new site for our second Riccardo's. Earls Court. Ground floor with a little garden at the back. We put out tables in summer, dining under the stars. Oh, it ees so romantic,' he said, his dark eyes wandering once more to Emily.

'It ees also London,' Sam said drily. 'Where it rains all summer.'

'What a killjoy,' said Emily, still glowering at Sam for his suspicions. She waved him away, and he left the kitchen rather readily, feeling out of favour with them both.

Vanessa and Rodney had arrived and were stamping around the public bar in their usual manner. Vanessa was drinking Guinness from a pint mug. 'Sam, old thing. Great to see you, jolly, isn't it?' She slapped his back and sent him careening against Rodney who said, 'Do tell,' apropos nothing.

'What a pity we're not at Hardacres,' Vanessa said loudly, putting her finger on a sore spot. Harry coughed and Sam looked uncomfortable but Vanessa continued gaily, 'Got a splendid bay mare the other day, suit you perfectly. Thought you'd try her out this weekend.' She tilted her head sideways, sympathetically, 'What with you being so busy these days, bet you haven't had a good ride in months.'

Terry creased up in unclerical delight against the far wall, pointing a finger at Sam and gesturing over Vanessa's back. Sam struggled to keep a straight face and conceded that a ride on Vanessa's mare might be just the thing. A few moments later he cornered Terry alone and said, 'Thanks a lot, brother,' punching him in the shoulder, 'I was having a hard enough time without your help. A little decorum from the Church might be in order.' Terry only laughed harder, enjoying himself.

'What are you griping about? *I* haven't had a good ride in seven years.' He wandered off to talk to Harry. He was having a wonderful time, Sam knew, remembering back to the way the sudden release from the orderly world of the monastery would also delight him when he too belonged within the walls of Ampleforth. As for himself, Terry's presence completed the evening for him; he felt totally at home, as if he was once more back in their school or army days, when they were always inseparable and every party was a joint adventure to be played through together, with their unique twinned solidarity, and laughed about afterwards. There had been one infamous occasion when the Hardacre brothers jointly seduced a young lady who was none the wiser that the twin who had nipped off to the hotel bathroom was not the same twin who returned, moments later, to her bed. In retrospect, they were both a little shocked at the memory, but it was an opportunity provided by their doubled lives that was simply too good to miss. It *had* actually only happened once, though rumours abounded of repeat performances. They had only to remind each other to be reduced to hysterical laughter, and the young lady's name alone was sufficient reminder. To this day, neither could speak the name with a straight face, and each had been terrified during more solemn moments of their lives that the other would pronounce the fatal syllables, 'Jeannette'. Terry had long threatened to save it for Sam's wedding, whenever that was, at which he would undoubtedly be best man. Sam was now keeping his sabotage for Terry's ordination, and they both knew that the dual threat would keep each in line.

Still, there were occasional backslidings. When, that evening, the family were solemnly gathered around the dinner-table, all present with the sole exception of Noel who wouldn't have come even if it were at Hardacres, half a mile from his cottage, and most certainly wouldn't come here; and Harry begged them, after the meal, to be upstanding for the Loyal Toast, Sam knew it was coming. Terry hated anything remotely resembling pomp and ceremony, except in Church, and as glasses were charged he stepped back from the table as if in search of another bottle, drifted in remarkably ecclesiastical solemnity past Sam and leaned briefly over his shoulder, gesturing across the table to Jan Muller.

'Get back to your place,' Sam hissed, seeing Harry's offended eyes upon them.

'If Jan had a little sister . . .'

'Shut up.'

'What do you think she'd be called?'

'Bugger off.'

'Jan-*ette*,' said Terry, giggling and topping up Sam's glass as Sam collapsed in helpless laughter.

'The *Queen*,' intoned Harry, sharply.

'God bless her,' Sam giggled, tussling with his brother, as the rest of the party looked on with their usual bewildered amazement.

'They've never learned how to behave,' Madelene apologized later, as everyone sat around over coffee, more relaxed, and Harry, mollified with port, had got round to forgiving his two nephews. 'I suppose it was growing up without a father.' She shook her head but didn't look in the least sorry. She was inordinately proud of them both and didn't care who knew it. At the moment, she had even forgiven Sam for his absences from Hardacres. It was just so nice being together again, all her family.

She looked only mildly disapproving as Sam and Jan Muller closeted themselves on a bench inside the inglenook and talked business, as they always did. After a while Terry joined them, glass in hand, and leaned lazily against Sam's shoulder, happily listening to their discussions of ships and shipping, subjects which he knew little about but found interesting enough. Madelene, watching them, thought them very alike, even with Jan's blond hair in such startling contrast to that of her two dark sons, and the incongruity of Terry's monastic dress. They could all three be brothers. She was pleased with the friendship and partnership between her son and that of Heidi Muller. Though Jan was hardly much older, he seemed to her always steadier than the twins, and she relied on him to provide the steadying influence to Sam's mercurial and inventive nature. It was a good combination; she had been in business, in her own way, for a long time, and understood the need for solidity to be balanced by imagination, lest it become stolidity, and likewise for the quickfire sharpness of the Sam Hardacres of the world to be anchored by the realism of someone like Jan. They sat together, the three of them, for the rest of the evening until Terry suddenly looked up, startled, from his drowsing by the fire.

'Good God,' he said, 'I'm going to turn into a pumpkin if we don't get back to Ampleforth smartish.' Sam looked at his watch, seeing it later than he'd imagined and got up as well. Rather hastily they made their farewells, Terry leaving the pub with one arm around his mother and the other around Harry's shoulders. Harry was much softened by the evening's gentle drinking and was exhibiting his amusement at Terry's slightly weaving steps.

'A drunk monk,' he cried, delightedly. 'Always wanted to see a drunk monk.' Harry was a bit tipsy himself. Terry grinned. He tossed the keys across to Sam.

'I'm plastered,' he said, flopping into the passenger seat. 'You drive.'

'Just as well I'm not, isn't it?' Sam said, climbing behind the wheel. Terry had closed his eyes and looked about to go to sleep. Sam started the engine and carefully backed the car away from Jane's XK 120, waving to the family gathered before The Rose as he did so. Then he turned the car into the village street, driving back the way they'd come.

He was, as he had said, thoroughly sober. He'd seen the way Terry was headed early on in the party, and knew he'd be driving home. Besides, he wanted Terry to relax and had deliberately curbed his own drinking so that his brother might freely indulge. It was something they had always done for each other, when out together, and driving together. Almost by instinct, one always maintained sobriety, though very rarely both.

The road was as dry as it had been in the afternoon and the night air faintly crisp with early summer chill. Above, the stars were bright, only occasionally veiled by thin wisps of cloud. Small curls of moorland mist crossed the road once they were up high, away from the village, but even those were frail streamers that broke harmlessly over the bonnet of the Jaguar. Sam drove hard, enjoying the invigoration of the night air and the emptiness of the darkness after the crowded hours of the party. Terry was asleep beside him.

He passed Sledmere and headed towards Malton. The roads were empty. He'd not seen another pair of headlights for twenty minutes. He was moving along, flooring the accelerator on the straights, his foot just flickering across the brake before the curves, slowing only slightly, changing down at the last moment, and up again as she cornered beautifully, his eyes already on the far reach of his headlights, striking the stone walls of the next bend. Ahead was a dark shadow of heavily foliaged trees, blacking out the stars, a stand of chestnuts. Something tugged at his memory from long ago, in the afternoon, but was fogged and lost behind the hours of talk and laughter, that lay between. There was a sharp bend. He took it well, gunned the car out of it, beneath the dark shadow of chestnut trees. The only warning he had was the flash of some light-coloured object by the roadside, a broken crate lying by the verge. A fish crate.

Oh God! He hit the fishy slime almost sideways, coming out of the bend, and it took the wheels of the Jaguar like a pool of oil. She broke free, losing all traction, and the steering wheel became airy and light in his hands. He fought it, but it was like fighting with water. The car slewed, he corrected, it slewed the other way, he almost won. 'I've got it, Terry, I've got it,' he heard himself shouting. But he hadn't got it.

She mounted the steep nearside verge with two wheels, as on to a ramp, and instantly was in the air. In a slow, impossible blur he felt her turn, bounce, strike something, turn again, and felt air take him, and suddenly his flight was not that of the Jaguar. He was apart from it, flung with ferocious force on to the grass verge to lie stunned and winded, as in a fall from a horse. He could not believe how easily she had flipped, how simply it was done. How quickly it all happened and how he was now lying on the same smooth blur of grass that seconds before he had driven by disdainfully at such graceful speed.

Sound reached him first; a distant, remembered crashing, dying away. Then a whirring sound, as one wheel of the overturned car still spun on in a phantom journey. And another sound, a dripping of liquid, water, or petrol. Then silence began to swallow it all. The wheel came to a whispering halt. The dripping faded. A night bird sang off on the moor. Pain crept in on its voice. Not bad pain. In fact, so little it had not occurred to him that he might be hurt. He tried to move, and found it difficult but not impossible. He was surprised to taste blood in his mouth, but knew it was not of consequence. He sat up, feeling winded yet, and remembered he had not been alone in the car.

'Terry,' he called. His voice was almost casual, expecting a ready answer from where Terry would also be sitting up, thinking the same thoughts of amazement he was thinking himself. That was *close*. And like a million times before, they'd been lucky.

'Terry,' he called again. Then suddenly terror seized him and he struggled to his feet. The headlights of the overturned Jaguar probed uselessly, frighteningly into the tops of the chestnut trees. 'Terry!' Silence came down on the black moorland, and with it a loneliness such as he had never, in all his life, endured.

CHAPTER
SIXTEEN

Everyone was so kind. The passing motorist who stopped
and summoned the police. The police constables themselves
who stayed with him until the ambulance came, and had not
the slightest interest in apportioning the blame that Sam so
desperately needed to shoulder. They praised his calm
behaviour after the accident, and said the accident itself was
unavoidable considering the state of the road. The ambulance driver and his assistant were kind. Not that they were
needed; Sam was not hurt and Terry was beyond all
helping. Jane, when she came to pick him up from the
casualty ward where they insisted on taking him, was
inimitably kind.

Jane held the family together. She was their rock. She
had been so before at other times of family tragedy, and
became so at once, as soon as they were notified. When it
happened, what Jane later called, 'what all families dread
and none should ever have to endure', the telephone call in
the night, the clutch in the darkness at the throat, there was
no one else capable of responding. Jan Muller had left for
London and was out of contact. Madelene collapsed in
numb hysteria and Harry became in an instant a frail,
helpless old man. Jane left them in the charge of Philip and
Emily Barton and motored to the hospital alone.

She drove Sam back to Hardacres. On the journey she
repeated those sad comforts that the police constables had
offered her. That there had been no suffering. Death had
been instantaneous; so quickly had it all been over that it
was more than possible Terry had never awakened, even,
before the overturning car had flung him, as it had flung
Sam, on to the verge of the road. Only Terry had been

unlucky, and the fall had broken his neck. Sam sat beside her staring straight ahead through the windscreen into the still pleasant May night. She could not be sure he was even hearing her.

'He wouldn't have known about it, Sam.' There was no answer. 'They said there wasn't a mark on him.' He knew that. He'd sat in the dim starlight beside him for half an hour before help came. 'He was just unlucky.' Unlucky. All their lives they had been lucky. So lucky. The scrapes they'd got through. London, the Blitz, the whole of the war. Unharmed. The famous Hardacre luck. They'd pushed it just once too often. And it ran out. 'Sam, it could as well have been *you*.' Would God, would God that it were. So fast, so fast. Before the spinning wheel of the overturned Jaguar had whispered to a halt, Terry was dead. He knew that because that was when the black cage of aloneness had locked around him, that held him still.

Three days later, it held him yet. The funeral bell at Ampleforth was still tolling when they drove away. Sam seemed to hear it for days. His entire being focused on it, as if it were his only voice. He had neither thought nor desire, wanting only to throw himself literally into the grave with Terry and, short of that, to prostrate himself at the feet of the abbot and beg to be taken back. But neither was a possibility, he knew. He was thirty-eight years old and the time had finally come to grow up once and forever. He would never be really young again.

They returned to Hardacres. Jane made him drive, an act as necessary as it was cruel. Later, he thanked her. At the time he simply obeyed. He was numb with grief and did whatever he was told to do. She watched, unspeaking, as he took the wheel with painful hesitance, handling the machine that so recently had been as a mistress at his command like something alien and fearful. His hands were white on the wooden-rimmed wheel, and he drove slowly and with terrible jerky uncertainty down the winding country roads. But she would not relent and in the end he got them home.

Jane was not at all sure that Hardacres was the best place for Sam to be. But she did realize that it was perhaps only at Hardacres that he would come to terms with what had happened, if he was ever to come to terms with it at all. Which was something over which, from the very beginning, she had haunting doubts.

He had not so much shown his grief as been visibly shattered by it. He had never wept. He neither sought people out to speak nor deliberately avoided speech. When spoken to he answered rationally and without emotion. When not spoken to he sat alone staring into space or walked about the house or gardens like a ghost. She imagined he was reliving his childhood with Terry, a necessary act of mourning if it were so, but could not really be sure of that.

Madelene could not reach him. Lost in her own grief, she was baffled by him. She herself had turned at once to her deep-rooted religion for comfort and expected him, logically, to do the same. When he did not, a wall of incomprehension came up between them.

Once or twice Jane, who had also felt that wall, felt herself about to breach it. They would talk; the usual pointless and essential litanies of regret that follow any death and, most particularly, a violent one. They were too obvious to be ignored. Nothing could change the fact that Sam was at the wheel of the car in which his brother died. Nothing could change the guilty circumstance that Sam's own, deliberate, self-interested change of venue for the party had been totally responsible for them being on that fatal road in the first place. Those were facts. They could talk around them, but not diminish them. When Jane, once too often, gently reminded him that Terry's death had at least been painless, he flared into anger and shouted back.

'He's still dead, though, isn't he?'

She retreated to silence, working carefully at a piece of needlepoint that she had picked up only to keep her hands busy. She said, slowly, 'Sam if you want to take it back to beginnings you have to take it right back to VE Day. If we hadn't had a party *then*, we wouldn't be sitting here now.'

'That's nonsense,' he said without feeling.

'*All* life is connected, Sam. *All* of it.' He was silent again, staring out of the window at her car parked by the ornamental cherry at the edge of the lawn.

'Would you like to see a priest?' she said, not for the first time. She knew he wouldn't get angry about that. But he just shook his head. Faith could not help him. It was lost somewhere, beyond the black circle of isolation into which nothing could break.

He said, bitterly, 'I was so damned proud of my driving.'

'With reason,' she responded at once, surprising him. 'You're good.'

'Oh, very.'

'The police constables said . . .'

'I *know* what they said. And I told them. It was all my fault. I *knew* about that patch of grease. We'd seen the damned lorry that caused it. I knew about it.'

'You forgot, Sam. Anyone could forget. Anyhow, what if Terry had hit that lorry in the afternoon,' she stood up clutching the needlepoint to her chest, as if it were the idea she was pursuing. 'Tell me that. What if he had . . .'

'He didn't.'

'He only *just* didn't. You told me. Supposing he had, and it was you dead, do you think he'd suffer like this?' Sam looked stunned. 'Would you *want* him to?' she demanded.

He shook his head, looking confused, with the hard lines softening slightly in his face. He looked out of the window again at her Jaguar. Then he said, 'Terry wouldn't have hit it. He was a better driver than me. He always was.'

Jane exploded in frustration, 'Well, if he was so damn good why didn't he damn well stay sober enough to drive you back?' She froze in saying it. Neither of the twins had ever tolerated a word spoken against the other. They'd close ranks like iron. Sam stared at her, with the anger in his eyes the first real emotion she'd seen there in days. He raised a fist and for an astounding moment she thought he was going to strike her. But he slammed it instead into the wall with a bone-crunching sound that caused her physical pain, and he ran from the room.

Half an hour later he came back. He was calm, and made no reference to what had been said. He said only, 'Could I have your car keys, Jane? I'd like to go for a drive.'

She looked up, stunned. She tried to meet his eyes, to read his intentions, but when for a moment she did catch his glance, she met nothing but the same dark, impenetrable wall. She nodded slowly, thinking, buying time. She could not refuse. He could well intend only to test his own shattered nerve and she must not prevent him or, worse, show lack of confidence. She stood, reaching for her handbag, withdrawing the Jaguar keys. She said, carefully casual, 'Would you like me to go with you?'

'No.'

She handed him the keys. She had worked herself into a corner that demanded no other action. Trust obliged her. He took them, thanked her, and left the room. She stood at the window, watching the car disappear down the drive. He had lowered the hood though the sky was threatening rain. She had watched him do it, methodically, almost as if it were a necessary ritual. She had noticed, in watching, how thin he had grown in the handful of days since the party, and thought suddenly that, although he had sat at table with them for most meals, she could not recall seeing him eat. The Jaguar disappeared into the rhododendrons, reappeared, vanished into the beech wood and was gone. She stood yet staring after and whispering, 'He must. He must.'

He drove quietly, even sedately to Driffield, and made his way through the town and out on to the Sledmere Road. He

271

found that Jane's therapy had worked; he was no longer nervous at all and he handled the car as well as he had ever done. The thought only touched him idly, as from a great distance. It did not really matter. Nothing really mattered.

When he reached, and passed, Sledmere, he felt a tightening, a tensing into readiness about him that seemed to flow actually from the car itself, as if it were a racehorse turned towards the post after a warm-up canter down the stretch. He flexed his fingers, once, against the worn wood-rimmed wheel. The car began to pick up speed.

Ahead he saw the tall stand of chestnuts that marked the site of the accident. He slowed, approaching them, and came nearly to a halt as he came abreast of them. The road had been, belatedly, scrubbed clean of the fishy scum on which he had skidded. There was a patch of oil on the roadside, and a battered-down section of hedge and brambles where the wrecked Jaguar had lain. His eyes went just once to the place on the verge where he had crouched in the night beside Terry. Then he looked straight ahead, eased off the clutch and floored the accelerator and the Jaguar gathered itself and leapt forward, roaring away with a skidding of rear tyres in the dust and a gravelly whine through second, third, and into top, so that he was doing sixty-five by the next bend, and seventy and then eighty on the straight without an ounce of deceleration for the bend ahead.

He made it, with a horrible squeal of tyres and a lurch up on to the verge, and hardly paused before he was off after the next. A stone wall loomed, grew huge, skimmed by his rear wing, and he'd made another. No matter. There were plenty more. He floored the accelerator again. A farm gate flew by, and a voice, shouting. He was deaf. Ahead, a small family saloon loomed up and he had a glimpse of a terrified white face before he flashed by it with inches of clearance. Something tugged at his conscience but was defeated.

He saw another bend, and begged the Jaguar for more

speed. She gave it, but she fought back, cornering so beautifully, fighting for her own life perhaps, if not for his. Bewildered, he skidded out of the next bend and into the next straight. No matter. There was one ahead. A vision of it sat firmly on his mind. He had been heading for it since he left the door of Hardacres behind. He had been heading for it since he left the side of Terry's grave. It was a true right angle, facing an eight-foot brick wall edging one of the many local estates. The wall had stood there for three hundred years, as solid as granite, and no doubt would stand another three hundred, when he and Jane's Jaguar were both dust. 'Sweetheart,' he whispered to the beautiful silver-grey machine, 'you'll not make this.'

He saw it ahead, at last. A long smooth straight, enough to get the Jaguar up to whatever impossible speeds she could undoubtedly do, and the brick wall a soft red blur, far away. He took one deep breath, tightened his hands on the wheel, but felt no need to tighten his resolve. He accelerated smoothly, feeling the wonderful surge of power as if the car was thrown forward from behind. He changed up into top, relishing, even then, the lovely smooth action. He felt reverent towards the car, preparing her for her end. His eyes flicked to the speedometer just as it touched the ton. Half the straight gone. Goodbye, sweetheart.

And then she failed him. Like a lover wilting away from the moment of embrace, of her perfection, she slipped from him, almost imperceptibly, then undoubtedly. She slowed, failed, the roar of the engine faded, thinned, and actually died. Suddenly he was coasting in silence and at such speed that even without power he nearly finished the straight. She came to a halt graciously at the inner edge of the bend, the brick wall a road's width away, and as far as heaven's gates.

'What's the matter, mate? Got problems?' The voice came like a clap of thunder. He looked up, startled. He had no idea how long he had sat there, unmoving, in the stalled

Jaguar. It could have been a minute, or an hour. He found his voice, sounding queer and distant after the roar of the engine and the tension of his absolute concentration.

'Guess I have,' he said, with the hopeless mundanity of the ordinary settling upon him without mercy.

His rescuer proved to be one of those mechanically adept gentlemen who carry full toolboxes and handbooks and assorted spares with them everywhere. He was also chatty and friendly, and kept up a non-stop stream of diagnosis and comments as he got his elaborate gear out and settled down to work. Sam let him. Another time, in the other world of normality he had once, too, inhabited, he would have done all that himself. He knew engines and even had, at the moment, a fairly good idea what was wrong. He just couldn't care enough to act, or even reveal his knowledge. He leaned, numbed, against the Jaguar's wing, watching his helpful companion work.

'Dirt in the carbs, probably,' the man said, poking about. He took something off and blew through it. Sam barely watched. 'Could be fuel lines,' the man went on. 'Bit of muck.' Sam said nothing. The man looked at him queerly. 'You all right, mate?' Sam nodded, looking into space. After a while the man finished over the engine and came back to him, leaning over him, studying him carefully. 'You sure you're all right?'

'I'm all right.'

'You want to try her now?' Sam looked blank. 'You want to start her up?' the man said, now looking at Sam as if he doubted his sanity. Sam nodded, dully. He got back into the car and turned the key. The engine came alive, smoothly and beautifully. He listened to its low mutter, numbly.

'Seems all right now,' the man said, with evident satisfaction. He was clearly waiting for some appreciation.

Sam looked at him with such emptiness in his eyes that the man looked away. Sam said, 'Thank you,' very softly and the man, encouraged by the first sign of civility he had met, smiled.

'No trouble. Just a bit of dirt,' he said. Sam nodded. The man asked, 'Aren't you going to put the top up?' Sam looked around. It was raining lightly, but steadily. He had not noticed. The grey leather was beaded lightly with moisture. 'Oh. Yes,' he said, climbing out again. The man helped him, still glancing queerly at him from time to time. When the top was raised Sam climbed back behind the wheel, staring out briefly through the rain-streaked windscreen. He remembered again to say 'Thank you', and the man nodded. He was backing towards his own car, glad to get away. 'Should be all right now,' he called. 'Just a bit of muck. You were just unlucky, that's all.'

Just unlucky. He put the car into gear, turned the corner by the brick wall and drove away. In his mirror he saw his rescuer driving off in the opposite direction into the rain. Sam drove another few hundred yards and then pulled into a lay-by at the side of the road and switched off the engine. The rain made a light pattering on the canvas top. He watched it stream down the windscreen over the stilled wipers, blurring his vision. Just unlucky.

'Terry, you smug bastard,' he cried, out loud. The loneliness broke apart, like a solid object, shattering, and the black circle that had encaptured him crumpled into light. He rested his forehead on his hands on the wooden wheel and, for the first time since Terry's death, he wept.

CHAPTER
SEVENTEEN

The knock came again at the door. Again, Sam ignored it.
He wondered distantly who it could be this time, but he
lacked the energy to care. Earlier, it had been Ruth Barton.
He had opened the door to her, angrily, because he thought
Emily had sent her. He had left Hardacres and come back to
his own flat in Bridlington, to be alone; but they would not
leave him alone. But it turned out Ruth had come of her
own volition, and he had been distantly touched by that,
though he could not rouse himself from his lethargy to feel
real emotion. Still, he had allowed her in. She had wanted to
do something; clean the flat, or cook him a meal. He let her
make coffee. She teetered on the edge of her chair while he
drank it, mystified by the change in him, unnerved by grief,
as the young often are, and he had gently sent her away.

Then he had gone back to what he was doing before,
which was lying on the sofa in the sitting-room, his
stockinged feet resting on the arm, with a packet of Senior
Service, and an overflowing ashtray on the floor beside him,
into which he occasionally flicked ash, when he could be
bothered. Otherwise he just let it fall on the floor. The flat
was in chaos, which was not at all its usual state. Hitherto,
Sam's solitary home had owed more to his monastic past
than to the bachelor years that had preceded it. It was
almost always well scrubbed and clean and scrupulously
neat. He cleaned it himself, having long held a private
belief that each human being in the world, regardless of sex
or social status, ought to clean up after itself. He never liked
clutter anyhow; his own mind, full of rapid, shifting
thought, and will-o'-the-wisp inspiration, was clutter
enough. His surroundings must always be simple, to ba-

lance it. He was no longer short of money, by any standard, but there was little sign of wealth about the flat. The furnishings were plain, sparse, and old. He didn't like new things. The sitting-room contained, aside from the sofa and a chair, a large desk, usually surprisingly neat, and now buried in unsorted papers and unopened mail, a wall full of home-built bookcases, the television set that he had got to amuse the Barton kids, and very little else. The only valuable things in the room were his collection of antique paintings, seascapes in oils gleaned from local sources, and a good gramophone on which the Barton kids had played Bill Haley all last summer and which now played only Handel's Messiah, over and over again.

Half-filled coffee cups, overfilled ashtrays, and an assortment of books, papers and articles of clothing were littered about wherever he had happened to drop them. The whole was only faintly visible, anyhow, since there were no lights on in the room and the curtains were drawn, as they had been for days. Here and there a stray band of strong summer sunshine crept through to light the dust, where he had failed to close the curtains fully when he had tugged them shut on the day he had arrived. Outside, the sound of children shouting and the endless calling of seagulls obliged him to remember it was summer, in a holiday town, and the world was bent on pleasure.

The knock came a third time, harder and more persistent. Sam stubbed out a cigarette and lit another. The knocking turned to a sudden impatient hammering. 'Sam. You in there?' It was Mick Raddley's voice, and belligerent, because he knew very well Sam was there and ignoring him. Sam gave up. 'It's open,' he said.

The door swung open cautiously, and Mick, bent over like a grumpy bull, plodded into the room. He looked around disbelievingly at the chaos and said only, 'Good morning. It's three in the afternoon.'

'What do you want, Mick?' Sam said. He hadn't moved

from the sofa, and continued smoking with his eyes shut, as if by not looking at Mick he could make him not be there.

Mick looked sourly at him, but said only, 'Jan called. He says he telephoned four times but he couldn't get through.' Mick's eyes went to the desk and the telephone, with the receiver off the hook. He grunted. 'I see why. He gave up and rang the pub and they sent round for me. Seems at t'moment the main line of communication between t'directors of Hardacre Salvage is the barmaid at the Ship's Wheel.'

'What does he want?' Sam said, his voice flat.

'He needs an *answer*,' Mick said, suddenly vehement.

'Tell him to make his own decisions,' Sam said, and then snapped angrily, 'can't any of you ever think for yourselves?' Mick was unperturbed.

'Aye,' he said. 'We can. 'Cept in the past whenever we've done anything without consulting Your Royal Highness there's been bluidy hell to pay.' Sam said nothing. It was true. Mick pursued, 'And Riccardo needs a signature on that lease.' Mick plodded across the room, and lifted up a couple of the myriad dirty cups and carted them through to the kitchen. 'What a shithouse,' he said.

'Tell him to sign it himself,' Sam said, still from the sofa in the living-room. Mick put the kettle on the cooker before he plodded back through and answered, 'It's the managing director they want. Happen you don't remember, but that's you.' He lifted a couple of books and set them back on shelves and began collecting used ashtrays and herding them on to one table.

There was another silence from Sam, and then he said, 'Tell him to sign my name to it.'

Mick stood for a moment by his stack of ashtrays. Then he lumbered across the room and sat down on the edge of the sofa, roughly shoving Sam's feet out of the way. He said, 'Now I'm just a working man, an' all, an' not that genned up on these things, but something still tells me that's not the best advice in the world.'

278

There was another long silence and Sam said, 'Mick, go away. I want to be alone.'

'Oh, aye? I'd never uv guessed.'

'I'm selling out, Mick,' Sam said then, more gently. 'It can all go to hell for all I care.' Mick took out his pipe and tobacco and, slowly withdrawing a flat slice of Navy Cut, began shredding it into the bowl of the pipe.

'Is that so?' he said, without emotion. Then he glanced across at Sam who was finishing his cigarette and lighting another without looking at either it, or Mick, and he said, 'Why's that?' Sam did look at him then, surprised. The question hardly needed answering. When he didn't answer, Mick said, still in the same, pleasant conversational tone, 'Because your brother's dead?' He looked right at Sam when he said it, which Sam appreciated. Mick was the only person other than Jane who would meet his eyes when Terry was mentioned. 'I don't rightly see the connection,' said Mick.

Sam closed his eyes and drew on his cigarette. It was a connection he saw all too clearly and did not wish to elaborate. But Mick showed no sign of moving and eventually Sam said, 'Everything, all of it, was one step or another that led to where I am right now. If I hadn't started any of it, I wouldn't have ended up on that roadside with Terry.' He shook his head suddenly, sharply, and stubbed out the cigarette. 'I'm sick of it all. I want out.'

Mick nodded. He just sat, smoking his pipe, considering, until he said, 'Happen you've never thought, lad, but every step of all our lives only leads to t' grave. It's a one-way ticket we all get. There aren't any day returns on this line.'

'Some things hurry it all up a bit, don't they?' Sam demanded, suddenly bitter.

Mick was unriled. 'You mean like parties and fast cars?' He glanced across, gauging how far he could go. Sam was watching him again, his dark eyes intent and unreadable. 'Nay, lad, you put too much weight on that. It were Terry's time, that was all. It were Terry's time to die.'

'It wasn't,' Sam shouted, sitting up, 'I *made* it his time. Don't you see?' Mick thought a moment, and then stood up, still chomping on his pipe-stem. He turned away, looking for something else to tidy up. He said, almost under his breath, 'Heard ye were gettin' a pretty big man around here. Hadn't heard you were God, yet.' Sam stared at him, anger giving his face more animation than it had shown since Mick arrived. But he said nothing, flopping down on the sofa again and willing Mick, with all his being, to go away. Mick didn't. He plodded about, shifting things through to the kitchen. Sam heard the water running as he filled the sink and noisily washed up, one-handedly. He came back into the sitting-room and drew one of the curtains.

'Leave the bloody thing,' Sam shouted, and Mick, slightly cowed, left the rest. One bar of pure sunlight lit one corner of the room, celebrating the squalor mercilessly.

Mick picked up a half-empty bottle of Scotch lying on the floor half under a chair and said, with real disgust, 'Oh you're not *drinking*, for Christ's sake.'

Sam shook his head, feeling sheepish. He had tried that actually, and failed miserably. Drink had always been a light, spontaneous pleasure in his life; as an antidote to pain it had proved useless. He couldn't even get himself properly drunk.

Mick made another one of his passes of the room, like a minesweeper, gathering up crockery, old socks and litter. He picked up Sam's ashtray and the packet of Senior Service and laid them on the desk.

'Leave those.'

'If you want them, you can get up and get them.' Mick was standing in the middle of the room, the way Sam had seen him stand facing the sea that he hated, full of belligerence and perverse, unswerving courage. He looked like a small, tough tugboat that had just turned into the wind.

'Mick, get out of my flat.'

'In a moment. One more thing I came for.'

'Oh, what now?' Sam closed his eyes and put the backs of his hands across them, fighting to retain the unthinking grey mindlessness in which, in the dark, he could bear to live. Mick's presence was as jarring as the bright beam of summer sun he'd allowed into the flat, and disruptive as the shouts of children on their way to the shore, outside. Everyone was rushing him so, even the natural world hurried him forward against his will.

'One more bit of business,' said Mick.

'Jesus Christ,' Sam exploded, 'can't anyone leave me alone? Give me some time, for God's sake.'

'You've had a month.' A month. Four weeks in which to undo, unravel the ties of forty years.

'It's not enough.'

'It has to be enough. The world's not waitin' for ever. And neither am I. I'm handing in my notice.' There was silence. Sam sat up. He swung his feet down to the floor and turned, uncertainly, to face Mick.

'What?'

'You heard me. I'm givin' notice.'

'Mick? Now?' He looked so uncomprehendingly hurt that Mick almost weakened; but there was no point in that.

'Why not now? For all that's been done lately, you certainly don't need me. Anyhow, what do you care? You're pullin' out as well.'

Sam got slowly to his feet, looking confused and bewildered, and he said again, 'Wait, Mick. Please. Give me time.'

'You've had time. I'm done. Not stoppin' here, any road. It's like workin' in t' bluidy morgue.'

Sam hit him. Mick had pretty well gauged what was going to happen, and was already fading back out of the way, but the blow still sent him careening off balance, and crashing back into the desk. The time it took for him to

281

awkwardly disentangle himself from the chair and the tangled wire of the telephone was enough for Sam to absorb what he had done. He stopped in his tracks and stood frozen there, unable to believe he had actually struck a one-armed old man, even if only with the flat of his hand.

'Mick,' he whispered.

Of course, as one-armed old men went, Mick Raddley was on the tough side. He bounced back genially enough, and seemed more amused than anything, rubbing his jaw. And he had a jaw like an unshaven rhinoceros. Sam's whole hand stung.

Mick said, pleasantly, 'You know, there was a time I'd uv wiped the floor with a skinny weed like you. An if'n you fancy holding one arm behind your back, I'll do it just now. If that's what you're wantin'.' Sam still stood unmoving and shocked.

'I don't want to *fight* with you, Mick,' he whispered.

Mick shrugged. 'Then what *do* you want?' he said. Sam shook his head. He reached for the arm of the sofa behind him and sat down stiffly, like an old man. Mick, after a moment, lumbered across and sat beside him. He let the silence drag out, while Sam stared numbly into space. Then he said, 'I'm not pretending I can properly understand. I never had a twin. Never had anyone I was as close with as you an' Terry. But I had an older brother died at eighteen of TB. And a younger one, died uv the same thing, t' year after.' He paused as Sam turned to look at him, surprised.

'I never knew about that,' Sam said. As he said it he realized he knew almost nothing about Mick. He hardly even knew his wife; a shadowy figure behind a half-open early morning door, who more often than not he had regarded merely as an obstacle to the useful presence of Mick. He felt ashamed suddenly.

Mick was saying, 'Funny, you don't hear much about TB any more. Plenty uv it about, when I were a lad. Reckon it's this new National Health or summat.'

'Mick, forgive me.'

'Still an' all. That's life. What we can't change, we got to bear.'

'I'm so lost I don't know what I'm doing.'

Mick just nodded. He puffed at his pipe. 'Fancy a sail, lad?'

Sam stood alone on the deck of the *Mary Hardacre* as she ploughed her way, in a stiffening breeze and below a patchwork sky of thickening cumulus, through the choppy waters of the Dogger Bank. They were en route to Stavanger in Norway from her home port of Hull, with the hulk of a salvaged freighter in tow. He glanced back over his shoulder. The dead ship rode low, but well. The patches were holding. He looked forward again, and then turned to let his gaze follow the whole complete circle of the horizon, but for the stretch blocked off by the clumsy superstructure of the tug and the low lines of her charge. He smiled spontaneously, feeling the wet salt wind on his face, and the surprising brief warmth of a patch of sun, through which they were passing. There was no peace, he reflected, like the peace of the sea beyond all sight of land. He had forgotten his own ever-recurrent amazement at the encircling blue emptiness. Perhaps, he thought, with a remembered streak of darkness, if you took all the land off the face of the earth, there'd be no sorrow left. He put the thought away; he was winning, he knew, and it was sabotage.

They'd left Hull in the late afternoon and thus were enabled to enjoy now the delight of waking to this landless horizon. It should be an easy job. The *Mary Hardacre*, like any tug, was built for towing, and indeed spent most of her time doing precisely that. Towing was the bread and butter of salvage; she filled in the time between the drama of rescue and shipwreck with her steady series of contract tows. This one was more personal. The hulk behind them had been their own job. She was a small Norwegian freighter that had collided with a tanker off Spurn Head and capsized in shallow waters, in February. Sam had won the salvage contract and they had proceeded to right, then raise her. It had not been easy; the weather turned against them, and they'd had a difficult time getting her upright. Twice she had dragged along the bottom towards the salvage barge, slackening their winch lines uselessly over the A-frames fastened to her side. On the third attempt a cable had snapped, triggering off a rapid series of explosive partings as the strain shifted intolerably along the length of all thirteen frames. A young lad had been hurt badly by a recoiling two-inch hawser, and Sam had been shaken. No one he employed had yet been killed, but he knew it was a state of affairs, considering the nature of the work, that could not possibly last. He thought at the time of Ernest Cox, who had raised a goodly part of the scuttled German Fleet at Scapa Flow, working for seven years at it, and quitting with instant finality when he lost a man. Sam had wondered, while the lad in question was recovering in hospital, whether he mightn't do the same. He pushed the thought aside now, fighting to keep his mood light, remembering Pete Haines saying gruffly, 'Own bloody fault. Shoulda run faster.'

Pete was Master of the *Mary Hardacre*, and towing master as well; he had the experience from wartime, and the qualifications, which Mick Raddley lacked. Though Sam was personally certain that Mick could have taken the big tug anywhere and done anything with her. Still, she was no Keel boat. She was 125 feet long, and carried a crew of ten to tend to the needs of both tug and salvage gear. Her powerful diesels could haul several thousand tons of dead weight at eight knots through hearty seas, and do so willingly. Sam loved her, an affection Mick Raddley found comical. He turned now, seeing Mick approaching, his lumbering gait more appropriate now, on the rolling deck.

'Aye, aye,' Mick said. 'It's bluidy Wijsmuller.' Sam grinned.

'In time,' he said, 'in time.'

Wijsmuller of Holland were the acknowledged masters of long-distance towing, tramping the seas with a fleet of twelve tugs. Sam had no serious pretence of matching the established Dutch company, but it was something to aim at and tease Mick with. He had his eye already on another tug, or had done, before 8 May. He winced involuntarily, remembering, and the uncertainties of the last month descended like a flitting shadow of a gull, and passed over. He shrugged it off. Mick was watching him with his steady, wise old eyes.

'I owe it to my Aunt Jane,' Sam said suddenly, forcing another grin.

'What? Name a bloody tug after her? I'd think she'd be insulted. Nay lad. You just like collectin' things. Nowt but a jackdaw.'

Sam shook his head, 'Jackdaws like shiny things.' He kicked at the rust-stained deck of the *Mary Hardacre* with the toe of his tall seaboot, grinning.

'Oh, yer wantin' her shiny now?' Mick grumbled. 'Bluidy hell. I'll get out my toothbrush, and scrub her up.' Sam was looking back along the length of the tug, at the tow, riding easily behind. 'She okay, Mick?'

'Can't you judge for yerself?'

Sam shrugged, 'I think she's okay. I'd like your opinion.'

Mick took out his pipe, filling it. 'Reeght gradely lad. Nay bother.'

'I was wondering if we oughtn't to put a riding crew aboard to man the pumps,' Sam said. 'Just in case.'

'Don't trust your patches?' Mick grinned. Sam shrugged. The freighter had been holed in the collision, but they'd patched her thoroughly with concrete poured into wooden coffer dams. She seemed dry enough, and rode well. He wondered briefly about the weather getting up, but he was glad in a way that Pete had chosen to leave her unmanned. If they lost her which, with the strains always present on tow-lines, was always possible, he'd far rather be hunting through a gale for an empty ship, even if it meant her springing leaks and foundering, than be searching for a stranded crew on a powerless vessel. Pete said he lacked nerve, and he knew it was true. But it was hard to have nerve with other people's lives.

He looked out to sea. Responsibility, life and death, were as persistent as the gulls that followed their wake, mewing and crying like lost souls. The wind was rising slightly, and white horses splashed the incredibly blue sea. 'God, it's beautiful, Mick,' he said, smiling.

Mick grunted. 'You're damned well always thinkin' it's lookin' beautiful, just afore she's gonna blow like all hell.'

'Is it, Mick?' Sam said, almost dreamily, leaning on the rail and drinking in the astonishing peace of it.

Mick grunted again. 'Still in love wi' t'old whore. Thought you'd be over that. A course she's gonna blow. Look at t' lie uv yon bank.' He was pointing up ahead to a heavy scud of grey cloud settling nearer the water, with a white translucence beneath, between cloud and sea. Sam looked; acknowledged it looked like a storm and yet, despite the small fortune of scrap metal behind him, could not totally regret it. Sunlight broke out of the cloud, skidded across the wet deck of the tug, and was gone. He felt the wind begin to rise, and the first urgent scatterings of rain.

The sea got up at once, in response to the stiffening breeze, and the squall hit them quite suddenly. Sam went below for oilskins and came back on deck, thus protected against the weather. He went forward and stood again by the rail. The *Mary Hardacre* began to pitch and roll as a proper swell developed, and was crossed by fervent wind-driven chop. The rain came in heavily, and horizontally, and when he turned towards the towed ship she was barely visible through a thick grey sheet of water. Hail, mixed with rain, bounced off the surface of his oilskins and rattled on the deck. He drew his hat down closer and remained where he was, enjoying the feel of the tug bucking and rolling over the waves with powerful sureness. Sam had never been seasick in his life; an unexpected and unearned blessing for which he was singularly thankful.

At noon, the Shipping Forecast broadcast over the BBC promised them a gale. Mick grunted they already had one. They were watching the tow carefully now, when they could see her, that was. Sheets of rain lashed in between, and at times visibility was down to a matter of feet, and the only sign they had of their charge was the tow-line extending steadily out into grey nothingness. The rain cleared momentarily, and the freighter slipped into view, hunkered down low and steady, rising up and over each swell in their wake. She was in ballast for the tow and presented very little obstruction to the weather, being virtually a bare hull. Her superstructure had been so damaged by the pounding she took during the two months it took to raise her that there had been nothing for it but to cut all her top-hamper off, above the main deck. Still, ninety per cent of her value was in the hull itself, and that was what they had contracted to bring to the breaker's yard in Stavanger.

A huge swell rolled under the tug, just as Mick Raddley staggered out of the wheelhouse to join Sam, who had gone aft and stood now at the leeward rail, watching the tow-line. The swell rolled beneath their stern and rose mountainous between them, and the tow and the steel cable tightened visibly over the arch of its watery back.

'Aye, aye,' said Mick, around his pipe-stem. They held their breath. The line held, the swell receding behind them. The *Mary Hardacre* pitched up, riding the next. 'Do wi'out any more uv those,' muttered Mick. The tow-line was fastened hard to bitts on the bow of the freighter, but on the tug was held by a constant-tension winch, which was capable of taking up slack and easing the strain, but even that had its limits. The freighter was seaworthy enough, under tow, but cut loose she would be a dead hulk in the water, broaching sideways to the heavy swells and in danger of capsizing, even assuming her ballast didn't shift and her concrete patches, under siege then by the full force of the seas, did not fail.

The *Mary Hardacre* ploughed into another swell, so large that her bows momentarily buried, and a rush of seawater poured down her decks, swirling about their boots before pouring back over the sides. Spray cast up in sheets cleared her stack. The swell moved beneath, throwing up their stern, and passed between the two ships, and again the tow-line tightened. Sam heard, over the roar of wind and water, a distinct, low hum of straining steel. Two men were on the winch now, ready in an instant to retrieve the line, should it break. Sleet, pounding the decks, made of them yellow shadows in their streaming oilskins. White heaps of hailstones built up behind every protection, and Mick's grey windblown hair was iced with them. It was July, Sam reflected, with a whimsical vision of the soft green lawns and rose gardens of Hardacres flitting through his mind.

''Ere she goes,' Mick grunted, as another swell lifted them. But it was smaller, and the line held without trouble, and the two that followed were smaller still.

'We're making it,' Sam said.

'Shut up,' Mick growled. He had less time for superstition than any seaman Sam had ever known, but there were moments when even Mick Raddley was canny. 'Ah, ye damn fool,' he added in disgust, as the bow of the tug slammed into another green swell of tremendous proportions. The gale was whipping the top off it, and showering them with spray. 'Well, hang on,' Mick shouted grumpily, as if the swell was actually Sam's creation, and he wasn't sure it shouldn't be allowed to sweep him into the sea. Sam grabbed for the rail, and a wall of water hit them, making them both scrabble for footing, drenched in tumbling foam. They staggered to their feet as the *Mary Hardacre* plunged into the trough, and the tow rose up on the swell. The mountain of green water stood between them, blotting out the freighter, and the tow-line itself was momentarily engulfed. Sam heard again the sharp, electric hum of straining steel and then the line parted with a thundering crack, like cannon-shot.

'Down,' Mick howled, reaching for him, but Sam was going down already, and the two of them hit the wet deck side by side. Overhead there was an eerie, airy shriek as the broken end of hawser whipped back in release, slicing through the air a foot above the rail at which they had stood. There was a ringing clash of metal as it struck the side of the wheelhouse and a tinkling of falling glass from a shattered port. Then it thudded heavily on to the stern rail like a sullen snake, and slithered off into the sea.

'Haul 'er,' Mick was shouting, already on his feet, but the winchmen, rising from their own bits of sheltering deck, were sprinting for their machinery already. They knew, as much as anyone, that the loose end of cable swirling into the sea could foul their propeller in an instant and leave them as helpless as the freighter in mountainous seas. The winch rumbled and hummed, barely audible above the wind, and the tug plunged forward yet, to keep the line outstretched behind. Its frayed and shattered end whipped up, dripping, on to the after deck. Mick signalled the wheelhouse and Pete Haines slowed the tug and brought her round in a lumbering circle, turning her blunt prow down wind, in search of her renegade charge.

It took a full half-hour just to find her. The search was visual; they lacked radar, and the visibility in the shifting sheets of rain and sleet was virtually nil. They had gone on some distance, while retrieving their tow-line, and even the manoeuvrable tug took a wide circuit of sea in which to turn. The freighter, when they sought the shortened horizon for her at last, was nowhere in sight. As they circled, bouncing and plunging across huge seas, Sam went around his crew, checking no one had been hurt by the broken cable and finding to his relief that they'd all run fast enough this time. The damage to the *Mary Hardacre* was cosmetic, a missing railing or two, a ten-foot scraping of her paint, and the broken port. They had been lucky, he knew, and he said nothing to Mick or anyone, grown at the moment as superstitious as all the rest. He was forward again, at the prow of the tug, when he saw her.

'There she is,' he shouted to Mick, three feet away, to be heard over the gale. Mick looked over his pointing arm and at first saw nothing. Then he grunted, nodded, and said, 'You've got good eyes, any road,' as if that were maybe Sam's sole contribution to the whole procedure so far. In a way it was. It was his tug, his salvage company, and his lost freighter out there, but he was still, at least in Mick's eyes, an amateur along for the ride. He didn't resent it, acknowledging it as true enough, though he had an itchy longing to prove himself to Mick, somehow. He wasn't likely to get the opportunity just now. The tow was in trouble, and there was no time for amateurs to play. The professionals, Mick, Pete, and the rest had their work cut out as it was.

They'd found the freighter now; but the question was, what were they going to do with her. As they approached, they found her lying, as they expected, dead in the water and broadside to the pounding waves. She rolled heavily with each strike, and though the heavy mist of blowing rain made it hard to see her clearly, Sam felt she was listing, if slightly, to port. Her ballast had shifted, perhaps, in her helpless state, or she'd begun to take on water from the patched hole in her port forward quarter. As they watched, a heavy sea took her, rolling her right over forty degrees, and she came up sluggish, her decks streaming. They'd need to get her into the wind, fast, and that meant getting her under tow.

The normal procedure, not easy in the best of conditions, and difficult in heavy weather, was to shoot a light pilot line aboard with their Lyle gun, and bend increasingly heavier manilas, and then steel cables to that. But that all presupposed that there was someone aboard the disabled ship to take the line. And there wasn't. Sam still only half-regretted the lack of riding-crew. They'd have been there now to take his line, but the unsteady look of the wallowing hulk made him more than half-glad he had no one aboard. They might not have found her, after all.

'We'll have to let the wind drop, afore we can board,' Mick said at his elbow, looking with a practised, anxious eye at the tumultuous sky. Sam nodded, wondering if it would. They circled the floundering freighter, looking for the lowest point, and then stood off and waited, praying for a break in the weather. It was squally, with luck it would give them a chance. Late in the afternoon the steady north-east gale backed slightly to north, and then north-west, and slowly moderated. The sky was no lighter, the rain only slightly lessened; it would be a brief respite, but the best they were likely to get. Pete brought the *Mary Hardacre* to windward of the hulk, and closed her bow in facing the bow of the freighter. At the stern, they lowered the dinghy, with a boarding party of five. Mick was at the tiller and he let Sam ride along, probably more because there wasn't time to argue than any other reason. They had grappling hooks and lines for scrambling up the side, and a heaving line of manila to lead in their cable. Mick headed the little boat into the wind and sent her plunging through the huge seas like a chip of wood. She skipped about and slid sideways, but he held her as steady as he could and brought her in as close as he dared. Above them, the side of the stranded freighter was huge and black, and their little boat was tossed a dozen feet up and plunged the same distance down with each swell.

'Now,' Mick shouted. One of the crewmen, a young Whitby lad called Kevin Hawes, stood, balancing on the lee rail, and swung the grapple once around his head and flung it. The dinghy dipped as he did so and the grapple clattered against the side of the freighter and tumbled into the sea. Kevin Hawes jerked it back and tried again. Sam took up the other grapple. This was something he could do; he was tall, and athletic. He swung the grapple and flung it, the manila whipping through his hands. It went over the freighter's rail, and he pulled it tight at once, feeling the hook slithering across metal and catching fast.

'Good,' Mick shouted. Then a heavy sea caught the freighter and dinghy, and they heeled over, nearly capsizing, their rail crunching to bits against the huge bulk of the dead ship. The rope whipped from Sam's hands. Mick revved his engine and scudded her away to safety. Sam picked himself up from the bilges, where the sudden roll of the dinghy had flung him, and looked back. Through the rain he could see the grapple still holding, and the boarding rope blowing uselessly free against the side of the ship.

'Go in again, we'll try the other hook,' Sam said.

Mick shook his head. 'She's getting up again.' The rain was slashing down so hard once more that the two men could barely see each other at opposite ends of the small boat.

'Once more, Mick. I'll get on her this time.'

Mick grinned, through the hail. 'No, sir.' He turned the prow of the dinghy back to the waiting tug; the dinghy might be just a little ship, but he was its master, no matter who owned her.

Soaked and exhausted, they climbed back aboard the *Mary Hardacre*, and glowered back across the gap of roiling sea that separated them from their tow. The afternoon was darkening; evening was coming on. There were many hours of daylight left in the long summer evenings of the North Sea, but the storm was bringing a darkness of its own. It was settling in for a night-long blow, the wind veering north-east again, and quickening as the light faded. They'd not launch their boat again before morning.

'She's listing, Mick,' Sam said, peering out into the horizontal sheets of hail. 'She'll go over.'

'Happen she will,' Mick said, chomping on his pipe-stem. 'Bugger eff-all we can do about it now.' It wasn't his first job to go wrong; nor would it be his last. Not unless he launched that bottle-cap of a boat again. He softened a little. 'Let her go, lad. She's just a hunk uv scrap iron.'

'Let's give it one more try,' Sam said. 'Before the light goes.'

'More sea now than there ever was. She'll flip that chip uv wood afore we get half-way.'

'I don't mean with the boat, Mick,' Sam said. He was still peering into the storm studying the height of the freighter's rail with careful intensity. Mick looked at him warily.

'What's on your mind?' he asked, with a canny narrowing of his salt-reddened eyes. Sam still studied the freighter, watching where her now-heavy list to port had brought her lee rail down near the crest of the rolling white-splashed waves.

'How close can Pete bring her in?' he asked, not taking his eyes from the freighter. Mick shrugged, water splashing from the shoulders of his oilskins as he did.

'Close as ye like, happen ye don't mind bumping into her. Mind, that's what she's built for.' He gestured to the padded prow of the tug. 'Long as we don't do it too hard, or get caught by a sea and smash our stern up against her, lose t'bluidy rudder.' Sam nodded. That wouldn't be fun, he knew.

'Ask him to do it,' said Sam.

'Just fer t'fun?' Mick asked, his bushy eyebrows raising slightly. Sam grinned.

'Give me a heaving line, up forrard,' he said. 'I'm going to jump it.' Mick just laughed, a big sound in the heavy wind.

'Oh no you're not,' he said.

'She's so low in the water now, I'll be jumping down. No problem Mick. I can do it.'

'Happen you could. Happen you couldn't as well. Eitherwise, you're not finding out.' But Sam was already making his way forward with a length of manila over his shoulder. Mick followed him. The young Whitby man, Kevin, watched curiously as Sam, his eyes hardly leaving the freighter, positioned his line by a forward bollard.

'What ye doin', Mr Hardacre?' Kevin Hawes asked.

'Nothing,' Mick snapped, from behind Sam's shoulder, but as Sam turned to explain, he caught sight of Pete Haines, down from the wheelhouse, making his way across the rain-swept deck.

'What's up?' he asked, eyeing the rope, and before Mick, who was occupied in discouraging Kevin Hawes from volunteering to join Sam, could intervene, he spoke quickly.

'Look, Pete,' pointing to the lowering port rail of the freighter, 'I've got to get aboard and get the pumps running if nothing else. I want you to bring her right in by that rail, just for a moment, and I'm going across with this line. There's a snatchblock on the bow, by the shed,' he pointed to the small wooden and sheet-tin construction that they had used as a shelter on the open deck while they were cutting away the superstructure. 'You bend a bight of manila on the end of this, as soon as I'm across, and I'll put it through the block, so we can use our own capstan to haul the cable across.' He might very well jump alone with the light rope, but there was no way he was going to haul cable aboard by hand. It weighed five pounds a running foot. The freighter was powerless, of course, though below decks they had left three portable petrol-driven pumps.

Pete, unlike Mick, listened carefully, and actually looked at the lowered deck of the freighter as he did so. He said, 'Risky jump.'

'Risky?' Sam grinned, raising one dark eyebrow. 'For the long-jump champion of Beaumont School, 1935? Surely you jest?' He was laughing.

Pete didn't laugh. He said, 'That was a long time ago. And I doubt they chucked you between two steel hulls in t' North Sea, when ye missed.'

'I won't miss,' Sam said, gathering his manila line in careful loops. He was confident. He knew his abilities, and his limitations. It was the corollary to what Pete had called lack of nerve. When he was unsure of things he left them alone. When he was certain, he had all the nerve in the world.

'Okay,' Pete nodded curtly. He was worried and showed it by quiet and lack of humour, the way Mick showed it by fuming and storming. But Pete, not Mick, was the Master of the *Mary Hardacre*, and it was his word, only, that was law. Mick gave Pete a filthy look but he said nothing. Instead, he gathered up the end of Sam's heaving line. Its tending was crucial. If it snagged, or caught, or simply dragged, it would break Sam's jump and pull him into the sea. Mick, even with his artificial arm, was the best hand with a rope around, and he wasn't trusting it to anyone else. Pete went back to the wheelhouse and the tug lurched into her new course, bearing down on the wallowing freighter. Sam shed his oilskins, too cumbersome to jump in, and climbed up on the rail, and as he did so Kevin Hawes did the same and scrambled up beside him.

'Get out t' way,' Mick grumbled, but Kevin said, coolly, 'I'll jump wi' ye, Mr Hardacre. Ye'll need a hand with t' cable.' Sam looked across. The lad was eighteen, long-legged and fit. He'd probably make a better job of it than he'd do himself. He grinned.

'Okay.'

'Oh, gradely,' Mick grumbled. 'Two idiots. Ye stay clear uv the line,' he shouted to Kevin, 'or ye'll both end up in t' drink.' Kevin nodded, unimpressed by Mick's temper, and moved a foot or two down the rail, to give Sam and his line more room. The freighter loomed up near, rain half-obscuring her yet. Sam glanced down at the white curl of

295

their bow-wave, foaming back through broken seas. The black gap between the two ships narrowed, and seemed to deepen as it did.

'What t' hell do I tell yer bleedin' family?' Mick shouted. The gap narrowed to nothingness, the rail of the crippled freighter skimming by with astonishing speed below. Sam waited for the moment when he felt the tug's engines go hard astern, and the whole vessel lurch as Pete, with stunning skill, sent her just skidding by, with a narrowing ten feet to spare. Ten feet across, ten down, and closing.

'Tell them it's all in my will,' Sam shouted back to Mick, and he jumped.

Brushes with death are notorious for their mental irrelevancies: the only thing in Sam's mind as he launched himself over the terrifying, narrowing black gap between the two ships was the sudden quixotic question, *would* the immediate inheritance of all his worldly wealth at last cure the daunting financial pains of Hardacres? Then his foot struck the rail, breaking his jump and throwing his balance out. He twisted in mid-air, flailing with his free hand, throwing himself forward, clear of the rail. He made it, barely, but landed all wrong, hard and awkwardly on his back and shoulder on the sloping wet deck. Still, years of Rugby at Cambridge and then at Ampleforth had at least taught him how to fall. He rolled over, frantically loosing the rope coils from his shoulder as he did so. If Mick failed to play the rope out fast enough, it would take him back into the sea. The deck of the freighter lurched as she rolled into her list, and he slid down it, grabbing for holds, trying to regain his footing. Beside him, he saw the eighteen-year-old Kevin, already on his feet, running to take up the rope. As Sam had thought, he'd jumped better and landed better. Sam got his footing, staggered down the pitching deck, and snagged the manila once round a bitt, letting it run out as smoothly as he could towards the departing tug. He could hear, over the wind, the roar of her engines, yet hard astern, as Pete tried desperately to slow her before she drew the rope to its limits and snapped it, undoing half their purpose. He and Kevin braced their feet against the railing, lying back on the deck which rolled to an angle of forty-five degrees before lumbering back to its list of twenty, and both fought to slow the flying manila as it played out through their burned hands. They had ten feet of bitter end left when it stopped. The rope slackened. The *Mary Hardacre* stood off, holding steady in the water. Sam got shakily to his feet and the lad Kevin bounced up beside him.

'Got the bugger,' Kevin exulted.

'Shut up,' said Sam, filling in for the absent Mick. He signalled to Mick with a wave of his arm, and saw the old one-armed fisherman set about securing their pilot line to a bight, or loop, of heavy manila, the lead-in for the cable. Together, in the driving rain, he and Kevin drew the loop across from the tug, over the roiling gap of darkening sea. The rain was heavier than ever and without the oilskins they were getting very wet indeed, but were too busy to feel the cold. When they had the bight of three-inch manila aboard, they hauled it across to the snatchblock at the bow, where Sam raised the hinged side of the iron sheets that held the pulley and they eased the loop into place. Again he signalled to Mick through the sheets of rain, and distantly heard the powered capstan start up and saw the double lines go taut. Mick would have run the manila through it and fastened the free end to the heavy U-shackle of the towing cable. They watched, huddled against the slight shelter of their work-shack on the bow, as the manila dragged the cable across the gap of water. The freighter rolled again, heavily, and seemed to regain less of her trim as she righted. She was listing worse with every swell, and Sam was desperate to get below and get her pumps running, and willed the cable to reach them faster. But there was no way the job could be hurried.

The cable thudded over the railing, flopping heavily on to

the deck, pulling up tight against the snatchblock. Sam signalled Mick again, and the capstan ceased turning. He and Kevin released the heavy hawser from the manila lead-in and wrestled its icy steel length towards the bitts at the bow of the freighter. It was immensely heavy, and they were both now very wet and very tired. Sam seriously doubted for a moment they could do it. The slanting deck of the freighter made their progress virtually a climb, and he felt his strength failing. But the youngster Kevin was tough, and heartily determined, and between the two of them they managed at last to make the cable fast to a forward bitt. For a moment they just sagged across it grinning at each other, and then Sam straightened up and made his final signal to Mick. He and Kevin got back out of the way. They'd broken one hawser on this tow already and, although this was a heavier one, the sea was heavier too. They went well aft, and watched the *Mary Hardacre* turn her nose north-east and take up the slack.

The cable rose, tautened, and held. The bow of the wallowing freighter came round into the weather and she quivered below them, if not with life, at least with purpose. She was again under tow, no longer mere flotsam on the sea. She still rolled with each wave and still listed, and after a moment more watching the steady length of hawser, Sam tapped Kevin Hawes on the shoulder and led him below.

The damage below was no worse than he expected. He was relieved to find the concrete patch holding, though two lesser holes, patched temporarily with steel, had been battered enough to let water in, and no doubt other damage of the original collision was showing up under the strain. Three of her holds were partially flooded, explaining the list. He and Kevin manhandled the pumps into position and with difficulty got two of them running. The third proved recalcitrant, and eventually they were obliged to give up with it. The two remaining chugged away faithfully, sucking up hundreds of gallons of water and cascading it over the side. By midnight she had righted to a mere ten-degree list to port and was riding easily, once more, under tow.

Sam and Kevin were back on her empty, spray-swept deck. Ahead, the lights of the *Mary Hardacre* were steady and reassuring, and in the dim summer light of the far north Sam could just make out the tow-line joining them across the sea. The gale was lessening, he felt, if only slightly, and the rain had, for the moment, ceased. It was colder though, as high pressure built up in their corner of the North Sea.

'Bloody freezing,' Kevin said, huddling into his woollen seaman's jacket. Sam nodded. Other than woollen jumpers and jackets they had no protection against the weather, and even below working with the pumps they had hardly managed to dry out.

'We'll get some shelter in the shack,' he said. Kevin looked mournfully at the so near and so unreachable lights of the tug. 'Aye,' he said, wearily.

'They'll get us off in the morning,' Sam said. 'The wind's dropping.' He wasn't sure it was, or that they would, actually, but felt Kevin needed cheering up. With luck they'd be able to launch their dinghy again some time the next day. One thing was for certain; they weren't going back the way they came on.

They found a couple of tarpaulins in the shack, and unfolded them, wrapping the uncomfortable stiff canvas lengths around themselves for warmth, and huddled in the shelter of the little structure, watching out through its open doorway at the tow-line and the lights. If they lost each other in the night, Sam wanted to know about it, though no doubt the recoiling hawser would remind them. And if they did part company, he was well aware there was nothing at all that he could do. Still, he watched. Kevin dozed beside him, waking up with sudden starts, nervous and uneasy. Sam realized that there were different kinds of nerve. At eighteen, challenge was everything. Kevin had jumped the six feet of ferocious sea without a thought. But the slow patience of the long, dangerous night; that kind of nerve came with age. The jump hadn't worried Sam either, at the time. His own confidence had carried him. Now, looking back, the dark chasm of water and the speeding weight of the *Mary Hardacre*'s hull came back to haunt him.

He shrugged into the tarpaulin, shivering, not choosing to think, and wishing he had a cigarette. The freighter lurched over a heavy swell, and the line tautened. Sam watched it, tense, waiting for the low hum that preceded danger, but it eased off, and the freighter ploughed forward. Kevin woke, grabbing the side of the shed, 'What was that?'

'Nothing. A swell.'

Kevin peered out into the dim light, at the tow-line. 'What if she breaks, Mr Hardacre?'

'We'll put another on,' Sam said, hoping Kevin wasn't going to ask how.

The youngster nodded, sleepily. 'D'ye think we ought to check t' patch?' he said.

'I did. Half an hour ago.'

'What if it goes?'

'It won't,' Sam said, with new confidence in his work.

'But what if it does? She'll roll right over, won't she?'

'Then we'll swim,' Sam said. 'Go to sleep. I'll wake you if she sinks.' Kevin grinned nervously, but in another moment he was snoring, leaning against the wall of the shed. Outside, dim night turned to grey, early, three-in-the-morning dawn. Sam thought of Scotland and summer mornings in Strathconon, fishing with Terry. He instinctively thrust the thought aside, but then, experimentally, allowed it room in his mind. He felt he was walking out on to thin ice on frozen water, feeling his way. The ice held.

It was midday before the weather cleared enough to allow Pete to send the dinghy across with a relief boarding party, and take Sam and Kevin back to the tug. By that time he felt he had seen more of the freighter than he ever wanted to see of any freighter again. Grey clouds still scudded across a white sky, but the wind was lessening all the while. A patch of blue broke free as they crossed to the *Mary Hardacre* and sun splashed them momentarily. It was hard to believe that only a day had passed since he had stood at the rail, with Mick, enjoying the sea.

They sat in the wheelhouse as the tow got underway again. Pete handed him coffee that seemed to be literally half rum, and gave Kevin the same. He was so cold he could not stop shaking. Mick came in and threw a blanket at him, which he caught gratefully and wrapped around his shoulders. Kevin finished his coffee and lay down on a bench and went instantly to sleep. But Sam sat, sipping the hot liquid and luxuriating in returning warmth, and feeling inordinately pleased with himself.

'You look like t' bluidy Cheshire cat,' Mick grumbled. Sam said nothing, leaning his head back against the cabin side still smiling. His eyes kept closing, but he stayed awake.

'Proud uv yerself?' Mick said.

'Yes.'

'Shouldn't be. Yer a bluidy fool. Happen you didn't notice, but you nearly got killed out there. It were stupid. Lump uv scrap metal ain't worth a life.'

Sam only smiled. He'd never felt in real danger. He knew he could do it. He said, 'Risking our lives for lumps of scrap metal is what the job's about. You and Pete do it all the time.'

Mick grunted. 'Ye'd never catch me doing a thing like that. Or Pete.' Pete, at the wheel, said nothing.

'Ah, you're just getting old, Mick,' Sam teased.

Mick growled, but Pete, letting his eyes rove just a moment from the sea ahead of the *Mary Hardacre*'s blunt, hessian-padded prow, said suddenly, 'Let me tell you something. Young salvage men do things like that. Old salvage men don't do things like that. That's how they get to be old salvage men.' He nodded briefly towards Sam with a look of knowing authority, and returned his eyes to the sea. Sam thought, momentarily, of the hungry black water beneath the rail of the freighter and shivered as much from memory as from the cold. He felt sleep closing in, but fought it, savouring the incalculable relief that the remembrance of fear brought to him. Death, that for so many weeks had appeared his only friend, had taken its rightful place as his enemy once again. The whole night was worth that.

He got up, went below and fell across a bunk. When he awoke they were in Norway.

CHAPTER
EIGHTEEN

From Hull, Sam drove directly to Hardacres rather than returning home to his flat in Bridlington. He had been nine days away in all, and in his new peace of mind he was suddenly aware again of duty to family. He could hardly credit, much less justify, that he had actually gone off by sea to Norway without telling anyone where he was going or when he'd be back. He wanted to see his mother and offer her the comfort he had failed to offer her before, and to see Harry and reassure him. That they had worried about him was something he could not have failed to realize, but until now he had been unable to care.

He was driving one of their lorries, a big grey monster of a thing, which he had liberated in rather cavalier fashion at the dockside in Hull, leaving a grumbling Mick and Pete to make their way back crammed into the other with half the crew. He had as yet no car of his own, and had not even considered replacing or repairing the Jaguar. He simply did not wish to see it and doubted he'd ever feel differently. It was dark when he made the Driffield road, but as he approached the black iron gates of Hardacres, which had stood open so long that he had always rather doubted they'd move, he was amazed to see them not only shut but padlocked and, more shockingly, firmly defended by two officers of the law. A police vehicle and several other cars were parked awkwardly along the narrow roadway. For an instant, the sight of the cluster of hurriedly parked vehicles, and the turning blue light, brought back wrenching memories of the accident, and he found his hands suddenly shaky on the wheel of the big lorry. But the moment passed and, with it, the nerves. There was something reassuringly casual about the stance of the constables at the gate, one of whom was chatting with a man in a trench coat. And the small crowd of onlookers, mostly men, mostly dressed the same as the constable's companion, in trench coats, against the light July rain, had nothing of the grim air of the scene of a tragedy.

Sam slowed the lorry and brought it to a halt in front of the gate, and sat staring. One of the constables straightened up from his comfortable slouch against the wrought iron and strolled across to Sam. Sam lowered the window with difficulty; the lorry was not in pristine condition.

'Can I help you, mate?'

'Yes, please,' Sam said, glancing at the gate. 'I'd like to get in, for a start.'

'Sorry mate, no chance.'

'What?' Sam only half-smiled; he was tired, and it was late and, whatever was going on, he didn't really feel like being delayed. 'What's happened?' he said then, getting concerned again. 'Has there been an accident?'

'Nothing to worry about, mate. Just a private family matter. You just move along now, and come back tomorrow.' The constable stepped back authoritatively, and gave him a businesslike wave down the road.

'Now wait just a damned minute,' Sam said, feeling his already frayed patience thinning. The journey back from Norway had not been much easier than the one across. Granted, they were free of the cumbersome tow, safely delivered to the breaker's yard in Stavanger. But the *Mary Hardacre* had got fussy, her diesels giving them trouble, and he'd spent a lot of the voyage below, struggling with recalcitrant engines. Once back in their home port, he'd been engaged for most of the afternoon, side by side with Mick and Pete, covered in oil and grime, trying to sort a persistent and intermittent fault. On top of that, the weather had been as unkind for their return as for the outward journey, and he had found to his annoyance that he could not seem to get warm again after the night on the freighter. His shoulder and back still ached from the fall he had taken on her deck, and whereas his young companion Kevin Hawes was, within half a day, totally back to normal, Sam was obliged to admit that he was not. For the first time the fact that he was nearly forty seemed significant and the thought did not please him. Now he was tired, dirty, cold and hungry and wanting very much to be sitting by the fireside in Harry's library with a large whisky. 'Just open the gates,' he said, struggling to remain cool before an officer of the law, 'and we'll leave it at that.'

The constable eyed him gravely, and his companion ambled over to join him. They stood shoulder to shoulder, and the crowd of men in trench coats perked up like a flock of sheep about to be fed. Sam realized suddenly they were journalists; recognizing one as the representative of the local *Chronicle*. He could not imagine what they were doing here, and didn't particularly care.

The second constable said, to his companion, 'Having trouble?'

'Gentleman wishes to go in,' said the first, formally.

'Sorry, sir, no one gets in tonight,' the second said politely. 'Nothing I can do. Orders.' He was obviously the team diplomat.

'Damn your orders,' Sam said. 'I live here. Now undo the gate and let me in.'

'Gentleman says he lives here,' said the diplomat to the other, in spite of the fact that they were standing side by side, just outside the door of Sam's lorry. The first constable, big and beefy with a look of real Yorkshire malevolence about his small eyes, said, carefully surveying Sam's lorry, and then Sam, 'Lives here, does he?' his voice ringing with incredulity.

'Yes,' Sam said, his own voice rising. 'I don't know or care what all this is about, but I'd very much like to go home.'

'Your name, sir?' said the diplomat.

'Hardacre.'

'Like the house?' said the diplomat, writing something down.

'Like the house,' said Sam.

'Hmm,' said the diplomat. He withdrew to the iron gate and stood talking with his companion. They both returned to the lorry. 'Would you mind stepping down, sir?' the diplomat said.

'Yes, I would mind. And in half a minute you'd better get all those people away from the gates of my house because I'm going to drive this lorry right through them.' The officers stared. Sam was a little chagrined. He hadn't meant to sound so vehement, but the tiredness was getting the better of him. 'Look,' he said, opening his door, and swinging down from the high seat, 'my name is Sam Hardacre. My great-uncle is Harry Hardacre, who lives in that house with my mother.'

'Your mother is Mrs Hardacre?' the officer said. Sam noticed one of the trench-coated gentlemen writing busily. 'Yes,' he said sharply. 'My mother is Mrs Hardacre.' It was true in its own way. He stood glaring at the gate, wishing someone from the damned house would get down here, explain everything, and let him in.

'Could we have some identification, sir?'

Sam looked blank. He said, 'Yes, of course,' and then remembered he had nothing remotely resembling identification on him. He was wearing worn and oil-stained dungarees, a torn navy pullover, and his navy seaman's jacket. His passport was on the *Mary Hardacre* and his driving licence was in his flat in Bridlington. If pressed, he wouldn't be able to prove ownership of the lorry, even, in spite of the fact that his name was written across the side. He shrugged and grinned suddenly, in exasperation. 'No, I'm afraid you can't,' he said. The constables studied him. The grin had softened them, but not enough. They were at an impasse and Sam suddenly realized that they really were not going to let him in, and he was genuinely going to be obliged to leave, either to find a telephone and ring the house and find out what was going on, or drive back to Bridlington through the night.

'Could you kindly tell me,' he said, controlling the tremendous urge to leap back in the cab and drive right through the locked gates, 'on whose orders you're keeping people out?'

But before they could reply, a man broke off his conversation among the cluster of onlookers in trench coats and made his way over to the lorry. It was the one Sam had recognized as a reporter from the *Chronicle*. He looked at the lorry, and at Sam and he said, suddenly, 'You're Sam Hardacre, aren't you?' Sam nodded. He had not met the man before, though he'd seen him about. The two constables looked up from their notepads.

'Can you identify the gentleman?' one asked rather eagerly, as if he wanted a way out of this now, too.

'Aye, I can that. Yon's old Joe Hardacre's grandson. You must be new in these parts, or ye'd know him.' Sam looked at the officers, who exchanged a glance and went off to the gates and began unshackling them.

'Thank you,' he said to the reporter, an elderly man with thinning grey hair and sharp, shrewd eyes. 'But I don't know you, do I?'

'Nay, lad, nor I you. But I knew your great-grandad. And old Joe. Figured anyone around here talkin' posh and dressed like a tink is bound t' be a Hardacre. Queer lot, t' bunch uv ye. Figured you needed helpin' out.'

'Thanks,' Sam said again. 'I really am who I said,' he added, as reassurance.

The old man nodded as Sam climbed back into the lorry. He watched solemnly, and then said, 'Damned sorry about your brother, Sam.'

Sam nodded, acknowledging the kindness, and put the

lorry into gear. A reporter of course; naturally he would know. He drove through the gates hurriedly, lest anyone else try to stop him, and because he did not want any other stranger to speak to him about Terry. Grief did not cure in a moment's revelation like in films or books. It took a damned long time.

The house was lit from one end to the other as he approached it through the beech wood. It looked beautiful, as if a wonderful party was going on inside and he felt a sudden surprising wave of emotion for it, his childhood home. He parked the lorry off to the side of the house by the empty conservatory, because the semi-circle of gravel above the balustrade and stone steps leading to the lawns was already packed with vehicles, some family, some he did not recognize. He climbed down from the cab, stiff and aching from the long day and the drive in the uncomfortable vehicle, and made his way round to the front door. It was shut, even the big heavy outer door that they never shut but, as he reached it, that was flung open and light spilled out on to the gravel. Someone had heard the lorry approach. Sam stepped into the light spill and Noel suddenly appeared, his grey hair wild and his face animated by real fury.

'Just get the hell out, whoever . . .'

'Noel? What?'

'Oh, it's you.' Noel's anger faded to his ordinary glower, touched slightly with surprise. 'How'd you manage to get in?' he asked curiously.

'With difficulty,' Sam said. On the drive up he had reflected that only his public school accent had got him through those gates. The thought had amused him; his great-grandfather who founded the whole line would have been locked out by his 'thees' and 'thous' and be standing there yet. 'Would you mind telling me what's going on?'

'All bluidy hell's going on,' said Noel, turning his back and stamping unhelpfully off into the house interior. Sam was left to follow, lightly shutting the door behind him. As he crossed the main hall, he heard Harry's voice, suddenly old and quavery, he thought, asking who was there.

'It's t' bluidy prodigal,' Noel's voice, sour-tempered, returned, and Sam heard his uncle's old, limping footsteps making hurriedly across the floor to greet him.

'Sam,' Harry said as they met in the doorway, his voice tinged equally with warmth and tension, as if he never knew what Sam was about to do next. They, all of them, had addressed him that way since Terry's death. 'I had no idea. I am so sorry. Did they stop you? Oh, I do hope they didn't give you trouble.'

'No trouble, Uncle Harry, no trouble,' Sam said, smiling, embracing his uncle with both arms and realizing with a start that the old man had shrunk somehow and seemed barely to reach above his chin. He rested his cheek briefly against the grey thin hair, and caught sight of his mother, across the room, watching him with uncertain hope. She, too, seemed years older than he recalled her, and he was aware that he had not seen either of them clearly since the accident. Its effect on all the family was written on the cluster of faces in the drawing-room, and he yearned to ease their mutual pain. He extended one free arm to Madelene and she ran sobbing across the room to him. He held them both, two old people, like two children in his arms.

When he released them, he looked carefully around and saw to his amazement that not only were Noel, Vanessa and Rodney present, but both the Bartons, all three of their children, Mary Gray, and Albert and Maud Chandler. Only Jane was absent, and for a moment he had a horrifying fear that the gathering, so like the funeral party of six weeks ago, was for an equally dire cause. But then, like a jester sent to amuse a royal court, a small dapper figure appeared who by no means would have any place in a gathering of family sorrow.

'Bernie?' Sam said, unbelieving.

'I remember you. You were the wise guy in Janet's

bedroom,' said the little man. 'Do me a favour, don't try any of that stuff again, please.' The entire company, jarred suddenly out of their concern for Sam, turned to face him, visibly wondering what that was about.

Sam said, 'What the bloody hell is going on?' He glanced instinctively towards his mother the next instant, and apologized.

Albert Chandler stepped forward. He looked excruciatingly uncomfortable. He said, 'Sam, had I any idea you would be here, I would never have allowed this to occur.'

Sam shook his head impatiently. He raised his hands in a gesture of placation and said, 'Look, everyone, please. I'm all right. I'm fine. I've just been away, working, and I'm fine. You're all terribly kind, but it isn't necessary. But will you please tell me what's happening?'

'*I'll* tell you,' Noel said. He alone of all the family had shown no great concern for Sam's feelings, and he had treated Terry's death like he treated all death, the natural summation of the rather raw deal he regarded life to be in the first place. He said, 'What's happening is that her Royal Bleedin' Highness is throwing a royal fit up in t' master bedroom and her loyal toadies are all tearing their hair out in sympathy.' Noel slammed down his tankard, from which he had been heartily drinking brown ale, and stalked out. 'Ye can all call me for t' bluidy curtain,' he announced, disgusted, as he slammed the drawing-room door.

Sam watched, mystified, and his Aunt Maud approached tentatively, touching his arm. 'Sam, I'm terribly sorry about this. My daughter . . . Janet . . . agreed to some publicity photographs at the house. It was all rather sudden. Naturally Harry arranged a family dinner . . .' she trailed off, and Sam nodded, remembering the crowd of reporters at the gate.

'Those people,' he said, gesturing behind himself towards the door and beyond, 'is that why they're here?'

'Miss Chandler has an immense following,' Bernie put in, remembering his job.

'I gather,' said Sam, drily. He was feeling more than a little resentful as well as bemused. Albert Chandler cast a miserable glance towards the hallway, and the main stairs.

'I'm sure in a moment or two . . .'

'Do you think perhaps she isn't happy in the room . . .' Harry ventured. 'There are others. Only, it is the biggest . . .'

'I'm sure she'll be all right,' Maud comforted Harry. 'The journey was wearing,' she added doubtfully, as if she didn't believe much of what she was saying.

'I wouldn't have planned the dinner had I known,' Harry apologized. 'Oh dear, I've made a mess of it, haven't I?' He looked plaintively for Madelene, who took his arm. Sam looked around the room, carefully, his resentment turning to anger.

Albert Chandler, his tall dignified form still elegant in his shabby evening dress, looking humiliated and weary, as any parent whose offspring was causing difficulties beyond his control, said, 'No, Harry, it's our fault. You've done your best. It's all just unfortunate, that's all.'

Bernie hopped around pouring people drinks and soothing everyone in sight. He turned briefly to Sam, who still stood in the centre of the room, his dungarees and oily jacket in stark contrast to the rest in their dinner-suits and long gowns.

'Miss Chandler, she's very high-strung. She's very tired,' he shrugged. 'You know.'

'Yes,' Sam said coolly, yet eyeing his embarrassed family, 'I know. You mean she's drunk.' There was a silence. Nobody would reprimand him; they were still a little afraid of his recent grief in spite of his reassurances. But they all slowly stopped talking, and stared. Bernie, like an agitated penguin in his dinner-suit, came to a halt.

'Mr Hardacre,' he said, with puffy dignity, 'Miss Chandler is tired.'

'That's right. Drunk,' said Sam again. Bernie glowered at

him but Sam suddenly looked dangerously angry and, in his working clothes, rather formidable, and Bernie stepped back. Harry stepped to intervene, but Sam whirled about and stalked out of the room.

'Where are you going?' Bernie shouted.

'Upstairs.'

'You can't.'

Sam stopped and turned around in the doorway and caught Bernie by his jacket lapels and lifted him half off his feet. Harry mouthed protest, but Sam just held the kicking little man there as he said, 'I can bloody well go upstairs in my own house.' He dropped Bernie, whirled about and slammed the door. He went up the stairs, despite his weariness, three steps at a time, turned down the first corridor, up the next and was at the door of the master bedroom before anyone downstairs had moved. He paused just a moment, and then slammed the thin panels three times with his grimy, oil-stained fist.

'Bernie, you bird-shit, I said leave me alone.' The voice was high, sharp and had the thickness of recent tears. Sam paused, hesitating only a moment, and then slammed the door open with his hand, knowing it wasn't locked. There weren't any locks in the house. Old Sam hadn't believed in locks. He'd thrown every key away the day he moved in.

'I said, stay *out*,' she shrieked, and then she saw him, or saw, at least, that he wasn't Bernie. She was wearing a white silk dressing-gown and standing by the mahogany dressing-table on which was prominent a large, open bottle of Scotch and a full ashtray into which she flicked desultory ash, even as she stared. 'Who in *hell* are you,' she breathed, in a mixture of shock and fury. Then, quite suddenly, she recognized him, which Sam found surprising considering how long it was since they had met, and how differently he was dressed. She nodded, a nod of assessment and said, 'Oh, it's you.'

'Yes, madam,' he said sourly.

She partly turned away, looking at her half-filled glass, and then she looked back, met his eyes and said, 'Look, I'm not very good at this sort of thing. I'm sorry about your brother.'

Sam was startled, and slightly unnerved. He feared her shaking his fragile equilibrium and said quickly, 'So am I. I don't want to talk about it.' She shrugged, annoying him with her apparent nonchalance.

'Okay,' she said. She drew on her cigarette and blew out smoke, and then abruptly shook her head, regaining momentum. 'Now kindly leave.'

'No.' She stared.

'Get out of my bedroom,' she said. She stared again, and then looked around, as if she were in a hotel, for a phone, or bell to ring. 'I'll call someone,' she said, defiantly.

'You can call the bloody Horse Guard if you like,' he said. 'I'm not leaving until you get yourself together, and downstairs.' She looked uncertain, partly frightened, partly furious, and mostly drunk.

She murmured, 'Bernie,' in a trembling voice, and then suddenly shouted, 'Bernie. Bernie, help!'

Sam had no worry of Bernie hearing her. Bernie, he suspected, was not likely to have followed him. But he said, 'If I *see* Bernie again I'll throw him out of that window,' and she, looking as if to believe him, stopped shouting.

'Good girl,' he said. 'Now, get your evening clothes, unless that *is* your evening clothes, and get your face washed, and get downstairs. I'll be waiting just outside your door, madam, and you have five minutes. Dinner,' he added, 'is served.'

He made a step towards the door, and she stood silent and open-mouthed. He thought he'd succeeded, but as his hand touched the knob she regained her voice. 'Now wait just a fucking damned minute, you pompous prick.' He turned around again, his eyes widening with amazement. 'Yeah, that's right. You listen. I'm not sure who sent you, or just

313

where you fit in around this circus, but I'm telling you for a start I am *not* going downstairs. I am *not* having dinner with that bunch of clowns in penguin suits. I am *not* getting sent off with "the *ladies*" for coffee or any of the other dumb things you stuffed shirts get up to. I *never* wanted to come here, it was all Bernie's bright idea, and I *never* agreed to any smart-ass dinner. So piss off and tell them that, and,' she gasped as he caught her upraised forearm which had been brandishing a small, decorative fist, 'let go of my arm and don't you dare touch me.'

She swung the other fist and Sam caught that one too, and she began to kick with her fluffy little slippers. 'Let me go,' she hissed. He did, afraid he would hurt her wrists if she continued to struggle, and she looked startled. She stepped back, her eyes blue and hard, and said angrily, 'Hey, you're really some smart-ass, aren't you?'

'Miss Chandler,' Sam said quietly, realizing everything was out of hand, 'I'm sorry. I'm sorry I broke into your bedroom, and I'm sorry I touched you. It was unforgiveable.' His anger was cooling rapidly into tiredness. He became suddenly, abstractedly aware of quite how stunningly beautiful she was, even drunk, tearstained and angry. The realization shook his confidence. He said, still quietly, 'Look, I've just spent nine days at sea, and I'm exhausted and I just want a quiet dinner with my family.'

'So who's stopping you?'

'You are,' he snapped, feeling the calm going again. 'Everything's impossible down there. My uncle is miserable that he hasn't pleased you, and your father is mortified.'

'I can't help that,' she sniffed. 'It's Bernie's fault.'

'Yes, you can damn well help it, you spoiled brat,' Sam said. 'My uncle's the sweetest man in the world and your father runs him a damn close second and I won't have you treat them this way.'

'*You* won't?' Janet Chandler whispered, as if she doubted her hearing. '*You*? And what are you, in all this, and what

314

for Chrissake gives you the holy right to set yourself up as judge and jury around here? I'm not going to be lectured to by some . . .' she looked him, and his oil-stained clothing, up and down with distaste, 'some dirty, ignorant lout.'

'I was at Cambridge,' he said, feeling a childish need to defend himself suddenly against her heavy scorn. He didn't mention that he'd not been there very long.

'Big deal. What did they teach you? How to be an asshole?' Sam shook his head, exasperated, and she said, 'You'd have thought they'd have taught you not to come into a lady's bedroom in filthy dungarees.' She looked at him again with disgust.

'I work for my living, madam,' he said.

'And you think I don't?' she exploded. 'Shittin' hell, I work my ass off, just *being* Janet Chandler, half the time. You think it's easy, you think it's fun? You dumb shit.' She grabbed for her cigarettes and lit another.

'You know,' Sam said, wonderingly, 'I've been at sea for nine whole days with ten Yorkshire seamen and every *one* of them has a cleaner mouth than you.'

She glared. 'Oh yeah? Nine days at sea with you, it's a wonder they can still talk.' Then suddenly she smiled round the cigarette, and a mischievous look caught her blue-green eyes, softening them. She turned towards him, and tilted her hip dramatically sideways, lowering one hand to it and giving an ostentatious little wriggle. She whispered, throatily, 'On the other hand, nine days at sea with *me*, and they'd have something to talk about.'

The fact that he knew she was acting did not stop him feeling the sudden devastating stirring of the loins that the vamping hip and the voice engendered. Physical exhaustion always brought with it, for him, a sort of weary renegade randiness, a flicker of rogue interest from a body that was no doubt too tired to perform. The room, warm from the flickering coal fire in the grate, and sensual with dim lighting, and her perfume, did not help. She saw the effect

315

she'd had in the uncertain way he stepped back from her and her smile broadened.

'Hey, how long did you say you were at sea?' she said, teasing.

'Too long. Madam, please get dressed. The family are waiting for dinner.'

She grinned, drawing on her cigarette, and pushing her luck a little. 'I bet they'd wait a little longer,' she said in the same throaty voice.

Sam, fully aware she was playing with him, said, quite quietly, 'Another time, madam, if you're that eager. Right now, I want you to move your selfish little arse and get downstairs, and stop playing havoc with my family.'

She was offended at his abrupt end of her game and said coldly, 'Me playing havoc? That's rich. The whole damned place is coming apart at the seams, as far as I can tell, with the strain of everyone tiptoeing around you . . .'

'Don't,' Sam said.

' . . . ever since . . .'

'Don't.' He stepped forward, willing her to silence, but she just flicked ash a little drunkenly from her cigarette and looked him coolly in the eyes.

'Ever since you killed your brother in that damned car.'

'No,' he whispered, and lunged for her, 'No, no. No.' He caught her upflung hand, oblivious of the sudden real fear on her face, feeling nothing but the need to silence her. He had come so far; he could not let her, anyone, plunge him back into that dark valley he had inhabited. 'Please,' he whispered, 'just be quiet.' He fought to not hear her words. But she was, after all, very drunk.

'It's the damned truth. The big damned truth no one's talking about. Time someone did.'

'No,' he begged, but he had both her wrists in one hand, and was fighting to cover her pretty, painted and frightened mouth with the other. He caught a glimpse of himself in the mirror of the wardrobe and was dimly, shockingly aware of

316

what she was afraid of. He looked dishevelled, unbalanced and dangerous. He paused, his big, dirty hand by her face, fingers outspread, and she took that moment of uncertainty to foolishly bring up a treacherous knee. He weaved out of the way and she missed, but he fell then, heavily, and had just time to twist enough so that he hit the floor first, with her landing on him, rather than the other way around. The fall stunned them both into sense. He gripped her tightly, where she sprawled across him, and whispered, 'Jesus. I didn't mean to do that. Have I hurt you?'

She was silent for a moment, her face buried against his shoulder, her white-blond hair spread over his face, and he was frightened for her. Then she said, adjusting her body quite comfortably so that she lay full length on his, 'No. And I hope I've hurt you, you bastard.' Her head came up and her eyes met his for a moment, malevolently, and then, quite suddenly, they filled with tears and she buried her face against him and whispered, 'Oh Christ, did I really say all those things. What a rotten thing to say. What a rotten thing. I'm a drunken bitch.' She sobbed so that her whole body shook, and he knew she was not acting, and knew, in the same moment, that the drink was no longer remotely a joke. The firelight fluttered in the room, making odd shadows about her tumbled hair. He stroked it, absently, and relaxed on the floor. It was soft, heaped with Persian rugs, one on top of the other, a century of flagrant wealth tumbled over Hardacre floors. He forgot his anger, and that he had hurt his back again in the fall. Weariness, grief and pain dissolved mercifully in the smooth honey of sex. When he lifted her wet face and sought her mouth she did not even hesitate but was instantly returning his kisses with hunger and passion. The drawing-room, the waiting family and dinner downstairs seemed very, very far away. It was she, not he, who remembered them.

'Oh God,' she said, pulling back. He released her

gently, and she slid from him and drew herself together, kneeling in her white dressing-gown on the floor.

He sat up. 'Do I apologize?' he said softly.

She shook her head, smiling a small, very real smile. 'No,' she said. 'I do. I'm sorry. I'm in a mess.' She waved somewhere near the whisky bottle, and shook her head. 'Please forgive me. I've . . . I've had a hard time lately. A personal thing. Lousy damn thing,' she said to herself. He knew she meant a love affair and was illogically hurt. 'I'm getting over it,' she said, 'only every now and then it comes back a little, you know?' Sam nodded. 'Oh Jesus,' she whispered. 'You'll know.' She shook her head again. 'Look, what I said . . . I didn't mean . . . it was drink talking . . .' Sam closed his eyes and held up his hand to her, to stop her, and she quite surprisingly caught the hand, taking his fingers in her own. 'Okay,' she said. 'Bigmouth will shut up.'

When he looked at her again she was smiling at him, gently and wisely and, whereas a short while ago he had thought she behaved like a twelve-year-old, now it seemed hard to imagine she was only twenty-seven. 'I think I'd better get dressed,' she said.

'So had I,' he answered, standing up and reaching to help her to her feet. 'If you'll excuse me, I need a bath.' She looked ruefully from his oil-stained clothes to her once white satin wrap which now was smudged darkly.

'So do I,' she grinned. Then she tilted her head and dropped her voice. 'Shall we share?'

He looked at her very steadily, and more than a little hungrily, then shook his head, 'Madam, with all due respect, I'm too tired just to play. You'd better mean what your eyes are saying.' She smiled and shrugged.

'Okay, separate baths. Separate beds. As you like it.' She grinned as he went to the door, and tilted her hip and made her Mae West voice, 'Come up and see me sometime.' He was half-way out of the door when she suddenly thought and came running after. 'Do you know where it is?'

'What?'

'The other bathroom.'

'There are eight, my dear, I'm sure I'll find one.'

He grinned, and she said, 'Do you live here, then? You know your way around, I mean?'

He shook his head. 'I did. I have a flat in Bridlington. That's on the seaside. I lived here most of my childhood.' She nodded, obviously trying to sort out the tangle of Hardacre family ties.

She said suddenly, 'It must have been nice, being a kid here.' He paused, reassessing her. She looked wistful.

'It was,' he said, remembering his lost twinned past.

'I spent my childhood in a theatrical trunk,' she said, laughing, realizing she'd touched something deep and offering a helping hand. 'Very romantic and all, traipsing from town to town with Mother and Father. All I wanted, all my life, was a house.' He smiled.

'Great-grandmother was like that. And this was what she got in the end. She hated it, of course.'

Janet grinned, ruefully. She said, 'Were you very alike?'

He knew at once she meant himself and Terry and smiled, and shrugged. 'Exactly alike. Of course.'

'I'm sorry, Sam. I really am.' She reached up and kissed his dirty and unshaven cheek. 'I'll meet you here in half an hour, and we'll go to dinner, okay?'

'Okay.' She smiled again.

'Truce?' she said.

'Truce.' He stood watching as she slipped back into her room and closed the door. He went off down the corridor to the room that had always been his. Harry kept it for his use whenever he wanted it, unchanged. An easy thing to do; there were more rooms in the old place than any of them had ever known what to do with. The bedroom shared a bathroom with the next, which had always been Terry's. He went in, switched on a light, and drew the curtains. He went through into the bathroom and turned on the taps, hearing the familiar protest of the ancient pipes. Distantly he thought the whole place would need replumbing and probably rewiring as well, in the near future. He added that potential expense without hesitation to the hefty rates bill, the staff wages, and everything else that he automatically paid for. He no longer even thought about it. He searched about the room for clothes, finding underwear and a reasonable shirt in a chest of drawers, and a lounge suit in the wardrobe. No dinner-suit. He shrugged. No one was likely to fuss much, if he just managed to get himself and Janet Chandler down there in reasonable order. He found a silk dressing-gown hanging in the wardrobe and brought it into the bathroom, where he undressed, dropping his oily clothes in a heap in a corner. The bathroom, like all in the house, was huge and antique in its fittings. He lay for a long while in the blissfully hot water, thinking about Janet Chandler, uncertain what he was to make of her. Gradually the ache in his back eased and he managed to scrub some of the pervasive scent of engine oil from his body. He felt sleepy and was half of a mind to go back into the bedroom and stretch out on the bed and forget dinner, but the thought of Janet awaiting him dissuaded him. Besides, the family would be less than pleased. He dried himself, wrapped himself in the dressing-gown and then, on impulse, went through the second connecting door to Terry's room, rather than his own. It was dark, but he knew his way around it, and found the wardrobe easily. He did not want to see the room, and felt about inside the wardrobe without the benefit of a light. He found what he knew to be Terry's dinner-suit and took it out, still on its hanger. They'd always swopped clothes; in fact, between them they had never really had separate wardrobes. He took the dinner-suit back to his own bedroom and hung it on the door. It was a bit old-fashioned, mid-forties and pre-monastic, so to speak, but naturally it fitted perfectly. It felt comforting.

He went back into the bathroom and stood before the

long, free-standing mirror, tying his black bow tie. He glanced in the mirror and then over his shoulder to the door to Terry's darkened room that he had left open. 'Thanks, mate,' he said, and went out, switching off the lights behind him.

She was waiting patiently beside her door.

'I'm sorry I'm late,' he said. 'I almost fell asleep in the bath.'

She nodded. 'You look nice,' she said. He looked at her. She was wearing the sort of gown that only movie stars wore; strapless, pale yellow satin, with a tight sheath skirt, and a sweep of fabric asymmetrically over one hip, so that a graceful, sexy ruffling fell all the way to her ankles. Around her throat was a wispy draping of pale yellow chiffon. Her hair was done in a smooth golden bun at the back, and she wore earrings that danced and glittered with a sparkle of diamonds when she turned her head.

His appreciation, he knew, was written on his face, but he said only, 'If that's what working at being Janet Chandler means, you're doing a frightfully good job.' She smiled, a short quick smile, and licked her glistening lips. He realized suddenly she was intensely nervous. She leaned towards him and said quickly, 'Just wait a moment, please.' He caught her arm as she turned back to her bedroom door, assessing her shrewdly. 'Just a moment,' she said urgently.

'You're going for a drink,' he said.

'Oh boy, here comes the lecture.'

'So you are.'

'Oh, don't be so damned pompous. Come and have one with me, for God's sake,' she laughed, trying to be light, but he kept his hand on her arm, restraining her, and she tugged nervously to be free.

'You've had enough,' he said.

'Look,' she said, 'I've agreed to be friends, but that doesn't mean you can start running my life.' He shook his head. 'I need a drink,' she said urgently.

321

'No, you don't.' He paused. 'You know, madam, I've never seen you sober.'

'Big deal,' she snapped. 'I've never seen you civil.'

'You should cut it out. Right out,' he said. 'You're in trouble.'

'And you should fucking well cut out telling people what to do,' she returned, her voice rising. Then she stopped, waving her hand in the air, as if pushing anger away and said, 'Hey, look. Let's not fight. We had a truce, remember?'

'I remember.'

She looked at him, suddenly a frightened little girl. 'Jesus Christ, I can't face all those people down there. Please, Sam, let me have a drink.'

'You?' he asked, amazed. 'Face *them*?' She shrugged. He said, 'They're in *awe* of you.' She shrugged again. Then he said quickly, 'Anyhow, they're just our family. Just our family. You can't be scared of them.' He saw at once that she was. He took her arm again and said, very gently, 'Would you like to hear about the time Terry and I flew Uncle Harry's drawers at half-mast from the roof?'

Her eyes opened wide, and she squealed with childish glee. 'Tell me,' she shrieked.

'Okay. While we go downstairs.' She looked up at him, and then longingly back at the door to her bedroom. Then she nodded, leaning trustingly on his arm as he led the way.

He bent over and whispered softly, 'You are so incredibly beautiful.' She smiled, and leaned closer, the fear leaving her eyes. They came down the sweeping curve of the main stairway, with Janet on Sam's arm, her pale dress and pale hair in sharp contrast to his black dinner-suit and dark handsomeness. The assembled company, having heard them laughing on the stairs, rushed to see and stood staring. Janet was animated and smiling, looking up gaily at her companion and turning once to bend her marvellous, intense smile on the audience below. Albert Chandler put

322

down his drink and stared. 'How the hell did he do that?' he said. No one had an answer. Sam and Janet made their way leisurely down the stairs and through the assembled company to the dining-room.

They made a stunning couple.

CHAPTER
NINETEEN

They made a stunning couple at Covent Garden, the next week. And at Simpson's the night after. They probably would have made a stunning couple at the new Riccardo's in Earls Court, but Sam, much to Riccardo Cirillo's annoyance, would not take Janet Chandler there.

'But, Miss Chandler, she is how-you-say, good publicity, she is good for the business,' he protested. Sam didn't care. Riccardo's wasn't good enough for her, even though he owned it. Business had no place in Sam's courtship of Janet Chandler. Except that he pursued her with the singleminded intensity that he always pursued anything in his life that he really wanted. And there was no doubt that he wanted her.

He won her as his lover within the month, not as soon, perhaps, as her vamping flirtation might have indicated, but sooner than he had seriously thought. Sam was a rather wise man where women were concerned, wiser than his bachelor life, and relative youth, inferred. He had been raised among women; his widowed mother, his much loved great-aunt Jane, his great-grandmother, Mary Hardacre, all had their influence. He liked and respected them, and in some ways understood them better than many men; such was the inheritance of his fatherless childhood. He had known, with no need to be told, that that high-pitched, sharp-witted flirtation that Janet so often displayed hid a nervous uncertainty about sex, the tense, prickly resentment of a sensual woman too often in the wrong male hands. He knew she wasn't going to be easy, and she never was.

He made no attempt to seduce, but played her game of frivolous teasing intermixed with moments of sudden passion. It was a not unpleasing game. When not tired out beyond all reason, as he was on the day they met at Hardacres, he was happily capable of being teased and played around by that lovely young woman, who brought nothing so much to mind as a frisking young filly running for company and, in a moment, kicking up nervous heels and galloping away. He was patient and willing, and able to wait. Years of religious celibacy had taught a surprising amount of control, though at the time he'd not expected to put that control to such use. He was also utterly determined.

He was pleased, in the end, that when he did win her at last, it was not in some gorgeous and anonymous hotel suite in London but at Hardacres, which was his home. Not that he flagrantly tumbled her into the feather bed of the master bedroom, more or less over the head of his unsuspecting uncle. Hardly. Harry Hardacre, in spite of the long years of his own infidelity, if that lifelong affair with Sam's mother could really be termed that, was not sexually liberal. It would not be fair to say he was old-fashioned. He was simply old. In the years of his youth, young unmarried women were not even informed of what was to become of them one day in the marriage bed, much less invited to partake of its pleasures in advance. If gentlemen found such pleasures themselves, it was only with ladies of a totally different class. Harry's older brother Joe, Sam's grandfather, had been such a young gentleman, and had begun his sexual career surprisingly enough with the youthful and randy wife of the headmaster of the run-down public school which Old Sam had bought to gain his sons places. He had begun it right here, in the Mews of Hardacres, actually, not that anyone, least of all his grandson, knew that. His grandson was about to follow him, however.

Harry would not know. He had been a virgin on the day of his wedding to Judith Winstanley, and to this day he held that such a state of affairs was not only right but wise. But he was not an idiot, and did not imagine his example to be much followed today. Besides, although Noel's romantic activities, if they ever existed, were indeed a mystery, the reputations of his twin nephews had been, before their monastic era, quite legendary in that regard. Harry had then turned a blind eye and turned one now. But he would have been grievously offended if the decency of his household were presumed upon in such a way. Sam would not have dreamed of it, any more than he would have thought to accuse his great-uncle of the hypocrisy one could read into such an attitude. For it was not that. It was not his reputation he sought to protect, but that of the gracious brick walls of which he was guardian.

'We can't,' Sam said to Janet at the door of her bedroom.

'What?' she demanded, blinking.

'We can't. Not here. I'm sorry.'

'Look pal, we damn nearly did. Or have you forgotten?'

'No. I haven't forgotten. But I was very tired and I wasn't thinking.'

'Damn right you weren't thinking,' she murmured, grazing him with her bony and sensual hip. 'What are you thinking now?' she whispered in her lowest, most provocative voice. Sam stepped back. 'Look, I *want* it!' she declared, loudly and indignantly.

'Shush,' he said, turning to look briefly over his shoulder. He kissed her. 'And you always get what you want,' he grinned.

'Not me,' she said shrewdly. 'But you do, don't you?'

He shrugged and smiled. Her eyes flared with anger. Nothing much had changed in the last month. Their romance continued precisely as it started. There were no miracle transformations. She was highly-strung and she drank too much. He was hot-tempered and very strong-willed. It was never peaceful between them, right from the start, and it never changed.

The Mews was the first place he thought of and, gently

taking her arm, and thanking the vagaries of English weather for granting them a night of rare, gentle warmth, he led her from the bedroom doorway, through the maze of corridors along which he had played as a boy, and down the back kitchen stairs. In the empty, late-night kitchen he paused once to kiss her again, with slight lingering attentiveness, and she squirmed and wriggled, and suggested they use the kitchen table. 'Mrs Dobson wouldn't like it,' he said.

'Mrs Dobson isn't going to get it,' she whispered breathily. Then she looked at him warily and said, 'She'd better damned not, anyhow.'

'She's sixty-five,' he said, taking her hand. He led her out of the back door.

'Sam,' she moaned. 'It's outside. Your shittin' awful weather, it'll rain. I'll freeze.'

He kissed her again. 'I promise you'll not freeze. And one more four-letter word and I go back to Mrs Dobson.'

'Sorry,' she said morosely. She'd come to understand that he really didn't like the language but the habit, which was what it had become from the affectation which had begun it, was hard to break. Also, she wasn't all that pleased about changing to please him. Curbing her drinking was one thing. Turning into an English lady was another.

The cobbled courtyard was silent and dark and smelling of honeysuckle. They crept across it, hoping the three Labrador dogs in their kennels would not wake. She giggled, enjoying the secrecy and he had to cover her mouth with his hand as they crept by the rear windows of the house, which belonged to Vanessa and Rodney's self-contained flat, overlooking the Mews. They made it into the shadow of the low, slate-roofed building, and Sam cautiously pushed open the door. Inside the air was warm with the breaths of horses, and there was a rich tang of manure and hay.

'Yeeuk,' said Janet.

'Joys of the country,' said Sam. There was a ladder into the hay-loft and he was considering how he'd get Janet, in her high-heels and long gown, up it when the dog began to bark. It was a loud, furious yapping, a non-Labrador bark, and he remembered with a groan Vanessa's shaggy little black and white sheepdog that slept, not in lordly style in kennels, but here, in the Mews.

'Tramp,' he called softly, 'hush, Tramp.'

'Oh, he's sweet,' Janet breathed, crouching down and extending a hand in the dim moonlight. But the dog kept yapping, and suddenly the pale light was deeply brightened, as lights switched on in the house.

'Trampsie?' shouted Vanessa's ringing animal-greeting voice. 'Trampsie? Mummy's coming.' And then an aside, 'Rodney, old thing, we've intruders!'

'Good Christ,' Sam said, grabbing Janet's hand and retreating rapidly through the heavy Mews door. 'Run.'

'Where?'

He knew where. The summer-house. It stood at the foot of the lawn, where the beech wood swept closest, by the small ornamental pond full of carp. He had played with Terry there, as a child, and he remembered the fascination of its viney darkness, hung heavily with wisteria. But that was years past. No one used it now, and the carp, too, were left to their own devices, to live out their golden lives in secret. There were so many other works to be done, and expenses to be met; repairing the summer-house and maintaining its vines was low on the list. Noel used it now as a hay store, convenient to his bottom field.

'Oh, Sam, I can't,' she gasped, but she was laughing with the delight of running with the dog yapping behind them, and lights coming on in the Mews. She kicked off her shoes and he carried them as she ran in her stockinged feet. The door, a trellis construction of ancient rotting rustic wood, was off its hinges, leaning against the jamb. He slid it aside and stepped up on to the softness of scattered hay, among

328

the stacks of bales. He reached a hand to her and she came after. The light within the summer-house was dappled through its thick clothing of vine leaves. The wisteria, heavily in bloom, trailed clusters of blossom, like grapes, casting lumpy shadows. The dim few lights of the house, over the tops of a line of elms, were remote and peaceful. He felt her tense against his body as he held her in that silent place.

'We don't have to,' he said.

'I want to,' she whispered, but her voice was frightened. He knew she wanted a drink, and was torn between exasperation and sympathy. At least she did not ask.

She sat down, cross-legged in the hay. He could only just see her and the glow of her pale hair in the soft light. He sat down as well, and leaned against the rough wall of the old building. Even the scent of it was powerfully evocative of the past. He suddenly began to laugh and she, tentatively hurt, asked why.

'I've never taken a girl here before,' he said, still laughing. 'It's the first place anyone thinks of, and I've never done it until now. I'm almost forty.'

'I'm glad you've never had anyone else here,' she said. She huddled closer to him and put her chin on his shoulder. 'You must think I'm awful stupid,' she said. 'All my wise-assin' around and I'm as scared as a half-assed virgin.'

'Why not?' he said, stroking her hair. 'We're all a little bit virgins again, with a new lover.'

'Do you think so?' she said, and then she sighed. 'God, Sam, I've screwed half the western world.' She whimpered slightly, 'What the hell's happened to my life?'

He could have told her. Too much work, too much drink, too many people wanting something from her, and too much frightful determination to be herself. He thought fleetingly of Ruth Barton, weeping in the cinema on the day of Janet's première. She was, after all, more like her idol than she could have dreamed. 'I love you,' he said. He did too. He loved her in many different ways, some that startled him. She had become his confidante, the one person in whom he ever confided, as he had once confided only in Terry. She had come into his life at the height of his struggle to overcome Terry's loss, and she quite literally took Terry's place. She was like his sister, he thought, which was an odd thing to think of a young woman with whom he was about to make love. But she was. They were always like a passionate brother and sister, intensely alike and tumultuous, from the beginning. And, from the beginning, he was always more in love than she.

'May I keep some clothes on,' she whispered. 'I mean, it's cold.' Then she said, 'No, fuck it, I mean I'm scared.'

'We don't have to do it,' he said again, 'I mean that.'

'Easy for you to say,' she snapped, then she buried her tense face against his throat and lay beside him in the hay. 'Oh, please, quickly, before I lose my nerve.' He gently put her aside, and sat up. He was smiling, though she could not see.

'You're angry.'

'No. Janet, I want to make love to a willing woman. I don't want to rape a frightened girl. I love you. Now, let's go back to the house. I'll make you some coffee. We'll talk.' She relaxed and reached for his hand, and when she drew him down to her, her mouth was open, seeking his, and her body was as soft and giving as the summer hay.

It was dawn before they returned to the house, and as they walked over the grey, empty lawn she leaned sleepily against him, as calm and peaceful as he'd ever seen her. She left the next day, because she was filming in London, and he expected to go about his work the same as before, with that slight feeling of added confidence that sexual conquest always imparted, and little change. But that wasn't the way it happened. He found alarmingly and quickly that he wanted, even needed, to see her again. The thought was strong, dominating, and even got in the way of his work.

There was plenty of that about, and after a week in Hull he went to London, ostensibly to see Riccardo, but in reality to see Janet.

He found her different when she was working, concentrated and distracted. She was filming at Pinewood and rising at five-thirty each morning to get to the studios in time for make-up. She did not wish to go out late, and she didn't want sex either. His pride was slightly hurt, but that was not his real concern. He sensed already that the relationship was one-sided, indeed top-heavy with his passion for her, only sometimes returned. It had never happened to him before; he had won, so to speak, every sexual encounter he had entered, and unwittingly left a trail of broken hearts behind him all his life. The tables had just turned.

Not that she rejected him. Far from it. She openly, demonstrably, adored him, but again much as one flagrantly shows adoration for a close male relative who is handsome and presentable. She liked to be seen with him, and when there was a first night to attend, or a theatrical party, she wanted him beside her simultaneously to ward off the public she feared and jointly attract the attention she craved. It was a dual role that was not easy to play. Sam, to his credit, played it well. He was not jealous when men fawned over her, but pleased for her. And when she took fright and yearned for the comforts of alcohol, he gave her the comfort of his love instead. And it seemed to suffice. She virtually quit drinking for the whole first year of their affair and, when she did lapse, it was never so violently as before. Janet spent much of that year in London. She did two films at Pinewood and a limited run of a play on the London stage. He liked to think that she took further work in England to be near him, but in his heart he admitted honestly that was not so. The work was good, so she stayed. A good offer from Hollywood, or New York, or Timbuctoo, and she'd be off. He understood that. Work was vital to him as well; and even in his most miserable days of passion for her, he never neglected it.

Of course, there are just so many hours in the day, and days in the week, and something had to go. So what he did neglect was rest; he slept odd hours, became more erratic in his daily life than ever, and ate whatever he could find when he found the time. It didn't do him any harm, though he gained a thin, ragged look at times, like an over-active tom cat, that rather suited him. What mattered more was that he neglected family.

The visits to The Rose at Kilham, to cheer Emily Barton, the time spent with the Barton children, now rapidly growing up, the weekends at home at Hardacres with his mother and Harry; all those went by the board. Occasionally he'd have pangs of conscience and make flying visits home, but they were unsatisfactory. His mother was resentful, and he found it hard to settle, hard to even sit still. The only time, indeed, Madelene maintained that he really spent more than a fleeting hour or two with them, was when he'd had a real row with Janet. Then he came home, cloistered himself in Harry's library, and was hell to be with anyway.

The rows were many and they were stormy. Their causes were myriad and mostly irrelevant. They rowed because their natures demanded it. Some people said they rowed because they loved to row. Whatever the truth of that, the world generally knew about it. Theirs was a flamboyant and exaggerated romance, screen-style and bigger than life. Janet's career demanded it, and probably profited from it, and besides she, in her faintly schizophrenic relationship with her audience, positively thrived on it. Sam, who was, and had always been, an essentially very private person, found himself living a very public love affair. But it wasn't only Janet's fault, nor her craving for publicity, nor even the omnipresent Bernie's shrewd manipulations, that won them spotlights. The real reason was the intensity of their multi-faceted devotion, an intensity that made them oblivious to their surroundings, much as it made Sam oblivious to family duty. They were known to have full-fledged battles in restaurants, famous or otherwise, and equally passionate reconciliations. They each walked out on the other from cocktail parties and theatre lobbies and, once, from an extremely elegant titled dinner-party, where Janet said 'shit' once too often and Sam threw the soufflé at her. They finally both left that one together, and were not asked back.

They'd laughed all the way back to the Dean Street flat and made happy love, thereafter.

'They're just a pair of show-offs,' Madelene sniffed, upon being told, and even Aunt Jane was mildly appalled. But it wasn't true. The fault was deeper, the simple nature of their love for each other. It had always a tension, an incestuous heat about it that had ironically enough nothing to do with the fact that they were actually first cousins. It was in their natures, not in their close blood, that they were too close, and they squabbled and fought like two who had been raised together, and each lost years of hard-earned maturity simply by coming into the presence of the other.

The obvious question was, of course, how long could it last? It lasted through the winter of 1955 and into the spring of 1956 and right through that summer as well. It wasn't, of course, without hiatus. There were three weeks off in November, when Janet was filming in Cannes. And there were two months in the spring of 1956, when she went briefly to Hollywood. Sam was glad of that. It enabled him to get through the anniversary of Terry's death in the company of his family, where he belonged. Otherwise, they'd maybe not have seen him. And there were, also, unplanned breaks in the partnership, periods of days and even weeks when they became suddenly combatants, gathering an army of supporters on either side. Janet would run to Riccardo for comfort, though not too often, because

Riccardo seemed to spend a lot of his time comforting Emily Barton on extended trips to London these days, to the family's bemused chagrin. More often, Janet retreated to the quiet, serious presence of Sam's friend and partner in business, Jan Muller.

From the very beginning, on the occasion of the fight with Mike Brannigan in Claridges that had ended her party, Janet had an unusual admiration for Jan. She seemed to sense something in him both remote and deep, a circle of mature peace for which a part of her chaotic nature secretly yearned. Even Sam noticed she was a different person whenever he was present. She didn't swear. She didn't drink. When she got excited, Jan would put his big broad hand over hers, and just smile his slow smile, and she would relax. It was something not even Sam could manage with her, but he did not resent it. Not yet. Janet had a way of winning loyalty from anyone, and Sam was more than once presented with petitions, earnestly voiced, from Riccardo, and more often Jan, on her behalf. Filtered through the screen of their loyalties, Janet's case drew much sympathy, and Sam appeared always the sinner. As for himself, he sought no followers, although Jane Macgregor remained his staunch ally as she always would. When Janet ran to her comforters, Sam went to sea. It was as good a solution as any.

In the meantime, they went their way, exactly as they had always done. He had with her probably the best times of his life, and undoubtedly the worst.

If the rows were shattering, the reconciliations were sweet, and they were batted from one to the other as if in some unholy tennis match. She got out of his car once, in the middle of Sussex, and walked six miles over open fields rather than ride home with him. He got out of her bed in a London hotel at three one morning and she didn't hear from him again for three weeks, and then from Oslo. But in the end he, or she, would soften. He would arrive at her door directly off a salvage tug, with two dozen red roses over his greasy arm. She flew once to New York on business, after an argument with Sam, and turned right round at Idlewild, to the amazement of Bernie, the press, and a waiting film producer, and flew straight back. Then, and still without sleep, she borrowed Jan Muller's car and drove all the way to Bridlington where, at four-thirty in the morning, she roused Mick Raddley and got him to let her in to the warehouse below Sam's flat. She camped cross-legged outside his door until he awoke and let her in.

When things went wrong, wherever she was, Sam was the only person she wanted to see and that, of course, was the source of half the trouble. She never, in all the time they were together, fully accepted the seriousness of his intentions regarding work. Nor could she comprehend his need to take physical part in the dirty and dangerous work it was.

'Jan doesn't,' she declared tearfully, after a resentful reunion following a five-day trip on the *Mary Hardacre* through the Irish Sea.

'Because I do,' he said. 'One of us must.'

'I doubt that.'

'You don't know anything about running a business.'

'Neither do you. Jan does. He knows how to manage people. What kind of a company director spends half his time covered in engine oil and bilge water?'

'This kind,' Sam said angrily, because he was by now (it was the mid-summer of 1956), getting tired of hearing Jan's name in her dulcet tones. But he didn't argue. She was half-right. He did what he did because he liked it; and he was not about to change. She, of course, was exactly the same. Sooner or later her needs, that is, those of her working career, and those of his must reach an inevitable impasse. And in the late August of that year, they did.

Janet had taken a part in another play. It was, for her, an unusual play and an unusual choice of role. She, who had been previously cast always as *ingénue* and romantic lead,

335

was to play a woman several years older than herself, for a start. Bernie was having a nervous fit about it; all his careful groundwork to protect her ever-youthful image seemed about to be thrown aside. But Janet was determined. In the May of that year, *Look Back in Anger* had burst upon the scene, and suddenly the London stage was a new and exciting place to be. The play Janet had chosen, a new work, *All Downhill Now*, did not deal with the angry young, but the bewildered old. She was to play a woman of the British upper-class, whose loving nursing of her war-crippled husband had quite suddenly reached a point of no return. Resentment, sexual disgust, drink and social decline were the themes; not themes typical of the previous *oeuvre* of Janet Chandler.

'Are you sure?' Sam had asked stupidly.

'Of course I'm sure, dumbie,' she snapped.

'But what about the accent?' he asked, tentatively.

'Actually, my dear, the accent is a trivial matter,' she said coolly, making his own essentially public-school tones sound just slightly northern and gauche by contrast. He gave up. So did Bernie. Later they both conceded she was right.

Sam attended a full rehearsal and was impressed. He sat alone in the darkened auditorium, having come in out of a rainy London summer afternoon, and almost instantly was swept into a convincing reality. He saw Janet middle-aged, even old. He saw her play her fatal dance around the whisky bottle on stage, and play it so effectively that it frightened him. He felt he watched her predict her own future destruction. He also saw her become British before his eyes, and the effect of that was so powerful that he was utterly amazed when, on going back to her dressing-room after the curtain, he was met with her big broad smile, both youthful again and sober, and her 'Whaddya say now, wise-ass?' in the bright tones of California.

'I think you're marvellous,' he said with conviction. She

was. She was so marvellous that it took him all the drive back to Hull to shake off the frightening false image she had created on the stage. He knew the play was good, and would be important. He knew it would reach out for critical acclaim, something none of her previous work, films or stage, had attempted. She was at a crossroads in her career, a compelling, important time. The pressure would be on, and she would need him. The wraith of the drunken woman on the stage haunted his mind and he thrust it worriedly aside. No matter, he would be there.

Only, he wouldn't.

There was little enough room for manoeuvre in the schedulings of a London stage play; theatre managements, ticket sales, advertising, cast commitments, all hemmed a production in to its precise allotted time. *All Downhill Now* would open on 7 September 1956, and there was precisely nothing Sam Hardacre could do about it, other than be there.

But on the other hand, though he couldn't tether time, he wasn't likely to be able to tether tide either. Nor would he outmanoeuvre the sea. On 13 August, a MacBrayne's steamer, travelling unloaded from the Minch to the Firth of Clyde for repairs, ran into trouble in a gale, lost power, and was driven ashore on the seaward coast of Tiree. Her crew was taken off by lifeboat and the steamer, holed on rocks, went quickly down, to lie in shallow water, her top hamper battered by waves. Before she fully settled on the floor of the sea, Jan Muller, on Sam's orders, had a bid in for the salvage contract, and by late afternoon the next day, Sam was on his way to Tiree.

Time was of the essence. They had to patch her and they had to raise her before the determined Atlantic took her apart before their eyes. There was a brief fortunate hiatus in the weather when, for a short spell, the West Highlands took on its almost magical rare air of summer. They worked in still air, in temperatures approaching eighty-five degrees, in burning sun, throughout the endlessly long daylight of the far north. The normally ferocious Hebridean sea was still as glass, broken only here and there by curious, watching grey seals. They patched her with wood and concrete, and prepared to raise her with a combination of compressed air, pontoons, and the helpful nudge of the tide. By now it was the first week in September and the weather was yet holding. Sam, who had spent weeks of his childhood in the North of Scotland, knew for certain it could not possibly last. September and gales went hand in hand up there.

On 4 September, with the work nearly completed, Sam left his crew in charge of Pete Haines and flew back to Glasgow from Mull, and then on to Manchester. From there he travelled back to Bridlington, to meet with Mick Raddley, whose job it had become to keep the rest of the activities of Hardacre Salvage alive while he was away. Age and a finally rebellious wife had more or less pegged Mick down in Yorkshire, somewhat to his resentment. Sam found him down at the Harbour, working on the old *Dainty Girl* which, like himself, was semi-retired these days, replaced by her larger sisters, the Hull-based *Mary Hardacre* and the new *Jane Hardacre* which Sam had bought in the spring.

'Aye, there?' Mick greeted him, as he always greeted him, as if Sam had been away an hour and not two weeks. 'Fancy doing some honest work for a change?' Mick was sitting on an overturned fish crate on the sun-baked deck, surrounded by black, oily bits of the *Dainty Girl*'s disassembled engine.

'Having trouble?' Sam said, jumping down on to the deck.

'Nay, do this sort uv thing fer fun,' said Mick. ''Ere, clean that.' He flung a piece of rust-encrusted metal and a stiff wire brush at Sam. Sam took them obediently, partly because his mind was on Janet and the play and how the hell he was going to get to London in three days' time and immediately back to Tiree, and partly because he still did what Mick told him to do.

'What is it?' he asked curiously, not recognizing the metal.

'Damned if I know,' Mick said. 'Found 'er in the bilge. Can't tell what it is until it's clean, can I? Happen it's important.'

'Happen it's rubbish,' Sam said sourly, scrubbing the rusty lump.

He looked idly around the Harbour. It was busy, with holiday excursion boats taking trippers out for spins to Flamborough Head and private yachts crewed by the crisply elegant young of the Royal Yorkshire Yacht Club. Crowds of frumpily dressed working-class women from the West Riding, with clusters of sunburnt children, crowded about the stalls selling shell trinkets and sticks of rock. The late afternoon sun, still warm in the same steady weather that had blessed them in the north-west, mellowed all with gentle summer kindness. As he sat working on the deck of the *Dainty Girl*, people passing greeted him, as they greeted Mick, familiarly; people of every class, fishermen, yachtsmen, arcade folk, trippers even, who knew him, or his family, from somewhere. It gave him great pleasure, a feeling of belonging that was, he realized, the essence of the word 'home'. London seemed far away.

'Eh, eh, lad,' Mick said, looking up idly to the sound of a distant throaty engine, 'happen yer in for some fun.' He looked down again, without further comment, to his work, and when Sam glanced up to see what he meant he was startled to see, arriving amidst a crowd of scattering trippers on the Harbour Top, his mother's bright red MG-TC and, at the wheel, driving with demonic determination, was Janet.

He was amazed. He had not told her he was coming down from Scotland; indeed would not have told her until he was certain he could actually get to London, which was something entirely in the hands of his salvage crew on the sunken steamer at the moment. When they were ready for the lift he was going to Tiree, and that was that. He had only faintly hoped it would be after the seventh.

He stood up on the deck of the *Dainty Girl* as Janet, in denim jeans, an old white shirt of his own and, incongruously, high heels, came running up the Pier. He smiled and waved, but she didn't smile back.

'Sweetheart,' he called.

'You bastard,' she shouted back. Several trippers turned to watch. Sam, still smiling, uncertain of his sins, reached up both arms to help her down to the deck, but she deftly avoided them, scrambled down herself, and stood her ground, one hand on a hip, and the other balling a fist around Madelene's car keys.

'I was going to call you,' he said. 'I've only just got here. Haven't I, Mick?' Mick said nothing, pretending he'd heard nothing. He had signed a non-aggression pact with Janet long ago, and would not participate.

'Jan said you left Tiree yesterday. I've been everywhere looking for you.' Of course, Jan in Hull, and his radio link with the *Mary Hardacre*. All kinds of information came that way.

'I did,' Sam said honestly. 'It takes a day to *get* here from Tiree. The first bit is in a twelve-foot launch.' Janet never quite believed him about the remoteness of Scotland.

'Well, how screwing long does it take to get to London?' she demanded. Sam put down his piece of rusty anonymous metal and the wire brush, and straightened up again to face her. He knew she was spoiling for a fight because she was swearing. But suddenly he didn't feel much like placating her. He'd thought of nothing for the last two weeks but how he was to get to London in time for her play and was, as often as not on her behalf, driving himself in circles trying to be in two places at once. He didn't mind, but he didn't like being shouted at for his efforts, or called a liar.

'I'll get to London when I get to London,' he said.

'Well, that's fine. If it's after the seventh you might as well not bother.'

'Then I shan't,' he said calmly, and sat down again, picking up his wire brush and Mick's lump of metal. Mick looked up and handed him something else.

'Take that apart, will you?' he said. 'You've got two hands.' Sam nodded and took a small bolt, stubbornly frozen on to its nut. He fiddled with it, and suddenly a small determined little hand grabbed it from him with a yelp of fury and flung it into the harbour. It made a bright splash on the dark water and vanished.

'You dumb bitch,' Mick howled, suddenly alive with fury. 'It'll take me a week to replace that!'

Sam stood up. He looked at Mick impotently fuming amidst his circle of oily engine parts. And he looked at Janet, glaring at him with little-girl triumph in her eyes. He took a step towards her and she got suddenly scared and backed off, down aft. Then he leapt for her; she dodged, but he caught her up in his arms with startling ease and with one smooth swing flung her in the harbour after the bolt.

'I'll be,' Mick marvelled, as she went under. She rose spluttering, and Sam watched in sudden horror. It wasn't exactly that he never thought that perhaps she couldn't swim, but more that he'd always rather assumed that, if pressed, she could probably walk on water. She couldn't. She gasped a little pathetic cry and went down like a stone, trailing small fingers after. Sam was terrified. The water was deep, and it was black. He leapt in instantly, after her, and with two strong strokes was beside her.

She waited, floundering helplessly before him, until he was within arms' length, and just as he reached to help her she suddenly rose up out of the water like a vengeful mermaid, shouted, 'Shithead', and thrust him under. When he came up, spitting oily water, she was swimming with sure, athletic strokes for the boat. He had forgotten she was an actress.

Mick displayed partisan interest only in that he offered Janet his hand to climb back up on deck, whereas he allowed Sam to find his own way up. Then he went back to his engine parts while Janet scrambled on to the Pier, with Sam in pursuit, both dripping wet and equally furious. He caught her after a dozen yards, with one big hand around her wrist.

Her shriek alerted any of the now large watching crowd of assorted trippers, yachtsmen and harbour regulars who might have thought the show was over that it still had some time to run. Mick looked up. Janet swung her free hand and hit Sam across the face. Sam hit her right back. Those two didn't fool around when they fought.

He wrestled her, with great difficulty to a nearby bench. He was obviously stronger, but concentrated outrage gave her powers of her own. She twisted round and sank her teeth into his arm and drew blood, which just made him that much more determined. Some serious-minded citizen stepped to intervene, thinking it had gone too far, but Mick stood up on the *Dainty Girl* and shouted, 'Leave be, you big twit. Yon's a private fight,' to which the waiting audience responded with a small hand of applause.

'Eeh, give it to her proper, Sam,' someone shouted, but Janet had her defenders among the tougher of the women who shouted advice, most of it obscene. Janet didn't need much; she was the dirtiest fighter in creation, and could have taught them all a lesson. Still, he got her across his dripping thighs and pinned her kicking legs long enough to get in three resounding smacks across the stretched wet denim on her bottom before she struggled free. It was no pretty play-spanking either; he meant to hurt, and he did. Only when she got free of him did some faint remorse strike him, both towards Janet, and towards Mick, his family, and indeed the rather respectable company of which he was a director, for making so public a spectacle of himself. The remorse was shortlived. He saw Janet heading for her borrowed car, and he wasn't letting her off that easily.

He sprinted after and caught her climbing behind the wheel. He picked her up under her wet armpits and lifted her bodily out, carried her right around the car and plonked her down in the passenger seat. Then he fought her for the keys, gaining another bitten wrist for his efforts, and, winning them, leapt into the driver's seat, and drove skidding away, with Janet yet screaming abuse and pummelling his head and shoulders, as he did so.

A ripple of applause followed them down the street.

Mick went back to work on the *Dainty Girl* and Sam and Janet's audience drifted away. He heard, in the distance, a small childish voice requesting, 'But what was the man *doing* to the lady, Mummy?' until the Mummy in question stuffed a sweetie into the curious mouth, for silence. The harbour was still and peaceful, as evening came on. Mick worked until the carnival lights down along the promenades came on, and then he packed up his tools and went home. As he passed the street in which Sam lived, he looked up at the old warehouse. The lights of Sam's flat glowed gently through drawn curtains, and the little MG was parked docilely below. Mick shrugged and walked on.

She left in the early dawn. She had to get back to London. Sam stood in the chill, crisp air of the deserted street, watching her drive away to a serenade of morning gulls. The air smelt heavily of salt. The warmth of her still surrounded his body. When he returned to the flat he lay down again on the rumpled bed which smelled of her perfume, remembering. In the middle of the night she had agreed to marry him. He let the thought play across his mind but did not dwell on it, instinctively aware already, perhaps, that it was counterfeit. In the middle of the night, in his bed, she'd agree to anything.

343

He slept again for a while, and then got up, with the morning still early, made coffee and sat down at his desk with a heap of awaiting mail. He was consciously waiting for the telephone to ring, with word from Jan that the lift was ready to begin. He prayed the message would not come; at the same time he prayed it would. The weather could not last for ever. The needs of work, and the needs of love had never been more in opposition.

When Mick Raddley came back down to the Harbour at nine in the morning to finish his work on the engine of the *Dainty Girl*, he saw that the MG had gone, and assumed one, or both of the couple had gone with it. Disgruntled, he went into the warehouse and climbed the stairs to Sam's flat. Sam was getting harder than ever even to find, much less do business with, which for Mick was a nuisance and for other people, like Jan Muller or Pete Haines, was a potential business disaster. Some day soon it was going to matter, and either Sam was going to have to grow up or Hardacre Salvage was going to fall apart. Mick, clomping up the stairs, wondered idly which was going to happen first.

He knocked on the door, and was happily surprised to be summoned in not by Janet but by Sam himself, sounding rather efficient at that. He pushed open the door and looked around. He could always tell when Janet had spent the night. Not, as the films would have it, by little touches of femininity, jugs of flowers or what-not, but by the fact that the place was suddenly a mess. Janet, whose own person was always immaculately groomed, yet trailed a small hurricane of chaos behind her wherever she went.

'Good morning,' Sam said. He was sitting at his desk, with a neat stack of papers at one side, and an equally neat heap of sealed envelopes at the other. He wore his reading glasses down on the end of his nose, and they looked incongruous and attractive on him, as such scholarly attributes do on a weatherbeaten face. He had the look of a man who hadn't slept much and was all the better for it.

'You're bloody cheery,' Mick groused.

'Just as well. You're obviously not. Go and make some coffee, I'll be done in a minute.'

Mick lumbered off to the kitchen, and shouted through in a moment, 'Like a bluidy pigsty in here. When are you going to teach that woman how to wash up?'

'Never,' Sam called back at once. 'She's too beautiful to wash up.'

'Aye, aye,' Mick muttered, ploughing his way through discarded wine glasses, and Janet's borrowed shirt which hung drying over the sink. 'Like to hear you say that in ten years' time.' Sam was silent. Mick made coffee and brought it through and leaned against the edge of the desk. 'Tell me something,' he said.

'Aye,' Sam said, not listening, reading a letter instead.

'You gettin' serious?' Sam looked up, startled and suddenly cagey.

'About what?'

'You and Janet. About each other.' Mick was not an easy person to be cagey with. Sam looked down at the letter, pretending to read it.

'Perhaps,' he said, almost to himself. There was no answer. He looked up. Mick was drinking coffee and looking at him. 'What's wrong?' he said.

'Nowt.'

Sam shrugged. He tried to read the letter again, but now his mind wasn't on it and he looked up again, irritated, and said, 'All right, Mick, say what's on your mind.' But Mick seemed now determined not to speak. He left the side of the desk and wandered about the room, looking at each of the seascapes on the walls, as if he had never seen them before. 'Stop walking around,' Sam snapped. 'You're making me nervous.'

'Yon's a pretty one,' Mick commented, pointing ingenuously to a painting of a full-rigged schooner, off Flamborough. Then he said abruptly, 'Happen you should think again.'

'About Janet?' Sam said. He deliberately kept his voice light and said, as a dismissal, 'I think I can sort out my own personal life, Mick.'

Mick turned to face him, his lined old face suddenly very wise. 'It'll not work, lad,' he said. He raised his one hand, fingers outstretched, a surprisingly strong gesture, silencing argument. 'Just a moment, afore you lose the rag. Just listen. You're like a match and dry tinder; look at t' pair uv ye, yesterday. You're fire and fire. It won't do. Lass needs someone steady, and if ye'll pardon me, so do you. Ye'll give each other nowt but misery, and in a dozen years ye'll burn each other out.' He lowered the hand, having said his say, and shrugged awkwardly, his voice more gentle, 'Find another, lad,' he said. 'Be better for ye both.'

Sam said nothing, staring down at the papers on his desk. After a long while he said, still without raising his eyes, 'And what in hell would you know?' He looked up suddenly, and Mick saw how very angry he was, and how he was struggling to control the anger, 'What gives you, what *possibly* gives you the right to judge me? To judge Janet?'

'Nowt,' Mick said, 'but forty years' experience uv marriage.'

Sam looked at him coldly and said, 'Really, Mick, this is something quite different.'

Mick smiled slightly, and shrugged again, 'Oh aye?' he said mildly. Then he leaned forward, put his hand down on the desk and, in a low voice, said, 'Now, I know what you're thinking. You're a different class uv folk, the two uv ye. I know that. An' I don't need remindin',' he added sharply. 'But I'll tell ye summat. There's nowt much atween the classes when it comes to t' ways uv a lad an' a lass. We're much uv a sameness, from the big house, or the fisherman's cottage.'

346

He straightened his back and looked Sam coolly in the eyes and Sam said, ashamed and a little sullen, having been caught out in a subtle snobbery he hadn't thought himself to possess, 'I didn't mean that, Mick.'

'Oh, I think ye did,' Mick said, unperturbed. 'Now I've had my say, and I'll not say further,' he added, stepping back.

Sam was angry again, with the petty anger that comes when someone comes bearing us a truth we're busy trying to fly from. He said, 'If you'll pardon me, Mick, I have some work to do.'

Mick smiled faintly, stepping towards the door. 'Aye, aye. One uv t' best things about bein' t' boss.'

'What's that?' Sam asked, testily.

'Ye can always chuck folk out, rather than listen to 'em.' He grinned, retreating.

Sam wasn't amused. He looked at Mick over the tops of his glasses. 'Damn it to hell, Mick, I'm your employer. Just once in a while I'd like some respect from you.'

'And ye'll get it. Ye'll get it.'

'I'm waiting,' Sam snapped.

'When you earn it,' said Mick. He stepped jauntily to the door, gave a little wave and walked out, leaving it ajar. Sam rose angrily to close it but, before he reached the door, the telephone rang. It was Jan Muller.

'Four o'clock tomorrow morning,' he said. 'Pete says everything will be ready, by the tide. There's a gale forecast for the end of the week.'

'I see,' Sam said, and Jan, waiting a moment returned, 'So? Are you going?'

'Of course.' There was really never any question about it. He was no longer an amateur, playing at the professional's game. He had used his years of apprenticeship, to Mick, to Pete, and to Jan himself, well. He probably knew as much as any of them, though he might lack their practical experience to some degree. What he had gained in the last two years, though, was confidence. He no longer turned to any of them to make his decisions for him. And in the end there was no one but himself in charge. He left the flat in half an hour, for Manchester, on the first leg of the long complex journey to Tiree. There was not even time to telephone Janet, and say goodbye.

Janet opened in *All Downhill Now* three days later to a crowded house empty of the one person she wanted most to be there. The play received a mixed response. Half the audience loved it and cheered it. The other half sat on their hands and a small noisy percentage walked out. It was controversial, if nothing else, and the critical response was equally mixed. But the one thing everyone agreed on was Janet Chandler's powerful performance, and so she underwent the peculiarly divisive experience of triumphing personally while the production collapsed around her. Within a fortnight it closed. The fanfares were still ringing in her ears and she was out of work. Still, it could not be doubted that, on the London stage, Janet Chandler had made her mark. She would never again be the image of blonde froth she had so long projected; that was over. What remained to be seen was whether she could climb up to the new image that needs must replace it. Bernie panicked and begged her to bolt to California and grab the first Hollywood film vehicle that was passing. Janet was uncertain. The one person who could bolster her confidence, make her judgements seem right, reassure her ever of her own deeply-doubted talents, was six-hundred miles away towing a patched, barely floating steamer through a gale, to the Firth of Clyde. It was precisely the scenario Sam had always dreaded, and its corollary he dreaded even more; that finding him absent, she would turn again to drink.

She did not. She did something far wiser, something that showed that she too was capable of shouldering her own responsibilities a little, if not completely. She turned to Jan.

When Sam learned of that, that Jan had attended her first night in his place, that Jan had seen her through that chaotic first week of the play, taken her to supper every night, seen that she ate and did not drink, he felt nothing but relief and gratitude. Later, when he was to learn how personally destructive, for himself, that week would prove, even then the gratitude did not entirely wane.

None of this was learned by the ugly voice of rumour, none of it was hidden from him. Janet was as honest as he was, and she told him everything herself. Had she seen what he had seen, she would have told him that as well. But Janet did not see it for months, whereas Sam knew almost at once that, between them, it was ending.

CHAPTER
TWENTY

When Harry came back from his midday walk through the beech wood gone luminous with October sunlight, he saw to his surprise that the library fire had been lit. He saw it, that is, from the soft whitish plume of fresh smoke from one of the myriad buff chimney-pots surmounting the high roof of Hardacres. Only one as familiar with every inch of the building as Harry was could have told which of those many chimneys belonged to his library, among the scores of rooms.

Harry's walk had been shorter than the old walk he once had taken regularly, down through the steading, across the bottom field, out along the border of the two pastures, as far as the edge of the moorland, and then back by a circuitous route to the beech wood, and home. These days he wandered as far as the summer-house, the over-grown fishpond, the edge of the rhododendrons and through the subtle brown light of the beeches to the small cottage, now empty, where his mother had spent the final years of her life, having forsaken the big house when her husband died. It was not a sentimental journey on Harry's part. She had been an old woman when she died, and he was an old man. He was no longer sentimental about death. It had become a familiar. Indeed, his journey was shortened, just as the shadows of the beech wood were lengthened, merely by time. He walked always with a stick now, and this small circumference of his land was all he could manage. It was, also, all he cared to manage. His world was closing in, with the closing shadows, to the fireside. As he approached the house, wondering why Mrs Bennett had lit the fire so early, he thought suddenly of the firesides of his childhood, campfires beside the itinerant pony cart, and kitchen-range fires in the rented rooms that were his parents' many homes. They would do him now, he thought. As one grew older the scope of the space one felt capable of occupying grew smaller. In the end, the deathroom and the nursery were one.

He saw, as he cleared the last of the rhododendrons, a large, work-used-looking lorry parked before the house, and quickened his limping steps gladly. Sam was home. Hence the fire, and the smoke from his library chimney. Harry was as pleased as a child, as the child he had once been on his own father's return. He glanced at the lorry as he passed. Sam always arrived in something like that, ungainly and businesslike, and he suspected he did not own a proper car. Or if he did, he rarely used it. Harry wondered if that was his way of making amends to Terry; by making driving, which he had loved, a matter of business that he must do, forbidding himself the pleasure it once gave him. He was sorry. There was no making amends. One simply had to get on with life, but that was something only Sam himself could learn, in whatever time it took him to learn it.

He had seen a lot more of his great-nephew in the last few weeks, indeed he had practically taken to living at Hard-acres once more. Harry was glad, but guiltily so, sensing the reasons were not happy ones. Still, Sam kept them to himself, and he no longer displayed the high tempers and childish moodiness that he did in the old days, with Janet. Harry knew from that alone that this time the split, if that's what it was, was real.

Harry was glad to get inside. The house was warm. Sam had put central heating in some years ago, and a big tanker with oil regularly arrived and kept it stocked. Harry never saw the bills, which was just as well, since he no doubt could not have paid them. He appreciated that more than anything. As one got older, cold became one's enemy, as if the grave was teasing already. In fact the whole place was looking better than it had in years. There was an extra woman from the village helping out, and many of the rooms had been redecorated. Of course, there was always more to be done, always carpets that grew tatty, furniture that sagged. It was like painting the Forth Bridge, keeping a place like Hardacres going; it was so impossibly big. 'What can Father have been thinking of?' Harry asked himself, not for the first time. But of course, in those days there was money, and staff worked for a pittance and, in the brutal 1880s, were glad of it.

Harry met Mrs Bennett in the hall. Over the years she had softened to him again, and finally even to Madelene, and indeed was known now loyally to defend in village gossip her new mistress's unorthodox arrangements with the master of the house. All things took time, Harry knew, and only time. 'Young Mr Hardacre is in the library,' she said. 'Shall I bring tea?' Harry nodded, making his limping way across the hall, his stick careful on the polished floor. He wondered what had become of the Boer farmer-soldier who'd given him the wound in his leg half a century before that had so plagued him ever since. Probably dead. Most of his generation were.

Harry pushed open the library door, feeling guiltily glad that Madelene was away at the dress shop. She had continued with her proprietorship of that establishment even after joining Harry at Hardacres, as his wife in all but name, and he had encouraged her. She was young yet, at least in his eyes, and she needed to be out and about and, though he was a little lonely now in the daytime in the big empty house without her, he would not have wanted her tied to his side. Their relationship had grown chaste and honourable, by force of the years, and he was grateful to her loyalty, and sometimes wondered at it. Still, he preferred her to be absent when Sam came to see him. She was hard on Sam, and the atmosphere was always charged with tension when the two of them were together. She seemed always to think he did not do enough in terms of family, whereas Harry thought he did too much. It was the difference that blood parenthood made; she regarded his attentions to them as a right, and Harry saw them as a gift. She was demanding of her son, and he, who was not the father, was forgiving. Madelene, he knew, felt she owed him a debt for his part in raising both her boys, and she would have Sam pay it. Harry thought nothing of the kind, and sometimes secretly suspected Madelene was punishing one son for the loss of the other, something for which, had he proof, he would have castigated her. But it was a thing made of subtleties, impossible to prove. Ironically, it was at times like this, in the companionship they shared when she was absent that any debts there might have been were paid.

Sam was sprawled comfortably across the floor in front of the big wood fire, surrounded by stacks of leather-bound ancient books. He was wearing dungarees and a fisherman's jersey, and had obviously come straight from work.

He got up as Harry entered, and stood, respectfully, as he said, 'I've rather helped myself,' indicating the books and the fire. 'I hoped you wouldn't mind.'

'Of course not,' Harry said, waving him back to his place by the fire. 'How very good to see you. I've asked Mrs Bennett for tea. You will stay, won't you?' he added. He'd not yet got used to the change from the old flying visits of the last year. He wanted to ask about Janet and knew he'd better not. He said instead, indicating the books, 'Looking for something particular?' Nothing suited Harry better than a chance to sleuth through his extensive library in search of information that only he was likely to find.

'Yes, I am, actually,' Sam said, slowly turning the fragile pages of a bound collection of Parish annals. 'I'm looking for a ship.'

'In there?' Harry said, settling down on the sofa with his bad leg held out straight before him.

Sam said, 'Your leg worse?'

'Winter,' said Harry.

'It's October,' Sam answered softly.

'When you're my age, you'll find winter begins in October.' Harry shrugged. 'Tell me about your ship.'

'Do you want the doctor to see you?' Sam said.

'When he's found a cure for old age,' Harry said, 'I'd be delighted. Stop tha fussin'.' Sam look startled, and faintly apprehensive. His great-uncle's childhood dialect had taken to creeping back into his speech as the past slowly advanced against the present in his mind.

'All right,' he said slowly, forcing his own mind back to the ship and off Harry's health, which worried him more and more. Harry had become to him an old man the year that Terry was killed. He was not sure if any real change had taken place or whether his own vision of life was utterly altered on that day. In the aftermath he had hardly noticed; when time allowed him to look more fully on other people he saw Harry suddenly aged beyond recognition. Harry had never recovered from that year, but remained ever afterwards sadly mellowed and resigned.

Sam said quietly, 'She was three-masted and a collier, there's still coal in the wreck. We found her out on the Smethwick, almost completely buried in sand.'

'We?'

'One of the divers and I. We've got some of this new scuba gear and we've been trying it out. It's quite fantastic.'

'*You're* doing that?' Harry said.

'Just for fun. The old wreck's not worth anything, of course, and coal's easier to get from the coalman, but she's interesting.'

'It's dangerous, surely.'

'No, it's not, Harry,' Sam said with a smile, 'I promise you.' He never told Harry about the things he did that *were* dangerous, only the things that were not. 'But I'd like to find out which she was. We found what looks like copper letters, along part of her bow. Says Ann something,

354

we think. I thought she'd maybe be mentioned. I have a feeling she's one that went down in the Great Gale.'

'Of 1871?' said Harry.

'That's right.'

'I remember the old wrecks on the shore. I used to play in them when I was a child.'

Sam looked up, startled, over the rims of his glasses. 'Surely not.'

'Of course. It was just a bit before I was born.'

'Good God,' Sam said.

Harry laughed. 'Aye, lad,' he said, amused. 'I'm really that old. And what's more, I bet I'm in better shape than your wreck, any road.'

'Much better, Uncle Harry, much better.' Sam rose and opened the door for Mrs Bennett who brought in tea on the silver tray. Unconsciously she treated him as the master of the house, as much as she treated Harry that way. Noel, ironically, who would one day, perhaps soon, really be master of Hardacres, she treated like a farm labourer.

They sat together drinking tea, and Harry from time to time remembered things, problems, about the house, over which he had meant to consult Sam. He saved them up, a little litany of troubles, mostly minor, occasionally major and to do with money, which latter he always approached with apologetic tentativeness for all Sam's reassurance. He had come to rely totally on Sam's judgement and his advice, and turned in every detail, like a child, to this man who, but a blink of his eye before, had been an unruly boy subject to his own rueful guidance. Now, whatever problem arose, he would say to Madelene, with contented trustfulness, 'Sam will sort that. Sam will know what to do,' and day by day he relinquished adulthood like a burden he was grateful not to have any longer.

Sam rose and went to the tall windows, looking out over the lawn. He leaned against them, his arms folded comfortably against the centre span of the sash, which made Harry suddenly realize how tall he was. He'd taken off his heavy jumper in the warmth of the room and was wearing only a light shirt with the sleeves rolled up to his elbows, in that way the young had of being warm all the time, when Harry was always cold. He stood a long time, watching something out of the window, and Harry studied him. His forearms were tanned and muscular, and Harry saw him suddenly as a big, powerful man, and was surprised. The image reminded him of someone, and he looked harder. Sam's hair was lightened now, from the intense black it had once been, by a scattering of grey. The lightness of the hair was what did it, he realized, completing the resemblance.

'Eh, lad.'

Sam half-turned.

'You're getting so like my father,' Harry said.

Sam grinned, pleased. He beckoned Harry to the window and Harry hobbled across. 'Look,' he said, pointing out across the lawn where a gap in the line of tall elms showed an expanse of green down to the summer-house, the pond, and the beeches ruddy with autumn. The small herd of fallow deer, inhabitants of that cathedral woodland, had crept to the very edge of their domain and stood now, on the edge of darkness, peering out into the brightness of the lawns to the big house beyond. They were pale and delicate, and unearthly beautiful. Harry stood beside Sam in silence, watching for a long while. He said, slowly, quoting,

> 'The trees are in their autumn beauty,
> The woodland paths are dry . . .'

Sam smiled, and answered softly,

> 'Under the October twilight the water
> Mirrors a still sky . . .'

Harry stood quite still, holding the moment out there on the lawns and the moment in here in the library, together. Then suddenly there was a distant flutter of motion among

356

the deer, and their heads came around as one as Noel, on his tractor, appeared at the edge of the vision. In an instant they broke, scattered, and were gone. The tractor rumbled across the edge of the lower pasture, ploughshares raised, black against the bright light.

'Damn him,' said Harry with a short, sharp intake of breath. He turned, shaking his head in sudden, old-age frustration.

Sam said gently, 'He has to plough, Harry. It must be done.'

But Harry would not answer, because it was neither the deer nor the ploughing that really angered him, and there was no way he could explain. How could he put, to the one who was not his son, the myriad failings of the one who was? He shook his head and limped away from the window, his anger cooling. Why waste what he had, lamenting what he had not? His relationship with Noel had gone wrong the day the boy's mother, Judith, had died, and Noel was then only a tiny child. It was probably all his own fault; he had been too young, and too self-centred with grief to play the devoted widower father. Hetty, as nanny, and later as his neglected wife, had raised the children, not he.

'Sins of the fathers,' he said, aloud. Sam turned from the window.

'What?' he said. Harry shook his head.

'I say,' he said brightly, 'sun's surely over the yardarm? Fancy a brandy?' Sam nodded, watching his great-uncle deliberately shaking off whatever mood of sour philosophy had struck him. Harry poured brandies from the decanter on his desk, and sat down again by the fire. Sam wandered around, sipping his drink, and looking at the books. Harry watched. It was, he knew, always a mistake to try to make people into a role simply because they are born to it. He probably would never have been close to Noel, regardless. He didn't like the man. And he was closer to Sam than many fathers ever managed to be with their own sons. The trouble, he realized, the trouble that was plaguing him more and more was that, although bloodlines did not determine love, they did yet, traditionally, determine inheritance. And tradition was deep in Harry Hardacre.

'You love it here, don't you?' he said suddenly to Sam, without bothering to look round to him.

'Of course.' He heard pages turning, and wondered if the answer had been genuine or casually unthinking. He couldn't always tell with Sam. He thought he knew him, but at times he was not fully sure. Ironically, that closeness he felt between them had grown there only since Terry's death. Before that, both the twins were unreachable by all; no one ever broached their paired isolation. They were utterly self-sufficient, and self-delighting. As children they had lived in a world apart, even, as many twins, speaking a private, self-invented language. He remembered them darting about the house and gardens, two quicksilver shadows. It had occurred to him early on that they were spared the great human burden of loneliness, a most unusual state that set them ever apart. Loneliness, he had realized then, is the one breach in the shuttered fortress of the human soul. Those who are not lonely cannot be reached, unless they so choose. Terry's death changed that. He knew Sam came here sometimes because now he, too, was lonely; he came seeking company like anyone else, and he had become thus reachable at last.

Harry toyed with his glass, wondering how to approach, and then abruptly lost his nerve. It was not easy. Sam spoke to him from his desk.

'What's this?' he said.

'What's what?'

'Newspaper cutting. From *The Times*.' There was a pause. '21 September. It's about mineworkers.'

'Oh yes. Yes, of course, I'd meant to show you that. Jane sent it down from Scotland. Look at the picture.'

'I am.' Sam was studying the cutting, holding it up to the fading light by the window.

'Recognize anyone?'

'No.'

'Neither did I. Look at the caption.'

Sam read, 'Newly elected local secretary, George R. Emmerson.'

'Mean anything?' Harry sipped his brandy.

'No. Oh God, yes, Geordie Emmerson. That's who it is, isn't it. RAF pal of Peter's; I think I met him.'

'Mavis's brother, Sam. That's why Jane sent it.'

'Of course,' Sam said. 'You know, I'd forgotten they *were* brother and sister. Mavis Emmerson, of course. Jane hadn't heard from her or anything?'

'No. No, she just saw the article in *The Times*. He's becoming quite the big panjandrum, I gather. Made his name last year in that dispute over faceworkers.'

'I remember he was pretty fiery.'

'Damned Bolshie,' grumbled Harry. Sam grinned. He stayed out of politics with Harry. His own were complex and disjointed. He had a sneaking sympathy for the working man, because he often worked as one but, on the other hand, he got annoyed when the government got in his way.

'She didn't think of trying to contact Mavis?' Sam asked.

'I think she thought of it, and thought better. Jane tends to give people credit for knowing what they want. Mavis knew where we all were, if she wanted us.'

Sam nodded. He didn't suppose they'd any of them gain by prying into a life that was abruptly closed to them all those years ago. Yet he'd never understood her sudden defection. They had had good times together, all of them, Peter, Mavis, Terry and himself, and whatever vanished wartime girls they had been courting then. Good, frenetic, wartime days and nights, all gone, and perhaps best left untouched by prying memories. Perhaps it had been simply her grief over Peter; grief took everyone in different ways. Perhaps she had run, as he had done, to the solace of solitude, and never returned. He turned the paper over, idly. The back of it was covered with a dissected article on Suez, which covered so much newsprint these days. It had been much on his mind, partly because Jan had been so disturbed by it and had even spoken of going back to Israel, to enter the armed forces there again. Janet had been almost hysterical. She had not, as they had done, lived through war, and did not believe it could be survived. He said abruptly, 'What do you think will happen in the Near East?'

Harry grunted, 'Don't know, old son, but I'll tell you what *should* happen. We should bloody well go in there and take it back. Never should have let that upstart take over in the first place.'

'I don't think we had much choice, Harry,' Sam said, reading bits of the truncated article.

'Rubbish,' said Harry. Sam smiled, and didn't pursue it. The days of Empire, so inexorably gone, were real yet to Harry. Sam, who lived in today's business world, and knew that Britain stumbled on as virtually a pensioner nation and would have no more empires, would not disillusion him. He looked again out of the window, to where evening had foreshortened the landscape to the gentle circle of lawns and gardens which had been tamed in Tudor times. His uncle's reflection was cast across the darkening glass, like a ghost floating over the shadows of the beech wood. He could not blame him for clinging to a world where all was so beautifully ordered.

'May I stay the night, Uncle Harry?' he said, as he always did when he so wished. Harry shook his head, exasperated.

'Why do you ask? It's your home.'

'It's your home, Harry. I've got my own. I've two actually,' he said, laughing. 'That's one up on you.'

'You know what I mean,' Harry grumbled. 'Pour me another brandy,' he said abruptly. 'Damn leg's so stiff.' Sam crossed the room, took his glass and refilled it. Harry took it, grunted his thank you and stared at the floor. He said slowly, 'I *want* you to regard it as your home. I want you to come here whenever you want, without asking my permission, or anybody's. I want to think you'll still come here,' he paused, waving a hand in space, 'in the future. You know.'

Sam did know and said, laughing, 'I daresay Noel will chuck me out. I don't think he particularly likes me.' Harry grunted again.

'Don't think he *dis*likes you, actually. Not any more than he dislikes any of the rest of us, anyhow.' He looked troubled, and Sam said, 'You're hard on him, Harry. We all joke, but he's not a bad sort. He just doesn't suffer fools gladly.'

Harry glowered into his glass. He said abruptly, 'What I don't understand is, why does he have to behave like such a boorish lout? He had a good education, good as any of you. He had all this. And yet, you watch, he'll come clomping in here in a couple of minutes, in his tacky boots, smelling of bloody cattle, demanding his damned brown ale . . .'

'He's been *working*,' Sam defended. He stood in front of Harry, and said, 'Look at me. I've come in the same, in my working clothes. So, I left my boots at the door, maybe, and I prefer brandy. But what's the real difference, Harry? It's not a sin to like brown ale. I've seen you drink it occasionally.'

'In the pub,' Harry defended peevishly. 'There's a time and place for everything. This is my library. I don't want a damned farm labourer in my library.' Harry had long passed the age when one hid one's snobberies.

Sam smiled, bewildered. He extended both his hands to Harry, palms upward. They were scarred and calloused. He said, 'Look, Harry. He's a farmer. I'm a salvage engineer, general labourer, scrap-merchant, and restaurateur. I think his profession has an older pedigree than any of mine. How's he really any different from me? And yet you blame him for the very things for which you praise me.'

Harry was silent, absorbing that. It startled him, because

there was truth in it that he had never seen. They both had that peculiar streak in them that actually desired and sought out physical labour by choice. They wanted to work with their hands. Now, of course, for Noel, it was essential, an economic necessity. But it wasn't so when he began. He had had laid before him the life of a country squire, and he took by choice that of a farm hand. But what of Sam?

'You're different,' Harry said stubbornly. And then he sighed. 'You're different because you love the place. And he hates it.'

'I'm not tied to it, Harry.'

Harry looked up; he met Sam's eyes and saw them suddenly guarded, even troubled, but he pursued. It would be his only chance. Noel would be here in minutes. 'What if you were?' he said quietly.

Sam shook his head. 'It's Noel's by right,' he said.

'Rights be damned,' Harry suddenly burst out with a vehemence that startled them both. 'What has he done, ever, to deserve it? What has he done in all these years but worry it like a damned terrier?'

'He's made it work, Harry.'

'*You've* made it work.'

Sam was silent, looking into the fire, his hand on the mantel, and the line of his arm and shoulder tense.

Harry said quietly, 'As far as I've noticed primogeniture's rather had its day. It's mine, Sam. I can give it to t' bluidy dustman if I fancy. I can give it to whoever I please.'

Sam looked up. Their eyes met, and he shook his head, almost imperceptibly, perhaps quite unconsciously. He said nothing but his eyes, dark and elusive, spoke for him, begging Harry not to lay upon him the intolerable burden of words.

Harry opened his mouth, and then closed it, chewing his thoughts over, like cud. He knew Sam would refuse him nothing, should he ask. He put his glass down and took up his stick. In the hallway he heard the clump of Noel's boots, and the boom of his intruding voice cursing at his dog, the only way he ever conversed with it. Sam turned instinctively to the sound, and Harry struggled to his feet. Sam offered his hand but Harry shrugged it off. He limped towards the door. Sam watched, his eyes questioning.

'*You* entertain the lout,' Harry grumbled. 'I'm going for a walk.'

It was cold outside, but he did not care. He wanted to be away from human company and, once out in the dark gardens he felt better. He limped down the long lawn, stumbling occasionally in the dark of the October evening, as far as the ornamental pond, the summer-house, and the beech wood, from which the deer had fled. He stopped there, leaning on his stick and looking back at the house. The lights of the library shone out on to the lawn, making a green-gold patch, broken by the shadows of the two men, who stood by the window, talking. He had been wrong, he realized. He had been twice wrong. Sam was not reachable. There were so many layers to the man. One could go just so far with him, and then be warned away. He was the same unfathomable will-o'-the-wisp he had always been. Harry had been wrong. He had no heir.

CHAPTER
TWENTY-ONE

She came to him unexpectedly one late winter night, at his flat in Bridlington. He was surprised, thinking her in London, and delighted, until she turned, shrugging awkwardly from his embrace. Still, he released her gently, without displeasure. She was edgy. He was used to that. It often happened. Her responses to him covered the whole range, from passionate sensuality to outright frigidity, sometimes all within the same day. Sometimes when she shrank from him he had to leave her alone; sometimes, conversely, she needed loving. It was a tightrope he was accustomed to walk.

She stepped away from him, walked to the other end of the room, and stood with arms folded, leaning resentfully against the bookcase, staring at the floor. When she looked up her eyes betrayed her with an odd mixture of desire and annoyance.

'I need to talk to you,' she said.

'Lovely. Let's talk in bed.' She shook her head with abrupt vehemence which seemed directed more to herself than to him.

'No,' she said. 'You're too damn good in bed. That's half the problem.'

Sam laughed with bemused delight. 'I've never heard *that* held against a man before,' he said.

But she was not amused. Nor did she come closer, and when he took a step, still laughing, towards her, she turned her back. She said, 'Sam, I'm going to say something, and you're not going to like it. But I'm right, and I know I'm right. So let me just finish.' He was silent. 'All right?' she said, her voice thick. He suddenly realized she was crying, and it shook him.

'All right,' he said softly, sitting down. He knew already, before she began to speak, what she was going to say. He listened, in silence. She never turned to face him, but spoke quickly, in a tired, unhappy voice, a speech she had long prepared. She did not present it well. None of the actress was working in her; love between them was long free of that. At the end, she turned slowly to face him, her face miserable and tear-stained, and the tears, he knew, were not for herself, but for him.

'Is that all?' he said.

'Sam, please try to understand.'

'I do understand. You love him. I know that. I've known it a long time.'

'Have you?' she said, surprised. 'I don't know how. I haven't known myself . . .' she paused. 'It was when he talked of going back to Israel. The war there. I couldn't bear it, Sam. I knew I couldn't live without him,' she shrugged, annoyed at the eternal cliché that was love. 'Or I didn't want to. Sam, I never felt that way about you. I'm sorry, but I never did. When I was with you, you were everything. When we were apart, I half-forgot you. It's not like that with Jan.' She started again to cry, and turned her face away. 'I wish I could make you understand what it is like.'

'I know what it's like,' he said.

'Oh, goddamn it,' she said. 'What a shittin' awful mess. I'm sorry,' she added, at once. 'I didn't mean it.' She looked at him like a tearful, morose child. 'I don't know how I got into this. You know,' she said with a dry, unhappy laugh, reaching into her handbag for cigarettes. 'I used to think I was helping you. I thought I was doing you good, at the beginning. You were so lost when it all started.'

'You did do me good,' he said. He tossed her his own cigarettes, and she took one and stopped fumbling for hers.

He reached to light it for her, but she shook her head, as if afraid to let him within some private line of defence.

'Sam, come on, get angry. I can't stand this.' He shook his head. He took a cigarette from the pack and lit it, and got up and wandered about the room. He settled at last, leaning on the edge of his desk, smoking.

'I can't, Janet,' he shrugged, and smiled whimsically. 'I wish I could. We'd end up in bed, like we always do, and I might change your mind.' He realized suddenly then why he couldn't feel anger. He couldn't fight with her because now there was no longer the chance to cure the hurts inflicted, with passion. Their fighting had always been a kind of loveplay anyhow. 'I think you'd better go,' he said with wisdom, rather than unkindness.

'Sam, don't make it end like this.'

'Like how?' he said. 'This is civilized enough, surely. There's no way you can finish with me and walk away from here feeling like you do when we've just made love. What you're saying, really, is don't make it end.' He paused and said softly, 'You just can't have everything. Love and freedom, both.'

'But I do love you, Sam.'

'I know, like a brother,' he said with a small smile.

'Yes,' she shouted suddenly. 'That's exactly what it's like. That's what it's always been like. You're the goddamned brother I wanted all my life.' She looked quite amazed at her own revelation.

'My dear,' he said, 'you don't sleep with your brother.'

She smiled very knowingly, and said, '*We* would have done, no matter what.' She drew on the cigarette, assessing him through the smoke, her eyes growing hungry even as she did. 'I was right, you know, that's really half the trouble. More than half. Sex is just fine, but between the two of us there's more than either of us can handle. We can't live like this. We'll kill each other, between the fighting and the lovemaking, and the fighting again. Come on, Sam, how could we marry? Can you really see us in wedded bliss, with children? The whole bit? *We* can't have children, Sam, we're two damned Peter Pans, whenever we're together we *can't* grow up. We'll be children ourselves all our lives.'

'Children have a lot of fun,' he said.

'And so we have,' Janet returned. 'So we have. Look, do you know when I knew I was in love with Jan?'

He shook his head and said, 'I don't want to hear all this.'

'Just a moment. It wasn't anything passionate, or moonlight and roses, pal. It was when I realized that for the first time in my life I wasn't acting like a twelve-year-old kid. When he was busy, or troubled or something, I understood. When you're busy, I throw a tantrum. Look, I'm not proud of it. It's my fault, I know that, but I can't change. Not around you, anyhow. And I don't think you can change around me,' she added shrewdly. 'Sam, we've never been in love, you and I. We've never had a love affair. We've just had the best damned fencing match in the world. So damned good that there isn't anyone, ever, going to win.'

He straightened up from the desk, crossed the room slowly and deliberately, against her half-mouthed protest, invaded her sequestered corner of the room. He put his arms lightly around her, without touching, and then drew both hands together so that they cupped the back of her blonde head in that beautifully controlled way he had, so that his considerable strength supported and protected her and never threatened. She stared at him, pleading silently to be released.

She said softly, 'There's never been anything like that between Jan and me, Sam. I want you to understand that. I want you to know I came here, first.' He did not doubt her. She would never lie to him about anything. Honesty was the deadliest of her virtues. He yearned to kiss her, not

367

out of any desire to possess, or even change her mind, but just because he loved her. He let his hands drop from behind her head, and smiled.

'Shall I make coffee?' he said. 'We can talk.'

He let her go then, without argument. He could have won her physically, he knew, and staved off the hour for weeks, or months. But he did not. It was not honourable, and he was essentially a man of honour. Nor would it have been a loving act, and he did indeed love her, always, as he had always known, more than she had loved him. From the beginning to the end, nothing had ever changed. She was reaching out for security, as she had always done, and now she was reaching out to Jan for that security she needed simply to survive. A security he could not give her. He could not deny it her, and so he let her go.

She left an hour later, and not a word of anger had passed between them. After she had gone, he sat alone, listening to good music until morning. For the first time in his life he had suppressed, totally, his own volatile nature, and let all that emotion go utterly underground.

A day later, he drove to London to see Jan.

He actually drove right by the gate of Hardacres, on his way. He had intended to stop, having promised his mother he would come that day to see Harry, who had not been well. He slowed the van but then kept going. He could not face them, or anyone until he had settled, and finished with Jan.

Still, when he reached London, he stopped at a telephone kiosk in Tottenham Court Road, and telephoned the house. He was surprised to hear Jane's voice on the line, having thought her to be in Scotland.

'Are you coming?' she said without preamble.

'I'm in London.' There was a silence. He added, 'I'll try to be there tomorrow,' and, when she still said nothing, he added, 'I didn't expect to find you there.'

'No,' she said slowly, dragging the word out over a thought. 'Sam, are you all right, you sound odd.'

'I'm fine. A bad line.' He paused, and said, 'There's something I have to attend to. Business. I'll come up as soon as I can. How is Harry?'

'Not very well, Sam.'

He paused, struggling with conflicting emotions and said quickly, 'Jane, should I be there?'

'Your mother would like you here.'

'My mother would always like me there,' he snapped, losing control of that anger he had carried for a night and a day. 'I'm asking you.'

'Use your judgement, Sam,' she said, with her voice, as always, beautifully restrained. He hung up the phone.

He got back into the van and drove quickly to Soho, to Dean Street, where Jan stayed when down from his permanent base at Hull. He was angry with himself for being short with Jane, and worried about Harry, but neither thought held much strength against the wave of pent-up anger now rising towards Jan. That none of it was in any way Jan's fault was a thought as useless as it was obvious. The anger had to go somewhere, and he would not allow it near its true target. Jan was his friend, but Jan was also his rival and, essentially, Jan was a man.

Still, he kept in remarkable control as he climbed the stairs to the flat. It had not even occurred to him that Jan might not be there. He was so singleminded that Jan's presence, for the confrontation he must have, was inferred by its simple necessity. As it was, he was right. Jan was there, on the telephone, to some unfortunate shipowner in Cornwall. Sam entered the room without knocking, crossed the floor without speaking, and took the receiver from Jan's hand and set it down on its cradle with a rude bang.

'What you do that for?' Jan said looking up, amazed. 'That man, he is an important client. What will he think?' Jan reached for the receiver but Sam caught his wrist and ground it down on to the desk top. Jan looked up astonished.

'My client, anyhow,' he said. 'Not yours.'

'What is this?' Jan protested, freeing his hand with a small gesture of annoyance, rather than anger. 'What are you doing?' Sam, with one sweep of his hand, cleared everything off the desk – books, papers, the telephone even, which landed with a jingling clang on to the floor. 'You going crazy?' Jan shouted, jumping to his feet. He bent instinctively to reunite the two bits of telephone, which were protesting with a loud dialling tone. Sam watched, saying nothing. Jan set the telephone on the desk and looked at the mess of papers on the floor. 'You would maybe explain?' he said.

'I want you out of my business, and out of my life,' Sam said. 'And I want it a fortnight from now.'

Jan stared. 'You're joking,' he said.

'Oh my God, I am not joking,' Sam said, his hands suddenly gripping the end of the desk, as he struggled to keep from violence.

Jan saw then how serious he was and he straightened up from the mess of papers on the floor. He said very slowly, 'You can't do that.' It was rhetorical, for he was well aware it was not so. Sam had been fair to Jan. He had been indeed generous, financially. But he had never relinquished one ounce of control. It had been instinctive, from the start, to keep that to himself. Hardacre Salvage was always legally his own, and the holding company, Hardacre Enterprises, which he had formed when Riccardo joined him, was totally under his control.

'Oh yes, I can,' he said, and Jan nodded as the true situation hit him.

'So. Janet has seen you.'

Sam was silent.

'Oh, come now, this is what we are talking about, is it not?'

'I'll not cheat you,' Sam said. 'I'll buy you out. You'll do quite well.'

He turned, as if to go. 'The solicitors will contact you tomorrow,' he said.

'No,' Jan said, so vehemently that Sam stopped, losing some of his momentum. 'No. You *won't* do this to me. Look,' he said. 'You will listen to me. You will do that. A moment. I have spent six years of my life in this, in a foreign country, for you; for me, too, but for you. I made this possible for you. I taught you everything. You knew nothing. You were a boy, playing. I taught you. Not just salvage; I taught you how to do business, how to deal with people. We all taught you. Mick Raddley and Pete, and myself. This is our company, too, no matter how much control you've always kept. And I've been well aware how closely you've kept it. Do not suppose you have fooled me. You would be none of this without us.'

Sam listened, looking down at the scattered books and papers on the floor. He raised his eyes and met Jan's and said, honestly, 'True. I won't argue. But the fact remains it *is* mine. And the fact also remains that if you leave, it will continue. If Mick, or Pete, or any one or any group of you leaves, it will continue. If I leave, it will fall apart. I cannot do what you all do by myself, perhaps, but none of you can keep it together. Only I can do that. That's why it's mine, Jan. Not because I kept control.' He was quite calm now, and turned again to walk to the door.

'Stay there,' Jan shouted. Sam only glanced at him, his hand on the knob. 'No, you will not walk out on me. I will finish first.' He moved closer and Sam shrugged and turned his back. He felt Jan's hand close on his shoulder and, in an instant, all pretext of rationality left him. He turned and went for Jan with a savagery he had not known himself to possess.

Sam was not a fighter. He disliked violence because he disliked inflicting pain, unless he was too angry to care. He had seen enough brutality in the war to do him for a lifetime; indeed what he had seen there was a good part of what had driven him to the monastery at the end of the war. But always, when truly angry, he would fight with total commitment and total lack of sense; he would turn on anyone, regardless of size or ability, without the slightest regard for personal safety. So he did now. Jan was a big man, a really big man, heavy and powerful, and he was a fighter, trained, and in his own day, and his own war, quite brutal.

But Jan didn't want to fight, and Jan, too, was flabby from years of sitting behind a desk, and Sam was fit. Even so, it was sheer fury that carried the fight for him, and at first, Jan was actually struggling. He dodged about, getting the desk between them, then a chair, still fending more than fighting, trying to talk, to argue, to win some sense from the opponent he still regarded as his friend. Eventually his own reluctance undid him. He emerged once too often from behind his shelter, stepping backwards, his hand only lightly raised in protest, and Sam caught him with a sharp right that sent him backwards over the overturning chair, and down to the floor. He sat up, shaking his head, and his expression changed.

'Enough,' he said. He got up slowly, his eyes never leaving Sam's, and took his stance in a sturdy, professional fighter's crouch. Sam didn't even notice the difference, he was so senseless with fury. He went for Jan once more, and met a fist that sent him into the wall. He just shook his head, almost satisfied, and went back for more. But Jan was alert now, and ready, and Jan was skilled. He threw punches from places Sam never thought of, and knew holds he'd never heard of, and had the skilful ability to use his own strength and momentum against him. In half a minute, Sam found himself on the floor, got to his feet with some difficulty, and found himself back there again, not even sure how it happened. Jan was standing over him, his arms outstretched, hands open.

'Enough?' he said hopefully. Sam shook his head. He got up, staggering, and swung once more, wildly. Jan just stepped out of the way. But he swung again, and connected, and Jan cursed softly, and took again his waiting, professional stance. Sam was losing and even knew now that he was losing, but he didn't care. He just kept going back for more until Jan had hit him so often, and so hard, that he was reeling. Then Jan turned the fight in an instant, going on the attack, and in moments had Sam from behind with one arm locked behind his back, and the other pinned to his side by Jan's arm around his waist. In truth he was so tired that Jan was as much supporting him as restraining him, but he fought yet, and Jan suddenly shouted, 'Idiot', and twisted the lock on his arm with sudden viciousness. Sam gasped and Jan said, 'Right. Enough. In a moment now, I break your arm. Enough, right?' Pain began to break through to rationality, where nothing else had done. Sam said nothing, but he stopped fighting.

'Right,' said Jan. 'Now we talk.' He eased the armlock to the point where it would not be painful, but did not let go. 'Now I tell you something,' he said.

'If it's about Janet, I don't want to hear,' Sam said.

'You,' said Jan, 'will hear what I want you to hear.' He tightened the armlock slightly for emphasis. 'But no, it is not about Janet. There is nothing to tell about that. We have been utterly honest with you. There is nothing more we can do, other than lie and say we do not love each other, and that we will not do.' He sighed slightly. 'You know,' he said, 'you make this difficult.'

'You pompous bastard,' Sam whispered, turning again to fight. The pain in his arm made the room go black.

He heard, from a distance, Jan's voice, deeply angry, 'Stop making me hurt you, for God's sake.' Sam stopped, he couldn't take any more. 'Now listen.' He listened. When Jan started to speak his words seemed to make no sense, an illogical blur that blended with the sickening spin of the room. His anger was fading and, with it, the last vestiges of his strength. He tried to concentrate and realized that Jan was talking about the war.

'France,' he said. 'We were dropped in to join the Underground. We worked with the British; the British whom we had fought over the Mandate. It did not matter then; we had worse enemies. I was useful to them; I was a good linguist, even then. German, French, English, Hebrew.' He shrugged slightly, loosening his hold, but Sam did not struggle. 'A network, fifty people, all tied together, tied with a thread, a lifeline, and for each that thread is like a noose, if ever any one of them should talk. Are you hearing me?' Sam nodded; he could see more clearly now. 'There was a girl. A pretty girl. Dark, like your mother when she was young, no doubt. French, dark, lovely. I loved her,' he said. He paused so long that Sam thought he would not continue. He said suddenly with great force, 'I loved her, Sam. I loved her. They reached her. Who knows? A word dropped foolishly, a little girl's bravado. She was seventeen. They took her somewhere. They threatened her. Perhaps they did things to her, perhaps not. They threatened . . . her young body, her pretty face. A child, Sam, a child with a child's simple vanities. But I loved her.' He sighed again, suddenly tightening the grip of his arm about Sam's waist, but not with violence, or to restrain, but as if he himself needed support. 'But she knew . . . she knew everything. And they turned her. They turned her. We knew, of course. We knew at once. Five men died because of her. And she, so foolish, she led us to herself with her child's protests of innocence. Oh, we turned her again, it was not difficult. She was like clay in my hands. But we could never trust her. A lifeline, fifty people, a noose and a lifeline, in her little hands. And not just us, but the whole Resistance. It was too important. It could not be risked. She begged me to trust her. I could not.' Again he was silent, staring straight ahead, over Sam's shoulder, into an emptiness of the past. 'I could not,' he said. When

374

he spoke again his voice was thin and distant. 'There was no one else I could trust to do it. No one who would do it so cleanly, so quickly, so there would be no pain. You see you came at me to kill me just now with your hands, because you were so angry. But it is not easy to kill with the bare hands, angry or not; it takes terrible certainty. You could not do that. Even if you were stronger than me, you could not do that. I know, Sam. I have done this thing.' Sam was silent. He felt cold all over, in the aftermath of Jan's words. Jan said then. 'Do you think, now, I do not know what it is to be betrayed in love? To betray?'

Sam said nothing. It had never ever occurred to him to question Jan's odd, solitary existence, without women, or love. Jan said, as if in answer, 'I thought for so many years I could not love. I told Hannah I could not love. She did not care. She asked nothing of the world. Most women are more demanding.' Again he shrugged, lightly. 'Now, you,' he said abruptly, his tone changing, 'you can put me out of your company, if you wish. I cannot stop you, though I will fight you. But you cannot put me out of your life. I am going to marry your cousin. We will be family, whether you wish it or no. You can tear this family apart now or hold it together. It is entirely up to you. But you cannot put people outside your life and make them vanish. You are a powerful man now, but you have not that power, nor that right.' He paused and said again, 'Are you hearing me?'

'Yes,' Sam said. He started to turn, but felt Jan's relaxed grip suddenly tighten, twisting his arm back into the painful lock, and pinning the other by his side once more, as if to once more demonstrate his victory.

When Jan spoke again, his voice was very hard. 'Now, I am going to let you go. If you come for me again, I will make an end to it. I have had enough now. I am tired, and I am not fit. I will make an end to it. Do you understand me? I know how to do this, Sam, I assure you. It is something one does not forget. Use your sense, now. You are not usually stupid. In this you are still the amateur; I am the professional. It is not love you are fighting for; only pride. It is not worth anyone's life. But if you come for me again, I will kill you.'

He released his hold and stepped back, dropping his arms to his side. Sam stood still, holding his left arm with his right. He was bloody and exhausted, a defeated man, and Jan was not happy seeing him like that, but it could not be helped. He started to turn away and then saw, out of the corner of his eye, Sam lunge for him again.

'Oh you bloody damn fool,' he whispered in dismay. He sidestepped and turned to defend himself, his hands spread open, his eyes desperate, when suddenly the ringing of the telephone broke into the bitter silence of the room like a voice from another world. They both stood dumbfounded looking at it, wrenched back to civilization by a comic bit of stage play, a bad joke.

'You'd better answer it,' Sam said.

Jan looked at him and nodded. They stood studying each other, dumbly, and he reached for the telephone, aware of the insanity of their appearance, both cut and bleeding, their clothing torn, and the room in a shambles. Jan raised the receiver and said, with businesslike formality ridiculous in that setting, 'Hardacre Enterprises.' He listened for a moment, nodded, and said, '*Ja,*' as he did under times of stress. 'He's here.' He held the phone out to Sam, 'For you,' he said. 'Your mother, from the North.' Sam took the receiver from him, conscious that his hand was shaking with exhaustion and emotion.

'Yes?' he said flatly.

'Sam?'

'Yes.'

'I don't want the reasons. I don't want the excuses. Just get here. Now. Just get here.' The phone went down with a click and he was left with the hum of the dialling tone ringing in his ear. Carefully he handed the receiver to Jan, who replaced it, watching him with cautious, questioning eyes. Sam brushed one hand across his face, distractedly brushing back his bloody hair.

'Harry's dying,' he said.

Jan raised both hands to the sides of his head, shaking away confusion. 'Oh, Jesus Christ,' he said. They both just stared at each other in mutual remorse. Sam was silent. The fight was gone out of him in an instant.

Jan shook his head again. He raised his hands placatingly in the air and said quietly, 'Go. Wash. Clean yourself up. I'll find you a clean shirt.' Sam just stood for a moment and Jan touched his arm lightly and said, quite gently, 'Come now.'

Sam nodded. He went into the bathroom of the flat and washed the blood from his face, conscious sharply of pain as he did so. He looked up into the mirror and was surprised to see his shirt, too, was liberally splashed with blood. He took it off, still looking in the mirror. There was no way he could possibly disguise the damage. He would simply have to explain it. His mouth was swollen and cut, both his eyes, he knew, would blacken, and the left, with a deep cut just above it, was already half-closed. The cut bled freely. He held a wet facecloth to it, soaking up the blood. Jan came in carrying a white shirt. He looked over Sam's shoulder at his reflection in the mirror and winced. His own face was relatively better, though scarcely unmarked.

'Wonderful,' he said, with another wince. He took the wet facecloth from Sam, studied the cut over his eye, and searched for a plaster to stop the bleeding. He said, 'That will need stitching.' Sam shook his head. 'It will scar,' said Jan.

'Good,' Sam said, and suddenly grinned. 'Whenever I look in the mirror I'll remember my limitations.'

Jan did not smile. He was bitterly remorseful, which, considering how little he was at fault, was not logical. Sam put on the shirt that Jan had given him, and came back into the main room of the flat. Jan was standing at the door, with his coat on, holding his car keys.

'Come,' he said, 'I will drive you.' Sam shook his head.

'No. I must be alone. Please.'

Jan looked at him doubtfully, studying his cut eye. 'Can you see to drive?' he said.

'I can see.'

Jan nodded. He looked reluctant but said slowly, 'All right.' As Sam passed him in the doorway he held out the car keys. 'Take mine,' he said. 'It will take you all night in that van.' Jan had no qualms about motor cars. He had a very nice Aston Martin parked outside the florist's shop below. Sam nodded and took the keys.

'Thank you,' he said. Jan smiled for the first time, a small, tired smile. He held out his hand. Sam willed himself to take it, but he could not. He turned, and went out of the door.

He drove out of London carefully, getting used to the car and his somewhat limited vision, and wary of tangling with some officious bobby who might question his appearance in conjunction with the luxurious vehicle. It didn't matter; he could explain, but it would slow him down. It was getting dark when he got out on to the A1, and then let the car go. He drove as fast and as well as he had ever done, effortlessly, without thought. He did not enjoy it, but only because his concentration was solely on getting to Yorkshire for Harry. He drove one-handed most of the way, changing gear with painful difficulty only when most necessary. His left arm, that Jan had refrained from breaking, still felt rather as if he had. He never looked at the speedometer, only the road ahead, and as he drove he unselfconsciously prayed aloud the decades of the Rosary. Not for himself, or his safety, neither of which occurred to him, but for Harry, facing eternity without that lifeline of faith that he himself had always held.

The Yorkshire countryside was silent and dark when he

reached the familiar roads of home, and yet when he switched on the radio for the time, he was amazed to find it nowhere near as late as he thought it must be. He had made such remarkably good time that, afterwards, when he had leisure to reckon it, there was no way he could work it out that did not end in an average speed that was downright terrifying. Still, he made it. As he drove up the driveway he saw lights on throughout the house, but his eye went at once to the windows of Harry's bedroom. They were lit, but dim. The library was dark.

He drove right up to the front door, switched off the engine and leapt out of the car, running through the always-open outer door and into the foyer, pushing the glazed doors open and blinking painfully in the light of the hallway. It was deserted. He did not waste time looking in the drawing-room, where he saw lights, but ran through the main hall to the foot of the stairs and bounded up them several at a time, and ran down the corridor to Harry's room.

It was not, as perhaps it should have been, the master bedroom of Hardacres, where he had once confronted Janet Chandler, but another, more modest room, at the corner of the house. Old Sam and Mary had been the last permanent occupants of the master bedroom. Harry had never assumed his natural sovereignty there, regarding it, until even now, as his parents' domain.

Sam stopped just for a moment outside Harry's door. He was breathing hard, and he wanted to look controlled when he entered the room, to offset the appearance of his face. He straightened the collar of his borrowed shirt and smoothed his hair down, trying to draw some of it over the cuts on his forehead. It was useless, he realized even without a mirror, but he didn't want to shock anyone. He knocked lightly on the door, and heard Jane's voice say softly, 'Come in.' She was always their authority in times of crisis.

Cautiously, Sam pushed open the door, standing just in

its shadow for a moment before he stepped into the room. It was, without doubt, a deathroom. Harry lay on the bed, a wisp of a white-haired wraith, propped up on pillows and breathing with audible difficulty. Sam's mother sat beside him, loyal as ever, and the closer members of the family, Noel, Vanessa, Rodney and Jane, were gathered in the room. Madelene looked up as he entered, her face registering first amazement that he could be here already, and then shock. Jane looked up as well and gasped, and Vanessa opened her wide mouth to speak out in, undoubtedly, her ever-ringing tones. Sam shook his head and silenced her with a sharp gesture of his good hand. He looked at once so commanding, and so vehement, that not only she, but the rest as well, kept silent. He was hoping that, in the dim light, in his frail condition, Harry would not see anything wrong. He met his mother's eyes as he approached the bed. They were, after their initial shock, stony and cold. He saw, but did not acknowledge. For Sam, there was no one in the room except himself and the old man on the bed. He came closer and leaned over to touch Harry's hand lightly with his own. It felt cold and dry, and immensely old.

'Harry?' he said. The old man at first did not stir. Sam had seen him just over a week ago, but the change was massive. He had always been thin, but now his face was all bony points and hollows and, when he did then open his eyes, they were murky, their colour gone indeterminate, and one lid sagged, still half-closed.

'That you, Sam?' Harry said, his voice surprisingly clear.

'Yes.'

'Took you long enough.'

'I'm sorry.' Harry peered at him in the dim light, and gestured him closer with one claw-curled hand, on the counterpane. Sam leaned closer, smiling gently.

Harry said, 'You been fighting again?'

'Yes.'

Harry made a small grunt of acknowledgement. 'Looks like you lost,' he said.

'I did.' Harry, quite suddenly, laughed, a dry sound that ended in a cough, but he looked intensely amused. 'You'll never learn, will you?'

Sam shook his head, still smiling. 'No, sir.' He knelt beside the bed, put his long arms around the old man, and buried his battered face in the dry hollow of his neck. Harry laughed again, lightly, absently stroking Sam's silvered hair as if he were yet the repentant child he had helped to raise.

He said suddenly, 'Now where the hell's Terry.'

Sam raised his head abruptly, looking straight into the old man's eyes. He heard a sigh go round the room, and again willed them to silence. He said clearly, 'Terry's been delayed. He'll be here soon.'

Harry lifted his head from the pillow, struggling up on one elbow to stare straight into Sam's face. Sam knew he realized he was being lied to.

'Rubbish,' Harry said sharply. 'What are you saying *that* for? You're the one who's always late everywhere, not Terry. Terry's not late. He was here before you. He was here just a moment ago,' Harry grumbled looking around him. He flopped back on the pillow. He looked exhausted, but his voice was still strong, and old-man querulous. 'The trouble with you two is, you still think I can't tell you apart. Well, I can.' Sam nodded, not knowing what to say. Harry's eyes roved round the room, from face to face, with quiet satisfaction. 'That's better,' he said at last. Then abruptly his tone changed. 'Now go away, the lot of you, I want to sleep.'

CHAPTER
TWENTY-TWO

The Hardacre family solicitor was a man called Appleby who resided in Driffield, a gentleman of some seventy years who was the professional descendant of old Sam Hardacre's legal adviser, the venerable Saunders. He had presided over family affairs since the latter's decease, which was coming up for thirty years now. Naturally, he knew all the family well and when, on the day set for the reading of Harry Hardacre's will, he was met at the door of the house by young Sam, he greeted him warmly.

Sam did not employ Appleby for his own legal needs, but used a big London firm. The complexities of salvage law were not for Yorkshire country solicitors. But he met him socially, often, over the years.

'Terribly sorry about your uncle, of course,' Appleby said, formally.

Sam smiled. 'An old man, dying in his own house, among his own family. Not a bad thing, surely.' Appleby nodded, still looking grave, as he thought the occasion warranted. But Sam only smiled again. He was at peace over Harry. It was not an unexpected death, though a little sudden, its suddenness only ensuring a relief from wearying descent into senility. He had known Harry was dying, all that autumn, and accepted it. He would miss him greatly, but that was all. No death would ever again affect him as Terry's had, he knew. When he had at last, and only very recently, accepted that death he had accepted also the will of God over life, the first step towards religious maturity, which wasn't too bad, at forty.

Sam showed Appleby into the library, where the family was gathered. He had become, in the intervening weeks since Harry's death, the acknowledged master of the house, which bemused him, since it was not really right. But he was the only one there among their men who knew how to behave in that manner. He was the only one comfortable in the place, easy with the staff, aware of social needs and priorities. Jane, of course, knew what to do but Jane was a woman from a generation who turned always to their men, even to do what they well knew how to do themselves. It was gracious and old-fashioned, and he loved it as much as he was exasperated by it.

Rodney, of course, was useless. Social events were things at which he arrived late so as to miss the introductions, and during which he depended on Vanessa to direct him to do and say the appropriate things. Philip Barton was not bred to this world, and Noel Hardacre, who most certainly was, couldn't care less.

Noel, actually, had been surprisingly subdued by his father's death, and had stood quite humbly in the deathroom, a shaggy gnome of a figure, and shambled out afterwards, lost into the night. He seemed like a man interrupted in the middle of a long acrimonious argument, suddenly without anyone left at whom he might direct his venom. He had responded to the situation in an old way that he had long abandoned. That is, immediately after the funeral he went on a bender that lasted a week. And it took another week to sober him up. Now he sat in a corner of his father's library, morose and silent, as if feeling yet the old man's resentment of his unseemly presence there.

Emily and Philip Barton were present, though Maud and Albert Chandler were not. They had taken brief winter employment aboard a cruise liner in the Mediterranean, a job less glamorous than it sounded, comprising as it did long evenings of work in a pitching, water-bound ballroom full of half-interested people, followed by nights in the cramped, noisy quarters up in the bow allotted to lesser performers. But they sent happy postcards, all the same, and even found the occasion to sun themselves quietly in a secluded corner of the deck. And it was better than Blackpool in February.

Paul Barton, therefore, who was with them more than with his own parents, usually, was also at Hardacres with his mother and father. Sam was surprised to see him grown suddenly into a tall and lanky adolescent, with his ever-cheery face quite unchanged. His voice had indeed dropped and, as his sister Ruth had predicted, indeed also kept its beautiful quality. Sam knew he was studying music seriously now, and Albert was excited both by his voice and his ability with the piano. But Paul's great love was his guitar, which Albert had somehow scraped the money together to buy for him; a really good guitar, too, which he played with absolute devotion by himself all week, and in the company of his three-man skiffle group at weekends in Scarborough and Brid. The other instruments were cheaper; a washboard and thimbles, and a home-made double bass constructed from a tea-chest and a broom handle. They played Lonnie Donegan numbers all night, and affected American accents, and Albert said they sounded like hell.

'Look at him,' Emily mourned in disgust, indicating her son. He was dressed in the fashionable drainpipe trousers, black shirt, and long, velvet-cuffed jacket of the coffee-bar set. 'I do apologize, Sam, but I couldn't get him to change.'

'He's young,' Sam said, laughing, but Emily did not laugh.

'I'm ashamed of him,' she said. He kissed her cheek.

'How's Ruth getting on?' he asked. She shrugged, suddenly evasive.

'All right, I suppose,' she said, and then added sharply, 'Frankly, I haven't heard.' Ruth was at drama school, in London. Not at RADA, or anything of that stature, but at one of those small drama colleges opened by failed actors to bring other future failures into the profession. Janet had told Sam it was a waste of time and money, and Albert

384

Chandler had said quietly to Ruth that if she couldn't make RADA, she should quit now, while she was ahead. But Ruth was determined, and her father was dutifully paying. She had been in London since the autumn but Sam, preoccupied with business and his own personal life, had not managed to see her, either there, or in the North.

'I'll try and see her, when I'm down,' he said now, with a twinge of remorse. 'What's her address, Emily?' Emily looked at him, sideways, as Appleby made his way to Harry's desk, which had been turned to face the company. She smiled suddenly, without humour.

'Ask Riccardo,' she said.

'What?' Sam whispered, but she shushed him, as the solicitor began to speak.

Jane Macgregor came in just then, quietly and hurriedly from the drawing-room where she had been sharing coffee with the ladies of the family. Sam rose instinctively as she entered and found her a place beside him. She sat down, and he took her hand for a moment and said, 'Are you all right?'

She squeezed his hand and released it and said, 'Of course, my dear.'

Jane had been calm throughout the whole three weeks; her attitude to death was marvellously serene, with a serenity based less in religious faith, which she did not really share with him, than in her aristocratic nature. One did not complain. One accepted. One made the best of things. He admired her immense control, just as he knew he could never emulate it, even if he lived as long as she. She was so British, and his half-French blood would always deny him that marvellous aplomb.

Appleby was making the sort of speech he had made at similar occasions for fifty years; regrets, and formalities, and professional respectfulness. Jane Macgregor, listening to him, could hear, as he carefully, reverently opened the seal of the will, the echoes of his predecessor Saunders reading her own father's will, in this very room. She smiled. Almost forty years ago, and it seemed like yesterday. That was what age meant, that the young could never understand, how the years, once spread so bountifully, folded up tight like a pack of cards, diminished, in a trickster's hand. Forty years. The tall greying man beside her, whose hand rested gently on her shoulder, had been an infant in the Hardacre nursery on that day.

Appleby read out the opening formalities, then quickly the instructions for the settling of debts, and the long, detailed list of small bequests to faithful staff, old acquaintances, more distant family. Sam glanced across to Noel, who was sitting yet in his corner, with one booted leg drawn up sideways across his knee. He peered at the solicitor as at some beast he was assessing for market.

Appleby reached the main part of the will, and read out Harry's provisions for Madelene, the cottage on the grounds that she had used for so many years; a sum of money as generous as he could afford, for her yearly support, of which she, with her own business and her extremely wealthy son, had no need. But that was the way it was traditionally done, and Harry was a traditional man. He had made small bequests, in trust with Sam named as trustee, for each of the family's children under the age of eighteen, again as generous as he could afford. There wasn't much free money about, and they all knew that. There were token, sentimental bequests to Jane and others, paintings, bits of silver, things admired over the years that Harry had not forgotten. There were small nods about the room, and a little laughter, and the occasion was warm, far different from the reading of old Sam's will in which Joe and Helen had been cut off without a penny. As for Helen and Mike Brannigan, there was no mention, and none expected. For Janet Chandler Harry had selected a Victorian oil painting of Edmund Kean. Heaven knew where it had come from, but it had been in the house as long as any of them

386

remembered, and Janet had once admired it, and Harry did not forget. Sam smiled, listening, remembering the occasion, a family dinner, early on in their affair, at which she and Harry had held each other in equal awe.

'I believe that completes most of the details,' Appleby said. He looked down at the paper before him, and up at Sam and Noel. He was as aware as anyone in the room who had really carried Hardacres for the past five years. The bills came through his office and he knew who paid them. He looked down at the paper again, running a finger behind the collar of his shirt. He cleared his throat. He was evidently, clearly embarrassed.

He coughed again and read, quickly, so as to complete the whole thing in a breath, if possible, and get it done.

'"To my great-nephew Samuel Hardacre I leave the contents of the envelope vested with this will, and the books of my library. With respect, he is the only one of all of you who could put either to proper use."'

The solicitor paused and looked up at Sam, who was smiling faintly. He looked down, and read, '"He well knows how gladly I would have given him more."'

Appleby looked up again, over his spectacles. He said, 'I really don't understand that last bit at all, Sam.' He was apologetic, and shrugged. Sam heard Jane next to him quietly sigh. His smile broadened.

He said, 'Never mind. I do,' and reached across the desk to take the envelope that had lain beside the will. It was unsealed, and his name, just his first name, his, and that of his great-grandfather, was written across it, in Harry's fine old spidery hand. He opened it, grinning, knowing what it was. The room watched. The contents of the buff envelope slipped easily into his hand and rested against his calloused palm as if it belonged there. It was a short, stubby knife, with a string-bound handle, the string sweat-stained from his great-grandfather's hand.

'Father's gutting knife,' Jane said, amazed. She had not

387

seen it for years, since her mother died and they cleared the old cottage. She had not known it to be yet in her brother's possession. 'Harry,' she whispered disapprovingly. But Sam closed his long hard fingers around the handle, and grinned with delight.

'Harry, God bless you,' he said. 'Who knows, I might need it yet.' The assembled company squirmed round to look at him, slightly unnerved by his illogical pleasure, and the solicitor looked as if he frankly thought Sam insane. Sam nodded to him to continue, still grinning. The solicitor shrugged.

He read quickly, '"As to the house and lands known as Hardacres, I choose to do as my father before me, and vest it in the trust and care of one, for the benefit of all. I realize it will leave some of you dependent upon the judgement and good grace of another, but so it must always be in families, and should such an arrangement fail, it will be, I regret, a judgement only upon myself and my failures as parent. Therefore I do bequest this property to my only son Noel, that it be his, by all rights, and with the wish that he will, perhaps, learn one day to love it as I have done."'

The solicitor stopped reading and removed his glasses, and waved a vague hand in the air. 'And then there are the usual signatures and witnesses.' He looked at Noel Hardacre, still sitting with one leg crossed lazily across the other, as if at his cottage fireside. Appleby studied him a long while and then turned his glance once to Sam and then he simply shrugged, and folded and stacked neatly the pristine papers on Harry's desk. There was a small murmur around the room, and Noel yet sat, unmoving. He raised his eyes from the floor, searched the room with their quick, canny and darting glance. They met Sam's for an instant and Sam lightly touched the fingers of one hand to his forelock of black hair where it lay across the healing scar above his eye. He grinned, and Noel grinned, and a look passed between them like that between two Border collies that was nine parts irascibility and one part sheer respect.

Noel got up, walked through the room, and stood for a moment looking out of the window of his father's beloved library. Then he turned back to the waiting family and said with a slow needling grin, 'Well, here I am. Master of all I bluidy survey.' He grinned again, and then, with the clomp of his heavy boots echoing on the polished floor, stamped out of the room, and out of the door.

The gathering began to stir and break up. Luncheon had been laid in the long dining-room, and Sam stood and turned to escort Appleby, since the now-confirmed Master of Hardacres was apparently not quite ready to take up his inheritance, and rightful role as host. But Jane caught his arm and stopped him, holding him there in the library until the room was emptied of all but themselves. He turned, questioning, towards her and saw to his astonishment that she, who was ever candid, was not able to meet his eyes. She looked away, absently, out of the window where thin February sunshine shone on frosted lawns. When she did speak her voice was, amazingly for her, both flustered and emotional. She said with a little laugh, 'Do you know, I'm really most annoyed with my brother. Most annoyed. When I see him next I'm going to have a very severe word.' She was smiling that wry smile she used for changing circumstances beyond her control. Her sanguinity about death was an integral part of her age, and he knew she really did mean to have it out with Harry in some very low-keyed, very British hereafter. But he did not know why.

'What's wrong?' he said, bending over her, trying to look into her face. She turned to him suddenly and he had rarely seen her look so angry.

'Oh, Sam,' she said, her voice very low. 'How could he hurt you like this?'

He stared at her, amazed, and then said quickly, 'He hasn't *hurt* me, Jane. What can you mean?'

'Oh really, Sam. I told him, years ago, he couldn't keep taking money from you, taking everything, if he didn't change his will.' She shook her head. 'The damned thing is, I thought he *had*. I was sure he had.'

'Jane,' he said urgently, 'I never gave anything to Harry that I didn't want to give. You know that.'

'Well, he had a hell of a way of saying thank you,' she snapped. She faced him, both her hands on his upper arms, smiling and shaking her head, 'I really *don't* understand, Sam. Really I don't. He loved you so.'

'Jane, why are you expecting me to be hurt?' Sam asked again. 'He gave me his two dearest possessions. I *know* he loved me.' Her chin came up and she gave one of her angry and scornful sniffs, looking at him down her long nose.

'His dearest possessions?' she whispered. 'You and I both know what his dearest possession was.'

Sam finally understood her, and slowly shook his head, 'No, Jane,' he said.

'For God's sake, Sam, we all knew.' She looked hard at him, trying to read emotions she assumed must be hidden in him somewhere. 'He should have given you Hardacres,' she said bluntly, at last. 'You know, as well as I.'

Sam shook his head again, and said, his voice serious, 'No, Jane. He should not have. Hardacres is Noel's. By right, Jane. By right. I'm not his son, Jane.'

She looked wearily about the room, and shrugged. 'More's the pity,' she said, at last. She turned to go, but Sam stopped her.

'No, look. You must understand about this. I never realized, or I would have explained. It is not like you think, and you mustn't blame Harry.'

'He's my brother, Sam, and I *will* blame him,' she said.

He shook his head again and took her arm, determined now to make her understand. But the door opened, disturbing their peace, and Madelene was standing there. She had obviously heard the end of their conversation, and she said, her voice brittle and barely controlled, 'No. You're not to blame Harry. Sam's quite right, Jane. Sam knows exactly who's to blame.' She stepped slowly into the room and closed the door. Sam's eyes met hers and saw in them the confrontation that had awaited him there in Harry's deathroom, and which had finally come to him now. She sighed softly, and tightened her lips momentarily before she spoke. She was still a beautiful woman, even with her face lined with grief for her lover of so many years. Her eyes were as dark and as beautifully expressive as those of her sons, but they had a hardness about them the twins had not inherited. It was something life had done, that could not be carried in the blood. They hardened more as she said, 'Are you quite pleased now?'

'I don't understand,' Sam said.

'Oh yes, you do.' She stepped closer. 'You've got what you want now, haven't you?'

Jane suddenly intervened, knowing it was not her business, but overcome by confused anger. 'Madelene, he has got *nothing* from all this. Nothing.'

'Exactly,' she said. 'And precisely what he wanted.'

Sam shook his head and raised his hands slightly, as if shielding his face. He turned to go, 'I want out of this,' he said.

'*Don't* you leave this room.' Madelene's voice dropped to a hiss and Jane was suddenly aware where Sam's famous temper came from. She thought for a moment that *she* wanted out of this, but she wasn't leaving Sam alone. Instinctively she even moved closer to him. He had frozen at Madelene's command. He also was of a generation that did not openly defy their parents. Madelene looked long and hard at him and whispered, 'He took me into this house when I was a widow of seventeen, a pregnant widow. He kept me all my life. He raised you and Terry like his sons;

he spared nothing. You sat at his table and slept under his roof for all your childhood. He put you through school, and to Cambridge. He gave you every start in life. He gave you as much of a father's love as your own father, God rest him, could ever have done. And the only thing, the *only* thing, he ever asked of you, you denied him.' She gasped, fighting tears of fury. 'How could you do this to him? How could you break him so?'

'Madelene,' Jane suddenly intervened, her voice indignant and hurt, 'please. What are you saying? Sam *has* given . . . he has given so much, he has done nothing but give . . .'

'Money,' said Madelene with distaste. Her eyes darted just once to Jane, knowingly, and then back to Sam, who was utterly silent. 'He knows,' she said bitterly. 'He knows.' Her face softened slightly but her mouth twisted as she spoke, and she never took her eyes from Sam's. 'He wanted to give it to you, Sam. He *had* to give it to you; it was all his life's work and purpose, and there was no one else. He wanted to give it to you, and *you would not let him.*'

Jane turned in amazement to Sam, but he was not looking at her. He was looking at Madelene, and he did not even look angry, only stunned. He said, very softly, 'I know.'

'How *could* you?' she cried impotently. He half-raised his hands, dropped them, turned to look away, and then made himself look back. His eyes met Madelene's and they were totally honest.

'I couldn't live his life for him again, Mother. I couldn't live his dreams. I can't live Terry's life for you. It's right back to that again. All I want . . .' he shook his head and covered his face momentarily with his hands, then dropped them, looking wildly about the room, as if for somewhere to run. 'All I *ever* wanted was just to live my own life, my own way. Why can't any of you ever understand?'

'No,' Madelene shouted, 'all you've ever wanted is to do precisely what you want, and when you want it, and God help anyone who gets in your way.' She paused, stepping back from him as if she would leave. 'And God help,' she added, 'the woman you marry, if you ever do.'

He looked down and said, almost to himself, 'Well, there's not much chance of that now.'

Jane stepped forward and took his arm. She said quietly, 'Madelene, we are all overwrought and overtired. I think we should leave this, please, now?' Madelene, exhausted by her own outburst, looked almost about to relent. She still glared at her son in a distorted mixture of hurt and anger, but she said nothing.

Sam said, again to himself, 'I loved Harry.'

She shook her head again, knowingly. 'No, Sam,' Madelene said, quietly wise. 'You did not. You've never loved anyone. No,' she corrected, closing her eyes briefly, 'you loved Terry. That was true. You loved Terry and you've never loved anyone else. Not Harry, not me, not any of your women. Not even Janet, though it may surprise you to hear it. You can't love people, because you are too selfish. You are a very selfish man.'

'No, Madelene,' Jane said, tightening her almost possessive grip on Sam's arm. 'I won't have this now. You are being hurtful without reason.'

'I am being truthful,' Madelene said with great composure. 'Actually, it's all quite amusing, because selfish is the last thing anyone who doesn't know you would think of you. They all think you're so generous, and the men who work for you think you're wonderful, and Mick Raddley worships you. I know all that. But they don't know you. I do.' She crossed the room, and absently lifted a log from the log box by the fire and set it, with another, across the lowering flames, exactly as she would have done had Harry yet been sitting there, with his books, by the hearth. 'You give. Of course you give. But you only give what you don't want anyhow. Money? What's that to you? It's never meant anything to you. Look at yourself. You are a rich man, but

393

you live like a poor man. This is the first time I've seen you in a decent suit for weeks. You live in a warehouse and you drive around in great wrecks like that thing sitting outside the door. What's money to you? All you care about, all you've ever cared about, is adventure. Even Janet was just the biggest adventure of your life.' She shrugged. 'You give,' she said. 'Of course you give. But you are only buying your freedom. From us, from responsibility, from having maybe once in your life to give something you care about. Time. A little of yourself. Love.' She paused. 'Sometimes, Sam, to give is to take. Sometimes it is a great sacrifice to take something. Something we don't want, that will tie us down, something someone wants us to have. You owed it to him, Sam. You *owed* him the acceptance of his quite beautiful gift.' She looked around the grand old room and shrugged, a shrug of Gallic mournfulness and despair.

Sam had listened all the while with his head down and no sign of either argument, or apparent remorse. But he looked up then and said clearly, 'Mother, it was not mine to take. I admit I did not want it. But it was not mine. It was Noel's. It was Noel's by right.' She looked round from the fire with utter impatient disgust.

'Noel?' she said. 'Noel will destroy it.' She shrugged again, studying her son. She said, 'Do you know, Sam, we love our children by instinct. And of course I love you. And I certainly loved Terry. But I haven't liked you for years, and I don't like you now.' She turned from him and walked out of the room.

Sam felt Jane's arm, which had held his, slip around his waist and join her other, so she quietly embraced him. She leaned her fine old head against his shoulder and whispered, 'Oh, Sam. I'm sorry. You shouldn't have had to hear all that.'

'Is it true?' he said.

'She is grieving. She is grieving and angry with grief. You know what it is like.'

He nodded but said again, 'But is it true?'

She stepped back a little so that she could look at him, yet keep her hands linked behind his waist. She smiled, shrugged her shoulders in her elegant way. Her eyes were warm with love. 'In part, Sam, I suppose. In part, it's true.'

He was silent, shaken, standing with his shoulders hunched and his hands in his pockets like a recalcitrant but guilty schoolboy. His fingers closed suddenly on the guttie's knife he'd slipped without thinking into his pocket, and it felt warm, comforting, as if it held yet the warmth of another's hand. He said, 'Why didn't you tell me?'

She smiled, released her grip, and drew his arms forward towards her. He took her hands, and she shrugged again, and smiled more broadly. 'Perhaps because I like you the way you are?' She leaned back, still smiling. 'I'm an old woman, Sam. An old, self-indulgent woman. You're my last indulgence, my dear.'

CHAPTER
TWENTY-THREE

'You've seen this, of course,' Emily said. Sam, sitting in the May sun coming through the kitchen windows of The Rose, nodded, and took up the stapled sheaf of papers that she had laid on the table before him, studying the top sheet idly. The photograph was not very clear, but he'd know the old place, even in silhouette. Beneath, the title, 'Watton Manor by Great Driffield', cleared up any doubts.

'I don't see why they didn't use our own name,' Emily said, faintly hurt.

'It's better known by the original,' he said.

She was busy making pastry at an edge of the table. Without looking up she said, 'Did you know he was going to do this, Sam?' He did not answer for a long while, riffling absently through the pages, only lightly glancing at each. He knew the details like the back of his hand, anyhow.

'I knew he was going to have to, Emily. He couldn't possibly afford to keep it going by himself. And he wouldn't take any help.' Her hands stilled on the pastry, and she looked up, her lined, strong face registering amazement.

'Help?' she said. 'Did you offer to help?'

'Of course,' Sam said.

'But *why?*'

'Because I could. I was quite happy to. I could have continued, just as I had with Harry.'

'Sam, I don't understand you.' Emily shook her head.

He smiled and sipped the tea she had set before him. 'Join the club,' he said, ruefully. Then he straightened up in his chair and set the cup down. 'He wouldn't take it. He's a proud man, Emily.'

'Sam,' she said, 'he's a *bastard.*'

She was expressing the family judgement, he knew, which he did not quite share. Two months to the day of his inheritance, Noel had put Hardacres on the market. He had retained, of course, the home farm, and his own cottage. The rest, as the particulars of sale Sam held indicated, was offered either as a whole, a major investment, with its gardens and policies and two large tenant farms, or in several variable lots. The beech wood was kept apart as a potential development site for housing, and as such was worth another small fortune by itself.

'He'll be the richest farmer in Yorkshire,' Sam said with a grin.

'Oh, it's not funny, dear.' Emily looked coldly at him over her pastry. He was still looking through the thick sheaf of papers.

'I'm not really laughing,' he said. He didn't meet her eyes.

'I don't know what will become of Rodney and Vanessa. I mean, it *is* their home.'

'Emily, I'm very fond of Vanessa and Rodney but they've lived off Harry, and off Noel, all their lives. Maybe it's time they stood on their own feet.'

'Sam, people like Vanessa and Rodney don't *have* feet to stand on. We're not all like you, dear. Maybe we should be, but we're not. I frankly don't know what they'll do.'

Sam tilted his chair back against the wall, stretching his long legs under the table. He reached in the pocket of the heavy cotton fisherman's smock he wore for his cigarettes and his hand closed instead on the guttie's knife that he carried everywhere. It was surprisingly useful. He ran his fingers along the worn string handle, and looked at the flagstone floor. He felt pressure from Emily to suggest some salvation for Harry's daughter and son-in-law, but he didn't speak. He hadn't any suggestions.

Emily suddenly turned, brushing flour from her hands and dismissing the subject. It wasn't as if they hadn't all talked about it a few thousand times before. She said, instead, 'Have you been to London lately?'

'No. I've been in Orkney for three weeks.' He'd been in Orkney when Noel had dropped his bombshell and he rather wished he was in Orkney now.

'Then you've not seen Riccardo.'

'No. But he's doing well enough. He's opening the new restaurant in June. A bit upmarket, Emily. I think I'll even take you.'

'No thanks,' she said coldly. 'Then you don't know, do you?'

'What?' He straightened up and tilted the chair forward again. 'What's the matter?'

'Oh, nothing. Except that he's living with my daughter. Or she's living with him.'

'Ruth?' he whispered.

'Well, hardly Olive. She's still at school.' He stared, his eyes narrowing, and then suddenly reached for her with both hands.

'Oh, Emily.'

'No, don't,' she said, holding her arms up in front of her in a funny tense gesture, the knuckles of her hands pressed together. 'I can stand everything but sympathy,' she said, trying to grin, shaking her head from side to side. 'One ounce of loving kindness and I'm going to break down.'

'I don't care,' he said, and he got up and pulled her towards him and held her while she began to shake and then she turned and buried her face against him and wept uncontrollably. He led her to the window-seat and sat with her, his arms about her, rocking her like a child, back and forth, stroking and kissing her hair.

'I'll kill him,' he said, so quietly that she believed him.

She looked up, shaking her head, suddenly mature. 'None of that, Sam,' she said warningly, and then abruptly she pulled away from him, patted her hair, and dabbed her face with the end of her apron. 'We're all too old for that sort of thing. Much too old,' she said grimly, wiping her eyes. 'Besides, why not? He probably loves her. He's apparently *begging* to marry her. You know, Italian, Catholic.' She paused. 'Sorry,' she said, 'but you know what I mean.'

'I know,' he said, still trying to absorb it. 'So when's the wedding?' he added stiffly. Emily shrugged.

'Oh, it's Ruth holding that up, not him. She's busy being Bohemian or something.' She smiled faintly. 'It reminds me of Maud, all those years ago, with Albert.'

Sam said, 'Well, if it goes the way that went, no one could possibly complain.' She smiled again, more composed, and straightened her back, turning briefly to look out of the window to the pretty gardens and the pond.

'Oh, I suppose not. Just think of it, I'll probably soon be a granny.' Her mouth twisted wryly, 'Won't that be nice.' Then quite suddenly she wrapped her arms about his neck again and sobbed, 'Oh God, Sam, I keep lying to myself and saying he's having her because he can't have me, but it's such a stupid, childish lie. How can I be such a fool?'

'Maybe it's true.'

'Of course it's not true,' she said with immense self-directed scorn. 'He's young. She's young. And I'm an old woman. *That's* what's true.' She sniffed. 'Oh, he made such a fool of me.'

'He *loved* you, Emily. It may not have been right, or appropriate, and it certainly had no future. But he loved you. You and I both know that.' She looked into his eyes and smiled, looking as if she wanted very much to believe him, but could not. He saw, in the softening of the hard ageing lines of her face, the warmth of past memories crossing her mind.

She shook her head and got up. 'No, Sam. I guess I'll just have to live out the rest of my life with Philip like I was meant to.' She paused. 'Ageing gracefully,' she laughed lightly. But when she turned to face him her face was as youthfully defiant as a girl's. 'And I know I should be sorry but, damn, I'm not. It was the sweetest thing in my life and I'll live on it for the rest of my days.' She brushed her hair back with the spread fingers of one hand, suddenly lithe and sexy. Then she composed herself, a look of nervous embarrassment crossing her face, followed by another of concern.

'Sam, you do know, don't you, there was never anything . . . I mean it was all terribly proper.' She reddened, not looking at him. 'It wasn't physical, Sam.'

'Emily,' he said clearly, 'I would not possibly care if it was.'

'But it wasn't, Sam, it wasn't.'

'All right. But it wouldn't matter. Not one whit.'

She studied him and said, 'Doesn't anything ever shock you?'

Sam thought it an odd question and was silent, thinking about it, before he answered eventually, 'Not much, I suppose.' He thought again. 'It's like judging really, being shocked. And I don't like judging.' He looked at her and smiled. 'I'm hardly in a position the way I've lived.'

She grinned wryly. 'You know,' she said, 'you're our only moralist. The family Thomas Aquinas. How nice.' She laughed and then said, 'Still, not judging can also just amount to not caring.' His eyes suddenly became guarded, in a way with which she was familiar, and she physically felt him slip out of contact into the depths of himself that nobody ever got near.

'Don't you start, please,' he said. 'I've really had enough of that from everybody. And it isn't so, anyhow.' His voice hardened and became slightly angry. 'I just believe in leaving people to be themselves. Just leaving them alone.'

'Like you'd like us to leave you alone,' she said bluntly.

'Emily.'

'It can't happen, Sam. You're born into a family. There's no way out, unless you lose them all like Heidi and

Jan. And you wouldn't swop with them, surely,' she said and then paused and added drily, 'or would you?'

'Emily,' he whispered. She looked sorry. 'Now I *have* shocked you,' she said.

'Yes. You have.'

She brushed her hands down her floury apron, a little remorsefully, and went back to the table and began rolling and cutting her pastry. He sat quietly at the window-seat, looking out at the ducks sunning themselves by the pond. After a long silence she said briskly, 'Anyhow, I didn't bring you down here just to moan about my troubles.' He still looked out of the window, and she wondered if she was going to have to leave this now. But he turned, and she said, 'Noel's had an offer.'

'Already?' he said, feeling suddenly chilled. He added cautiously, 'A good offer?'

'Every penny he was asking.' Sam was silent. He was, or thought he was, prepared for it, but not quite so soon.

'Well, that's that then,' he said flatly.

'I suppose so. Would you like to know who it's from?'

'Not really.'

'Oh yes, you would,' she said. He looked startled. She said, watching his face. 'It's from Mother. And Mike.'

He stared, not comprehending. 'My *grandmother*?' he whispered at last. Emily nodded, looking faintly satisfied. 'But *why* for God's sake? What do they . . . what does she possibly *want* with it?'

'The same thing she's always wanted all her life,' Emily said mildly. 'Revenge.' Sam stood up and turned away from her, his arms, in the loose sleeves of the smock, wrapped around himself as if he was terribly cold. 'Are you all right?' she asked suddenly.

'Of course I'm all right,' he said. He turned back to her, a complex of emotions crossing his face, the uppermost being confusion. 'Surely no one spends *that* kind of money out of vengeance.'

401

'I don't see why not,' Emily said, still mildly. 'People sell their souls for it, St Thomas.'

He walked about the room restlessly, ducking his head under the low central beam. He seemed unable to stand still. He said at last, 'Has he accepted?'

Emily shrugged. 'He wouldn't tell me, likely, would he? But I don't see why not. He should be delighted. He'll be rich as Midas and he'll be able to sit back and watch the fun. And it's bound to be just super fun.' She glared at him, and he knew she, like the rest of them, held him responsible.

His hands closed on the guttie's knife in his pocket again, and he said abruptly, 'I'm leaving.'

'Thought you would,' she said.

He was outside, climbing up into the cab of his lorry, when she came out. She had taken her apron off, to appear in the street, and her face was remorseful. She said, 'I thought you might like to know they're coming up to see the place tomorrow.'

'I'll be in London,' he said.

She shrugged and turned away, angry again, but she stopped. 'Look, Sam.'

'I'm off, Emily,' he said, starting the rough old diesel engine.

'All right. I'm sorry. I wasn't going to speak about that. It's about Riccardo. And Ruth.' He switched off the engine, softening to her visibly. She said, 'Don't be hard on them. I want them to be happy. I do. Really.'

He nodded. 'He'll make her a good husband, Emily,' he said gently. 'He's generous and warm-hearted.' He nodded towards the dilapidated inn, and grinned suddenly. 'He'll be able to keep her in the style to which she's grown unaccustomed. He's going to be a very rich man.'

Emily smiled. 'Thanks to you,' she said.

He shook his head. 'No. Thanks to his own hard work. I just gave him a break. I was to him what Erasmus Sykes

402

was to me. That's all. Nobody can do it all alone.' She nodded wisely, and raised her hand in a wave of farewell.

'Some of us keep trying, though,' she shouted as he drove away.

He didn't go to London, though, the following day. He drove to Hardacres instead. He wasn't expected, but he knew it didn't matter. Since Harry's death and Madelene's removal to the cottage, the place had become rather like a railway station, which people wandered into and out of, always on their way somewhere else. He stopped down the drive and climbed out of the cab of the lorry, standing and looking at the house in the soft early summer sun. They had been in snow and gales for the three weeks in Orkney, and the gentleness of the English countryside always came, at such times, as an unexpected gift. He stood looking at the house, wondering what it was going to be like when he could no longer come here.

He was wearing dungarees and the fisherman's smock which he more or less lived in when he was working, which was all the time. He had spent the morning in a scrap-yard outside Whitby. He thrust his hands in his pockets and turned suddenly away from the house, and walked, head down, across the lawns, towards the summer-house and the ornamental pond. He wasn't ready suddenly, to go within.

Helen Hardacre Brannigan, standing coolly at the window of the master bedroom which she had been carefully examining, saw him, and took him for a tradesman whom she dismissed with no thought. She had other things on her mind. One of them was Mike, who was still trying to talk her out of it, and whom she could not let out of her sight lest he try to talk Noel out of selling, as an alternative.

Also, he was inclined these days to be a simple embarrassment. Age had caught him at last, though he didn't realize it, and in an oddly loving, motherly way, she felt bound to protect his foolish ego from himself.

'Aw, come on, honey, haven't you seen enough?' he complained. 'I mean, it's not like the place were new to you.' It wasn't. She had known it well, so many years ago, and it wasn't very different. Leave it to Harry, she thought, to keep everything forty years out of date. But she was enjoying this, savouring it. There wasn't much Helen enjoyed any more. Money had long ago ceased to excite her. There were just so many things one could buy with it, without simply starting over again and buying the same things twice. She didn't enjoy travel much; she was an old lady and liked having things in the same place, and not shifted around by alien staff in hotel bedrooms. Mike was manageable in New York, where they had a set ritual of restaurants, theatre, house-parties, and only the right people were ever present. She didn't like surprises any more; pretty blondes placed at his elbow by some over-generous host, or that extra martini slipped his way out of the perverse kindness that those not married to drunks can feel for them. Evenings alone together, conversely, were no great joy either. And evenings really alone, when, rarely, she allowed him out in selected company without her, were a terror. Memory, that solace of the contented old, drove her as a whipper-in drove hounds.

She'd begun to dream a lot, sometimes when she was not even properly asleep, but sitting in her chair and only dozing. All sorts of people came back, and most of them – people from her past – were naturally from England. Coming here was like coming to joust with a legion of ghosts. It was madness, perhaps, as Mike said, and yet Helen Brannigan had never run from anything in her life, not from the day she met Joe on the great liner, on which she herself was a stowaway, and bargained with sex to keep her crime secret. She'd met all life head-on. So had Joe. She thought of him often, with almost kindness. He'd been a man at least, not a perpetual, now-ageing, flabby boy, like Mike. She looked round the room, slowly and thoughtfully, remembering Joe confronting his father here, one day. She had not even noticed that Mike had slipped away.

Mike found his way downstairs. He was looking for a drink and thought he knew where to find one. There'd always been booze in the library, where the men of the family always gathered. If he could just remember where the library was. He groped his way down corridors, peering in doors. He wanted that drink badly and his hands were shaking. When he found the library, he was so desperate he didn't even stop to knock, but pushed the door open and strode right in, and was half-way to the Jacobean sideboard by the hearth, where he had spotted already a tantalus containing two filled decanters, when the girl spoke.

'Excuse me,' she said in a low, pretty and surprisingly mature voice. She sounded slightly surprised, and slightly proprietorial. 'Can I help you?'

Mike looked to the voice. The girl was sitting at the large desk that filled the area before the tall windows. He realized that she must logically be Vanessa and Rodney Gray's daughter, Mary, but was surprised to see her so grown up. Faintly he remembered her as the little child whom he had met on that Festival year visit with Helen. She looked about sixteen, he thought, but British children of the public school variety were deceptive. Mike, long accustomed to checking out young ladies with the age of consent in mind, was not usually deceived. He remembered when she was born, late in the war. She couldn't be more than twelve, he acknowledged, with faint disappointment.

'Hello, sweetheart,' he said, in his best paternal voice. She looked a little uncomfortable, sitting there before her schoolbooks which were spread out on the desk. She drew her feet together in a modest gesture of tightened security. He noticed she was wearing knee-socks and that, above, the small band of visible leg below her short, plain school-

405

girl skirt, was bare. He saw her fidget, and realized he had been staring. 'Just getting myself a drink,' he muttered, crossing to the decanters.

'There are glasses in the sideboard,' she said politely, accustomed no doubt to family friends helping themselves. Then she said, 'You're Mr Brannigan, aren't you?'

'Yeah, sweetheart,' he said, surprised at her adult tone again, and her awareness, 'that's me.' He waited for her to say something else, but she didn't, dropping her head to her books again. She began to write in a notebook. He poured himself a large whisky, added soda from the siphon by the tantalus, and stole another look, while she wrote.

She was slim and graceful, and developed already. He loved the way they began, so literally like budding flowers, everything so hard and firm yet, just a step from childhood. She wore a neatly buttoned blouse and a cardigan with her plain grey skirt, which would have been stodgy on an American girl but which suited her, somehow. Her hair was very black and straight, cut at chin length, and her eyes, he had noticed at once, were deep blue-green and very large and expressive. He wished she'd look up so he'd see them again.

The drink went down too fast. He poured another. The girl glanced up at the movement, but glanced down again at once, conscious of her good manners. Mike settled uneasily on the arm of a sofa, trying to make the next drink last. He half-wished Helen would hurry up, and half-wished she'd not. She was a long time. The girl worked away at her schoolbooks, oblivious apparently of Mike, who found himself on his third whisky and soda and suddenly conscious of the heat of the room, in which a fire had been lit, perhaps better to show off its qualities to the prospective buyers. The family solicitor, Appleby, was obviously astounded that anyone had so quickly met Noel's outlandish price, and was making the best of things. He needn't have tried so hard, Mike knew. No one, but no one, was going to talk Helen out of this. He had tried hard enough, himself.

'Whatcha going to do?' he asked the girl, suddenly. She looked up, perhaps startled at being spoken to, perhaps also startled at the blurring of his words, which had rather surprised him. It didn't seem to take much, these days. Three Scotches and he was in a thick haze. He must be getting old, like Helen kept saying. The thought angered him in a sad, frustrated way. It was ironic. He was so used to Helen being the one who was old, he hadn't realized it could happen to himself as well.

'Do when?' she said, meeting his eyes with her own, clear and candid.

'You know. When you grow up,' he waved a hand in the air, uncertain of why he'd asked the question, except that it was the sort of paternal question adults were supposed to ask of schoolchildren. And it was a lot better than the other question in the back of his mind, which was something more like, 'Can I touch that strip of bare leg, please?'

'I'm going to read law,' she said with confidence. 'At Cambridge. If I make it.'

'Oh, you'll make it, honey,' Mike muttered boozily. She blinked and did not answer. It was when she bent her head to her books again, exposing the soft feathery down on the back of her neck, as the cropped hair swung forward, that he found he couldn't sit still. He got up from the arm of the sofa and wandered around the room, glass in hand, in concentric circles that closed on the desk. Then quite suddenly he settled his bulk on the edge of its broad surface, just brushing the edge of her Latin text. She looked up, surprised, her eyes clouding at the intrusion into her private space. 'My God, you're a winner,' he mumbled. And then, without his really directing it, but by an old familiar instinct of its own, his hand came out across the desk, and trailed down the side of her cheek. Her face came up as if he had struck it.

'What?' she said aloud, confused and unhappy, as if the gesture had been somehow a misunderstanding.

'Now, it's all right, sweetheart,' he muttered. 'It's just me. You know me.' He fumbled to pat her hair. She leapt up from the desk, suddenly frightened, and he jumped after her so she wouldn't start shouting, and grabbed her clumsily and apologetically about the waist. She froze. Her eyes became very adult and aware, and considerably angry.

'Let me go,' she ordered. But his rebellious hands were doing their old familiar things. They'd stopped consulting his head years ago. She suddenly became not just angry, but terrified, and shouted, 'Let go of me. Help, someone, please.' Embarrassment and refinement kept her voice down, but then she panicked and suddenly shrieked, in a child's voice, 'Daddy! Daddy, where are you?' and struggled to get away.

Mike tripped over the desk-chair, lost his grip and fell heavily to one knee. The chair went over with a crash, and she broke free and ran for the door. But as she reached it, it was flung open and an angry masculine voice demanded, 'What's going on in here?'

She met him at the door, and his anger seemed directed at her. She shrank back. She was, and had always been, afraid of him. But she needed his protection. She forced herself to go and stand beside him, where he stood glaring at Mike. 'Get my Daddy, please, Sam,' she said.

Sam saw the girl, frightened, embarrassed, indignant, the way young girls are when their new vulnerability is shown to them. He saw Mike. He saw the overturned chair, the scattered schoolbooks on the desk, the spilled whisky glass on the floor. What had happened in the room could not have been more obvious to him if someone had stood in a corner and read aloud a resumé.

'It's all right,' Mike was muttering, waving an apologetic hand over the disorder in the room, 'it's just me. You remember me, Sam, don't you? Mike. Mike Brannigan . . .' he extended his hand convivially. 'Didn't know you were around.' He stood weaving, uncertain of the expression

Sam's face, reading it as a lack of recognition. 'I'm Helen's husband,' he said baldly. 'Your grandmother's . . . hey Jesus Christ, what are you doing?'

Sam could not have told him. He didn't know what he was doing. The room had become suddenly a blurry, unreal place in which he was aware only of Mike's face, inexplicably terrified, mouthing words he seemed not able to hear. Dimly he heard the child shrieking again behind him, and heard voices shouting. But nothing meant anything, only Mike, retreating across the room until he was cornered, with widening eyes, in the ell of two walls of books. He was conscious of his own hand on Mike's shirt collar, and of shaking the burly man so vehemently that his jowly face shook in folds around his terrified moving mouth. Even his own voice sounded distant, saying, 'Not in my house, you filthy bastard, not in my house.'

Then suddenly Mike's eyes reflected a vast desperate relief as he looked for a moment over Sam's shoulder and, suddenly also, the shouts and sounds that were distant were imminently upon him, voices clamouring, directed at him, illogically, not at Mike Brannigan, as if he, himself, were the trespasser.

Rodney was there somewhere saying repeatedly, 'Good God, Sam. Good God,' in his short, stuttery way and Appleby the solicitor was pawing uselessly at the arm by which he held Mike, spluttering prissily inane requests that he stop. But it was Noel, little tough Noel, who was incredibly strong, who physically wrenched him off Mike and shouted in a voice that finally reached him, 'For the love of Christ, man, what are you doing?'

The blur faded; he saw Mike clearly, sweating and terrified, pinned against the bookcases; he saw the cluster of worried frantic family, even Vanessa valiantly braying, 'She's all *right* Sam. You don't have to . . .' And then, for the first time, he saw, too, the guttie's knife in his hand, held inches from Mike Brannigan's throat.

Slowly, numbly, he lowered his hand, feeling Noel's arm come over his with a kind of firm authority as he did so. Everyone was still talking, except Noel, who was just watching him with his head tilted sideways in his squinting, quizzical way. Sam looked down into Mike Brannigan's face, the astonishment in his own eyes meeting the fading terror in Mike's. Noel said, 'Go and sit down, Sam.' He did, slowly, ignoring the baffled questions of Vanessa and Rodney and the solicitor. He sat on the sofa in front of the fire and laid the guttie's knife on the inlaid Indian table before it. The family clustered round, still clamouring, while Noel, doing the only sensible thing among them, took a not-unwilling Mike by the elbow and propelled him out of the room, out of the house, and to his waiting car, before Sam changed his mind.

Appleby settled himself on the sofa next to Sam and peered at him over his spectacles. He had shown signs of doubting his rationality ever since the reading of Harry's will, and now his face reflected a hardening conviction that Sam was insane. He was saying in deeply offended tones, 'I don't know what you were thinking of. You would have been facing a murder charge.' Sam ignored him.

Rodney was still stuttering about, between his daughter, who was sobbing yet, and his wife. He leant over and said, his voice shakily helpful, 'Why don't you just get in that lorry and go away somewhere for a while, please, Sam. Just go off and cool down. We're quite all right, really . . .'

Vanessa came closer, still holding the trembling girl, her voice as always echoing in the wood-lined room, 'I mean, it was jolly decent looking out for Mary, but he didn't really *do* anything, did he, love?' The girl turned her face away, cringing in embarrassment, and when Vanessa came closer with her, towards Sam, she tugged to be free. He saw to his dismay that she was more afraid of him than she'd ever been of Mike. He shook his head, and waved Vanessa back.

'Take her out, Vanessa,' he said. 'She's afraid.' She nodded, uncertainly, but led the girl away.

Noel passed them in the doorway, returning from outside. He looked around the room with a wry grin, which settled on Sam. He said, 'I thought I was bad, but you're a *real* maniac.' There was genuine admiration in his voice. He looked around the room, startlingly cheerful, his grey straight hair falling in wild chunks about his ears. 'Anybody like a drink?' he said.

Before anyone could answer there was the sound of sharp, high-heeled footsteps at the door and a dry, hard, feminine voice said, 'So *here's* the party then. Aren't *we* all having fun?' Helen Hardacre Brannigan stepped into the room, wrapped in black mink, her shrewd eyes wrinkled up with sour amusement. Behind her, red-faced, stood Vanessa, still clutching her unhappy daughter, and it was as evident from her blushing face as from Helen's words that the whole tale had been told.

Rodney said again, his hand on Sam's shoulder, 'Come on, old son, just go out for a drive. We'll see you later.'

But Helen said, 'Oh, don't. We're just leaving anyhow.' The solicitor got to his feet, glared once, unamused, at Sam, and hastened to Helen's side.

'I do hope, Mrs Brannigan, that this unfortunate incident . . .'

She merely waved him away. 'Go on,' she said crustily, 'all of you. Just before I go, I want a word with my grandson. Alone.' They all filed out, obediently. Helen Hardacre Brannigan was accustomed to being obeyed. Sam stood up as they did so and turned to face her. She turned briefly, and pushed the heavy door of the library closed until she heard the click of the latch. Then her face broke into an ancient, crêpy smile, cracking the weight of powder on her rouged, ravaged face. 'Tell me something,' she said, her eyes mischievous. 'Why are Catholics so violent?'

Sam shook his head, raising his hands in a helpless gesture of remorse, 'Helen, there is nothing I can say . . .'

'No, I'm serious. I'd really like to know. You, Mike, both of you, just alike. What *is* it . . . ?'

Sam shrugged, and smiled slightly, also. 'Perhaps we get forgiven too often. I don't know, Helen, but I am most grievously sorry.'

She dismissed that with a quick wave of her gold-laden hand. 'Oh, please, don't be. You've done me a favour. That'll keep him in line for at least a week.' She glanced down at the inlaid table and saw the guttie's knife. Her eyes lit. 'Oh my dear, this is rich. So you've won the family heirloom.'

Sam nodded. He said, 'I don't think that was quite what Harry intended when he gave it to me.'

She smiled. 'Oh, I wouldn't know about that,' she said, laughing to herself. 'Ah, Sam, your grandfather would be disappointed in you,' she said. He looked at her curiously, wondering where Joe Hardacre fitted into this. She smiled again. 'He had a saying, you know. If a thing's worth doing, its worth doing right.' She grinned and picked up the knife, running her perfectly manicured claw-like nail along its razor edge. 'You should have slit his stupid throat,' she said. There was such disgust in her voice that Sam felt illogical remorse now towards Mike.

'He was drunk, Helen,' he said. She raised one eyebrow, her fingers still fondling the knife.

'When a man spends his whole life drunk, it ceases to be an excuse,' she said. She turned the knife over in her hand, studying it. 'What delicious justice,' she said. 'The best use anyone ever put it to.' She extended her hand, with the knife in it, handle first, to Sam. He hesitated and she said, 'Go on, take it. You might have to defend the Faith again some day.' She grinned, her ancient, watery eyes still sharp. He took the knife from her, still uneasily, and slipped it back into the pocket of the fisherman's smock. He realized two things suddenly, about his grandmother, one of which he should have realized long before. She was, firstly,

412

extremely intelligent. And secondly, under the right, radically different circumstances, he would have liked her.

'Why are you doing this, Helen?' he suddenly said. She made no answer, but half-turned away, as if she had suddenly grown coy. 'Surely you don't intend to live here?'

She turned back and her eyes took a stony glitter. 'Oh yes,' she breathed, 'I'll live here. For a while, anyhow, I'll live here.' She stalked to the window, her mink darkly enfolding her, and stared out with her old eyes squinting against the bright light. She waved distractedly across the lawns with one hand, on which diamonds flashed rainbows in the sun. 'Long enough for me to hear the bones turning over down there,' she indicated the family mausoleum, just out of sight behind the beeches. 'That long, anyhow.'

'Just for that, Helen?' he said gently. She turned to face him, her eyes narrowing slightly and her mouth made a small defensive pout amid its spiderweb of wrinkles.

'No,' she said slowly, her voice thin and crackly, suddenly very old, 'I've got other reasons. It's a good investment. You wouldn't argue that.'

He shrugged. 'Then you'll sell again?'

She wrapped her mink tighter, as if the room, warmed by fire and May sunshine, were not warm enough. Her voice dropped, and hardened. 'Oh yes. I'll sell. I'll sell it into so many little pieces, scraps; I'll cut it up, and divide it, and undo it all, until no one will ever *know* there was an estate here at all. I'd put a damned factory right in the middle if I could, but the damned planners won't let me, I don't suppose.' She looked questioningly at him.

'I don't suppose,' he said softly, his eyes sad.

'That,' she continued, pointing to the grey and green glory of the May beech wood, 'I will turn into a housing estate.' She grinned her malicious grin. 'Maybe a *council* estate. That would be appropriate. I'll ring their graves with the pride of the working classes. How's that?' She grinned again, almost playfully, but he did not return her smile.

'Why look so sad?' she said. 'That should please you, after all. Aren't the poor supposed to inherit the earth?'

Sam said, 'The people you speak of are the people I live and work with every day. I have absolutely nothing against them. I am only sad to see something beautiful destroyed, for whatever good purpose.' He turned from her, his eyes sweeping hungrily over the grey, still trunks of the beeches, and their perfect shadows. 'And,' he said quietly, 'it's the meek who inherit the earth. The poor get the kingdom of heaven. That's not the same thing. The poor in *spirit*,' he added. 'That's not the same thing, either.'

'A theologian,' said Helen wryly.

'I've read the Bible.'

She was quiet. 'Yes,' she said eventually, 'I daresay you have.' She looked at him carefully. It was always hard for her to regard him as one of her own. He was so different from all of them. The twins had always seemed to her as changelings among the blue-eyed, fair-skinned Hardacre clan. The Hardacre men were all either big and solid, like old Sam, and her Joe and Arnold, or thin and craggy, like Harry and Noel. This one with his warm dark eyes, and lithe French grace, had no place among them. And yet he was her grandson, the only surviving child of her only son. Helen had not been a model mother; her children were largely an interruption and an annoyance in her life. The girls had not interested her at all. But she had been proud of her son. Like many strong women she preferred, and identified with, men. And an element of that long ago affection remained. She said, 'Don't be angry at me, Sam. I'm not trying to hurt *you*, you understand.'

'If you hurt my family, you will hurt me.'

She wavered, just for an instant. But she had not come all this distance, both in years and miles, to soften at the end. 'I'm sorry then,' she said, her face going rigid in a fixed, painted smile, 'but that can't be helped.' Then she shook her head, petulantly, tiredly. She had had enough.

414

Vengeance was less sweet than she had imagined, and more exhausting. She was an old lady. 'I must go now, Sam. I'm tired. It's time for my nap,' she added, like a peevish worn-out child. He smiled gently and took her arm, leading her out from the library and into the hall.

'And what of the house?' he asked quietly.

'What of it?'

'When you sell.'

She waved her free hand, with distracted annoyance, in the air. She was weary now; the discussion had ceased to interest her. 'I don't know,' she mumbled. 'Maybe it will make a hotel, flats . . .' her eyes brightened suddenly, catching sight of the two great portraits of Sam and Mary Hardacre that hung side by side in the galleried great hall, lit from the skylights above. They had been painted, almost as a ritual, in the first year of Hardacre residence at the house known previously as Watton Manor. They showed a man and a woman, quite handsome really, caught in an eternal embarrassment of unaccustomed dress and uncertainty of place. 'Or maybe,' Helen said with her old mischievous smile, 'maybe I'll just raze it to the ground.'

Sam led her to her car, bent to give her a filial kiss, his eyes avoiding Mike sitting in the dark of the vehicle, making himself small. Then he turned and, as they drove away, walked with bowed head back into the house.

Mary Gray knew he had gone back into the library. She had been watching from the corridor that led past the stillroom and gunroom to the kitchens, and had seen him. In a way she was glad. Her books were still in the library, and they gave her the excuse she needed. In another way, she wished he had just gone out and driven away in his big lorry, the way her father had asked him to, and spared her the ordeal of approaching him. Still, Mary was determined and, even at twelve, Mary Gray knew her mind. She crept down the corridor and through the entrance to the two-storey hall, off which the library door opened. She glanced around, making sure no one was in sight. She expected no one. Her parents had gone back to their flat at the back of the house when the Brannigans left and Noel was in the courtyard, working on the tractor. She wanted no interruptions and was confident she would get none. But she paused still, outside the door. It was all the more frightening approaching him in the still and empty house. As she hesitated, she glanced up, once, to the portrait of the woman who was her namesake. She was supposed by everyone to resemble that woman; certainly she had the same blue eyes and black hair; but Mary always felt that the oil portraits looked like no real people at all, but lifeless statues. She raised her hand to knock on the door and then lowered it again, glancing again to the portrait as if the woman there could give her courage. The painted eyes did look gentle, as if she too, had known what it was like to be young, and afraid.

Mary had always been afraid of Sam. As a small child she had hardly known either of the twins. They were away when she was born, in the army and, by the time she was old enough to be aware of people, they were away again, at Ampleforth. Their rare visits home were her first memories of them, exotic figures in their black Benedictine habits, so tall and dark, and confusing, there being two of them exactly alike. True, they laughed a lot, and offered to play with her, but she had been too awed to play.

Then there had been that brief, confusing spell when one of them, Sam, would appear at the house, no longer dressed in black, but looking like anyone else. But even then she was confused, being yet very young, and was never sure if she was seeing only one of them, or each of them on different occasions. That confusion ended, or perhaps reached its height, on the occasion of the first really clear memory she associated with them; a memory of detail and an exact event, rather than an amalgam of many. That was the day of Terry Hardacre's funeral at Ampleforth. She had been ten; she was brought along because all the family were going but, as often happens to children at funerals, she was more or less ignored throughout the day. The minds of all the adults were too filled with their own concerns to bother with her. That in itself added much to the fearfulness of that day; the awful unsettling she felt in the presence of so many of the staple figures of her life, suddenly turned aloof, irrational, distracted and strange.

She remembered her mother sitting weeping on the stairs that day, or a day just before, and her father who was so restrained, cursing quietly to himself, over and over again, saying only, 'Oh damn, damn, damn,' in a voice of immense sorrow. The funeral itself, with the monks of the abbey like black ghosts in their habits, the terribly sad plainsong, and the tolling bells, made an impression that would never leave her, that she associated ever after with Sam.

That, and her earliest clear picture of him, standing between his weeping mother, and tall old Aunt Jane, neither looking at, nor speaking to, anyone, was the foundation of her fear of him. It was fed too by the undeniable uncanniness of there having once been two, and there remaining now but one. She was never precisely sure which one of them had died. And, too, as a smaller child, she wondered how she would know if she was seeing the living one, or the dead one's ghost. The anxious tense concern, the desperate caution, with which the family had treated him at that time was reinterpreted in her childish mind as an extension of her own fear. She would run, hiding in the gardens, whenever she saw him come near.

Later, the fear modified, became more adult, more akin to shyness perhaps, but it never fully left her. She was at boarding school now and rarely home, so she had seen little of him in the last year or more and then only as a fleeting glamorous figure with his beautiful woman friend or, more recently, as a moody inhabitant of the library whom nobody much wanted to approach. She would, just now, have given

417

anything not to knock on that door and enter that dark, book-lined room. But she needed Sam, because only Sam could help her get what she wanted.

She knocked, lightly, but quite firmly. He was a very long time in answering, and when he did say, 'Come in,' his voice was quiet and reluctant. Still, she pushed open the door, entered, and closed it behind her. He was sitting slouched down once more on the sofa in front of the big fireplace, and he did not turn to see who had entered. She could see over his shoulder that the fire was dead, white ash.

She stepped a few paces into the room, nervously tugging at the edge of her school cardigan. She saw her books on the desk, and made towards them with a quick jerky action, colliding with a small table as she did so, nearly overturning it and its vase of flowers on to the faded Persian rug. He twisted sharply round at the sound and she gasped and froze, reminded frighteningly of the terrible suddenness with which earlier, he had lunged at Mr Brannigan.

'I've just come for my books,' she said in a small, squeaky voice. She hurried to the desk. The books, and her papers and notebooks, had been scattered by Mike's clumsy bulk and were yet splayed across the floor.

'Let me help you, Mary,' Sam said.

'It's all right. I can do it.' She began hastily gathering them shoving loose papers inside her folder with abandon. But he stood and crossed the room, and knelt down on the floor, carefully collecting her scattered schoolwork. Cautiously, she too got down on the floor, and began stacking up papers.

He said, 'Please don't be afraid of me, Mary,' without looking up. She was startled. She had not realized her fear showed to anyone, least of all him, whom she doubted had ever noticed her.

'I'm not,' she lied. He looked up. He was still kneeling, and she had stood to lay her stack of papers on the desk. He was less frightening that way, since she was looking down to meet his eyes.

'Yes, you are, dear. Please don't be. I'm sorry I frightened you this afternoon.' He paused, and said carefully as if he were a teacher explaining something, 'I have a terrible temper and sometimes I can't control it very well and I do things I don't intend. I must,' he paused again, 'I must *learn* to control it,' as if he were speaking to himself, rather than to her. He smiled. 'Does that ever happen to you?'

'Oh, yes,' she said eagerly. 'Sometimes I get so mad I throw things,' she added helpfully.

He smiled again. 'I'm sure you'll outgrow it,' he said. 'It doesn't matter when you're a child.' He was looking at her books. 'Your mother tells me you wish to read law.'

'Yes,' she said, surprised that her mother had spoken of her to him.

'I did that,' he said. She was again surprised.

'Why don't you practise law?' she said, with an adult awareness.

'Oh, I didn't finish my studies, Mary. I left.'

'Why? Didn't you like it?'

He laughed softly. 'I'm not sure if I liked it or not,' he said, 'I was too busy getting in trouble with my brother to really find out. I'm afraid we didn't study much.'

'Did they throw you out?' she asked candidly.

'No,' he smiled, 'I daresay they might have, if there'd been time. No. The war came. And that was that.'

She nodded, accepting that all-inclusive fact of life that all the adults she knew so often referred to. The war had finished the year she was born, but its shadow, in the form of ration cards, and utility clothing, and a thousand adult reminiscences hung over her childhood, as it would for all her generation. She relaxed a little. Hearing him speak of his brother in terms of ordinary human mischief was comforting. She gathered her nerve to approach with her question.

He was still looking down at her Latin text. He had paused, thinking. When he looked up their eyes met. He said, with infinite care, 'Mary, please understand. I thought he had . . . I thought he had hurt you. I misjudged. I never meant to frighten you so.'

She thought suddenly that he had the most beautiful eyes she had ever seen. It startled her. She had never been that close to him before. She said, 'He didn't do anything, really. I,' she paused, 'I know about old men like him.'

Sam blinked, rubbing one hand over the white scar over his left eye. It gave him a permanently quizzical look which was emphasized now by his confusion. 'Do you?'

She smiled, a smile of surprising awareness. 'I'm not a *little* girl.'

He nodded. 'I guess not,' he said, reconsidering. He smiled to himself, deciding he was getting old when little girls of twelve were more sophisticated than he. He lifted the Latin text and two others and handed them to her.

As she took them, for the brief moment in which the old books joined their hands, she suddenly said, 'Sam, I need your help.'

'What, Mary?' he whispered uncertainly.

'I need you to help me,' she said, with more conviction.

He was silent for a moment and then, releasing his hold on the books, he said clearly, 'All right, Mary. What can I do for you?' He got to his feet slowly and sat down at the desk on which she had piled her schoolwork, and motioned that she too should sit, on the chair nearby.

She didn't, preferring to stand, free to run if he should suddenly again change. But she wasn't really afraid now. She said, 'Do you know the money my grandfather left me? In his will?'

'Of course, Mary,' he said, still baffled.

'I want it,' she said. He tilted his head sideways, studying her earnest, but determined face. He decided not to discuss the relative possibilities before he had the reasons. It was the way he would have responded in business.

'Why?' he said.

She went cautious. 'Does it matter why?'

'I should think so.' That had thrown her. She had her ideas very clearly laid out. But they were laid out in sequence. First was getting the money. Second was letting her intentions be known.

'It's mine,' she said, a little defiantly.

'It's yours when you're eighteen, dear. That was the stipulation of the will.'

'But you're the trustee. It's up to you really, not the will.'

He shook his head. 'No, dear. I am the trustee but I am meant to follow your grandfather's express wishes, which were that the money be properly invested for you until you're eighteen. I've done that.'

She looked dismayed, 'Can't you get it back?'

'Of course. But to what purpose?'

'Because I need it now.'

'Mary, if your grandfather had thought it wise for you to have that amount of money at your age he would have said so in his will.'

She shook her head, impatient with his slow thoughtfulness, and said, 'But everything has *changed* now. Surely grandfather would understand. Everything's *different*. Surely if things change, then it's up to you to decide what he might do now. That's why he made you trustee.'

Sam studied her. He was impressed with her thinking. He said, 'It would be terribly risky for me to attempt to assess what he would have done. What a man puts in his will is his clear last intention. I think it's all we have to go on, and that I'm morally bound to follow his wishes.'

She shook her head again, and twisted one foot against the other on the carpet, tugging at her cardigan nervously.

He leaned forward, over the desk and said, 'Mary, what do you want this money for?'

She looked up from the carpet and met his eyes, and she knew she must tell him. Reluctantly she sat on the chair he had offered her. She said, speaking slowly, 'Do you know the Mews flat?'

'The ostler's flat?' he said. 'At the far end? Of course. What of it?'

'You see,' she began again, 'it's been empty for years, but it's in quite good shape, really. I mean, it has to be, the rest of the Mews is. We used to have parties in it, birthday parties when we were little, me and Paul and Olive, and our friends. It was lovely because we could make a great mess and nobody cared.' She grinned, suddenly a child again. But she was serious at once. 'I want to buy it,' she said. 'I want to buy the whole of the Mews, and the flat. For us to live in when the house is sold.'

'Oh, Mary,' he said. He leaned back in the chair and closed his eyes.

'But it's a good idea,' she said, insistently. 'There's plenty of room. We'd all fit. It would be quite jolly really,' her voice was tinged with a self-willed enthusiasm that he found pathetic. He was filled with a sudden bemused wave of annoyance for Rodney and Vanessa, a mixture of love and anger for their charm and their fecklessness. The little girl in front of him had more sense and initiative than both of them put together, but it hurt him that she had to have it.

'It is,' he said. 'A very good idea. A good, intelligent idea.'

'Will you help me, then?'

'A good idea. But there are some things wrong with it, Mary,' he said gently. He saw the flicker of hope fade, and wished he did not have to continue. But he did; she was no little child to pat on the head and send away. She had approached him as an adult. The least he could do was respond in kind.

'Mary, it's unlikely that Noel would be willing to sell the Mews separately or, more to the point, if the Brannigans would agree to it being sold apart. That's the first thing.' He looked at her; she was watching him intently. 'The second thing, Mary,' he smiled gently, 'the second thing, I'm afraid, is the money. Even if I could release it to you, and I don't frankly know if I could . . . Mary, it's not enough. The money your grandfather left . . . there wasn't that much. Not for that kind of thing, not really.' He shook his head, feeling a strange disloyalty to Harry, to have to disillusion his granddaughter about his attempts to provide for her. 'I'm sorry, Mary,' he said.

She stood quietly, stunned. He said softly, 'Sweetheart, you wouldn't want to live in the Mews with the Brannigans in here. I know you wouldn't. Your Daddy will find somewhere else, somewhere nice, to live. Quite nearby, no doubt. You'll be happy there.' As he spoke he wondered deeply if Rodney would find anything, ever, but it was a doubt he could not show to her. But she only shook her head. Perhaps she knew, already, what he knew; perhaps she shared his doubts. He wished she would cry, and become a child that he might comfort. But she just slowly nodded, absorbing it all, and then straightened her back, and stood up.

'Thank you, Sam,' she said, and turned as if she would go. He held out one hand to her, but she did not notice. She was looking blankly out at the late afternoon sun on the lawns and gardens. Then she whirled to face him, her face distorted but her eyes quite dry. 'I don't want those people to live in my home,' she cried, and then she began at last to sob, like a woman, holding the back of the chair, one hand over her mouth, her eyes closed, as Janet had done in the depths of the miseries of drink.

He leapt up from the chair, and her hand flew from her mouth in sudden renewed terror. She started to cry out, but he swept one arm roughly around her, holding her to him for a moment that passed before she could be fully afraid. He kissed her hair and let her go, leaving her stunned behind him.

'Excuse me, sweetheart,' he said, and strode out of the door.

He found Noel in the cobbled yard behind the house. He was in overalls, bending over the tractor engine, a spanner in his hand, his wild grey hair spattered with grease. He half-looked round as Sam approached, and grunted.

'Oh, it's you.' He glowered briefly at Sam and returned his glare to the tractor. 'Want a job, salvage-master?'

'What's on offer?'

'Take this bluidy piece of rubbish out and dump 'er in the sea.'

Sam laughed. 'I think you'll be able to afford a new one, anyhow, Noel.'

Noel grinned, straightening his back, his eyes narrowing with private satisfaction. 'Aye, I might.'

'You're taking their offer?'

'They've met my price.'

'What can dissuade you?'

Noel looked around briefly, toying with the spanner. 'More money, obviously,' he said.

'How long will you give me?'

Noel's eyes opened wide, and he almost dropped the spanner. 'What?'

'How long will you give me to top their offer?'

'You want to *buy* it?' Noel said. '*You* do? You were offered it on a bluidy silver platter six months ago and you turned it down.' The vagaries of Harry's will and his intentions were no secret. Madelene, in her anger, had seen to that. Noel was remarkably sanguine about it; nor did he resent Sam's place in his father's affections. People's affections didn't seem to mean much to him anyhow.

'I've changed my mind,' Sam said.

'You *are* a maniac.'

'How long will you give me?' Sam said again.

Noel shrugged, studying the spanner, squinting against the late, low-angled sun. 'A week,' he said, yet eyeing Sam cagily over the spanner's tip.

'All right,' Sam said slowly. 'A week. And you'll accept? If I top their offer?'

Noel smiled slightly. 'Aye,' he said, 'I'll accept.'

'Okay,' Sam said, nodding slowly, looking away over the slate roof of the Mews. Then he turned back abruptly to Noel. 'One thing,' he said. 'I want an assurance that you'll not play me off against them.'

Noel grinned. It was evident from the whimsical light in his eyes that the thought had crossed his mind. After a good half-minute's consideration he said, 'No. I won't do that.'

'You're sure?'

'Want it in writing?'

Sam smiled slowly and shook his head. 'No,' he said. 'You're a sod, Noel, but you're an honourable sod.' He turned and walked back to the house. As he reached the kitchen door, Noel called after him.

'Sam?'

'Aye.'

'Top it by a pound, and it's yourn.'

CHAPTER
TWENTY-FOUR

Sam's accountant was based in York. He was a man called John Cranswick, and Sam had employed him ever since he first founded Hardacre Salvage to raise the cargo of the *Louisa Jane*. A man in his fifties, of Yorkshire farming stock, he was precise to the point of fanaticism, which was what Sam wanted from an accountant, but singularly lacking in humour.

Sam went back to the library after speaking with Noel and, finding Mary Gray fled, he went in and shut the door. He sat down at Harry's desk and telephoned John Cranswick. The telephone was answered by Cranswick's wife who, after reluctant hesitation, fetched her husband. John Cranswick had been enjoying a gin and Italian in the garden with friends, and was not pleased to be disturbed.

'John. Sam Hardacre. Something's up. I need to talk with you.'

'Sam,' came the slightly aggrieved voice at the other end, 'it's five o'clock and it's *Saturday*.' There was momentary silence from both parties and when Sam spoke again his voice was very businesslike.

'John, I've employed you for six years and I've given you a fair amount of trade. I've never called you on a weekend before. You don't have to say yes, obviously, but if you say no, Hardacre Enterprises will have new accountants on Monday.' There was a sudden noise on the other end of the phone, as if Cranswick had straightened suddenly and shifted the phone, coming to some sort of attention.

He said testily, 'All right Sam. Don't get sore. What can I do for you?'

'I want you here tomorrow morning with every file you have on both companies.'

'That'll take a bloody lorry,' Cranswick wailed.

'I'll send a lorry.'

'And tomorrow's *Sunday*,' he protested further. Sam was silent. Sundays had a way of following Saturdays.

He said, very formally, 'I beg your pardon, John. I didn't realize you attended church.'

'Well, Sam you know . . .'

'You do attend church?'

'Well, Christmas, Easter, you know.'

Sam was silent again. He looked at the calendar, on Harry's desk. 'Maybe you'd like to check your diary, John. But as far as I can see, I don't think it's Christmas or Easter tomorrow.'

'All right. All right. I'll be there. Will nine o'clock do?' he added with a thin touch of sarcasm.

'Thank you,' Sam said. Then he paused. 'Make it ten.'

'Ten?'

'Yes, please, John.' He paused again. 'I'll be at church.'

Sam stayed the night at Hardacres. He didn't ask permission. Noel didn't give a damn who slept there. In the morning, he went to mass in Beverley as he had said he would, and was back in time to greet John Cranswick at the door upon his arrival. He took him into the library and plied him with sherry and coffee until his aggrieved crustiness softened slightly. Then he seated the accountant in a chair before Harry's desk and sat down himself behind it, folded his hands, and smiled.

'Reeght Sam,' John Cranswick said, reverting to his country past, as he got down to serious business. 'What's this about?'

'I want to buy a house,' said Sam.

Cranswick looked up at him from under thick grey brows, his crustiness returning. 'Wouldn't that have waited until Monday?' he said sourly.

427

'No. It wouldn't.'

Cranswick sighed. 'All right, Sam. What house? Have you got something in mind, at least?' He leaned back in his chair, crossing his legs with evident overstretched patience.

'Yes, I have,' said Sam. 'The house sitting all around you.'

Cranswick straightened in the chair, putting both feet back flat on the floor. He stared. 'This?'

'This.'

'Oh, Sam,' he said, lightly shaking his head with new seriousness. 'This is not just a house, Sam.'

Sam laughed. 'Oh, I know it's not. It's the family millstone, but it appears I'm elected to wear it.' He laughed again, but John Cranswick stayed serious. He leant forward.

'But, Sam, you can't afford *this*. Of course, the figure he's asking is ridiculous and he'll have to come down, but . . .'

'He's got it,' said Sam.

'You mean there's an offer? At that price?' Cranswick shook his head, and waved the whole matter away with both hands. 'No, Sam. That's out. We'll never find that.'

Sam bowed his head and looked at his hands, lying flat on the desk before him. 'I'll find it,' he said. 'Come on, John, get the stuff,' he indicated the boxes of files he'd helped to carry into the library, 'and let's get to work.'

They worked over it all day Sunday. John Cranswick stayed to lunch and to dinner, because the alternative was starving. Sam wasn't letting him out of there until they'd reached the beginning of a solution, and he knew it. There was certainly money around; Sam was not an extravagant man. He lived almost frugally, because that was how he liked to live. Only during his courtship of Janet had he really spent money lavishly, on dinners and theatres and flowers and all the playthings of romance. And even that was not really a great deal. Almost everything he'd ever made, aside from what went to Harry, he'd simply put back into the company, which was why it was as successful as it was and which, conversely and ironically, was also why money was hard to find. Or rather, cash was hard to find. Everything he had was more or less wrapped up in the fabric of Hardacre Enterprises. He owned property in Bridlington, Hull and London, but all of it was thoroughly in use. He owned virtually a small fleet of seagoing craft; the two deep-sea tugs, the *Dainty Girl*, several other workboats, a dredger, a floating crane, and all their ensuing tackle. But it was all matériel. It was all the basic structure of his company, and he dared not dismantle it, or leave it too stretched for operating capital. For if he did so, he might well be able to buy Hardacres but, without the solid backing of a sound financial enterprise, he would no more be able to maintain it than Harry had been. Of course he could borrow against it, and of course he would, but how much?

'I'll see the banker tomorrow,' he said at nine, while a weary Cranswick was petulantly and unhappily sipping a small brandy. Sam was drinking coffee and smoking cigarettes. He needed every ounce of his wits, and he'd only allowed Cranswick the brandy in the last half-hour, because he was about to let him go home. 'If you'll call Jan, and let him know the situation,' he added. He was glowering at the paper before him which listed his property, possessions and investments and suddenly he shook his head with sheer annoyance. 'Damn it all, John, there's so damn much of it. Surely I'm worth something?'

'Certainly,' said Cranswick. 'Walk in front of a bus tomorrow and you'll be worth a fortune. What you haven't got is cash.'

'Thanks,' Sam said, 'I'll try another way.'

He tried a lot of other ways.

On Monday morning, at nine-thirty, his bank manager arrived. He was a man called Bill Strathers, a round, soft, kindly individual in complete contrast to the accountant, Cranswick. A few years older than Sam, he was balding and middle-aged and had been so for a decade. His head was surrounded by a fringe of dark hair, neatly tonsured like a monk's. He had intelligent, bright small eyes which reflected his emotions vividly. They lit up as he entered the library with Sam.

'What a lovely old house,' he said shyly.

'Surely you've been here?' Sam said, but then realized it was unlikely. He rarely did business from Hardacres, and Harry's own banking had been in Driffield, not York.

'No, but what a pleasure. I certainly can understand your wish to own it,' he said with innocent kindness.

Sam laughed and said, more to himself, 'That's more than *I* understand, then,' but he wouldn't explain when the banker looked at him, the bright little eyes mirroring confusion. He only motioned him to be seated in the chair that Cranswick had occupied, and resumed his own place behind the desk. They went, together, over the same territory that he had covered with the accountant the day before and, at the end, Sam laid the difference between the assets they had freed, and the sum required, before Strathers.

Strathers's eyes went mournfully sad. 'That's an awful lot of money, Sam,' he said.

'You'll get it back. I *make* an awful lot of money.'

The banker did not argue. 'Yes, you do,' he said, but his voice was uneasy. 'Things *can* change,' he said cryptically. He looked uncomfortable.

'Of course they can. Shipping has ups and downs. Scrap values vary. It may all fluctuate, but salvage isn't going to vanish. Ships will always sink,' he added drily, feeling rather as if he was on one, doing just that.

'Yes, yes, Sam.'

'The company's *existence* is collateral,' Sam insisted. The banker squinted his little eyes shut and leaned forward.

'Sam, the company is *you*. Without you it's a bunch of rusty tubs and three Italian restaurants.' He leaned forward

430

again, glancing over his shoulder to see that the door to the library was shut to any of the family. 'I know the way you live, Sam, the work you do. Anything happens to you and the whole thing will come down like a house of cards.'

'I've got life insurance.'

'Not to that tune, you haven't. Anyone insuring *you* to that level hasn't got his head screwed on right.' He looked down at his small pudgy hands, and up again, and said gently, 'I'm sorry, Sam. I'll give you what I can.'

Sam nodded, glancing down at his figures again. 'Thanks, Bill,' he said, with sincerity, 'I know you will.' His mind was already elsewhere, as he rose to see the banker out. 'Thanks. We'll work from there.'

There were other banks. He tried them all. He spent most of the day on the telephone, and the rest of it over his books. But he was not entirely alone. Jan Muller rang from Hull, having just spoken with the accountant. His voice was oddly strained. He said, rather than asked, 'Sam, you will call on me. There must be some way I can help.' He paused, and then said vehemently, 'I want you to understand, I will do anything, *anything* to keep that man out of your house.'

'Thank you, Jan. I *will* call on you. I'm going to have to.' He thought a moment, still chastened from his own confrontation with Mike Brannigan. He said, 'I say, Jan, just keep it financial, okay? Nothing physical.' He was remembering too, that day in the Dean Street flat. 'I don't want my future cousin-in-law, or whatever the hell you'll be, in Wormwood Scrubs.'

'No problem,' Jan said, laughing. 'I am here when you want me.' He hung up the phone. An hour later, it rang again, and Sam lifted it absently.

'Hello?'

'Sam?'

The voice was thin and crackly over the Atlantic cable, and furious. It was Janet, from New York.

'I've just heard what that armour-plated bitch of a grandmother of ours has done,' she shouted.

'Sweetheart,' he said, delighted, forgetting the house and his columns of figures in an instant. It was so good to hear her voice. 'How are you?'

'Are you going to stop her?' Janet said, not bothering with inconsequentials.

'I'm trying, sweetheart.' There was a silence, filled with the whisperings of a weight of ocean.

Her voice came again, fainter, 'Sam, Bernie thinks I spend every penny I make, but I've got money stashed away he hasn't even heard of.'

'No, sweetheart.'

'Come on, Sam, don't be an asshole.'

'You're as charming as ever,' he said, 'but no. Not from you.'

'Why not?' she demanded, ready to fight.

'No, dear. Please. I'm grateful, but no.'

'You'll take it from Jan,' she said, sounding hurt.

'Jan and I are in business together.'

'You mean, he's a man.'

'Maybe I mean that.' She could hear in his voice that she wouldn't change him.

She said, regretfully, 'All right darling. You know where I am if you need me.'

He laughed, delightedly. 'I'll keep that in mind.' He said goodbye and put down the phone, and felt the distance between them come in like a wave from the sea. For a moment he sat sadly quiet, and then he returned to his work.

The family rallied round in a discreet, quiet way. Meals were provided, odd words of encouragement dropped his way, some rather comical, coming as they did from Vanessa and Rodney, whose necks he was trying to save. But he appreciated it. He held court, more or less in the library, for three days, and most of the nights as well. He did make progress. He persuaded his various banking establishments to raise their backing drastically, which was a considerable achievement, but one which unfortunately did not yet meet his needs. He made an arrangement with Riccardo which would result in a larger share of the future restaurant profits going to Riccardo, in return for ready cash for Sam just now. It wasn't a particularly good deal, but he was pleased with Riccardo for being so tough with him, and he wrote it off as a wedding present to Ruth. He was getting there, but there was a long way to go, and it was Wednesday.

At odd intervals, Noel stuck his dishevelled grey head round the door and offered his compliments. Noel was laughing at him, laughing at all of them, he knew. But he didn't care. He liked Noel, and even admired him. His action, taken abstractly, was the best bit of Hardacre wheeling and dealing since old Sam's day. Only, unfortunately for himself, he was at the receiving end.

He spent much of Wednesday morning on the phone with Jan, simultaneously discussing a job they were involved in, in the Solent, and the possibility of selling one of their many and varied boats. Jan was, if anything, more determined than Sam, and aside from volunteering a really sizeable personal loan, at a comically low rate of interest, he was enthusiastically dismantling Hardacre Salvage in his head, and Sam was finding himself the one to put the brakes on.

'Hey,' he finally said. 'Hold on. It's my problem, not yours.'

'My friend,' Jan said in that solemn European way of his, 'Mr Brannigan was my problem before I ever knew you. You give me only an excellent opportunity for a little settling of scores.'

'You're getting like my grandmother,' Sam said suddenly, seriously. 'Vengefulness isn't good for people.' He meant it, and was getting sorry he had got Jan involved.

Jan laughed softly. 'That is very Christian and forgiving,'

he said 'but today, if you will excuse me, I choose to think with Moses. An eye for an eye, Sam.' He paused for a long while and added quietly, 'He is getting off lightly if he loses only a house.'

Sam put down the phone and sat thinking before he called the next name on his list. He wondered briefly what precisely had happened between Mike and Jan in Palestine, and decided quite abruptly that he never wanted to know. There was a knock on the door, and he absently said, 'Come,' as he yet sat thinking, toying with his glasses on the desk before him.

Vanessa came into the room, walking in her overgrown schoolgirl way, a lanky, long-striding woman, leaning forward hesitantly as if to make herself less of an intrusion. 'Sam?'

'Aye, Vanessa. What is it?' His eyes were already on his papers before him, as he put his glasses back on.

'Sam, have you a moment?'

'Aye,' he said, still not stopping to look at her. She didn't speak, and he realized she wouldn't until he appeared not to be working. So he leant back in the desk-chair, took his glasses off again, and waited.

'Rodney and I, well, we had an idea. We thought we might be able to help.' He said nothing, and she, after another awkward pause said, 'Well, it *is* our home you're fighting for . . .' He looked up, faintly surprised that that fact had got through to her. She smiled her jolly-hockey-sticks smile. 'So we thought, Rodney and I . . .'

'Vanessa, please, could you just get to the point.'

She shuffled nervously. 'Of course, old thing, sorry to bother. We decided maybe we . . . we'll sell the horses.' She spoke the last in a great rushed mouthful.

'You'll *what*?'

'The horses, old thing. I mean, they're very good stock. They'd fetch a tidy packet. Naturally we'd be sorry, after all the years . . . but we could build up again . . .' she shifted

434

from foot to foot, her big candid eyes filled with willingness and misery.

'Vanessa,' said Sam, 'I'd quite seriously rather see you sell your daughter.'

'No, but I mean it. We *will* do it. We must help, mustn't we?' she said, with unhappy sincerity.

'No.' He waved her away.

'But Sam . . .'

'*No*. Besides,' he said leaning back, his eyes mischievous, 'whatever would we do without them? I haven't had a good ride in months.'

Vanessa looked startled, and blank. 'Well,' she said uncertainly, 'we can soon fix . . .'

'Out, Vanessa,' Sam said, laughing and waving her away again.

'But Sam . . .'

'Out.'

He picked up his pen again, but the phone rang. It was Pete Haines, from Hull.

'Aye, Sam. I've got a buyer for t' *Dainty Girl*. Jan says we can sell, if it's all right wi' you. She's not much used anymore, anyhow.'

'No,' Sam said, suddenly hasty.

There was a long silence, before Pete, uncertain, said, 'It's a good offer, Sam. She's not really worth that much, but t' lad wants her.'

'He can want. I'm not selling her.'

'Understood you were looking for money.'

'I am. But not that hard.'

'I don't understand,' Pete said slowly. 'You don't need her, Sam.'

'She's my luck. I won't sell her.' There was a long slow laugh from the other end of the phone.

'Well, well, lad. It comes to us all in t' end.' Pete laughed again, and put down the phone. Sam shrugged, and offered up a quick Ave of apology for his superstition before he went back to work. But he wouldn't sell the *Dainty Girl*.

Late in the afternoon be began to wonder if between scruples and superstition he wasn't walling himself into a corner. He was beginning to have an inkling that it wasn't going right, but he wasn't about to admit it to himself yet. At ten o'clock that night, after he had eaten sandwiches at his desk rather than waste the time that dinner in the dining-room would have taken, there was another knock on the door. Before he could respond, the door swung open and Noel appeared, grinning in his old way.

'Come in and shut it, there's a draught,' Sam said, by way of greeting.

Noel ambled into the room, shutting the door behind him. He was dressed, as always, in his rough tweeds and farm boots. He wandered about the room, while Sam worked, and eventually arrived at the desk. He perched on the end of it and prodded at the stacks of paper. 'Having fun, lad?'

'Aye. In a way, I am.'

'Bluidy fool,' said Noel, amiably.

'We're all entitled to our own aberrations, Noel. Get off your father's desk.' Noel grumbled, but he got off. 'Have a whisky,' Sam said, 'and pour me one, please.' He was adding up a column of figures and not looking at Noel. Noel crossed the room slowly, his heavy boots making solid thuds on the padding of carpet. He paused at the sideboard, before the tantalus.

'May I touch the sacred vessels?' he said. Sam made the sign of the cross in Noel's direction without looking up.

'*Ego te absolvo.*'

Noel poured two whiskys and returned with them to the desk. He handed one to Sam.

'You're mad as a hatter,' he said.

Sam took the glass and saluted Noel with it. 'No worse than you.'

Noel grinned, downed his whisky in one, and stamped off into the night.

On Thursday morning, he dearly would have loved to stay in bed and sleep half the day. He'd been averaging four hours of sleep a night since Sunday and he was beginning to get very tired and, when tired, he was less able to fend off the logic of the situation, which told him he was losing. But he'd promised to call John Cranswick at nine, so he got up and dressed and went down to the kitchen to have coffee with Mrs Dobson, who insisted he have breakfast as well before he went back to work. He ate it to please her, but his mind was already too busy to let him feel hungry. He went back to the library, with a longing glance out of the front door. The day was beautiful and he ached to be outside. He'd been within walls for five days running, the longest such stretch in years. He saw Noel striding off over his fields and both envied and understood him. But he turned and went back to his desk and rang John Cranswick. Cranswick was grumpy at that early hour, and not in a mood to ease the blow.

'Forget it, Sam,' he said.

'Why?'

'Because you can't do it. I've been over everything. It's not possible. Look, Sam, I'm the accountant, not you. You know salvage, I know figures. Believe me, you're wasting your time.'

'It's my time; I'll waste it as I please,' Sam said. 'I've got till Sunday, and I'll use till Sunday.'

'Please yourself,' said Cranswick, and hung up.

Sam listened for a moment to the dialling tone and laid the receiver on its cradle. He sat looking across at the wall of books, their shapes, colours, sizes, outlines, familiar from his childhood. Then he put his head in his hands and prayed, 'Please, just this once. I know I shouldn't ask, but it isn't really the money, and it isn't really for me.' He kept his head down for a moment then raised it, straightened his stiff back, picked up the phone and rang Jan to see what else he might possibly sell.

As he was talking, he saw a familiar flash of silver-grey as a car, long and low, swept up the drive and past the library window. He half-stood to watch it and said, suddenly, 'I'll call you back, Jan, someone's just arrived I've got to see.' He dropped the phone on its cradle and ran from the room, crossing the great galleried hall in three long bounds, and met her at the door.

'Jane!'

'Hello, Sam,' she said. She turned her cheek for him to kiss, but he threw his arms about her tall, bony body instead and held her to him, 'Oh, Jane. I am so glad to see you. You can't imagine.' He stepped back, holding her at arms' length. 'What are you doing here? I thought you were in Scotland.'

'I was,' she said; she glanced at her solid old, leather-strapped wristwatch, 'precisely eight hours ago.' She grinned with satisfaction, glancing over her shoulder at the silver Jaguar. 'Not bad, eh?'

'Jane, you terrify me,' Sam said honestly. 'At night as well?'

'Oh well, my dear, I couldn't sleep. Anyhow, I like driving at night. The roads are nice and clear, not all jammed up with nasty little Morris Minors.'

'You're becoming a dreadful snob,' he said.

'Just to tease my egalitarian nephews,' she grinned. 'Anyhow, I promised Emily I'd come down. It's cheer-up time. She's facing the season, and getting over Riccardo and Ruth. I thought she could use some moral support.' She paused, eyeing him wisely, 'Thought you might use some as well.'

'Oh, my dear,' he said, smiling wanly. 'If you but knew.'

She took his arm. 'Come now, find me some coffee and then we'll take a turn around the gardens and have a little talk.' Sam glanced over his shoulder to the library and she said, 'Yes, you have the time, dear,' for him.

Jane's arrival hadn't really changed anything, but by the time he returned to the library, he had hope again. He remembered a man in Manchester for whom he'd been able to do a favour; a good, honest man who'd made him swear at the time that he'd come, in time of need, for the favour's return. It was something he had never intended to do, but he had learned something in the last weeks, and developed a new humility about taking offered gifts. The man, a self-made shipowner with a fortune that made Sam's look like pocket-money, was delighted, as thrilled as a child to have been remembered. His cheque was in the post within half an hour and it took all Sam's effort to make him regard it as a loan, and not a gift. He added the figure to the credit side of his financial balance. It was a long list of dribs and drabs, loans, repaid debts, small sales of property, realized investments, and plain old-fashioned cash. He felt he was building a castle out of matchsticks.

So he continued, throughout the day, even at one point rewinning John Cranswick's guarded confidence, at least for a little longer. He took time off for dinner so that he might join his family now that Jane was here. And then once again he returned to work. At eleven o'clock that night he was talking once more to Jan. And at two in the morning he found a couple of thousand pounds he'd quite forgotten he had. He made coffee in the silent kitchen to celebrate, and found a packet of Rodney's cigarettes lying on a window-sill, which he liberated, having smoked all his own.

He went back to the library, drank the coffee, black, so that he could keep awake, and lit another cigarette. Then, with a sudden shake of his head, he sat down to make a final tally. He had decided it was time to stop fooling himself, as well. He laid everything out in order, and began to combine figures, feeling as his columns grew and multiplied, rather as he did at the moment in salvaging a sunken vessel when one waited in desperate tension to see if the force of one's lift, cable, or compressed air, or pontoons, was going to

439

break the powerful suction of the ocean bottom and set the vessel free. He was very calm, very patient, and it took him forty minutes. At the end he sat staring quietly, then slowly and without emotion he drew a long black line diagonally across the lot. He leaned back in his chair, took his glasses off, and closed his eyes. There was then, quite softly, a knock at the door. He sat up, startled, and called, his voice sounding loud in the silent house, 'Yes?'

The door opened slowly and quietly, and a tall figure appeared just inside. It was Jane. She was wearing an old-fashioned nightgown, buttoned up to her fine, strong old chin, and a long woollen dressing-gown. He stared, uncertain why she looked so different, then realized that, for the first time in his life, he was seeing her with her hair down. It hung in a long grey braid over her right shoulder.

'You're still here,' she said, softly disapproving.

'Why are you up?' he said. 'It's three in the morning.' She shrugged and smiled, stepping properly into the room and softly shutting the door.

'I couldn't sleep. I came down for some milk and I saw the light.'

'Are you all right?' he asked anxiously.

'Oh, of course. It's just age. I often can't sleep, these days.'

He leaned back in his chair, and closed his eyes again. 'Oh, I could,' he said.

'Go to bed, Sam. You've done enough.' He shook his head.

'I haven't. I can't yet. I just can't get it to work.'

She was still standing at the door. She said, 'Excuse me a moment,' and half-turned from him. She had suddenly remembered her hair, and was quickly winding it up round her head and securing it with hairpins, the old-fashioned kind, from her dressing-gown pocket. She was suddenly shy of him, and he remembered that she was of that generation of women who were not seen publicly with their hair loose. He turned away until she was done.

She came then and stood behind his chair, her strong old

440

hands light on his shoulders. She looked down at the sheets of paper on the desk.

'Having second thoughts?' she asked.

'About what? Taking this on?'

'About saying no to Harry,' she said. She smiled. 'It *would* have been easier.'

'No. I still think I was right. And I still think Harry understood. Noel had to have it. First, anyhow.'

'No regrets?'

He paused, thought for a while, and then said, 'I don't, Jane. I don't have regrets about things. I like life the way it is. Most of the time. If I had my whole life to do over, the War, Ampleforth, all this,' he waved one hand over the paper evidence of his years of work, 'Janet, even,' he smiled wryly, 'there's only one thing I'd do different.'

'Be born into a different family?'

'There's an idea!' He laughed. 'No, not that. No. I'd just have taken that bend at thirty-five.'

She was silent, her fingers gently smoothing the long grey streaks of hair back from his temples. 'Still with you, Sam?' she said.

'Every day. For the rest of my life.' He leaned against her and said, 'I wish I was at sea.'

'Go to bed, love. You're so tired.'

'I won't manage it, Jane. I've done my best. My level best. It's not enough.' He paused. It had never happened to him before. 'It's beyond me,' he said.

Still, he didn't give up yet. The next morning he left the house and drove round the whole of the East Riding, seeing people. Some things were always better managed face to face. He tried other angles, other ways, other friends. He would even have approached Erasmus Sykes again, but Erasmus was dead, since the spring. He felt better for being out and about, but he made no progress. It was Friday. He had two days left yet, but he knew in his heart it did not matter. He'd run out of options before he ran out of time.

And so, late on Friday afternoon, he was once again sitting in Emily Barton's kitchen of The Rose at Kilham. It was exactly a week since he had last been there. It felt like a month.

Emily was making broth, chopping vegetables, swedes, carrots and onions from her garden, and scooping them up in handfuls and dumping them in a huge pot bubbling on the Aga. The kitchen was warm with the smells and steam of cooking and the afternoon sun pouring through the window on to the slate floor and well-scrubbed deal table. Sam was sitting on the window-seat, his legs drawn up and his long body folded comfortably, leaning against the wall. He said, 'The damn thing was, Emily, I got so close. But I couldn't. When you're talking about money like that, it seems madness to be stopped by a few thousand pounds. But there comes a point when you just can't go any further. I just couldn't do it.' His voice was flat, and tired.

Emily said, 'It doesn't matter, Sam.' She paused, her chopping knife stilled. 'What matters is, you tried for us. Thank you.' He didn't answer. Emily went back to her broth, chopping feathery spring greenery off young carrots. She watched him as she worked. He sat quietly, his head resting back against the plastered wall, his eyes closed. The sunlight was harshly strong, reflecting a gleam of silver from the St Christopher at his throat and showing clearly the familiar weatherbeaten lines about his eyes. There were other lines, too. For the first time, Emily saw age on his face. He looked exhausted, as if he would sleep there, sitting in the sun.

Emily felt guiltily that she had goaded him into doing something she'd never intended for him to do. She'd never intended that he do anything. She'd only been working off some of her own anger, against him. She wasn't angry any more, only remorseful. The kitchen was peaceful, sun-filled. Emily liked the kitchen. In fact, she was beginning to like the Inn a little, though she'd not told Philip.

She thought Sam was asleep and worked very quietly. But suddenly he said, 'Emily, why is it that all the things I really care about in life are the things at which I fail?'

She looked sadly across the room. 'If I had the answer to that one, Sam, *I'd* be Aquinas,' she said. She turned away, and noticed the small envelope that she had left lying by her earthenware jug full of wooden spoons. 'Oh, Sam, I forgot,' she said. 'Jane was in this morning. She left this for you.' He looked across politely and, before he could move from the window-seat, she quickly crossed the room and handed it to him. He took it from her, a plain buff envelope with his name on the outside, unsealed.

He opened it and slipped out the contents. It was a small, good-quality sheet of notepaper which he carefully unfolded to reveal a little note in her lovely old-fashioned hand.

> My dear,
>
> > I never thanked you for the rose that day in Dean Street.
>
> > Love,
> > > Aunt Jane

Clipped neatly to the note was her cheque for ten thousand pounds.

CHAPTER
TWENTY-FIVE

They met on Monday morning, for the transfer of monies and deeds, in Driffield at the offices of Noel's solicitor, Appleby. Sam's own solicitor travelled up from London for the occasion, and he was accompanied by the accountant, John Cranswick. Cranswick still looked faintly stunned at their success, and Appleby looked intensely suspicious, of Sam, Sam's solicitor and, indeed, of Noel. He looked a little as if, had the Hardacre family chosen just then to take their legal business elsewhere, he would have been just as pleased.

'You're quite certain this will be satisfactory, Mr Hardacre?' he said to Noel. Noel didn't say anything. He never answered questions that struck him as extraneous.

Appleby was very formal and old-fashioned about the proceedings, the more so for their taking place in his formal and old-fashioned wainscotted offices. He wore a pin-stripe three-piece suit, as did Sam's London solicitor and, indeed, Cranswick. Noel was dressed as always in his habitual tweed plus-twos and some sort of canvas-appearing army-surplus jacket. He had green wellington boots on his feet. Sam was wearing dungarees, a Navy-surplus jumper unravelled at the sleeves and, over that, his oil-stained fisherman's smock. The two of them, in the dignified surroundings of Appleby's office, looked like a third-rate rag-and-bone man and his mate dragged in off the street.

'Shall we proceed?' said Appleby.

'Aye,' said Noel. 'Get bluidy on with it.'

Cranswick opened his briefcase and began carefully laying out his rather complex collection of bank drafts, cheques and promissory notes. There'd hardly been time to even co-ordinate it, but as Sam's solicitor pointed out to Noel's grunting agreement, it was all, more or less, money. It took a while. Appleby, with Noel looking over his shoulder, went through everything with a jaundiced, indeed suspicious eye. John Cranswick, made nervous by the pressured rush of the week, fidgeted. Sam's solicitor looked out of the window politely. Sam sat on the edge of Appleby's desk, his arms folded, and looked at the floor. He heard a whispered comment from Appleby, a shuffling of papers, and Noel's sour grunt. There was a silence, in which he waited, smiling slightly. Noel tapped his shoulder and he looked up.

'You're short, Sam,' he said.

Sam's solicitor turned round sharply from the window, surprise on his face, and John Cranswick let out a small sigh, and looked faintly green. Sam straightened up from the desk. He glanced at the stack of paper on the desk and looked up to meet Noel's eyes. They both just looked at each other for a long moment, while the rest of the room held its breath.

'Thought you'd say that,' said Sam. He reached slowly into the back pocket of his denim trousers and drew out his wallet, which he opened with great care. Slowly he withdrew a single, rather battered pound note. Without expression, he handed it to Noel.

Noel took it, eyed it carefully, perhaps checking it wasn't counterfeit. He folded it once, and then unfolded it, and his craggy face twisted in a lopsided grin, 'I think these gentlemen can take care of the rest. Fancy a beer?' He waved the pound note lightly before him. 'Happen this should cover,' he said.

'Aye, Noel, that'll be fine.'

They turned together, and walked out of the door, leaving behind them two baffled solicitors, one stunned accountant, and an awful lot of money and the title deeds to Hardacres lying on the desk.

Sam parted with Noel at the pub, leaving the latter to return on his own to his farm cottage and his now extremely solvent farm, relieved at last of the deadweight of the house which had so long held it down. He got back in his lorry and drove, alone, to Hardacres. Rodney and Vanessa, his mother, the Bartons, Albert and Maud, the staff, and anyone else who was passing, were planning a champagne celebration, supplied by Harry's yet willing cellar, of his success.

Success was, he knew, an odd word to describe what was undoubtedly the worst deal of his life. The house and its policies had cost him a considerable fortune, and six months before he could have had them for free. As it was, he was deeply in debt in many directions, and drastically over-stretched. It would take years of hard work to recover. He did not mind. He liked to work. Still, it was going to be something of a struggle. Jan Muller would later maintain that that one purchase, coming as it did at a crucial time in the development of Sam's business empire, would make the vital difference for him between wealth, and *real* wealth, which he would never now attain.

Again, he did not care. Money never had, and never would, mean anything to him. What mattered a little, and gave the property, for him, something of a new value, was that he had fought for it, and won. But what mattered far more, he knew, as he drove up the driveway and the house came in sight on its rise as he cleared the shadows of the beech wood, was that he had saved it. He stopped the lorry for a moment and sat looking out through the dusty windscreen at the eccentric old brick structure softened by summer sun. The love he felt for it was a composite of effort and annoyance, memories and hopes, past joys and past sorrows. Everything he was had its roots there, all the people he had loved had set foot within its walls. He shrugged and restarted the rough diesel engine. He had, like Harry before him, taken on a duty he would maintain for the rest of his life. It was safe now, as long as he lived, and it would shelter his family as it had sheltered so many throughout its ancient years.

He parked the old lorry squarely in front of the open door. The house was not exactly graced by it, but it might as well pay a little homage to what earned its bread. He went in slowly, and alone, thinking with a smile that, as always, he still had no keys, because Hardacres had no locks. But keys or not, it was his.

Inside there was a tremendous silence and he knew, by a deep-rooted instinct, that there was no one at all within. Such an occurrence was so rare that the house actually had a different, virginal feel about it when it happened. Vanessa and Rodney and Mary were out on their horses; he'd seen them in the bottom field. And he had passed Mrs Dobson, with Mrs Bennett in the front seat of her Ford Popular, as he came up the drive. No doubt they were out for some late provision for the party. His mother, of course, no longer stayed in the big house, but in the cottage that Harry had left her. Within an hour the house would be filled with people, but right now it was his alone, and he was rather pleased.

Feeling suddenly reverent, he walked slowly into the great hall and stood, his hands in his pockets, looking up around him in a slow circle, at the two-storey walls filled with paintings in their heavy gold frames, at the graceful sweep of staircase and gallery, and up to the skylights lit bright with blue summer sky above. His fingers in the loose pocket of the smock closed automatically on the guttie's knife he yet carried, and he looked up to the portraits of his great-grandparents and suddenly grinned.

He wandered through, slowly, to the drawing-room, a formal and beautiful room, infrequently used, but festive now with freshly cut flowers and a table spread with white linen, on which glittering rows of crystal glasses were set out in anticipation of the party. There were silver trays covered

447

with crisp damask napkins. It was evident that Mrs Dobson had been half-way through her preparations when she dashed off to the village.

He circled the room, his fingers still wrapped around the string-bound handle of the knife in his pocket. He stopped and stood before the huge fireplace with its heavy carved mantel and marble pillars, its brass fender and fire-irons, and screen. On the mantel, below the ornately-framed mirror which reflected the entire room, was the assortment of family photographs in varied, silver frames that had gathered, and stood there, for generations. There was Harry and Hetty on their wedding day, and beside them a small oval daguerrotype of Judith Winstanley. There were photographs of most of the children, as babies, now looking so alike as to be hard to tell apart, though a generation or two might separate them, pictured there in the same family christening robe. There was a wartime portrait of Peter in RAF uniform taken six months before he died. And one old, badly-faded picture of Jane Macgregor and her husband, Sir Ian, stalking in Scotland. At one end of the mantel was the slightly blurry photograph Harry had taken of himself and Terry a year after they entered Ampleforth. They were standing before one of the grey stone walls, laden with Virginia creeper, the two of them together in their solemn, graceful black habits, laughing eternally at some private joke. He could not, looking at it, tell which was himself and which was Terry. He glanced over the rim of the photograph at the older, greying man alone in the mirror, and abruptly turned away.

He went through to the empty, silent kitchen, his footsteps suddenly loud on the stone floor. The fridge was neatly packed with bottles of champagne, patiently chilling. He took one out and carried it back to the drawing-room, setting it down carefully on the white linen of the table, beside the glasses.

He undid the gold foil, and began slowly levering off the

wire from the cork. He heard Harry's voice saying, '*Don't shake it up, you damned idiots,*' as he and Terry sprayed champagne froth gleefully and wastefully all over the dining-room ceiling at countless family parties. He did not shake it now, but gently eased the cork out with his thumbs until it slipped free with the subtlest of pops and an airy breath of wine smoke.

With quick expertise he tipped the bottle over one wide-mouthed glass and caught every frothing drop. He filled the glass and walked with it into the centre of the galleried hall. He stood alone, an incongruous figure in his working clothes, holding the bubbling glass. He looked up and grinned once more at the portraits of Sam and Mary and toasted them, smiling, drinking from the glass.

'Well,' he said, 'I'm home.'

He turned and went back to the drawing-room, and stood once more before the mantel, looking quietly at the photographs and sipping the champagne. He finished the glass and set it down beside the open bottle. Then, very carefully, he chose a second, clean glass, and with equal care he poured the champagne again, filling it right to the brim. He set it, still without spilling a drop, on a small table in the centre of the room. Then he turned and walked to the door, looking back once at the full glass with its tiny haze of bubbles, alone on the dark table. He heard Harry's voice again, quoting

> . . . *A ghost may come;*
> *For it is a ghost's right . . .*
> . . . *To drink from the wine-breath . . .*

He went out, leaving the glass on the table, and shut the door.

Sam didn't move into Hardacres for over half a year. He wasn't in a hurry. It had waited forty years for him and could wait six months more. When he did leave his

Bridlington flat, in October of 1957, it was more because he was obliged then to vacate it for the new owner coming in. He had sold the flat, and the entire building, as part of his efforts to raise money. He didn't really need it now, anyhow. He was really based in Hull where the deep-sea tugs were berthed, and where he kept most of his work-boats. Still, he felt a strong tinge of nostalgia as he dismantled it, removing what possessions would go with him to the big house. It had been his first real home and it was rich with memory, much of it of Janet Chandler. Her wedding was set for 20 December, in London. He was to be Jan's best man. It was a situation at once ridiculous and obvious. Jan had no family and he was, despite everything, Jan's closest friend. He had threatened he might change places with him at the last moment, and make off, like Lochinvar, with the bride. But Jan wasn't too worried. Janet was the sort of bride nobody made off with except by invitation, and they both knew, Sam most of all, that the invitation would not be forthcoming. He was no longer angry, or even hurt. He was wistful and would probably remain ever so slightly romantically in love with her all his days, but it was nothing he couldn't live with. He knew very well it was possible to live with almost anything.

He sat on the edge of the desk, smoking, looking around at the boxes and crates on the floor. All he was taking were his books, his clothing and his paintings. Hardacres hardly needed his auction-room furniture to grace its halls. He heard a solid rap on the door which he recognized as Mick Raddley's, and called, 'Come in, you old bugger,' and then hoped he was right. He had been. Mick clumped into the room and looked around at the chaos of packing without comment. He took his pipe out and began to fill it, as Sam got back to his packing.

Sam said, 'If you're going to be here, you might as well be useful.' He indicated a stack of his extensive library and a paper carton. Mick grumbled but got down on his knees and began packing books, one-handed, in place. He paused now and again, looking at titles and puffing at his pipe.

'You read these things?' he said suddenly.

Sam looked up over the painting he was carefully wrapping in hessian. 'No, I just use them to prop the walls up,' he said with a grimace, wiping dust from his face. 'Of course I read them.'

Mick nodded, resuming packing. 'You're brighter than you look,' he said, finishing the box, and reaching for string to tie it. Sam grinned and said nothing. He was getting used to Mick.

Mick rocked back on his heels, looking at the next stack of books. He said, 'Aye, lad, we're going to miss you.'

Sam was busy. He spoke mildly, still carefully packing the painting. 'I'm not going that far.'

Mick laughed softly, chomping his pipe-stem, 'Yes, you are. Further than you think.'

He caught Sam's attention then, and he said slowly, getting to his feet, 'It's just a house, Mick.'

Mick smiled wisely, looking up at him, 'Aye, lad. Just a house. An' your sayin' that says just how far you're going.'

He seemed quite unperturbed, but Sam was deeply disturbed because there was something unbudging and final about the way it was said. Eventually he asked softly, laying the wrapped painting on the desk, 'Mick, do I have to lose my friends because I'm going home?'

Mick was very thoughtful. He wasn't about to make a ready kind answer that he couldn't keep to. At last he said slowly, 'Nay, lad, happen not.'

'Will you come to see me?'

Mick laughed, waving his one hand in a light-hearted gesture of fending. He said, 'Hold on, I didn't say nothing about that.'

'Will you come to see me?' Sam said again. He was not laughing, and his eyes were immensely sad.

Mick nodded again, softening, 'Aye, I'll come. If 'n you let me sit in t' kitchen, like we done once before.'

Sam agreed. He knew he had to, and that was as far as Mick would ever come, and then but rarely, to the kitchen door of Hardacres, but no further. He returned, saddened, to his work, thinking how every step of his life seemed to cost him some unexpected price that he had found hard to pay.

'When's the big wedding?' Mick asked then, lightly, as if unconsciously to underline the point.

'December,' Sam said, distracted yet, bent over his books.

'Where'll it be?' Mick said. He seemed not to notice, or not to acknowledge, Sam's change of mood.

'Oh, London, of course.'

Mick puffed at his pipe. 'Wouldn't uv thought uv course,' he said.

Sam looked up, startled. 'What?' he said.

'Who lives in London?' Mick said. 'Bride? Bride's parents? Groom?' He shrugged, refilling his pipe. Sam hadn't exactly thought about that. London had seemed obvious. Janet was a London person, when she wasn't being a New York or a Hollywood person. She belonged to big places, with big names and bright lights. But her parents, Albert and Maud, did maintain a small house outside Scarborough, for when they weren't on the road. Jan's mother lived in Scotland. Jan himself made his home in Hull, when he wasn't in London at the Dean Street flat, which was really Sam's anyhow. He had to acknowledge then that London was only logical by default.

'There didn't seem to be anywhere else,' he said. 'It's to be a Register Office wedding anyhow and they'll have the reception in one of the big hotels. Claridges, I suspect. It's Janet's favourite.'

Mick relit his pipe. He was sitting on the floor amongst stacks of Sam's books, occasionally placing another in a crate. 'Didn't think your kind uv folk had weddings in hotels,' he said.

'What do you mean, *my* kind of folk,' Sam said testily. Mick was unimpressed.

He said, 'Big house folk. Now don't get uppity. That's what you are an' that's what you've always been. Never mindin' this little sabbatical you've taken the last seven, eight years.'

'Where'd you learn words like that?' Sam said, surprised.

'Talking to you. Answer the question.'

Sam leant back against the clawed feet of the big old desk and said slowly, getting Mick's jist at last, 'Now wait just a minute. I know what you're aiming at and the answer is no. I've done my bit for King and Country where this little love-match is concerned. I think I've behaved pretty damned well, if you don't mind me saying. I'm even standing up for him at the wedding, like the perfect gentleman you say I'm supposed to be. But that's it, final. No more.'

'Gentleman, my arse,' said Mick. 'You went harin' down to London like a bat out a bluidy hell, all set to beat the hide off uv Jan when you found out. An' don't deny it, because I know all about it. And t' only reason you didn't was because he beat the hide off uv you first. So don't tell *me* you've done yer honourable bit. Happen you owe him a favour yet.'

'Happen I damn well *don't*,' Sam said. He picked up the nearest book at hand and threw it at Mick, who caught it agilely in his big hand. He dropped it on to his broad knee and turned it cover upwards. He grinned devilishly and read aloud, 'Thomas à Kempis, *The Imitation of Christ*. Guess you haven't read this one yet.'

'Go to bloody hell, Mick. Get out of my flat, and come back when you've learned to stay out of other people's affairs.'

Mick just sat, grinning, waiting perhaps to be thrown out.

'God *damn*,' Sam said. He reached up to the desk and pulled down the telephone, setting it on the floor. He dialled the London number of the Dean Street flat where he suspected, correctly, he'd find his business partner. 'Jan,' he said, 'yes, fine, thank you. Jan, I've been thinking,' he looked murderously at Mick. 'Seems a damn shame to spend money on hotels and all when I've got so much room at Hardacres. It is rather a lovely house for a party . . . of course I mean the wedding, Jan, what else?' He waved an angry fist at Mick who was laughing so much he could barely hear Jan's response. 'Of course you can. You must,' he said, with sudden conviction that had nothing to do with Mick. 'You're family.' There was a silence while Jan spoke and Mick chortled behind his hand. Sam said finally, 'Well, treat it as a wedding present. You're damned well not getting another, you know. I mean, I've already given you the bride.' He laughed then, softly, at something Jan said, and quietly hung up the phone.

'Right, you lopsided bastard,' he said to Mick. 'Now get out.'

Mick got to his feet, grinning. 'Was going anyhow,' he said ambling to the door. 'Too damn much work around here, any road.'

'What are you laughing at?' Sam asked sourly.

'Nowt,' Mick said, still grinning. He raised his one hand and lightly touched his forelock. 'Mr Hardacre. Sir.'

He went out and closed the door behind him with a respectful, gentle click.

Three days before the wedding a foot and a half of snow fell on the East Riding. No one minded, other than Noel, who spent the time trudging up to the hills bringing feed to stranded cattle and sheep. Most of the rest of the family were already gathered at Hardacres for Jan and Janet's wedding, and for Christmas, and those that weren't were ferried in from the nearest unsnowy railway stations and airports by a fleet of varied Hardacre vehicles. The old house was graced with a magnificent blanket of white, and the beech woods were a fairy land.

Sam found a fir tree on the estate to decorate for Christmas and he and Jan went out for it through the snow, with Janet gamely driving the tractor, unbeknownst to Noel. They felled their tree and dragged it home, stopping along the way for a three-sided snowfight that left them as snow-caked and delighted as playing children. The tree was tall enough to reach half-way to the roof of the galleried great hall, and they set it up there with immense difficulty, burying the fine old rugs in left-over snow, and nearly wiping out the ancestral portraits in the process. Vanessa, busy draping holly around everything like a deranged woodland muse, stopped and stared as the tree swung, swaying, into position and said, surveying the general damage, 'If Father could see this he'd be turning in his grave.'

Sam was on a ladder half-way up to the roof, draping electric lights around the tree. He thought a moment and shouted down. 'That would take real talent, Vanessa.'

She sniffed, shocked, and hung holly over the portrait of her mother over the hall fireplace, eyeing it morosely. Christmas always made Vanessa wistful, a turn of sentiment hard to imagine with her pink-cheeked hearty face. Christmas, likewise, made her brother Noel thoroughly bloody-minded. But then, almost everything did.

Janet came in, drying her blonde hair with a towel and cast a critical eye at the tree. 'Sam,' she said, with shocked disappointment, 'not *artificial* lights. You can't have artificial lights. We *must* have candles. They're so traditional. I insist.'

He paused in draping the lights and looked at the tree and briefly around the hall. He said, 'My dear, if you'd just paid for this house what I just paid for this house, I don't think you'd fill it full of candles and dry tinder.'

Jan leaned against the wall, assessing the slight list of the tree as if it were a troubled ship and said, 'Have the candles, my friend. You're thoroughly over-insured. It might be the best solution.'

'You been looking at the books again?' Jan nodded, smiling. Sam said, 'Okay, maybe candles.' He thought a moment, still adjusting the cable, 'Or maybe a little gelignite along the west wing. Think you could drop her nice and even, Jan, not ruin my great-grandmother's roses?'

Vanessa stared, and whispered in a little-girl voice, 'Sam? Are you serious, Sam?'

He laughed, climbing down the ladder, eyeing his tree. 'Serious as death and taxes, my love.'

But he wasn't. He was loving his house as he had never loved it, filling it full of people so that at nights the windows blazed gaily out over the dark gardens and woodlands, and that mystical sense of secret revelry hung over it all. It was meant for that, he knew. To be filled with people, and music and celebration. It should shelter as many as its rooms would allow: all its fires should be lit and burn every day, every one of its myriad chimneys should be blessed with smoke. It was impossible, of course, but he would try. It was a house meant for many and, without many, working together to keep it warm and living, it would slowly, and surely, die.

Janet Chandler's wedding was the sort of social event so renowned that it must be secret. Janet was a very famous young woman, which fact, seeing her now in faded dungarees and an old jumper of Jan's, Sam found a little hard to imagine. From the moment that he and she had become lovers, he had lost that screen image of her that was the only way she existed for so large a world of strangers. But that world of strangers was still out there, and at times like this she must be shielded from them.

The banns had been posted in Driffield three weeks

before, which rather made secrecy impossible, but they had come upon a plan to switch to the Register Office at Beverley at the last moment, and send a decoy party of guests to the wrong one, for good measure. Understanding authorities, and a little family influence, had done the trick, and Vanessa had volunteered to undertake the sub-terfuge, warming to the idea of 'throwing them off the scent', with huntswoman's verve. Sam kept envisioning a pink-coated and mounted Gray contingent leading a can-tering clutch of journalists and movie fans over the hedgerows. The wedding itself was, of necessity, to be strictly private; the bride and groom, their witnesses, who were Sam and Emily Barton, and no one else. The real party would be at home afterwards, with the essential and secretive formalities finished. Sam had thought he would have to lock the wrought-iron gates at the foot of the driveway for the second time in a hundred years, and both because of Janet Chandler. In the end, the snow sorted all that.

On the morning of the wedding Noel came stomping in, shaking a shower of white off his coat and announced, with his usual malicious delight, 'Better you than me, mates. No one's getting down that road today.'

'You're not serious,' Sam said. He went out and stood at the back of the house, watching the snow pile up in the courtyard, softening the lines of the Mews and garages.

'Fancy a run up hill with a few bales of hay like I been doing, to find out?'

Sam grinned, for once equally malicious, 'If you'd kept the house and sold the farm, maybe that's what I'd be doing. Right now, I'm going to sit by the fire.'

'Bastard,' said Noel, and went stamping off, work-dogs yapping at his heels, into the snow.

'He's right,' Sam said to Janet, re-entering the kitchen. She was sitting by the big Rayburn, warming her toes. She was in a dressing-gown, a sensible one made of wool, not

457

the sort of filmy thing she used at one time to wander through hotel bedrooms. 'He can't be right,' she said sharply, glaring out of the windows at the falling snow.

'It can't do this. I'm getting married today.'

Sam grinned, 'It looks like an Act of God, my dear. I think you'd better just come to bed with me instead.' She straightened slowly and put her feet on the floor. She stared at him for a long time and he fancied he saw for a moment a flicker of the old passion, but it vanished in an instant and he knew he'd not see it again.

'Aside,' she said, 'from being blasphemous, that was in lousy taste. I'm getting married today. If you say that tomorrow morning, it will be an invitation to adultery. And that, my dear, is where I draw the line.' She was deadly serious and he looked down at the floor, chastened.

'Sorry,' he said. He leaned over her and gave her a brotherly kiss on the cheek. 'I stand corrected. Anyhow, tomorrow you'll be on your honeymoon, and you've not told me where you're going.'

'Can you blame me?' she said. She rose and stared out of the window, with growing desperation. 'Why doesn't it damned well stop?' she demanded. 'We'll never get there in this.'

'I'll get you there,' he said.

And he did, too. He got them there in the Hardacre Land-Rover, with Jan and himself digging it out at intervals of every half-mile or so, and Janet at the wheel. The bride wore dungarees and wellington boots and the groom wore the same. Nobody carried flowers, though Sam did tuck a sprig of mistletoe into Janet's woollen fisherman's cap, to give him an extra excuse to kiss the bride. All their elaborate plans and evasions were totally unnecessary; theirs was the only vehicle moving in the East Riding that day. They got back to the house at five-thirty in the afternoon, to find their guests already thoroughly cheerful, having broached the champagne an hour before out of boredom. Albert Chandler, aside from providing his daughter, provided the music as well, and the central core of his once-famous band, now an aged but well-weathered group, performed in the great hall. It was all very late-thirties, with an adventurous leap occasionally up to about 1944. The young stood around amazed, and everybody Sam's age and over got frightfully sentimental. But Paul Barton, to his uncle's worshipful delight, stood up in front of the dinner-jacketed ensemble and sang every old number in the book, in the crooner style his parents adored. Paul could sing anything. Emily and Philip got so drunk they fell briefly in love again and went off to a bedroom to celebrate.

They weren't the only ones. It was rapidly apparent that, since every road in the county was blocked, nobody was going anywhere that night, not even the bride and groom. Sam didn't care. There was room for everyone. In the end, Jan and Janet spent their wedding night under his roof, and she would ever afterwards cheerfully, and publicly maintain he'd come along on their honeymoon out of spite.

Jan was a little shocked at that, as he would always be a little shocked at times by his wife, who came floating down the beautiful staircase, after changing from her snow-covered trousers, in a magnificent gown of brilliant red. 'I'm an honest tart,' she said to anyone passing. 'And it's Christmas, anyway.' Sam danced with her in the galleried great hall of his house, beneath the Christmas tree, and they made, as always, a stunning couple.

He saw his mother watching him with a faintly suspicious eye, but he only grinned and circled the floor with his lady again. She knew, and he knew, that there'd be nothing more between them as long as they lived, whatever the world might suppose. In the end, he got immensely but cheerfully drunk, less out of past sorrows than in celebration of Harry's still splendid stock of champagne, and had no recollection at all of climbing the stairs to bed.

He woke, some time in a late winter dawn, in the old

four-poster bed in the master bedroom of Hardacres with, to his amazement, a young lady in his arms. He drew back from her and stared, at first not even knowing who she was. But then he recalled her as a girl from the village who had served the wedding supper. She was very young, very pretty, and she certainly looked contented enough. He lay for a moment, bemused and sleepily guilty. Then, begging the pardons, simultaneously, of Harry Hardacre and Holy Mother Church, he stretched lazily, wrapped his arms about her soft warmth, and went luxuriously back to sleep.

It was, after all, a country house tradition of its own.

CHAPTER
TWENTY-SIX

The small car, a bright red Austin Mini, slowed carefully as it approached the break in the high brick wall that fronted the Driffield road at the edge of the great estate. It came to a halt as the driver studied the big black wrought-iron gates that stood open before the driveway, long grass grown around the rusty hinges. Had the gates been closed she would have just continued, but they were so casually open. Cautiously, like an inquisitive puppy, the little red car nosed its way through the gates and started up the drive. It was November, and the tall elms were shedding their leaves in a soft brown rain. Here and there one stood stark and bare, tribute to the elm disease spreading over England. She looked at them sadly as she drove.

The driver was a pretty woman in her thirties, wearing a thick red woollen jumper that matched her little car, and a flat, peaked tweed cap. She had honey-brown hair, tumbling out beneath in a tangle of short curls, and a face of surprising strength in one so young. Her cheekbones were prominent, and her slightly stubborn jaw firm, over a long, graceful but strong neck. She was the sort of woman who improved with age, and was prettier now than she'd been as a girl.

Suddenly, she spotted a flash of colour on the road and drew the bouncy little car to a halt. A great bird, a peacock with trailing tail feathers, made a slow and deliberate progress across the road. The woman smiled. 'Well, look at you,' she said, and waited for it to pass. She drove forward cautiously, lest there were more. Ahead she saw a beech wood and, before it, a break in the trees and a broad, grassy field.

There were a horse and rider in the field, cantering easily across. They caught her eye, and she slowed the car again and brought it to a halt. She turned to watch. There are few more lovely sights than a fine horse, finely ridden. She smiled in appreciation. She'd loved horses, and riding, all her life, but it was a wealthy pleasure she had never remotely been able to afford.

The rider was a man, dressed casually, and hatless, and he rode beautifully, as one who has ridden from childhood. As the horse came into the thin November sun, beyond the shadow of the trees, she caught a flash of grey hair, incongruous with the lithe and youthful body of the horseman.

Abruptly the man reined the horse in and she realized he had seen her. He turned and trotted the horse towards the car, and she rolled down her window, suddenly nervous, expecting she was about to be sent away. However, as he came closer, she saw the rider was smiling, and he didn't really look about to send anyone away. He rode right up to the fence and leaned down over the horse's withers to see into the window of the little car.

'Can I help you?' he asked. The woman just stared, silent. He waited a moment, then kicked his feet free of the stirrups and jumped down from the horse, bringing the reins over its head. 'Were you looking for someone?'

'Sam?' she said, and he just stared. She smiled shyly, and said, 'You don't remember me, do you?' Her voice was very low and soft, and rolled over her northern vowels in a surprisingly attractive way, making them a thing of some delight. Her smile broadened, became faintly mischievous and she added, 'I thought you never forgot a female face.'

'Mavis Emmerson,' he said.

'Thought it was time I came to apologize,' said Mavis.

By the time she got the little car up to the great house at the head of the drive, he was waiting already for her. The gravel roadway was winding and narrow and she'd been

462

afraid of hitting any of the beautiful peafowl or one of the pretty deer that wandered freely there. He had set off at a slightly hair-raising gallop, jumping fences and hedges in a short-cut across the grounds to get there before her. When she drove up to where he stood waiting, the rather well-sweated horse was being led away by a miffy-looking woman in jodhpurs. He ran forward at once to open her door.

She smiled, thinking it had been a while since anyone had done that for her. 'You'll stay to lunch,' he said, as he helped her out.

'Oh Sam, I couldn't,' she returned, at once, carefully dropping the keys of the Mini into her handbag. She had earned every penny of its price herself, and the car was a proud and precious possession. 'I just came to say hello, honestly,' she said.

'After eighteen years,' he said, 'hello takes at least as long as luncheon. Maybe even all afternoon.'

She looked at him cannily, not quite sure if she was reading that familiar teasing smile correctly. 'You know,' she said, 'I expected to find you very changed, but I have this terrible feeling you're exactly the same.'

She came shyly into the big house, at his side. She had been there before, with Peter Macgregor, during the war, but only once. Their life together, brief and fleeting as it was, was lived in the narrow world of the RAF, and blitz-bound London. There was little time for visits home, anyhow, even had Peter the inclination. And Peter, God rest him, she always knew had not too much of that. She didn't blame him. She was a working-class girl from Newcastle and he was a Scottish lord. With due respect, she readily, gladly admitted that his family, and particularly his gracious mother, had made her most welcome. But it was wartime, and so many boundaries were stretched in those days. She could not have blamed him had he been slightly, so slightly, ashamed to bring her here.

'Oh, Sam,' she whispered, as he led her into the drawing-room. 'It's bonny.'

'Do you think so?' he said with delight, as if it were quite possible people often didn't even like the magnificent place. 'I'm so glad.' He sounded so genuine that she looked hard at him in amazement. 'Sherry, or madeira?' he said.

She accepted sherry and waited quietly alone in the room while he went away into the house to speak to the cook about lunch. She still felt she should refuse, but he had been so insistent and, to be honest, she was very slightly afraid of him and not inclined to argue. As she had said, he had changed less than she had expected knowing, as she did, so much of what had happened in his life in the intervening years. The Hardacres were a well-known family, better known these days because of Sam himself, and Mavis lived, after all, only a relatively short distance away, in Halifax. But there was yet a mature assurance about him now that was slightly awesome.

She stood before the fireplace, which was bereft of fire and filled with white wood-ash, looking at the room reflected in the big mirror, and her own self contained so incongruously in the picture. Her eyes dropped to the framed photographs along the high mantel, falling first of all on a wedding photograph, unusual in that the bride was dressed in red, and she recognized the woman at once, as indeed anyone who ever went to the pictures would. She sighed faintly, studying that beautiful face. Who could have blamed him for loving that? Her gaze crossed the mantel, and suddenly struck Peter Macgregor's RAF portrait. It was so strange to see it there; its identical companion sat on her worn old dresser at home, as it had for the past eighteen years. She smiled at it, and her gaze moved on, coming finally to the photograph of the twins in their Benedictine habits, at Ampleforth. Her eyes suddenly stung. They had been so beautiful together, so gay, so reckless, romping through wartime London as if the whole war were a vast

464

joke. She had sat at her bench in the factory and shut away tears as one of the girls read that sad story aloud from the tabloids, with ghoulish outsider's sympathy. She wouldn't let them know she'd ever known the twins. They, and all the Hardacre clan, were a private part of her life, kept precious to herself alone. Still, though she had never expected to see any of them again, much less the twins, shut away in their monastery, the knowledge that they were there yet, and presumably, though amazingly, content, had always pleased her. Indeed, it had been hard for her to imagine one of them gone until, today, she had at last seen the other, alone.

'Paying your respects?' he said softly, and she turned, amazed and a little embarrassed, having not heard him enter. He was gently smiling. She did not know what to say, whether one talked to him or not about it, and remembered how, after Peter's death, each meeting with an old acquaintance brought the whole thing back. 'It's all right,' he said, knowing just what she was thinking. 'I've made my peace.'

'I was so sorry when I heard, Sam,' she burst out, 'I almost . . . I almost came to see you.' He smiled again, and took her arm, leading her to a chair and seating her with a small table before her for her drink.

'I wish you had,' he said spontaneously, and then laughed. 'You might have saved me from some chaos about that time. Who knows?' Mavis nodded, uncertainly. She had a fair idea who that chaos was. *That* was all in the tabloids too, a great deal of the time. But she had no idea what it might have had to do with her.

She tilted her head suddenly sideways and nodded towards the mantel and the photographs with a wise smile, and said boldly, 'She's very beautiful, that chaos of yours.'

'Oh, my dear, she is that.'

She suddenly wanted to know if he was still in love, and suspected he was, but she would naturally not ask. But she did say, in her candid way, 'The wedding was here?'

465

'Amazing, wasn't it?' he grinned. 'Don't worry, I was trying to talk her out of it right up the aisle, so to speak. Stabbing my best friend in the back with happy aplomb.' He was laughing but she wasn't precisely sure he was joking.

'Sam,' she said. He nodded, turning briefly towards her. He was on his knees before the huge fireplace, with kindling and newspaper, lighting the fire as if he did it all the time, and she wondered suddenly about all the staff she had remembered here. He was thinking that she pronounced his name exactly as his great-grandmother had, and he liked that.

He said, 'What is it?'

'Why'd you do that?'

'What, the wedding?' She nodded, and he saw she was perceptive, or his own romantic nature was easily read, or both. He laughed, 'I never argue with Thomas à Kempis,' he said.

Over lunch she was still considering that. 'You always *were* mystifying. Who's real, Sam, that playboy I knew, or the monk? Or whatever you are now?'

He looked away, slightly evasive and laughed lightly. 'Monasteries are full of ex-playboys,' he said. 'Actors, all sorts of extroverts; the more contemplative the order, the wilder souls they draw. St Francis was a wealthy rogue once, too, you know.' He sipped his wine again, studying her face. She had a way of tossing her chin up and flicking her beautiful eyes sideways as she spoke that put his mind in unseemly haste on the thought of bed.

'And now?' she said again.

'Now?' He smiled slowly, looking once quickly round the oak-panelled dining-room where they were seated, with delicious formality at opposite ends of the great long table. 'Now I'm just a working man.'

She did end up staying for a long while after lunch, if not the entire afternoon. They'd sat for ages over coffee in front of the drawing-room fire, and then he had walked with her around the beautiful gardens, graced with the sad peace of autumn. They talked in the rambling, dissociated manner that one talks with friends absent for extraordinary lengths of time. She told him snatches of her life; that she had worked as a factory girl for years, but recently obtained a much better position managing a small canal-side hotel in Sowerby Bridge, which had even enabled her to buy the red Mini. She told him that she had lived in Halifax for some years in a rented house. She even mentioned the district and he remembered it as a worn and tumbledown neighbourhood of small two-storey brick dwellings with scraggly patches of garden. But she had not, in all that time, truly told him anything of herself.

Eventually she said she must, really, go. He walked her to her little car, and then said suddenly, 'You haven't done it, you know.'

'Pardon?' she said.

'What you said you came to do,' he reminded. He looked solemn. 'You haven't apologized.'

She was silent, and looked nervous. 'I suppose I just meant that coming here was an apology.' She looked down, drawing her keys from her handbag, and when she looked up her lovely eyes were quite defiant. 'Do you want more?'

'No. But I want an explanation.' She looked away. 'Why did you just walk out of our lives, Mavis? Why not even a telephone call to say goodbye?' He was reproachful, but gentle, and he had been so gracious to her that she hated to leave him with no answer.

Still she just shook her head and said, 'I'm really sorry, Sam. I have to go now. I'm late, you see. I have to meet my son at four.' Her eyes came up suddenly to meet his, and were fiercely defensive. He had been leaning forward, his hand lightly on her arm, and he straightened and visibly withdrew from her.

'I'm sorry,' he said quickly, apologizing for thoughts he

467

had entertained throughout the afternoon, thoughts that she didn't even know about. 'I'm terribly sorry. I had no idea you were married.'

He felt a total fool. He had addressed her by her maiden name and naturally she had responded to it, the only name by which he would know her. And from that alone he had drawn a simple, wrong conclusion. And yet he had been sure she'd not worn a ring. He was too much a gentleman to look, now, but she saved him the trouble.

'Oh, I'm not, Sam,' she said. And before he could make any more mistakes she added, with a feisty touch of annoyance, 'and I never was, either. It's quite possible to have children anyway, you know,' she added. She got hurriedly into the car and slammed the door.

'Mavis,' he said urgently.

'I have to go, Sam.' She turned the key, and the little engine started like a puppy's playful growl.

'Wait,' he said.

'No.' She gave the pudding-stirrer of a gearstick an angry shove, and cursed as the gears ground. It gave him time to run round the tiny vehicle and jump in the other side, folding his long legs awkwardly to fit himself in.

'What are you doing?' she demanded, less angry than amazed.

'I want to see the peacocks. Drive me down the driveway. Go on.'

'You're mad,' she said, almost laughing.

'We've got to talk.'

'Nothing to talk about,' she said, suddenly stiff and cold once more. She started down the driveway. 'I've never been married and I have a bastard son called Geordie. Curiosity satisfied?'

'Named after your brother,' he said.

'Sam, you don't usually name bastards after their fathers,' said she. She slowed the car. 'Now would you like to get out? I don't think the peacocks will much care.'

468

'I'll get out,' he said. She stopped the car staring straight ahead. 'If you'll come to dinner with me on Saturday,' he said.

'Impossible.'

'Looks like I'm going to Halifax.'

She smiled slowly, switched off the engine, and turned to look at him. She looked very wise. She said, 'You know, I'm really glad I came here. And I'm really glad to find you so much the same. And every bit as attractive, I assure you. But no, Sam, believe me. Leave well enough alone. We're from two different worlds that never should meet. I know, I've been here before.'

'I've always *liked* Halifax,' he said.

'You are *stubborn*,' Mavis half-shouted, staring amazedly at him. 'Anyhow, I'm not even going to Halifax. I'm going to Scarborough. That's where my son is. He has a job. I'm meeting him for tea.' Her son, and his job in a Scarborough hotel, were precisely the reasons she was over in the East Riding in the first place.

'How *old* is he?' said Sam slowly.

She got suddenly cagey and said only, 'Old enough to work.'

'Tea in Scarborough is such jolly fun. Particularly in winter,' he said.

'What do you mean?' she asked warily.

He was looking at her very, very carefully, and there was something new in his eyes, a wary calculation, and it wasn't entirely friendly. When he spoke there was an edge to his voice that she found frightening.

'I want to meet your son,' he said.

She tried to get out of it. She even eventually, in desperation, agreed to dinner on Saturday, if he'd let her go now. But he only said, 'And you'll walk out like you did eighteen years ago, won't you? You'll not turn up and I won't know where to find you. And then I'll really not see you ever again.'

She was angry, nervous and frustrated. She asked him to get out of her car and he flatly refused and she said, 'Are you always like this? Do you always pursue people like this?'

'Almost never,' he said. He was lighting a cigarette after having offered her one which she briskly refused. 'Only when I really want something. That's not very often,' he added, 'but right now I want to meet your son. And I want to see you again after I do.'

'I don't want you to meet him.'

'I know that, Mavis. And I think I even know why.' He leaned back in the small seat and relaxed, as much as he could in the little car, and smiled slightly. 'When you're ready,' he said.

She drove him to Scarborough. She really didn't know what else to do. She supposed she could have screamed and made a fuss, but there wasn't anyone to hear, and it wasn't as if he were kidnapping or raping her, only coming along to where she was going anyway.

'How will you get home?' she said sharply. 'I'm not going out of my way again.'

'I'll walk,' he said, and she thought he meant it.

It was a moderately-sized, seafront hotel, facing the grey November water, not many doors from the one in which, not so many years before, he had taken his mother to lunch on the proceeds of his job in the chip shop.

As she parked the car outside, she said, 'He isn't expecting me to be with anyone.'

'Just tell him I'm an old friend.'

'Just now,' she said angrily, 'you're not. And besides, he won't be able to sit with us, he's *serving* tea. It's his first week. I'm giving him a little moral support.'

'You're a good mother,' he said. 'I'll give some moral support as well.'

She looked down at her hands, ringless, and fiddled nervously with her keys. When she spoke, her voice was pleading, 'Sam, he's had a hard row to hoe. And I've had a hard row to hoe, as well. Folk where I come from don't forget. And they don't let us forget, either. Don't make it harder for us. Please go away and leave us in peace.' He was silent. He knew he was hurting her, and he did not enjoy it. But there was more at stake than his feelings, or hers.

'I'll be discreet,' he said.

She turned on him, fiercely angry, 'Discreet. Oh, your kind are so discreet. Damn you rich bastards, all of you. My brother's right. I never thought so, but he is. He's right.'

Sam only nodded, without emotion or expression. 'I'm waiting,' he said.

They went in together and sat down at a table in the lounge, where other parties were engaged in sipping tea and nibbling scones and cakes from tall, three-tiered silver cake-stands. It was a pleasant room, faintly worn, in the Victorian tradition of elaborate flocked wallpapers and heavy wood furniture. The boy was dressed in black trousers, white shirt and black bow tie and, with the help of a young girl in a black dress and white apron, was busy bringing pots of tea and hot water to the tables. Sam knew him at once. But he said nothing, and waited for Mavis, nervous and unhappy, to catch the young man's eye. She signalled to him and he looked over with an engaging lopsided grin, proud of himself and yet relieved to see his mother all the same. Then he saw the man with her and surprise came over his face and was followed by wary uncertainty. Sam saw a familiar long, aristocratic nose and dark blue-green eyes. He smiled when the boy approached and the youngster returned the smile.

Mavis said, 'Geordie, this is Sam. I knew him during the war.' She didn't mention his last name and she didn't say anything about friends. Sam stood and shook hands with the boy, who called him 'sir'. Then Geordie went back to waiting on tables and Sam and Mavis drank the tea he had brought. They didn't talk much, and when the bill came and Sam reached for it, she said, 'I'll pay for mine,' with such vehemence that he felt obliged to let her. It was not a happy occasion.

Once outside she said abruptly, 'All right, you got what you wanted, now I hope you enjoy your walk.' She turned towards her car. He stopped her, with his hand about her wrist, and her eyes were murderous when she looked up to meet his.

'Now look,' she said, her voice low and cold, 'you're not on your bloody great estate any more. You're in the middle of an ordinary English town full of ordinary English people. Let me go or I'll shout for help. I mean it, Sam. I'm sorry I ever came near you, God help me, I am.'

'That's Peter's son,' he said.

'What a good guess,' she returned, wrenching her arm free. But he grabbed both her shoulders and backed her against the railing overlooking the sea wall. She didn't like the look on his face and remembered suddenly that the gay and laughing Hardacre twins had tempers like the devil.

'A guess? Why in the name of God should I have to guess? Why didn't you tell me?'

He was so fiercely angry that she was momentarily cowed, but not for long. She had stood up to the buffetings of working-class morality too long to be subjected long to his.

'And what is it to you?' she demanded. 'Who are you that I have to answer to you?'

'He's my cousin's son.'

'No. He's *my* son,' she replied. She said the words in that proud way that working-class women speak of their male offspring. The way his great-grandmother spoke of hers. It touched him. But she flew at him then in a rage equal to his, 'He's my son, and he's a bastard. I know. I don't have to be told. I've been told for seventeen years. And I'm done apologizing for it. Yes, Peter fathered him. Yes, we were engaged and we didn't wait. And Peter was killed and I had his bastard. But *I* raised him, *I* worked to keep him. *I* stood

472

up to all the bloody pointing fingers and wagging tongues, and I made all the apologies. Happen by now he's mine. All mine. I've bloody earned him, a dozen times over.' She turned her back and stared out to sea to hide from him the sudden weakness of tears. When he spoke it was over her head, with his hands suddenly on her shoulders, his fingers lightly protective, soothing her sudden anger.

'Please,' he said. 'Please. Do you think any of that matters to me? Of course you didn't wait. Which of us did in those years? We all carried death around in our back pockets. We took what we could. Why shouldn't you have done the same?'

'Because I was a woman,' she snapped, 'and had the misfortune to survive.'

'Oh, no, no,' he said sadly, 'don't talk like that.' She softened slightly towards him and said, 'I don't understand. Why were you so angry, then?'

He waited a while before he answered but even so, when he did, the kindness was gone from his voice and the anger had returned, beyond his control. He said, 'I'm glad you loved my cousin. I'm glad you gave him a son. *Something* for that handful of years he had of a life.' He paused and said bitterly, 'God *damn* that war, it took so much from us all.' He was silent again and she almost turned to face him, but then he said, 'But why didn't you bring him to us? Why all those years on your own with him? Why didn't you come to us instead of running away to a Halifax slum?'

'No!' she shouted suddenly, whirling about. She raised her right hand and struck him across the face with stinging force. 'No, you rich bastard. You'll not call my home a slum. It's rough, but it's not a slum. It's clean and decent. And it's my home and I've kept it for him all these years while you've lived in your bloody mansion. But I didn't *run*. I didn't run from anything. I've never *run* from anything in my life. I took my son because he were mine. I raised him. My way. I didn't come running, begging after Hardacre

473

money and t' Macgregor title or your big house or any of it. I took what was mine. My son. And whatever you want to think, he's had a good life with me. I couldn't give him money, but I gave him love. And if you'd not lived your life among rich bastards like yourself, you'd know that counts for summat, yet.' She drew a deep breath, while he still stared, quietly stunned by her anger and the viciousness of her hand, and she said, 'He *weren't* deprived.' Her eyes met his, daring him to oppose her. He only shook his head.

'No,' he said, 'he wasn't. But we were. You deprived us. He was ours too. You had no right to take him from us.' He spoke so softly that she misread his emotions and saw only regretful sorrow in them.

She was a little shaken and said, 'Did it matter to you?'

He grabbed her shoulders again and shook her. 'Did it *matter*? What do you think we are? Of course it bloody mattered. My aunt, Peter's mother, whom you once knew well, has no one. No one. The First War took her husband, and the Second, her son. She has no one. Only for seventeen years she's had a grandchild, and she's never known. That's what you did. That's what matters.' He closed his eyes briefly, as if fighting to control his own anger. 'Oh, maybe you can make amends now. Maybe a little. But you'll never give her back those seventeen years. She's an old lady now, Mavis. How long has she left to enjoy him?' Abruptly he let her go. He turned and walked from her but stopped and looked back over his shoulder.

'I'll never forgive you,' he said. 'I'll never forgive you those seventeen years.'

He walked away down the street in the November twilight without looking back again, as if he could not tolerate even to see her face. She thought surely she would never see him again, and savagely regretted the whole ill-conceived day. Whoever had said one can't go back had been very, very wise. She got in her small red car and drove away, wondering sadly how he'd ever get home.

She never did find that out. But she did see him again, after all.

She came home one night, about ten days later, from work, not in the best of tempers since one of the kitchen maids had announced a previously undeclared pregnancy and walked out, and found, to her annoyance, a large lorry parked directly in front of her house. It was a working-class neighbourhood and there were no garages, for there were indeed very few cars. So Mavis was accustomed to keeping her favourite acquisition on the street before the house, and indeed in precisely the position now filled to overflowing with lorry. Grumpily she nosed by it in the narrow street and nipped in right in front of it, hoping to display, by parking the Mini virtually on the front bumper of the lorry, that it was in her place. The gesture was aimed not at the vehicle itself, which was more or less an innocent, but at the driver, a tall man leaning against the near side of the vehicle, smoking a cigarette.

He was obviously waiting for someone, but she didn't see why he had to wait in front of her house. She got out of the Mini, carefully locked it and gathered up her handbag and some late shopping off the roof where she had laid them. The man watched her curiously, the while. She could not see him that clearly in the light of the street lamps, but clearly enough to be aware of his attention, that sort of disinterested attention of people with nothing better to do. She didn't look round. She had noticed him first as she drove up the street and seen he was dressed like a trades-man, in dungarees, heavy boots and a thick jumper. She wanted to say, as she struggled with her parcels, 'Well give me a hand, you lazy sod,' but she didn't, partly because she didn't really want a conversation with a stranger. There were always men about with an eye out for a woman alone. She'd spent seventeen years fending them off, both the kind, thoughtful ones, and the out-and-out rogues. She wanted no more complications in her life.

She managed to get all the parcels together and her key in her hand, and turned towards her door, walking past the cab of the lorry as she did so. She was aware of, rather than actually saw, his shift of position, as his eyes followed her. As she stepped around him he said, 'Any old scrap iron, Ma'am?' Her head spun round and she dropped the parcels. He bent, laughing, to collect them.

'What are you doing here?' she demanded, almost afraid. 'What do you want from me, Sam?'

'Dinner?' he said, adding after a moment, 'it's Saturday. A Saturday, anyhow.'

In the end, they had fish and chips from the local chip shop, at her plain, scrubbed kitchen table. She said, smiling wryly, 'Bet you haven't had these for a while.'

'No,' he said, 'I have not.' He hadn't had fish and chips since the day he walked out of Mr Ormsley's chip shop down near the harbour in Brid. After cooking them every night for four months he'd never been able to stand the sight of them again. However, he revised his judgement that night. They were good, and the company was excellent. It was a lovely evening. Mavis, after an initial shyness, had shown him her home. She didn't apologize for it, for which he was deeply glad, but she was a little touchily defensive all the same. She wouldn't let him light the coal fire, but insisted on doing it herself, on her knees before the tiled hearth. He liked the house. It was like Mick Raddley's in Bridlington, which he had always liked as well, though Mick's wife would flee into the kitchen if ever he came through the door.

'I'm sorry for my behaviour last time,' he said at last. 'I should not have walked away.'

She nodded. She sensed he was not, however, forgiving her, only regretting his own bad form. In fact, as long as she knew him, she always sensed he had never forgiven her for keeping Geordie from his grandmother, just as he had said he would not. It was, she came to learn, so unlike him, the

476

only bitterness she ever saw in his warm and forgiving nature, and all the more impressive for that. Twice she tried to raise the subject, and twice met a sudden, dark wall, as he dodged her and became unreachable. She learned not to raise it again. Just now, she hadn't the nerve. She said only, 'How do I make amends?'

'What?'

'You said I could make amends, a little. To Peter's mother. How?'

He got up from the table and walked slowly about the kitchen, ducking his head under the washing airing on the rack hung on pulleys from the ceiling. He held the mug of tea she'd given him with both hands, sipping it thoughtfully. He said, 'Let me take him to Scotland, to meet her.'

She turned away, with a soft sigh. After a long while she looked back, studying him. It was hard, seeing him dressed like that, and in her own kitchen, to imagine him as the same person as the gentleman she'd met riding over the gracious grounds of his estate. It was hard, even, to see him as a threat. She said at last, in a small voice, 'He's all I have, Sam.'

'We won't *take* him from you,' he said, astonished at her fear. 'What do you imagine us to be?'

She shrugged. 'He's young. Impressionable. You, all of you, are very impressive. I could lose him, anyway.'

He said suddenly, 'Mavis, does he know who we are? Does he know who *he* is?'

'Sure he knows. He's an Emmerson, that's who he is. He's my son. And Geordie Emmerson's nephew. And Geordie's going to be in Parliament next time, when we throw your lot out,' she added defiantly.

'What makes you imagine you know how I vote?' She shrugged, and he pursued, 'And he's not only an Emmerson. He's a Macgregor. And he's a Hardacre. Does he *know* any of that?'

She looked down at her tea, idly pursuing a chip across the crumpled newspaper.

477

'He knows all he needs to know. That his father was a fighter pilot and a brave man, and he died for his country. A little too soon,' she added with almost a smile, 'to marry his mother.' She looked up sharply, and said, 'It's hard being a bastard around here, Sam. I know. I'm one too, and I grew up in just this kind of place, in Newcastle. So's my brother. It's made us both learn to fight. It's made my Geordie the same. I don't think he needs to know *whose* bastard he is, as well. That just makes it harder. It just draws the line under the fact that you don't belong. Not here, there, or anywhere.'

'Oh, he'd belong,' Sam whispered, 'if you'd give him half the chance. So would you. If you'd get down off that damned working-class high horse of yours and treat people as people. Sometimes the damnedest snobs are the ones working from bottom to top. And as for your brother, I wish him well, if he stands for Parliament. Maybe he'll have my vote. But I won't apologize to him, or you, or anyone for who I am. No one chooses the way they're born.' He set the cup on the table and said, 'May I help you wash up?'

'Of course not.' She stood. 'Are you going?'

'I think I'd better,' he said, quite solemnly.

'We're only going to argue. I used to do this kind of thing for fun,' he said, laughing and remembering. 'But with you it just makes me sad.' She nodded, faintly remorseful, and saw him to the door.

As she stood there, looking out at the lorry on the street, she said suddenly, 'How did you find me, Sam?'

'I drove around half the night, last week, until I found your car.' It was the truth.

She said slowly, 'Was it that important to you? I mean, to find Geordie again?'

'It was. But I did it, actually, to find you.'

She studied his face in the lamplight, unable to read his subtle eyes, nor to untangle truth from teasing. She said slowly, 'I'd need time, Sam. To tell him about it all. To let

478

him get to know you, first. He's just a boy, Sam. I can't send him off with a stranger.'

He was silent for a moment and then suddenly he reached for her with both arms, and embraced her with tremendous warmth, 'Oh, God bless you,' he said.

It took time; it took a lot of time. It was eight months before Sam took Geordie Emmerson to Scotland. But it was time enjoyably spent. He left to her the explanations and let her make all the first moves. When she was willing, he took them both out, to dinners, once to the pictures, another time to York to the theatre, another, out for a run on the *Dainty Girl*. That was undoubtedly Geordie's favourite outing. The time came when Sam could stop in at the hotel in Scarborough to take Geordie out for a beer, just the two of them together. Sam enjoyed it all immensely. In fact, winning Geordie's friendship and confidence was the easy bit. Unlike his mother, Geordie was not impressed by Hardacre money, or style. He liked the big house, but it didn't worry him. Indeed the only reason he went there, but rarely, was his mother's wary objection. She didn't mind her son mixing with Sam on what she considered neutral territory, but within the brick walls of his estate was another, more doubtful matter.

But Geordie had no such concerns. He was of another, new generation, the post-war generation, aware in a new way of social mobility, and the first children of the Welfare State. Perhaps their confidence that they would shake the old bastions down was ill-placed, but it did not change the fact that they felt it. Ironically the only member of the Hardacre clan of whom Geordie Emmerson was in any awe was his own contemporary, Paul Barton, whose little skiffle band had matured into a highly professional group playing the clubs and dance-halls of the North. Geordie was every bit as enamoured as Paul with the throbbing new music of the young, and drove his mother mad at weekends with his own banjo and guitar, but Paul was leagues ahead of him, and a hero in his own right.

As for Sam, Geordie adored him. Not because, as Mavis feared, he was wealthy, but because Sam treated him like a man. He took him out on salvage tugs and let him do things that would have stood his mother's hair on end, and Geordie worshipped him accordingly.

It was Mavis, then, who he found he must win, and that was a far more difficult task, but no less enjoyable. He had always found her attractive, an attraction he'd been a little hard put to suppress when she was yet his cousin's fiancée. Indeed hers was one of those female faces that never left him throughout the years, and would come to him at times, in dreams. But she had not been, then, as beautiful as she was now. There had always been a shy uncertainty about her, a vaguely beaten-down look, inheritance perhaps of her rough childhood with a brutal mother and her drunkard common-law husband. And Peter Macgregor, he sadly admitted, had not always helped, with his slick, thoughtless public-school aplomb, dragging her, too hastily, into situations with which she could barely cope.

But now she'd made her own way in the world for too long to be so deeply impressed by anyone, or so he thought. He never fully realized quite how much she was impressed by him. Her response to her own awe was to come out fighting; she put him in his place so many times that *he* began to feel the social misfit, beside her.

She was fiercely, even savagely independent. She would accept his paying for meals and theatres, because he was the man and, in her world, that was how men were to behave. But she shied from coming again to his home, and she rarely allowed him to hers. Sometimes he wondered if she feared seduction. At others he suspected she was, out of habit, carefully protecting her reputation. He was aware, as no doubt was she, of the twitch of lace curtains along the street whenever he arrived at her door. They were watching, as they had watched for so many years, and they were aware now that her son no longer lived at home. And yet he doubted they'd condemn as quickly as she expected. Nor would he cause much stir among them; they didn't know who he was. Mavis told anyone who really pushed too hard that he was a friend, a scrap-merchant from Bridlington and they all accepted that. He looked like a scrap merchant and he drove a succession of battered vans and lorries. The fact that his name was on them would cause no stir. They didn't know his name, and they didn't expect the owner to drive lorries. As long as he spoke to no one, and was not thus undone by his accent, they would regard him as just one more tradesman courting a local lass. Surely they would forgive that?

'Those bitches forgive nothing,' she said, and it was only later he realized her unpardonable sin was not what she'd done, but that she wouldn't crawl back into the fold, marry a local chap, and be forgiven. It was her feisty independence they hated, her refusal to engage in the endless gossip behind those lace curtains, the interminable discussion of sex and more sex at the factory bench, the lively and harmless street squabbles over children. She'd set herself above them, and that was mortal sin.

Still, the result of that independence was a long succession of meetings on some sort of no man's land, half-way between Hardacres and Halifax, in country pubs and small hotels for long, leisurely dinners, after which he would go his way home, and she, hers. The sight of her little red Mini bouncing away defiantly alone down the road was a sight he grew to detest. But she would have it no other way.

It was in the midsummer of 1959 that he took Geordie, at last, to Scotland, to meet his grandmother. In all that time he had made no mention of what was happening to Jane. He could not bear to tell her of him until he was certain they would meet. He drove up to Strathconon with Geordie in an old van. The boy had never been north of the Border, indeed never been anywhere much further than Leeds, and was thrilled with the journey. He had a provisional driving licence and Sam, who was teaching him, allowed him to drive on the empty Northern roads. They reached Jane's home late at night, but it was still light enough in the long Highland twilight to make out the shape of the house with its high, narrow gables, a house Sam had always loved. He went to the door through the dim garden, sweet with fresh rain on the lavender hedges, and rang the bell. Geordie hung behind, a little shyly, by the van. Jane answered the door herself; she had only a daily woman to help in the house. She peered out into the dim light and suddenly recognized him. She was utterly amazed.

'Sam? Whatever are you doing here.' He just grinned and half-turned, waving to the boy to join them. Geordie came forward, only slightly shy now and stood beside Sam for reassurance. Sam put his arm over the boy's shoulders.

'I've brought someone to meet you,' he said. It was the sweetest moment of his life.

CHAPTER
TWENTY-SEVEN

It was only after that summer meeting that he and Mavis
Emmerson became lovers. Even then, it was not like any
affair he had carried on before. He was not even certain, at
first, that he wanted it to happen. He wanted *her* of course.
He had wanted her from the day she drove up his driveway
in her damnable Mini. But there was no way he could
possibly pursue her, and certainly no way he could seduce.
She was a mother, and an unwed mother, doubly vulnerable. He could not possibly endanger her hard-won reputation or, worse yet, risk the faith of the boy he had
befriended. He felt with Mavis, as he would always feel over
one issue and another, that his rights were few, if any, and
his desires must always come last. He would never have
used his not inconsiderable romantic talents to persuade her
into his bed. Even were she persuadable, and he had his
doubts. He did generally know his limitations, and he'd
never met a woman like her before.

She had her way of meeting him half-way, not just
literally, but emotionally as well. She insisted always on
pulling her own weight, and she refused to lean on him one
whit. It was both refreshing and infuriating. She certainly
won his respect, but she frustrated his need to look after
people, particularly the women in his life. He was a little
old-fashioned that way, anyhow and, particularly once he
was her lover, he wanted to be her protector as well, and she
wouldn't let him.

She didn't consult him about things. She made her own
decisions. Even when it became necessary to leave her job
at the hotel and take another similar job elsewhere, she only
told him when the matter was settled. All the women in his

family, even Jane, who had more sense and more strength even than he, always turned to him for advice. Mavis didn't. It was unnerving. And it was tantalizing.

Yet had she not made the first move, they would have remained only friends, though they may have been friends for life. And it was a move, when she did make it, of sheer spontaneity, a split-second decision and a reaction to the sheer undeniable pull of romance and, had a dozen different things been otherwise that evening, he knew it might never have happened.

They had been to dinner in a country pub, one of their many neutral meeting grounds. It was a filthy wet night in September and the red Mini, his arch-enemy, had chosen that occasion to develop an intermittent fault with its lights. Just occasionally, when Mavis would dip her beams, they'd go out entirely, leaving her alone in an unhappy little dark shell. It was scary, and since it had happened twice on her journey from Halifax and the second time had required a good several minutes fiddling with the recalcitrant switch to get the headlamps back on, she arrived at the pub nervous and unhappy. After dinner he offered to drive her home, but she wasn't about to leave the Mini in the middle of Yorkshire alone. Eventually she agreed to let him follow her back to Halifax as an escort, to make sure she got home. He felt a malicious delight in keeping the fleeing little red car at the edge of his headlights all the way, like a recaptured lost sheep.

Outside her house he dutifully said good-night. She kissed him, she turned, and then suddenly she stood straight, still in the middle of the street, as if the weight of seventeen years of celibate respectability had suddenly landed on her at once. 'God damn you buggers, just watch me now,' she said aloud, to the silent closed curtains of the street. She took his hand and led him defiantly to the door, through it, inside her little house and up the narrow stairs of the old two-up, two-down, without ever releasing her hold.

She took off her coat and threw it on the floor, and shoved open the bedroom door. She turned and grasped him about the waist. 'I want *loving*,' she said, in a whisper as fierce as a growl. And she got loving, too. He went home in the morning, a bemused, but happy man.

And so it began. They continued, naturally, since it's a step that generally only goes one way. They conducted their affair, and themselves, with infinite restraint and respectable dignity. They were not children, not even young, and the whole thing seemed to have greater significance to Sam than he'd ever felt before about it. Besides, there was Geordie, whom he felt a tremendous need to shield and protect. They met at her house, and occasionally for a stolen night away in the countryside where no one knew either of them. Even so, they did not meet too often, and even then, she would not come to Hardacres and would certainly never spend the night beneath his roof. That saddened him, but he respected her need to stand alone, and found the cramped room in the little brick house in Halifax as romantic and lovely as the master bedroom of Hardacres with its ancient four-poster bed. As always, he walked his familiar tightrope with the morality of his church, though with something less than the old reckless ease.

Still, he was quite contented with it all, as was she, both of them a little too adult and worn by life to even consider further commitments. It might have continued like that for years, but an incident in February of 1960 brought it all to a sudden end.

They were working in the North Sea, off the coast of Scotland, on a small coaster that had gone down a fortnight before after her cargo shifted. She had tried to make her way to Aberdeen, and failed, capsizing eventually and sinking in eighty feet of water midway between that port and Stonehaven, with the loss of two of her crew. The rest had been taken off by lifeboat, and the ship now lay on her side in shifting sand. Pete Haines had taken the *Mary Hardacre* up to Aberdeen from Hull, after Sam won the salvage contract, and Sam had gone with them. They were attempting now to send divers down to see what could be done to raise her.

It was, for February in that part of the world, a nice day, in that it was marginally above freezing, the wind was brisk but not savage, and it was only snowing part of the time. In between the sun actually shone. They'd done a good day's work, mooring a barge over the site and making ready a diving platform aboard it, and were about to head back into Aberdeen for the night. Sam was standing at the lee rail, watching the crew prepare to raise anchor. He was tired and pleased with himself and the day, having done a hard day's work and got a lot done, which is a lot nicer than doing a hard day's work and getting nothing done which, in the nature of things, often happened. He was thinking that he would telephone Mavis from Aberdeen. She was not hysterical about his work, nor did she resent it, as Janet had done, but she was healthily concerned, and he found it the decent thing to do to keep in touch. Two young lads were fooling around at the stern, capering, enjoying the same relaxation that he was. He watched them, good-naturedly, but Pete Haines, who had absolutely no sense of humour over work, shouted down a warning, which they either did not hear, or ignored. He came right out of the wheelhouse then and waved his fist. Sam thought him harsh, but he was wrong, in the next few moments would learn how wrong.

Somehow, he was never sure how, they ended up half on the rail, and half off, and in a moment of silly confusion one of them overbalanced the other, and a man went in the sea. It took two seconds, and in the third second Sam went after him. It was not heroism, but immediate instinct. He was nearest, and he knew, too, that the man, in the inexplicable tradition of some members of the maritime community, could not swim. There was nothing else to do.

486

Sam could swim, and very well. And he'd taken the moment's pause to kick off his boots, so he had that advantage, too, over the crewman floundering in the choppy sea. But it was February, and the water in those near-Arctic latitudes was a handful of degrees above freezing. It shocked and numbed his entire body the instant he hit it, and he went right under before he could make his limbs move. He broke surface, angry with himself for losing sight of the man in trouble, but glimpsed him over the top of a wave, and struck out for him.

Swimming in that water was not like any swimming he'd done ever before in his life. It was almost impossible even to breathe. But he reached the man, taking more energy to do it than he'd ever imagined, and was confronted with the desperation of the drowning and found it difficult to fend off the grasping hands that would draw him under too. Eventually he got behind the man, calmed him with his voice, and managed to hold him above the surface while the crew aboard the tug cast a life-ring and lines.

Even that was difficult. The man was a lot heavier than he was himself, and a dead weight in the choppy shifting sea, though at least now he was not struggling. Sam realized quickly that the other's calm was not reason, but shock, and the effect of the freezing water. He was already barely conscious. Sam got a line about him, with tremendous pains. His hands were too numb to manage the simplest knots without a struggle and the man himself was now incapable of helping, or holding on.

The distance between them and the tug seemed to have widened greatly, and he wondered dimly if they were being blown away from it, or if it was only imagination. The side of the boat was dark and very high above them suddenly, and the sky was darker too. In a handful of minutes it had turned from afternoon to the edge of early northern night. He was, just for an instant, afraid, not of the sea, but the darkness closing in.

He heard voices shouting, and the line was pulling them both towards the tug, and then they were within the reach, almost, of arms from above. Other lines were thrown down and he strove to reach one with his free hand, but had to give up because he could not stay afloat and do so, as well. The sea buffeted them against the metal side of the *Mary Hardacre* and he kicked away from it for safety. It is incredibly difficult to get a man out of rough water on to a sea-tossed vessel. Disinterestedly, almost, he began to assess their chances and was finding them diminishing. But between himself supporting the near-comatose seaman from below and those above drawing up the line he had secured about the man, they finally got him within arms' reach and, with the effort of several strong hands, hauled him dripping and near-frozen on to the deck.

Sam felt himself relax, as if the whole thing were finished, which was terribly foolish, and he heard Pete Haines's voice suddenly insistent, 'Come on; now you,' as if he needed reminding, as perhaps he already did. Cold is the most deceptive of enemies, the closer it comes to killing, the kinder it gets. He was already feeling lazily uninterested in the whole affair. He did actually reach the side of the tug again, and grasped the extended lifeline with stiff, frozen hands. The solid feel of it in his hands gave him purpose, and in a moment's alertness he realized he was in danger, and struggled to use the line to get himself aboard. He was within a foot's reach of help when a sudden swell tipped the tug savagely towards him and cast him, free of the line, back into the sea.

When he broke surface again, reality was fading. He heard shouts, distant over the sound of the water and wind, and something swished by him in the sea. He knew it was a line and tried for the rope with one hand, but it slithered, wet and icy, free of him. He tried again, but it seemed not worth the effort any longer. He wasn't afraid, but out of a dim sense of duty he tried for the line once more, grasped it, hardly aware he was holding anything with his numb hands, and felt it slipping free. He let it go. He had done his best and the sea seemed suddenly gentle and kind. What stunned him briefly into a last action was the sudden desperation in Pete Haines's voice shouting, somewhere far away, 'Get him out of that water, for the love of God!'

He struggled for a moment to stay afloat, so that he could see where Pete was. The dark hull of the tug was a dim outline, washed in a watery mist. He wanted to see him, to let him know somehow, as he knew, that it didn't really matter at all. But he could not. And then suddenly there was someone in the water with him. He heard a voice nearby, and glimpsed the arm of a swimmer and knew someone had gone in after him, as he had done after the first man. He was momentarily angry at Pete for allowing it, and putting yet another life at risk, but the anger faded with the flash of rationality that had preceded it.

It didn't matter either; the sea was kind to all.

The swimmer reached him. He was dimly aware of the strength of arms around his numbed body, supporting him in the sea. Over his shoulder he heard the voice of Kevin Hawes, the Whitby lad he had cheered through the long night on the towed freighter, say with young authority, 'All right Mr Hardacre, I've got you now.'

Consciously, gratefully, he relinquished the burden of survival to that strong young voice, closed his eyes, and let the watery darkness win.

He had no real awareness of being brought aboard the *Mary Hardacre*, only the fleeting distant sensation of the exhausting weight of his own body unsupported by water, and the oddity of feeling snow-blowing wind as warm. There was darkness after that and then, some time later perhaps, a realization that he was below deck, lying on a bunk, mercifully dry, someone having taken his wet clothing from him, and wrapped in swathes of blankets which seemed only to wrap tighter the ungodly cold around him.

Pete Haines was beside him, talking to him, trying to hold his attention, but he couldn't understand what it was he was saying. And yet he was again aware of reality, and the true state of things. He knew Pete was trying to help him, was extending yet to him a lifeline, but he could no more reach out and grasp it now than he could in the icy sea. Again he wanted to thank Pete for trying so hard, and to let him know he had done enough. But he could neither speak nor listen. And then the cold began peacefully to fade, and with it Pete's voice. In the last conscious remnant of his mind he sought the words of the *confiteor*, but they eluded him, like the ill-studied prayers of a child.

CHAPTER
TWENTY-EIGHT

He awoke, sick and confused, in hospital in Aberdeen, having no recollection at all of how he got there. Later he learned that Pete had brought the *Mary Hardacre* into harbour there, and sent all three of her casualties into the Royal Infirmary, suffering from cold and exhaustion and Sam, eventually, from pneumonia as well. They had all been in the water far too long, and he'd been in far longer than either of the others. He was, for a while, extremely ill.

His first awareness was of Jane Macgregor sitting beside his bed. Her presence there seemed, at the time, as natural as the cool touch of her lovely old hands. His sense of time vanished for a while, but she seemed always to be there, whenever he awoke. It was only later that he was stunned by her loyalty. True, he was in Scotland, and relatively, if not particularly, near her Strathconon home, but he knew she would have done the same had he, or any of the family, been in a similar state in Cornwall. He wondered who would hold them all together when she was gone.

He was ten days in hospital. It was an odd and chastening experience. He had never before, in all his adult life, been ill, and it took him as much by surprise as it did his stunned family. He was not, after the first night, in any real danger; it was the initial exposure, not the subsequent illness, that had threatened his life. But he was quite miserably sick with it, all the same. And when, after the ten days, he was released only on the agreement that he would go with Jane to Strathconon to convalesce, he did not argue. He was weak and still very tired, and he wanted only to sleep.

Jane drove him to her remote and beautiful home and he was there almost another fortnight. The clear Highland air was wonderfully refreshing and he slept twelve hours a night and spent the days lying on a sofa in front of her fire. She was a most attentive nurse. She spoiled him and protected him, answering the telephone always herself and letting no one but Mavis Emmerson even speak to him. She was quite severe and strict, but he did not mind. It was comforting to be looked after, for a little while, rather than always looking after everyone else.

He was, at just forty-three, the acknowledged patriarch of the family, simply by virtue of capability. It was to him they all turned if anything was wrong and, considering the number of them and their various quirks, there was usually something wrong somewhere. Between family and business, he got little peace. Ordinarily he did not mind at all, but just now he was tired, and content to let everything go.

It was all quite marvellously peaceful, like a spiritual retreat, and an occasion for a great deal of thought. One or two thoughts, born out of the experience in the icy water, came to rest with him with considerable force. Foremost in his mind was that he had come within a hair's breadth of dying and had been quite cheerfully oblivious of it at the time. Death was an unpredictable bastard; he flashed no lights and gave no warnings, but waited where he chose to wait in odd nooks and crannies of one's life. A moment's ill-conceived boyish horseplay on the deck of the *Mary Hardacre* had very nearly cost three lives.

He understood now at last, why Mick Raddley hated the sea, and why Pete Haines treated work with such cold, humourless intent. The sea was merciless to error. She was a whore, as Mick had always said, and a vengeful whore as well. He had used her to his great advantage, and like any whore she would demand, one day, to be paid. The only open question was when.

And the second, most pressing thought, that went hand in hand with the first, was that he had nearly walked out on Mavis Emmerson through the same door as Peter

Macgregor, and left her, as he had done, without station or rights.

He telephoned her from Jane's house every day, and she called him as well, whenever work permitted a moment free. Partly, he felt the need to tie himself to her with words, as if in apology for almost leaving her. But, also, he simply missed her, and needed to talk. They always talked a great deal and, oddly, when he remembered his romance with Janet Chandler it was difficult to recall any long conversations. They must have been there, and yet they faded from memory. He remembered long and lavish arguments, but that's not the same thing. And he remembered action, going places and doing things, and being in bed. What he did not remember was words.

And yet, with Mavis, words were everything. It was doubly odd considering that she was by no means an erudite person, and her education was extremely limited, particularly compared to his, which, though erratic, was considerable. But there was never a subject, from marine engines to the complexities of the great Church philosophers, that he could not discuss with her. If she did not understand something, or a word was new to her, she would stop him and ask, with the candid curiosity most people leave behind as children. And thus, as children do, she learned, and he never would meet with her that blank wall of bored incomprehension that he met often from more educated, but less inventive minds. She was a delight, and he courted her mind as much as her body.

Jane always left the room when he telephoned Mavis. After bringing the phone to him and setting it on the table by the sofa she would hurriedly, and discreetly depart. He tried to tell her it was not necessary, but she was adamant that he have his privacy. He felt guilty though, because they talked so long, and on the first Sunday he was there they spoke at such length that the fire had nearly burned to ash by the time he hung up. And he'd done so then only because the talking had made him cough so much that Mavis got worried and refused any longer to speak.

Jane came back in when she heard the phone ring off, carrying a silver tray set with her tea service. She put it down on the table and removed the telephone to its proper place.

'I must pay for the call,' he said. 'We talked for an hour.'

'Yes, dear, and bed and breakfast besides. How is Mavis?' She poured tea and handed him a cup, and knelt by the hearth to restore the fire.

'Let me do that, please,' he said, guilty again.

She gave him her most imperious look. 'Shall I drive you back to Aberdeen?'

He gave up. He sipped his tea, watching her and said, 'She's fine. Marvellous.' Finished with the fire, Jane rose and settled on the arm of the sofa behind him, balancing her own cup on her knee. He was staring into the reviving fire, dreamy and distant. 'Geordie and Paul are playing together again in Scarborough. I think it's going to be every weekend. Mavis says they're using every penny on new equipment. It really costs, all that electric stuff they use.'

'You mean people are paying to listen to that cacophony?' Jane sniffed.

'Paying very well, my dear. And *you're* getting old-fashioned,' he said, with a grin.

'I've a *right* Sam. I'm nearly seventy. I got as far as jazz and swing, and a little of this skiffle they were doing, but I'm calling a halt.' She paused. 'Is Albert still with Paul in this?' she asked curiously.

'Oh, right behind him. Steady as a rock. He's the best of us. You know that. Noel's a bastard. A delightful bastard, but a bastard all the same. Philip's an ass. Rodney's beneath mention. And I'm a rogue. But Albert's a gentleman. Like Harry.' She laughed, but he was quite serious. He said suddenly, 'You should have them up here.'

Jane had absorbed her new-found grandson into her fold

just as she absorbed all the others of the young. They got on beautifully. Indeed, she had welcomed Mavis back into her life after eighteen years with warm grace, as if she had only slipped out a moment for a breath of fresh air.

'Up here?' she said. 'To make that noise?'

'No. Just to be here. They'd love it.'

She shook her head. 'It crossed my mind,' she said. 'But no. This is for the *very* young and,' she paused, adding slyly, 'the mature. Like you and me. The young are bored up here in a trice. At that age, they want bright lights.'

'Terry and I loved it here at that age.'

'Oh well,' Jane said softly, remembering. 'That was a while ago. You were different. We all were different. You were quite innocent, you know, the two of you, compared with the young today.'

He laughed suddenly, a laugh that ended in a fit of coughing that brought her anxious eyes to him at once. He waved her away. 'Just thinking,' he said, 'of Willie Campbell's daughters down the way. Whenever you'd send us down for eggs, they'd take us behind the byre. They taught me everything I know.'

'Sam!' she said, shocked. 'I was not aware.'

'You weren't meant to be,' he said, laughing and coughing again. She told him to be quiet then and he obeyed, relaxing back against her heap of cushions while she reached across him, leaning over his shoulder, and wrapped the tartan rug more firmly around him. The pneumonia had frightened her; she was old and remembered it as a killer. She laid the long cool fingers of her right hand against his forehead, as she did a dozen times a day, guarding against a return of the fever. He said, in her father's voice, 'Stop tha fussin' woman, I'm a' reeght.'

She laughed, dropping her hand and linking it with her other loosely around his neck.

'Oh, I suppose, Sam,' she said. 'I'm sorry. But you gave me a scare.'

'Nothing to be scared about,' he said, 'I just got too cold, that was all.' He felt her linked arms tighten against him, and said, 'You're a worrier. See, you're getting edgy now.' He lightly patted her hands.

She said, drily, 'Well, my dear, when they let me in to see you first in Aberdeen, the hospital chaplain was giving you last rites. That sort of thing always makes me edgy.'

'Somebody was being a little excitable,' he said. Actually, he had no recollection of any of that, and no way of knowing if any of that caution had been justified. He did know, however, that he was all right now. Still, he understood her fears, and let her fuss. It was the least he could do in return for all she'd done for him. He closed his big hand over both of hers, holding them gently, and said, quite suddenly, 'Would you mind if I married Mavis Emmerson?'

She was quite silent for a moment and he waited, a little uneasily, for her answer. Then she said, 'Mind? Why should I mind?'

'Peter?' he said softly. She shook her head.

'Oh, no, dear. On the contrary, nothing could give me more pleasure.' She felt him relax and lean his head back slightly against her, and was surprised at how much her response had mattered.

'Are you going to do that?' she said.

He was a long while in answering and then he said, 'I don't want it to happen to her again.' He still held her hands, but he felt her straighten, almost pull away, and after a while she said in her unassailably direct way, 'You mean, you want to leave her a rich widow.'

He shrugged, 'If I must leave her, yes. I'm not expecting . . .'

'No, no,' she said. 'Of course you're not. But that's what's on your mind, is it not?'

'It's on my mind.'

'Sam,' she said slowly, 'that is very kind. But it's no reason to marry.'

He had half-turned his head, but he could not see her face, for she sat yet, straight and regal, behind him. 'Well that's not all, for God's sake,' he said hurriedly.

'Do you *love* her, Sam?' asked Jane. She was smiling with bewildered affection down on to his grey head.

When he answered, he spoke very thoughtfully and said only, 'There are so many kinds of love.'

'Does that mean yes or no?' she said bluntly. She was thinking simultaneously of Janet Chandler and of Harry and Hetty. She had her own opinion of marriages of kindness. He did not answer at all, but stared into the fire. She offered him more tea and he refused. She tried another tack.

'Tell me,' she said. 'Who did you think of when you thought you were drowning?'

He laughed. 'Did my whole life and all my mistresses pass before my eyes? No. I'm afraid it didn't. There wasn't time. One moment I was fine, or I thought I was, the next I was really in trouble. That's what the sea is like.' Her arms tightened around him again. 'All I thought of was sleep.'

She was silent for a while after that, but then she said brightly, 'All right then, who do you think you asked for, when you were in hospital?'

He was wary suddenly, 'Is this a test?'

'Maybe.'

He took his hand from hers and brushed back his hair, uneasily. He said, 'That's unfair. I won't be held to that.' He paused and said slowly, 'There's a kind of woman a man dreams about when he's young, and maybe remembers when he's dying. It doesn't mean she's a woman he could live with.'

Jane laughed, delighted. 'Oh, jolly well done. I took two years trying to get that through to you, and never managed it.'

'What I'm trying to say is, it isn't significant. It's passion and passion guides us at times like that. It's not significant that I asked for her.'

'No,' said Jane wisely, 'but it's significant that you thought you did.'

He half-turned again, looking around to see her face, but she avoided his eyes. 'Didn't I ask for Janet?' he said.

'No dear,' she shook her head. 'You asked for Terry, of course. Just like Harry did. That was what scared me Sam, not the chaplain.'

He nodded slowly and then asked, suddenly curious, recalling Harry outfoxing him on his deathbed, 'Whatever did you say?'

'I said he'd gone out to the pub. It was what first came to mind.' He laughed. 'You said something indecent and went to sleep. I thought I handled that quite well, actually.'

He laughed again, 'Very. Better than I did with Harry, anyway.'

She said suddenly, 'You're not certain, Sam. That's why you were afraid you'd said the wrong thing when you were ill. You don't know your inner mind, or you don't trust it. Or both.'

He got suddenly angry. 'Are you trying to make this hard on me?' he said.

'Oh yes, dear, I am. I want you to be certain. Marriage isn't a kindness to bestow, dear, nor a place to run to hide. It's a commitment of love, and with you it's a commitment for life.' He leaned against her again, his anger gone.

'I don't understand love,' he said. 'I never have. I'm certain of one thing only. I want her with me for the rest of my life, however long that is.'

'That will do,' said Jane. She sat with him until he slept, and then rose and drew the curtains on the fading winter day.

Mavis met him in her red Mini at York when he returned by train from Scotland. He had done all he could do to persuade Jane to let him travel that way, since she was ready and willing to drive him the whole distance. But it was still

February, and snowy, and half the roads in the North were blocked. Eventually he won her round by convincingly demonstrating, by chopping a stack of firewood for her, that he was perfectly well, which he was. She drove him as far as Inverness, and he parted from her there, on the grey station platform, with snow blowing by. He found himself suddenly too emotional to thank her, or even say a proper goodbye. She just smiled, kissed him, and walked away, her tall old figure dignified and appropriate beneath the Victorian glass-arched roof of the station. It had been, in an odd way, two of the best weeks he could remember. There were times he thought quite seriously that she was perhaps the only person, other than Terry, he had ever really loved, without complexity or doubt. It bemused him, because it was virtually what his mother had rather bitterly accused, three years before.

At York railway station Mavis forgot all her reserves and restraints and embraced him publicly and passionately, clinging on to him like a child. He was surprised and delighted, and only regretful that she eventually pulled away. She took his hand and walked with him to her car.

'Oh God, I was so worried about you,' she said. She was studying him carefully as they sat together in the Mini before she drove off, as if to be quite certain he was as well as he outwardly appeared.

'You needn't have been,' he said. 'I told you on the telephone. I was fine. Just tired, a little, but fine.'

'Oh, not then,' she said, starting the car. 'Before. When I talked to Jane. She rang me, you know, right away from Aberdeen. The first night. I didn't even know she had my number.'

'Pete had it,' he said. 'He was still there then. He waited in Aberdeen a couple of days, for the other two.' He laughed. 'He said he was going to take them out as soon as they were released and throw the first poor sod back in the sea. He was fuming, I gather.'

'I was surprised,' Mavis said. 'I didn't know she was that aware . . . you'd not told her anything?'

He shook his head, 'Not then love. I wasn't talking to anyone just then.'

'So I gathered. I was so frightened. I wanted to come right up there, but there was no way . . . I felt I couldn't.'

He looked at her oddly, but said only, 'I think Jane must have exaggerated a bit.'

'Jane never exaggerates,' she returned at once. 'She just gets more and more restrained. She was so restrained that night from Aberdeen, I was terrified.' She paused. 'Your mother's at the big house,' she said. 'I went to see her the day after Jane rang, and she was terribly upset. I took her up to stay with Vanessa. I hoped you wouldn't mind me interfering, but it seemed the best thing.'

He smiled gratefully, and said, 'I'm sure if you thought of it, it was the best thing. That was terribly kind.' He was surprised, actually, to imagine his mother that concerned; her whole attitude to his choice of profession, if he could call it that, had been that whatever dangers might befall him eventually would be both inevitable and well-deserved. 'I'm sure she'll recover,' he added drily.

'She's really concerned,' Mavis said sharply. 'She's waiting for you there, right now.'

'Take me to Halifax,' he said, with a grin.

She glanced across, not particularly amused, and she took him to Hardacres, anyhow.

They met Noel half-way up the driveway. He was coming down to the bottom field, in which he had the heifers, with the tractor and a barrow laden with hay bales. Mavis had to squeeze the little Mini on to the grass verge to get round him. He recognized the car and halted the tractor, staring glumly down at them.

Sam wound down the window and said, 'Aye, Noel, how goes it?'

'I see you're alive.'

'Sorry about that.'

'On the contrary. I'm delighted. Another lot of death duties and this family's going under. Then I'd end up feeding t' bloody lot.' He glowered again and then touched his grey forelock, 'Afternoon, Mavis,' he said.

'You could always send them to market, Noel,' Sam shouted as Noel clattered away.

Mavis stared at his disappearing figure, hunched up on the tractor seat, and drove back on to the drive and continued on her way. She looked at Sam, and at Noel's reflection in the mirror. 'He *is* joking,' she said nervously.

'He means every word,' Sam said, with a grin. 'I assure you. Underneath that crusty exterior is a heart of pure lead.'

'Why do you *like* him so much?'

He laughed. 'Would to God that I knew.'

When he arrived at the house, he paused for just a moment before the door, suddenly terribly glad to be home. Then he went in with Mavis, the slightest bit reluctant yet, at his side. His mother was half-way down the stairs when he entered the great hall. Perhaps she had heard a car, perhaps she was simply coming down anyway. She stopped, on a step several up from the bottom, and stared silently. In spite of Mavis's protests of her concern, she looked not one whit happier to see him than Noel had. She said, in her usual sanguine way, 'It is not good enough that you must be an idiot. Now you must be an heroic idiot as well?'

'Mother, I assure you, it wasn't that. If I'd had a moment to think I'd have let the silly bugger drown. It was his own fault anyhow,' he heard himself suddenly sounding like Pete Haines. 'The trouble was, I didn't think.'

'When have you ever?' She paused, and then said perfunctorily, 'I'm glad you didn't drown.'

'You sure now?'

'That's not funny, Sam.' He shrugged. The one person in his life he would always fail to amuse or charm was his

501

mother. Then suddenly she ran down the stairs and flung herself into his arms, tearfully clutching him to her and sobbing, 'Oh God, I can't lose you both. I can't lose you both.' He stopped teasing then, and held her close, stroking her yet beautiful hair, now blacker than his own.

He kissed her face and said, 'Nor shall you,' but even as he embraced her he felt the familiar, subtle distancing, even within the circle of his arms. He let her go. She composed herself, and became in another moment as calm and controlled as before.

'Tea is waiting in the drawing-room. You'll join me?'

He nodded, and as she went on before him, he turned to follow her. Out of the corner of his eye he saw Mavis slip towards the door. He stopped. 'Where are you going?' he said.

She smiled. 'I'll see you later, tomorrow perhaps.' She turned to leave.

'No,' he said quickly. 'I want to see you now. I've not seen you at all for three weeks and I've missed you terribly. Come in and have tea with us. I want to talk.'

'Later, Sam.' She looked towards the closed door to the drawing-room. 'Go on, your mother's waiting.' And before he could protest further she said, 'Your family need you with them now.' She smiled gently once again.

He stared at her, then turned quickly and strode to the drawing-room door, opening it half-way. He leaned in and said, 'I'll be five minutes, Mother, there's something I must do.'

Mavis didn't hear any reply Madelene may have made, because he shut the door almost at once. He crossed the room with such purpose that she was a little frightened, but he only took her hand and led her out of the door. Once outside, he continued walking down to the steps that led in a graceful sweep to the lawns. He yet held her hand, and she was obliged to follow. He walked quite a long distance so that they stood eventually in the midst of a great sweep of green, with the big red-brick house dreamy behind them in frosty winter sunlight.

'If *anyone*,' he said fiercely, 'is my family, it's you.'

She shook her head. 'Family is the tie of blood, Sam.'

'Family,' he said, 'is the tie of love.' He was still holding her hand, and she'd drawn back from him so they stood at the lengths of their two arms. He was looking down on her, his eyes solemn.

She nodded slowly. 'She's your mother Sam. She does love you, whatever you think. And she's had a hard time. She was terribly, terribly distraught. She needs to have you to herself, just for a little while. You owe her that. Now go back and don't tease her. You're cruel, without realizing it, but you're cruel.'

'We understand each other,' he said, with solemnity.

'You *don't* understand her. She was desperate over you.'

'She was desperate, my love, because I'd become the lost sheep for a little while. In a week she'll be back to normal. We all know, after all, who the lost sheep really is.' She stared at him sadly, and he said, 'She'll never forgive me, you know.'

'Oh, surely she has. Surely now.'

He shook his head. 'Oh, no. Why should she? I killed her son.' He said it calmly and rationally, with no trace of bitterness.

'How can you *accept* that?' She was suddenly hostile to Madelene, on his behalf.

'Accepting is the art of living.' He looked up at the house and back to her. 'And of loving.' He smiled. 'Will you marry me, please?' he said.

She twisted round so the link of their hands was broken. She stood with her back to him, facing the beech wood. After a long while she spoke and her voice was deliberately light.

'Let's talk about it next week,' she said. 'You've been ill. People get sentimental when they're ill.'

'I'm not being sentimental,' he shouted illogically. 'I love you.' He glared at her. 'And I'm perfectly well now, anyhow.'

She folded her arms and studied him, faintly belligerent, as she always got when he shouted. 'All right, I suppose you are. The answer's no.'

'What?'

'You heard the first time, Sam. No.'

He blinked. 'You can't just say "no",' he said disbelievingly.

'Oh yes I can. And if you think not, you've not been said no to enough lately. That's what happens when you get rich and important.'

'I'm neither rich nor important,' he returned at once. 'I'm in debt up to my eyes and everyone I employ still tells me what to do. Now give me a reason.'

'All right,' she said, cocking her head sideways in that devastating way of hers, and pointing over his shoulder to the big red brick house. 'That.'

He turned round slowly to look at it, as if it had just arrived there and suddenly caught his notice. Then he looked at her. '*That*,' he said slowly, 'is my home. And I'm not apologizing for it, to you, or to anyone.' He was beginning to get angry, which was a side of him she, unlike Janet, rarely saw. When she did see it, however, it produced in her a slightly nervous rebelliousness.

She glared at him and at the house with equal resentment and said, 'You know, my brother says when his lot get into Parliament next time, they're going to nationalize all that sort of thing.'

Sam was very quiet. He folded his arms and looked down at the velvety grass, tinged with frost. He looked up at her through narrowed eyes. 'You tell your brother, whom I like and respect, by the way, that I've earned every penny I have, and *furthermore* if he or *anyone* attempts to *touch* that, I'll break his bloody neck, Parliament be damned.'

She smiled, a long cool smile of satisfaction, 'Aye,' she said, on an outward breath, 'so blood will out. Happen I hear the old robber baron at last.'

Their eyes met and locked, and they teetered a moment between fury and humour, but neither of them would budge. She was every bit as headstrong as he, in her own quiet, unassuming way. At last he looked away. When he spoke his voice was serious, and a little sad. He said, 'My great-grandfather, if that's who you mean, was neither thief nor lord. He was a working man. Like me.' He smiled wryly and held out to her hands more calloused by far than those of her brother, who carried the labour banner and spent his days behind a desk, 'And if,' he went on, 'you're too much a snob to marry me, so be it. I've been turned down before.' He turned and walked away from her to his lovely house, alone. When he reached the stone steps, she shouted after him in her old-fashioned voice, 'Sam.'

'Aye.' He turned to face her.

'I love thee,' she said.

CHAPTER
TWENTY-NINE

Sam gave Mavis the engagement ring that Harry had given Judith Winstanley before their wedding in South Africa at the close of the Boer War. It had gone to Jane in Harry's will and she insisted Sam have it for his future wife. It was a very beautiful antique and worth marginally more than her rented house in Halifax. She looked at it on her ring finger, gently shaking her head.

'This is going to play havoc with the story about the scrap-merchant,' she said.

'Tell them I nicked it,' he replied, which was precisely what she did.

Still, secrecy was not easily maintained. Not that it really mattered, only Sam wanted a week or two to get his family used to the idea, before the whole world knew. The family actually were remarkably co-ordinated in their response. They were universally delighted, which slightly surprised him, if only because he'd never seen them so united on any single issue. Madelene's response was the most startling, and also the most gratifying. She was thrilled. Later, he realized he should have expected that, but he'd grown so accustomed to her disapproval since the day he left Ampleforth that he had long regarded it as the only possible form of communication between them. As Noel cursed his dog, his mother opposed his every action. But not this one. Madelene was a conventional lady in some ways, and an unconventional one in others. Madelene was not the slightest distressed at either Mavis's bastard son or her own illegitimacy. Madelene had long held, with Gallic frankness, that had timings worked out only marginally different, Sam and Terry would have been bastards as well. In any event,

506

they were born a scant seven months after her wartime wedding to Arnold Hardacre. Such things did not disturb her. What did disturb her was having a son of forty-three wandering about the world thoroughly unmarried. She liked Mavis anyhow, but she no doubt would have liked any woman who promised to turn Sam into a family man. Just as, years before, when the twins had made their religious profession, her one regret had been the lost possibility of daughters-in-law and grandchildren, now the one circumstance that would have her forgive Sam's defection from the religious life would be a daughter-in-law and grandchildren.

He happily accepted his partial return to the fold. A daughter-in-law he would indeed give her. Grandchildren were another matter, and he dodged the question for reasons of his own.

As for the rest, Emily Barton got frankly sentimental, Jan Muller was delighted and perhaps ever so slightly relieved, Vanessa waxed lyrically romantic, which was enough to make Sam reconsider the whole thing, and Noel actually bought him a beer to celebrate. He thought he'd pulled it all off beautifully when a day or two later the telephone rang and when he picked it up there was the familiar airy crackling of the transatlantic cable. He said hello.

'Bastard!' shouted Janet from New York, and hung up. He sat looking at the receiver for half a minute, wondering about women, life, love, and why he'd ever left the monastery in the first place.

When the telephone rang again, a few minutes later, he was almost afraid to answer it, but eventually did. The caller introduced himself as a reporter from the *Chronicle*.

'Sam?'

'Aye?'

'I've been hearing some rumours, Sam.'

'Not good journalism, surely, listening to rumours.'

'Where there's smoke, there's fire.'

'Call the fire brigade. Goodbye.'

507

'Eh, hold on, Sam.'

'I don't think so.'

'Happen you don't recall, but we've met, you know.'

'Not likely.'

'Oh, but we have. It were outside t' gates uv a bluidy great house. Gates were locked, I recall. Bloke in a lorry, looking like a bluidy tink, havin' a spot uv bother gettin' inside.'

'What a memory.'

'Never let a journalist do you a favour, Sam. They never forget.'

So he gave him the story, thinking it was time enough, and the following day put his own announcement in *The Times*. It was four days later that George R. Emmerson, ex-miner, labour stalwart, and brother of the bride-to-be rang.

'Sam Hardacre?'

'Yes.'

'George Emmerson.'

'Geordie, how delightful, I've not seen you in years.'

'Stuff that, Sam. We've got some talking to do.'

Which was how he realized that his family's happy accordance was not about to be matched by that of hers. George Emmerson, one-time RAF mate of Peter Macgregor, was not Mavis's only living relative. Both her parents were yet alive, but they'd thrown her out on the day she'd told them of her pregnancy, nineteen years before, and she'd seen neither since. But her brother George had been faithful, loyal, and fiercely protective all her life. Nor had he forgiven Peter Macgregor his unfortunate, and innocent defection.

'All right,' Sam said, 'come to dinner.'

'Don't need bluidy dinner in your bluidy big house.'

'Geordie.'

'George to you, mate.'

'George. Today's Thursday. On Monday I'm going to be a hundred miles off Fair Isle, with any luck. You can meet

508

me for dinner here tomorrow, or you can hire yourself a boat and meet me in the middle of the North Sea. Which is it going to be?'

George Emmerson decided to come to dinner. Mavis was visibly shaken when Sam told her. She admitted that George's response to her wedding plans had been less than gracious, but she'd hoped he would cool down before he and Sam had occasion to meet.

'Seems the occasion has just arisen,' he said.

'Must it be dinner?' she asked nervously.

'Most people are more civilized sitting down at a table over a meal, than just standing in the middle of the street.'

She shook her head, 'You don't know George that well.' She looked around the drawing-room as she spoke. 'And I don't think any of this is going to help.' Mavis had conceded slightly on her reluctance to visit Hardacres, and she had even spent a night there, after a family party a few days before. But she had spent it chastely in a guest bedroom and Sam, even engaged, had not the effrontery to knock on her door. She still clung so fiercely to her independence that he had once, only half-jokingly, asked if she intended maintaining her house in Halifax even after they were wed.

She said now, 'Will it have to be terribly formal?'

'Not terribly. Black tie, that's all.' He was grinning.

'Couldn't we do something casual. I mean, just for George?' she asked uneasily.

'Fish and chips in the summer-house?' He laughed. 'No, Mavis. He's meeting me on my terms, not on his. And let's not get carried away with his common-man's simplicity. George is a politician, not a miner. He's attended more formal dinners than I have. You know that.'

She sighed. 'Am I hostess?' she said in a small voice.

He was more gentle then. He said, 'My mother will be here. She always does that for me. She'll be quite happy to, if you'd rather not.' He bent and kissed her. 'It's just a game, like any other, once you've learned the rules.'

She smiled gratefully, and in the end she agreed she would take her rightful future role, with Madelene's discreet assistance gladly offered. Young Geordie wandered in then, with Paul Barton in tow.

'Saw that,' he said, slyly. 'You were snoggin'.'

'You didn't,' Mavis said angrily. 'You've just come in. Besides, we're engaged.'

'So I was right,' he said, grinning. He was amused and delighted by his mother's marriage plans, and in the way of the young found the whole matter far funnier and far less significant than did the principal participants. It was ironic, because they had been intensely concerned about breaking to him the news which he received with the cheerful concession that it was about time.

Geordie had none of his mother's qualms about Hardacres. He and Paul Barton had taken the major step, some months earlier, of quitting other forms of employment and taking up their embryonic musical careers in earnest. They were getting plenty of work, and still using most of their earnings to improve their expensive stock of equipment. Rehearsals with their five-man group were naturally noisy affairs and they had been thrown out, virtually, from both their homes, trailing plugs and wires, and Sam had given them refuge. The upper corridors of Hardacres now echoed incongruously with the vibrant throb of electric guitars. Sam didn't care. The house was big and he could, and did, like Harry before him, retreat to the library and shut the door.

There were limits however, and on the Friday evening, with George Emmerson and his wife due in fifteen minutes for dinner, Sam stood in the middle of the central staircase, tying his tie and glaring down the corridor, which shook with the steady drum-beat so much that he thought the plaster would fall.

'Geordie,' he shouted loudly, so as to be heard.

'Aye, Dad.'

'I'm not your bloody dad yet. Turn the damned volume down. The ceilings are falling and my guests are due.'

'Reeght, Dad.' Sam stood listening, but the sound continued undiminished.

'Geordie, I'm going to throw the mains switch. We can always eat by candlelight.' There was another un-silence for several bars of music, and then down the corridor a figure appeared, shuffling amiably towards him, snapping fingers and swaying with the rhythm. He was tall and slender, wearing tight trousers and a peculiar-looking jacket with no collar. His hair was smoothed down in an even circle, like a pudding basin, and hung an inch and a half over his ears. Sam had never seen him before in his life.

'Who the hell are you?' he asked curiously.

'I'm t' drummer, Dad,' he said.

'Jesus Christ, I'm not *your* Dad, whatever.'

The drummer shrugged, unperturbed. 'I'm Bill,' he said. 'I came with Greg and Taffy.'

'Who are *they*?' Sam said.

'Paul said it would be all right,' Bill said hopefully.

Sam thought a moment and shrugged. 'Fine. Just put the volume down, please.'

'Geordie says it won't go any lower,' said the unfortunate drummer, who clearly had been sent as sacrificial lamb. Sam looked at him, thought about throwing him down the stairs and decided he rather liked him, instead. 'Shut some doors, please,' he said at last.

'Sure, Dad,' said the drummer, with a happy freckled grin.

Sam waited until the music marginally diminished then gave up and went down the stairs, where Mavis was already greeting their guests at the door.

George Emmerson was a short, solid, tough-looking man nearing fifty. His hair was cut short and stubbly and was something the colour of his sister's with a redder tinge that came out noticeably in his small, bristly moustache. He

511

wore a dinner suit with an aggrieved air, though it was well-tailored and had seen plenty of wear. His wife followed him through the door, looking around with cool, assessing eyes. She was younger, no older than Mavis, and tall, slender and attractive in a clear-eyed, intelligent way. She was a dustman's daughter with a degree in economics, and she was nobody's fool.

George Emmerson shook Sam's hand as a concession to good manners, and little else, and introduced his wife as Maureen. She also shook Sam's hand, abruptly, and met his eyes for one cool moment. She was that sort of well-educated woman whose manner had grown abrasive through struggling in a man's world. Her response to any man who had the misfortune to be found attractive by her was clever and witty aggression. And she did find Sam attractive, which was not surprising. He was, without doubt, in the prime of his life. He had lost, over the years, the rakish playboy look that George Emmerson remembered. He had been through a lot, and it showed on him. His face was lightly lined and weathered, wind- and sun-tanned from his life out of doors. His hair was now totally grey, but as thick and luxuriant as ever and seemed always incongruous with his otherwise youthful appearance. He was forty-three and apart from the hair looked thirty-three. He was light on his feet and as athletic as he'd been as a boy. He was also happy, which does wonders for anyone's appearance, and his always expressive eyes, though no longer boyish and playful, were no longer sombre either, only faintly chastened and wise. Maureen Emmerson took one careful look and decided she could understand Mavis falling for that, and decided as well she'd cut him down to size.

George Emmerson, not to be outdone, walked into the middle of the great hall, turned around in a careful circle and said, 'Bluidy shocking, place this size housing one bluidy damn family.' Even Maureen who was, if aggressive, thoroughly refined, looked shocked.

Mavis said, 'George, please,' and looked on the edge of real anger, but Sam just quietly grinned and said, 'Never mind, I've got half a Barnardo's Home upstairs, for a start.'

There was a sudden ringing electronic chord echoing down the gallery and both Sam's guests jumped and said, 'What was that?'

'Your nephew and my cousin courting their muse,' said Sam. He led his baffled and reluctant guests into the drawing-room.

Actually, it went better than he could have hoped. Maureen Emmerson cornered him over sherry, which was not entirely unpleasant, and certainly nicer than being cornered by George. Mavis decided meanwhile to ignore her brother, who stood around looking disgruntled and talking in turn to Vanessa and Madelene who, out of her new good-nature to Sam, was being as French and charming as possible, which even softened the Red menace a little. After three sherries Maureen had decided that Sam was not half as stupid as she'd have liked him to be, and after the fourth she decided she didn't even care. They were yet crossing swords, but she was parrying more gently and in her sharp, quick eyes there was the rarest hint of flirtation.

George Emmerson circled the room, studying the portraits and looking for signs of ostentatious wealth to despise, and trying to ignore the fraying carpets. He was on his second circuit when he came face to face with a thin, craggy, wiry little man, inappropriately dressed in tweed plus-twos and a pullover with a hole in the elbow, who had appeared out of nowhere. He had spiky grey hair hanging over his ears and he was looking around the room disgruntledly over a full whisky glass. George couldn't imagine he was a guest but, since his host hadn't turfed him out or confiscated the whisky, he assumed he couldn't be either a passing gatecrasher or a rebellious member of staff. What he did appear to be, both from his dress and his cynical eye, was a compatriot.

'Geordie Emmerson,' George said, extending his hand. The other grunted something, nodded, and neither shook his hand nor gave his own name. He did however seem to acknowledge George's presence, so George continued, getting in stride. 'You see a place like this,' he said conspiratorially to his fellow member of the downtrodden class, 'and you see the real crime of inherited wealth.' Like all politicians, George Emmerson thought in rhetoric. His companion said nothing but sipped his whisky and after a very long time, when George had assumed he was never going to answer he spoke suddenly.

'Sam didn't inherit it.'

George blinked, surprised at having his rhetoric taken so personally, but he said, 'Of course he damn well did. He's a Hardacre.'

The scruffy man sipped his whisky non-committally, watching Sam and Maureen across the room, leaning against the French windows, talking with great animation. He was thinking that, if he had a wife like that, he'd keep her shackled to his wrist around a man like Sam Hardacre, but he didn't say that. He said instead, 'He bought it.'

'Impossible.' George Emmerson narrowed his eyes, fascinated by this information, but doubting it thoroughly. 'Who are you? How would you know that?'

'I sold it to him.'

'You?' Emmerson stared.

'Aye.' The other suddenly extended a crusty, calloused hand. 'Noel Hardacre,' he said. '*I* inherited.'

George Emmerson stared again, as Noel walked away, and he was still in a faint daze when his hostess and sister asked him to come through to dinner. She took his arm. His wife, laughing a little giddily, was ahead, on the arm of his host.

George behaved himself over dinner. He was still a bit bemused by Noel's revelation. Besides, the food was good, and Madelene Hardacre was fussing over him so attentively that it was hard to be ill-natured. By the end of the meal he was gently soporific, so much so that three choruses of the Red Flag might well have failed to get him to his feet. The company was cheerful, his host was very charming, and his sister, radiant in a white dress, looked stunning and oddly appropriate at the foot of that long mahogany table. She also looked very happy and Geordie loved her and, if he could really believe that Sam Hardacre would genuinely keep her happy, he might actually relent. But then she got up and asked the ladies to retire. That's what did it. It was that damned medieval country-house performance. He saw Maureen give him a sharp, cynical glance, but it didn't stop her from letting Sam Hardacre teasingly kiss her hand as he rose to stand as the ladies left.

Geordie glowered as the table was cleared, trying to work up a feeling of solidarity that would communicate to the two plump Yorkshire countrywomen who busied themselves with that task. They looked disappointingly content, and ignorant of a comrade in their midst.

Sam passed the port. Geordie took the decanter, poured for himself, and passed it on. It was not exactly the first time. Labour conference dinners sometimes ended that way, too, he had to admit. He even stood and drank the health of the Queen, which Sam, loyal to Harry and apologetic to Terry, always carefully included in every such evening.

'And now,' said George, without preamble, 'I'm having my say.'

'But of course,' said Sam.

'Our Mavis,' said George, 'went through a lot of suffering on account of your family. A lot of suffering, and a lot of humiliation,' he added.

'It was never our intention,' said Sam solemnly. But George Emmerson was not to be mollified.

'Damn your intentions, your cousin made a mess of her life.'

'Well the Luftwaffe rather made a mess of his,' said Sam very calmly. 'He wanted to marry her, and he would have done.'

'That's as maybe,' said George.

'No,' Sam said. 'You can say what you like to me, or about me. But you'll not slander a dead man's honour at my table.' He was suddenly terribly serious. He had taken George Emmerson's needling all evening, though admittedly George had been restrained, and his wife, after the initial onslaught, was positively charming. He had been prepared for worse, and he'd sworn he would not be riled. Partly because he would do nothing to hurt or shame his fiancée, and partly because, ever since the episode with Mike Brannigan, he had made a solemn vow to himself that he would not lose his temper again. He had scared himself as much as he had scared Mike.

But George Emmerson, like any good politician, knew how to seek and find the nerve. He'd found it now and he went purposefully back for more.

'I suppose a gentleman's honour means more then, than the honour of a working-class girl?' Sam set his glass down on the table. He leaned back in his chair and closed his eyes for several seconds. When he opened them George Emmerson was almost grinning.

'Right,' said Sam.

His hands came down flat on the table and he straightened in the chair, but Noel, who had watched, silently amused, over his port glass the while, said suddenly, 'Sam, I can't stick this stuff. Get me a beer, old son.'

'What?' he said.

'There's some round the back of the still-room.'

'Ring Mrs Bennett,' Sam said, his eyes yet on George Emmerson.

'She'll never find it. Go on, mate, nip out and get one for me.'

Sam looked round at him, puzzled. Noel was watching

him in that funny quizzical way of his, his head slightly on one side. He was surprised that Noel had even attended though, naturally, he was, as always, invited. Noel's insistence now surprised him more. It was more like him to simply get up, without excusing himself, and clump out for his beer himself. But Sam was a good host. He nodded and got up from the table and, with another, curt nod to George he left the room.

George Emmerson grinned.

'Bet that's the first time anyone asked him for a beer with the bloody port,' he said with a comradely nod again to Noel. Whatever the truth about the inheritance of Hardacres, Noel was clearly a man of the earth.

'I don't want his bloody *beer*, mate,' said Noel.

'Then what?'

'I wanted him out of the room,' said Noel. George Emmerson blinked. 'I wanted him out of the room because I'm about to make my first after-dinner speech ever,' he said. 'And it's not for Sam. It's for you, mate.'

'I say, what's this?' said Rodney, having just come to an awareness that something was happening. Noel just waved a hand at him that meant for him to shut up. He faced George again.

'Now, you, working man,' he said. 'You ever taken a salvage tug out in a Force Ten gale in the middle of the night?'

George shrugged, faintly annoyed. 'Of course not, it's not my line.'

'You ever chased around the Irish Sea in a hurricane trying to get a line aboard a crippled freighter? Ever patched up a leaking hull with the bloody ship sinking all round you?'

'I'm a miner, damn it,' said Emmerson.

'You *were* a miner,' said Noel. 'You haven't been a miner in years. You were a union man and now you're a politician. Don't be ashamed of it, it's a good dishonest trade. But it's time you bloody hang up your flat cap and give over. And lay off Sam because he's done all those things, and more.' Noel sat back and finished his port with satisfaction. George Emmerson opened his mouth to protest, but Noel continued, right over his words.

'Now, that much was for your information. This next lot's for your protection.' He got up, stalked across the room, and drew the curtains shut suddenly on the evening, which had darkened suddenly into night, with rain lashing down against the windows. It was late May, but hardly summery.

He turned from the draperies and said, with an almost cheerful grin, 'You ever seen Sam angry?'

'I hardly know the man.'

'Oh, you've got a treat in store, then. Because let me tell you something. You've been pushing him all evening and by my reckoning you're about a half-inch to go. You say you don't know Sam. Well, I know him very well indeed. And I happen to know that when he leans back and closes his eyes he's saying an Ave to keep from hitting someone. You see, you have to understand Sam. He's religious. That means he gets sorry when he hits somebody. Not like me. I don't get sorry at all. But *you're* going to be sorry. Because if you push him once more, either *he's* going to hit you or *I'm* going to hit you. Only difference is, tomorrow he'll go to confession and I'll go to the pub. Either way, you'll go to hospital. So wise up, mate, and lay off.' Noel sat down, poured himself more port, and downed it in one.

'I won't be threatened,' said George Emmerson stiffly.

Noel shrugged. 'Nobody's threatening you, mate. I'm just telling you the truth, and Sam never threatens anybody. He'll just sit there smiling and then he'll snap. I know. I've seen it. Now if that's what you want, go ahead. I think it's stupid. He loves your sister and he'd love to be your friend. And he's a good friend, believe me.'

He shrugged again, hearing Sam's footstep in the corridor. 'Now, mate, you're on your own.'

Sam came in then with Noel's beer and a glass on a tray, which he offered to his cousin. Noel took it with a grunt and poured the beer into the glass, watching as Sam, his anger temporarily forgotten, sat down again. He sipped it briefly and set it down.

'It's flat,' he said with a grin. He tilted his head sideways, glancing once at Geordie Emmerson, who was sitting quietly thoughtful for a change. Noel finished his beer in a couple of hearty gulps, slapped the glass on the table with cheerful rudeness and said to Sam, 'Shall we join the ladies, old son?'

They had scarcely done so and Mavis, graciously and a little proudly had only just begun to pour from Mary Hardacre's silver coffee service, when Sam was called away to the telephone. He returned after a short interval, hurried and apologetic, looking round the roomful of guests with remorse.

'I'm most terribly sorry, but something has come up. I'm afraid I'm going to have to leave you on your own.' He glanced quickly round and his eyes settled on Noel. Noel grinned.

'I'll pour your booze for you, if that's what you mean,' he said. Sam nodded gratefully, avoided his mother's accusing eye and signalled to Mavis to join him in the corridor.

'What is it?' she said.

'That was Jan. There's a freighter in trouble off Spurn Head. We're going out for her.' He paused, 'I'm sorry, I'm so sorry, I hate to leave you like this.'

She only shook her head distractedly, her eyes on a distant set of windows in the open hall, on which the wind-driven rain was slashing in watery sheets. 'It's blowing a gale,' she said.

'That's why she's in trouble, sweetheart.' He kissed her lightly and said, 'Give them coffee and send them home. Mother will arrange everything. I'll see you when I get back.' She nodded, and did not ask when that might be.

Mavis accepted his work; its disruptions and its dangers. She watched as he ran upstairs to change his clothes, his mind already far from her. She went back into the drawing-room and poured coffee for her guests.

Sam appeared a few minutes later at the door of the room, in his dungarees, fisherman's jumper and heavy Navy jacket. He looked an entirely different person. He leaned in and waved, grinning at George Emmerson, turned and ran lightly out through the hall and into the night. Mavis followed slowly, watching the tail-lights of his van as he drove off into the rain. She turned then, facing the awesome splendour of the house, suddenly alone and suddenly terrified. But she straightened her shoulders, nodded to the portraits that looked down from every wall, and walked determinedly back to the beautiful drawing-room. Mrs Bennett was waiting outside the door.

'Mr Hardacre's been called away,' Mavis said, 'but we'll have some more coffee, please.' She smiled pleasantly and the woman returned her smile, almost shyly, and went away. Mavis entered the drawing-room.

Noel and her brother were standing by the darkened windows, from before which Sam had just driven away. Noel was grinning. He said, as in some private joke, 'Fancy going with him, working man?'

George Emmerson bridled, just for a moment, and then his tough, belligerent face relaxed slightly. He looked round the room and his eyes settled on his sister and, as Noel pulled the great floor-length drapes over against the storm, as he'd done in the dining-room, he said, 'May I get some wood for that fire, Mavis? If you'll show me the way.' The party went on until the late hours, and it was just after midnight when Mavis stood at the door of Sam's house, beside his mother, and waved good-night to her departing guests. Then she went in and shut the door behind her, against the stormy night.

* * *

At the same hour Sam, himself, with Pete Haines and eight of a quickly-gathered crew, set off into the teeth of an on-shore gale, aboard the *Mary Hardacre*, from Hull. He had already forgotten his guests, and to some degree his lady. It was the only way; the work required full concentration, and full commitment, and there was no one to whom he might delegate his authority. Jan was there, of course, but Jan had become a desk man. In the years they had been together, Sam had overtaken him and passed him by in knowledge and experience. The only person he really turned to now was Pete Haines and, of course, to Mick. But that last was for reasons of emotion rather than logic. Mick had never been a salvage man at all, but a fisherman, handy with engines, and the sea. He'd learned a bit, but not that much. But Mick was Sam's mentor, as the *Dainty Girl* was his luck, and his relationship with both remained the same. As long as they knew each other he would turn to Mick Raddley in times of trouble and seek his advice, nor would he ever feel happy about anything of which Mick disapproved.

And yet, for all that, Mick would step but rarely into his world, and there was nothing he managed to do about it. He tried, many times. And he tried again that summer before he was wed, coming home from that long May night at sea.

The *Mary Hardacre* was one of a fleet of three tugs, now. The second, the *Jane Hardacre*, was busy that night with a tow in the Channel, and the third had been working off the Cornish coast, on a beached trawler. He had added that third tug to his fleet late in 1959. He had intended then to name her for his mother, but her response had been less than gratifying.

'You name one of those filthy things after me and you may leave home,' she said, with a sniff. The fact that Sam owned Hardacres made Madelene none the less inclined to throw him out of it. So he'd given up and called the tug, instead, simply *Hardacre's Luck*, with a personal irony that no one else would likely understand.

521

On that rainy May night, Sam stood beside Pete Haines in the wheelhouse, searching for the lights of the stricken vessel, a Danish coaster that had developed engine difficulties and was in danger of being driven ashore. The lifeboat was already out, in readiness, and the *Mary Hardacre* ploughed her way through heavy seas until they sighted her through the rain. They stood off at a respectful distance, like a patient vulture, and Pete Haines radioed his willingness to assist.

The Dane wasn't having it, just yet. He was communicating with the master of a sister ship, hoping to pick up a tow from him, keeping it in the family so to speak. And meanwhile he struggled with his engines. They waited, and Pete said, as the lights of the freighter drifted shorewards, 'Bugger gets himself on the rocks, I'm sure as hell not joining him.' But he spoke without emotion. The waiting was part of the game. Twice the coaster got under way, twice her engines failed again. At dawn they could see her still powerless, and being battered broadside by the waves. But her master was stubborn, and still refused their tow. And in the end he was right. In the grey light of a storm-lashed early morning, he finally got under way and the coaster battered her way off northwards on her journey under her own power. The sight of her rusty transom disappearing gamely into the rain made Sam think of nothing so much as Mavis's red Mini going on its feisty independent way.

He went out on deck to watch and met Mick Raddley, standing glowering in the rain. 'What you grinnin' for,' Mick grumbled, watching the Danish ship go. 'Silly bugger'll break down again in half an hour and be shouting for help. We ought to bloody leave him.'

Sam laughed. 'Come on, Mick, if she were your ship you'd do the same. Not let some bloody salvage tug haul you off and make himself a fortune.'

'Aye, fine, but he better be right. Lot uv lives lost by folk tryin' to save someone money.'

Sam just shrugged. 'Well, we'll just go and get him if he does.' He was still thinking of the ship as Mavis's little car, and said, 'In the meantime, good luck to him.' They watched the lifeboat return to her port, and the *Mary Hardacre* turned herself round in the sea and made for her own.

'Yer gettin' soft,' said Mick. 'It's all this romance.'

He still found quite hysterically funny the fact that Sam was, at long last, getting married. He was pleased too, Sam knew, like he was not pleased over Janet, and that approval meant a lot to him, even though it was never expressed.

'Tell you one thing,' Mick continued. 'Things are going to change in your life. No more traipsin' out over t' North Sea whenever you fancy, for a start.'

'We'll see about that,' Sam said with a grin. 'Anyhow, you manage well enough.'

'Aye, but you don't see t' scenes when I get home. Nay lad, a married man's lot is another thing entirely.' He was smiling slyly, standing in the lessening rain and lighting his pipe, shielding it against the wind.

'Trying to put me off?'

Mick shook his head, suddenly serious. 'No. You marry your lass. Marry her, and treat her well.'

Sam nodded. He was looking out to sea, and thinking. He said, very tentatively, 'Mick?'

'Aye?'

'Will you stand up for me?'

'Eh, lad?'

'In church. Will you stand up for me at my wedding?' He paused, turning to face the old fisherman, his eyes a strange mix of teasing and pain, 'Terry was meant to do it, but he's got a prior commitment.' He laughed lightly.

'You mean to be t' best man, enall?' Mick asked, faintly incredulous.

Sam nodded. 'That's what I mean.'

Mick was silent. He fiddled with his pipe, knocking ash

out on the rail of the tug, watching it blow in the rain, into the sea. He sighed slowly, and shook his head. 'Nay, lad. Don't ask that of me.'

'Why not?'

'It wouldn't be right. Really it wouldn't. Besides,' he said, 'I'd feel an awful fool.'

Sam said sharply, 'Well, *feel* a fool, for me, then. You've made enough of a fool of me, one time or another, over the years.'

Mick laughed softly. 'Now don't get het up,' he said. He sucked at his pipe-stem contemplatively, in that infuriatingly slow way of his. Finally, he said, 'Sam, let me teach you a little lesson.' He suddenly indicated a bunker on the deck that stored ropes and gestured that they were to sit down. Sam obeyed, as he always did when Mick got serious about something. 'Now look, lad,' he said, 'sometimes we have a gift to give, and there's a right person to give it to, and a wrong person. Sometimes the person we *want* to give it to, for whatever t' reasons are, isn't the right person. T' trouble is, a gift to t' wrong person can end up no gift at all. Now, I'm thankin' ye for your gift. I know the honour it is, don't get me wrong. But I'm the wrong person. The right person is Jan. Now, he's not Terry, lad. Neither am I. Neither of us, nor anyone, will ever be Terry. But he'll come close one day, if you'll let him. One day you'll be as old as me, lad, and I'm sure as hell not going to be here. But Jan will, and by then you'll be brothers, if you let it happen.'

He paused, looking steadily at Sam with his rheumy old eyes tearing from the salt wind. 'Now you give your gift to Jan. He'll be happy, and do ye proud. I'd make a fool of myself. Oh, I'll come to t' church a'reeght, and see ye wed your lass. But that's all, Sam. There's just so far your kind and mine can go together, and we'd both be fools to go further.'

Sam shook his head slowly, and Mick just laughed.

'Aye, lad, ye'll change a lot with your own hands, but ye'll never change that. Accept it. We'll work together, all day, every day uv t' year. And if we make a mistake, we'll maybe die together. But until then, at t' end uv t' day we go our own ways.' He stood up suddenly, laughing, and tousled Sam's grey hair with an affectionate hand.

'Go on, lad. Ask me to t'bluidy christening. I'll be t' godmother, instead.'

Sam smiled, and knew he'd not win. He also suspected that Mick was right, and knew already that he would ask Jan. He did really owe it to him. But he said now, 'You'll wait a long time for that, I'm afraid.'

'Oh, aye,' Mick said, his eyes widening, as Sam stood up, 'why's that?'

Sam laughed again, ruefully. 'This lad and lass you're always talking about are pretty well middle-aged. I don't think there'll be any christenings, Mick.' He smiled as he said it but he was sad, all the same. Still, he was sure he was right. Mavis was thirty-eight and had raised her son to manhood. He honestly felt he had no right to ask her for a child. He had accepted it already. He would be father to his cousin's son now, as Harry had been to his brother's grandsons, and that way, perhaps, a debt would be paid. It was their way of doing things, anyhow. They held together. Mick grinned broadly, and slapped his back.

'Getting too old for it, are ye?' he chortled. 'Never ye mind. I'll nip round t' back door uv that bluidy great house uv yourn, an' fix things up. Ye'll have bonny twins by July. Happen ye'll not mind them lookin' a bit like me.'

CHAPTER
THIRTY

In August of 1960, three weeks before the date of the
wedding, Mavis Emmerson was received into the Catholic
Church. She had been under instruction since the spring. It
was one of the many things she did without ever consulting
Sam. She did it because she knew both that he dearly
wanted it and that he would never ask. It was her wedding
gift to him, and his to her, though she did not realize that at
the time. It gave him tremendous happiness and peace, and
was the one single thing that cemented their relationship
into certainty and cast away what remained of his doubts.

They were to be married in the Catholic Church at
Beverley in the first week of September. Sam did, in the
end, ask Jan to be best man, and Jan accepted with alacrity
and gratitude. By the day before the wedding most of the
more distant members of the family had gathered at Hardacres, or at The Rose at Kilham, with the sole exception of
Janet Chandler, who was filming in London, having recently returned from New York. She and her husband
passed each other, like ships in the night, appropriately
enough, but their long separations seemed in no way to
harm their marriage. Janet had been quite correct in her
assessment of herself. Like many other people she was a
different person, subtly, to every person she knew. The
tempestuous child she had been with Sam had vanished
when she married Jan. She was a mature and understanding
woman in his company, though from time to time, on the
rare occasions she was again in the company of Sam, she was
known to revert.

They did not precisely avoid each other; neither of them
was bitter and neither of them ever lost the heady delight

they felt in each other's company. But they dodged each other a bit, and arranged never to be alone together. Sam called it avoiding the occasion of sin; Janet called it not looking for trouble; Jan called it simply wise. And there they left it.

Janet was due on the midday train from York, and Sam had promised to meet her. He was in the library at Hardacres hiding from the musical genius of his cousin and about-to-be stepson when the telephone rang. It was Janet.

'Where are you?' he said, suddenly suspicious.

'London.'

'What the bloody hell are you doing in London? I'm meant to be picking you up in York in an hour.'

'Darling, forgive me, but please let me off.'

'From what?'

'The wedding.'

'No,' he said, furious, and then, 'why?'

'Because I'm going to be so damned jealous I can't stand it.'

'Jealous? That's ridiculous. *You're* married already.'

There was a pause. Then her voice came again, chastened. 'Oh, I don't mind you *marrying* her,' she said glumly, 'I've gotten used to that. But I suddenly realized there's going to be someone else in your bed and I can't stand it.'

'You *suddenly realized*? What were you expecting? Abelard and bloody Heloise?'

'C'mon, Sam.'

'No,' he said again. 'No, really, what did you want me to do, for God's sake, live like a bloody monk for the rest of my life?'

'Well, why not? You've had the practice.' She paused and said offendedly, 'You could have gone back, even, and prayed or whatever, and been wistful over me.' She sounded really hurt.

'With due respect, sweetheart, I doubt the good brethren would want me on those terms.' He was silent for a

527

moment, exasperated and then suddenly got furious again. 'Now look,' he said, 'you get here. I'm meeting the next train at York and if you're not on it I'm coming to London after you. If you don't show up, Jan will be ashamed. No one will *ever* believe there's nothing between us, again. And when I catch you I'll belt your bloody little arse.' He hung up the phone, and met the next train. She was on it.

George Emmerson agreed in the end to give the bride away. It was an abrupt turnabout, and done in an abrupt and bluntly honest way that Sam respected. When he returned from Hull, late on the day after that dinner, and just before he set out once more on a towing contract to Oslo, he received a telephone call from George Emmerson in which he gruffly, but sincerely, apologized for his behaviour, wished Sam and his sister well, and offered to pay for the wedding. That latter was difficult to handle, because Sam rightly realized that, whereas accepting was difficult, refusing could well cause offence. The reconciliation, like a union-management discussion, nearly broke down before it was properly under way. But in the end Sam won by appealing to George's economic logic. The wedding party was at Hardacres, the wines from their own cellars and half the food was home produce. Its value would be difficult to assess and, besides, since it all really was coming from the home farm, the person to consult was really Noel. George balked at that suddenly, for reasons, like the reasons for his sudden about-face, Sam never fully understood. But he conceded then to good sense, much to Sam's relief.

The other thing Sam didn't really understand was Noel himself, whose willingness to provide from his harvest seemed suspiciously out of character. He was uncertain whether to thank him, or wait and see if he sent a bill. He decided on the latter because it was a distinct possibility, and because thanking Noel was always, so to speak, a thankless task.

Sam left the arrangements of the wedding entirely to

Madelene, acknowledging in doing so that it was an unfair and totally cowardly act for which he refused to apologize. Nor was it the normal course of events but, as the bride's parents had opted out of arrangements nineteen years before, Madelene was the only candidate. She complained, but cheerfully, enjoying stage-managing the event, loyal to Mavis, and too delighted about getting her son within the bonds of holy matrimony to really care. It was to be a large and formal wedding; large because even were it limited to family it would be large, and formal because Sam wanted it that way. There was that much of Harry in him, yet.

In keeping with tradition, as well, Jan Muller arranged a stag party the night before at The Rose at Kilham that was almost the undoing of it all. Geordie Emmerson the younger, having just received his new driving licence, volunteered to play chauffeur since everyone too readily assumed that Sam was not going to be in any condition to drive on his return. Geordie was pleased because, even if it meant he was going to have to stay cold sober, he was ever after going to be able to say he attended his own father's stag night. He was enjoying the incongruities of his mother's wedding more than Mavis would have liked. He'd even, before his uncle stepped in, volunteered to give the bride away, an offer which Mavis rather quickly declined. She didn't trust anyhow that he and Paul Barton wouldn't get up to something terrible, like the twins would have done at their age and, besides, as she pointed out to her son, she'd never exactly hidden him, but this was one occasion where she'd rather not advertise him either. He had conceded with good grace, and was getting his own back on the wedding eve.

'Can I come on the honeymoon, Dad?'

'Just drive, Geordie.'

'Where you going? Scarborough?'

'Watch the road, please.'

'Fab place, Scarborough.'

'Blackpool, Geordie. We're going to watch the Illuminations. All night. Watch that *bloody* van.' Geordie grinned, concentrating on his driving, which was better than Sam was willing to admit.

They arrived at The Rose, safe and sound, with Sam wondering if murder of a would-be stepson really qualified as infanticide or not. Philip was waiting outside the pub, in the September sunshine, wearing his 'mine host' smile. He actually had customers, even regulars, at the pub now, though one of the reasons they came so regularly was to listen to Philip's Yorkshire accent and see if it was still as bad as ever. There was a new, younger set, too, that sometimes turned up on mopeds from the coast. They looked a bit peculiar but they behaved well enough, and they were usually either friends of Paul Barton or some of his increasing band of fans. Emily had, much to her annoyance, put her pincurled head out of the window one morning to find herself, and the pub, being photographed by two giggling long-haired girls.

There were none in evidence that night, to Geordie's faint disappointment. Rodney was there, with Noel, who had amazed everyone by turning up. And Jan was there. Emily was also briefly there but she took one look and said, 'I'm closing the bar and going out. You're on your own.' She glanced briefly at Sam and at the assembled company, and said, 'Now look. Nothing too funny. He's getting married tomorrow. And if he's not at that church, safe and sober, by ten o'clock, I'll have your guts for garters, Philip Barton.' She glared once at her husband and walked out, slamming the door.

'I think she means it,' said Sam.

'She's been waiting for an excuse for years,' said Philip morosely. But then he grinned, turned the key in the latch of the front door, and headed for the bar.

It was the best party that Sam could remember since the war. The sort of party that he and Terry had once so adroitly created in those long past and lost days when they were young and life, with Hitler's bombs pulverizing London around them, was not serious at all. In the end he got so drunk that, had Terry walked in through the door, he would not have noticed anything amiss. Nor, likely, would anyone else, other than Geordie Emmerson, who was as sober as a judge.

Noel looked sober, but then he always did when he was drunk. Or perhaps, conversely, he looked drunk when he was sober. The relevant point being, he never changed. He just sat in a corner of the inglenook, not saying much, and knocking back pints of ale alternated with nips of whisky, until he eventually, and quite suddenly, slid down the bench and went to sleep. There wasn't much need for Noel to say something; everyone else was saying too much already.

Philip had forgotten his Yorkshire accent for the evening and begun reminiscing about his past in the London police force, and how he had rescued Emily from a raid on the somewhat notorious nightspot at 43 Gerrard Street and carried her off to Hardacres by force, like a latter-day, if at the time unpopular, knight. He would have been more unpopular had Emily found out he'd been repeating that story, but there was no one there capable of remembering but Geordie, to whom it could mean nothing at all.

Rodney had got giggly, which was an extraordinarily disconcerting state of affairs, and Jan Muller, pleasantly responsible through half the evening, like everyone's older brother, suddenly settled into a nostalgic mood of boozy sentiment, and ended up doing a little German folk-dance in the middle of the room.

As for Sam, he was drunker than the proverbial skunk. He went through most stages, from light and witty, to affectionately cheerful, to pedantically serious. Fortunately he was too happy to get maudlin and, fortunately too, he never got angry when he was drunk or drank when he was angry. He was a pleasant enough drunk, as they go, actually, and was, at the end of the evening, when Emily finally returned, carefully, logically, and extremely pointlessly explaining Anselm's ontological argument to Geordie who, though patient enough to listen, would probably not have understood it had Sam been sober enough to make sense.

Emily entered slowly, looking once around the room at Noel snoring in the inglenook, Rodney giggling in a corner, Philip expounding the virtues of real ale to Jan Muller, who was humming an old German melody and swaying happily on a bench, and the theological debate in the corner. She picked up a jug of water, threw it over Noel, kicked her husband in the shin and said to Geordie, 'I don't care how you do it, but get him home. Goodnight.' She turned her back and walked out, slamming the old door so that a small rain of disintegrating plaster fell in her wake.

'Eh, Dad,' said Geordie nervously.

'I'm not your bloody damn Dad,' said Sam, 'and you've missed the point.'

'It'll have to wait. I think we've got to go.' He had a terrified feeling that Sam, like Noel, was going to pass out at which point the cause, and his mother's wedding, would be lost. Fortunately Sam got to his feet instead, still arguing about Anselm, and Geordie managed to sling Sam's arm over his shoulder and his own about Sam's waist, and staggered with him to the van. He dumped his future stepfather unceremoniously across the front seat, slammed the door, went around to the driver's side, and got in. Sam was already thoroughly asleep.

Geordie shrugged, and drove slowly and carefully home, feeling the oldest and most sensible person around. When he reached Hardacres he managed to revive his companion enough to get him on his feet, and through the front door of the house. Sam was as cheerful as ever and re-embarked on his discussions on Anselm.

'Sure, Dad,' said Geordie, looking hesitantly at the broad

sweep of stairs up to the gallery, and again at his charge, leaning drunkenly and happily on his shoulder. He decided the stairs were probably impossible and certainly dangerous and headed for the library. He didn't know whether the best course, at four in the morning, was to get coffee and start the long process of sobering the groom now, or let him sleep for an hour or two first. Either way, Geordie had his work cut out for him tonight.

They made the library, Sam still talking as intently, and senselessly, as ever, and Geordie manoeuvred him past the desk to the sofa by the hearth. Then Sam solved the dilemma for him. He said suddenly, with a look of real discovery, 'You know, Anselm was an idiot,' and passed out cold. Geordie leapt forward, caught him, and deflected his fall enough so that he ended draped across the sofa and not the floor. Though it hardly mattered; Sam was so relaxed by then he could have fallen down the stairs without feeling it. Geordie stood rubbing his head, looking at the clock on the mantel and adding up the hours until the ceremony in Beverley. It made five and a half any way he tried. He shrugged, dragged Sam's feet on to the sofa and then searched around, found Harry's old laprug that yet lived in the library, and spread it dutifully over him before going to the kitchens in search of coffee. Somewhere he heard a cock crow and thought of Noel lying yet on the floor of The Rose at Kilham.

Sam got three hours of sleep on the morning of his wedding, and those only because he was so thoroughly sodden drunk that Geordie simply could not wake him, and doubted he'd have woken if the house fell down. Geordie thought of getting his guitar, plugging the amplifier into a socket in the library, and playing the Wedding March, but decided that if Sam did perchance wake, his own life wouldn't be worth much in consequence. So he tried tender loving care and the offer of coffee and, at seven in the morning, with the house, frighteningly enough, beginning to stir, he finally got a reaction.

'Fuck off.'

'Sam?' Geordie said, deciding it wasn't wise to try the Dad routine just now, 'Sam, you've got to wake up.' There was no answer. 'Sam?'

Sam opened his eyes a fraction and immediately drew the rug over his face and said, 'Pull the damn curtains, there's sun in here,' as if sun were somehow poison.

'You've really got to wake up.'

Sam rolled over on the sofa and buried his face in a cushion and put his hands over his head, blotting out sound and light. 'Do you have to shout.'

'I'm whispering. Do you want some coffee?'

'I want a priest.'

'Sir? You're getting married today, sir.'

'Married, hell, I'm bloody dying.'

Geordie rocked back on his heels, where he crouched by the sofa and wondered what to do. He could call someone for help, but he felt too loyal to do that. All the male members of the household were *hors de combat*, no doubt, and to call any of the female members just now would be like throwing Sam to the Amazons. He tentatively touched his shoulder and suddenly Sam turned and sat up, blinking, and said, 'Jesus Christ, what time is it? I'm getting married today.'

Geordie collapsed in giggles of relief, and handed him coffee. 'It's all right,' he said, still laughing, 'you've got all day.'

They hadn't actually. They had a very short, fleeting morning, but it was, somewhat miraculously, enough. By ten o'clock Sam, immaculately turned out in grey morning-dress, and nearly steady on his feet, was standing, with a more-quiet-than-usual Jan Muller, at the altar rail, awaiting his bride. And then suddenly, as he stood there, there came from nowhere a fleeting rogue remembrance of a young lady called Jeanette, upon whom, long ago, he and Terry Hardacre had played a most unforgivable trick. The solemnity of the occasion was suddenly assailed by a wave of hysterical humour, and he turned quickly and buried his face in his hand against Jan's shoulder.

'Hey, what's with you?' Jan whispered. 'Why you laughing? This is Church you are in.' He sounded shocked.

'Nerves,' Sam gasped, giggling yet. 'Say something serious. Please. Quickly.'

'I get yesterday the tax demand from Her Majesty. You cannot pay.'

Sam grimaced, straightened, and faced the altar, nodding gratefully. 'Fine. Excellent,' he muttered to Jan. He looked at the altar again and thought of Terry, and addressed him in the silence of his heart. *I'll sort you out later, mate.*

The music began then, and he turned towards the aisle, and saw approaching him in a soft, flowing dress of peach-coloured silk, a young girl with honey-brown curls surmounted with flowers, smiling shyly. A girl no older than the young WAAF he had flirted with in the London of another world lost in time. He stared, hardly knowing her, this pretty stranger who could surely not have raised to manhood the son who had somehow got him to the church on time. He did not take his eyes from her throughout the ceremony, as if afraid that she might yet take fright and run, gathering peach silk around her, and leap into her red Mini and escape. But she didn't, but made her vows to him, as he made his to her, and then knelt beside him for the blessing of his church, to the edge of whose forgiving boundaries he had so often strayed, and whose invisible walls comprised yet his one true home.

The wedding breakfast was laid out in the long, oak-panelled dining-room of Hardacres, overlooking green lawns and Mary Hardacre's rose beds, still bright with summer colour. Long tables, covered in white linen, were set up in a U-shape, with Sam and Mavis at the head with Madelene, Geordie Emmerson and his wife, and the best man and matron of honour, Vanessa Gray, beside them. Vanessa was pink-cheeked and gawky, wearing the sort of hat usually reserved for Victorian pantomimes. But the favourite sight of the day was Noel Hardacre, who had not only sobered enough to actually turn up, but had arrived in formal finery dragged from the recesses of some forgotten cupboard, wafting the scent of mothballs after him.

Janet Chandler wore black, looked utterly stunning, and aside from that, behaved herself impeccably.

When Sam rose to say grace over the meal, looking down the long tables with their extraordinary mixture of humanity, all ages and types, each with their own histories, quirks and enchantments, he found himself almost too emotional to speak, so dear were they, suddenly, to him.

Before he could begin, Vanessa suddenly brayed, 'Oh look, what jolly luck,' and pointed out of the window.

Everyone turned, and Sam, turning with them, saw the little herd of half-wild fallow deer, choosing their moment to perfection, suddenly step out of their shelter of woodland and pick their way carefully, with delicate weightless steps, across the green lawn. They approached until they were scarcely a hundred feet from the house and stood for a moment, their fragile legs poised for instant flight, gazing into the tall windows of the room. Somebody suddenly cheered, seeing them as an omen, and the sound, even through the glass, sent them fleeing like a memory clasped too hard from the ungraspable illusion of time. Sam watched them until they were gone into the beech wood like shadows, thinking of Harry the while. Then he spoke his benediction over his wedding meal, quickly, and in Latin, so no one would hear him stumble over the words. He sat down again, put his arms about his wife, and buried his face in her sweet-smelling hair.

He felt blessed and sheltered by the old house, and was

glad to bring his bride home to it, as Harry had done before him.

After the meal, and the speeches, Albert Chandler again provided music, as he had done for Jan and Janet, and there was a little dancing, with Sam and Mavis leading the first waltz. There was champagne, and the makings of a good party, though Sam was not quite up to another just then. Anyhow, the bride and groom left early, with her son sniggering cheerfully at their haste, but their reasons were less romantic than mundane. They had a long way to go that day.

No one other than Jane Macgregor had the faintest idea where they were going. She knew, because she had given them the keys to her home in Strathconon, and announced she was going to the South of France and wouldn't be back for a month. So Mavis went off to change and stopped long enough to throw her wedding bouquet from the gallery of the great hall. It was caught by Ruth Barton, in attendance with Riccardo. He beamed, happy Italian paternalism, and Emily looked relieved, and Ruth looked sour. Sam was relieved as well, because he thought that Ruth, as well as sour, looked pregnant, and he was confidently relying on Riccardo to do the decent thing, assuming he wanted to live a little longer.

When Mavis returned, lovely in a tailored suit of bright green, with a small, matching hat, they made their farewells and left the house through the kitchen door, since Sam insisted on saying goodbye to the staff as well. Mrs Dobson got frankly tearful and kissed them both, and the little kitchen maid hired for the day from the village met Sam's eyes with a look of remembrance and shock which was reflected in his own. She blushed, giggled and looked at the floor, and he leaned down just for a moment, and whispered 'Happy Christmas' as he passed. She blushed again, and showered him with a handful of rice, as he went out of the door.

They were suddenly alone, except for Jane Macgregor, who had walked with them through the house and out into the courtyard, thick with yellow falling leaves from the old ash tree. She had one arm around Mavis's waist and put her other around Sam's, and she said, as they walked in sudden silence, 'Well, children, you're on your own.'

Sam suddenly embraced her fiercely, and said, 'Thank you for everything.'

'For what?' she laughed, lightly. 'I've not even given you a wedding present. Surely you've noticed?'

Sam hadn't noticed. 'You've given me enough for a lifetime,' he said.

'Oh, but that's all very well, you still must have something from me, for your marriage.'

'You've given us the honeymoon,' Mavis said.

Jane sniffed. 'I'm charging B and B for that. Seventeen and six per night. That's the going rate. No, my loves, that's what I had in mind.' They had rounded the corner of the house and she pointed with one long, regal finger towards the grey Jaguar which was parked directly in front of the door of Hardacres, festooned with white streamers of ribbon.

They stared, and Mavis said, 'I thought Jan was lending his car?'

Jane sniffed again. 'That was only to keep our favourite son from driving you off in his damnable lorry, with "Just Married" on the tailgate. But I had a better idea. The registration is in the glove compartment, Sam,' she said, holding out to him the keys. She paused. 'It's in your name.'

Sam, who had thought she was merely lending it and had strong reservations about even that, stared, and then shook his head slowly.

'Oh, no, Jane. No.'

'What do you mean "no",' she snapped. 'When are you going to learn how to accept a gift?'

'I can't, Jane. I can't. It's yours. I can't imagine you ever without it.'

She shrugged, elegantly. 'What else do you give someone who's got everything including three tugboats? Of course it's not *new* or anything, but it's in fair nick. And anyhow, you like old things.' She turned briefly to face him and said, 'Besides, I know how you and your brother always loved a good car.' Her eyes met his, and held them until she saw the sudden flicker of shock in them fade. She kissed the keys, impulsively and extended them to him. '*Ego te absolvo*, my dear.'

He stood for a long moment before he reached out a hand to take them. Their fingers touched around the keys for an instant and he nodded slowly, and faintly smiled. He took the keys from her, and then carefully helped Mavis into the low seat of the open car, and walked, with Jane at his side yet, around to the driver's side. He opened the door, and hesitated once more. 'Jane, I can't take this from you,' he said.

'Of course you can. I'm getting a bit past it, anyhow, dear. A bit long in the tooth, you know.'

'Oh, no, please. Don't even think it,' he said, with real anguish. She was the one, the only member of his family he couldn't conceive of being without, and the thought of her advancing years was something he would not face.

'Well, it's true,' she said as he, yet reluctantly, got behind the wheel of the beautiful motor car and started the engine. She admired the sight of them there, and said, 'Perfect, it matches your hair.' She leaned over him and caught Mavis's hand and bent and kissed Sam, as she did.

'Anyhow, I've just ordered an E-type,' she said.

CHAPTER
THIRTY-ONE

The two young girls brought their matching red motor scooters to a halt at the side of the tall brick wall and dismounted, taking off their brightly-coloured helmets and shaking out their long hair. One was fair, the other dark, and both pretty in the elfin way fashionable now with the young. Their hair was worn smooth and straight, and as long as they had managed to get it to grow, with a long, silky fringe, so that each of them peered out with black-rimmed, heavily-lashed eyes, through a veil darkly. They giggled and looked at each other, and looked at the red brick wall.

'We'll never get over,' said the fair one.

'I'll give you a leg up,' the other said, eagerly.

'But what of you, then?' The fair one shrugged, touched the wall slightly reverently and said, 'Perhaps we'll find a gate.'

The girls trudged along beside the red brick wall for a while, pushing their scooters along the grassy verge of the road. Eventually they did come to a gate, tall and elaborate of ingeniously decorative wrought iron, but the gates were closed and padlocked. There was no one in sight. The fair girl leaned her red scooter against the curve of the wall and sank disconsolately down, cross-legged, on the ground.

'Should have guessed,' said the other. 'People like that don't leave gates open.'

'I bet he isn't even here,' the fair girl said. 'We've probably come all this way for nothing. He's probably at Kilham.'

'They're *never* at Kilham any more,' her companion said, 'everyone knows that. I'm sure he'll be here. They're probably all here. Nick says they live here.'

'Not likely,' the fair girl said. 'Bloody rich place like that.'

She cast an unkind glance through the locked gates, as she chewed thoughtfully on a grass stem. The dark-haired girl sat down as well. She was wearing a little short skirt of corduroy, an inch or two above her knee at the hem, and lacy patterned tights. She, too, sat cross-legged, oblivious of the length of long leg revealed.

'Geordie lives here,' the dark girl said. 'His father owns it.'

'His *step*father,' the other corrected. She paused, running the grass stem through her teeth. 'It's really weird, Geordie having a stepfather like that. I mean Geordie's so *natural*, you know. I mean, just like an ordinary person. The way he jokes between numbers, you feel you could really know him.' She paused. 'His stepfather's *really* weird. He was a priest or something and ran off with this film star. It was really grotty.'

The dark girl was silent and then she said, 'My dad met him once, in Hull, down at the harbour. He said he was really nice.'

The fair girl looked up wisely over her blade of grass. 'Nobody,' she said, 'with that kind of money, is nice.'

'Maybe we should go home,' said the dark-haired girl.

Her companion shrugged, but said, 'Let's wait. If we stay by the gate, we'll see them come in.'

'If they're not in already.'

'Well, let's wait anyhow. It's a beautiful day.' The blonde stretched out in the grass, spreading her long hair out over the wild flowers. She closed her eyes, and did not see the man approach, but her companion did.

'Hey, Cathy,' she said. 'We'd better go. There's someone coming.'

'Oh, fab,' said the blonde lazily. 'Is it one of them?'

'Hardly. And he looks really furious. Come on.' She jumped up, and Cathy joined her, staring through the black gates. A man, short and wiry, and wearing old-fashioned tweed knee-breeches, was walking purposefully down the driveway from a parked car beneath the June shadow of the tall elms. He had a bunch of keys in his hand which rattled as he walked. He was grey-haired, with a spiky dishevelment about him that looked vaguely lunatic, and he looked to the girls terribly old.

'Yes?' he demanded. The dark-haired girl was terrified, but the fair one was bolder.

'Can we see Paul Barton?' she asked, grinning cheekily.

'Not from here you can't.'

'Is he in there?' the dark girl said, finding her courage.

'Not to my knowledge.'

'Is he with the family?' the blonde Cathy said, bolder yet.

'Damned if I know.'

The dark girl relaxed, realizing the man was only hired help, obviously, and said, 'I'm sure it'll be all right if we wait here. We just want to see him when they come home.'

The man shrugged. 'Please yourselves,' he said. He left them and wandered off again to the old black shooting-brake in which he had driven down, and got in, leaving the door yet open, put his feet half-up on the dashboard and appeared to go to sleep.

'Friendly, wasn't he?' said the blonde. But she saw then another pair of girls walking up the road and, behind them, a small giggling group of four, and decided they'd come to the right place, after all.

They waited an hour, as their little group slowly became a small crowd, before the first car appeared. It was followed immediately by another, as what amounted to a small cavalcade came up the road from the direction of Beverley. The man with the keys got out of the old black shooting-brake and ambled unhurriedly to the gates as the first car drew up. He scrutinized its occupants, who looked a little nervous, and shouted something, perhaps a name, to him. He seemed to be enjoying holding the keys to the kingdom and only let them in with a slow, teasing grin. He stopped the next car as well, with the grim stare of a traffic warden, but eventually let it, with its flower-hatted ladies in the back seat, through. A red soft-top E-type Jaguar suddenly roared up behind it, and the girls squealed, thinking it would be their awaited heroes, but the driver was a tall old woman with a stern grey bun of hair. The gatesman ran, grinning, to let her in, so she barely had to slow down, and bowed elaborately as she roared by, and up the drive.

Another few cars made their mundane, closely scrutinized way past the gaoler. The next likely candidate for Paul Barton's vehicle was an antique red MG roadster, but it contained no handsome long-haired young men, only a pretty dark woman of indeterminate age and, beside her, another woman, younger, with lovely soft-coloured hair, holding a tiny baby wrapped in mountains of antique lace. One or two of the more motherly of the girls leaned over and stared as it passed, momentarily forgetting their heroes in favour of a more timeless delight.

'Where *are* they?' Cathy moaned.

'There, surely,' said her dark-haired friend.

Behind the MG, a silver-grey Jaguar, of considerable age and immense style, pulled discreetly up to the gates. The little crowd of girls momentarily surged forward, but relaxed back in a moment with a small sound of disappointment. The driver of the car was a man, but he was neither Paul Barton nor Geordie Emmerson. He was tall, greyhaired and very distinguished-looking, rather handsome actually, Cathy thought, as older men go. Beside him was a beautiful woman, in a striking black suit that set off her long, waving white-blonde hair. She too, was holding a shawl-and-lace-wrapped infant, and looking down on it with an expression of some amazement. The keeper of the gate put on his biggest grin, and leaned, unmoving, against the gatepost, nodding to the barrier as if it were nothing to do with him.

'Open it,' the grey-haired man shouted.

'Any ID?'

'*Open it*, you sod.'

'Driver's licence? Credit cards?'

'Open the damnable gates, Noel, or I'll give you back the bloody title deeds.'

That did it. The gatekeeper tugged his forelock and rubbed his hands together obsequiously and hurriedly unlocked the gate. The cluster of long-haired girls leaned closer, staring, momentarily won over by a new attraction. The blonde woman looked around and flashed a stunning smile.

As they passed through the gates, Janet said, 'Do I wave regally, or do you?'

'I somehow feel it's not for us,' said Sam.

'I do *know* that,' she said tartly. 'You don't have to rub it in.'

He smiled, gently. 'Do you mind, sweetheart?'

She laughed, 'Ladies who get Oscar nominations for best supporting actress don't mind.'

'Good,' he said slyly, 'maybe next time you'll even win.'

'If I weren't holding a baby, I'd hit you.'

'You be careful of that baby.'

'I *am*. But why worry? You've got a spare.' She looked down, still bemused.

Behind them a thin, squealing cheer suddenly arose, far down the driveway.

'Looks like the boys are home,' said Sam.

'I hope they make it with their trousers intact. Those girls don't fool around.'

'I somehow doubt they'll care.' Sam grinned. 'Ah, to be young,' he said.

Janet snapped, 'Include me out of that, please. Just because you're getting paternal, doesn't mean I have to leap blind into middle-age with you, you know.' She looked down at the baby again and said, 'Thank God *I* didn't marry you. Catholics *breed*.'

'Non-stop,' said Sam. 'We're going to have fifteen.'

'Don't laugh. You've had three in three years.'

'Wait a minute. Two in one go doesn't count.'

'Oh, pardon me. You've only done it twice.'

'That's right, sweetheart.'

Janet studied the baby again and said, 'Which one is this anyhow? Peter or Michael?'

Sam glanced across and shrugged. 'Damned if I can tell. Ask Mavis.' He paused. 'You'd better get it straight, though. You're the godmother.'

'Yes,' said Janet, drily. She wasn't quite sure whether she was honoured or insulted by that. 'I hope you don't expect me to look after their spiritual welfare for real, Sam,' she said, suddenly serious. 'I'm not up to it. You've got the wrong lady.'

He reached over and patted her hand. 'No, pet. Gerry will see to that. He's a good Catholic.'

Gerry Flannigan was First Mate on the *Jane Hardacre*, a solid, steady Irishman who took his religion seriously, and he was godfather to Sam's twin sons, as a solemn counterpoint to Janet.

'Not all that good,' Janet sniffed, 'from the way he was looking at me in Church.'

'You, my dear, would tempt a saint. He's a good family man. Keep your hands off him.'

She grinned and, in answer, slid her free hand down his thigh. 'Come up and see me sometime,' she whispered throatily, but she withdrew the hand at once and wrapped it innocently about the bundle of lace in her arms as the grey Jaguar arrived at the front door of Hardacres. He gave her one, quick, warning look and she said, 'I'll behave. Promise. Cross my heart and hope to die.'

The christening party was held in the gardens. A marquee had been set up on the lawn by the summer-house, and there were tables with platters of smoked salmon, bowls of strawberries, and cases of champagne. The conservatory doors stood open to the garden, and the ladies of the house had gathered there. It was Mavis's private retreat, as the library was Sam's. She had restored it from the sad, empty shell it had been throughout Sam's childhood and youth, to the rich, tropical splendour it had boasted in the days of Mary Hardacre. There were figs and grapes and peach trees, and a wealth of tropical palms, and wicker chairs and tables set out on the ancient tiled floor, in the warm sheltered sun. Mavis had kept the pram there, for her little daughter, and now for the twins, as Mary Hardacre had done with her own daughter's pram, seventy years before.

Mavis had not, as Mick Raddley confidently predicted, given Sam his twins by July, but she had indeed given him a daughter within a year of their marriage, and now, a year and a half later, his two sons. None of the three children looked the slightest bit like Mick, though he never relented an inch on his claims of paternity. The children, like her entrance into the Church, were another of the many things Mavis did without consulting him at all. He had, about them, the delight that only a man who has abandoned hope of ever having his own children, and indeed, abandoned it twice, can possibly have. He was understandably thrilled by the twins, for obvious reasons, but it was his little daughter, barely two years old, who was without doubt the chief joy of his life. He had called her Jane, of course, and the only sorrow in his world now was that he must, at times, be apart from her. He would willingly have taken her with him everywhere, had Mavis and good sense, allowed. He would return from a trip to sea, late on a winter night, tired and cold, and run directly from his car up the great stairs to the nursery before he would even stop to speak to anyone else. Mavis did not resent his devotion; no one could; though at times the sheer fierce strength of it was frightening. Still, she accepted it, and let it pass. The man had enough love in him to share with many.

Now, he got out of the car and carefully helped Janet out with her lacy burden, and escorted her with great propriety down the lawn to the gathering by the marquee. He could see the slender figure of his mother carrying the other twin around, showing him off to everyone in sight. They were dressed in the same ageing christening robes in which Sam and Terry had been brought out of heathendom into the Church, and Madelene was as proud of them as ever she'd been of her own sons. They were the last, fated chink in the wall between them; on their birth the barrier had fallen, and his mother had, at last, welcomed him home. It was as if only a life, and another male life, could pay the price of the son he had taken from her. Whatever, he was glad the price was paid. As he grew older, disruptions and sorrows in the family of which he was head, brought him increasing pain. He wanted them together, and at peace with each other, as Harry had wanted before him. He smiled, seeing Ruth Cirillo leading her own toddling daughter across the lawn to the waiting arms of her deliriously proud Italian father. He was not sure Ruth was totally happy with the marriage, but she couldn't be that displeased either, because there was no doubt that she was pregnant again. He shrugged. There was a kind of Hardacre woman, like Emily, like Ruth, indeed like Janet, he would never quite understand.

Janet walked placidly beside him as far as the summer-house. Mavis had had Noel restore it, a remarkable trick, indeed, winning unnecessary labour from that savagely practical man. But he'd done it for her. Sam was a little sorry. It had memories like it was that he would have gladly left untouched, but there was no way he could tell that to his wife. Janet eyed it, perhaps thinking the same. It was full of wrought-iron chairs and tables now, rather than bales of hay, but the wisteria grew as ever. Janet smiled, and rocked the baby, who yawned and looked up with dark long-lashed eyes.

'God help it,' she said. 'It's going to look like you.'

'You know, that suits you,' he said, watching, 'and Jan was looking positively wistful in Church. I think you're going to have to do something for him.'

Janet gave him a stony stare. 'Fine,' she said, 'I'll get him a cat.'

There was a distant beeping of a shrill horn, and the small red Mini suddenly appeared out of the beech wood, with Geordie and Paul Barton in the front seat. They parked it and leapt out, laughing, with two long-haired girls tumbling out of the back seat after them, and came running across the green lawns to the marquee. The girls squealed and chased and the boys didn't run all that fast for such long-legged, athletic young men. They got caught somehow, and had to slow down to a walk, burdened as they were with the clutch of female arms about their necks, and the silky weight of long, loose hair. Geordie, thus encumbered, arrived at the marquee by Sam and Janet and the baby. He said, 'Can we keep them, Dad, they followed us home?'

Sam smiled wryly, at the big-eyed girl peering uncertainly at him around Geordie's neck. She was clearly terrified of him and it always bewildered him that anyone could be. Like everyone else of forty-six, he still felt eighteen in his heart, and didn't see why he should so strike awe into the young. 'As long as they don't eat too much,' he said. 'You'd better find your Uncle Albert,' he said to Paul. 'He's looking for you, I think.'

Paul nodded. He was the more serious of the two, and he was always very responsible about family, and most particularly his uncle, Albert Chandler, whom he worshipped. 'I'll find him,' he said, wandering off into the crowd, holding his new young friend by the hand.

Mavis, with little Jane in her arms, found Sam then, and began directing him to gather the strays among his guests, but he only caught up his little daughter from her, and said, 'Where's my darling,' and was at once lost in his own world with her.

So Mavis went off and organized his family for him, for the christening photographs which would sit, one day, with all the others, in silver frames on the mantel of the drawing-room. Mavis was terribly good at organizing things, in her quiet-spoken unobtrusive manner. Like Jane Macgregor, she held everyone together, and created peace and harmony, while her husband went his erratic and cheerful way.

After the photographs, Paul Barton found Albert sitting in the summer-house with Maud, holding hands and talking with Emily and Philip about London, long ago. He knocked on the rustic wood doorpost before he entered the open, airy little building, as if it were somehow a private room. Albert stood up to greet him. He was still tall, and straight as ever, and looked rather appropriate in the antique grace of morning-dress beneath the soft shadows of wisteria. Sometimes, looking at him, Paul got a little ashamed of his own generation, with their rough and scruffy clothes, and their sloppy manner on stage. Sometimes, although he knew it was not possible, he wanted it all to be more like Albert Chandler in the ballroom of the Savoy. He said, politely, 'Sam said you wanted to see me.'

'Ah, yes.' Albert put his hand on Paul's shoulder and looked down at the wooden floor. 'Just a thought. You playing tonight at the club?'

'Yes, sir.'

'Usual time?'

'Yes, sir.'

'Ah good. Friend of mine, up from London. Like to take him in to see you. Just for a little, if you don't mind.'

'Of course not, sir.' Paul paused, thinking, and said tentatively, 'You sure, Uncle Albert? I mean, it's awful noisy, and all. You know what it's like in there. You sure he'll like it?' Albert smiled, distantly, his thin moustache twitching.

'He'll like it,' he said.

Paul wandered off and found Geordie and his find from the crowd at the gate, and they went into the marquee and introduced the girls to champagne, which neither had ever tasted before. They liked it, after an initial suspicious wrinkling of noses like small puppies. Which was not surprising, seeing as how it was from Harry Hardacre's cellar, and quite splendid; Sam was liking it as well. As the afternoon progressed, warm, sunny, and soporific with the rare splendour of a perfect English summer day, he got gently plastered, and wandered around the gardens contentedly with his little daughter on one arm, and a bottle of champagne in his free hand, with which he topped up any glass he passed. He was quite resplendent in morning-dress, and looked every bit the aristocrat that he occasionally was.

Mick Raddley approached with some trepidation, a wary Pete Haines at his side. The advent of the twins, as predicted, if a little late, had given Mick such devilish delight that he'd actually overcome all his wary restraint and attended the christening, in battered, rented, formal attire. Sam was delighted and he smiled happily as he met them, poured champagne into Pete's glass, and over Mick's head, and said, 'No, he's not the bloody father, so don't ask.'

'Weren't going to ask that,' said Pete.

'Nay,' said Mick. 'We got summat else on our minds.'

'Oh, aye?' Sam said. 'It's not bloody work, is it? Because if it is, it can go to hell. I'm getting drunk today.'

'Aye, we've noticed. No. It's about the names.'

'Don't you like them?'

'Fine. We like them fine,' said Pete.

He rocked on his heels and Sam said, giggling, 'My God, you look a proper toff, Pete. There must have been some blue blood on the wrong side of the blanket in *your* house once.'

'Nowt but good Yorkshire stock,' said Pete sourly. 'Now I know there was a Peter in the family somewhere, but it's the Michael we can't figure.'

'Lovely name,' said Sam.

'A'reeght, stop beatin' round t' bluidy bush,' said Mick. 'Did you name t' little bastards after us?'

550

Sam stared, as well as he could with the slight lack of focus caused by the champagne, and shifted his little daughter carefully so that she was more comfortable, leaning over his shoulder. He said, with a look of imperiousness worthy of his great-aunt Jane, 'After you? You two? You're getting ideas above your station, the pair of you.' He paused, swaying slightly, and said, 'They're after the archangel. And the bloody saint.' He poured more champagne over Mick's head and walked away.

'Reeght,' Mick shouted after him. 'As long as we all know our place.'

'The Club' – it had no other name – was a cellar beneath a shopfront, in a less attractive corner of Scarborough. It opened its doors when the pubs closed theirs, serving no alcohol, of course, but its customers didn't come for that kind of intoxication. They sipped cokes and drank endless coffees and smoked too many hand-rolled cigarettes, so the atmosphere was thick and sour, full of the scent of tobacco, a faint trace of marijuana, and the unabashed stench of sweat. The Club was packed from ten until two, with young, healthy dancing bodies, and all they came for was the music that had no end.

On the night of the June day on which Sam Hardacre's sons were christened, Paul Barton and Geordie Emmerson Hardacre, with Bill, Taffy and Greg, the three supporting players, held the stage at The Club for four hours straight. It was a stunning feat of energy and musical resource, but at midnight, when they'd played steadily for two hours already, Paul wasn't even tired. He was lead singer, and Geordie lead guitar, and between the two of them was a rhythm and understanding that was almost mystic.

Offstage they were just pals, two young men with a tenuous family link, who went their own ways and chased their own women. But on that stage they were brothers, more than brothers, they were twins, two minds and bodies so close as to share one soul. They never had to plan a performance, nor even hint which song came next, or when they would make that devastating slip into the minor key that made the girls shriek and grow faint. It just happened; like with the old black jazzmen Albert had told him of, they improvised and teased, flirting with each other through the tangle of melody and rhythm, never a note out of step. The Guttie Boys were a good group, five good competent musicians, but it was that pairing of the two leads that set them streets ahead of the rest.

Paul could just see Geordie out of the corner of his eye, over the edge of the mike; swaying, his eyes half-closed, lost in the sound, feeding back the musical seduction that Paul threw to him, and tossing it, like crumbs to the hungry, to the audience below. The girls shrieked; white, upturned faces, huge eyes made huger by great splodges of eye shadow and cakes of mascara; all hunger and desire. Paul grinned, and they shrieked again; he could play them all as if they were all in his bed. And yet he did so with no pride. That they took sex from him was an accident; what he was giving was music. And as always, music was his whole being. He stood and sang, and forgot everything, just as he had eleven years before on the sands of Bridlington beach. *Oh, for the Wings of a Dove*. Paul needed no wings; he was flying and music alone was the source of his flight. Albert Chandler came in in the middle of a number, and Paul didn't even see him until the last chord came crashing through his soul. Then he stopped, breathing in great gasps, his face and body coated with sweat, as the real world of boys and girls and cokes and coffees and fags came suddenly jarring back.

They rested a moment, and Paul caught Albert's eye. He went to step down from the stage, suddenly cast down into a world of family and duty, but Albert made a curt little nod and a small smile, said something to his companion, a stranger in a trench coat and hat, and after another few moments, they quietly went away.

'Hey, who's the gear old guy?' a girl asked suddenly.

'He's Albert Chandler,' said Paul stiffly, knowing that would mean nothing, and suddenly resenting it. Then he said, 'He's my uncle.'

'Hey, keep cool, man,' she said shyly. 'I like him. He's,' she paused, 'he's, you know, sort of real.'

Paul was sorry that Albert had left without speaking to him, but he was not too surprised. The Club was pretty grotty, in its way. He really hadn't expected Albert's London friend to like it much. Still, it was nice of them to come. He ran his fingers down the strings of his guitar, fretting lightly, with an imaginative left hand, teasing out the next song, and a soft moan went about the room.

Paul didn't see Albert until the next day. He had not expected to see him at all. But Albert rang him, unexpectedly, at the crash-pad of a flat off the harbour side that he shared with three of the Guttie Boys when he wasn't at Hardacres or, rarely, at Kilham. They'd only recently put a telephone in, and done so because the need to be available and reachable for gigs had become important. Albert asked to meet him at a café down on the Promenade and, yet surprised, he agreed.

He dressed hurriedly, washing sleep from his face in the ghastly bathroom of the flat. Greg was asleep in his own room and Geordie was tucked up in a corner of the sitting-room, if you can call a bare floor with three cushions and an Indian durry a sitting-room, with a young lady with knee-length red hair. Geordie woke, blinking, as Paul stepped over them.

'Sorry,' he said, trying not to wake the sleeping girl as well, 'I need my jacket.'

He lifted it, a heap of worn denim, from the floor by Geordie's head. Geordie stretched, his hands under the blanket exploring the unexpected pleasure of his companion's young body beside him. 'Hey, look, you're not going home, or anything?' he said.

553

'I'm going to meet Albert. He just rang.'

Geordie was silent. He looked through squinting eyes about the morning light of the flat, staring at the peeling wallpaper.

'You're not bringing him here, are you?' he said, with sudden concern.

'Of course not.' Geordie looked relieved and closed his eyes. 'Hey, look, mate, don't, you know, *say* anything, okay?'

'Jesus Christ, do you think I'm an idiot?'

'Maybe. You've an awful big mouth sometimes. I mean,' Geordie hoisted himself up on one bare elbow, suddenly serious, 'I really don't want anyone . . .' he paused, 'I don't want my Dad to know about this, you understand. I really don't want him to know.'

'You must think I'm a *total* ass,' said Paul. 'Relax, the last person I'd tell would be Sam.'

He went out into the misty, salty air. The day was grey, but would clear. He knew the type. After he saw Albert he'd maybe go down to the beach and lie in the sun. It had been a hard night, with another ahead. He could use the rest. Maybe he'd go down to the harbour and cadge a lift on someone's boat. He liked the sea.

Albert was waiting for him at the café. He was sitting, inappropriate and dignified as always, at a little Formica table, on a little tubular metal and plastic-padded chair. Paul wished in his heart he could somehow create the world anew, or again, rather, for Albert, and surround him always with oak panelled walls, brocade upholstery, velvet draperies. Like at Hardacres, he thought suddenly, wishing Albert would just move in with Sam and Mavis and knowing, though welcome, he never would. Paul smiled as he entered, and saw to his surprise that the trench-coated gentleman was sitting by Albert's side.

They stood up as Paul entered. Albert said, 'I'd like you to meet an old friend, Paul. Matt Goldman. Matt, this is my nephew, Paul Barton.' The man shook his hand and smiled and they all sat down. He was Albert's age at least, but he didn't dress like Albert. Under the trench-coat he wore denim jeans and a roll-neck sweater and a silver medallion hung around his neck. His glasses were the old rimless kind that were suddenly fashionable again, and shaded faintly green. 'Matt's in the music business,' said Albert then. He smiled and said, 'Coffee? Breakfast maybe?' He looked understanding, as well he might have been. Musicians, like all stage people, worked late, and rose with some difficulty.

'Just coffee, please, sir. Let me get it. And for you.' He always hated taking anything from Albert. He knew how broke he was.

'You paid last time,' Albert said, and Paul knew he had to let it rest.

'Albert tells me you've not signed with anyone yet,' said Matt Goldman.

'Signed?'

'Your recording rights. You've not signed . . .'

'I don't record, sir,' said Paul, with something of the ingenuous modesty that had always marked his uncle's career.

Matt Goldman grinned, amused. 'Yet,' he said. 'The word is "yet".'

'Sir?'

'I think, Paul, that we have here the East Riding's answer to the Beatles.' Paul laughed and shook his head, but he wasn't modest about his ability; he knew he was good.

He said, 'Give me time,' laughing again.

'All the time in the world, son. Come to London on Monday. I'll meet you off the train Bring all your gear, and be ready to stay a while.' Paul blinked. The man drew a card from his pocket, and handed it across the coffee-stained Formica table.

'United Studios, Shepherd's Bush,' he said.

Paul just looked at the card. His eyes came up slowly as

555

he understood. He said in a whisper, half-looking at Albert, 'Did you come all this way just to hear us, sir?'

'Every step of it.' The man leaned back, sliding his shaded glasses up on to his forehead. 'To tell the truth, son, I came because your uncle asked me. Your uncle gave me my first job, when I was the worst damned trombone player in London. He had no taste, but a big heart,' he grinned at Albert, a grin of their own generation that passed metaphorically over Paul's head. 'I came up to say thank you. But I don't offer recording contracts out of sentiment, you can be sure. And I'm damned glad I came.' He looked at his watch. 'Albert, I have to go. I've a train to catch.' They stood, shook hands again, once more in their own adult world and Matt Goldman, with a brief nod to Paul, went out of the door.

Paul turned to his uncle, his eyes filled with amazed gratitude, but before he could speak, Albert said, 'Now, you're sure this is what you want? Not Italy, and Puccini?'

Paul smiled and shook his head. 'Puccini's been around a while, Uncle Albert. He'll wait for me. Just now, this is my way.'

After he parted with his uncle, Paul Barton walked, as he had planned, down to the strip of yellow stony sand facing the summer blue waters of Bridlington bay. He walked along Beaconsfield Promenade, and went down on to the sand below the Victoria Terraces, and sat in the sun leaning against the seaweed-smelling stone wall, looking out at the yachts on the sea. Then he got up, stretching, went and bought himself a hot dog and ate it as he wandered along to the Harbour. He went out on the North Pier, to its end, and then made his way back, looking at the boats, passing Sam Hardacre's *Dainty Girl* moored in her usual place. He smiled. He'd had fun out on her, over the years. He made his way to the Harbour Top, where the fishermen gathered in the early mornings, walked round to the South

Pier and went out along that. He was basking, not just in the sunshine, but in his sudden, extraordinary fortune. He knew, for certain, that he was on the edge of a momentous step in his life. He felt he should go and tell Geordie, but he didn't, not yet. Anyhow, Geordie was happy enough with his redhead, and besides, Paul wanted just a little time alone, to savour in solitude a moment that would come but once.

He sat on a bench in the sun, aware of two young girls looking at him, pointing and giggling. He smiled, but did not invite their company. It always amazed him that they sought him, and watched him, and treated him as some odd sort of hero. He knew he was none of those things. He was just Paul Barton who, by the grace of God, could sing. That was all.

Across the Harbour he saw a familiar long grey open car arrive, its driver waving to someone as he brought it to a halt, his grey hair, silvery in the strong sun, matching the motor car rather pleasantly. The man got out, lifted a small dark-haired child out of the car and carried her on his arm as he walked up the Pier. He stopped every few feet to point to one or another of the boats in the water. As he got closer, Paul smiled. But the man stopped then, meeting an old fisherman in a worn cotton smock, who extended his one good arm to the little girl, and took her from her father, grinning and making faces. The two stood together, the child between them. Paul got up suddenly to wave, but heard a voice behind say with sour envy, 'Eh, look. There's bluidy Sam Hardacre, takin' time off from countin' his money.'

'Aye,' said an invisible companion. 'Bluidy great house in t' country. Drives a bluidy Jaguar. Some folk have all the luck.'

Paul froze. If it had been Geordie, there would have been a fist fight. Geordie had pasted a good few for remarks about his stepfather. That was Geordie's way. But not Paul. He

557

just rose, straight-backed and stiff, like Albert Chandler, and walked with dignity away towards Sam. But as he went, his eyes on his cousin yet, he heard behind him words that chilled him more.

'Oh aye, true enough. But yon's the one to really watch. Aye. There. Young Paul Barton. T' bluidy songbird. He's the one with a fortune at his feet, a'reeght. Yon's the one with the *real* Hardacre luck.'